ANGEL IN SCARLET

Angel in Scarlet

Jennifer Wilde

INNER CIRCLE

Copyright © 1986 by Tom Huff

This edition first published in
Great Britain in 1987 by
Judy Piatkus (Publishers) Ltd of
5 Windmill Street, London W1
by arrangement with
Corgi/Avon Books, London W5

British Library Cataloguing in Publication Data

Wilde, Jennifer
    Angel in scarlet.
    I. Title
    813'54[F]   PS3573.I422

    ISBN 1-85018-064-4

Printed and bound in Great Britain at
The Bath Press, Avon

For Kerry, Kathy and Janelle
and for their grandmother
with all my love

Book One
Angie
Kent

Chapter One

As I walked across the field toward Greystone Hall with my basket of eggs, I told myself I wasn't at all afraid of The Bastard. Oh, he was bound to be a bad 'un, probably scary as all get out, but I didn't believe half the things they said about him. Eppie Dawson swore she had seen him with her own eyes, claimed he was a giant, claimed he had actually breathed fire! A great pack of lies, that. I might be a year younger than she was, but I had a lot more sense than that silly goose. Eppie Dawson was thirteen and thought she was so bloomin' superior just because she'd already started bleeding. Couldn't talk about anything but hair ribbons and boys, that one. Gettin' the curse once a month might thrill her to death, but I was *glad* I didn't and hoped I never would. Who needed the aggravation?

Across the field I could see the high gray stone wall that enclosed the grounds and gardens of Greystone Hall. I could see lofty green treetops beyond the wall and even caught glimpses of the uneven, multileveled blue-gray slate roofs studded with tottering orange brick chimneys and a forest of sooty black chimneypots. Grey-stone Hall was two miles beyond the village, and I'd never had a proper look at it before. The Merediths kept themselves aloof from the common folk, although naturally they were the chief topic of conversation in the village. I'd heard about 'em ever since I could remember, felt I knew 'em, though I'd laid eye on nary a one.

Lord Meredith was fifty-seven, a grim, sullen soul who pinched every penny till it squealed and cared for nothing on earth but his greyhounds. He had married Lady Meredith after he came back from Italy with his bastard son, and she was said to be a mite too fond of her liquor, as well she might be, married to a man like that. The Nephew, who would eventually inherit, was a rake, recently expelled from Oxford—spent most of his time in the gambling halls and brothels of London, they said, spent precious little time in the noble halls of learning. Master Clinton was nineteen—today was his birthday—and no comely lass was safe from his clutches, one heard. His features could be clearly discerned on the faces of any number of bastard babes in the area, Eppie informed me. She said he was ever so handsome with fair blond hair and smoky gray eyes and a wonderful, muscular physique. Seen him herself, she said, though I suspected she was probably making it up. If she didn't watch out, our Eppie was likely to end up with an unwanted babe herself, though Master Clinton wasn't likely to look twice at *her* silly face. Bleedin' she might be, buds she might have, but she still resembled a gawky giraffe.

Lord Meredith loved his greyhounds. His lady loved her brandy. Master Clinton loved his card games and wenches. And then there was The Bastard, and *he* loved torturing little children. Loved to catch 'em trespassing on Meredith property, they said, and after he'd tortured 'em to his heart's content he fed 'em to the greyhounds. All the children in the village were terrified of him—except me. I wasn't afraid of anyone. I might be just twelve years old, my chest might be flat as a board, but

I was smart enough to know people loved to make up outlandish tales about their Betters. The Bastard wasn't a Better, of course, being born out of wedlock, but I guessed you could call him one by association. He *was* Lord Meredith's son, even though his mother was an Italian woman no better than she should be. She had died when The Bastard was born, which was why Lord M. had brought him back to England.

The Bastard was sixteen years old, three years younger than the heir, and he had rooms over the stables because Lady M. wouldn't allow him in the house. He was rough and dirty and surly as a bear, I knew— my stepsister Solonge had seen him walking down the lane and told us he was utterly un*couth*—but he didn't breathe fire and I seriously doubted he had ever tortured a poor mite. No one had actually *seen* him doing any of the foul things he was supposed to do. That was all just talk, and ignorant people dearly loved to talk. Not just the children. The adults were even worse. They talked about *us*, too. We weren't gentry—though my stepmother made preposterous claims about her aristocratic French ancestors—but my father was an educated man and educated folk were the brunt of almost as much talk as the bluebloods.

No, I wasn't afraid of The Bastard. Not at all. Didn't feel the least bit of apprehension as I crossed the field, swinging my basket of eggs. I had seen the fancy carriages passing through the village yesterday, marvelous carriages filled with marvelously attired gentry coming to stay at the Hall and celebrate Master Clinton's birthday, and I was determined to have a closer look at those elegant creatures in satin and lace. There was to be a garden party this afternoon, and I intended to climb the wall and climb up in one of the trees and spy for a while. Wouldn't do any harm. Wouldn't hurt anyone. No one would be any the wiser—except me. I read about those people all the time, in books and in the newspapers and magazines that flooded our cottage every month, shipped from London at great expense,

and now I would see for myself how they looked and
how they acted.

There was a Big World out there. My father was
always telling me that. I had never been to London,
never been more than a few miles outside the village,
but I knew all about that Big World and one day I
planned to be part of it. Eppie Dawson and her ilk might
be content to live and die in the country, rusticating,
never knowing about the Big World, never caring, but
I was different, always had been. All that reading had
ruined me, my stepmother claimed, though no one was
more eager to shake the dust of the country from her
skirts than Madame Marie. If it were left up to her,
we'd all leave for London tomorrow. Me, I was content
to wait, to read and observe and prepare myself.

The field was lavishly strewn with wild daisies, like
tiny gold and white heads peeking up out of the grass,
and I was tempted to put my basket down and gather
daisies and forget all about spying. Not that I was afraid.
Of course not. The Bastard would probably be cowering
in the stables—they wouldn't want *him* in evidence
with all those beribboned aristocrats traipsing around
the gardens—and the greyhounds would undoubtedly
be leashed, but ... well, it *was* a bold plan, terribly risky,
and if I got caught there'd be hell to pay. My father
would grin and shake his head and go back to his reading, but Madame Marie would have conniptions and
rave and rail for a week. Marie was always looking for
an excuse to criticize me. Never had to look very far,
either. I had always been a Thorn in Her Side. With
two perfect, perfectly gorgeous daughters like Solonge
and Janine, she hadn't much patience with a skinny,
scrawny, feisty and unruly lass like me. Maybe if I'd
been pretty it wouldn't be so bad, but I was plain as a
mud fence, as she was never loathe to remind me.

A bunch of daisies would look lovely in the book
room, I told myself. Father would appreciate 'em. He
loved flowers. Loved trees, too, and sunsets and long,
dreamy walks. When he wasn't reading he was taking
long walks and dreaming and contemplating *ideas*. Ideas

were all well and good, Marie grumbled, but they never once put food on a table or clothes on a back and here she was working her fingers to the bone in this hideous, uncivilized village no one had ever heard of while her Dear Husband idled away, teaching classes at the local school, scribbling on a history of the Assyrians that would Never Be Finished and Not Caring what happened to his impoverished, put-upon family. Marie had married Beneath Herself, as she was never loathe to remind *him*.

Maybe I would just pick some flowers and carry 'em back to the cottage and not spy on the gentry after all. Marie would have one of her fits if I was late, she needed the eggs, and I'd learned a long time ago that it was better not to deliberately rile her. I had already been gone almost an hour—it was a long walk to Granny Clempson's farm, but Granny had the best eggs, brown, speckled, always fresh, the best cheese and butter, too, and Marie would buy from no one else. I could pick the daisies and take the eggs on home and... and maybe I could slip back out later on. The party was sure to last for hours, and there were even to be fireworks tonight. Everyone in the village was talking about it.

Come on, Angie, I told myself. You ain't gettin' cold feet now. *Aren't* gett*ing* cold feet. If you were going to talk and act like a bumpkin, Father informed me, you might as well *be* one. I might live in the country, but I bloody well wudn't a bumpkin. *Wasn't* a bumpkin. It was bloody hard to remember always to speak properly when Eppie Dawson and everyone else you knew talked like hayseeds. Much easier to drop your "h's" and final "g's" and use words like ain't and wudn't. I was forever slipping.

Taking a deep breath, I crossed the rest of the field and set the egg basket down carefully at the foot of the wall. It was quite high and made of rough gray stones all piled together, half covered with moss and lichen. Climbing up it was easy as could be in my bare feet. I never wore shoes unless I had to. Scampered up it in no time, I did, then pranced along the top until I came to one of the big trees with limbs reaching out in every direction. Swung up into the tree nimble as an acrobat, crawled along a limb until I could get a good look at the gardens through the thick leaves. Felt at home in trees, I did. I'd been climbing them ever since I could remember. My legs were always scratched from bark and twigs, and I was always tearing my skirts. Marie grumbled about that, too, of course. *Her* daughters had never climbed a tree in their lives. It wasn't ladylike, and Solonge and Janine were perfect ladies, ever so refined. At least Marie thought so. I could have told her a thing or two about her little paragons.

Peeking through the leaves, I was bitterly disappointed. The party was obviously being held in the gardens on the *other* side of the house, and although I could hear distant titters and muted laughter I couldn't see a bloody thing but the house itself and the empty gardens below. The house was enormous, grand and gray, kinda run-down lookin', impressive nevertheless with all of them—those—leaded glass windows and the fancy white marble portico in front. Just caught a glimpse of it from where I was perched. Bleedin' waste of time, I thought. All this trouble just to see the house and a bunch of gardens that sorely needed attention. All shaggy and overgrown, they were. Shrubs needed pruning. Flower beds needed thinning. The marble bench beneath the white wicker trellis was stained with moss, too, and the trellis itself was drooping from the weight of the climbing pink roses.

Might as well go home, Angie, I told myself, and then I saw the lady in blue velvet. She was strolling toward the bench, coming from around the back of the house, and she was the most beautiful creature I had ever seen, even more beautiful than Solonge or Janine. Scooting forward a little, gripping the limb with my knees, I stretched out flat on the wide limb and peered through a hole in the leafy canopy, the lady and that part of the gardens framed in pale, hazy green.

She was a little older than either of my stepsisters. Solonge was fifteen, Janine seventeen, and this woman looked at least eighteen, quite mature, but maybe that was because of the cosmetics. Her eyelids were a shadowy blue-gray, her cheeks cleverly flushed, her lips a deep shell-pink. A small heart-shaped black satin patch was pasted on her right cheekbone, and her lashes, I saw, were much longer, much darker than nature permitted. Her eyes were a clear, lovely blue. Her rich, abundant hair was black, piled carelessly atop her head and caught up with a blue velvet ribbon, two long, thin tendrils curling over her temples and a cascade of waves spilling down in back. I recognized at once that her careless coiffure was the ultimate in style, painstakingly perfected by fashionable hairdressers in London.

Her blue velvet gown had a very wide skirt, a very snug waist and a bodice cut so low you wondered what held it up. The long, tight sleeves were worn off the shoulders, leaving them bare as could be. Never saw so much naked flesh, so much bosom exposed. Why, if she happened to sneeze she'd pop right out! Stylish women in London must catch a lot of colds. The lady paused by the trellis and sighed, toying with one of the drooping pink roses, looking a bit nervous, as though she were afraid someone would jump out and yell "Boo!" What a gorgeous, exotic creature she was, like something out of them—those—magazines Solonge and Janine were always porin' over. You could tell she was gentry, near naked though she was. She sighed again and her bosom heaved. I held my breath, expecting those full, milky white mounds to escape their velvet prison.

Footsteps approached. The lady turned, gnawing her lower lip, more nervous than ever. She tore the pink rose from the trellis. Loose petals showered over the walk. I could smell the heady fragrance perfuming the air. The lady lowered her lashes and straightened up and looked ever so demure, pretending she didn't hear the footsteps. A moment or so later the man strolled into sight. I caught my breath, so excited I feared I'd fall out of the tree. Clinton Meredith *was* handsome, so handsome you could scarce believe it.

I knew who he was at once, of course. Couldn't be anyone else—not with that thick, pale blond hair, as shiny as silk, heavy waves pulled back from his face and tied at the nape of his neck with a thin black ribbon. Not with those glorious gray eyes the color of smoke and those broad, flat cheekbones. He had a long aquiline nose and very full pink lips and his eyelids were heavy, drooping low, giving him a lazy, sleepy look. At least six feet tall, he was built like one of those Greek athletes I'd seen in picture books, lean and muscular, all supple grace. Never saw a man so fair. Looked like a bloomin' prince, he did, in those elegant clothes. His polished black pumps had silver buckles and his stockings were the finest white silk. Knee breeches and frock coat were of pale sky-blue satin. His white satin waistcoat was stitched with tiny flowers of sapphire, black and silver, and white lace ruffles cascaded from his throat, frothing over his wrists.

"Ah, the fair Laura," he said. "Fancy finding you here."

His voice was deep and throaty, reminded you of thick honey. A voice like that'd make a girl lose her senses, I thought. Made you think of bodies. Made you think of bedrooms. Made you think of those erotic engravings in the French books Father kept on the top shelf—Boucher, Fragonard, Watteau. I loved to pore over 'em, turning the pages in amazement.

"Looking lonely and a bit pensive," he continued, seeming to caress each word. "We'll have to do something about that."

"I shouldn't have come," she said.

Her voice was flat and tony and rather nasal, a proper aristocratic voice. Reminded me of metal scraping. Not at all pretty. He didn't seem to mind. He grinned and moved closer and lowered his lids even more and looked like he wanted to eat her up. She stepped back, bumping into the trellis. More pink petals scattered to the ground. Clinton Meredith chuckled. The snug fit of his sky blue satin breeches left no doubt about his feelings for her.

Rarin' to go, he was, bulgin' against his breeches like a randy stallion and hard as a rock.

Some people might wonder how, at twelve, I knew so much about such matters. Well, raised in the country you couldn't help knowin' about 'em with bulls and cows and stallions and mares and other animals copulatin' all over the place. A person'd have to be blind. Too, country folk are a lot more frank about sexual matters than town folk. Right bawdy, they are, always talkin' about who's doin' what to whom and how often. In addition to that, I read every chance I got, and Father had never tried to keep me from reading certain books. We owned all the novels of Samuel Richardson and Henry Fielding and Daniel Defoe—I'd read *Roxana* and *Moll Flanders* before I was ten, *Tom Jones*, too, and you got quite an education from books like that. We also had the complete works of Aphra Behn, and there were things in there that'd make you blush right to the roots of your hair. I'm not sayin' I under*stood* it all, but I knew what was what and then some. Eppie Dawson couldn't hold a candle when it came to such knowledge, even if she *was* already bleedin'.

"I'm very glad you *did* come," Clinton Meredith crooned. "It's my birthday, you know. I deserve a special present."

"I—I really must get back," the lady protested, though I could tell wild horses wouldn't have made her budge an inch. She was breathing rapidly, breasts heaving against dark blue velvet, and her shoulders were trembling slightly. Oh, she was every bit as excited as he was. It just wasn't as obvious with a woman. I clutched the tree limb with arms and knees, peering down through the frame of leaves. Both of 'em were all primed up for humpin'. *Would* they? I could hardly believe my luck.

"No one'll see us here," he said. "They're all on the other side of the house, drinking champagne, eating cakes. Don't be shy, Laura love. Here, give us a kiss."

He took hold of her arm and pulled her to him and Laura looked horrified and tried to pull back and he chuckled again and wrapped his arms around her and gave her a rousing kiss, bending her at the waist, fairly devouring her lips with his. I'd never actually *seen* anyone kissing like that, except in the erotic engravings, and it was something to see, I can tell you. She kept struggling and trying to get free and he kept tightening his arms around her and swinging her to and fro, their lips glued together the whole time, and it was more like they were wrestling than showing affection.

When he finally let her go she looked all weak and helpless and he looked triumphant and pleased with himself and she sank down on the marble bench and stared at her lap and he moved around behind her, smiling to himself, his eyes full of . . . of something I couldn't quite recognize. It was like he was the hunter and she was the prey and he had her in his sights and was ready for the kill. He leaned down and curled one arm around her slender white throat, drawing her back, resting his cheek against hers, and his free hand reached around and slid into the bodice of her dress and one of those large, milky teats popped out with his fingers curled around it, squeezing the soft flesh. The nipple was bright pink and seemed to grow, seemed to strain as his thumb and forefinger pinched it.

Jemminy! It was exactly like one of them engravings come to life: him in satin and lace, her in velvet, him leerin', her pantin' with lips parted, eyes closed, long silky lashes flutterin' against her cheeks like tiny black fans. He squeezed her nipple harder and she moaned and arched her back and it looked like they were going to start copulatin' any minute now. Eppie Dawson was going to be pea green with envy when I told her about it!

"Clinton—" she moaned. "No—no—it isn't—"

"It's what you want," he told her.

"No. I—I'm not—"

"Don't give me that malarky," he said harshly, and his handsome face was suddenly hard, predatory. "Jon Hartley told me all about your little sessions in London—how you slipped off to meet him, how you couldn't

get enough. Don't try that virginal act on me, Laura
love. I know better."

"Jon—Jonathan Hartley is no gentleman!"

She was angry. Her face looked hard, too, no longer
soft and dreamy. He laughed, curling his arm tighter
around her throat, holding her down there on the bench
even though she was trying to get up. His hand was
still holding her teat, squeezing it savagely now.

"You—you're no gentleman, either!" she cried.

"You knew that before you agreed to slip off and meet
me. Jon isn't the only one who's mentioned your name.
William Brandt said the two of you had a jolly time in
Bath last month when you were there with your aunt,
said he was damn near worn out before you finally went
back to London."

"Lies!" she protested.

"I think not, love. I think it's all true—and I think
it's delightful. I'm a better man than Jon Hartley or
William Brandt, love—know a lot more ways to make
a woman happy, make her squeal with pleasure."

"You—you invited me and my aunt here just so—"

"Right," he said, grinning.

He let go of her then and stepped back, and Laura
frowned and tossed her head and stuffed her teat back
beneath the blue velvet. She stood up, looking all sulky
now, looking like a spoiled child. Clinton Meredith put
his hands on his thighs and leaned back a little, grinning at her.

"I've heard all about you, too!" she snapped. "Raping
serving wenches is more your style, I hear. I heard
about those escapades in Oxford, how you raped the
wrong wench—turned out she was the daughter of one
of the dons. Cost your uncle a fortune to get you out of
that jam, and he still couldn't keep them from booting
you out."

"I don't deny a word of it," he said amiably.

"And then there was Lady Milburn. Forty years old
if she's a day! You just seventeen at the time. Quite a
scandal that was."

"Lady M. was a magnificent instructor. Taught me everything I know."

"You're a cad! A rake!"

"And you, Laura love, are an aristocratic little whore. It's obvious we were made for each other."

Jemminy! I exclaimed to myself again. This was better than *Tom Jones*, better than *Roxana*, a hundred times better than that dreary *Clarissa*. Eppie was going to die.

"Tonight," he said. "Leave your door unlocked."

"I may," she said haughtily, "and then again I may not."

The grin widened on his beautifully chiseled lips. His gray eyes gleamed with devilish amusement.

"You'll leave it unlocked, all right," he told her. "You can hardly wait. We'll have a lovely time, love. Now I'd better go join the other guests."

And he strolled casually away, just as though nothing had happened. Laura tossed her head again, raven curls spilling loose, and then she scowled and adjusted her deep blue velvet gown. I expected her to stamp her foot. She didn't. Instead, she smiled, looking as satisfied with herself as he had looked a few minutes before. She plucked one of the pink roses and sniffed it, and then she strolled away, too, and I found myself looking at the empty marble bench and thinking these bluebloods, beneath their fancy facades, weren't at all different from other folks, just richer and better dressed was all.

I was a little disappointed, truth to tell. I had expected 'em to be . . . well, kind of unique and rare, like those porcelain figurines they made in Sèvres, elegant and exquisite and beautiful to behold. Clinton Meredith was beautiful to behold, sure, I granted that, but he wasn't one bit better than Bertie Anderson who'd laid every lass he could, got three of 'em pregnant and finally had to run away to sea to keep from bein' beaten up by Mary York's four brothers. Laura might wear sumptuous blue velvet and paint her face cleverly, might speak in a flat, tony voice, but those were the only things that set her apart from Masie Brown who took on four boys at a time in the haystack behind her father's barn. As I thought about all this, I realized I'd learned an important lesson, one I'd remember always. Never, ever would I be intimidated by anyone just because they happened to be better born than me. I wouldn't even be intimidated by the King himself, and Lord knew *he* was a randy buck, if half the things they said about him were true.

Clinging to the limb with my knees, stretched out flat, my cheek resting on the rough bark, I watched sunlight dapple the trembling green leaves and thought about all this business of humping and roiling about on mattresses and in stacks of hay. I knew what they *did*, of course, had since I was nine—the man got hard and stuck his thing between the woman's legs and they wiggled around and thrashed their limbs—but what I didn't understand was *why*. Seemed kind of clumsy to me, seemed kind of silly as well. Eppie claimed it was supposed to be fun, but what did she know? Me, I'd rather be curled up in a big leather chair with a book in my hands and the cat in my lap, a dish of lemon drops nearby.

Not that I ever had much chance to do *that*, I added to myself, not with all the chores Marie was always finding for me to do.

Better be on your way back, Angie, I told myself, and I began scooting backward, the bark scraping my knees a little. The limb wobbled, seemed to sway, and the leaves rattled. I lost my balance, swung around, and then I was hanging from the limb with my knees and my hands and the limb swayed wildly and I heard loud padding noises and then snarls and then savage barking, directly beneath me. I looked down and saw three ferocious greyhounds leaping up high and snapping, trying their best to sink their fangs into my backside which was just barely out of reach. Jemminy! I clung to the limb and felt my face turning white and knew I was a goner for sure unless I could swing back up onto the limb. The greyhounds leaped higher and higher, yowling fiercely, and one of 'em got his fangs into my faded pink cotton skirt that was dangling down and I felt it tearing and then a big patch of it was gone and the dog had it on the ground, shaking it in his jaws like it was a dead rabbit. The other two tried to take it away from him and they all began to fight.

Holding my breath, closing my eyes, summoning every ounce of strength I had, I swung my body up until I was stretched out flat on the limb again, looking down at the beasts, and then I seemed to freeze. I couldn't move. I could only stare in horror at the yowling, scrambling, snapping animals tearing that scrap of pink cotton into shreds. I had to get out of the tree, get onto the wall, get down to the ground on the other side, but my body was locked into place and I could scarcely breathe, much less scoot back along the limb. The dogs finally abandoned the cloth and started leaping at the limb again, fangs bared, eyes gleaming fiercely, lithe, nimble bodies leaping higher, higher still.

"Stay!" a voice roared.

The three greyhounds promptly sat back on their haunches and looked as innocent and harmless as lambs, wagging their stumps of tails playfully. I saw a man approaching—dirty black boots, soiled black breeches that clung to his long legs like a second skin, a coarse white cotton shirt with full bell sleeves gathered at the wrist, opened at the throat and all stained with sweat. I saw the dark, unruly hair on top of his head, and then he looked up and I saw his face and gulped, knowing I was *really* a goner this time. The Bastard scowled, staring up at me with savage eyes so dark a brown they seemed almost black. The dogs were whining and thumping their tails, waiting for instructions. I knew he was going to feed me to 'em, me just twelve with my whole life ahead of me.

"Come down out of that tree!" he ordered.

"Not on your life," I told him. My voice was surprisingly firm.

"Come down this instant!"

"Up your arse, you bleedin' sod!"

That incensed him. He balled his hands into fists,

scowling even more. I was still paralyzed with fright, but there was a curious excitement as well now, a bold, jaunty feeling inside that was almost pleasant, strange as that might be. He glared at me. I stuck my tongue out at him. I would have given him the finger, too, something I rarely did, but I was afraid to let go of my grip. He was breathing heavily, his chest rising and falling, angry as a bear, and here I was up in the tree, out of his reach, looking directly into those angry eyes. Eppie wouldn't believe a word of it.

"Little girl—" he began.

"I'm just four years younger than you, you sod. You ain't so bleedin' old yourself, so don't try patronizin' me."

"You got a tongue on you, don't you?"

"I ain't—aren't— I'm not afraid of *you*, that's for bloody sure."

I was lying, of course. I was scared spitless, but at the same time I was actually enjoying myself. Didn't make sense, I know, but that tingling excitement grew and grew until it was almost as strong as the fear. I suppose I was feeling what soldiers are said to feel when they are in the thick of battle and bullets are flyin' all around 'em, a curious elation in the face of mortal danger.

"I want you to come down," he said.

"So you can hang me by the thumbs? So you can put me on the rack? So you can feed me to the greyhounds? Fat bloody chance."

"I won't hurt you," he promised.

"Expect me to believe that? I know all about you. I know what you do to poor, innocent mites who fall into your clutches—" I was going good now, really beginning to get into it. "You take 'em to the stables and tie 'em up and stuff a gag into their mouths and get out the hot pincers and thumbscrews and laugh maniacally as you torture 'em for hours on end."

I thought I saw him smile. I couldn't be sure. He was as tall as Clinton Meredith and much leaner. Looked like a beanpole, he did, with his thin, foxlike face and wide, cruel mouth and those sleek black eyebrows that slanted up from the bridge of his nose and then arched and swept back down. *He* wasn't no beauty, that was for sure. His face was deeply tanned, and I could smell sweat and manure all the way up here.

"Will you come down if I send the dogs away?" he asked.

"I might," I said.

"Get!" he yelled.

He clapped his hands together smartly and the greyhounds yelped and scampered away. He stood there beneath the tree, ever so casual, waiting for me to swing down, but I wasn't about to be taken in by his tricks. He was a sly one, sure, thought he could sweet-talk me into lettin' my guard down. I was enjoying myself immensely now, not at all scared since the dogs had gone. I knew he didn't *really* torture poor mites, but it was fun to pretend he did. Gave me a cozy thrill.

"Are you coming down?" he asked. His voice was testy.

"What'll you do to me if I *do?*"

"I'll lead you around to the back gate and see you safely off the property."

"No thumbscrews? No hot pincers?"

"If you don't come down *this minute* I'm liable to choke you to death with my bare hands!"

"Go grab yourself," I taunted.

And then his dark eyes glittered and his wide mouth curled up at one corner and he jumped up and caught hold of a low-hanging branch and began to pull it savagely and the limb began to shake violently and it was like I was riding a bucking horse. I flopped and flipped, hanging on for dear life, my body banging against the rough bark, and then suddenly I was tumbling through space and a pair of strong arms caught me and both of us crashed to the ground as he lost his balance. The Bastard grunted loudly and blinked, stunned by the impact, and I tore free from his arms and leaped to my feet and he grabbed my ankle and gave it a jerk and I fell back down—splat!—landing flat on my chest.

I was dazed and dizzy and beginning to see black clouds all around, and then steely fingers clamped around my wrist and I felt myself being hauled to my feet. The clouds evaporated and I knew real terror when I saw the look in his eyes and knew the stories about him were probably *true*, and I balled up my hand into a tight fist and slammed it into his jaw and kicked his shin with my bare feet and tried my best to knee him in the groin, but he merely scooped me up under his arm and hauled me over to the marble bench and sat down on it and pulled me across his knees.

I screamed. He clamped a brutal hand over my mouth. He whipped up what was left of my skirt and whipped up my cotton petticoat and I squirmed furiously as I felt the cool air on my bare bottom, for I was wearing no underpants. He slammed his palm down and there was a loud popping noise like a gunshot and a hot stinging pain that made me jerk and squirm all the more. He spanked me thoroughly, viciously, all the while smothering my screams with his other hand, and while the pain was awful it wasn't nearly as bad as the humiliation. When he finally stopped, when he finally moved his hand from my mouth, I scrambled up and adjusted my clothing and looked at him through a silvery blur of tears I couldn't control.

He didn't say anything. He looked perfectly calm now, sitting there on the marble bench.

"I hate you!" I cried.

"I'm not surprised," he replied. "Most people do."

I rubbed my bottom and glared at him through the tears. They were spilling over my lashes now and streaming down my cheeks. Hugh Bradford was totally unmoved—for that was his name, Hugh Bradford. They weren't likely to call him Hugh *Meredith,* were they? My bottom was smarting something terrible, but it wasn't hurt nearly as much as my pride. No one had ever spanked me before, and I felt curiously weak and vulnerable, not myself at all.

"Come," he said, getting to his feet. "I'll take you to the back gate. Why aren't you wearing shoes?"

"I never wear shoes. I hate 'em."

"Don't wear underpants, either, do you?"

"You're a brute!"

Hugh Bradford grinned to himself. I flushed.

He took hold of my wrist and started walking through the gardens, tugging me along beside him. He was awfully tall—I barely came up to his chest—and he was as lean as a whip. You wouldn't think anyone so thin could be so tough and powerful. One thick black V-shaped wave slanted across his brow, the point just above his right eyebrow. I'd never seen anyone with such a dark tan, such wicked eyebrows. His nose was long and thin, his mouth much too wide, the lower lip full and curving. He wasn't no beauty, true, but that foxlike face was striking. You weren't likely to forget it.

"What were you doing up in that tree?" he inquired.

"Spyin'," I said, "and I saw plenty, too—I can tell you for sure."

"It's not nice to spy on people."

"Who said I was nice? Ask anyone you know about Angie Howard and they'll tell you I'm a terror. I got—have—a dreadful reputation for gettin' into mischief, gettin' into scrapes. I'm as tough as any boy," I added.

"I don't doubt it," The Bastard replied.

He sounded bored, and that aggravated me. Even though he was a mere four years older than me, I could see he considered himself an adult, considered me a child, unworthy of serious notice, and for some reason I wanted to look important in his eyes. I wanted him to see me as something more than a pesky brat. Even though he had spanked me—hard, too—and even though his fingers were digging into my wrist and he was jerking me along beside him not at all gently, I wasn't angry with him anymore. Maybe it was because, when they weren't smoldering with anger, those dark brown eyes of his looked so sad and . . . resigned. Couldn't be much fun bein' a bastard, havin' everyone know it.

"Howard," he said. "Any kin to Solonge Howard?"

"She's my stepsister. You *know* her?"

"I've met her," he said dryly.

Now *that* was interesting. Solonge had come home one day a few months ago and said she'd seen him walking down the lane and said he was utterly un*couth*, but she hadn't said she'd *met* him. Solonge looked like a vision and acted ever so refined, just like Janine. She was always bringing home stockings and ribbons and perfume and such. How she came by 'em was a mystery indeed.

"Solonge is a beauty," I said. "So is Janine. I'm the plain one in the family."

He didn't disagree, and that riled me a bit. He could have at least said I had nice eyes. Solonge was right. He *was* uncouth, a skinny, gawky lout who smelled of sweat and manure and be*longed* in the stables. I stubbed my toe and stumbled. He gave my arm a rough jerk, almost pullin' it out of its socket. I cried out in protest, but he kept right on walking, tugging me along like I was some kind of unwanted baggage.

"I may not be a beauty," I said tartly, "but I'm smarter'n either one of 'em. Read all the time, I do. When I'm not doin' chores or climbin' trees or gatherin' mushrooms in the woods, I'm always readin' books—grownup books, too. I ain't—I'm not interested in ribbons and laces and attractin' a rich man like those two. I'm gonna *do* things with my life."

"Shouldn't wonder if you did," he replied, voice dry as dust. "You're Stephen Howard's daughter."

That startled me. What did *he* know about my father? His face was as cool and bored as ever, and he gave my arm another jerk as he led me through the back gardens. The greyhounds came leaping out again, prancing all about us as friendly as pups, and Hugh Bradford spoke to them sharply and they looked woeful and disappointed and loped away. From the distance came the merry, tinkling noises of the garden party.

"I wanted to see the swells," I said suddenly. "That's why I climbed over the wall and up in the tree. I saw 'em passin' through the village in their fancy carriages and—and I wanted to get a better look at 'em."

"And did you see them?" he inquired.

"I—I saw two of 'em," I replied, thinking it best not to identify them. "They were dressed ever so grandly—velvet and satin and laces. Me, I'd love to wear velvet and satin. I'd love to be beautiful."

My voice was wistful, rather sad, not like me at all. Why was I telling these things to him? Why did I feel so...well, *close* to him? Didn't make a bloody bit of sense. He was as ugly as sin and mean as hell and my bottom still stung and I had every reason to *hate* him, but instead I felt this curious sympathy and *kin*ship like him and me—he and I—were somehow two of a kind, like neither of us belonged. Get hold of yourself, Angie, I scolded. That fall must've addled your brains.

There were a lot of big, thick shrubs in back of the gardens, all green and overgrown, and The Bastard led me through them and to a rusted iron gate in the back wall. He opened it and spread his right palm against the small of my back and gave me a brutal shove. I pitched forward and stumbled through the gate and almost fell down. I whirled around and glared at him with angry defiance, and Hugh Bradford gazed back at me with bored indifference as though I were a worrisome but harmless gnat. Stood there like a gawky scarecrow, he did, tall as a beanpole, thin as a whip, boots muddy and breeches too tight, loose white shirt sweaty and soiled, that dark wave dipping across his brow like a lopsided V. I gave him the finger. His wide mouth curled slightly at one corner in what might have been another grin.

"Don't ever let me catch you around here again," he told me. "Next time I just might *use* the thumbscrews."

"Sod you," I said hotly.

The Bastard *did* grin then, no mistake, and I glared at him for another moment or so and then tilted my chin and marched haughtily away. I heard a clang as he closed the gate, heard leaves rustling as he moved back through the thick shrubbery, and then there was just the sound of the breeze rustling the grass and making the daisies dance. I went back around the wall and

retrieved the basket of eggs and started home, daw-
dling, lost in thought. I decided I wouldn't say a word
to Eppie Dawson. Something *strange* had happened to
me there in that garden. Silly goose like her wouldn't
understand at all. I wasn't sure I understood it myself.

Chapter Two

As I sauntered down the lane with elm trees making
shadowy patterns on the sunny road, my bottom still
throbbed, still felt warm and prickly, but the sensation
wasn't at all unpleasant. My knees were scratched and
my face was probably dirty, but that didn't concern me.
I was worried about my torn skirt which, I knew, would
give Marie conniptions. Marie wasn't cruel, just bitterly
disappointed with her lot, buried alive in a rustic back-
wash, she felt, but her sarcasm could be devastating.
Shrewd, shrewish, she faced life with a tight mouth and
glittering yellow-green eyes that missed nothing. My
ruined skirt would be just another example of the sad
lot she had to bear.

My own mother had died from complications three
days after I was born, and six months later my bereaved
father had left me with a wet nurse and gone for a
much-needed holiday in Brittany, and it was there that
he met the French widow with two young daughters.
In her early thirties, Marie de Valois was vivacious,
attractive and quite desperate. Although she claimed

an impressive aristocratic background, she was completely impoverished, living in cheap lodgings and taking in sewing in order to pay for food and rent. The handsome English schoolmaster must have seemed a godsend to her. My father extended his holiday. When he returned, he had a new wife and two beautiful stepdaughters whom he legally adopted shortly thereafter. The chic, sharp-tongued Frenchwoman had detested life in our village from the first, always contemptuous, always an outsider, and though her husband provided a secure, comfortable home, he provided none of the frills and fripperies she felt essential for civilized living.

Passing the bank of rhododendrons with their lush purple blossoms and dark green leaves, I turned and started toward our cottage. Of mellow golden-beige stone with a thick, grayish-brown thatched roof, it was the largest in the village, which, as Marie pointed out, was hardly a distinction. It was on the outskirts of the village, actually, with pleasantly ragged flower beds in front and two large oak trees that provided bountiful shade. Our fat gray tabby was lazing on the front steps and waved her tail idly as I passed. Snug, comfortable, mellow with age, the house seemed to welcome me as I stepped inside the shadowy front hall with its worn oriental carpet, murky mirror and worn but lovely rosewood table.

I heard Janine and Solonge talking as I passed the parlor on my way to the kitchen in back of the house. Marie was at the counter, wearing a dark garnet silk dress and a black apron. She was kneading dough, intent on her work, her lips pressed tightly together. There was a wonderful smell of spices and freshly baked bread. Three golden-brown loaves were cooling on a rack placed on the window ledge. Marie might be testy and shrewish, but she was a marvelous cook, preparing the fanciest meals with little or no visible effort. Grand pastries. Delicious sauces. Not for us the bland meat and vegetables that sustained the rest of the village. I set the basket of eggs down. Marie turned, scrutinizing me with those shrewd yellow-green eyes.

Tall and bony, my stepmother had faded orange-blonde hair that had once been a lustrous red-gold, worn atop her head in a stack of waves with short, curly ringlets spilling over her brow. Her thin, sharp-featured face was invariably painted, and the cosmetics she skillfully—and generously—applied only stressed her years, the blue-gray lids and rouged cheekbones and scarlet lips giving her the somehow pathetic look of all middle-aged women who strive to look younger. It was a harsh, waspish face, the glittering eyes alive with bitter discontent. Marie longed for London, longed for activity, longed to be among people who could help her daughters get ahead, but in eleven and a half years she had been unable to pry my father away from his snug nest here in the country.

"You took your time about it," she snapped, eyeing the eggs.

"I hurried as fast as I could," I lied.

"And you've torn your dress! Another expense. Climbing trees again, I suppose. Running wild through the woods like a red Indian, always covered in dirt, scratches on your knees—I despair! I despair!" She shook her head, the dangling jet earrings she always wore swaying to and fro. "Don't run off again," she cautioned. "I'll be needing you to set the table in half an hour or so."

Got off lucky, I did. That tongue of hers wasn't nearly as scathing as usual. It wasn't that Marie was vicious—she wasn't, nor was she particularly malicious—but I was merely someone whose presence she tolerated, without affection, without interest, a nuisance to be endured as she endured the dreariness of country life. Marie gave an exasperated sigh and turned back to her dough, and I scurried out of the kitchen, snatching an apple off the counter as I did so, relieved she hadn't bombarded me with questions. I moved back down the hall and peered into the parlor where my stepsisters were idly chatting, Solonge standing at the window, Janine stretched out on the sofa as was her wont, a glossy light-blue box of bonbons beside her.

Ordinarily being plain wasn't so bad. Most of the time I didn't think about it, but when I was in the presence of two exquisite creatures like my stepsisters, I was painfully aware of my mousy-brown hair, my too large mouth and the light freckles scattered across cheekbones that were much too high. I couldn't help feelin' gawky and awkward with those two so lush and opulent, so sleek and lovely. Solonge was only fifteen, but she already had a body that made all the boys pant and a face usually referred to as piquant. Her hair was a glistening pale red-gold, tumbling to her shoulders in thick, glossy waves. Her eyes were a lively hazel, more green than brown, her nose a dream, her mouth perfect, pink as a rosebud. Solonge had freckles, too, but hers were pale gold and only made her face all the more enchanting. She reminded me of some gorgeous, vivacious pixie, though Solonge was much worldlier than any pixie I ever heard about. Wearing a dark pink dress cut almost as low as Laura's, she gazed out the window, the sunlight turning her hair to molten gold.

If Solonge was lively and restless, full of energies she found hard to repress, Janine was just the opposite. With silver-blonde hair and limpid blue eyes and a complexion like cream, she was as lethargic as she was lovely, always lolling about in placid indolence. Taller than her sister, with a large, voluptuous body, she was so beautiful you could scarce believe it with her delicately flushed cheeks and generous pink mouth. If Solonge made the boys pant, Janine made them stare in awe, but, unlike Solonge, she seemed totally unaware of their interest. Solonge thrived on masculine attention, encouraged it with capricious abandon. Janine found it utterly tiresome. Her sky-blue skirt rumpled, lacy petticoat showing, she idly reached for another bonbon and popped it into her mouth.

"If you keep stuffing yourself with those, you're going to get *fat*," Solonge informed her, turning away from the window. "Statuesque is one thing. *Plump* is quite another."

"Who cares?" Janine inquired lazily. "*You* brought the chocolates home, sister dear."

"I have the good sense not to eat them. I could scarcely refuse them—Johnny Martin felt he was doing me *such* a favor, giving them to me. I thought Angie might like them, didn't know you were going to make a pig of yourself on them."

"Johnny Martin, was it?" Janine yawned. "*Maman* know about it?"

"His father is one of the richest men in the country and Johnny is going to Oxford next year. *Maman* knows. *Maman* approves. All hands and mouth, he is, never knew a man quite so horny."

"And?"

"I told him I wasn't that kind of girl. A little white lie never hurts now and then."

"You're incorrigible, Solonge," her sister scolded.

"I also have a drawer full of stockings and a solid gold locket. *Maman* doesn't know about the locket, so keep your mouth shut."

"Johnny?"

"William Randolph."

Janine lazily elevated one brow. "He's little better than a hooligan, not a penny in his pocket. Must have stolen the locket."

"But he has *such* shoulders," Solonge said.

Both girls looked up as I took a bite of apple and munched it. Solonge frowned. Janine smiled faintly. I sauntered into the parlor, taking another bite of apple.

"How much did you hear?" Solonge asked sharply.

"Enough," I replied, "and I think William Randolph's a dolt, always showin' off, thinkin' he's God's gift just because he has blond hair and smoky-blue eyes and a body by Michelangelo."

"What would *you* know about it?" Solonge snapped.

"Eppie Dawson and I spied on him last time he went swimming in the river. We were hiding among the willows. He wudn't wearin' a stitch. His thing's as big as a stallion's."

"That explains it," Janine said wryly, reaching for another chocolate. "Who is this Michelangelo?"

"He was an artist, you ninny," Solonge informed her, "sculpted a lot of naked men. If you say *one word*, Angie—"

"I never tattle," I replied airily, "you know that. Eppie Dawson says girls who chase after boys like you do always end up in trouble."

"Girls who end up in trouble are inexcusably careless, and Eppie Dawson is a smart-mouthed little brat who doesn't know beans. I brought these chocolates home for you. You'd better take them before Janine makes herself ill."

"You don't have to bribe me. I won't squeal."

"They're not a bribe. I thought you might *like* them."

I took a final bite of apple, chucked the core out the open window and removed the box of chocolates from Janine's reach, placing the glossy blue lid on top and setting the box on the mantelpiece. Janine yawned again and stretched out full length on the gray velvet sofa, her silvery-blonde hair spilling heavily over the cushions. Her sky blue skirt and lacy petticoats slipped back to reveal a considerable amount of naked calf.

Solonge still looked testy, not at all pleased that I had overheard their conversation. She knew I wouldn't squeal, though. Solonge was wild and worldly and had a tongue almost as sharp as her mother's, but she was genuinely fond of me and treated me with what I could only call bitchy affection, as opposed to Janine who lazed through life with sleepy indifference and was fond of nothing but naps.

"What's the matter with Marie?" I asked. "She seems to be off her mettle this afternoon, didn't snap at me nearly as bad as she usually does, and I was at least an hour late with the eggs."

"She's out of joint because Solonge and I weren't invited to Master High and Mighty Clinton Meredith's birthday party," Janine said wearily. "We're gentry, you know. Our *step*father might be a mere schoolmaster, but our father was the great grandson of the Marquis de Valois."

"So she claims," Solonge said. "I, for one, am bored to tears with her incessant babble about our supposed genealogy. Our father was an underpaid advocate who died without leaving her a sou. I'm not even sure she was *married* to him."

"Probably wasn't," Janine agreed, burrowing against the cushions. "She can be so tiresome at times. Who *cares* who our grandfather was?"

"Ridiculous of her to think we'd be invited to Greystone Hall. We've never been asked before, and it's not likely we'll be asked in the future. Families like the Merediths don't associate with the hoi polloi, and, supposed genealogy aside, that's what we are in their eyes— hoi polloi, two flashy trollops from the village."

"Speak for yourself, sister dear."

"I was at Greystone Hall this afternoon," I told them.

That got their attention, all right. Janine actually sat up, and Solonge stared at me in patent disbelief.

"Well, I wudn't actually *there*," I added, "but I climbed up the wall and into a tree and *watched* for a while. I saw Master Clinton—he looks just like a prince, much better lookin' than William Randolph, ever so elegant. He was wearing satin and laces and spoke in a voice like thick honey."

"You *spied* on him?" Solonge exclaimed.

"For quite a while. He was cuddlin' up a lady named Laura—she was wearin' a dark blue velvet gown, and he popped his hand into her bodice and pulled her teat out and squeezed it until her nipple got hard as a cherry pit."

"Lady Laura Troy," Solonge said, "I've read about her in the society columns—heard she was coming down to Greystone Hall. She's a tramp."

"I thought maybe I'd get to see 'em copulatin'," I continued, "but they decided to wait until tonight. He's going to her room."

"This perpetual spying of yours is going to get you into serious trouble one day," Janine informed me.

"It already *has*," I confessed. "Soon as they wandered off these three huge greyhounds came galloping up and started barking and leaping at me and I almost fell out of the tree. One of 'em got hold of my skirt, that's why it's torn. They would've had me for sure if Hugh Bradford hadn't come along."

At the mention of his name, Solonge's greenish hazel eyes lighted up with new interest, but she strove to hide it, idly brushing her dark pink skirt and pretending to be indifferent.

"What did he do?" Janine asked.

"Shook the tree till I fell out. Then he spanked me."

"*Spanked* you!" Solonge exploded.

"Hard," I said.

"That son of a bitch! How *dare* he lay a hand on you! I—I'll take a horsewhip to him, that's what I'll do! If he thinks he can brutalize *my* little sister without paying for it he's due a very big surprise!"

Janine smiled another faint, secretive smile, and I suspected she knew something I didn't about her sister and Hugh Bradford. Solonge's cheeks were a vivid pink. Her eyes were snapping green-brown fire. She looked absolutely gorgeous all riled up like that.

"I guess I deserved it," I told her. "He was—well, kinda nice afterwards, in a funny sort of way. I didn't really *mind* the spanking."

"The man's a brute!"

"I'd leave it be, sister dear," Janine said languidly. "He may be tall and dark and terribly attractive with those quirky, brooding good looks, but he's no William Randolph, he's no Johnny Martin you can wrap around your little finger. He's a primitive, crude and rough and totally without scruples. You may have a yen for him, but a boy like that could only spell trouble for a greedy little girl with more hunger than sense."

"Go to hell!"

"Just thinking of your welfare, love."

"I wouldn't give Hugh Bradford the time of day."

"The time of day, no."

"Bitch!"

"It runs in the family."

Solonge glared at her sister, and Janine yawned and nestled her shoulders against the cushions, sinking deeper into the sofa. Yen? How could a gorgeous creature like Solonge have a yen for a surly brute like The Bastard? And what did Janine mean by "with more hunger than sense"? How could you be hungry for someone unless you were a cannibal? Puzzled me.

"I'd love another chocolate," Janine drawled.

"You're not gettin' one," I snapped. "You've already eaten half of 'em."

"Stingy gut."

"Sod you!"

"Angie, dear," Solonge said sweetly, "I'd like for you to do a favor for me."

I was instantly suspicious. I always was when she employed that particular tone of voice.

"You know that new dress of mine—the one Marie had made up for me?"

"The turquoise silk with all the beige lace and pink velvet bows?"

"That's the one. You're such a wizard with needle and thread. I'd like for you to remove all the lace, remove all the bows. Marie's idea of fashion is looking like a wedding cake. Could you do it for me?"

"Easy as pie."

"I'd also like for you to take it in two inches at the waist and lower the neckline two inches as well."

"Two inches! You'd never be able to wear it in public."

"That needn't concern you."

"Takin' in the waist, lowerin' the neckline—that'd involve an awful lot of work. It'd take me hours and hours."

"I'd make it worth your while."

"Oh?"

"That set of books at Blackwood's, the one you've been eyeing every time you pass the window. I'll buy it for you."

Blackwood's was our village bookstore, directly across

the square from the amber-brick schoolhouse where Father held classes, and I had indeed been eyeing the Strawberry Hill Press edition of Horace Walpole's *The Castle of Otranto*. I knew a bargain when I heard one, and I agreed to alter the dress for her. Two inches tighter at the waist, neckline two inches lower! Marie would have conniptions for sure, but then I doubted Solonge intended to model it for her. I wondered if she planned to wear it for Hugh Bradford.

"Just *one* more chocolate?" Janine asked plaintively.

I took the box of chocolates from the mantel and held them firmly, ignoring her question. "Father home?" I asked.

"He hasn't any classes this afternoon," Solonge said. "He's in his study, poring over the parcels that arrived from London this morning. Where *else* would he be? I'll bring the dress up to your room after dinner, pet."

Leaving them to their gossip, I took the box of chocolates up to my room and put them away, then hurried back downstairs and went to my father's study. The door was closed. It always was. In a house overrun by women, constantly, perpetually surrounded by them, harried by their moods and whims and bored by their chatter, Father had to have a retreat, and he sternly forbade any female to step foot inside the study without his express permission. Janine and Solonge hadn't been inside it in years, which distressed neither of them. Marie wasn't even allowed in to tidy up. Despite this I opened the door and stepped inside without a moment's hesitation. Father didn't consider me one of the "females." We had a special relationship, Father and I. We were friends as well as father and daughter, allies against the female tyranny that prevailed throughout the rest of the house.

The study was my favorite room, too, small and sunny with windows looking out over the oak tree and shaggy gardens at the side of the house. There was a huge, battered old desk, two comfortable chairs covered in worn green velvet, a stool, a globe of the world that stood in one corner and a small tan marble fireplace. The room was awash with books and journals, papers and pamphlets, books crowding the shelves that covered the walls, stacked on the floor in untidy heaps, papers, pamphlets everywhere. Father had recently opened the parcels from London—books, of course—and the floor around the desk was littered with crumpled brown paper and coils of twine. The room smelled of ink and glue and dust and old leather, a heavenly smell I savored.

Father sat hunched over the desk, examining a new volume, a precarious pile of books at his elbow. Immersed in print, which, like me, he loved and needed as an addict his opium, he hadn't heard me come in, and I paused for a moment to look at him, feeling that great rush of love I always felt whenever I saw him again after a few hours. The feisty, smart-mouthed Angie became a different person in his presence, sedate and adoring.

In his early fifties—he had married late, had been married some time before I was born—my father had thick, tousled hair that had faded to a pale gold, liberally streaked with silver now. Though still handsome, his face was worn, his skin like fine old ivory parchment, and his intelligent gray eyes always seemed a bit bemused. Wearing an old, once splendid brown frock coat, a rumpled yellow neckcloth and an ancient tan vest, he looked every inch the genteel, distinguished scholar he was.

Father looked up and saw me and sighed, reluctantly pulling himself away from the pages he found so immersing.

"Well, Pumpkin," he said, "I see you've survived another day. There are a number of new scratches, I observe, and your skirt appears to be torn. I'm sure your stepmother was delighted to discover that."

"She was less than elated."

"I assume you've been getting into mischief again."

"A little," I confessed.

"Pumpkin, Pumpkin—" Father shook his head. "What am I to do with you?"

I grinned. He grinned, too, and closed the book, carefully marking his place with a piece of paper. Father and I rarely hugged. It wasn't necessary. The love and affection was like a palpable thing between us, enfolding us both in its cozy warmth.

"Anything interesting?" I asked, examining the pile of new books.

"Mostly dull history tomes. Nothing bloody or bawdy enough to suit your fancy, I fear."

"What about this?"

I pulled a book from the pile. It was entitled *A General History of The Most Famous Highwaymen* by a Captain Charles Johnson and was extremely battered, the pages thumbmarked and threatening to fall loose. Sunlight streamed lazily through the windows and made wavering patterns on the floor as I turned the pages and looked at the crude but fascinating engravings.

"I forgot about that. It was sent along by mistake, apparently got mixed up with the titles I requested. It was published in 1734, looks it, too. The binding's in tatters. I suppose I'll have to send it back," he added, and he sighed again, as though the task were completely beyond him.

"Let's keep it," I suggested. "I've always adored highwaymen."

My father smiled his vague, indulgent smile, the one he reserved exclusively for me. "Handsome, dashing creatures in long black capes and rakish black masks," he said, "wielding pistols with aplomb. A romantic image, I confess, but the reality would fall far short."

"Have you ever *met* one?"

"Haven't had the privilege," he admitted, "though I'm sure they're a vile, bloodthirsty lot, pockmarked and puny and far from a maiden's prayer. Keep the book if you like, Pumpkin. It's probably no bloodier than some of those thundering melodramas Solonge sneaks home to you."

"I read *good* books, too!" I protested.

"Sometimes I fear you read altogether too much," he said, though I could tell he didn't mean it. "What kind of wild, unprincipled prodigy have I sired? You're twelve years old and far, far too knowing for your age, and far too mischievous, too, I might add. No wonder your step-mother is always in a state."

"Would you like me to grow up to be like Solonge and Janine?" I asked.

"God forbid."

"Janine's a slug," I confided, "but Solonge is not so bad."

"Solonge is destined to bring ruin and destruction to any number of unfortunate men. It's in her blood, though she's singularly lacking in malice or spite. No, Pumpkin, I wouldn't have you grow up to be like either of your stepsisters."

"At least they're *beau*tiful."

"They're gloriously lovely, yes, and I fear that will be their downfall. You, my darling, have your own kind of beauty."

"I'd rather have glossy blonde hair and blue eyes," I informed him.

Father chuckled, shuffled some papers aside and stood up. He was tall, a bit stooped, a bit overweight, though far from fat. In his youth he must have been glorious himself, I mused, but all the years of living with Marie, all the years of trying to drum a smattering of knowledge into the heads of recalcitrant schoolboys had taken their toll. I loved him with all my heart and soul and saw him through a haze of rapt adoration, but even so I knew he was not a happy man. The wry humor, the amiability and gentle, distracted manner failed to conceal the aura of sadness and lost dreams. Strange though it might be, I often felt I was the adult, he the child, and I felt a strong protective feeling toward him. I took his hand and squeezed it, expressing emotions mere words couldn't convey.

Father smiled again and patted me on top of the head, and then, looking at the litter of paper and twine as though wondering how it got there, he began to place the new books on the shelves, wedging them in wherever he could find an inch or two of space.

"And what particular mischief have you been getting into today?" he inquired.

"Nothing much. I—uh—I was with The Bastard today, Father."

"Indeed? I assume you're referring to Hugh Bradford?"

I nodded. "He—he *spanked* me."

"Oh?" He wasn't at all perturbed. "And how did this shocking event occur?"

"I—well, I guess you could say I was trespassin', but the sod still didn't 'ave—have—any right to blister my backside."

"I would imagine you were quite taken aback," he remarked, shoving one of the books into a space much too small for it. "First time you've ever been spanked, I assume. Why don't you tell me about it?"

I sighed and gave him a carefully expurgated account of the event, leaving Clinton and Laura out completely, embroidering the rest of it quite a bit, presenting a most satisfactory drama with myself as wronged heroine. Father continued to put up the books, apparently giving me only half his attention. When I finished he sighed and lifted a long, graceful hand to shove an errant pale gold lock from his brow.

"That's done," he remarked wearily. "One of these days I'm going to be forced to *do* something about all these books."

"Don't you *care* that he spanked me?"

"I'm sure you deserved it, Pumpkin."

"I guess I *was* awfully cheeky," I confessed. "I—strangely enough, I didn't—I didn't really *mind* it, not—not afterwards. For some reason I felt—felt kinda *sorry* for him."

"Hugh's lot has not been a pleasant one, Pumpkin."

"You—you *know* him?"

"Quite well, though it's been a long while since I've seen him. He's a very intelligent young man, polite and mannerly, far better bred than Master Clinton. Offhand I would say young Hugh was far and away the most satisfying student I've ever had."

I was dreadfully shocked. "Surely he didn't attend *clas*ses," I exclaimed.

"I fear the good people of our region would never tolerate anything so unseemly," my father replied. "Righteous fathers would have yanked their sons out of school posthaste—there would have been a mass evacuation, I assure you. No, I tutored young Hugh privately, after hours, when everyone assumed I was grading exams. I saw him hanging about the schoolyard one day, looking sullenly but longingly at the fine-scrubbed, fine-dressed young gentlemen trooping out after classes. He must have been eight or nine years old at the time, unkempt and dirty, quite the young ruffian. No shoes, if I recall, a wretched looking specimen indeed."

"And?" I prompted.

"And I noticed him several more times during the weeks that followed and I saw the hunger in his eyes, hunger for knowledge. Late one afternoon I was alone in my classroom—the school was quite empty—and I saw him outside and went out and brought him in."

"What did he do?"

"He kicked my shin."

"Sounds just like him," I said, plopping down on the low round leather stool near the fireplace. I was still holding Captain Johnson's book on highwaymen, and I cradled it against my nonexistent bosom, watching Father wedge the last book onto a shelf.

He sighed and moved back over to the desk, idly peering at the piles of paper, seeing instead a dark, dirty little boy with a sullen mouth and brown eyes hungry for knowledge.

"I sat him down at one of the desks and gave him a severe lecture on behavior and he scowled fiercely and looked as though he might hurl the inkwell at me. Lad reminded me of a cornered animal—I was quite touched, I must confess. When I saw him eyeing the books longingly, I became very brusque and asked if he would be willing to come in every afternoon after the others had gone and help me tidy up the room—sweep the floor, clean the chalkboard, straighten the books and papers. It was a ploy, of course, but I knew the lad was far too proud to accept any kind of charity."

"He agreed?"

"And in return I gave him private lessons. He snuck down the alleyway in back of the school, came in through the back entrance so no one would see him. He tidied up the room while I graded exams, and then we had our lessons."

"Could he read and write?"

"Barely, but he was amazingly quick. *Amazing*ly quick, far outstripping all my other students in curiosity, native intelligence, aptitude. We had a most pleasant relationship for several years, Hugh absorbing learning like a sponge absorbs water. No one ever knew. It was our secret. I grew quite fond of the boy. He was always borrowing books, asking for more. Alas, he had to stop coming a year and a half ago—his duties at Greystone Hall left him no more time for the luxury of learning. He informed me of the fact with no little bitterness. I was sad to see the last of him."

I was sad, too, deeply touched by what my father had told me. He shuffled some more papers and sat down at the desk, a wavering ray of sunlight touching his brow, gilding his pale gold hair. He looked older then, weary, almost frail, and I felt a moment of terrible panic at the thought of someday losing him. The panic stabbed me, sharp as a knife, and I bit my lower lip, longing to rush to him and hug him and beg him never to leave me, then he looked at me fondly and smiled and everything was all right again.

"A pitiful case," he said, "a pitiful case indeed. Poor Hugh hasn't had much chance."

"It—it must be dreadful to be a bastard," I said quietly.

"I shouldn't imagine it would be pleasant, people being what they are. Ours is a hypocritical age, Pumpkin. A hypocrite is something I trust you'll never be."

I felt guilty then, for I had talked about The Bastard and made fun of him like everyone else. I shifted uncomfortably on the stool, holding the book tightly. Father looked at me with those lovely gray eyes, as though he could read my mind. I looked at the littered floor, studying the crumpled brown paper and bits of twine with apparent fascination, a slow flush tinting my cheeks. Father sighed and shook his head.

"There's some question as to whether or not Hugh actually *is* illegitimate," he said. "When Lord Meredith first came back from Italy with the boy, everyone assumed he had married the Italian woman. He was treated as a grief-stricken widower by one and all, and then he went to London and met the current Lady Meredith—a lovely thing she was then, cool and patrician and haughty as they come. But lovely, a vision of loveliness. When Lord M. brought her back to Greystone Hall, everything had changed. She was expecting a child, you see, and she wanted *her* son to inherit. Talk was that she had made his disowning Hugh one of the conditions of her marrying the noble Lord M."

"But that—that's dreadful," I said hotly. "Disowning his own son, pretending he wasn't his rightful—"

"All this was just talk, Pumpkin. No one knows for sure if there was a wedding in Italy or not. Hugh was given the name 'Bradford' and when Lady M. gave birth to a son he was declared heir. Hugh, perforce, was a bastard. People forgot all about that hypothetical wedding in Italy, assuming quite naturally that it had never taken place."

I found this quite fascinating, a bit confusing as well. Father picked up a paperweight and toyed with it as the sunlight grew dimmer and hazy shadows began to fill the room. I could smell Marie's cooking and knew I would soon have to go set the table.

"The baby died a month later," Father continued. "Lady M. was never able to bear another. Her looks faded fast. Drink had a lot to do with it, I fancy. When his brother and sister-in-law were killed in a boating accident in Cornwall, Lord Meredith brought his young nephew to Greystone Hall. Master Clinton will inherit the estate."

"And Hugh sleeps in the stables."

"As I said, a pitiful case indeed. The boy is rightfully bitter. Legitimate or no—and he probably isn't—he has been treated most shamefully, but Lady Meredith took an intense dislike to him from the first—Hugh was three when Lord M. married her. Lord M. never had a great deal of character to begin with, and women—" He hesitated, a delicate frown creasing his brow. "Beautiful women can exert a—an inordinate amount of influence on a weak man."

He fell silent, a curious look in his eyes, and somehow I knew he was thinking of Marie. Marie had been very beautiful when he married her. Had she exerted "an inordinate amount of influence" on him? Had he been forced to abandon dreams, give up plans of scholastic glory? That history he was forever scribbling on—perhaps he could have finished it long ago had he not taken on a wife and two more daughters to support. He turned to stare out the window where a translucent blue-gray haze was filling the gardens, and then he sighed heavily and moved some papers about on his desk. Marie called me from the kitchen, her shrill voice clearly audible through closed doors. I got up and thanked Father for the book and told him I would see him at dinner and moved toward the door.

"Angie—"

I turned. "Yes?"

"What I've told you is—between us. There's no need for anyone else to know I gave young Hugh private tutoring. And Angie—" He frowned again, looking quite stern. "The boy has endured a lot of grief. I don't ever want to hear you call him 'The Bastard' again."

"I—I won't," I promised.

"Good. Now off with you. I want to get a little work done before facing the Gabbling Pack."

The Pack did indeed gabble during dinner. Solonge went on and on about a perfectly cunning bonnet she had seen with the most fetching green ostrich plumes dripping over the wide brim, it would look perfectly smashing on her, with her eyes, and Janine told her it

should be easy enough to acquire, like the locket. Solonge shot her a warning look and Janine smiled lazily,
refilling her plate. Marie said it was a shame, a wretched
shame her girls had to languish away in a stultifying
place like this when we could all be happily ensconced
in London, enjoying life. Father could easily get a post
there at one of the schools or he could take private
students and her girls could get out and *meet* people.
She gave full vent to her bitterness, and Father merely
shrugged, immune to her complaints after all this time.

I helped Marie clear the table and then she joined
her daughters in the parlor to complain some more. I
could hear her shrill, unhappy voice as I washed the
dishes and tidied up the kitchen, a task I really didn't
mind too much. Father was shut up in his study again,
scribbling away on his history of the Assyrians, and
later, after I fed the tabby, I trudged back up to my attic
room to discover that Solonge had already brought the
turquoise silk gown up, tossing it carelessly across a
chair.

Solonge and Janine had comfortable rooms on the
second floor, but I much preferred my snug, cozy room
up here under the eaves with its bare hardwood floor
and slanting ceiling and low, odd-shaped windows that
looked over the back lawn. A feather comforter and
faded sky-blue counterpane covered the old four poster.
The ancient overstuffed blue velvet chair was in de-
plorable shape, the nap worn to threads, one spring
broken, but it was large and seemed to enfold me when
I snuggled up in it to read or sew. There was a sturdy
table beside the bed with white porcelain pitcher and
pot, a small bookcase filled with my favorite books, a
tall wardrobe. Flickering candlelight washed over the
bare brown walls with a lovely golden glow. It began
to rain as I curled up in the chair with sewing kit and
turquoise gown, and the pleasant patter-patter made a
soothing background as I nimbly removed velvet bows
and rows of fussy beige lace.

As I worked I thought of all that had happened today,
all I had learned about Hugh Bradford, the sod. Sure,

I felt sorry for him, but... but he was still a crude lout with that striking, foxlike face, all sharp angles and planes, not at all handsome, not like Clinton, but... I couldn't forget that face, couldn't forget the strange, bewildering sensations I'd felt when he manhandled me so roughly. Bleedin' sod! My bottom no longer stung, but I felt a curious prickling feeling down below and my legs seemed to be growing numb. I shifted position in the big chair and, bows and laces removed, began to snip loose the tiny stitches that hemmed the neckline, the turquoise silk rustling and sliding over my lap. Solonge found him exciting, had a yen for him, she did, would like to wrestle with him in a stack of hay, have him stick his stiff thing in her, and him a beanpole smelling of sweat and manure. Couldn't understand it. Didn't make sense, not when she could have any man she wanted—and usually did. The prickling sensation down there wouldn't go away no matter how many times I shifted my rump and moved my legs. Wudn't really that worrisome just... just slightly irritating. I tried to ignore it, tried to think of something else besides the stableboy who had smacked my bottom so forcefully.

I worked for an hour or so in the candlelight and decided that Marie's rich sauce hadn't agreed with me tonight. I began to feel strange, strange indeed, kind of aching all over like... like an upset stomach, only lower down. My legs ached, too, but that wasn't unusual, climbing the wall, scooting along the tree limb like I did. Felt almost like I was coming down with some kind of fever, only it was different. I put the turquoise silk aside and stood up. My legs felt kinda shaky, the backs of my knees weak. I took off all my clothes and washed myself with water from the pitcher and dried myself off, then slipped on my thin cotton chemise, shivering now but strangely flushed. That ache down below was turning into an itching sensation that made me want to rub my private parts. I'd never felt so peculiar in my life. No more of Marie's fancy sauces for a while, I decided, and I intended to be extra careful climbing trees, too, if it was going to cause my legs and thighs to ache like this.

I blew out all the candles except the one by my bed and climbed under the covers and picked up Captain Johnson's book and started reading. Nothing I loved better than reading in bed, particularly if the rain was pattering on the roof and making slippery silver-gray patterns on all the windowpanes. I got caught up in the book immediately, but, curiously enough, I kept seeing Hugh Bradford in sweeping black cape, pistol in hand, his lower face covered with a black silk scarf. Ruffian like him would make a dandy highwayman, all right. I had been moved by everything Father had told me about him, but...he was still a ruffian, sullen and savage.

I read about Jacob Halsey, a dreadful rogue indeed, and he had Hugh Bradford's face, those dark brown eyes, those wicked eyebrows, that dark tan complexion and unruly black hair. "My pretty lamb," Halsey told the maiden he was about to rape, "an insurrection of an unruly member obliges me to make use of you; therefore I must mount thy alluring body, to the end that I may come into thee." The Bastard...Hugh...was saying that and his eyes were glowing and I was the maiden, shivering with fear and aching all over, particularly down below. My free hand slipped under the covers. I couldn't help it, that tingling ache was driving me barmy. My thighs tingled, too, like the skin was flushed and stretched too tight over my flesh.

I read on, rubbing, trying to assuage the ache, and came to the passage about Patrick O'Bryan, another rogue, even worse than Halsey. He looked like Hugh, too, and there I was, trembling at the side of the coach, and he turned to his confederates and grinned. "Before we tie and gag this pretty creature I must make bold to rob her of her maidenhead," and then he led me into the woods and I put the book down and stretched my legs as far as I could, writhing, rubbing, harder now, not really understanding what was happening to my body, what was happening in my mind. There I was and I was wearing the turquoise silk gown and I was on the ground, writhing, and he was standing over me with his cape blowing in the wind like black silk wings and the scarf was over his nose and mouth and chin and his brown eyes were glowing darkly and he was chuckling, legs wide apart, fists planted on his thighs, me helpless and all atremble.

I rubbed, eyes closed, and it felt... it felt good, like a thousand tiny needles jabbed my skin lightly, not really hurting, just irritating it pleasantly. Something was happening inside, too, something frightening I'd never felt before, and I stretched my legs until the tips of my toes touched the foot of the bed and something seemed to snap inside me and I could feel a flow and my hand was suddenly wet. I pulled it out from under the covers quick as I could and cried out when I saw all the blood. Scared me something awful, it did, thought I'd wounded myself, and then realization dawned and I caught my breath.

Jemminy! So that was it! I threw back the covers and dashed over to the pitcher and took off the chemise which was spotted with red. I washed myself, but there was still a trickle flowing. What did one do? Rags, Eppie Dawson had told me. You use clean rags. I folded one up and put it down there and climbed back into bed, shivering again, feeling awful, feeling frustrated. I hated it. I didn't want it to happen. I wanted to cry. I wanted to curl up in Father's lap and have him stroke my hair and tell me it would be all right. I wanted... I wanted to be in Hugh Bradford's arms. I wanted to look up into those smoldering brown eyes. I wanted him to... to do to me what Patrick O'Bryan did to his poor, defenseless victim.

No! No, it was disgusting! I hated him, the lout, and I wasn't ever goin' to let a man do that to me. I wasn't goin' to change. I wasn't goin' to be like Janine and Solonge, always thinkin' about men. Not me. I blew out the candle and listened to the rain and watched thin, thin rays of moonlight seeping into the room, all murky and making watery pewter reflections on the floor and

ceiling. I didn't want to start bleedin' every month. I
wanted to be like I was before this happened, before I
started havin' these disturbin' thoughts about the stableboy who might or might not be a bastard, who probably was, who had held me tight and spanked me soundly
and made me...made me feel all peculiar.

Time passed, hours probably, and the rain stopped,
just dripping from the eaves now, patter-patter, soft and
gentle, and the moonlight was brighter, making blurry
silver patterns that danced against the blue-black walls
and ceiling. I was feeling a little better now but still
strange and disoriented. My chest felt funny, the tiny
buds no bigger than beans aching, like flesh pushing
against warm skin. Next thing you knew I'd have
breasts, too, bloody inconvenient when you were climbing trees or scooting under shrubbery to find a smooth
round pebble. Thunderation! Wasn't anything I could
do about it, not a bloomin' thing. I wasn't going to let
it make any difference, though. I was going to go right
on being myself, just like before, and...there *was* a
bright side. I could hardly wait to see Eppie Dawson.
She wouldn't be so bloody superior when I told her *I*
was a woman, too, now.

Chapter Three

It was a warm spring afternoon and the village was peaceful and placid, too peaceful, too placid. At fifteen I had an inordinate thirst for high drama and excitement, something completely missing in my life. There had been no real drama since that day I had scrambled over the wall at Greystone Hall, and that had been three years ago. It seemed even longer. The feisty, rambunctious child had vanished, transformed into an awkward, too-tall fifteen-year-old subject to all the moods and contradictions of that age, silly as a goose one moment, silent and wistful the next. I hated being fifteen, hated it sorely. When *she* was fifteen Solonge was already a woman, mature and alluring. Me, I was like a gawky, skittish colt.

Eppie Dawson and I sauntered idly down High Street, warm sunshine washing the old brown cobbles and the rows of weathered tan shopfronts. Painted signs hung over the doorways, colors faded with age. Through the bakery window we could see the baker kneading his dough, a heavenly smell wafting out onto the pavement, and up ahead the knife sharpener was turning his stone, sparks flying as he honed the blade of a knife. A little boy with flaxen hair was playing with a dog across the street, tossing a stick the mutt fetched with a noticeable lack of enthusiasm, and a few village women were shopping, faces grim as they examined the bins of vegetables in front of the greengrocer's. Eppie kept an eye out for boys, but nary a husky lad appeared. I paused to look at the books in the window at Blackwood's but saw nothing of interest. I wanted splendor, spectacle, sensation, anything to relieve the tedious monotony that seemed to mark each day.

"I was hopin' Will Peterson might be hangin' around," Eppie said. "He lounges about the square sometimes when he idn't busy at his father's farm."

"Will Peterson's a dolt," I informed her.

"Oh, Will's all right. He's randy, always thinkin' about tail, true, but he's got a lot of charm."

"And a vocabulary of approximately twelve words," I added.

Eppie gave me an exasperated look and clicked her tongue, looking more than ever like a giraffe with her straw-colored hair piled up on top of her head, her enormous brown eyes, her long neck and tall, angular body. Eppie was a bore at times, but we'd been friends most of our lives and she was the only person I could really talk to. Eppie was a simple girl who never had a serious thought in her head, never worried or wondered about life, perfectly satisfied with her lot. Give her a shiny new hair ribbon and a rousing tryst with a muscular oaf like Will Peterson and she was blissfully content. Sometimes I almost envied her.

"You know what your problem is, Angie? Your problem is you need to get laid. *That*'d cure you of what ails you quick enough, I promise-ya."

"Bull," I said.

"It's ever so excitin', Angie, and much better than any silly tonic you might take. Can't tell you how wonderful it makes you feel—warm and cozy all over, like you're glowin' inside."

"I'm not interested," I told her.

"All the boys find you fascinatin'," Eppie continued. "They're always askin' me about you, askin' why you're so aloof and distant. Will Peterson said he'd love to ask you out, said he was scared to, scared you'd give him one of your cool, haughty looks and freeze his balls off."

"Someone should," I said.

"I often think you really *are* a snob, Angie," she replied. "The boys all say so."

"I haven't the faintest interest in what the boys say."

"Bosh! You're interested all right, you just won't admit it. They're certainly interested in *you*."

I sighed, bored, and Eppie gave me another one of her exasperated looks and told me that if I wanted to spend all my life moonin' around and readin' dreary books and bein' a tragic princess that was fine with her, *she* intended to have a good time before she got too old. I pinched her. She pinched me back. We both burst into titters of laughter then, and Eppie grinned and said I was still her friend even if I *was* a snob. We sauntered on down the street, full skirts swaying.

Eppie's dress was faded pink cotton, mine pale lavender with a ruffled white cotton petticoat beneath. My low-healed soft black leather shoes were scuffed, and I wore no stockings. Hated stockings. Still hated shoes, too, for that matter, but I always wore them now, however reluctantly. My dress was old, the hem too short, revealing my ankles, and it was too tight at the waist, too tight across the bosom, too. That bosom was the bane of my existence, my breasts full and round and, to my way of thinking, much too large. The low cut bodice left a goodly amount of them exposed. It wouldn't be so bad if the *rest* of me was rounded, but I was skinny as a rail everywhere else and felt like a freak.

"Don't you ever *think* about doin' it?" Eppie inquired as we approached the square.

"Never," I lied.

"That ain't even *natural*," she protested.

"I've more elevating things to think about," I said airily.

"Bosh! You're lyin' through your teeth, Angie Howard. I'll bet you do think about it, too. I'll bet when you're alone in bed at night you think about it a lot. Every girl does."

"Not me."

"Liar!"

"I don't happen to be obsessed with boys like *some* people I could name. There's more to life than—than wrestling with a sweaty lout in a haystack, letting him kiss you, letting him in*vade* you."

"Maybe so," Eppie retorted, "but I can't think of anything more *plea*sant."

I had to smile at that. Eppie giggled, pleased with herself as we sat down on the bench in the square. Sunlight brushed the pale green grass and gleamed on the old bronze cannon that had been here since Cromwell's time. Eppie spread out her pink skirts and gazed down High Street, still hoping to see a pair of shapely masculine shoulders appear. The sky was a pale, pale blue, cloudless. The apple tree at the edge of the square was abloom with fragile blossoms that filled the air with fragrant perfume. I felt I was in some strange kind of limbo, suspended, waiting for something to happen. I felt that way most of the time these days.

"Not much goin' on in the village," Eppie said. "I wish it were market day. Things'd be hummin' then for sure."

I didn't answer. I watched a robin hopping on the ground, looking for a worm. It finally flew up to perch on the cannon, its throat vibrating as it warbled a song. A bell tolled in the steeple of the old church beyond the square. The robin flew away, and a few minutes later a rowdy group of boys poured out of the school, laughing, shouting, larking about with boisterous glee. They filled the sleepy village with vitality for a short while, then dispersed, going their separate ways. The village seemed quieter than ever after the brief explosion of youthful exuberance. Most of the women with their shopping baskets had disappeared, and High Street was almost deserted now, deep gray shadows spreading across the sun-washed cobbles.

My father no longer taught at the school. He had given up his classes a year ago, on Doctor Crandall's advice. Father wasn't *ill,* of course, not really, but he had begun to lose weight, begun to grow tired, had developed a bad cough. Doctor Crandall told him he should take it easy. Father quit teaching and devoted all his time to the History. He still had his private income, a legacy left to him by an aunt who had died years ago, so we weren't strapped for money, but there were fewer new dresses for Solonge and Janine, less household money for Marie. She considered it a woeful hardship, grumbling more than ever, saying things would be much easier if we sold the cottage and moved to London and took a flat.

I sighed, not wanting to think of the situation at home. Eppie looked at me intently with narrowed eyes, her mouth pursed.

"You know, Angie," she said, "you really aren't all *that* plain. I've been studyin' you, tryin' to figure it out."

"Oh?"

"You have something. All the boys notice you. There's something about you that intrigues 'em. I'm not sure what it is."

"My winning smile," I suggested.

"If you weren't so cool and standoffish, you could have your pick of 'em."

"I'll keep that in mind."

"Of course you're too tall," she continued, "almost as tall as I am. Your cheekbones are too high, and your eyes are that peculiar shade of gray with just a touch of violet. You're too skinny and your legs are too long, but you've got glorious hair, so rich a brown, like gleaming chestnuts, so long and thick and glossy."

"Glad there's something you like," I said wryly.

"Your mouth's too wide, but it's so deep a pink, a de*lec*table mouth the boys say. You're not beautiful like Janine or Solonge, haven't got the coloring, haven't got the shape, but you're strikin', Angie."

"I'm plain as a mud fence and you know it."

"You just *think* you are. Me, I *know* I look like a
giddy maypole, but I never let it keep me from havin'
fun. Boys like all *kinds* of girls, and if you know how
to flirt, know how to please 'em, they come flockin'
around in droves even if you *do* have a long neck and
hair like a haystack."

"There are more important things in life," I informed
her.

"Like what?"

"Like—like making something of yourself. Like
learning."

Eppie raised her eyes heavenward and treated me
to one of her exasperated sighs, clearly finding me beyond help. The only thing girls like Eppie needed to
learn was how to attract boys, and she was already
expert at that. She'd continue to play around and dis-
pense favors with merry abandon and in a year or so,
maybe less, she'd get into trouble and get married
quickly and end up on a farm or in a tiny cottage with
a loutish husband and a passel of kids and never *know*
anything about the world out there. Or care. That was
the sad part. I wanted more. I wanted to *do* something
with my life, and me a female and plain to boot. It was
ever so frustrating.

Eppie sat up straight and gave me a sharp nudge,
suddenly atremble with excitement. Startled out of my
reverie, I looked up, frowning. Eppie nudged me again
and pointed. To the right of the square a road led into
the village, circling the square before turning into High
Street. A man on a powerfully built chestnut stallion
was slowly approaching the square. The horse's sleek
coat gleamed. The man in the saddle exuded virility
and a casual, lazy confidence. Sunlight burnished his
thick blond hair.

"It's him!" Eppie whispered. "It's Clinton Meredith!"

I had to admit that his appearance was a remarkable
event indeed. The Merediths eschewed the village, almost never coming here, sending a servant if they required anything from one of the shops. Constantly

gossiped about but rarely seen, the Merediths held themselves aloof. Seeing Clinton Meredith in the village was like seeing a Royal Prince consorting with the commoners. I hadn't laid eyes on him since that afternoon I had climbed over the wall and seen him wooing the beautiful Laura under the rose trellis, and though I was filled with curiosity about his sudden appearance, I refused to show it, assuming a bored, blasé expression unlikely to fool anyone.

"I wonder what he's *do*ing here?" Eppie exclaimed under her breath, too excited to speak in her normal voice.

"Who cares?" I said blithely.

"I'll bet he's on the prowl! I'll bet he got bored at the Hall and decided to come lookin' for a bit of tail!"

That was very likely, I thought. If all the stories about him were to be believed, Clinton Meredith spent the majority of his time pursuing sexual conquests. When he wasn't prowling the gambling halls and drawing rooms in London, he was roaming the countryside on his stallion searching for a complaisant wench to assuage his appetite. Handsome as a god, imbued with potent masculine allure, he was rarely refused, rumor had it. Farm girls and the like considered it a privilege to service the dazzling heir, and women like Laura probably offered only token resistance, just enough to maintain a pretense, as she had. Clinton Meredith was one of the golden lads, rich and powerful, heir to a grand estate, spectacularly good-looking as well.

"He's just back from London," Eppie confided breathlessly. "There was a frightful scandal—something to do with an older woman, married to a cousin of the King! Janie Yarbro's mother knows the sister of the cook at Greystone Hall and she gets *all* the gossip. Came home in disgrace, he did, just two weeks ago. They say the woman tried to *kill* herself, swallowed a whole bottle of some kind-a drug she'd got from an apothecary. I wonder if— Oh, Angie, he's goin' to stop!"

The man on horseback pulled on the reins and slowed the stallion to a walk, eyeing us with lazy interest. He circled the square, rode past the cannon, was momentarily obscured by the frothy blossoms of the apple tree, and then he came to a halt on the road, directly in front of the bench, only a few yards of grass separating us. Eppie caught her breath and flushed a bright pink, her eyes as wide as saucers, it seemed, and though I felt my pulses racing I somehow managed to maintain my bored expression.

"What are you girls doing?" he asked in that honeyed, melodious voice I still remembered so well.

Neither of us replied. Eppie couldn't have uttered a word if her life depended on it, and I didn't deign to speak. Clinton Meredith grinned, his full pink mouth curving up at one corner. Beneath the heavy, drooping lids his gray eyes were filled with amusement...and idle speculation as well. He sat casually in the saddle, one hand holding the reins loosely, the other resting on his thigh. He wore shiny brown knee boots, snug tan breeches and a tan frock coat with deep-brown velvet lapels and cuffs. The coat was unbuttoned, revealing a pale-golden satin waistcoat embroidered with brown and tan fleurs-de-lis. Though elegant, the clothes looked as though he had been wearing them a couple of days, and his tan silk neckcloth was definitely rumpled. Somehow this made him all the more attractive, more human. I found it hard to believe a man could be so beautiful, and that he was, as beautiful as any painting and virile as a ram.

"Cat got your tongues?" he inquired.

"Any fool could see we're taking the sun," I said. "We're minding our own business. I suggest you mind yours."

Eppie gasped at my boldness. Clinton Meredith grinned again.

"You're a cheeky one, aren't you? What's your name, wench?"

"None of your bleedin' business, and I'm not a 'wench.' Why don't you just sod off."

"Hostile, too. I don't often encounter hostility from one of the village lasses. Most of them are more than eager to be amiable to the heir of Greystone Hall. That's who I am, you know."

"I know," I said dryly.

"You're not impressed?"

"Not a bleedin' bit."

Clinton Meredith turned his attention to Eppie, his handsome face suddenly stern. "You!" he snapped harshly. "What's your name?"

"Ep—Ep—Ep-pie Dawson," she stammered.

"What's hers?"

"An—Angie Howard."

Those seductive gray eyes met mine again. Having provided the information he wanted, Eppie had ceased to exist. I found it difficult to control my breathing, for, defiant manner aside, I was really quite intimidated and amazed at my own cheek. I knew what he was up to, all right, knew what he wanted, and it frightened me. Glorious he might be, but he was still a man on the prowl, looking for a lay. He must be hard up indeed to pick on someone plain as me, I thought. Must be my bosom.

"Well, Angie," he purred, "I must say, I find you quite challenging. Did anyone ever tell you you have gorgeous brown hair?"

"Not bloody likely!"

"Rich and thick and shiny as silk, it is. You've got a very provocative mouth as well."

"Save your breath," I told him. "I'm not interested."

"No?" He arched one brow.

"Not in the least."

"I find that hard to believe."

"Conceited, aren't you? And superior and arrogant and—and a despoiler of innocent girls."

He smiled at that. Couldn't blame him. It sounded like something out of one of the novels I'd read, but it was true nevertheless. Nothing a man like Clinton Meredith liked better than popping a cherry, and he wasn't going to get anywhere *near* mine. He was handsome, sure, like a Prince out of a storybook, but that didn't mean a thing to me. Neither did the fact he was a bleedin' aristocrat. I was as good as he was any day of the week, I told myself, and I wasn't about to cower and curtsy like most of 'em did when he deigned to notice 'em.

"You're innocent, are you?" he crooned.

"I know what's what."

"I'll bet you do at that."

He gazed at me, eyes amused, a smile curving on his full mouth, and I returned his gaze with cool hauteur, wishing my breasts weren't so large, wishing they weren't about to pop out of this old lavender dress I should have altered a long time ago. My bravado was about to give out and I was afraid I might start trembling, might let him see how uneasy I really was. Clinton Meredith continued to look at me, and I could feel the color tinting my cheeks despite all my efforts to prevent it. After what seemed an eternity he sat up straight in the saddle and thrust his feet more firmly into the stirrups.

"Sure you don't want to play?" he inquired.

"Quite sure," I retorted.

"Don't know what you're missing," he said.

"A case of the pox, probably."

"You've got quite a mouth on you, Angie Howard. Don't know that I've ever met a cheekier lass."

"Go sod yourself!"

Eppie almost went into convulsions beside me. Clinton Meredith gave me a mock-polite nod, eyelids drooping, a half-smile playing on his mouth. He sat there in the sunshine on his powerful stallion, one of the Lords of the Earth amused by a saucy village brat who ordinarily would have been beneath his notice. I despised him, despised everything he stood for, and as those smoky gray eyes looked into mine he must have sensed what I felt. His manner changed. He frowned, a deep furrow above the bridge of his nose. Cold as ice he became, aloof and superior, but that couldn't conceal his anger. Men like Clinton Meredith weren't used to being bested by their inferiors. Didn't sit well with him. Didn't sit well at all.

He looked at me for a long time, seething, and finally he pressed his lips together and jerked the reins and turned the horse around, riding off the way he had come. Eppie gripped my hand so tightly I thought my fingers would snap. She still wasn't able to speak, wasn't able to manage it until he was completely out of sight, and then she had to take a deep breath before she could control her voice.

"I thought I was goin' to *die!*" she exclaimed.

"Whatever for?" I asked coolly.

"The things you said to 'im! Never knew you *had* so much brass. Me, I was shakin' like a leaf the whole time."

I stood up and casually brushed my skirt and she popped up, too, enormous brown eyes sparkling with excitement. A gentle spring breeze caused the apple blossoms to rustle, a few delicate pink-white scraps falling slowly to the grass. I wasn't nearly as calm as I pretended to be, but Eppie wouldn't ever know how shaken I was. I had my pride to maintain.

"He *wanted* you!" she cried as we started back down High Street.

"Why don't you talk a little louder, Eppie. I don't think the butcher heard you."

"I *told* you you had something," she continued. "You may not be beautiful, but Clinton Meredith was sure ready to pleasure you—and I hear he does it *good.*"

"He's had a lot of practice."

"And you cool as could be—and cheeky! I'd never have the nerve to speak to 'im like that. Isn't he the handsomest thing you ever set eyes on! If it'd been *me* he'd wanted I'd've *leaped* at the chance."

"I don't doubt it."

"Sometimes I *worry* about you, Angie. I really do. I can understand you not bein' interested in Will Peterson and his kind, you're too refined for 'em—but Clinton Meredith! I suppose you think *he's* not good enough for you either?"

"As a matter of fact, he isn't," I replied.

Eppie shook her head and said I was the most bewilderin' person she'd ever met, she'd never be able to figure me out. We walked past the school, past the greengrocer's and the bake shop, then Eppie sighed and said she guessed she'd better be gettin' on home. We parted company, and I left the village, walking slowly down the shady lane. Sunlight seeped through the limbs overhead, dappling the lane with shimmering flecks of gold. I could smell leaf and bark and pungent soil, rich country smells, and I longed to tear off my shoes and run through the woods and feel the wind on my cheeks and be carefree, a child again, climbing trees, gathering mushrooms, getting into mischief, not fifteen and too tall and prey to all the emotions constantly churning inside.

Clinton Meredith had wanted to lay me, me, plain and gawky, not beautiful like my stepsisters, and that frightened me, but ... I had to admit that it excited me, too. I was a good girl, a virgin, and I intended to stay that way, but it was exciting to ... to think a man found me desirable. Even Clinton Meredith, sod that he was. I could appreciate his good looks, his sensual mouth and those seductive gray eyes under the heavy lids, but he hadn't stirred a single tremor in my blood, not *that* way. He was too conceited, too sure of himself by far, and his superior air put me off, but ... he had wanted to lay me, said I had gorgeous hair and a provocative mouth. Maybe ... maybe one day the right man would find me desirable, too.

With these long legs? With this skinny body and too big breasts and high cheekbones? Not bloody likely, Angie, I told myself. Clinton Meredith was lookin' for tail and anything with a heart murmur would do, long as he was able to spend himself. Don't go gettin' smug. Take a good look at Janine, take a good look at Solonge, then peer into the mirror and see how bloody pleased with yourself you are.

A week passed, two, and I was restless as a kitten, unable to concentrate, unable to take an interest in anything. I snapped at Eppie and we quarreled and made up the next day and then quarreled again. She called me a snooty little bitch and I called her a hateful little slut and vowed never to speak to her again. I performed my chores with lassitude, clumsy as could be, incurring Marie's wrath when I broke half a dozen dishes. My father kept to his study, scribbling away or just staring into space, and I rarely saw my stepsisters. Janine was napping most of the time, and Solonge was busily occupied with her many suitors. April turned into May, and May was opulent, the air soft and fragrant, the trees all full of sap, flowers luxuriantly abloom. That only made me feel worse. Marie claimed I needed a good strong dose of tonic and said she was glad *her* girls hadn't gone through such an awkward stage.

Each day seemed to stretch out, endlessly long, woefully empty, each marked by that feeling of suspension. I felt I was waiting for something, but what? I had no idea. If the days were bad, the nights were worse. I tossed and turned in my bed up there under the eaves, windows opened to let in the soft night air and the hooting of owls. My body seemed to ache for no reason, "growing pains," Marie called them, and despite what I had told Eppie I *did* think about it. I thought about it a lot, and the man was always tall and thin with a dark complexion, moody brown eyes, unruly black hair, like Hugh Bradford. Sometimes I was in danger and he rescued me and then held me close and stroked my hair and murmured comforting words and I felt secure and happy in his arms and drifted to sleep with a smile on my lips, and sometimes he was dressed in black and wore a black silk scarf over his lower face and he wasn't gentle at all and I thrashed about restlessly on the bed and tried to think of something else and the dreams that followed were vivid and tense and exhausting.

I made up with Eppie, of course, and we took walks or wandered around the village, but I couldn't talk to her about all the things that bothered me, knowing full well she wouldn't understand, and I found her lively chatter irritating. Eppie was one of the lucky ones, simple and uncomplicated, a stranger to the doubts and fears and dramatic moods that plagued my days. Most of the time I preferred to be alone. Then I could be blithe and carefree or tragically sad according to mood, never knowing in advance which it would be. I was like an actress playing a role, but the role was always entirely real to me, and, in a perverse way, I almost *enjoyed* being sad, just as I enjoyed racing through the woods like a colt, elated by the sheer joy of being alive.

May was halfway over as I wandered across the fields one Monday afternoon under a clear blue sky that seemed to arch into eternity. I was wearing the old lavender dress again, the full skirt fluttering in the breeze. I still hadn't altered it, but I wasn't likely to encounter anyone and today I didn't care if my breasts *were* too big. The sun was warm on my bare arms, and the breeze was laden with the delicious scent of new-mown hay and caused silken skeins of hair to blow across my cheeks. I strolled aimlessly, and in the distance, beyond a line of trees, I could see Greystone Hall silhouetted against the sky, just the top stories and rooftops visible from here. It seemed another lifetime ago that I had climbed over the wall and scrambled along the tree limb to spy on the gentry. I was a young lady today, and today I was content to be a young lady, serene and demure, a role I rarely played.

I wasn't wearing the old lavender dress that was too small for me. I was wearing something much finer, cream-colored silk with a dark blue velvet sash, and I had on a wide-brimmed cream-colored hat with a blue ribbon and a long blue plume that draped over one side. I was the beautiful Lady Angela and spoke in a flat, tony voice without a trace of country accent. I was on my way to tea and I would chat pleasantly with all the attractive gents while I poured from a silver pot and they would all be charmed by my wit and poise. I wasn't fifteen. I was twenty, maybe, maybe twenty-two, all grown up, without a care in the world. The field was dotted with wild daisies, and I stopped to pick some, gathering a handful and holding them up to my face to smell their scent. They were roses, gorgeous pink roses, given to me by a handsome, courtly young man whose manners were flawless, whose voice was tender, whose eyes were...were brown and moody, whose hair was dark and unruly, who smelled of the stables.

I heard the barking then. I dropped the daisies. I whirled around, paralyzed with fear as I saw the three sleek greyhounds racing across the field toward me, barking fiercely. My throat went dry. My heart started pounding. I cried out as they leaped and lunged, sailing over the ground like shiny gray arrows in the sunlight, nearer and nearer. They were going to tear me to pieces! I closed my eyes tightly, terrified, expecting to feel fangs sinking into my flesh at any moment. The barking grew louder. They were upon me! I trembled, bravely opening my eyes. All three of them were crouching only a few feet away, ready to spring and growling now, fangs bared.

I didn't move. Neither did they. They crouched there on their haunches, growling savagely, and I felt my knees growing weak and felt my head growing dizzy and knew I was going to faint any second now and when I fell they would leap upon me and rend me to pieces. I took a deep breath. One of the dogs snarled angrily, edging nearer. If I made the slightest movement they ...they would kill me and I was too young to die and ...and I was going to faint, I was going to fall, I was going to be torn to pieces right here out in the open and Father would never know how much I loved him because I hadn't told him and...Fuzzy gray clouds seemed to close in on me and I started to reel.

"Stay!"

The voice seemed to come from a great distance, from the end of a tunnel, and I barely heard it over the pounding of my heart. I closed my eyes again and blackness swallowed me and through the blackness I could hear the dogs whining and hear a rough voice thundering orders and then black turned to gray and then to blinding white and my eyelids fluttered and I opened my eyes to see long blades of greenish-tan grass and merry white and gold daisies. My cheek was resting on the ground. My body felt bruised. A strong tan hand seized my arm, jerking me to my feet.

It was him. I wasn't dreaming. He had rescued me, just like in those dreams I had, but his eyes weren't filled with tender concern and he wasn't murmuring soothing words. He was glaring at me angrily, like *I* was to blame for what had happened. I hadn't seen him since that day in the gardens, but I knew him at once, of course. Who could mistake that sullen, foxlike face, those wicked eyebrows, those glowing brown eyes? He was very tall, at least a foot taller than I, and I was far from short, and though still thin as a whip he no longer looked like a beanpole. He'd filled out, lean now instead of skinny, his body well-muscled and suggesting tightly coiled strength. He was wearing high black knee boots, but they were neither muddy nor scuffed, and while his snug gray breeches and the loosely fitting white linen shirt were hardly elegant, they were clean and smelled of soap, not stables. The shirt was tucked carelessly into the waistband of his breeches and open at the throat, the full sleeves gathered at the wrist.

"You all right?" he asked harshly.

"I—I don't know—"

"Did you hurt yourself?" he demanded.

"The dogs—"

"I sent them home. You seem to have fainted."

"I did not faint!" I snapped.

"No?"

He was still holding my arm. I pulled it free. "I merely tripped," I said tartly. "I'm not one of those stupid girls who're always swoonin'. Can't stand that type."

"Neither can I," he confided. "When you—uh—tripped, did you hurt yourself?"

"Of course not," I said, and then I put weight on my right foot and winced at the pain, almost crying out.

Hugh Bradford saw the wince and frowned. "Your ankle?" he asked.

"It's all right. It's none of your concern!"

"Better let me look at it," he said sternly.

Before I could stop him he had dropped down on one

knee and was reaching for my foot. He raised it up and took it in his hand and I tilted forward, wobbling dangerously. I had to rest my hands on his broad shoulders to keep from falling, and I could feel bone and muscle and warm flesh beneath the cloth of his shirt. I stared at the top of his head and saw how thick and black his hair was, black as a raven's wing and smelling almost as nice as the new-mown hay, only different. He flexed my foot. I let out a shriek that must have been heard all the way in the village. Hugh Bradford put my foot back down and stood up, taking hold of both my arms as he did so, holding me steady.

"No real damage done," he curtly informed me. "More than likely it's just a light sprain."

"It hurts like hell!"

"That's what you get for trespassing."

"I wasn't trespassing!" I said hotly.

"This happens to be Meredith property."

"Big bleedin' deal! You think I was going to *steal* it? That why you turned the dogs loose on me?"

"I didn't," he said. "We were on our way back from one of the tenant farms and they saw you and bounded away before I could stop them."

"In another minute I'd've been mincemeat!"

"They never bite unless I tell them to, just growl and hold intruders at bay."

"I might have died of fright!"

"Big brave girl like you? I doubt it."

"Let go of my arms!" I demanded.

He did. I toppled immediately, landing with a thud smack on my backside. Hugh Bradford chuckled, looming there above me tall as a tree, and I longed for a pistol so I could blow his bleedin' brains out. I made no effort to get up. Angry tears brimmed over my lashes, and I was afraid I might start sobbing any second now. I gnawed on my lower lip and blinked away the tears, and he stepped back a few paces, thrusting his hands into his pockets and examining me with his head tilted to one side. Silhouetted against the clear blue sky from my vantage point, he was a detestable sight. My rump was sore as could be from the fall and I longed to rub it, but I was a young lady and rubbing one's rump in the presence of someone else was definitely declassé. To hell with it! I pulled up my knees and shifted position and rubbed it anyway, wishing it weren't so boney and flat. Hugh Bradford didn't bother to avert his eyes. Sod like him wouldn't. I rubbed briskly and finally eased my bottom back down on the ground and spread my skirts out.

"Feel better now?" he asked.

"Not much," I snapped. "Why don't you get back to your stables!"

"I don't work in the stables any longer. I've come up in the world. Now I supervise the tenant farmers and tend to their needs. My father is too old to do it. My cousin is much too noble to soil his hands with any kind of work. So I do it. I'm actually paid wages."

"Get back to work, then," I said hatefully.

"And leave you stranded here? My conscience wouldn't allow me to do that."

"Sod like you wouldn't have a conscience!"

He smiled. "Still as cheeky as ever, I see," he observed. "Still as foul-mouthed, too. Someone ought to wash your mouth out with soap. Folks say that's very effective."

"Go to hell!"

His dark brown eyes gleamed with amusement, but somehow, even when he smiled, that lean, tan face still looked grave. Smiling was something he rarely did, I suspected, and I was livid that he smiled now, the smile rueful, resting lightly on his wide, thin lips. He remembered me. He still considered me a child, despite ample evidence to the contrary. I wished I *were* that cool, patrician young lady in cream silk gown and beplumed bonnet. Then I'd be able to snub him with frosty dignity. Hard to be dignified when you were skinny and gawky and sprawlin' on your backside among a clump of wild daisies.

"How's your ankle?" he asked, the smile gone.

"Throbbing," I said.

"You'd better let me help you get home."

"I don't need your help!"

Hugh Bradford scowled. "Don't be difficult," he said, impatient now. "I've wasted enough time as it is."

He took two long strides and reached down and took hold of my arms and hauled me to my feet. My bodice twisted, revealing half an inch more of my bosom, and I quickly adjusted it, then brushed a heavy chestnut wave from my cheek. I cautiously put a little weight on my right foot. My ankle throbbed something awful, but it wasn't anything I couldn't handle. I could get home if I took it easy. Might hobble a bit, but I could make it all right. I told him I wouldn't require his help. He merely scowled, caught my wrist and slung my right arm up around his shoulders, curling his left arm tightly around my waist.

"This isn't necessary," I protested.

"Shut up!" he ordered.

"You—you're just as nasty as you were three years ago."

"Afraid so," he replied, "and if you give me any more lip I'll spank you soundly, just like I did then."

"Sod!"

I didn't say anything after that, didn't dare, for I could see he was serious. His left arm was wrapped around my waist like a steel band, holding me up against his side, and he kept a strong grip on my right wrist so I couldn't move my arm from around his shoulders. He took measured strides, altering his normal walk to accommodate me, and I put most of my weight on my left foot, hobbling carefully when I had to use my right. I felt smothered, crammed so close to him, felt uncomfortable and uneasy, felt something else as well, something I didn't care to identify. I could feel the strength in his lean, muscular body. I could feel his warmth, smell the smell of him, and it made me all weak and trembly.

We slowly crossed the field and then another and then came to a wooden stile that spanned the low gray stone wall. He informed me that I would never be able to manage it like this and swung me up into his arms and carried me across, did it without effort, as though I weighed nothing at all, and then he set me down and wrapped me against him like before. We continued across another field and then started through the woods. Birds warbled overhead, darting among the leafy branches, and a hare scurried across our path. The woods smelled of moss and mud and lichen.

I was exhausted when we reached the lane, and my ankle was starting to hurt badly now. Hugh Bradford saw the pained expression on my face and set me down on the grass on the side of the lane. I rested my back against one of the tree trunks and began to rub my ankle. He scowled and tore a piece of bark from a trunk, impatient, sullen, no longer in the least amused. I told him he could go on back to his tenant farms, I could easily make it the rest of the way home without his gallant assistance. He gave me a surly look and propped his shoulders against a tree trunk, twirling the piece of bark in his hand, finally chucking it away.

Wavering rays of pale yellow sunlight slanted through the leafy limbs that met overhead and made a canopy over the lane. A hazy ray touched his face and bathed it with softly diffused light. It was so tan, so lean, so harsh and uncompromising, the mouth wide and thin, lifting slightly at one corner, the dark brown eyes moody, full of bitter reflections. It wasn't a handsome face, far from it, yet it had plagued my dreams for three years. I found it fascinating and found myself longing to brush that heavy black wave from his brow and rub the ball of my thumb along the firm curve of his lower lip. He was gazing moodily into space, shoulders propped against the tree, hands jammed into his pockets, and I continued to observe him, remembering all that Father had told me. I felt a curious empathy for this tall, sullen man who, at nineteen, had nothing of the boy left about him.

He turned his head to look at me. I quickly averted my eyes, suddenly absorbed in the weave of my lav-

ender skirt. I could feel those eyes on me and was afraid
I might blush.

"I hear your father no longer teaches at the school,"
he said.

"That's right. He—he retired a year ago because of
his health. He isn't really ill," I hastily added, "but—
the doctor said he needed to take it easy and the classes
were becoming a strain. He—he has lots of time to work
on his history now. It keeps him very occupied."

"He's a fine man," Hugh Bradford said.

"Thank you."

"How's your ankle?"

"Much better now. Rubbing helped. I'm sure I can
walk on it."

"We'd better not take any chances."

He helped me up and I put weight on my foot and
took a couple of steps and found that I could indeed
walk on it, albeit with considerable discomfort. He made
me put my arm around his shoulders again and then
curled his arm around my waist as before, holding me
close, holding me tightly. As we continued on down the
lane I was acutely aware of his body next to mine, of
that strong arm supporting me. I recalled the dreams
and tried to put them out of my mind. He was already
a man. He seemed much more mature than his cousin
Clinton, who was three years his senior. I was a mere
child in his eyes, the same cheeky brat he had spanked
in the gardens. I frowned, wishing I were older, wishing
I weren't all tongue-tied and ill at ease. As we passed
the rhododendrons Hugh Bradford took a deep breath,
finding this all very tiresome.

"How are your stepsisters?" he asked.

"They're fine," I said.

"Still unmarried?"

"No one around here is good enough for them. Their
great-great-great-grandfather was the Marquis de Valois, you see. My stepmother has ambitions for them.
They're much too beautiful to waste away in a dreary
country village like *she* has."

"I see."

"She keeps after Father to move us all to London. Never gives him a minute's peace. She's convinced that once we're in London Janine and Solonge will take it by storm and both nab wealthy, aristocratic husbands."

"Shouldn't doubt it," he said. "What about you? I suppose you want to find yourself a rich husband, too."

"I'm not interested in husbands!"

"No?"

"I'm going to *make* something of myself," I told him. "I don't *need* a husband."

Hugh Bradford didn't say anything, but his lips curled in a wry smile and I could tell he thought I was a silly, prattling child. That irritated me immensely. The cottage was in sight now, mellow amber stone brushed with shadows from the oak trees, the thatched roof a deep tannish-gray in the sun. The shabby flower beds were in full bloom, a patchwork of violet, blue, purple, pink and pale golden-orange. I pulled away from him when we reached the flagstone walk leading up to the porch. He thrust his hands into his pockets again, slouching as he stood, observing me with indifferent brown eyes.

"You're too big to be roaming about the countryside alone like that," he said in a bored voice. "A pretty girl like you could get into bad trouble."

Pretty? He was mocking me. He must be.

"There are a lot of rogues around these parts nowadays—gypsies and vagrants, thieves and country toughs looking for excitement. You're lucky it was me who happened upon you today."

"I can take care of myself," I said frostily.

"I doubt that. Stay at home, Miss Howard. Read your books. Take up needlepoint. I wouldn't want your father to have any more worries than he already has."

I flushed, trying to think of a demolishing reply, and Hugh Bradford looked past me, gazing at the cottage, his brown eyes thoughtful now.

"By the way," he said, "does Solonge still have that turquoise silk dress?"

I stared at him, horrified, and then I slapped him

across the face as hard as I could. He caught my wrist, twisting it, glaring down at me with a murderous expression. I was afraid, really afraid, but I fought valiantly to hide it, wincing as his powerful fingers squeezed my wrist, twisting it even more. A long moment passed, and then he frowned and shook his head and let go of my wrist. Hugh Bradford looked down at me and scowled darkly and finally shook his head again and left. I watched him stride back down the lane, tears in my eyes now. I sobbed and hobbled to the porch and sat down on the steps, hating him fiercely, hating Solonge, too, hating myself as well as the tears spilled down my cheeks.

Chapter Four

Summer seemed endless, each day dragging on, empty of sensation or splendor or spectacle of any kind. It was unusually warm, and I was almost as indolent as Janine, seeing little of Eppie, reading without enthusiasm, filling each lengthy day as best I could and trying not to think of the loathsome Hugh Bradford who had slept with my stepsister. Solonge had probably instigated it, I knew, but somehow it still seemed like ... like a betrayal of sorts. I hated him, I really did, and I never wanted to see him again. He was vile, almost as vile as his cousin. I could understand why Lady Meredith detested the sight of him and wouldn't allow him inside the Hall. Although, according to Eppie, the tenant farms were prospering mightily under his supervision, he still stayed in his old room over the stables. Serves the sod right, I told myself.

Autumn came and the leaves turned and the air grew crisp and the days were shorter but as empty as ever. I did quite a bit of sewing, refurbishing my stepsisters' winter wardrobes, even sewed some for Marie who begrudgingly admitted that I was an absolute marvel with needle and thread. I had to alter several of my own things, too, for, wonder of wonders and at long last, I was gradually beginning to fill out in other places besides my bosom. My straight, bony frame was taking on flesh and the flesh was shaping itself into soft, pleasing curves. I was still too tall and far from voluptuous, but at least I no longer felt such a freak. Gazing out the window at the vividly hued leaves, my lap full of sewing, I wondered if I might finally be growing out of "that awkward age" Marie referred to so often. It was certainly high time, I thought wryly.

For Christmas my father gave me a complete set of the works of John Dryden, including those scandalous plays generally kept under lock and key. He said he assumed I knew all about those things anyway and Dryden was a masterful writer, even when pandering to the tastes of Restoration theatergoers. Solonge and Janine got splendid new cloaks, Marie a bottle of very expensive perfume from her native France. Hair newly dyed, face vividly painted as always, she sniffed disdainfully and said she'd have no reason to use it here in this dreary outpost. Father merely shrugged, admiring the ivory-handled magnifying glass I had bought for him and wrapped in red paper.

January was very cold, icicles hanging from the eaves, snow covering the ground, and I worried about Father. He seemed to be even thinner now and his cough was much worse. Once, in his study, I saw thin red flecks on his handkerchief after one of his coughing spells, and he hastened to tell me it was nothing, nothing at all. Doctor Crandall had given him a potent new medicine and it was working wonders, he'd be as fit as ever once this cold weather was over. I tried very hard to believe him, but the worry was always there in the back of my mind, niggling away, and I was always bringing a lap rug for his knees and making sure there were plenty of logs on the fire. Father shook his head at my concern and called me his silly pumpkin.

I turned sixteen in February and no one remembered

my birthday except Solonge. She gave me a bolt of exquisite sky blue muslin sprigged with tiny violet flowers and tiny green leaves and told me it was time I
made myself something really fetching. I was sad that
day, not because Father didn't remember, he was much
too busy with his history, but because I was growing
older and life seemed to have no direction. Day followed
day and nothing happened and I saw nothing ahead but
more of the same.

I made the dress and it was fetching indeed, with
short puffed sleeves worn off the shoulder, a modestly
low neckline, formfitting bodice and full, flaring skirt
that belled out over my petticoat. Modeling it in front
of the mirror as the March winds roared outside, I was
amazed at the transformation I saw in the glass. The
tall, slender young lady with the rich, abundant chestnut hair and violet-gray eyes certainly wasn't beautiful, not even pretty with those high, sculpted cheekbones
and that wide mouth, but she bore little resemblance
to the skinny, gawky adolescent who was all elbows and
legs. My breasts were full, yes, but they no longer seemed
terribly out of proportion now that I had filled out elsewhere.

I tied the violet velvet sash around my waist and
turned to make sure the ends trailed properly in back,
looking over my shoulder into the mirror. Sunlight an-
gling through the window gave my long, wavy hair a
luxuriant sheen. I sighed and turned back around, examining the young lady anew. Not the lovely, demure
young lady in cream-colored silk and plumed bonnet I
had imagined when I was strolling across the fields
almost a year ago, but not ... not entirely plain either.
I wished Hugh Bradford could see me now. Wouldn't be
so quick to treat me like a child. I'd snub him royally,
I would, and he would scowl and look at me with those
dark brown eyes and they'd be filled with desire and
... I made a face at my reflection.

I wasn't likely to see Hugh Bradford again, and if I
did he'd be rude and sullen and I'd probably give him
the finger or slap his face again or do something equally

outrageous. He was a lout, a bumpkin, rough and uncouth and a complete sod. I wasn't interested in men,
but if I ever *was* the man would be genteel and polite
and charming. Certainly wouldn't be a surly country
ruffian who spent his days inspecting farm equipment
and making certain the manure was properly spread.
I took off the dress and hung it carefully in the wardrobe. It was a lovely dress, the finest I'd ever had, but
where was I going to wear it? Downstairs to dinner? To
the village on my errands? When I entertained one of
the countless beaux who swarmed around vying for my
favor? I slipped on my old blue cotton frock and went
downstairs to peel the potatoes for dinner. Marie would
have one of her snits if I didn't have them ready in
time.

The winds continued to roar throughout most of
March, making Marie testy and making me restless.
When finally they died down it was almost April and
the skies were a pure, pale white with only a touch of
blue and the sun was a pale white disc. The trees were
bare, the earth brown, but all the snow was gone and
a faint green haze was beginning to appear. Spring
would be here in no time, the flowers abloom again. A
decade seemed to have passed since that spring day last
year when I had picked the daisies and sprained my
ankle and slapped Hugh Bradford across the face. That
might almost have happened another lifetime ago, I
thought as I came back from the village with the groceries Marie had sent me to buy.

Marie wasn't in the kitchen. She was in the parlor
with my stepsisters, and all three of them fell silent
when I entered. Janine was on the sofa as usual, but
she wasn't stretched out. She was sitting up, and her
large blue eyes weren't as placid as usual. They looked
worried. Marie was sitting by the window in the familiar garnet silk dress and black apron she always
wore when she was working, her thin, sharp-featured
face painted as usual, orange-blonde hair stacked atop
her head with ringlets spilling over her brow. Her eyes
were glittering brightly, full of angry determination.

Solonge stood by the window, breathtakingly gorgeous in a lime green frock. Her red-gold hair glistened like pale fire in the sunlight streaming through the window behind her. She looked defiant, I thought, looked impatient, too, all that vivacity and temperament held carefully in check. I had obviously stumbled in on one of the fierce arguments Marie periodically had with her daughters.

"I put the groceries in the kitchen," I said.

"Go to your room, Angela!" Marie ordered.

"Let her stay," Solonge said. "She'll have to find out sooner or later."

"This isn't—"

"Angie's no longer a child, and she happens to be a member of the family, though you're so busy clucking over us you seem to forget it most of the time. Sit down, Angie," Solonge told me. "We're in the middle of an earthshaking crisis."

"Crisis?"

"Janine's pregnant," she said dryly.

I stared at her, stunned, certain I must have misunderstood her. Janine pregnant? I could hardly believe it. Solonge, now, that wouldn't have surprised me, although she always bragged about being so careful, but Janine was so indolent she could scarcely stir herself enough to go out with any of the youths who came calling. I couldn't imagine her having enough energy to perform the gyrations necessary for pregnancy to occur.

"Janine?" I said. "Pregnant?"

"Unquestionably."

"How did it happen?"

"Between naps," Solonge said bitterly.

Janine sighed wearily and leaned back against the pillow, idly rearranging the folds of her pink and blue striped frock. Silvery blonde hair atumble, cheeks a delicate pink, she looked at her sister with resentful blue eyes and said there was no need to be *bitchy* about it, accidents happened all the time, and then she swung her legs up and stretched out full length on the sofa, making herself comfortable.

"I don't know what all this fuss is about," she added. "Teddy wants to marry me."

Marie drew in a sharp breath, her long jet earrings swaying as she jerked her head around to glare at her oldest daughter.

"He would!" she snapped. "It would be a coup for him, winning the hand of one of my daughters. A book-seller! A pitiful clerk in a bookstore! Yes, indeed, that would be just *dandy*. The two of you could move into his elegant rooms over the store and live luxuriously on his generous salary. What does he make? Ten pounds a year? Fifteen?"

"Teddy?" I said. "Teddy Pendergast?"

"The same," Solonge told me.

"He isn't a clerk," I said. "He's the manager. He's very nice, always smiles at me when I come in."

"He smiled at me, too," Janine said. "He has a very nice smile and the warmest brown eyes."

"What in the world were *you* doing in Blackwood's?" I asked.

"Browsing," Solonge said.

"It was starting to rain and I just stepped inside to stay dry and there was no one else in the shop but Teddy and he was very polite, very attentive. I love that thick bronze hair of his. I love his soft, caressing voice, too. He asked if I'd like some tea and I said yes and we had the tea and ate cakes I'd just purchased—those tiny iced cakes I'm so fond of. That's why I had walked all the way to the village in the first place, to buy the cakes. Teddy is thirty-two," she added. "I think that's a lovely age for a man."

"He's a vile seducer!" Marie exclaimed.

"Hardly, *Maman*," Janine informed her. "I asked *him* to take me upstairs to his rooms. He was very nervous, almost forgot to put the 'Closed' sign on the door. I had to remind him."

"I can't believe it!"

"You could if you met him. He's much nicer than any

of the boys you're always encouraging me to go out with, the ones with wealthy fathers and money to spend."

"You slept with him! And you kept going *back.*"

"Not that often," Janine replied. "It's a long walk to the village."

"And now the whole village knows one of my daughters—"

"I only went at night, *Maman,* after the shop was closed, and I used the back door, the one that opens onto the alley. I always wore my long cloak, too, with the hood pulled up. I'm not a *complete* ninny."

"How could this have happened?" Marie wailed. "All my work, all my plans, and then you—" She shook her head, eyes pained. "I just can't believe it."

"Teddy's not an aristocrat, you see," Solonge explained to me. "He's not Oxford educated, doesn't have a title, doesn't have a private income or a father who owns a great deal of property. Hence, he's not good enough for a great-great-granddaughter of the Marquis de Valois."

"I've had enough of your sarcasm, Solonge!"

"It's true, isn't it, *Maman* dear? If Teddy were *some-*body, if Teddy had money, you'd have *shoved* her into his bed."

"I want my daughters to take their proper station in life."

"When are you going to give up that fantasy?" Solonge asked. Her hazel eyes flashed, and her voice was sharp. "Janine and I are never going to marry into society, *Maman.* We're *not* aristocracy. I doubt seriously we're even legitimate. If there *was* a de Valois in your life I feel sure he kept you stashed away in an apartment on the back streets of Paris. You should thank your lucky stars you found a perfectly respectable English schoolmaster to take us in and give us his name."

"You—you have no idea what you're saying. You—you—how could you speak to me this way? I've struggled and struggled, I've worked my fingers to the bone, trying to bring you both up properly, trying to instill in you an awareness of who you *are,* and—"

"We *know* who we are, *Maman.*"

Marie said nothing for a long while. Her face had gone white, making the paint and the dyed hair seem all the more garish. Her thin lips quivered at the corners, and her eyes were filled with bitterness and something very like defeat. I knew that Solonge had struck a raw nerve, knew what she had said cut very deep and was undoubtedly true. I felt a curious sympathy for this harsh, unhappy woman who had clung to a fantasy for years because the reality was too painful to bear. Her long fingers clutched and unclutched her black apron, wrinkling the cloth, and then, after several long moments, she stood up, her back stiff. The defeat was gone now, a hard, determined expression on her face.

"I won't have it," she said. "I won't have a daughter of mine marrying a clerk. I won't have either of you wasting away like I have. You're going to have things. You're going to have everything I never had."

Janine and Solonge exchanged glances. Janine's limpid blue eyes were full of indecision. She sat up and brushed a silvery-blonde wave from her temple. I could see that the idea of marrying Teddy suited her nicely. I also knew she hadn't the ability to stand up to her mother.

"I *like* Teddy," she protested.

"Shut up, Janine. I'm trying to think."

"You'd better think fast," Solonge said dryly. "The blessed event is scheduled to occur in eight months, perhaps sooner."

"I don't see *why* I can't marry Teddy. I'm twenty-one years old. I'm already an old *maid.*"

Not technically, I said to myself, but I didn't dare say it aloud. I stood near the hall doorway, and all three of them had forgotten I was present. I felt like an intruder, an outsider, but that wasn't at all unusual when I was with them. Marie pursed her lips, thinking hard, her eyes glittering. Solonge perched on the arm of the sofa beside Janine and began to tap her fingernails on the edge of the end table. How beautiful they were side by side like that, Solonge all fire and vitality, Janine indolent and lethargic, a vision of placid loveliness.

"We'll go back to Brittany for a visit," Marie said. "I still have a friend there—Clarise Duvall. We've kept in touch through letters all these years. She'll know what to do. She'll help us."

Janine pouted. "But—"

"I've put aside a little money—not quite enough to finance the trip, but your stepfather will provide the rest. I'll see to it. The three of us will go back to Brittany for a long holiday. We'll leave as soon as possible, and when we return no one will be any the wiser."

"Does Father know about Janine?" I asked.

Marie looked at me, irritated at my intrusion.

"Does he?" I insisted.

"We haven't told him," Solonge said. "Janine hasn't even told Teddy."

"I don't want Father to know," I said. My voice was firm.

"He'll have to know," Marie said tersely.

"No. He has—he has enough to worry about. I don't want him upset. You can ask him for the money if you must, but you aren't going to let him know why you want to go to Brittany."

Marie elevated one thin brow. "I'm not?"

"You're not," I told her.

She smiled then, a vicious smile. For a moment, for the first time, I actually hated her.

"Because if you do," I continued, "I'll tell Eppie about Janine and Teddy and her pregnancy. If I tell Eppie, the whole village will know before nightfall."

I meant what I said. Marie could see that. The smile faded from her lips. Our eyes met and held, my own level and determined. I had never defied her before, and although my childish mischief had caused her to bewail her lot in years gone by, I had never questioned her authority or deliberately given her any trouble. Her yellow-green eyes were filled with anger, but there was a new respect as well. For that brief moment we might almost have been equals, and then she grimaced and lowered her eyes.

"I suppose there isn't any reason why he should know," she said, and I could imagine what those words cost her.

"None whatsoever," Solonge agreed.

"I must get to the kitchen. Dinner will be late tonight. I'll speak to Stephen afterward. I'll need your help in a few minutes, Angie. I do hope you remembered everything on my grocery list."

She left then, garnet skirt rustling, and Solonge gave me an admiring look.

"The kitten has claws," she said.

"I—I couldn't let her tell Father. He—it would upset him dreadfully. He admires Teddy, thinks of him as his friend. Teddy's always ordering books for him. He—he'd feel betrayed."

"You're absolutely right, darling."

I sat down in the chair beside the door, suddenly exhausted and feeling drained from my confrontation with Marie. I was amazed at my boldness and surprised by my easy victory. I vowed to be extra-nice to my stepmother. I wasn't proud of myself for blackmailing her that way. I felt very bad about it. Marie might be harsh and bitter, might be sharp-tongued and frequently shrewish, but she wasn't the evil stepmother I sometimes encountered in novels. She was unhappy and disappointed in her life, and I could understand why she wanted more for her daughters.

Solonge got up from her perch on the arm of the sofa. "Well, sister dear," she said, "you've gotten yourself into quite a mess, it seems. I hope Teddy Pendergast was worth it."

"I don't know what I'm going to tell him," Janine sighed.

"Not a bloody thing, love. If you have any sense at all you'll never go near him again."

Janine's blue eyes looked regretful. "I suppose you're right," she agreed. "He did have a beautiful, soothing voice, though, and the nicest smile."

"Do you love him?" I asked.

"He made me feel good all over," she said dreamily. "When I looked at him I felt hungry—like I feel when I see a box of creamy chocolates. I just couldn't resist him."

Solonge gave her sister a thoroughly exasperated look. "Jesus!" she snapped. "You really shouldn't be allowed outside without a leash. There are a number of things you need to learn, love, the first one being that a girl *always* takes precautions. Men are too bloody anxious to think about such matters."

"I'm going to miss Teddy," Janine confided in a sad voice. "It was so sweet of him, asking me to marry him like that, and he didn't even know I was pregnant. I wish *Maman weren't* so difficult."

"In this particular case she's dead right, much as I hate to admit it. After you got your fill of chocolates you'd be trapped, living in two tiny rooms over a bookstore with a man who couldn't afford to give you a bloody thing. Next time you feel hungry, love, make sure the man has enough money to keep you in style."

"I thought you were on *my* side."

"I am," Solonge said. "You're never going to marry into society, nor am I, but you can bloody well do better than Teddy Pendergast."

"If we're going to Brittany we'll need some new clothes," Janine said, stretching out again. "I really would like a new bonnet, one of those straw ones trimmed in taffeta ribbons like we saw in the magazine from London. I think blue ribbon would be ideal—"

Janine didn't get a new bonnet, but she and Solonge did get new frocks. I spent endless hours with scissors, needle and thread, making them up in my attic room, a watered blue-gray silk for Janine, trimmed with pale blue lace, a golden-yellow taffeta for Solonge. I studied the London magazines in order to give the garments a modish look, and Solonge said I had a natural sense of style and was much better than the dreary old seamstress who used to sew for them. She slipped me two pounds and told me to treat myself while they were gone.

"Don't *ask* where I got the two pounds," she added wryly.

"I wouldn't dream of it," I replied.

"You're growing up, darling. Thank God you're not growing up like Janine and me. I fear both of us inherited very bad blood, but you—you're intelligent and gifted and kind. Make the best of it, love."

Though I wasn't really envious, knowing the purpose of their trip, I was wistful on the day of their departure. It would be lovely to take a trip, I thought, to see new places, meet new people, to have an adventure. A private carriage had been hired to take them to the nearest post station, and a husky footman in brown hoisted their trunks up on top of the vehicle, Solonge watching with an appraising eye. Marie wore a black silk dress and a black bonnet with garnet trim and looked chic indeed as she snapped orders and hustled her daughters into the carriage. Father and I stood on the front porch. I never learned how Marie got the money from him, but I did know he hadn't an inkling of Janine's condition.

We waved as the carriage pulled away with the pyramid of trunks strapped onto the roof, and then Father sighed wearily and said it looked like the two of us would have to make do with each other's company for a while. I said it shouldn't be *too* taxing. Father smiled and patted me affectionately, smiling again when I said I wasn't sure what kind of *meals* we'd have as I wasn't very handy in the kitchen. I'd probably set the house afire, I added, and he said he supposed we'd just have to risk it. He curled his arm around my shoulders and led me back into the house. It seemed very still and quiet. That afternoon Father left the door to his study open for the first time I could remember.

April was a lovely month, warm and pleasant. Flowers bloomed riotously in the gardens, as did the weeds, and Father and I spent many hours outside, raking and weeding and cutting back. He tired easily and often just sat out in the sunshine while I crawled about on my knees and got dirt under my fingernails and soiled my old cotton dress. It was nice to dig in the soil and pull up the weeds and clip the rose shrubs, nice to be out in the fresh air and smell the loamy earth and flowers and listen to the birds making fluting noises in the boughs of the oak trees. Father enjoyed it, too, and I felt it did him good. Many times he dozed there in his chair with a book in his lap, rays of spring sunshine bathing his face.

I did a lot of house cleaning, too, throwing open all the windows to let in the air, polishing the furniture with beeswax, scrubbing the kitchen floor with lemon juice and water. The house smelled wonderful afterward, all airy and fresh, and I took considerable satisfaction in my work. I took considerably less in my cooking. The huge old stove Marie used with such aplomb was a terror to me, always got too hot or not hot enough, always emitted billows of smoke when I opened the door. I burned several meals, burned my fingers as well, but Father was the soul of patience and always complimented me even if the baked chicken was brown as mahogany or the joint of roast so pink and runny it almost lowed when you stuck a fork in it. I got our bread from the bakery, and we had a lot of fresh fruit and cheese and vegetables cooked in butter. My Yorkshire pudding was a disaster. Father tactfully suggested we save it and use it to put up new wallpaper in the pantry.

"I'll never be a good cook like Marie," I complained.

"Afraid that's true, Pumpkin."

"Some women have the *knack*. I don't."

"You have a point there."

"I'll never be able to cook fish till it's tender and whip up a delicate sauce to go over it."

"But your heart's in the right place," he told me, "and you've done wonders with the house and garden. I'm proud of you."

"Thanks," I said glumly. "I think I'll attempt an apple pie tomorrow afternoon."

"Uh—why don't you just buy one from the bakery, Pumpkin. There's no sense in your going to all that trouble."

We got a letter from Marie in early May. They had arrived safely and were staying with her dear friend Clarise Duvall and the girls were having a wonderful time, she said. It was so lovely there and Clarise was so hospitable that they might just stay longer than planned, she wasn't sure just *when* they'd be home. Father said he was glad they were having a nice holiday and didn't seem a bit perturbed that they might not be returning any time soon. I longed to know what was really happening and how Janine was, for I knew being pregnant could sometimes be difficult indeed. What were they going to do with the baby when it arrived? I wished Solonge would write to me privately and tell me what was really going on.

Father had a bad spell toward the end of May. He coughed and coughed and grew so weak he could hardly climb the stairs. I fetched Doctor Crandall, and the two of them were closed up for a long time in Father's study. Doctor Crandall looked cheerful when he left, but I could tell he was putting on an act for my benefit. Father told me there was absolutely nothing to be concerned about, he had new medicine now and would have to rest for a few days but he'd be as fit as ever in no time. He *did* seem to get better, although I thought he looked thinner, his frock coat seeming to hang loosely on his once sturdy frame. His cheeks seemed thinner, too, but they were no longer pale, were, instead, a healthy pink. I told myself the new medicine must indeed be working, and if he didn't eat as much as usual that was because of my wretched cooking.

We took several short walks as the weather grew warmer, strolling leisurely, talking about books we'd read, Father questioning me about my reactions to them. He was warm and amiable and gently humorous, making wry remarks, slashing the shrubbery with his fine polished oak walking stick with its ornate silver head. We both enjoyed the walks, although he was always

tired afterwards. He insisted the exercise was good for
him, and, he added, the company was superlative. I
glowed inside when he said that. How I loved him. How
glad I was we had this time together. We were closer
than ever before, and I realized I was wonderfully blessed
to have so handsome, so special a father.

He continued to get better, continued to grow stronger,
and one afternoon in July he suggested we walk to the
village and stop in at Blackwood's and see what they
had in stock. I was hesitant, not sure how I would react
when I saw Teddy. I asked Father if he was sure he
wanted to walk all that way and he informed me that
he had walked to school and back for more years than
he cared to remember and wasn't completely decrepit
yet. He was wearing light brown breeches and a handsome brown frock coat and a rather dapper waistcoat
of bronze and beige striped satin, his frilly white neckcloth dapper, too. Silver-streaked pale gold hair neatly
brushed, gray eyes full of wry good humor, he looked
heartier than he had looked in some time, and I felt he
was fully recovered at last.

It was a warm day. I was wearing a white cotton
frock with narrow violet stripes, the full skirt billowing
as we strolled toward the village at our customary pace.
The sky was a pale blue, awash with silvery sunlight,
and the air was filled with all the smells of summer.
Father was in an unusually good mood and looked forward to visiting the bookshop. I decided I would be very
polite to Teddy. It wasn't *his* fault Janine had taken a
fancy to him, and I really couldn't blame him for suc-
cumbing to her blandishments. What man wouldn't?

"How's your little friend Eppie?" Father asked as we
neared the village. "I haven't seen her around for a
while."

"She's preoccupied," I said.

"Oh?"

"She's spending all her time with Will Peterson. She
isn't really all that fond of him, she just wants to make
Jamie McCarry jealous. Jamie just moved to the area,

he bought the old Marshall farm. He's twenty-four years old and looking for a wife. Eppie's mad for him."

"I see."

"All the girls are, he's quite good-looking, but Eppie has a *strategy*. She feels if he sees her with Will Peterson enough times he'll realize what a prize she is and snatch her for himself."

"Seems perfectly logical," Father said, "men being what they are."

"What *are* they?" I asked.

"Utterly helpless when confronted with a determined female. Jamie McCarry doesn't have a prayer."

It was market day, a fact I'd forgotten, and the village was bustling. The square was filled with wagons and stalls, and there was the squawking of chickens, the baaing of goats, the lowing of cattle and a veritable din of robust voices bartering for cabbage and squash, carrots and beans, handmade quilts, farm implements, used dishes, a plethora of merchandise. It was always festive and fun with children dashing about the stalls and matrons congregating to gossip while their husbands drove their bargains and exchanged news about crops and cows and the vagaries of weather. The pavements were crowded as Father and I strolled down High Street, and there were dozens of warm greetings from people whose sons he had taught over the years. All of them were genuinely delighted to see him, and it made me realize what a respected, even beloved figure he was in our small community.

Blackwood's, alas, wasn't crowded at all, only two other customers in the shop as we entered. I loved the place, loved the neat stacks of tempting new books on the tables, the leather-bound sets gleaming on the shelves, the wonderful smell of ink and glue and crisp new paper, but this afternoon I was nervous about seeing Teddy again and speaking to him. Father stepped over to the history section and began to examine the new titles. I looked at the new novels, watching Teddy out of the corner of my eye. He was helping a plump matron select a book on herbs, wearing the black frock coat and

breeches and dark maroon waistcoat he always wore.
His thick bronze hair gleamed richly in the light
streaming hazily through the front windows.

The matron left with her purchase, the bell over the
door tinkling merrily. The other customer left, too, and
Teddy went over to speak to Father. They shook hands
and talked for several minutes, and then, while Father
perused a new edition of Herodotus with a critical eye,
Teddy came over to see if he could help me. His smile
was as amiable as ever, his voice as warm as he said
hello, but those lovely brown eyes of his seemed darker,
seemed sad. I had always considered Teddy Pendergast
frightfully old—he was thirty-two, after all—but now
I saw him in an entirely new light. His face was lined,
true, but pleasantly so, and his nose was a bit too large,
but those expressive eyes and that full lower lip were
definitely appealing. I could easily see why my stepsister had found him so delectable.

"See anything you like?" he inquired.

"Not really," I replied.

"It's been a while since you've been in to see us."

"I've been busy," I told him.

Teddy smiled again, but I thought he seemed
strangely ill at ease. His shoes, I noticed, though highly
polished, were quite the worse for wear, and his black
broadcloth suit had the greenish sheen of age. He wasn't
a wealthy man, no, couldn't keep a woman in luxury
or ply her with expensive presents, but if... if one were
in love those things wouldn't matter. Janine was a fool
for letting her mother bully her out of marrying him,
I decided. A man as gentle, as warm as Teddy could
give a woman something far more satisfying than material things.

"I—I hear your stepmother has taken her daughters
to Brittany for a holiday," he said. His voice was ever
so casual.

"That's right," I said.

"I—I imagine they're having a very pleasant visit."

"They are indeed."

"When—uh—when do you expect them back?" he asked lightly.

There was hope in his eyes, and I realized that he loved Janine, genuinely loved her, that he was hurt and bewildered by her sudden departure without a word to him. He had asked her to marry him. She had probably led him to believe she would. Teddy Pendergast was one of the good people of this world, destined to be wounded by those harder, more selfish, less sensitive than he. I wanted to take his hand and tell him how sorry I was for what my stepsister had done to him.

"They won't be back for—for some time," I said kindly. "I'm afraid it may be months."

The hope died in his eyes and the pain appeared and he tried his best to hide it. He smiled a shaky smile and began to tell me about various new novels he thought I might enjoy, and I purchased two, plus a new edition of *Duchess Annie* by Miranda James, which I had read and loved several years ago. My father bought the Herodotus, a book of engravings and two books on old Egypt. Teddy was amiable and chatty as he wrote up the sales and wrapped the books in stiff brown paper, but the pain never left his eyes.

If that's love, I thought, if that's what love does to you, I don't want any part of it. I'm not ever going to let anyone hurt me like that. I'm not going to give them a chance. I took the parcel from Teddy and thanked him politely and then Father and I left the shop. Other folks can fall in love all they like, I told myself, but not me, not Angie Howard. I've got much better things to do with my life. I'm not *ever* going to fall in love.

I was lost in thought as we left the village and started toward the cottage, and after a while I sighed, gazing at the wildflowers growing alongside the road.

"I'm glad I'm not pretty," I said firmly.

"Not pretty?" Father inquired. "What's this?"

If you're not pretty, you don't have to worry about men wanting to make love to you all the time and you maybe wanting to do it, too, I thought, but I didn't say that to Father, of course.

"I'd much rather be smart," I told him.

"Pretty is as pretty does," Father said, repeating the homily with the utmost seriousness, "and you, my dear, are as pretty as they come. In fact, my gawky little colt has turned into a lovely and graceful young woman."

"You're my father. You see me with a father's eyes."

"And fathers are supposed to be blind?" he asked wryly. "It happens to be true, Pumpkin, but you'll never have to rely on your beauty. You're going to achieve remarkable things through your own intellect and gifts."

"I don't have any gifts," I protested.

"On the contrary, you've an abundance of them."

"I'd like to be able to write, like Miranda James. She grew up in London's worst slum, yet she wrote *Duchess Annie* and *Betty's Girls* and became a great lady. I can't write, though, can't paint or sing, either, and I certainly can't *cook*. All I can do is sew."

"Astonishingly well, incorporating your own ideas. You may grow up to be a renowned seamstress with your own exclusive shop, like Rose Bertier in Paris. She makes all Marie Antoinette's gowns and is one of the most famous women in the country."

"Sounds dull," I said.

Father chuckled softly. "You've plenty of time, Pumpkin," he told me, "but when the time comes—" He paused, and when he continued his voice was serious indeed. "When the time comes, you're going to excel. You're going to leave as strong a mark on our age as Miranda James has—or any other woman. It's something I feel," he added, so quietly I could hardly hear him. "It's something I know."

He fell silent then, and I smiled to myself.

Achieve remarkable things? Me? What a preposterous idea. I was just a country girl without a scrap of talent. It wasn't bloody likely I'd leave any kind of mark on our age, but ... but it was wonderful to have someone believe in you just the same, I thought. I took Father's hand and squeezed it tightly. I might not achieve remarkable things, but I was going to make him proud of me one day. I was going to make him very proud of me. I made myself that promise as we continued on down the lane in the splendid afternoon sunlight.

Chapter Five

Marie's dream had finally come true, and tonight Solonge and Janine would be mingling with real aristocracy, dancing in the famous gilt and marble ballroom of Alden House, wearing the sumptuous gowns it had taken me three weeks to make up. Marie had wanted gowns from London, from the best, most fashionable dressmaker, but there was neither time nor money for anything so elaborate and Solonge insisted I make the gowns, claiming they would be as lovely as anything from London and every bit as modish. She would be wearing pale yellow satin completely overlaid with frail gold tissue, Janine silver-gray brocade appliquéd with minuscule sapphire blue flowers. The material alone had cost the moon, but Marie had insisted it was imperative both girls make a good impression, their future *depended* on it, and Father had wearily given in and given her the money.

It was four o'clock now. A splendid carriage had come for them at one, sent by the Duke of Alden himself, for Alden House was a good distance from our village, at least fifty miles. A tall footman in blue-and-silver livery had helped them into the carriage. Another had taken charge of their gowns, carefully folded in large white boxes. They would change at Alden House, in the guest rooms assigned to them. Marie was in ecstasy, of course, had been ever since Solonge had met the Duke's son and heir, Bartholomew, in Brittany last year. Though the Aldens were rarely in residence at Alden House, spending most of their time in London, young Bart had come to call on my stepsister three times during the intervening months, and he had persuaded his father to invite both girls to the ball tonight. Marie was convinced it was only a matter of time before her daughter became the Duchess of Alden, as Bart was clearly infatuated and the present Duke, at fifty-seven, was already doddering.

Standing at the window, I had watched them leave, Solonge blasé and not at all impressed by the dazzling carriage or the cool, imperious footmen, Janine looking as though she'd much prefer to be taking a nap. They had come back from Brittany last September, and now it was September again, unseasonably warm, and the miscarriage Janine had had thirteen months ago might have happened to someone else. She was as indolent, as lovely as ever. The miscarriage had been a blessing as far as Marie was concerned, much tidier than leaving an infant with the nuns in Brittany, as they had originally planned. Clarise Duvall had made all the arrangements, but fortunately it hadn't been necessary to carry them through. Things had all worked out for the best, my stepmother declared, and if they hadn't gone to Brittany Solonge would never have met the future Duke of Alden, who happened to be visiting there. Janine would meet someone just as impressive at the ball tonight, Marie was sure of it, and soon both her daughters would have attained their proper stations in life.

She had been so excited at seeing her daughters drive off in the crested brown and gold carriage that she had developed a splitting headache. She had already gone upstairs to her room and was presently in bed with a cologne-soaked handkerchief over her eyes. She had left a platter of cold sliced ham for dinner, but Father had declared he wasn't a bit hungry after eating such a large lunch. He had gone up to his room, too, telling me that I really should go to the fair, it was bound to be amusing. He'd take me himself, he said, but he was worn out after all the excitement. The house seemed unnaturally quiet now. I could hear the clock ticking in the parlor. I was restless and on the verge of feeling sorry for myself, but I didn't have any desire to go to the fair.

It came to our village twice a year, in April and September, and it was always rowdy and colorful with gypsy caravans and rides for the children and dozens of gaudy stalls. There was a wooden dance floor, too, with Japanese lanterns strung over it on wires. I'd gone several times with Eppie in days gone by, but Eppie was married to Jamie McCarry now, living on his farm, and I rarely saw her. Going by myself wouldn't be any fun, and I really wasn't interested in seeing the calf with two heads or the dancing bear or to have my fortune told or toss the wooden hoops at a stake trying to win a gaudy painted doll. I was seventeen years old now. Such foolishness was beyond me.

I sat in the parlor and read, not really concentrating on the book. I was genuinely pleased for my stepsisters and glad they were going to have an exciting and glamorous evening. Wouldn't want to go to a silly ball myself, of course. Not for a minute. It was after five now. They would already be at Alden House, probably having tea in the gold drawing room before going up to their rooms to change. They were going to look gorgeous tonight in their new gowns. Me, I'd look silly as a goose in anything so elaborate, and I'd be nervous as could be surrounded by all those haughty swells with their powdered hair and diamond studs and lacy frills. Glad I was staying home, even if... even if I did feel so restless I was near to jumping out of my skin. Maybe I *would* go to the fair for a little while, I decided. It would be better than sitting here in the parlor, turning the pages of a book without the least idea what I'd just read.

I went upstairs and took a sponge bath and brushed my hair until it fell to my shoulders in glossy chestnut waves, and then I put on the sky blue muslin dress printed with tiny violet flowers and tiny green leaves. This would be the first time I had ever worn it anywhere, even though I had made it some eighteen months ago, right after my sixteenth birthday. It was already a bit snug at the waist, and the bodice seemed much lower than I remembered, or was it that my bosom was even fuller than before? I tried the violet velvet sash, adjusting the trailing ends in back, then turned to study myself in the mirror. Too tall, slender but pleasingly curved now, not skinny. My cheekbones were too high, too sculpted, and my eyelids were etched with faint mauve shadows.

You're never going to be pink and blonde and pretty, Angie, I told myself. You're always going to look odd with those cheekbones, that full pink mouth, those violet-gray eyes. You're never going to be petite and soft and fragile, either. It's just as well. Who *wants* to be pretty? I fetched the violet velvet reticule Solonge had given me, checked to make sure I had some money in it and then left the house, feeling a little better now, if only because I was *do*ing something.

The sun was beginning to go down, the sky all smeared with pink and gold banners that grew blurry as the light gradually faded. My stepsisters would be wearing their gowns now, mingling with the other guests, and I felt certain Bartholomew would be making calf eyes at Solonge and trying to get her alone. Marie might think him the grandest thing that ever walked the earth, but Solonge had confided that he was somewhat less than exciting. His father might be one of the Peers of the Realm and positively groaning with wealth, but Bart was a rather dull young man, nice-looking enough if a bit too stout. He had a slight stammer and a shy, apologetic manner, these because he had always lived in the shadow of his domineering father.

His father had been a notorious rake in his youth, and rumor had it that he hadn't reformed one jot with age. I wondered what *he* thought about Bart's infatuation with the stepdaughter of a country schoolmaster, or did he believe the fantasy about her aristocratic blood? At any rate, he had invited both of my stepsisters to the ball, and that signified something. Maybe Solonge *would* snare his son, though she was less enthusiastic about the idea than Marie was. Poor Bartholomew would hardly be able to satisfy her, but then ladies in that particular circle were not noted for their fidelity. They took lovers by the score, one heard. Solonge would fit right in, I thought uncharitably.

I sighed, strolling idly through the twilight haze that was beginning to thicken the air. The fair had been set up in the vacant field beyond the village, and I could hear the music as I walked down a deserted High Street, all brown and shadowy now, shops closed. Teddy Pendergast was no longer at Blackwood's. He had left a year ago, without ever seeing my stepsister again. She had forgotten all about him, but I often thought about him, thought about that terrible pain I had seen in his eyes. He was working in a bookstore in Coventry now, I knew, and I hoped one day soon he would meet a nice young woman who would erase that pain. Crossing the square, I saw the lights in the distance, bright blurs of color against the haze, and the music was much louder now, almost drowned out by the din of boisterous voices.

I wouldn't stay long, I told myself. I would have a glass of pink lemonade and maybe one of the sausage rolls smeared with tangy mustard, and I might toss some hoops just for the fun of it. I might even have my fortune told, although you could never believe a word the gypsy woman said. I wouldn't look at the dancing bear, that always made me sad, the poor, shaggy creature so mournful as it went through its paces with a pink skirt around its middle. Perhaps I'd run into Eppie, but it wasn't very likely. Jamie McCarry was a sober chap who had no time for frivolity. He kept Eppie extremely busy on the farm, but she didn't seem to mind in the least. Jamie was *won*derful in bed, she had confided the last time I saw her. It was a pleasure to cook his meals and scrub his floors, milk his cows and feed his chickens. Soon there'd be a *little* McCarry as well, and she could hardly wait. I feared Eppie was lost to me, but she was happy with her lot, and that was the important thing.

No one paid the least attention to me as I mingled with the noisy crowd. I strolled past the stalls and colored tents, pausing now and then to look at an exhibit or contemplate a particularly tempting treat. The roasted peanuts looked delicious, but they were always too salty, and the spun sugar, so pretty to look at, always tasted like dry cotton. The candied apples were bright red and tasted divine, but they were terribly sticky. I strolled on, jostled by noisy, irritable children who had been here too long, had had too much excitement and too many treats. Parents were beginning to lead them away now as the sky grew darker, as torches blazed like ragged orange banners and a rougher atmosphere prevailed.

I bought a lemonade and sipped it at the stall, watching the crowd swirling about in ever-shifting patterns. Wrestling matches were being held in a roped-off area, and spectators cheered hoarsely as sturdy, bare-chested youths grappled furiously on the ground. A fistfight broke out in front of the Petrified Man's tent. The gypsies were prowling about furtively in their shabby, garishly colored attire, eyes out for a likely mark, and hefty country boys in ill-fitting jackets made lewd remarks at lasses in their best attire, the latter giggling with delight. The air was charged with an ugly tension I had never noticed before, but then Eppie and I had always come during the daytime. I set down my empty glass, deciding I'd best leave soon, although I was perfectly capable of taking care of myself.

I passed the fortune-teller's tent, wincing at the reek of grease and garlic. A tipsy lout with tousled red hair staggered over to me and asked if I'd like a good time. I gave him the finger. He reeled away, appalled. I paid a pence and stepped into the tent to see the Geek in his iron cage, but he wasn't frightening this time, only pathetic. The other spectators gasped with anticipation as his keeper handed him a live chicken through the bars. The stench of sweat was so strong I almost reeled. I shuddered, hurrying out of the tent as the Geek stuck the chicken's head into his mouth. I felt dizzy, wondering how Eppie and I could ever have found such horror fascinating.

It was definitely time to leave, I decided, moving purposefully across the grounds. It was night now, much too warm for September, and the heat from the blazing torches made it worse. The music was playing loudly. Dancers stomped and shuffled enthusiastically on the wooden planks of the dance floor as Japanese lanterns swayed overhead, showering them with colored shadows. Foamy mugs of ale were being sold at half a dozen stalls. A tall, muscular youth in snug brown breeches and coarse linen shirt and unlaced leather jerkin reeled toward me, calling my name. He had broad, peasant features and shaggy blond hair and green eyes flecked with brown, and I didn't like what I saw in those eyes, didn't like it at all. His wide lips curled into a leering grin as he lurched in front of me, blocking my way.

"If it isn't Miss Angie Howard!" he exclaimed. "Fancy meetin' you 'ere among the common folk. Come to snub us, 'ave you? Come to look down that cool nose-a yours."

"You're drunk, Will Peterson," I said icily.

"I'm 'avin' me a 'igh time, that's what I'm doin'. That's somethin' you wouldn't know nothin' about, always 'oldin' yourself aloof. Think you're too good for th' likes-a me, don't you?"

"I think you're disgusting," I told him. "I don't know what Eppie ever saw in you."

"It ain't what she *saw* in me, it's what I *done* to 'er. Ain't no one better at doin' it than me," he bragged. "I make 'em purr, make 'em beg me for more."

I stared at him with cool disdain as the crowd bustled around us, as another fistfight broke out nearby, and Will Peterson shifted his weight from one foot to another, his heavy body weaving. I wasn't afraid of him, not for a minute, but I really didn't want to knee him in the groin. I firmly intended to do just that if he laid a hand on me. His brown-flecked green eyes narrowed. His lips lifted at one corner.

"'Bout time you tried some of it," he said.

"Let me pass, Will."

"You're gonna love it," he promised. "Yeah, you're gonna love it a lot. 'Adn't 'ad me a virgin in quite a spell."

"I believe you're bothering the lady," a dry voice said.

It came from behind me. A strong hand clasped my arm, pulling me aside. Hugh Bradford stood in front of Will now, tall as a tree and utterly nonchalant, his dark brown eyes filled with boredom. Will flushed, glaring at the intruder. Hugh Bradford stood in a lazy slouch, his hands hanging loosely at his sides, the fingers curling inward. There was nothing at all intimidating in his manner, but Will hesitated just the same, clearly uneasy.

"This ain't none-a your affair," he said belligerently.

"I'm making it my affair," Hugh Bradford drawled. "It would give me a lot of pleasure to break your neck. In fact, at the moment I can't think of anything I'd enjoy more."

His voice was lethargic, totally devoid of menace, yet Will turned pale, the color visibly draining from his face. He stumbled back a step and almost lost his balance, his eyes wide. He muttered something ugly under his breath and then turned and stumbled away as fast as his wobbly legs could carry him, soon disappearing with weary exasperation.

"You didn't have to do that," I told him. "I could have handled him by myself."

"It seems I spend an inordinate amount of time getting you out of trouble," he said in a bored voice. "Every time I see you you're in some sort of scrape."

"No one *asked* you to interfere," I snapped.

"Don't get testy with me, Miss Howard. It would give me even more pleasure to wring *your* neck."

"It probably would, you sod."

"You've no business being here," he said. "Half the men here have been swilling ale all afternoon. Most of them are even drunker than Peterson and they're beginning to turn nasty. It's no place for a respectable young woman with no escort."

"I know that," I retorted.

"Then why did you come?"

"I—I was lonely," I confessed. "My stepsisters went to a ball and I felt—It's none of your bleedin' business! If *you*'ll get out of my way now I'll go on home."

"Since you're here, you may as well enjoy yourself."

"A respectable young woman like me?"

"You've got an escort now," he informed me. "No one's going to bother you with a vicious chap like me at your side."

And then he curled his left arm around my shoulders and casually guided me toward a stall where cold apple cider was being sold. I was too startled to protest, and I stood by meekly while he purchased two glasses of cider and handed one to me. He drank his quickly. I sipped mine, looking at him with new appreciation. He really wasn't all that unattractive, I decided. He was too lean, of course, and his features were too sharp, but there was something undeniably fascinating about those moody brown eyes and those wickedly arched eyebrows, that long nose, those wide lips. I began to understand why Solonge had chased after him. He noticed me studying him. I lowered my eyes and felt a blush tinting my cheeks.

"Are you vicious?" I asked.

"I can be," he replied, "if the need arises."

"Will was afraid of you."

"So are a lot of people."

"I—I suppose you've been in an awful lot of fights," I said. "I suppose you had to learn to be vicious. They—they must have taunted you terribly when—when you were younger."

"The Bastard was taunted, yes. The Bastard learned to fight dirty. After bloodying a number of noses and breaking a couple of arms and dislocating a few shoulders, The Bastard wasn't taunted any longer. Is that what you wanted to know?"

His face was expressionless, his voice flat, but he still wasn't able to conceal the bitterness that must have been gnawing at him from early boyhood, that consumed him still.

"I'm—I'm sorry," I said.

"A well-brought-up young lady like you shouldn't even be seen in my company. Tongues will wag. People will talk."

"They can go sod themselves," I told him.

A faint smile curled on his lips, so faint it was barely discernible. I felt a poignant emotion welling up inside me, a tenderness I never believed I would feel for him. It took me completely by surprise. For years I had told myself I detested him, and now ... now I wanted to be kind to him. I wanted to alleviate the pain he had lived with ever since he was old enough to realize he didn't belong. An accident of birth had made him an outcast, a pariah, and I wanted to make it up to him. What I felt was more than mere compassion. It ... it was much stronger than that.

"Finish your cider," he said sternly.

I did, and he set the empty glass on the stall and curled his arm around my shoulders again as we walked away. The night was beautiful, everything bathed in a soft glow—the tents, the stalls, the people around us— and the glow came from within me. Never, never had I felt so safe, so secure, so happy. Never had I felt so complete. It was ... it was as though a vital part of me had been missing until now, and now, at his side, his arm wrapped loosely around my shoulders, now I was truly whole within. This feeling had come over me all at once, it seemed, and I was slightly dismayed, slightly bewildered, but I reveled in it nevertheless.

"Have you eaten?" he asked.

I shook my head. "I'm—I'm not hungry."

We passed in front of the fortune-teller's tent, and now it seemed lovely with the faded gold and silver

symbols sewn onto the ancient purple cloth. He asked
me if I'd like to have my fortune told, and I shook my
head again, for I already knew what my future held in
store. It hadn't happened all at once. I realized that as
we strolled past the dance floor with the soft colors
swaying above. I had been in love with Hugh Bradford
for years. I knew that now, and the realization filled
me with a tremulous joy.

"Want to see the Petrified Man?" he asked.

"It's really just a rock," I said, "carved to look like a
man. They've been using the same rock for years."

"Want to watch the dancing bear?"

"It always makes me sad."

The faint smile flickered on his lips again. "You don't
want anything to eat. You don't want to have your fortune told. You don't want to see any of the exhibits.
Why did you come?"

"I told you. I—I was lonely."

"I know the feeling well," he said.

"Why did *you* come?" I asked.

"Same reason Will Peterson did."

"To get drunk?"

"To find myself a woman."

"I—I see," I said.

"Looks like I succeeded," he told me.

He tightened his arm around my shoulders and the
glow inside spread until I could feel it in my fingertips,
in my toes, coursing through my veins like a glorious
elixir. He no longer thought of me as a child, a noisome
brat always getting into mischief. He saw me as a
woman, and I was truly a woman at last. The Angie I
had been all these years had been miraculously transformed, seemed but a distant memory, and I was filled
with new emotions, new instincts, a new wisdom as
well.

We strolled past the gypsy caravans, the gilt and
garish colors bathed in flickering orange torchlight,
shadows dancing on the ground. Cooking utensils rattled. A dog barked. Hugh scowled as a dark gypsy man
approached us with a cap in his hand. The gypsy mut-

tered a curse, retreating. Hugh seemed lost in thought, silent and content to stroll aimlessly with his arm curled so casually, so naturally around my shoulders. He had been so very unhappy for so many years, but that was going to change now. I was going to make him forget those bitter years. He belonged now, and neither of us need ever feel lost or lonely again.

I smiled as we passed the booth where one tossed hoops at the stake, hoping to win one of the gaudy dolls propped on the shelves in back. Hugh asked me why I was smiling and I told him how in years gone by I used to toss the hoops and never once got them all around the stake, never won a doll. He sighed and slowly uncurled his arm from around my shoulder and asked me which doll I wanted. I told him I was much too big for dolls now and he scowled and ordered me to pick one. I smiled again and pointed to the prettiest doll of all, a porcelain lady with blonde hair and a blue hat with tiny blue plume and a blue gown spangled with tiny gold stars.

"That one? It's yours," he said.

"She's very special," I told him. "You have to get *all* the hoops around the stake three times in a row, you can't miss even once. No one's ever been able to win her. She looks a bit dusty, poor thing."

Hugh stepped over to the counter and spoke to the man behind it and gave him some money and the man handed him a big pile of narrow wooden hoops. He moved back a few steps, squinted, tilted his head to one side and then tossed the first hoop. It sailed smoothly through the air, whirling around the tall stake ten feet away, as did the second, the third, the fourth. He was utterly relaxed, didn't seem to concentrate at all, seemed bored, in fact, yet all the hoops went spinning around the stake.

Several people had gathered to watch, and the number of spectators grew as the man behind the counter retrieved the hoops and gave them back to Hugh. Hugh nodded and began to toss again. The man stepped back, forcing a hearty smile onto his plump lips. "'Ey, look!

It's Th' Bastard!" someone shouted. "'E's tryin' to win th' special doll!" Hugh's spine stiffened and he hesitated a moment, but he didn't turn around. He tossed the next hoop. It hit the top of the stake, shimmered, almost went over the other side. I sighed as it toppled and rattled noisily down over the stake. The spectators cheered, and Hugh continued to toss and ten minutes later the plump man behind the counter reluctantly handed him the doll. Several people applauded. Hugh scowled and thrust the doll into my hands and then walked briskly away, shoving a man out of his path.

I hurried after him, afraid, upset. He didn't slow down, didn't say a word when I finally caught up with him, didn't even acknowledge my presence there at his side. Panic welled up within me as people streamed past us in noisy swarms, as music blared and raucous laughter rose. I tripped and almost fell and he stopped and grabbed my arm and looked down at me with dark brown eyes full of anger and bitterness and pain. His fingers squeezed my arm with bruising force, but he wasn't even aware of it. He looked into my eyes with frightening intensity, and a long moment passed before he frowned and relaxed and released my arm.

"Go away, Angie," he said, and his voice was stern. "I'm no good for you. I don't want you to be hurt."

"You—you heard what that man—"

"I heard. Take your doll. Go home. Find a good, respectable man and marry him and have a good, respectable life."

"I—I don't want that. I don't want the doll, either."

My voice trembled. A merry young girl in a sprigged yellow dress moved past on the arm of a husky lad with flaxen hair and roguish blue eyes, and I turned and gave the doll to her. Her eyes widened in surprise, then filled with delight when I told her I didn't want the doll, it was hers. She stammered effusive thanks and then she and the lad moved on and I looked at Hugh Bradford. He stood there, silent, frowning again, the frown digging a deep groove above the bridge of his nose. The air between us was charged with an entirely new kind of tension.

"I—I told you earlier," I said. "I'm much too big for dolls."

His mouth curled at one corner. He looked at me for a long time before answering. Those brown eyes studied me, darkening almost black, and I knew what he was seeing, knew what he was thinking. It frightened me just a little, but I didn't lower my own eyes.

"Yes," he said at last, "it seems you're all grown up now. Go home, Angie."

"I love you. I think I've loved you for years."

"You shouldn't," he warned.

I didn't reply. My silence, my level gaze said more than words, and he finally shook his head and the frown disappeared and his face was expressionless again. In his tall black knee boots, his snug black breeches and loose white shirt with full, flowing sleeves gathered at the wrist, he looked like a pirate, I thought, that raven wave spilling over his brow like a slanted V, that lean, sharp face so deep a tan. The decision was mine, I knew that, and I knew that I should leave, now, while there was time, while there was still a choice. I knew that I should let him get on with his life and get on with my own, without him, but I couldn't do that. There really wasn't any choice. I looked at him. He knew.

"Shall we go?" he said.

I nodded, and he curled his arm around my shoulders again and we continued on past the tents and stalls, past the vendors, past the dance floor. I was nervous now, trembling inside, the old Angie longing to be safe at home, longing not to know the meaning of these new emotions that held me in thrall, but my step didn't falter as I moved toward my destiny, for that was what it was...my destiny. I was destined to love this man, and I knew it would be futile to try to resist. I shouldn't love him. He had told me so himself, but that didn't matter. Common sense told me this was dangerous folly, but what I felt for him was too strong, too compelling, and I refused to listen.

We left the fairgrounds and started across a field, walking slowly, and I didn't ask where we were going. I really didn't care. I was with him, and the trembling ceased and the magic began anew, light and lovely inside me, a wonderful effervescent feeling as though I had imbibed the finest, the lightest champagne. I felt joyous and jubilant and might have been walking on air instead of over a vacant field brushed a soft silver by starlight. There was a light summer breeze, and my skirts billowed, as did the sleeves of his thin white cambric shirt. It was very warm. I could smell the faint perspiration on his skin, a musky male scent, could smell his thick hair and the scent of woodsmoke and leather.

The lights of the fair were far behind us now, a mere blur of colors on the horizon, the music so faint it was barely audible. The summer sky above us was a misty purple-gray shimmering with pale-silver stars, the earth silver-gray streaked with velvety-black shadows. A bell tinkled somewhere nearby. A cow lowed. There was a scent of hay and damp soil. Hugh still hadn't said a word, and that was fine with me. I was content to walk beside him and feel his warmth and strength, his body lean and long, moving slowly in long, lazy strides. I rested my head against the arm curling across the back of my neck, reveling in the beauty of the night and the beauty inside. We came to a low gray stone wall and he stopped and caught me around the waist and lifted me up and over, and a moment later we started across another empty field. I could see haystacks in the distance and, on the horizon, the silhouette of a farmhouse.

"No one's home," he said.

"This is one of your tenant farms?"

"The Rawlins'. They've gone to spend a week with his brother in Surrey. I feed their livestock every day."

"Father says you've done a wonderful job with the tenant farms. Do you like your work?"

"Someone has to do it."

"I—that was tactless of me."

"I'm sorry. I was terse. I shouldn't take my bitterness out on you. I can be a real sod sometimes."

"I know. I remember."

"I remember, too. I remember a lively and saucy child with huge violet-gray eyes and dirt on her face and the vocabulary of a stevedore. I remember a moody, awkward adolescent ill at ease with herself and bewildered by the emotions inside her."

"I—I must have been awful."

"I thought of you often," he said.

"Did you?" I asked quietly.

"I couldn't get you out of my mind," he told me. His voice was flat and matter-of-fact. "One day I saw you in the village with your father. You were coming out of the bookstore. It was market day, I remember, and I was supervising the sale of some of our produce. I saw you and I stared and I said to myself you had grown into a very fetching young woman."

"But not as fetching as Solonge," I said.

"Solonge?"

"Surely you remember Solonge."

"Yeah, I remember."

"And how often did you think of her?" I asked. I couldn't resist it.

"Not once," he said. "That's why you slapped me that time, isn't it? You knew."

"Not until you mentioned the turquoise dress."

"She—"

"You needn't explain," I told him.

He didn't. We sauntered on until we reached the haystacks, and then he stopped and uncurled his arm from around my shoulders and stepped back, resting his hands on his thighs. He looked thoughtful there in the starlight, a small frown furrowing his brow, his mouth spread wide, indecisive. His face was bathed in soft silver, lightly shadowed, and I could see the doubt, the hesitation in his eyes. I reached up and touched his cheek, resting my fingertips against it, and then I ran my forefinger along the curve of his lower lip, smiling a quiet smile, loving him so, longing to love him even more. He scowled. I loved his scowl.

"You're not Solonge," he said gruffly.

"I know."

"I should take you home immediately."

"But you won't," I said.

He folded his arms across his chest, scowling still, and he was silent for a long while. In the distance a cow lowed. The light summer breeze caressed my bare arms and cheeks like warm, invisible fingers, and a tendril of hair blew across my temple. He was brooding. He might have been alone. His face was harsh. The beauty of the night and the beauty inside me was so poignant I was near tears, but I didn't cry. I smiled instead. The future had been a vast void before, an emptiness yawning before me, but now it beckoned, full of marvelous promise.

"There's something I want you to know," he told me. His voice was grim. "I'm not a bastard, Angie. My father married my mother in Italy. I know it. One day I'm going to prove it. There was a nurse—her name was Maggie Clemson, I remember her well, although Lady Meredith discharged her when she came to Greystone Hall. 'It isn't true, lamb,' Maggie told me. 'Your mother was a lovely lady and she married your father in the church, and this—this is a scandalous outrage. That woman has bewitched your father. A grave injustice is being done. A grave injustice.' I was little more than an infant at the time, but those words were burned into my memory. 'A grave injustice.' Maggie left and I never saw her again, but—"

He cut himself short, staring angrily across the silvered field. Several moments passed before he spoke again.

"Greystone Hall should be mine, not Clinton's. My own father has cheated me out of my inheritance. Better he should—better he should have given me to the gypsies than keep me on the estate so I could nourish my bitterness and hatred. How many times have I longed to kill him, kill her? There's murder in my heart still."

"Hugh—"

"One day, when I have the means, I intend to prove the truth, and then I will be worthy of you."

"Worthy? You *are* worthy, Hugh. I don't care about your birth, that isn't import—"

"It's important to me!"

"Of—of course it is," I said quietly. "I—I didn't mean—" I hesitated, groping for the right words. "It's *what* you are that matters, not who you are or where you came from."

"I'm taking you home, Angie."

I shook my head. He was suffering. He was in pain. He had grown up as a pariah, an outcast, and he had never known love. I had love to give, sweet balm for those wounds, and I would not turn away from him now, even though he might try to drive me away. I took his hand. I held it tightly. He made no response. He might have been carved from stone. I wished I were experienced like Solonge, wished I knew what to do, what to say. I felt helpless, filled with longing, filled with love, not knowing how to express it. I stood there on the threshold, and I was frightened, trembling inside, but I knew I would take that final step, knew I must if I was not to lose him.

He took a deep breath and looked down at me and saw the love in my eyes. His face was like granite in the starlight, the V-shaped wave slanting across his brow. I let go of his hand and touched his cheek again. His chest rose as he took another deep breath, and his mouth tightened. His eyes were dark, full of indecision. I reached up and brushed the wave from his brow. It was heavy, silky to the touch, the hair spilling through my fingers and tumbling back into place immediately. He hesitated a moment longer, and then his eyes filled with tenderness and I knew he loved me, too, fight it though he might. He put an arm around my waist and pulled me to him and tilted his head. His lips parted, but he didn't kiss me, not at first. He peered into my eyes, and in the soft starlight his own told me all those things he couldn't bring himself to say aloud.

The arm around my waist tightened, drawing me closer still until my body was molded against his, and I curled my arms around him and ran my palms over his back, exploring the sculptured curves of muscle as they moved up to rest on his shoulders, feeling the warmth of skin beneath the thin white cloth of his shirt. My legs felt trembly, the back of my knees aching, and I clung to him as ivy might cling to oak, and the strength in that hard, lean body gave me strength and gave promise of pleasure I had never imagined. His dark eyes glowed. He touched my cheek with his fingertips and wrapped his long fingers around my chin and tilted my head back more and leaned forward, bending me at the waist. Lips still parted, he covered my mouth with his own, and the sensations inside were like tight buds that burst into blossom, filling me with splendor.

Often I had dreamed of such a kiss, but this, my first, made those insubstantial dreams seem the shadows they were, the reality of flesh on flesh causing a delirium of delight. Warm and moist, his lips tenderly caressed my own, pressing gently, probing, firm, growing more and more insistent, demanding the response I instinctively gave. He made a sound deep in his throat, a guttural moan, and then he slung his free arm around my back and held me tighter still, swinging me in his arms as his lips continued to caress and then crushed, his need aroused, tenderness turning to torment he must assuage. I seemed to soar into a void of violent pleasure, and the delirium mounted moment by moment until nothing existed but this man, this magic, this miraculous new world of sensation exploding within me.

An eternity passed, yet all too soon he withdrew his lips, and I caught my breath, gasping, and then he buried his lips in the soft curve of my throat and my fingers clutched the cloth of his shirt at the shoulders and my knees seemed to buckle beneath me and I would have fallen had he not held me tightly against him. I threw my head back, my hair spilling behind me in heavy waves, and the pale silver stars shimmered in the sky above and seemed to shimmer inside me as well.

I ran my fingers through his hair and clutched it, tugging at the strong silky strands until he lifted his head and looked at me with burning black eyes and then slammed his mouth over mine once more, the second kiss a savage expression of need now bursting its bounds.

He leaned forward and curled an arm around the back of my knees and scooped me up into his arms and cradled me against his chest and I wound my arms around his neck and hid my face in the curve of his shoulder and he carried me over to the nearest haystack and set me down in the hay and then stepped back. The hay rustled noisily, so soft, smelling so sweet, welcoming my weight, and I sank into its softness and looked up at the man who stood before me with hands on hips, silhouetted against the misty purple-gray sky full of pale silver stars. I was limp, had no will, no strength, seemed to have melted, and I closed my eyes and still saw the stars etched against my eyelids as I reeled in darkness and cried silently for a surcease of these sensations that surely soon would tear me asunder. I caught my breath and opened my eyes and he was still there before me as tall as a tree, looming there, and my throat tightened and I was afraid, terribly afraid, fear eclipsing all those other emotions as he hooked his thumbs under the waistband of his breeches and tugged and the breeches slid down and his manhood sprang free, throbbing with a life of its own, it seemed, ready to rend and ravish.

No, no, no. I must run. I must flee. I mustn't let it happen for it wasn't a dream, not this time, no, it was real and he was real and I was trembling with fear. I loved him, yes, yes, and yes, I wanted him, but the fear took over and drove away the magic and the limpness left and I felt my body tightening and I grew stiff all over, my limbs like wood, and I felt cold, very cold, as though my blood had turned to ice. I wanted to cry out and tell him to stop, to leave, to let me be, but my throat was tight and constricted and it wasn't possible to squeeze the words out. Icy, immobile, I looked at him and looked at that throbbing, swollen tool and somehow managed to shake my head and utter a cry that was a wordless whimper, barely audible.

He did not remove his clothes. He spread his legs wide and then he kneeled over me, a knee on either side of my thighs, and I was like wood, like ice, and he looked at me and saw my fear and frowned but it was too late now, he couldn't draw back, not now, not with that urgent need, swollen and throbbing, demanding release as, before the fear, a like need had filled me. He leaned back on his knees, his face harsh, and then he touched my cheek and I cringed, hay rustling, and he was angry, determined. Cold tears brimmed over my lashes. He touched them with his fingertips and then he leaned over and kissed them away. His lips were moist, warm, gentle, moving over my face, brushing my brow, my lids, my cheeks, finally resting lightly over my own. He was there hovering over me, hard and brutal, and the tender kisses were but a ploy, a prelude to that horror that would inevitably follow. I didn't respond. I couldn't. Every vestige of warmth had ebbed away and there was nothing now but ice and wood and fear.

He kissed my throat and murmured soft words but the silent cries inside made them meaningless to me. I tried to sit up, tried to get away and he scowled and shoved me back into the hay and held me firmly by the shoulders and then continued to brush his lips over my throat as his hands tugged at the cloth of my bodice, pulling it down, tugged at the petticoat beneath, pulling it down, too, and my breasts were exposed and he touched them lightly with his fingertips, exploring their shape. Lightly, gently, and with the greatest of care, he squeezed my nipples and they began to throb and swell and tiny threads of warmth began to radiate from them, spreading, growing, melting the ice. He scooted down and began to kiss my breasts, his lips brushing, burning my skin, and of its own accord my hand lifted and touched the back of his head as the thaw continued and the fear began to recede, slowly, slowly, bit by bit.

He sat back up on his knees again and looked down

at me and smiled and then shifted position again and removed my shoes and lifted my skirts as the hay made music beneath me, rustling softly, as the warm summer breeze caressed my breasts as he had caressed them moments ago. He took my left foot in his hand and began to massage it, flexing it, caressing the instep with his other hand, and then he made a circle with his hands and moved it up my calf, palms and fingers warm and leathery as they moved up, up, squeezing, encircling my knee now, then spreading and caressing my thigh, fingers pressing, fingertips digging into the soft flesh that began to glow and tingle, and the tingle spread throughout me, in my blood, in my bones, a delicious, delectable torture that grew and grew and grew until I could feel a warm fountain within, brimming, brimming, soon to brim over, I knew, soon to drown me in a flood of pleasure.

Fear was gone now, gone completely, and I made a soft moaning noise as his hands continued their sweet torture. I writhed on the hay and it made more music beneath me and there was music inside me too as his fingers fanned out, tenderly touching that secret area. I closed my eyes and listened to the music and drifted in a blissful void, reeling, it seemed, floating far, far away, and then I heard him move and felt his knees on either side of my thighs again and he was atop me then and I felt his weight pinioning me and there was another moment of panic and I struggled but he held me fast with his body, crushing me beneath him with brutal strength. He shifted again and forced me to spread my legs and then I felt his manhood as it touched the opening, entering carefully, slowly, slowly, becoming a part of me.

Panic possessed me anew and I opened my eyes and flung out my arms and made a violent effort to throw him off and I saw his face, saw him grimace, his mouth a tight, determined line, and he pressed down with the full weight of his strong body and I gasped for breath and felt him move deeper, deeper, brutally impaling me and meeting resistance. I was a tiger, fighting him, but

it was futile, completely futile, and there was a terrible
pain as I was ripped asunder and I knew I was going
to die as the magic had died, as the music had died,
and then I felt something new, something incredible,
and the pain turned to pleasure and I began to move
as he moved and beauty came, shimmering beauty,
shattering beauty, and I wrapped my legs around his
and lifted my thighs and caught his hair in my hands,
pulling it, throwing my head from side to side as the
fountain welled within and began to brim. I was no
longer a tiger, I was a kitten clawing, purring as the
beauty became unbearable and I was lost, lost, soaring
into oblivion that loomed just ahead, awaiting with
shuddering intensity.

Closer it came, closer and closer, and he filled me
fully and I held him inside me and clasped him and
caressed him and expressed my love with all my heart
and all my soul and all my body and love made us one
now and then he pulled back and almost left me and I
cried out as he filled me again and yet again, our bodies
molded together, straining to come closer still. The glory
grew, and he was mine and I was his and never, never
would either of us be alone again. I lifted and he lunged
and both of us moved to the music of love, and then I
felt a bliss so bright, so blazing I knew I couldn't possibly endure it, not possibly, not a moment more. He
shuddered, shouted, shooting, and I felt the life jetting
out of him as life left me, too, and I was torn into a
thousand shimmering shreds and cast into the abyss of
ecstasy.

Chapter Six

Sunlight spilled and splattered through all the windows and filled the house with light. It was a gorgeous day, a glorious day, and I hugged myself and smiled and wondered how I could contain my happiness. Father was in his study and Marie was in the kitchen and Solonge and Janine would be returning soon now, for it was after four, and I knew Hugh would come to call and speak to my father and ask if he would consent to our marriage, and Father would give his consent, I knew he would, and the future would be ours to shape and share. Was it really possible to be so happy, to feel such joyous elation shimmering inside? I smiled again and stepped into the hall and looked at myself in the mirror there and was surprised to see I still looked the same although there was a sparkle in my eyes and a delicate pink flush on my cheeks and my lips couldn't seem to stop smiling.

I moved on outside into the garden and smelled the soil and the flowers and hugged myself again and strolled in the sunshine and the shadows of the oaks and thought about last night and smiled once more. After we made love he held me in his arms for a long while and stroked my hair and kissed me tenderly and then we had made love a second time and it was even better, leisurely and lazy and lovely, each of us savoring the splendor, and it was almost dawn when finally we got up and adjusted our clothing and brushed off the hay. Slowly we strolled across the fields and past the sleeping village and down the shadowy lane, Hugh holding my hand, silent. The first pink-orange light of dawn was staining the sky as we reached the end of the lane, and there was the cottage, all shrouded in shadow, the pinkish light reflected dimly in the windowpanes. He pulled me into his arms and kissed me for a long, long time and then released me and left abruptly, without a word, and I slipped silently into the house and upstairs to my room and the sky was a pale yellow-white when finally I slept.

Neither of us had spoken during that slow stroll home, both lost in thought, remembering the bliss, the beauty, but words weren't necessary. We would be married, for he loved me and I loved him, and he would leave Greystone Hall and find some other work and I would be beside him to help him and encourage him and there would be hard times, true, but we would succeed and even the hard times would be good because we would be together. I strolled under the oak trees and daydreamed about the future until Marie called me in to help her with dinner, too impatient for her girls' return to notice my mood. I peeled potatoes and sliced them thin, grated cheese for the sauce, washed the asparagus and set the table, dreaming all the while. Marie was testy, snapping irritably, but I paid her no mind. She was going to be surprised when Hugh showed up to ask for my hand, but I doubted she'd make a fuss. She'd probably be glad to get rid of me, I thought, though it would mean hiring a servant to help in the house.

It was after five when the fine carriage returned with Solonge and Janine. A footman brought their things into the hall. Both of them were tired, Janine yawning, Solonge exasperated with her mother's questions and asking her to wait until after dinner for details. Dinner was strained. Father wasn't feeling well. His face was drawn. Marie was put out with all of us, tapping her fingernails on the table. Janine continued to yawn, and Solonge was silent, looking put out herself, her beautiful face hard. I suspected the ball had not been a huge success, but I wasn't really interested. I kept listening for Hugh, waiting to hear his step on the porch, his knock on the door. Marie had prepared a fancy dessert, but no one wanted it. Father excused himself and went to his room, and I heard him coughing behind the closed door. Marie told me to clear the table and then took her girls into the front parlor.

I cleared the table and washed the dishes and tidied up the kitchen. He did not come. Marie began to argue with her daughters in the parlor, her voice growing more and more irate, and finally she swept into the hall and went to her room and slammed the door. Janine and Solonge went to their rooms, too, and the house was quiet then and the clock ticked loudly, eight, eight-thirty, nine. I waited, and he didn't come. I stepped onto the front porch and watched the play of moonlight and shadow on the ground, not really worried, not allowing myself to worry, telling myself there was bound to be a good reason why he hadn't come to call. I went up to my own room at eleven and tried to read but couldn't, and it was after two before I put out the light and tried to sleep.

I was standing at the window in the front parlor the next afternoon when Solonge came into the room, looking bored and restless and lovely in a pale salmon orange frock with thin tan stripes. Marie had one of her excruciating headaches and was shut up in her room, the inevitable cologne-soaked handkerchief over her eyes, and Father was shut up in his study. Janine, of course, was taking a nap, and the house was very still. Solonge sighed and looked at me and, seeing my expression, asked if something was wrong. I shook my head and tried to smile, but I couldn't quite manage it. My stepsister frowned. Never openly affectionate, often hard and bitchy, Solonge was nevertheless fond of me in her way, and she was genuinely concerned.

"Something *is* wrong, Angie. You're pale. There're smudges under your eyes. You look like you've just lost your only friend."

"I—it's just the heat, Solonge."

"If I didn't know better, I'd think you were having man trouble. I'd think you were in love. God forbid," she added.

"Was the ball a success?" I asked, changing the subject.

"Everyone was very, very polite to us, very tolerant and very condescending and grand. The men were very attentive. They were very intrigued. Janine made a number of conquests and received a number of interesting invitations, as did I. Both of us could have made a small fortune had we been willing to slip out to the gazebo throughout the evening. Neither of us did. I suppose that's to our credit. We were quite respectable. For once."

"I'm sorry it wasn't—pleasant," I said. "I don't suppose you'll be seeing Bart any more."

"It isn't likely," she replied.

"I suppose his father made it very clear he didn't want any part of you."

"On the contrary, he made it quite clear just what part of me he *did* want." She sat down on the sofa and picked up a fashion magazine, idly flipping through the pages without looking at them. "Shortly after midnight he took me aside and informed me that I hadn't a prayer with Bart, that he was sending him on a long tour of the Continent, and then he made me a very attractive offer."

"He wanted to—to buy you off?"

"He wanted to take me to London," she said dryly. "He wanted to set me up in a grand apartment and give me a carriage and horses and servants and a monthly allowance."

"He's almost sixty!" I exclaimed.

Solonge smiled at my naïveté and told me I had a lot to learn, then turned back to the magazine.

As Marie was still indisposed with her headache, I cooked dinner that night and was grateful to have something to keep me busy. After I had cleared the table and washed the dishes, I went upstairs and changed into a pale lavender cotton frock and brushed my hair until it fell to my shoulders in lustrous chestnut waves, and then I went back downstairs to wait for Hugh. I was certain he would come tonight, even though... even though it was after eight and Father had already gone to his room. I waited, patient, forcing myself to be patient, and as the hands moved slowly around the face of the clock I assured myself there was a good reason why he... why he was so late. Hugh loved me, I knew he did, just as I loved him. We were going to be married. We hadn't discussed it, we hadn't discussed anything, but it was... it was understood.

He didn't come that evening, nor did he show up the next day, nor the next, and after a week had passed a terrible fear gripped me and it was all I could do to hold it at bay. I mustn't give in to it. I mustn't. I was very, very calm, going about my duties with a cool demeanor that belied the fear and anguish raging inside. I slept very little. I grew pale, my face drawn, but no one seemed to notice. I smiled and pretended nothing was wrong, but something was terribly wrong. I knew that now. Men took advantage of foolish, innocent girls, and after they had what they wanted they sauntered away without the least remorse, but Hugh... Hugh wasn't that way. Not Hugh. Hugh loved me. Steadfastly, I kept hope alive and held the fear at bay and continued to make excuses for him.

He hadn't come yet because he... because he was busy making arrangements for our future. We certainly couldn't live in the stables at Greystone Hall, nor would he continue to work there. He was finding suitable employment, hiring on as bailiff at some other estate, finding a cottage for us to live in. He hadn't come yet because he wanted to have everything set up before he spoke to my father. Yes, that was it, and such things took time, certainly more than a week. I must be patient. I mustn't give in to the fear and panic that surged just below the surface, waiting to tear me asunder. He loved me, he had shown it in a hundred different ways that night under the misty purple-gray sky, and I must have faith in him. He would come soon now, maybe this afternoon, maybe tomorrow, and Father would give his consent and we would be married.

I tried very hard to believe that.

Three more days passed, each an eternity, it seemed, and it had been a week and a half now. Marie needed some things from the village, and I was glad to go for them. Any distraction was welcome. The sky was a dark blue. Although September was almost over, it was still unseasonably warm and the leaves hadn't yet begun to fade. I walked to the village with grief in my heart and the shopping basket on my arm, nodding to passersby on High Street, even smiling at a few of them, very calm, very natural, no one suspecting the emotions inside. I stopped at the fishmonger's and selected the salmon Marie would poach, then stepped over to the greengrocer's and carefully selected lettuce and carrots and vivid yellow squash. I was putting peas into the basket when I heard a cry of delight behind me and turned to see Eppie hurrying toward me. She gave me an exuberant hug and told me how marvelous it was to *see* me and said she had just come in to purchase a few provisions and wasn't it grand we'd run into each other. Then she grinned and stepped back, proudly displaying her thickening waist.

"February," she confided. "I'm not really showing all that much. What do you *think?*"

"I—I think you look glorious, Eppie."

And she did. Her cheeks were fuller and tinted a delicate pink, her eyes a deep, velvety brown, aglow with contentment. Her straw-colored hair, piled up on top of her head as usual, had a glossy sheen, like silk, not straw, and, no longer skinny, Eppie bore no resemblance to a giraffe. She was pretty, almost beautiful in her dusty rose cotton frock. Love and incipient motherhood had brought about this transformation, and it was a wonderful transformation indeed. I took her hand and squeezed it affectionately, glad Eppie, at least, had had her happy ending.

"I'm ever so excited!" she continued. "Jamie is, too. He didn't want me to walk all the way to the village and back but I told him that was nonsense and informed him I simply had to pick up some things. Sugar. Flour. Beans. That charming boy who works behind the counter is going to deliver them after he gets off. Are you almost finished? I'll walk part way with you."

I put a few more things into my basket and paid for them, and then Eppie and I left the greengrocer's and strolled down High Street. I shifted the heavy basket from one arm to another as Eppie, vivacious as ever, regaled me with details of life on the farm with Jamie. She was becoming an accomplished cook and Jamie simply adored her trifle and Yorkshire pudding. Beeswax worked wonders on furniture if you didn't use too much and rubbed it in good, it gave wood a rich gleam. The chickens were laying more eggs now that they'd changed feed. She was still a bit nervous when she had to reach under the hens to get their eggs but she hadn't been pecked in ever so long, they were growing used to her. The cow was a sweetheart and stood so still while she did the milking and she churned her own butter and it took for*ever*. Jamie had tilled a patch of ground for her behind the house and she had started her own vegetable garden. I tried to show a proper interest, but it was difficult when I felt so bleak, so empty inside. Eppie's blissful contentment only emphasized my own unhappiness.

We left High Street and were nearing the side road where Eppie would have to turn off to get to the farm. Lost in thought, I was paying very little attention to her chatter and didn't catch the first part of her question.

"—*aw*ful about Lord Meredith?" she said.

"What? I—I'm sorry, I didn't—"

"Of course *I* don't believe The Bastard was responsible for his death, but I suppose he was, in a way. They did have a fierce argument and Lord Meredith had his stroke immediately afterward, just dropped dead on the spot, he did, but you couldn't call that *mur*der!"

I stopped. I seemed to grow cold all over.

"Eppie, what—what are you talking about?" My voice sounded strange to my ears.

"You mean you haven't *heard?* No one's been talking about anything else for the past four days! Where have you *been,* Angie! Four days ago The Bastard went storming into the house and into his father's study and they had a furious argument, both of them yelling at each other, and then Lord Meredith hit The Bastard with his cane and The Bastard tried to wrest it away from him, and Lord Meredith dropped dead!"

"I—I hadn't heard," I said. Could that be my voice?

I was standing there on the road and the sky was deep blue and the sunlight slanted through the limbs overhead and made shadowy patterns on the ground and I was holding the basket by its handle and it was heavy and Eppie was standing beside me and I knew who she was, of course, but I seemed to be somewhere else and nothing was familiar, everything was curiously distorted and diffused and I was seeing it through a haze.

"Lady Meredith came rushing into the room and started screaming at the top of her lungs and Clinton came rushing in behind her and yelled for the footmen. They overpowered The Bastard and he was carted out to the stables and locked up and put under guard! Janie Yarbro's mother got all the details from the Merediths' cook and Janie came tearing out to the farm to tell *me* all about it. I was stunned, just stunned. You could have knocked me over with a feather!"

How many times have I longed to kill him, kill her? There's murder in my heart still. He had said those words that night, under the pale silver stars, but he hadn't killed his father. His father had dropped dead as Hugh was trying to wrest the cane from him. I stared at Eppie through the haze and felt a dizzy sensation and was afraid I might faint. I didn't. I shifted the basket from one hand to the other, perfectly composed, so calm on the surface. Eppie clasped her hands together, caught up in the excitement of the drama she related with such gusto.

"Lady M. claimed he had *killed* her husband and said she'd see he *hung* for it! They sent for the doctor and sent for the authorities and the doctor came immediately. He said it was death from natural causes, Lord Meredith had been in poor health for some time, but Lady M. wasn't satisfied with that. The authorities arrived late that evening, they had to come from a long way off, and she had calmed down some by that time and knew she couldn't have him hung for murder so she told them The Bastard had stolen some of her jewelry and Lord M. had caught him in the act and that's why they were fighting. She showed them the jewelry— a diamond necklace, a diamond and emerald bracelet— she said he had them in his pocket when the footmen overpowered him."

"They—they took him away," I said.

Eppie shook her head, brown eyes aglow with excitement. "They locked him up in the stables, like I said, a burly footman standing guard over him with a *pistol*. It was two in the afternoon when they took him out there and well after eleven when Clinton took the men out to the stables with a lantern—" She paused for dramatic effect. "It was *empty!*" she exclaimed. "The Bastard was *gone* and they didn't find the footman till the next afternoon. He was trussed up like a hog, on his stomach, his hands and feet tied behind him and the rope looped around his neck so he couldn't struggle without stranglin' himself. He was under the hay. The Bastard had jumped him and grabbed his pistol, knocked him out with the butt. That poor man was tied up there under the hay for over twenty-four hours! He heard the men come into the stables, of course, but he couldn't move because of the rope around his neck, couldn't cry out because he had a gag stuffed in his mouth. The Bastard got away!"

She described it all so vividly, completely caught up in the story, that I seemed to be there, seemed to see it happening. I closed my eyes for a moment and took a deep breath, willing myself to remain steady.

"Did they—catch him?" I asked.

"He just *van*ished, Angie! No one's seen hide nor hair of him! Of course they're still lookin' for him, but it's not likely they'll find him, not after all this time. Cook told Janie Yarbro's mother that none of the servants believe he actually tried to steal that jewelry, but Lady Meredith *claims* he did and no one's going to contradict her. The Bastard's a fugitive!"

"I—I see."

"I can't *believe* you didn't know anything about it. So much excitement! They had Lord Meredith's funeral day before yesterday and the lawyers came to sort everything out and *Clin*ton's Lord Meredith now. He's taken Lady M. away to Bath to recover from her grief. You—you look a bit peaked, Angie. Your face is white."

"I have—I just have a slight headache. It was so lovely to see you," I said. "I've missed you."

"I've missed you, too, Angie. You must come out to the farm and see the improvements we've made."

"I'll do that," I promised.

We hugged, and she started down the side road, turning to wave, so pretty in her dusty rose frock. I waved back. I even managed to smile. I could feel it on my lips. Eppie walked on, disappearing around a curve, and I knew I had to get home, but how? How? I smiled again. I shook my head, alone on the lane, and the haze seemed to thicken and there was a whirring noise in my head. I have no memory of that walk home. One minute I was standing there, and then I was in the kitchen and Marie was giving me a peculiar look as she took the basket from me. She asked if I was ill. I didn't answer. I left the kitchen and started up the stairs and then I blacked out.

Time had no meaning, none whatsoever. I was whirling in a void, and my skin was burning, burning, and there were voices in the darkness and I shook all over and something cool was placed on my forehead and everything receded and I saw Hugh and the haystack and the stars and I saw him running, running away from the authorities, and I would never see him again and I didn't want to live. I wasn't going to live. I was going to burn, so warm, so warm. I drifted in the dark and there were voices again, so dim I could barely hear. Something was held to my lips. I swallowed, and then the darkness swallowed me and I tossed and turned and my hair was wet and my chemise was soaked and I opened my eyes and saw Solonge standing at the side of my bed, all blurry, standing in the haze, and then I was dry and shivering and there were covers over me and I tossed them off and cried out and opened my eyes again and saw Father.

"You're much better, Pumpkin. You're going to get well. Doctor Crandall left some more medicine. You must take it."

"I—I can't. I don't want to—to—"

"You've had a bad fever, my darling."

He said something else, but I didn't hear him. I drifted away into the darkness, and when I opened my eyes again the room was dark and an owl hooted in the night and I was ravenously hungry. I tried to sit up, but I couldn't manage it. Sunshine warmed my eyelids and they fluttered and opened and the room was bright and the owl was gone and birds were twittering in the trees. I heard footsteps on the stairs. The door opened and Solonge came in carrying a tray. The haze was gone. I could see her clearly now, see the relief on her face when I sat up and brushed a limp wave from my brow.

"Thank God," she said. "I've brought some more of Marie's soup, and I do hope you can eat it without assistance. I've been spooning soup down you for the past week, and it's bloody boring work, love."

"You—what day is—"

"You've been in bed eight days. Doctor Crandall said it was a fever of some kind. We were very worried. You

look a sight, love. I wasn't cut out to be a nurse," she
added, setting the tray on the bedside table. "Can you
eat it yourself, or shall I spoon feed you again?"

"I—I think I can manage. Solonge—"

I hesitated, afraid to ask the question, afraid of the
answer. My stepsister arched one smooth brow, waiting.

"Did—did they catch him?" I asked.

"Catch who, love?"

"Hugh—Hugh Bradford. Lady Meredith claimed he
tried to steal some of her jewels, and—and—" My voice
broke. I gnawed my lower lip, turning to look out the
window.

"They haven't caught him," Solonge said. "He's probably already left the country by this time."

"He—he probably has," I whispered.

She looked at me, and I knew she suspected, but she
didn't ask any questions. She sat down by the side of
the bed and put the tray across my knees and chatted
about inconsequential things as I ate. Father came up
later on, puffing a little from the climb. He looked very
old, very tired, I thought. He smiled and handed me a
bunch of flowers he'd picked from the garden and a box
of sweets.

"You had us all scared there for a while, Pumpkin,"
he told me. "How are you feeling?"

"A—a little weak," I confessed.

"Doctor Crandall's coming by again later on this
afternoon. You'll be right as rain in no time."

The doctor came and said I was making swift improvement and left a bottle of foul-tasting medicine
which I had to take every four hours. I stayed in bed
for the next three days, though I was able to bathe and
change into a fresh chemise. On the fourth day I was
able to go downstairs and sit out in the garden for a
while. My face looked drawn. I had lost weight. I was
extremely weak, and then I saw a calendar and realized
it was past my time and I grew even paler. I hadn't
thought about that. It hadn't entered my mind. I was
filled with dread as another day passed, then another,
and still there was no flow. I was five full days overdue

now, and I knew I couldn't endure seeing Father's face when he found out. What was I going to do? Why hadn't I died? Why hadn't I just slipped away during the fever?

Hugh Bradford was gone. I would never see him again. He had never intended to marry me, I realized that now. That had been mere illusion on my part, and all my illusions were gone now. How could I have been so foolish, so incredibly naive? He had had to flee, yes, but one full week had gone by before that fatal argument with his father, and he had made no effort to see me during that time. I loved him. Oh yes, I loved him still, I felt sure I always would, but I knew now that as far as he was concerned I had been just...just another lay, so easy, so very gullible, and now I would pay dearly for it. I tried to tell myself that he would get in touch with me somehow and ask me to join him, but I couldn't delude myself any longer. He was gone, and I had no one to blame but myself for what had happened.

You've grown up at last, Angela, I told myself, and it was true. Sometime, perhaps during the fever, that naive girl with her head full of childish fancies had vanished forever.

The next morning I felt miserable, aching horribly, and the flow finally came. For once I welcomed the cramping and discomfort. I was vastly relieved, of course, and that particular anguish was lifted, but the other was still very much alive inside me. I got better. I grew stronger. Color returned to my cheeks and I was doing my chores again and life resumed its normal pattern, but the anguish was there and at night, when I was alone in bed, when I no longer had to pretend, I didn't think I could possibly go on living without him.

It is said that time heals such wounds, but time passed, and I felt little lessening of grief. That part of me that Hugh Bradford had brought alive had shriveled away. I was no longer whole. I tried to hate him. I couldn't. I couldn't cry, either. I was a woman now, no longer a sensitive, naive girl, and I knew I would go on and make a life for myself somehow, but I would never get over Hugh Bradford, nor would I ever fall in love again. I was certain of that.

October came and the leaves took on autumn hues and it grew colder, skies more gray than blue. Solonge received an engraved invitation from the Duke of Alden, requesting her presence at a dinner party at Alden House, and Marie was very upset that Janine hadn't been invited as well. Solonge tossed the invitation aside. Marie had one of her fits and said of *course* she must go, even if Janine *wasn't* invited. Janine stifled a yawn and said she found all that lot at Alden House dreadfully tedious. Marie told her to shut up. Two weeks later the elegant carriage came for Solonge. She returned late the following afternoon and coolly informed Marie that she could forget all about the Aldens. There would be no more invitations.

"What *hap*pened?" Marie demanded.

"Nothing," Solonge said.

"What do you mean?"

"Precisely that, *Maman* dear."

Solonge refused to discuss the dinner party, but I knew Bart had already left on his Grand Tour, and I strongly suspected she had been the Duke of Alden's only guest. She confirmed this suspicion a few days later when she and I happened to find ourselves alone in the front parlor, Janine having gone up to her room for a nap before dinner. Solonge informed me that she had indeed been the only guest, that her host had served a fabulous meal with oysters in wine sauce and pink roast beef thinly sliced and eggs in aspic, all this with the finest champagne.

"And?" I inquired.

"And then he handed me a long black velvet box and I opened it to find a diamond bracelet the like of which I've never seen. The dazzle almost blinded me. I've rarely felt such temptation."

"You—gave it back?"

Solonge nodded. "He's remarkably virile for a man his age. Tall, lean, bony, with thick silver hair and piercing blue eyes and a small goatee. He's an elegant

dresser and has courtly manners and, of course, an immense fortune, but I prefer to select my own men. I
thanked him for the invitation, thanked him for the
meal and told him I was flattered by his attentions but
not interested in becoming his mistress."

"What did he do?" I asked.

"He smiled a thin smile, told me I should give it
more consideration and suggested we have some more
champagne. Later on I retired to my own room and we
had a late breakfast the next morning and he ordered
a servant to have the carriage brought round to take
me home."

Solonge smoothed down her pale yellow skirt and
settled back against the sofa cushions, observing me
with careful scrutiny. I got up and stepped over to the
fireplace to turn the logs with the poker, for it was late
October now and already quite chilly.

"You're looking much better these days," she remarked. "I suppose it's safe to assume you're not pregnant."

I felt my cheeks pale. "How—"

"I spent a lot of time watching over you when you
had the fever, and you babbled quite a lot about Hugh
Bradford and the haystack and the stars, love. I didn't
need a crystal ball to know what happened."

"Did—did anyone else hear—"

"That's one of the reasons I spent so much time playing nurse. I didn't want Janine or *Maman* or your father
to hear any of those extremely indiscreet phrases you
kept muttering in your delirium. No one else knows.
You'll survive it, Angie," she added, and her voice was
unusually kind.

I put the poker back in its holder and brushed a
chestnut wave away from my cheek. "I suppose I will,"
I said.

"And you'll be much better off, darling. Believe me.
I know you aren't able to see it now, but—men like
Hugh Bradford bring nothing but anguish to any woman
foolish enough to love them. I know whereof I speak.
They're devilishly appealing, yes, but they're danger-

ous, destructive. You're no longer your own person. You get so caught up in their moods you—" She cut herself short, frowning.

"You loved him, too," I said.

"I thought I did. You're too good for a man like him, Angie. One day you'll be able to see how lucky you were things—turned out the way they did."

"I—I thought he meant to marry me. I was— Oh, Solonge, I was such a fool."

Solonge stood up and came over to take my hand. "We're all entitled to make our mistakes, darling," she told me. "Even you."

She let go of my hand then and grimaced, as though disgusted with herself for stepping out of character. She sighed and became the cool, self-confident beauty, all worldly poise, and neither of us ever referred to the conversation again.

November came, then December, and although the terrible grief was there, aching inside me, it wasn't nearly as pronounced as before and I found myself actually smiling, laughing as I watched a big brown dog skittering about over the ice outside. Heavily bundled up against the cold, I went to gather holly and ivy to decorate the house for Christmas. I actually forgot about him for several hours, and I took that as a very good sign. Maybe . . . maybe soon I would be able to go to sleep without seeing that face, without remembering that night under the stars.

Shortly after New Year's Day I was in the kitchen, helping Marie prepare dinner. Solonge and Janine were spending the weekend with friends at a house party, and we were going to have a simple meal. Marie took the meat pie from the oven. I was finishing up the salad. I heard Father coughing even though he was in his study, the door closed. I paused, listening. It was a dreadful cough, much worse than usual . . . louder. There was a cry then. Marie dropped a plate. It shattered on the floor. I was already rushing into the hall.

I flung open the study door. Father was at his desk, his face as white as chalk. He was clutching a handkerchief soaked with blood, and there were flecks of blood all over the papers in front of him. He was trembling. Marie rushed past me and yelled for me to go fetch Doctor Crandall, as quickly as possible. I stared at my father, stunned, too stunned to move, and somehow he managed a weak smile. Marie was helping him to his feet. "Go!" she yelled, and I raced down the hall and grabbed my heavy cloak and hurried out into the night, running through the darkness and the cold toward Doctor Crandall's cottage, praying fervently, possessed by panic, and then I was pounding on the door and when the doctor opened it, I couldn't speak, words wouldn't come.

He wasted no time trying to question me. He got his coat and his black bag and then we were walking rapidly back toward the cottage. My stepmother had managed to get Father into bed in his room, and the doctor said he needed to be alone with his patient and ordered both of us out of the room. Marie protested, but he placed a palm on the small of her back and gave her a gentle but firm shove toward the door. We went into the parlor and waited, and Marie's face was sharp and shrewish, pale beneath the heavy makeup, her thin red lips pressed into a tight line. Her eyes glittered with anger, but I knew that was merely a defense. She clasped and unclasped her hands, genuinely worried.

It seemed hours before the doctor finally came into the parlor, his expression grave indeed.

"How bad is it?" Marie asked.

"Bad," he said. "Very bad. I gave him some medicine, and he's sleeping now, but—" He didn't finish the sentence.

"He's going to get well," I said. "Isn't—isn't he?"

Doctor Crandall didn't answer. He and Marie exchanged looks. I knew I had to face the truth. My father had consumption. I had known it all along, of course, but I had refused to acknowledge it. Like Father, I had pretended nothing was seriously wrong. There could be no more pretense now. Tears streamed down my cheeks in tiny rivulets, but I didn't sob. I didn't give in to the terrible grief. I was going to be strong. I had to be, for Father's sake.

"There's nothing more I can do now," Doctor Crandall said. "I'll come back tomorrow, Mrs. Howard."

Marie nodded. Doctor Crandall left. I made a pot of strong tea and insisted my stepmother have a cup. I told her I would sit up with Father, and she nodded again, for once letting someone else take control.

January was bitterly cold, a hard crust of ice covering the ground, icicles hanging from all the windowsills. Father was very, very weak, his complexion like thin, pale parchment, but he ate all his broth and drank his liquids and smiled at my light, pleasant remarks. We kept his room as warm as possible, and I spent hours with him each day, sitting at his bedside, talking to him, holding his hand. Often I read aloud to him. He enjoyed that a great deal, although he always grew weary and drifted off to sleep after I'd read no more than a few pages.

Marie spent hours with him, too, and Solonge and Janine made brief, polite visits to his room each day. He seemed to grow stronger after a while. Some of the color returned to his cheeks, and his eyes seemed brighter. His coughing spells weren't as bad as before, nor did they last as long. He was able to sit before the fire for short periods while we changed the bed linen and tidied up, and he began to eat a few solids. Doctor Crandall came three times a week, and he agreed that there had been a definite improvement. I began to hope.

Although the ice remained and it was still cold, the sun began to shine in February, sparkling brilliantly on the ice. I came into his room one afternoon to find him sitting up in the big chair by the fire. Marie had been with him earlier, and he was wearing his favorite tan frock coat and a neckcloth of faded yellow silk. His hair was neatly brushed, gleaming pale silver gold in the sunlight slanting through the windows. His cheeks were soft pink, his gray eyes sad yet full of warm affection as he watched me set down the tray I'd brought.

"My," I said, "you're all dressed, and looking quite handsome, I must add."

"In your honor, Pumpkin."

I was puzzled. "My honor?"

"Unless I'm terribly mistaken, today is your birthday."

"I—why, yes, I suppose it is. I'd forgotten all about it."

"You're eighteen years old today," he said. "I'm sorry I don't have a present for you, Pumpkin, but I—uh—" He paused and smiled a wry, gentle smile. "I've had very little opportunity to shop of late."

"Having you look so fit and handsome is the best present I could possibly have," I told him.

I poured him a cup of the hot raspberry tea Doctor Crandall said was so good for him. The cup rattled slightly in the saucer as he took it from me. He was still very weak, and he looked unusually weary, as though getting into his clothes had sapped what little energy he had. I adjusted the blanket over his knees, put another log on the fire and then sat down across from him.

"Would you like me to read to you?" I asked.

"Not—not this afternoon, Pumpkin. I'd rather just—chat for a while. It's been a long time since we've had a really good talk."

"We'll have lots of them," I promised. "You're getting so much better you'll be—why, any day now you'll be in your study, working on your history again. You'll be able to finish it at last."

He shook his head, and a sad smile rested briefly on his lips. "I fear not, Pumpkin."

"You will," I assured him. "I know you will."

"I'm never going to finish it. I never started it."

"But—"

"Dreams," he said quietly. He shook his head. "I had such dreams, my darling, but I fear I hadn't the determination, the stamina, the will. All those years shut up in my study, and what do I have to show for them? Notes. Thousands and thousands of notes. I realized a long time ago it—it was too late, but I continued to pretend. I continued to dream." He paused, gazing thoughtfully at the fire. After a moment he sighed. "Dreams aren't enough," he added.

"Father—"

"Remember that," he told me, and there was quiet urgency in his voice. "Dreams aren't enough. You must follow them through. And you will, Pumpkin. You have character and intelligence and spirit and you'll never be satisfied with hollow self-delusions. You'll never use your dreams as an escape, as I did. You'll look life in the eye. You'll never make—compromises."

"You didn't either," I protested. "You—you were a marvelous teacher who inspired hundreds of boys. You—you're loved and respected by everyone in the community. You made a great contribution."

"I settled for less, my darling. I gave up. I gave in. That's something you must never do."

He looked at me with those sad, resigned gray eyes, and I could tell he expected some kind of reply.

"I—I won't, Father," I said, trying to sound bright. "I'm going to make you proud of me. I promise."

"You will, Pumpkin. I—I feel sure of it."

He smiled a weak smile then. I could tell he was too tired to talk any more. I asked him if he wanted more tea, and he shook his head and asked me to send Marie in to him and asked if he might have a birthday kiss before I left. I went to him and leaned over and kissed his cheek. He reached up to touch my hair, ever so tenderly, and then he put his arms around me and held me to him.

"Take care, my darling," he whispered.

I fetched Marie, and she went to him, and I knew. I found myself waiting, consciously waiting, my throat tight, a strange, tremulous feeling inside. I prowled restlessly around the house, unable to concentrate, and after a while I went into the kitchen to prepare dinner and heard my stepmother call out and I stood there in front of the stove clutching the handle of a saucepan, and I couldn't move, I couldn't breathe. If I made the slightest movement I would fall apart, I would start sobbing and never be able to stop. Several minutes passed and then Solonge stepped into the kitchen and took the saucepan out of my hand and put her arms around me, and I clung to her and sobbed and tears too long unshed spilled down my cheeks.

Somehow I managed to get through the next four days. I seemed to be in a trance, functioning correctly, doing everything I should do but completely unable to associate myself with any of it. It was happening to someone else and I was watching it from afar. I remember the church and the organ music, and I remember all the people who came to speak to us and tell us what a wonderful man my father had been. I remember Eppie taking me into her arms and wailing, and I remember the churchyard and the ice and that long black hole. I remember them lowering the coffin into it, and I remember Solonge holding my hand so tightly my fingers felt broken. It was all happening to someone else, so I didn't give way. I told my father good-bye and dropped the first handful of dirt onto the coffin, and people said I was being very brave and talked about how well I was holding up.

My stepmother was calm and efficient, making all the arrangements, attending to all the details before and after the funeral with superb control. She showed no outward signs of grief, but her face was lined and she looked older, despite the makeup. In her widow's black she received all the people who came to pay their condolences and had a conference with the lawyers and received the new schoolmaster who was interested in buying our cottage, should she be interested in selling. It belonged to her now, as did all my father's possessions, and she was my legal guardian until I turned twenty-one. She busied herself making inventories, black skirt rustling crisply, and I felt something like a stab wound when she sold all Father's books to a dealer who quickly carted them away.

A week after the funeral a majestic black and silver carriage drew up in front of the cottage and a footman in white velvet livery held the door open as a tall, lean gentleman with silver hair and goatee stepped out. I was watching from a window upstairs, and I knew at once who he was, for he was exactly as Solonge had described him. He wore white satin knee breeches and a matching white satin frock coat with huge diamond-studded buttons. The long white satin waistcoat beneath was embroidered with tiny silver and sky blue flowers. Fine white lace cascaded from his jabot and spilled over his wrists. If the Duke of Alden intended to impress my stepmother, he was certainly dressed for it. I went downstairs in time to see Marie usher him into the front parlor. He had not asked to see Solonge.

He and Marie were closed up in the parlor for over three hours, and it was after six before he left. Marie stood in the hallway, watching through the open door as his carriage pulled away. There was a very determined expression on her face, and her green eyes were full of greed. I could easily guess what the Duke must have proposed to her, and, seeing that venal expression, I knew she had already reached a decision. If she couldn't marry her girls into society, she would settle for something less respectable but far more remunerative. Somehow that didn't surprise me. I felt I was beyond surprise at that point. She and Solonge had a furious argument that night. I learned the results of it the following morning.

"Well, girls," Marie said at breakfast, "it seems we'll shortly be on our way to London."

Janine yawned, too sleepy to show much interest. She gazed at her coffee cup with limpid blue eyes, silvery-blonde hair spilling to her shoulders in a luxuriant tumble. Solonge gave her mother a sharp, resentful look, and Marie smiled a tight smile. That avaricious gleam in her eyes was even more apparent this morning. She looked hard, very hard indeed.

"All the arrangements are being made," she continued. "It will take a few days to settle things up here, and then we can leave this dreadful place forever."

Solonge came up to my room a short while later. I

was sitting in front of the window, gazing out at the sun-splashed ice, seeing the past. I heard the rustle of her yellow silk skirt and smelled her exquisite perfume, but I didn't turn around.

"You're going to do it, aren't you?" I said.

"I haven't much choice, love. Your father left no money at all. What we'll get from the house and the furnishings wouldn't last a year, not with four of us to provide for. According to *Maman,* it's my duty to come to the aid of my poor, penniless family."

"I see," I said.

"*Maman* drove a very shrewd bargain. Not only will the Duke keep me in most lavish style, but he'll also set her up in her own business. It seems she's finally found her calling."

I turned to face her at last. "As a procuress for her own daughters?" I asked.

It was a bitter remark, and it hurt, I could see that, but Solonge didn't reply, not at first. A faint smile curled wryly on her lips. The beautiful, vivacious girl with piquant features and lively green-brown eyes had grown up into a worldly, disillusioned woman, and I knew she was lost to me, too. She would move in a different world, and she would no longer be there with her caustic remarks and bitchy affection. That saddened me.

"I intend to see that you're taken care of," she said quietly.

"I can take care of myself!"

"Yes," she said, "I imagine you can, when the time comes, but for now don't—don't judge us too harshly, love. Life isn't always as clear cut as it might seem."

And so, ten days later, I found myself saying good-bye to the empty cottage where I had spent my first eighteen years. I wandered through the bare rooms. All the furnishings had been sold at auction, and the new schoolmaster and his wife would be moving in tomorrow, bringing their own things. It was very cold, for the fireplaces were empty, too, and I shivered in my long blue cloak. I stepped into the small, sun-filled study where I had spent so many hours with my father and whispered a final good-bye, and then I went out to the coach where Janine and Marie were waiting, our bags strapped securely on top. Solonge had departed two days earlier with the Duke of Alden.

I climbed into the coach and closed the door. In a few moments we were bowling down the lane, Marie lost in speculation, gloved hands folded neatly in her lap, Janine already beginning to grow drowsy. As we came to the main road and rounded a curve I glimpsed Greystone Hall in the distance, rooftops bleak above the bare trees. The new Lord Meredith was rarely there, preferring the distractions of London, and his aunt was living permanently in Bath, drinking more than ever, it was said. I thought of the surly stableboy who had stolen the heart of a saucy child and broken it five years later, and my eyes were dry. I felt a hard resolve inside. There would be no more tears. The past was behind me now, and an uncertain future loomed ahead. I was going to face it squarely in the eye, and somehow, I knew not how, I was going to keep that promise I had made to my father on the last day of his life. I was going to make him proud of me.

Book Two
Angela
London

Chapter Seven

Church bells pealing woke me out of a sound sleep, and I rubbed my eyes, sitting up against the pillows. There were so many marvelous bells in London, I reflected, each with its own distinct sound. Marie said they drove her crazy, pealing all the time, but then the only sound Marie liked was the clinking of gold, and there had been plenty of that particular music these past two years. A shrewd, crafty businesswoman, my step-mother. There was no denying it. The terror of the Royal Exchange, constantly expanding, and in more ways than one, I thought uncharitably, visualizing my stepmother's new girth. The dress shop the Duke of Alden had set her up in had been a huge success, particularly with me working like a slave behind the scenes, but that hadn't been enough for her, no indeed, not for the new Marie.

Sighing, I climbed out of bed, performed my ablutions and began to dress. The bells had stopped pealing now, but through the open window came the rumble of traffic, the cries of street hawkers, the hooting of barges floating up the Thames. London was never silent, but one soon grew accustomed to the constant noise, just as one grew accustomed to the smells. Stinking, it was, the fetid odors enough to knock you down till you learned to ignore them. Didn't notice them at all now that we'd been here so long. Well...hardly at all. I put on the ruffled white cotton petticoat and slipped the new sky blue linen frock over it. It was printed with tiny amethyst flowers and miniscule brown leaves. With snug waist, modestly low bodice and small puffed sleeves, it was a fetching garment, and at least it was *new.* After dealing with used clothes so many months I was able to appreciate that.

Six months after our arrival, with the dress shop doing a brisk business, Marie had decided to sell used clothes as well, eventually ending up with four separate stalls. Kept me busy, that did, for guess who sorted the old clothes and took them to the stalls? I ran one of them, too, learning to barter sternly with foul-smelling fishwives who avidly pawed over the faded silks and napworn velvets. Marie had made a huge profit from those stalls, and without any help from the Duke. Didn't satisfy her though. Not Marie. She was restless, bored with the dress shop and stalls and looking for new horizons. Gambling. That's where the real money was, she declared. If she could run her own gambling house, she'd make a fortune.

Mr. Theodore Gresham had been most helpful there. Stout, middle-aged and beginning to go bald, Mr. Gresham was a textile merchant who had stores in the Royal Exchange and all over England. Marie had met him several months ago and had promptly noticed his interest in Janine, who had done nothing but sulk and complain ever since we arrived in London. Solonge was living in splendor with her own town house, with three carriages, a magnificent wardrobe and more servants than she could count, not to mention her dazzling collection of jewelry. It wasn't *fair,* Janine pouted. Mr. Gresham was decidedly plebeian, not an aristocratic bone in his body, but he was even wealthier than the

Duke, and he and Marie soon came to terms. Mr. Gresham agreed to invest an enormous amount of money in Marie's new venture, and Janine finally left the nest. As his business required several long buying trips a year, Janine was able to nap to her heart's content, and in surroundings even more luxurious than her sister's.

Marie had promptly leased this building and spent a frantic six weeks renovating it—dozens of workmen creating a bedlam of noise and confusion, Marie in the midst of them, shrieking orders, driving them mercilessly—and Marie's Place, London's newest gambling house, had opened three months ago. Decorated in a sumptuous blue and silver decor, with crystal chandeliers, a white marble bar and an elegant white marble staircase, it was already an immense success, thanks in part to the aristocratic customers the Duke of Alden had sent round. All the tables were run by very attractive young women, all blonde, their low-cut silver gowns matching the decor, and there were a number of private rooms upstairs for more intimate games. Marie knew how to turn a profit. No question about it.

Marie's living quarters and office were downstairs, behind the main room, and there was a large kitchen and lounge in the basement. I had a bedroom and sitting room upstairs, well removed from those private rooms where Jen and Sally, Lucille and others frequently retired with a well-heeled patron. Marie insisted I keep away from the girls, but I had gotten to know them nevertheless. Although none of them lived here, they were usually hanging around during non-working hours, and they had taught me how to shuffle, how to deal, how to play even the most demanding game with skill. I could easily run a table myself, I reflected, though I had no desire to do so. Marie kept me strictly behind the scenes, running errands, checking supplies, helping with the book work, and in three months' time not a single paying customer had caught a glimpse of me. A dark-haired stepdaughter with too-high cheekbones and a wide mouth wouldn't be good for the image.

Smiling ruefully, I stepped over to the mirror and

began to brush my long chestnut hair. My looks, or lack of them, hadn't mattered in the least when I was working behind the used-clothes stall, but here it was different. My stepmother still saw me as the gawky, tiresome adolescent who was plain as mud compared to her splendid pair of daughters, and I had no doubt she'd be delighted were I to start wearing a sack over my head. I wasn't blonde and languid and seductive like the girls who worked at Marie's Place, true, but as I looked at my reflection I doubted a glimpse of my face would frighten the paying customers. Some men might actually like violet-gray eyes and glossy chestnut waves. Not that I cared, of course. Not that I was interested in men. I had learned my lesson the hard way two and a half years ago, and I wasn't about to let myself in for that kind of pain again.

Setting down the brush, I sighed, fluffed my hair a bit and then left the bedroom, passing through the small, pleasant sitting room with its large bookcase crammed full of the battered volumes I had picked up at Miller's on Fleet. I could rarely afford new books, not with the pittance Marie reluctantly doled out to me. I received no salary, but Solonge had insisted I have a weekly allowance for pocket money. As we rarely saw her, she had no idea just how little that allowance was. My stepmother squeezed every penny until it squealed, and even then she hated to part with it. She provided food, clothes and lodging for her late husband's daughter and wasn't about to squander good money on anything else. A few shillings a week should be more than ample, she decreed, and I rarely received more.

I stepped into the spacious hall and made my way to the elegant white marble staircase that led to the main gaming room below. I had endured two years and two months of my stepmother's gracious charity. I could endure ten months more easily enough. I would be twenty-one then, no longer her legal ward, and I intended to leave this charming establishment with its "private" rooms quick as a wink. If I couldn't find work as a seamstress's assistant, I was certain to find re-

spectable employment at the Royal Exchange. I had
made many friends among the shop owners there, and
I felt sure one of them would give me work.

I would have a hard time of it, sure, I realized that—
being on your own in London was going to be scary—
but I had become considerably tougher during the past
two years. You had to be tough in London or you'd be
swallowed right up in its hungry maw. The sensitive
girl of days gone by had become shrewder, sharper,
worldlier, too. No more romantic illusions. Grim reality
surrounded me on every side, and I faced it with shoulders squared.

Moving down the stairs, I passed through the spacious main room. It was elegant indeed with its dark
blue carpet and pale gray walls and crystal chandeliers.
Dark blue velvet and cloth-of-silver drapes hung at the
windows, and bottles of the very best wines and bran-
dies were arranged on shelves behind the long white
marble bar. They were served to customers free of charge,
my stepmother maintaining that the more they drank,
the more recklessly they gambled. Hepplewhite had
made the gaming tables with their superbly carved legs
and ivory finish. The chairs were ivory, too, with seats
and oval-shaped backs upholstered in the same blue
velvet used for the drapes. Marie's Place was a grand
establishment, all right, even if Marie had had to sell
her own daughter in order to acquire it.

Not that Janine minded, I thought as I moved down
the small enclosed stairway to the basement. Gresham
made very few demands on her, his pride of ownership
much stronger than his libido.

"Good morning, Miss Angela," Bennett said as I
stepped into the kitchen. "Although it isn't rightly
morning, now is it? Well after eleven by my clock. Almost noon. No one gets up early around here."

"We stay open quite late," I reminded him. "Is that
fresh coffee?"

"Just made it. Made some honey and cinnamon rolls,
too. Your favorites. Could I persuade you to eat a decent

breakfast? Wouldn't take me any time to make some eggs, some bacon, some stewed mushrooms."

I shook my head. "Just coffee, Bennett, and one of the rolls."

"You'll eat two," he said sternly.

Tall, lean, with a fierce demeanor and gruff manner that belied his genial nature, Bennett was our cook— Marie referred to him as "the chef"—and he was a treasure. Though born in Liverpool and as English as fish and chips, he prepared the fanciest French meals with the flair and aplomb of a native Parisian, meeting even Marie's exacting standards. Bennett had his own quarters behind the kitchen, with his own private entrance from the mews, while the other servants Marie employed had tiny rooms in the attic. I was surprised I wasn't up there as well.

"Is my stepmother up yet?" I inquired.

"Came storming in here half an hour ago, out of sorts because the liquor supply is low and the wine merchant hasn't called, upset because the new playing cards haven't been delivered, distressed because one of the footmen had to oust Lord Brock last night when that young gentleman got altogether too rowdy. Her usual charming self," he added.

Bennett was an independent soul, confident of his skills, and he was completely unintimidated by his dragon of an employer, nor would he take any guff from her. Marie tolerated his "insolence" because she knew full well he would be impossible to replace.

"Here's your coffee, Miss Angela. See that you eat both these rolls."

"They look delicious, Bennett," I told him.

"Bound to be," he said. "I made 'em, didn't I?"

I had to smile at that. Bennett permitted himself a wry grin.

I carried coffee and rolls into the adjoining lounge where the girls took their breaks, gossiped about customers and flirted with any male employee who happened to be around. With its pale lime green carpet, ivory walls and sofas and chairs done in flowered pastels and beige, it was a pleasant, comfortable room with a number of low tables finished in ivory. Gentlemen not playing at the tables frequently came down to smoke, enjoy their drinks and compare winnings and losses. Sinking into one of the chairs, I leisurely sipped my coffee. It was delicious, strong as could be, and the rolls were delicious, too. I wondered what Marie had planned for me today. Would I be doing book work or running errands or supervising the maids? Marie's Place must be spotless every night, the chandeliers carefully lowered on their chains, fresh candles inserted in the holders and pendants cleaned. I usually ended up doing half the work myself.

"Here you are!" Marie exclaimed, marching into the room. "I sent one of the maids up to fetch you and she told me you weren't in your room. I suspected I'd find you lolling down here."

"Lolling away," I admitted.

"Don't be impertinent, Angela!"

I longed to stick my tongue out at her, but I didn't. Marie resented the "responsibility" I represented, and I resented her tyranny, but open hostility between us was rare. Much easier to endure, ignore and count the days. I had determined that a long time ago.

"I've had a dreadful morning," she declared. "The wine merchant hasn't delivered the new stock. We're almost out of fresh playing cards—the printer *promised* they'd be here. And on top of that Blake took it upon himself to throw out one of our very best customers last night."

"Lord Brock? I heard about that."

"Such a charming lad," she remarked. "Blake is *paid* to keep order, but he was entirely too rough with Lord Brock."

"That charming lad tried to rape Jen in the foyer, I understand. So unpractical of him."

"Unpractical?"

"For ten pounds he could have taken her upstairs and had her without any fuss at all."

Marie didn't care for that observation at all. Her

green eyes glittered dangerously, but she held her tongue, marching across the room to pour herself a brandy from the decanter on one of the tables. She had become quite fond of her brandy these days. Fond of her food as well. Once slender, my stepmother was now frankly stout, her hair dyed a brassy, improbable red and stacked atop her head in a tumble of curls that fell coyly across her brow. Her face, once so sharp, was now decidedly plump, jowls very much in evidence, and the black satin beauty mark she stuck on her cheekbone didn't help at all. In her black silk dress and diamond earrings, she looked coarse. She looked like what she was, I thought.

"What goes on in those rooms is none of your affair," she informed me in a sharp voice.

"Definitely not," I said.

"You're growing quite impossible, Angela!"

"I'll try to be better," I promised.

"Are you *mock*ing me?"

"Of course not, Marie. I wouldn't dream of it."

She gave me another of her dangerous looks and finished her glass of brandy, then ordered me to follow her up to her office. I obeyed, dutiful as could be. Her office was the very heart of Marie's Place, a huge iron safe standing in one corner, bills and receipts piled in neat stacks on top of the desk, each to be scrutinized with an eagle eye. Marie ran her domain with the stern precision of a general, and she brooked no insubordination from her troops.

"Sally was late again last night," she complained. "I intend to dock her salary. *That*'ll teach her."

"Maybe so," I said.

"Jen tore her gown last night. Those gowns cost me a fortune! She's going to have to pay for it herself."

"Why don't you send the bill to Lord Brock?"

"I'm in no mood for your sarcasm, Angela! Here's five pounds. I want you to go to Underwood's print shop off Fleet and pay the man for the cards, and if they're not ready you're to *stay* there and stand *over* him until he has them all printed up."

"Certainly, Marie."

"We'll need them tonight. Don't come back without them!"

"I wouldn't dare," I said sweetly.

Marie scowled and waved me out of the office, and I put the five pounds in my pocket and left, delighted to see it was a lovely April day with the sky all cloudless and blue. Not that you could see that much of it with rooftops crowded together and slanting out over the streets, sometimes almost touching in the middle. A housewife on one side of the street could borrow a cup full of sugar from her neighbor across the street simply by reaching out the front window upstairs. Needn't go out at all. Must be real handy in inclement weather, I reflected as I strolled down the street.

I kept close to the wall to avoid being splattered by the slops frequently emptied out of the windows above, and often I had to duck to avoid crowning myself on the painted wooden signs that hung over the pavement in front of shops. London was a fascinating maze of streets and alleys and courts and squares, all jumbled together with no apparent rhyme or reason. Had to know your way around if you didn't want to get lost. Had to keep your guard up, too, with pickpockets and rogues abounding on every side. Young women, in particular, were tasty prey for villains with evil intentions, but this young woman knew how to handle herself on the streets. Learned it early on, I had. If a scathing remark didn't do the trick, teeth and claws and a knee to the groin were invariably discouraging.

No villain tried to accost me today, although a husky butcher's apprentice gave me a lewd grin and a drunken old fop in a soiled blue satin frock coat attempted to block my way as he ogled me through his quizzing glass. I gave the butcher's apprentice a stiff middle finger and shoved the old fop out of my way. A shower of water and potatoe peelings rained on him from above as he stumbled into the edge of the street. A trio of gin-soaked fishwives applauded drunkenly, and one of them snatched his wig. Turning a corner, I noticed that bright yellow daffodils were blooming in the tiny park across the way, blue hyacinths, too. Lots of flowers in London, which was surprising with all the soot, smoke and cinders in the air.

I strolled on, moving down a busy thoroughfare now. Street hawkers shouted their wares, lustily proclaiming the virtues of roasted nuts and nice fresh oranges and sausage rolls fit for a bleedin' king. Carts, carriages and drays rumbled down the cobbled street, creating a perpetual congestion, and there was an occasional sedan chair, too, the bearers shouting angrily as they made their way through the tangle. Street sweeps darted hither and yon with straw brooms, sweeping up the dung, and dogs barked. As I moved along, a horse reared in the street and a small cart overturned, a barrel of eels tumbling off and splitting open on the cobbles with a noisy bang. Traffic was momentarily stalled. Pandemonium prevailed.

Whips cracked. Horses neighed. A fistfight broke out between the driver of the cart and a burly footman who leaped down from one of the carriages, both of them yelling furiously. A swarm of urchins spilled into the street, snatching up the eels, and a plump dame with a beauty patch stuck on her rouged cheek pulled back the curtain of her sedan chair and peeked out to see what was causing the delay. Another exciting drama taking place right before my eyes. Happened all the time in London. Never knew what you were going to see. The color and noise and vitality of this huge, bustling metropolis was always fascinating, I thought, watching as impatient drivers bounded down to set the cart back up and separate the fighters. The footman's jacket was torn, the cart driver's nose bleeding profusely. He scrambled back up onto the seat, clicked the reins and drove on, leaving pieces of barrel and flopping eels to be ground under the wheels of vehicles that followed.

Underwood's print shop was in a dingy court off Fleet Street, crowded between a stationer's and a shop with windows displaying heaps of dusty pottery, a cat snoozing contentedly amidst them. A bell over the door jingled as I entered Underwood's. The place was filled with dust and clutter, boxes of paper stacked against the walls, ink-smeared rags on the floor, but there was a wonderful smell of glue and grease and old linen. Underwood's was shabby, true, but the work produced in its back room was of the finest quality. The playing cards we used had glossy blue backs, bordered with a rim of silver, a silver *M* in the center of each. Elegant, indeed, and designed by Underwood himself, a cantankerous old recluse who, it was said, hadn't left the back room in over a decade. Slept on a pile of rags beside his printing press, he did, food and necessities brought in by a series of assistants.

"May I help you?" a hearty voice inquired.

His current assistant stepped through the curtains leading to that mysterious back room, a tall, muscular blond with merry brown eyes and a most engaging grin. He wore a thin black leather bib apron over his coarsely woven white shirt and tan cord breeches. The sleeves of his shirt were rolled up, displaying forearms and biceps, and a wave of that thick blond hair dipped down rakishly over his forehead. His eyes filled with male appreciation as he studied me, and his grin broadened. I rarely saw that honest, good-natured appreciation in a man's eyes. Couldn't help but be flattered.

"I've come for some playing cards," I said. "I'm Angela Howard."

He arched an inquisitive brow, still in the dark. I could hear the printing press grinding away in the back room, its clatter punctuated by an occasional hoarse oath.

"Marie's Place," I added. "Two dozen decks of playing cards were to have been delivered today. My stepmother sent me to see about them."

"Oh," he said. *"Her!"*

I smiled. The youth smiled, too, and then, his voice full of apology, informed me the cards wouldn't be ready for several hours. My distress was clear, and my expression caused him no small amount of concern. He explained that they were terribly behind, with a huge number of back orders to fill, and I gave him a woeful look and said I quite understood. He took a deep breath, made a decisive nod and promised me he would get right on them himself.

"Tell you what," he added, "since you'll have to make another trip and as you've gone to so much trouble already, why don't we take a pound off the price? My way of making it up to you for the delay."

"That—that would be very generous," I replied, thinking hard. "I wonder if it would be possible for you to give me a receipt for the full amount? I'd be ever so grateful."

He gave me a conspiratorial wink. "Sure thing," he said, and a few minutes later I left the shop with a receipt for five pounds, a pound to spend as I pleased and a promise that the cards would be ready by five o'clock this afternoon. Pulled a fast one on Marie, I had. Didn't feel the least bit of remorse, either. My step-mother would undoubtedly have the vapors and go into a swift decline if she knew someone had done her out of an entire pound, but I had bloody well earned it. I had earned myself a holiday, too, and I had the whole afternoon to do whatever I wished. Might go gaze at Westminster Abbey. Might stroll through the park and throw bread crumbs to the ducks. Might even visit one of the waxworks that were so popular—Mrs. Salmon's was said to be a wonder, with all the Kings and Queens in full regalia and hair-raising tableaux featuring savage aborigines.

I'd love to see the aborigines, but first, of course, I must pay a visit to Miller's on Fleet, just a short walk from here. Rarely had more than a few pennies to spend there. Who knew what treasures I might find today, with a full pound in my pocket? I turned onto Fleet and hurried past the booksellers' shops and printing establishments and cozy-looking coffee houses. Newsboys raced past, waving the latest broadsheets, shouting the news. Poets and journalists stood in front of doorways, ardently discussing literary matters. Plump gentlemen in wigs and frock coats idly examined the volumes piled up on tables in front of the bookshops, but I wasn't going to waste my time looking for bargains, not when Miller's was up ahead.

Miller was an enormously fat, lethargic chap who loved to read and, as a youth, hadn't been able to afford new books. Coming into a small inheritance some years ago, he had decided that there might be a great many people unable to buy new books, a great many others who would eagerly sell volumes they had already read, and he had gone into the used-book business, eventually opening the shop that had become a mecca for book lovers of every stamp. Miller sold everything, the finest classics, the most sensational thrillers, journals and magazines, too, all for a fraction of their original cost. Shopgirls flocked to Miller's to find vicarious romance for a few pence. Scholars searched industriously through the dusty stacks hoping to locate a rare tome long out of print. Oliver Goldsmith was a regular customer, and even the great Dr. Johnson was said to frequent the place on occasion, though he had harsh words to say about the dog.

The smell of dust and mildew assailed my nostrils as I stepped into the shop. Strong enough to knock you flat, it was, but that was all part of the charm. The gloom, too. The front windows were so dirty only feeble rays of sunlight seeped in, and Miller had a terror of candles. You had to be really passionate about books to frequent Miller's, for the shop was like a labyrinth, shelves covering all the walls and most of the floor space with only tiny aisles between. Books everywhere. Cramming the shelves. Piled on the floor. Stacked on the wooden steps leading up to a gallery that was itself so stacked with reading matter one feared it would come toppling down on one's head. The dog Dr. Johnson so detested thumped its heavy tail and yawned lazily as I came in. As big as a pony and as shaggy as a sheep, it was curled up comfortably on a nest of yellowing medical journals, its head resting on a battered copy of Dr. Johnson's famous dictionary. Perhaps *that* was why

Johnson detested the beast, I thought, smiling to myself.

"Hello, Hercules," I said warmly. "Remember me?"

Hercules thumped his tail a couple of times, yawned
again and settled his heavy jowls on the enormous com-
pilation of words. I entered the maze of bookshelves and
was soon caught up, my eyes greedily searching out
titles. Greek drama. Latin grammars. Volumes of ser-
mons. Books on crime and punishment and botany and
boats and every subject imaginable. Novels by the thousands, blood-and-thunder thrillers brazenly sharing the
shelves with the finest prose, tepid romances leaning
timidly against the bawdy works of Fielding and Defoe.
Stacks of books on the floor made progress hazardous,
but I moved deeper into the maze and soon came upon
Miller himself, lolling heavily in an overstuffed chair
with bottom sprung and nap threadbare, the poems of
John Donne in his hands.

Miller looked up, blinked and shifted position, no
more eager to stir himself than Hercules had been.
Round face pasty, spectacles covering watery blue eyes,
thin brown hair splayed over his brow in a monkish
fringe, Miller brushed a fleck of lint from the lapel of
his rumpled brown frock coat and adjusted his soiled
tan neckcloth. A cup of cold tea sat on a stack of books
at his side in a chipped saucer, a half-eaten bun beside
it.

"Miss Angela Howard, isn't it?" he drawled lazily.
Miller remembered the names of all his customers, even
those, like me, who rarely came in and weren't able to
spend much. "Haven't seen you in a while," he continued.

"I've been very busy," I replied.

"Browse on," he said, waving a plump hand at the
shelves. "Ring the bell up front when you want to pay."

He took a sip of cold tea and immersed himself in
Donne, and I wandered on down the narrow aisles, turning, finding myself near the book-laden steps leading
up to the gallery. A title caught my eyes. I stopped,
startled, unable to believe what I saw. I reached up and

touched the dusty, faded blue binding, my fingers trembling. *A General History of The Most Famous Highwaymen,* by Captain Charles Johnson. My eyes were moist as I took down the battered volume and examined the thumb-marked pages. Yes, it was the very same copy Father had let me keep that afternoon over eight years ago when I had come home after my first encounter with Hugh Bradford in the gardens at Greystone Hall. Marie had sold it along with all the other books after Father's death, and it had turned up here, through some miracle, to be reclaimed at last.

I brushed away the tear that trailed down my cheek. No, I wasn't going to give way to the grief still in my heart, nor was I going to entertain the flood of memories the book brought back. My father was gone, and I had come to terms with that loss in my own way. Hugh Bradford was gone, too, not a single report of him since he had bound and gagged the footman and fled the stables two and a half years ago. The pain was still in my heart, the love as well, unreasonable though it be, and I tried never to think of those wickedly slanted brows, those moody brown eyes, the emotions and sensations he had stirred that evening under the stars.

The noisy rustle of skirts and clatter of heels shattered my reverie, and I was amazed to see a radiant, attractive young woman hurrying down the aisle toward me. Stumbling over a pile of unshelved books, she uttered a very colorful curse, her vivid blue eyes full of exasperation. Her long auburn waves bounced wildly about her shoulders. Her white silk frock had bright cherry red stripes and was cut extremely low. The heels of her cherry red slippers were extremely high. Something told me she was not one of Miller's regular customers.

"Quick, luv, I've got to hide!" she exclaimed. "Show me *where!*"

Without a moment's hesitation I took her arm and led her over to the wooden stairs and told her to crouch under them. She obeyed promptly, disappearing among the shadows. I caught a whiff of exquisite perfume and heard a sneeze as I turned back to the shelves, examining the titles with studied nonchalance. A minute or so later I heard heavy footsteps stumbling about the maze of shelves. "Megan!" a husky voice called. "I know you're in here somewhere!" There was a thud, a crash, the sound of books toppling to the floor, followed by a groan and an expressive *"Damnation!"* I listened, fascinated, as the footsteps began to tromp again, drawing nearer, and then a tall, ruggedly attractive chap with dark bronze hair and angry brown eyes appeared at the end of the aisle where I stood. He was wearing a superbly cut brown broadcloth frock coat and a yellow silk neckcloth, both garments decidedly the worse for wear and both quite dusty at the moment. The fingers of his right hand were ink-stained, I observed, and there was a smudge of dust on his cheek.

"You're not Megan," he said. He looked thoroughly out of sorts.

"Definitely not," I informed him.

"Where is she?" he demanded.

"Who?"

"Girl who popped in here not more'n five minutes ago. Perky little thing with long auburn curls and saucy blue eyes, wearing a frock with red and white stripes and a pair of preposterous red shoes."

"Haven't seen anyone like that," I lied. "In fact, I don't think anyone has come into the shop since I've been here."

"You're *sure?*"

"Certain," I said.

"Damn! I could have sworn I saw her come in here. Maybe it was the shop next door—I was halfway down the street when I spotted her."

"It seems you've made a mistake, sir."

"Yeah, guess I have," he grumbled. "Damn. Left me flat, she did. Just up and left three months ago because I had to spend so much time working on my articles and couldn't squire her about town. Disappeared, she did. I've been looking for her ever since. London's a big city," he added.

"I know," I replied.

He shook his head, looking very unhappy now, and then he turned back into the maze, stomping about the place until he finally located the front door. I heard it open, heard it close, and then I stepped over to the stairway and informed the girl it was safe to come out. Skirts rustling crisply, she emerged a moment later with dust on her cheeks and cobwebs in her hair. Her blue eyes were full of admiration.

"You were *mar*velous, luv!" she cried. "I heard everything, and I couldn't have carried it off better myself. I've had *train*ing, too. Do yourself a big favor, luv. Never fall in love with a journalist."

"I'll try not to," I promised.

"Larry's actually rather sweet," she confided, "but the moment he asked me to marry him I knew I'd better clear out while I still had a chance. Journalists are all a bit mad, you see. Think they're geniuses, the whole pack of them. Think a girl should sit at their feet in rapt admiration. I left him a *note*," she added. "Some men just never give up."

She pulled a mirror out of her reticule, let out a cry of horror when she saw her face and began to remove the dust from her cheeks with a handkerchief. This done, she brushed the cobwebs out of her hair and told me it had been terribly *spooky* under there, and then she smiled a lovely smile.

"Megan Sloan, luv," she introduced herself, "late of the Drury Lane Theater. Very late, actually. I had a tiny, tiny walk-on in one of Mr. Garrick's productions last season and haven't worked since. On the stage, that is."

"I'm Angela Howard," I said.

"That's a lovely name. I can't tell you how grateful I am to you for helping me out. I owe you a huge debt of gratitude. Seeing Larry again would have been quite tiresome. He can be very persuasive, believe me. I might even have weakened and gone *back* to him."

"He was very good-looking," I observed.

"They all are, luv. That's the danger of it."

With her full pink lips, that pert nose and those vivid blue eyes, she was really extremely attractive, I thought, though one would never call her a beauty. Her long auburn hair was thick and wavy, a luxuriant reddish-brown glistening with rich highlights. Not quite as tall as I was, she had a superb figure, admirably displayed in the red and white striped frock with its tight waist and low bodice. Megan Sloan exuded vitality and good humor and a jaunty self-confidence I couldn't help but admire.

"Fancy all these books," she said, gazing around at the towering shelves. "What would a person *do* with them?"

"Read them, of course."

"Oh," she said.

Miss Sloan was clearly not of a literary bent, I reflected.

"I don't know about you, Angela, but I haven't had lunch and I'm positively starving. Why don't we buy some things and take them to the park and have a picnic? If you'd *like* to, that is. You may have other plans."

"I'd love to, Megan."

The girl was clearly delighted, and I suspected that, for all her vitality and good nature, she had very few friends. We made our way to the front of the shop and I rang the bell and Miller eventually shuffled up in his felt slippers to take my five pence for Captain Johnson's book on highwaymen. Megan was happily stroking Hercules, whose tongue hung out in ecstasy. Miller looked at her with considerable bafflement. I doubted many women in striped silk and outlandish red shoes frequented this particular shop.

We left, and Megan kept a nervous eye out for the ardent Larry, not relaxing entirely until we had turned off Fleet. We strolled to the park and bought sausage rolls and oranges and gingerbread and lemonade from various street hawkers, and I bought a loaf of bread as well. A strapping blond sailor followed us into the park. Megan turned around and put him off in language so salty it brought a blush to my cheeks. The sailor blushed, too, scurrying away as though he'd been stung. Megan sighed and said a girl had to know how to deal with men in a wicked city like this, else she'd be whisked away in no time at all. She was clearly an expert.

The park was lovely, multicolored flowers abloom in the beds, the grass a soft green, the trees beginning to bud. Children played noisily, romping about with reckless abandon, and lovers strolled hand in hand. Others, less inhibited, lolled on the grass, pant legs and petticoats all entangled. Vendors shouted, hawking roasted chestnuts, paper kites, a variety of goods, and plump blue-gray pigeons perched on the edges of the fountains. Several men looked us over as Megan and I sauntered along, admiring her lovely form and gleaming red-brown hair, but none of them accosted us, which was just as well after what had happened to the sailor. We finally located a spot near the edge of the pond for our picnic and sat down on the grass, spreading our skirts out and leisurely eating our food in the warm rays of sunlight.

"I love sausage rolls," Megan declared. "The sausage is always so spicy, the mustard so tangy."

"I love them, too, though I rarely have an opportunity to eat one."

"What do you do, Angela?" she inquired. "You're beautiful enough for the stage, talented enough, too, if your bit with Larry is any example, but I haven't ever seen you around Covent Garden."

Beautiful? Megan was very kind, I thought.

"I work at—at a gambling house," I told her. "Marie's Place. Perhaps you've heard of it."

Megan lifted an eyebrow, clearly surprised. "I thought she only employed blondes."

"I don't run one of the tables. I—work behind the scenes. My stepmother owns the place."

"How nice for you," she said.

"Not at all," I replied.

And I found myself talking to this friendly, engaging girl as I had never talked to anyone before, not even Eppie. Before an hour had passed I had told her about my life in the country, about my father and Hugh Bradford, about the trials and tribulations of being Marie's ward here in London. There was something about her that inspired trust and put one completely at ease. Megan ate a gingerbread man and peeled an orange, and when I finally lapsed into silence she told me her own tale. The daughter of a fishmonger, she had lost her father when she was thirteen and her mother had immediately remarried. When Megan was fifteen her stepfather had raped her and vowed to kill her if she breathed a word about it. She lifted his wallet the next morning and struck out on her own, making Covent Garden her turf, working in the flower markets and eventually going into the theater, without resounding success, she was quick to inform me.

There had been a multitude of men in her life, she couldn't seem to avoid them, and she was always making mistakes, like Larry, and hoping to find a man who would be *the* man but he hadn't turned up yet. They were rogues, the whole lot of them, handsome and delightful and ever so cozy to be with, yes, but always rogues in the end, treating a girl like she was his personal property and expecting her to dance to any tune he chose to whistle. She guessed she would always be a fool for a boyish grin and a pair of merry eyes, never seemed able to resist them, alas, but a girl needed room to breathe and she'd rather be on her own than be some man's plaything and drudge.

"It's all roses at first, luv," she confided, "and then they expect you to darn their stockings."

"Indeed?"

"And woe unto any girl who has ideas about having a career of her own. I could have been a super in Garrick's last production if Larry hadn't been such a menace about it. Not having other men ogle *his* girl, he wasn't. Flatly forbade me to take the job. That's one of the reasons I left him."

"What's a super?" I inquired.

"A walk-on. Someone who hasn't any lines. You stand around in the background and look decorative while the leads emote. I've been a super dozens of times. Once I carried a spear in a play about Boadicea, and next season I was an Egyptian slave girl, wore a long black wig."

"It sounds fascinating," I said.

"Helps pay the rent, luv, and a girl needs all the help she can get. I'm currently resting—that means between engagements—but there are several new productions opening soon, and my friend Dorothea Gibbons lets me work for her when I'm not otherwise employed—this is my afternoon off. Dottie makes most of the costumes for all the managers. I don't *sew*," she hastened to add. "I help in the stockroom and go fetch laces and velvets and such from the suppliers. It's not bliss, but at least it's honest work."

It all sounded wonderfully colorful and exciting, I thought, particularly when compared with my own bleak life. Lost in reverie for a few moments, I was startled to see Megan whipping off her outlandish red shoes. Then I heard the little boy crying. He had been playing with a toy sailboat at the edge of the pond and the boat had floated out of reach, moving slowly to the center of the pond. Leaping to her feet, holding her skirts up to her thighs, Megan charged into the water, retrieved the boat and gave it to the child, telling him to be very, very careful because little boys had been known to drown in this particular pond.

This small incident spoke volumes about my new friend. Megan Sloan might be fast, even wicked in the eyes of some, but in this age of brutality and indifference she had a kind heart and a caring nature, and these were rare. Probably went far to explain her failures with men, too, I thought, men being what they were. Other women might have become hard, calculating and mercenary given her experiences, but Megan retained an honest, open outlook on life, even a kind of innocence, though she hadn't a naive bone in her body. Drying off her legs with a handkerchief, she plopped back down on the grass and pulled on her shoes, sighing a deep sigh.

We talked for a while longer and then, gathering up our things, sauntered across the stone bridge and tossed small chunks of bread to the ducks paddling among the water lilies. They squawked with delight, flapping their wings and greedily fighting over the bread, and both of us laughed. Bells chimed, and I was surprised to find it was already five o'clock. I told her I would have to go now, and Megan looked wistful, as reluctant to part as I was.

"It's been a lovely afternoon," I said. "I—I don't know when I've enjoyed myself so much. I feel we've been friends for years."

"I feel the same way," she confessed. "It was destiny, luv, me hurrying into that strange shop, you being there. Now that we're friends, we've got to *stay* friends."

I agreed, and we made tentative plans to meet one week from today here by the bridge. There were long shadows on the grass as we strolled slowly out of the park.

"I've got a large flat over Brinkley's Wig Shop in Covent Garden," Megan informed me, "right across from the arcades. It isn't grand, but it's roomy, much too large for one person, actually. If—if you should ever need a place to stay, luv, I'd be delighted to have you room with me."

"I'll keep that in mind," I promised.

"I could probably help you find work, too," she continued. "I know dozens of people in Covent Garden. My friend Dottie's always looking for someone who can sew."

"I sew like a dream," I said. "I was thinking of trying to find employment with a seamstress when I leave Marie."

"Then it's settled!" she exclaimed. "As soon as you leave, you'll come room with me and work for Dottie. She'll be thrilled to have someone re*spon*sible, and you'll love her. She's an old dear—fussy as can be and a bit absentminded, but she's got a heart of gold."

We said our good-byes at the entrance to the park, and Megan gave me a hug before she trotted off on her

high red heels. Shadows were beginning to gather as I
made my way back to Underwood's for the cards, and
a thick purple-blue haze was settling over the city as
I started home, colors gradually fading, everything
brown and gray. It was after six-thirty when I got back,
for I'd had to wait a short while for the cards, and Marie
was in a tempest when I carried them to her office.

"You've been gone all day!" she cried.

"You told me not to come back without them," I reminded her, "and they weren't ready until a little while
ago."

"Where did you get that book?"

"I bought it with my own money. I browsed for a
while at Miller's while I was waiting for the cards."

Marie paid no attention to my reply, probably didn't
even hear it. She had had a very bad day, that was plain
to see, and something was definitely bothering her now.
Her green eyes flashed. Vivid red curls spilled untidily
over her brow. Her fingernails made an impatient rap-
tap-tap on the edge of her desk, and she seemed to have
forgotten my presence. She stood up after a moment
and scrutinized me with narrowed eyes, frowning deeply.

"We've got problems," she said. "Big problems. Jen's
sprained her ankle and that slut Sally hasn't shown
up. Two girls short, and this one of my biggest nights!
You're going to have to run one of the tables tonight,
Angela, and don't tell me you can't. I know the girls
have taught you everything about it."

"But—"

"I don't like it any more than you do!" she snapped.
"You're not even blonde—but there's no way around it.
Sally's gown should fit you, and you can put your hair
up. Get upstairs. Take a bath, wash your hair. Tess can
take Sally's table and you can take Tess's—she does
nothing but deal cards for Twenty-One. Hurry up, Angela!"

"Marie, I—"

"None of your lip! Customers will be arriving within

the hour. You're going to have to do it, and God help you if you mess up! Go on now, get upstairs and start making ready. *Merde!*" she exclaimed. "Why do these things always have to happen to *me!*"

Chapter Eight

I wasn't nearly as brave as I pretended to be. Oh, I
made a lot of noise and acted cool and intrepid and
sometimes it worked, sometimes I even tricked myself
into believing I wasn't nervous, but much of the time
it was just a pose. Couldn't trick myself tonight. I was
so nervous I felt I might jump out of my skin if someone
said "Boo!" It wasn't that I was intimidated by all the
aristocrats I'd be nobbing with—I'd learned a long time
ago they were just like other folk, only richer and snoot-
ier—it was just that at the moment I couldn't remember one card from another and knew I was going to
mess up dreadfully and probably make a complete fool
of myself. Marie would just love that. Sod Marie, I told
myself. This wasn't *my* idea. If I messed up she would
have no one to blame but herself.

I stared at myself in the looking glass. Didn't know
who the fancy creature was, but she certainly wasn't
me. The silver gown was gorgeous, with off the shoulder
puffed sleeves and a neckline so low you could almost
see my nipples and a waist so tight I could barely

breathe. The skirt spread out like a shimmering silver
bell. I'd never worn a dress like this before and doubted
I ever would again. Wasn't my style, not by a long chalk.
My hair was different, too. The girls had helped me get
ready and Betty knew all about styling hair and had
stacked mine on top of my head in glossy chestnut waves,
leaving three long ringlets to dangle down between my
shoulder blades. Since I wasn't a blonde, we might as
well call at*tent*ion to it, she declared, and she had affixed a cunning bow of cloth of silver and amethyst
velvet above my left temple. Looked rather nice, it did.
I had to admit that.

Judy was a wonder with cosmetics and had "done"
my face: mauve shadow on my lids, pale pink rouge
brushed lightly on my cheekbones and shaded to em-
phasize them, a darker pink rouge on my mouth, making it seem wider than ever. I had put my foot down
about the tiny black satin beauty patch. Flatly refused
to let her stick it on. I looked like something, all right,
but not like Angela. Their work done, the girls had "oh-
ed" and "ah-ed" and claimed I was a veritable vision of
loveliness and I knew they were lying through their
teeth just to make me feel good.

They had given me advice, too. Smile a lot, Tess
informed me, always be warm and friendly, no matter
what they say, you'll get far more tips. Flirt a little,
Betty advised, but discreetly. Don't try to cheat them,
Judy warned, you're not skilled enough for that and
might get caught, just deal your cards and leave the
sleight-of-hand to those of us who know what we're
doing. If a man asks you to go upstairs with him, be
polite and make some excuse, Anne informed me, don't
act offended, that'll put him off and be bad for *our* business. Jesus, Sonya said, sending a green kid like her
into that nest of rakes. Marie must be out of her bloody
mind. Don't worry, kid, we'll keep an eye on you.

The wide silver skirt swayed as I descended the white
marble stairs, and I winced as the silver slippers pinched
my feet. Wasn't used to walking on heels this high,
either. I'd probably fall flat on my face before the eve-

ning ended. Marie stood at the bottom of the stairs, watching me with glittering green eyes that clearly didn't care for what they saw. She frowned, curling her thin lips up at one corner. I looked like a fool and both of us knew it. For a moment I thought she was going to send me back upstairs and tell me to forget the whole crazy scheme, but I had no such luck. Marie shook her head, disgusted.

"I guess you'll have to do," she said.

"I could always put a sack over my head," I told her.

"I'm in no mood for your smart remarks, Angela!"

"I feel naked. This gown is two inches too low. If I were to sneeze I'd pop right out for all the world to see. The waist is so tight I can't breathe, and these shoes are ruining my feet."

"What's that perfume you're wearing?" she asked sharply.

"I don't know. Judy dabbed it on me."

"Judy never did have any taste. Just do your job and try to be incon*spic*uous about it, and don't speak unless you're spoken to. Keep that smart mouth of yours under firm control. Do you understand?"

"I could pretend to be mute," I suggested. "Maybe I could use sign language. That would be novel."

Marie looked like she might explode, lips pressed tightly together, eyes flashing green fire, but the door opened then and the first customers arrived and she forced a smile and hurried over to greet them, waxing ever so friendly and warm. She was wearing black velvet and pearls and her hair looked redder than it had when I'd seen her earlier. She had obviously touched it up while I was dressing. I moved over to the table assigned to me and stood there like one of Mrs. Salmon's wax dummies, praying the men who had just come in didn't want to try their hand at Twenty-One.

"Here, kid," Sonya said. "This'll help."

She handed me a glass of champagne and I gulped it down like it was water and I felt warm all over, felt dizzy, too, and I plopped down in my chair and before I knew it the room was crowded with men in elegant

frock coats and powdered wigs and lace, some of them
young, some of them old, some not even wearing wigs.
Every chair at my table was taken and I was dealing
cards and smiling pleasantly and finding it easy as
could be. An old roué with diamond buttons on his
waistcoat told me I was a tasty little piece and squeezed
my knee under the table. I slapped his hand and told
him he was very naughty, and he laughed and lost
twenty pounds on the next hand. I dealt the cards and
looked regretful when someone lost and smiled when
they won and even when they lost a lot they didn't seem
to mind.

"Why don't you get one of the other girls to sit in for
you for a while," a handsome young Lord suggested.

"Why should I do that?" I asked sweetly.

"So the two of us can go upstairs," he said.

"I'd dearly love to go upstairs with you," I told him,
"you have *such* a nice face, but unfortunately I can't."

"Oh? Why not?"

"I'm having labor pains," I said.

The other men at the table hooted with laughter and
the young Lord said I was a caution and grinned and
tipped me five whole pounds when he left the table a
short while later. The old roué with diamond buttons
tipped me big, too, and I reckoned I'd likely be rich
before the evening was over. The chandeliers burned
brightly, crystal pendants shimmering with rainbow
hues, and it was warm as could be, the huge room
jammed now, all the tables full and . . . Lord, men standing around *my* table, watching, laughing, promptly taking a seat as soon as a chair was vacated. They actually
liked me, even if I wasn't blonde, even if my cheekbones
were too high and my mouth too wide. One of the men
opened up a gem-studded snuffbox and offered me a
pinch and I shook my head and told him I didn't dare
because I might sneeze and wouldn't *that* be a treat for
them. This caused roars of laughter that fairly shook
the walls.

Marie came over to the table once or twice, a strained
smile on her lips, and I could tell she was both puzzled

and irritated by my popularity. My table was undoubtedly the busiest in the room, not because I was so clever and witty, certainly not because I looked like a dream, but merely because I was a novelty, a new face. That's what attracted them. Had to be, I told myself. I wasn't that skillful with the cards, even made a mistake now and then, but the men didn't seem to mind at all. There were no clocks in the place—Marie believed it bad for business for the customers to be reminded of the hour—but I knew I must have been at the table for at least three hours when Tess came over to relieve me.

"Time for your break," she told me. "I'll take over for a while."

"Just a minute," I said. "Let me get these bloody shoes back on."

The men laughed again and told me to hurry back. I struggled into the two tight silver slippers and got up and made them a pert curtsy, and Sir Basil almost fell out of his chair when I leaned over. Couldn't understand why until I remembered my extreme decolletage. "Whoops!" I said, and I straightened up as fast as I could. The shoes pinched my feet dreadfully as I made my way over to the enclosed staircase leading down to the lounge, and my head was aching, too. The glass of champagne that had given me such a lift and made it all so easy to do was causing an adverse reaction now. Another glass would probably fix that, but I'd rather have something to eat.

Passing through the lounge, I stepped into the kitchen and closed the door behind me, leaning against it for a moment. Bennett was at the counter, chopping something up, and he gave me a dour look that expressed his disapproval of the way I looked far better than words could have. I was Bennett's pet, and he wasn't at all pleased to see me garbed up like the blondes.

"It's only for tonight," I told him. "Sally didn't show and Jen sprained her ankle. Marie said I'd have to fill in. It hasn't been nearly as bad as I expected it to be."

"Sure," he said. "I heard some of them chattering in

there about what a success you were. Next thing you know she'll have you working the table every night."

"Not a chance," I replied. "It's rather fun, but I shouldn't want to do it again."

"You look like a strumpet," he grumbled.

"I think that's the *idea*."

"Any of those high 'n mighty toffs up there give you any trouble, you let me know. I'll come after them with my butcher knife."

"You're a darling, Bennett. I'm starving. Is there anything to eat?"

"Knew you'd missed your dinner," he said, "so I saved some cold chicken for you. I baked a chocolate cream cake this afternoon, your favorite with cream icing and cream filling between the layers. Guess you can have a piece of that, too."

"I *love* your chocolate cream cake."

"You'll want coffee, too, I suppose."

"At least two cups. I think I *need* it," I added.

Bennett knew I adored drumsticks, and he placed four drumsticks on a plate along with several asparagus stalks that just happened to be steaming hot. He poured his special white wine and cheese sauce over the asparagus, then handed me the plate. I got knife, fork and a large linen napkin while Bennett sliced an enormous piece of cake and put it on a smaller plate with another fork. I carried both plates into the lounge and placed them on a table and returned to the kitchen for cup, saucer and the small silver pot of coffee Bennett had prepared for me.

"See that you eat every bite," he ordered.

"I shall."

The lounge wasn't at all crowded, only two or three gentlemen standing in front of a sofa, bewailing their losses, and Betty chatting cozily with Blake, the stern-faced, muscular footman who had thrown out the unruly Lord Brock the night before. Like Reed, the other tall footman hired to keep order and guard the money, Blake wore white stockings, dark blue velvet knee breeches and coat, silver waistcoat and a powdered wig.

The elegant attire accentuated his tough demeanor and sturdy build. I gave Betty a wave and sat down at the corner table to eat my food, exhausted now, the earlier exhilaration worn off.

The coffee was hot and strong, just the way I liked it, and I sipped it gratefully. The cold chicken was extremely tasty, baked with spices, the meat tender as could be. Fancy folk might slice the meat off a drumstick and then eat it with a fork, but that was altogether too bothersome, took too long, too. I just picked mine up by the handle and gnawed away, tearing the meat loose with my teeth. Only way to eat it if you were as hungry as I was. Bennett was indeed a treasure, I thought, slicing my asparagus and taking a bite. Heavenly, it was, the wine and cheese sauce divine. I could hardly wait to try the chocolate cream cake. It was always scrumptious.

Easing off the shoes, enjoying my food, I thought about the events of the evening and decided that, yes, it had been rather fun, but it wasn't at all my sort of thing. All that attention was flattering, sure, but I'd rather be upstairs rereading Captain Johnson's book on highwaymen. If Marie had any ideas about having me run a table regularly, she was in for a big surprise. I wasn't about to do it again after tonight, even if I *had* already made over thirty-five pounds in tips. Bleedin' fortune, it was, with more undoubtedly to come before the evening was over, but it wasn't really honest money, I told myself. I hadn't done anything to *earn* it, just put on a vulgar dress and joked with a bunch of dissolute gents who had so much money they could throw it away.

I was eating my second drumstick when I got that spooky, unnerving feeling you get when someone is staring at you. The sensation was so strong I could almost feel the eyes on me, and I looked up and saw him standing there across the room. For half a moment I thought I must be hallucinating. He was wearing sky blue satin knee breeches and frock coat, just as he had over eight years ago in the gardens at Greystone Hall, and his white satin waistcoat was delicately embroi-

dered with tiny blue and silver leaves. A fine lace jabot
spilled from his throat in a frothy cascade, and lace
ruffles dripped down over his wrists, too. He was much
older, must be almost thirty now, but he still looked
like a bloody prince, even more handsome than I remembered.

Lord Clinton Meredith stared at me, a small frown
making a furrow over the bridge of that fine aquiline
nose, and I could tell that he was trying to place me,
trying to remember where we had met. So far as I knew,
he had only seen me once, the afternoon Eppie and I
had been sitting on a bench in the green and he had
come riding up, but I doubted he would recall that. Still,
the sight of me stirred some vague memory, and it bothered him. Maybe he would go away. Maybe he wouldn't
come over. I was surprised to find my heart palpitating,
surprised to feel my knees grow weak. Bloody hell! No
reason to be nervous about seeing Clinton Meredith
again, I told myself, no reason at all. He wasn't anything to me, just a spectacularly handsome rake who
once, a long time ago, had wanted to seduce me.

Still, I caught my breath as he started toward me.
The picture of him and the lovely Lady Laura flashed
in my mind. I saw him scooping his hand into her bodice
and pulling out her round white breast and squeezing
it until the nipple grew bright pink and firm. I saw him
pulling her into his arms and kissing her so passionately it was like an erotic engraving come to life. I
forced the unwelcome images out of my mind and tried
to compose myself. When he reached the table I managed to give him a cool, indifferent glance. I was still
holding the drumstick.

"Excuse me," he said. "I'm Clinton Meredith, and I
have the distinct impression you and I have met before."

"Afraid not," I replied. "This is my first night here."

"We didn't meet here—I would have remembered. I
have the feeling it was some time ago."

"Must be mistaken," I retorted.

"I don't think so. Your face, your—uh—I've seen you

before, I'm quite sure of it. That hair, those eyes—yes, I'm sure of it, I just can't remember the circumstances."

His voice was deep and throaty, as I remembered. Like thick honey, it was, a seductive voice that made you think of bedrooms and bodies and highly improper things. It seemed to caress each word as it came out, I thought, and I knew there weren't many women who could resist a voice like that, not if the man who was speaking looked like Clinton Meredith. Not if he had a full pink mouth and glorious gray eyes the color of smoke and heavy eyelids that drooped down, giving him a lazy, sleepy look. Not if he was over six feet tall and lean and muscular and built like a Greek athlete of old. His pale blond hair was thick, as shiny as silk, the waves pulled back from his face and tied at his nape with a blue silk ribbon. He was dazzling, all right, no question about it, but fortunately I knew him for what he was and was completely immune to that potent masculine allure.

"We *have* met," he said. "I can tell by the way you look at me."

"Maybe we have," I admitted. My voice was cool as ice.

"And—yes, and you were very impudent to me. I'm beginning to remember," he told me. "It wasn't in London. It was in the country, and I was sitting on my horse and—help me, lass."

"I'm trying to eat, Lord Meredith."

"There! You do know me. I didn't use my title just now. I seem to remember a small park—no, a green, and there was a cannon and you were sitting on a bench, it seems, and—yes, I have it now."

"Bully for you," I said. I took a bite of my drumstick, pretending to ignore him.

"Angie. Angie Howard. The schoolmaster's daughter. Of course. His widow runs this place. I remember it all now. You were with your little friend and I tried to be friendly and you told me to go sod myself."

"Why don't you?" I suggested.

Clinton Meredith smiled then, and oh, it was a won-

derful smile, the kind of smile that would melt any
woman's heart if she didn't know him for the arrogant,
superior sod he was. It curled beautifully on those chiseled pink lips, and his gray eyes were full of amusement
as he pulled a chair over and seated himself at the table.
I glared at him, my cheeks coloring.

"I didn't invite you to sit down, sir!"

"I know. I took it upon myself. Always was impetuous."

"I told you—I'm trying to eat."

"I'll join you," he said.

And he reached across the table and took one of the
drumsticks off my plate and began to eat it, tearing the
meat from the bone with strong white teeth. I was mor-
tally offended, so incensed I couldn't speak. Stunned, I
watched him devour the drumstick, and when he finished he laid the bone neatly back on the plate, gave
me a questioning look, hesitated just a moment and
then took the remaining drumstick and devoured that,
too. Furious, I handed him the napkin, and he wiped
his fingers, ever so dainty.

"Delicious," he declared.

"See that man over there?" I said.

"Which one?"

"The big, strong footman in blue velvet and
powdered wig. If you don't get up from this table and
leave me alone in precisely ten seconds I'm going to
yell at the top of my lungs and he'll come over here and
beat the bejesus out of you. Ten seconds. One. Two.
Three—"

"You mean Blake?" he asked. "Blake's a good chum
of mine. I tip him five pounds every time I come in. I
shouldn't count on his rushing to the rescue, Angie.
More than likely he'd report you for being disrespectful
to one of the paying customers."

"My name is Angela. No one's called me Angie in
years."

"I'm not such a bad chap, Angela. Really I'm not. I
enjoy the company of beautiful women, true, but is that
such a crime?"

"I know all about you and women," I told him.

"Indeed?"

"It was an open scandal years ago, and I don't imagine you've improved any with age."

"On the contrary, I've improved a great deal. I could give you any number of references."

He reached across the table again, deftly slid the plate of cake over and began to eat it with the fork Bennett had provided. I couldn't believe it. He smiled and took another big bite and shook his head slightly, indicating his delight. I longed to slap him. I watched in silent fury as he ate every bite of it and scraped dabs of icing up with the fork and licked it off the tines. His impudence knew no bounds.

"Magnificent," he said. "My compliments to the chef."

"That was *my* cake, you son of a bitch."

"Sorry. It looked so tempting I couldn't resist."

"Just what are you trying to prove, Lord Meredith?" I asked in my haughtiest voice. "That you're a complete and total ass? If so, you've succeeded beyond your wildest expectations."

"You know," he said, "you have a unique distinction, Angela."

"What's that?"

"You have the distinction of being the only girl who's ever told me to go sod myself. Most of them find me pleasant, even charming. Some of them actually enjoy being with me."

"And live to regret it, no doubt."

He smiled again, and oh yes, it was a wonderful smile. Lord Clinton Meredith exuded provocative charm, could probably charm the birds off the trees if he had a mind to, but this particular bird wasn't about to tumble for that husky, honeyed voice, those drooping eyelids, that wonderful smile. I finished the drumstick I'd been holding all this time and then ate the rest of my asparagus, pretending he wasn't there. I could feel him watching me, and that didn't help one bit. I found it quite difficult to swallow, but I ate it all nevertheless, and then I poured another cup of coffee.

"I find you an immense challenge," he said.

"Do you?"

"Indeed I do. Years ago when you were—what? Fourteen? Fifteen?—You were a challenge then, too, and I remember being quite put out that I had been rebuffed by a mere village girl. A skinny one at that. For a couple of weeks afterwards I entertained the idea of tracing you down and nabbing you and making you pay for your impudence, but I gave it up."

"How noble of you," I said.

"I kept thinking about you, though. I thought about you a great deal. I couldn't get you out of my mind for weeks on end. And then I walk in here tonight and see you again—no longer a skinny adolescent with gorgeous hair and lovely violet-gray eyes, but, instead, a superbly beautiful woman."

Lord, he did have a lying, flattering tongue on him, I thought. He almost made you believe you *were* beautiful. I took a sip of coffee, not in the least moved by his persuasive lies. Women must fall for him like dominoes in a row, helpless in the warmth of that charm and allure. There were a lot of very silly women in the world, I reflected.

"Why don't we settle this amicably?" he suggested.

"There's nothing to settle," I told him.

"We'll go up to one of the private rooms. The going rate is—what? Ten pounds? I'll give you twenty."

I could feel the color burning on my cheeks again, and I stood up abruptly, gazing at him with pure loathing.

"I'm not for sale, Lord Meredith."

He arched a brow. "Oh? I thought all Marie's girls were."

"This one isn't, I can assure you."

I marched across the lounge with all the dignity I could muster. When he called my name I didn't bother to turn around, and then I realized I was barefoot. I turned to see him smiling again, dangling the two silver shoes from his fingertips. I marched back and took them from him and put them on, balancing myself with one

palm resting on the tabletop. He got his eye full when
I leaned down, he did.

"You haven't seen the last of me, Angela," he promised.

"Go—"

"Sod myself?"

"Go to hell!"

Somehow I managed to make it back upstairs. I
paused for a moment at the top of the stairs and took
a deep breath and wondered how I could possibly get
through the rest of the evening. I took another deep
breath and tried to stop the angry trembling inside,
and then I went back over to the table and thanked
Tess for filling in for me and smiled at the men and
took the seat Tess vacated. I dealt the cards and made
pleasant remarks and the men were happy, but I was
in agony, certain Clinton would appear at any moment
and take a seat and continue to taunt me. An hour
passed, two, and I thought I saw a glimpse of him going
over to Betty's table, but the room was so crowded I
couldn't be sure. He was dreadful, dreadful, even more
dreadful than I recalled, and I detested him thoroughly.
For what he was. For . . . for what he had done to Hugh
as well. I hadn't forgotten that, either. Not for a moment.

I was invited upstairs three more times, and each
time I put the man off with a pleasant quip that gave
no offense, and I earned another twenty pounds in tips.
I was growing very tired, and I had to force my smiles,
had to concentrate hard in order not to make mistakes
with the cards. The candles were beginning to sputter.
The noise was beginning to grate on my nerves. Sometime around one I happened to glance up and see Marie
standing at the door of her office, deep in conversation
with a tall blond man in sky blue satin, and yes, it was
Lord Meredith, all right. Marie wasn't smiling. Neither
was he. He said something and she glanced over at my
table, and then she led him into her office and closed
the door. Sod them both, I told myself. I didn't *care* what
he told her, but my hands shook slightly as I cut the

cards, and I couldn't remember how many cards I was to deal to whom.

At last, at long last, customers began to leave, and finally I was alone at the table, exhausted, gazing at the cards and the empty glasses. Tess and Betty were having a glass of champagne at the next table, discussing the evening's events, and Judy was rubbing the back of her neck and telling them all about her tryst upstairs with "that dreadful Lord Duff." Bloke wanted to eat *oysters* and they sat there on the sofa and he stroked her leg and ate oysters and had a dandy time and tipped her lavishly, he did, for nothing but her company, easiest money she ever made. Sonya came over and told me I looked like I'd been through a war. I managed a weak smile and she patted my hand lightly and said I'd done a smashing job.

The girls drifted away to change into their street clothes and the maids came in and the great chandeliers were let down almost to the floor, the candles put out. A few were left burning in the wall sconces, and the huge room was dim, spread with shadows. I sighed and put my shoes back on and stood up. My head was aching terribly, and there was a pain in the small of my back. I might as well get it over with, I told myself. No sense waiting for Marie to come to me. Wearily, I went to the door of her office. Blake and Reed stood guard on either side of it, so I knew she must be counting tonight's take. I opened the door and went inside anyway, and there she was at her desk, separating stacks of bills, stacking gold pieces in neat piles.

She looked up, and I expected those green eyes to narrow when she saw me, expected those red lips to tighten. They didn't. She looked at me as though she were seeing me for the very first time and then like she wasn't seeing me at all, seeing something else instead, lost in thought. After a moment or so she frowned and shook her head and looked at me again, carefully, critically. The frown deepened.

"I've been blind," she said to herself. "Blind."

"I hope you're satisfied," I said. "I *told* you I didn't

want to do it. I don't know what he might have said to
you, but—"

I cut myself short. She sighed again, and her lips did
tighten up then. She looked irritated, the Marie I knew.

"I'm extremely busy, Angela, as you can see."

"I'm not ever going to work one of the tables again,"
I told her.

"I agree," she said. "It would be a waste."

"I'm going to keep all my tips, too," I said defiantly.

"That's the standard practice," she replied, and although her voice was crisp, as usual, it wasn't angry.
"You look tired, Angela. Go on up to bed. We'll talk
later."

I was extremely puzzled as I went upstairs and removed the detested silver shoes and gown. Expected
her to tear into me with a vengeance, I had, and she'd
been ... almost absentminded. Maybe Clinton Meredith
hadn't tattled on me after all. Maybe they'd talked about
something else when they went into her office. I took
the fifty-five pounds I'd received in tips and slipped
them between the pages of Captain Johnson's book for
safekeeping. They would come in handy when I finally
left this place. I'd be able to help Megan with the rent
right away, and I'd have enough to live on until I found
employment, in case Dorothea Gibbons couldn't use me.
Utterly exhausted, I got into bed, and I was sound asleep
in no time at all.

While it was clearly beyond her to be kind, Marie
was unusually considerate of me during the next three
days. She didn't snap. She didn't complain. She didn't
criticize my work. Didn't make me work nearly as hard
either, and when she *did* have me do some chore, she
always *request*ed I do it and smiled a tight, fake smile
that made me uneasy as all get out. Had me completely
baffled, it did. Wasn't like her at all. People in novels
might undergo sudden transformations of character, but
it didn't happen that way in real life. My stepmother
was a shrewd, calculating old harridan, fond of nothing
but money, and I was convinced she had an ulterior
motive. Did she think she could soften me up and get

me to run one of the tables every night? That must be it, I decided, and I kept waiting for her to bring it up.

Shortly after noon on Saturday a footman from one of the finest shops in London arrived at the front door, carrying a number of large white boxes, and I was startled when Marie told one of the servants to take the boxes up to my room. Marie saw the puzzlement in my eyes, and she smiled her fake smile and reached up to pat her vivid red curls.

"Some new clothes," she told me. "We're going to have a guest for dinner tonight, Angela, and I decided you really had nothing appropriate to wear. I want you to look your best."

"A guest?" I inquired.

"A—friend of the family, you might say. Someone who is very interested in your welfare. After seeing you at the table the other night, I decided this—really wasn't the proper atmosphere for you, and this friend will help find you—another position, one more suitable."

"I don't understand," I said. "Who is 'this friend'?"

"You needn't bother your head about it just now," she said. "We're going to close a bit early tonight, and we'll dine at twelve. Take the rest of the day off. Relax. Have a long nap. I want you to sparkle tonight."

I was even more puzzled, and I was suspicious, too, but I had to admit I was excited when I opened the boxes and saw the new clothes. I never had anything anywhere near as fine as these. They must have cost Marie a huge chunk of money, I thought, and that made me suspicious, too—she never spent a penny without good cause. She wanted me to look my best. She wanted me to sparkle. Something was up. I was extremely curious about this mysterious friend and wondered just what kind of "position" he intended to help me find. Was I to be hired out as a governess? It would certainly be far more suitable than working at Marie's Place, and I was undoubtedly qualified after years of private schooling from my father, but somehow I doubted that was what Marie had in mind. No profit for her in something like that. Well, I would just have to wait, and in the meantime it was lovely to have the day off.

I curled up in a chair in my sitting room and read for a long time, and then I took a walk and came back and had a lavish tea at five—Bennett gave me cold sliced ham and turkey and wonderful buttered scones and a huge slice of almond cake with raspberry paste between the layers and a pot full of tea. I took a nap after that, slept for four hours, and then I had a hot bath and washed my hair and dried it and brushed it till it shone, and then I began to dress for our late dinner, very wary about the whole thing and, I had to confess it, considerably intrigued as well.

The petticoat was of thin creamy white silk, with half a dozen billowing skirts. Fit me like a dream, it did, and so did the gown. It was of exquisite cream white satin with very thin amethyst and pale gray stripes, the cloth rich and lustrous, and it had tight, elbow-length sleeves and a scooped neckline that was cut quite low. The tight waist was accentuated by a narrow amethyst velvet band, and the very full skirt spread out over the underskirts in shimmering folds. Jemminy, Angela, I thought, studying myself in the mirror, you look like a bloody duchess. Looked even more like one after I had put on the high heeled amethyst slippers and arranged my hair in an elegant stack of chestnut waves, leaving three ringlets dangling down in back. My face looked better without all that makeup, I decided, but I did smooth on a bit of pale pink lip rouge.

Although all the chandeliers were still burning brightly, the tables had already been shut down and the girls were leaving as I reached the top of the white marble staircase. Marie closed the door on the last of them and turned to watch me descend the stairs. The full satin skirt swayed and made a delicious rustling noise, and I held my chin high, cool and composed, feeling extremely grand and grown up. Although Marie didn't say anything, I could tell she was pleased with what she saw. I might not be a breathtaking beauty like Solonge or Janine, but I knew I looked appealing tonight, high cheekbones and all.

Marie was still wearing her customary black velvet and pearls. That surprised me.

"Aren't you going to change?" I asked.

"It isn't necessary," she told me. "I see the dress fits nicely. Mrs. Hammond made it up to my specifications, a rush job, but she was paid a handsome fee, I can assure you. Are you ready to go up?"

"Up? We always dine in the lounge."

"It will be much cozier in one of the rooms upstairs. I had the footmen set a table up. Bennett has prepared a wonderful meal. His own pâté. Caviar. A bottle of the best champagne."

"Doesn't sound like much to eat. I'm awfully hungry."

"There'll be other things as well," she said impatiently. "Come along, Angela!"

Something was definitely afoot, and I didn't like the feel of it, didn't like it one bit, but I followed her up the stairs nevertheless, and we turned and moved down the hall. Marie opened a door at the end of it and ushered me into the grandest private room, one I'd never been inside before. It was all cream and gold and pale blue, dark blue carpet on the floor, cream walls with pale blue silk panels framed with gilt designs, more gilt on the ornate cream ceiling. It was like being inside a jewel box, I thought, admiring the small crystal chandelier that hung over the table. There was a large sofa as well, covered in sky blue velvet, and *that* gave me a turn.

"You wait here," Marie instructed me. "Our guest will be arriving in a few minutes."

She left the room then, closing the door behind her. By that time I was beginning to feel very jumpy, beginning to feel exactly like a goat staked to a tree to lure the tigers. I moved nervously over to the table and inspected the silver dish of caviar, the dish of creamy goose-liver pâté with truffles, the plate of thin toast, the tall green bottle of champagne cooling in a bucket of ice. The table was set for two. Two. Not three. Two exquisite china plates. Two slender crystal glasses. Two pale blue linen napkins with forks and knives and spoons laid out. I gazed at the table, and I knew, and I felt like an absolute ninny for not knowing from the first.

I was shaken to the core, and I was angry, too, angrier than I had ever been in my life. The anger blazed for a few moments, possessing me completely, and then it turned cool and hard inside me and gave me a steely strength, and that was what held the panic at bay. I could feel the panic springing to life within, a tremulous, twitchy thing, bubbling up beneath the anger, and I knew I had to keep it under control. I knew I had to stay calm and face this with shoulders squared or else I would be well and truly lost.

Well, Angela, you brought it on yourself, you did, being a complete fool and playing along and putting on your fancy new clothes and letting her bring you up here. Thought you were ever so worldly and wise, didn't you? Thought you were knowing and smart, sure, and here you've been duped like the dimmest innocent fresh from the farm. You're in for it now, and you're going to have to brazen it out. No use running away at this point.

I took one of the knives and dipped it into the pâté and spread it thickly over a slice of the thin toast. Might as well eat something. I'd probably need the strength, I thought wryly. The pâté was delicious, rich and creamy, the tiny bits of truffle giving it a marvelous flavor. Hadn't ever eaten any pâté before. Hadn't eaten caviar either. It looked quite appetizing, glistening gray-black. Might as well sample that, too. I finished the toast with pâté and heaped four spoonfuls of caviar on another piece of toast, and I was eating that when the door opened and Clinton Meredith came in.

He closed the door behind him and stood there for a moment, gazing at me with a half-smile curling on his lips, and I took another bite, paying him no mind.

"Good?" he inquired.

"It's all right," I said. "A mite too fishy for my taste. The pâté is divine."

"Oh?"

He strolled over to the table and took the knife and spread some pâté on a piece of toast and took a bite.

"You're right," he agreed. "It *is* divine."

"I suppose you're paying for this meal," I said.

"In a manner of speaking," he replied. "I had the caviar ordered especially for you. I'm sorry you don't care for it. It's frightfully expensive, you know."

"Still tastes too fishy."

"Your stepmother has talked to you?"

"As a matter of fact, she hasn't, but I think I get the general drift of things. If you've already given her money, I suggest you get a refund. You're wasting your time."

"You're going to be difficult?" he asked.

"I'm going to be impossible," I said.

He smiled at that, not in the least discouraged. Tonight he was wearing black pumps with silver buckles and fine white silk stockings and knee breeches and frock coat of deep navy blue brocade, the frock coat richly embroidered with delicate black silk flowers. His waistcoat was navy blue, too, and lace dripped profusely from his throat and cuffs. Handsome as a fairy-tale prince, he was, that thick blond hair glistening silver-blond in the candlelight, his smoky gray eyes full of mischievous delight as the smile played on those full pink lips.

"Am I so repulsive?" he inquired.

I spread more pâté over another piece of toast. "To me you are," I informed him.

"Are you frightened of me?"

"Not by a long chalk."

"Then perhaps you will at least agree to dine with me tonight and listen to what I propose."

"Since I'm here I might as well eat," I said, "but you're not going to say a word that could possibly interest me. My stepmother might—might have made whores out of her two daughters, but she's not going to make a whore out of me, I can assure you."

"Relax, Angela. Here, let me help you into your chair. A glass of champagne?"

"No thank you. I want to keep all my wits about me."

Lord Meredith smiled again and opened the bottle of champagne and poured some into his glass, and then he sat down across the table from me and lifted the glass, looking at me over the rim. The champagne sparkled, pale gold and full of tiny bubbles. I longed for a glass of it, but I didn't dare risk it. He sipped his slowly, gazing at me all the while, and then there was a rap on the door and Blake came in, pushing a small trolley laden with silver-covered dishes and another silver bucket with a second bottle of champagne nesting in ice. His face impassive, Blake removed the covers from the dishes and placed them on the table and placed the bucket on a small folding table he took from under the trolley and set up at Clinton's right. Clinton nodded with approval as the footman stepped back.

"That'll be all, Blake," he said. "I'll summon you if we need anything else. We're not to be interrupted again."

"I quite understand, Milord."

He left, removing the trolley, and we were alone again and Lord Meredith was looking at me with those seductive gray eyes with heavy eyelids drooping, and I felt the power and provocation of that gaze and felt very uncomfortable and wished I hadn't agreed to stay and dine. Sheer bravura, that. Wanted to show him I wasn't afraid. At least I would get a fine meal out of it. There was a marvelous-looking aspic and thin slices of pink-orange salmon and golden-brown pheasant on a nest of wild rice and my favorite asparagus with sauce and a cake with creamy white icing and flakes of chocolate swirled on top. I heaped my plate. He poured another glass of champagne and continued to watch me as I ate.

"You've bewitched me, Angela," he confessed. "Completely and entirely. I've never met a woman quite like you."

"You should try this pheasant. It's wonderful. The wild rice, too."

"I haven't been able to get you out of my mind. I haven't been able to think of anything else since I saw you five nights ago. No woman's ever had this effect on me—and I've known a lot of women. I must have you."

"Try some aspic instead. It's very tasty."

"I'm usually quite nonchalant about these things— I take a woman and I enjoy her and all too quickly I'm bored. I've a feeling you'd never bore me, and that's why I'm prepared to spend a fortune to have you. Will you please stop stuffing yourself and listen to me?"

"I'm not stuffing myself. I'd never do anything so inelegant. I'm eating with perfect decorum, using my knife, using my fork, taking small, polite bites. The salmon's heaven, has a wonderful flavor."

"I had a very long talk with your stepmother, and, I must say, she drove a very shrewd bargain."

Solonge had used those identical words over two years ago. I ate another slice of salmon and finished my pheasant. Lord Meredith poured yet another glass of champagne. He hadn't touched a bite of food.

"You'll have your own town house," he told me. "A small one, admittedly, but quite elegant, in one of the best neighborhoods. You'll have a maid, a butler, a footman, your own carriage and horses. You'll have a monthly allowance, and I intend to smother you with presents. I'm always most generous with my women— love to see the glow in their eyes when I give them some expensive bauble."

"I don't care for baubles, Lord Meredith."

My voice was icy and indifferent. He frowned. I sliced a piece of cake and placed it on the small plate provided. It was lightly flavored with some kind of liqueur and was rich and buttery, the icing sheer ambrosia. I offered some to him. He shook his head, irritated now, and that pleased me. Probably never been turned down before, I thought. With his incredible good looks, with that husky, honeyed voice and that potent male allure, he had undoubtedly been fawned over by women all his adult life, and they had spoiled him rotten. Thought he could just snap his fingers and they'd tumble into his arms. Most of them probably did, I admitted.

"There's no coffee," I said, finished with my cake.

"Forget the coffee."

"I'd really like some. Will you summon Blake?"

"I told you to forget the coffee. We have things to discuss."

"I'm afraid not, Lord Meredith."

I stood up. That surprised him. He stood up, too, frowning again.

"Your stepmother and I came to terms. She insisted we put it all down on paper. Both of us signed it. I've already given her a very large sum of money. You're not leaving, Angela."

"You intend to hold me here by force?"

"If necessary," he said.

He moved over to the door and turned the key in the lock and then dropped the key into his waistcoat pocket. The panic I had suppressed earlier started welling up inside again, but I staunchly refused to acknowledge it. The anger came back, too, and I knew that I was never going to spend another night under this roof. My stepmother had...had *sold* me, like I was a piece of property, and I actually longed to kill her. What joy it would give me to shove her down the stairs. I must leave. I must leave tonight.

"You're trembling," he said.

"Does that surprise you?" I asked crisply.

"I'm not going to hurt you," he said, and his voice was deep and throaty. "I think I'm in love with you, Angela. I've never said that to another woman. Never. I never thought I would."

"You—you don't know what the word love means."

"I think I do now."

He was very convincing, he was, made you actually believe he was speaking the truth, but then he had undoubtedly had a great deal of practice. He moved over to me and placed his hands on my bare shoulders and looked deeply into my eyes and his own were tender, filled with lies, and I trembled more than ever, unable to control it. His hands were warm and soft and strong, gently massaging my flesh, and he lifted one of them up and curled it around the side of my neck and squeezed gently and parted his lips and lowered his heavy eyelids and then wrapped his fingers around the back of my neck, squeezing more, and I was not nearly as immune as I thought I was, as I wanted to be. He was a magnificent male and I was human, I was flesh and blood, and his sexual magnetism was overwhelming, loathe him though I might.

"I'm going to love you, Angela," he murmured, and his husky voice seemed to ache with longing. "I'm going to be so good to you—make you so happy."

I stiffened and tried to pull away and his fingers tightened on the back of my neck and he curled his other arm around my waist and drew me up against him and held me tightly and his body was strong and muscular and warm and the contact caused me to shudder and again I tried to pull away and he chuckled, holding me fast, and then he tilted his head and kissed me and I was stiff as a board, refusing to yield, refusing to bend, and his lips caressed mine ever so gently and he made sounds deep in his throat and began to kiss me ardently, passionately, his mouth devouring mine, and I struggled and he pulled me closer, rough now, masterful, holding me so tightly it hurt me, but the pain wasn't nearly as disturbing as the pleasure, pleasure I couldn't deny. Images of that erotic kiss in the garden of Greystone Hall flashed through my mind, but it wasn't Lady Laura he was kissing, it was me, and sensations I never wanted to feel again flooded my being and I wanted more, still more, and I longed to curl my arms around him and give way, give in, my own body threatening to betray me.

I threw my arm out and the back of my palm touched something cold, and I realized it was the second ice bucket, sitting on the small table near his empty seat. My fingers groped and finally found the neck of the unopened bottle of champagne. I gripped it and pulled the bottle out of its nest of ice. The sound of half-melted ice clattering in the bucket caused him to draw back, his lips momentarily abandoning my own. He loosened his hold on me, puzzled, lifting his head, and when he

did I swung the bottle up with all my strength, slamming it against the back of his head. His eyes shot wide
open, closed, and his knees buckled. He crumpled to the
floor, landing with a heavy thud, and I was surprised
to see that I was still holding the bottle. It hadn't broken. I put it back into the bucket and looked at the
man on the floor, so still I wondered if he was still
breathing.

My God, I thought, I've killed him! I kneeled down
and took his wrist between my thumb and forefinger
and yes, there was a pulse, and I leaned my cheek over
his nose and yes, the son of a bitch was still breathing,
but he was likely to be out cold for some time and he'd
have a frightful headache when he came to. Served him
right. I slipped my hand into his waistcoat pocket and
got the key and got up and unlocked the door and pulled
it open. I paused for a moment, looking back at the
handsome blond lord in navy blue brocade and lace
sprawling on the floor beside the table with its gleaming white cloth.

"Good-bye, Lord Meredith," I said.

I hurried down the hall then, quiet as could be, and
reached my room without being seen. Quickly, quickly,
I took clothes out of the wardrobe and made a bundle
of them and then I put on a long cloak and pulled the
hood up over my head. I'd have to leave everything else,
the rest of my clothes, all my books, all of them but
one. I fetched Captain Johnson's book on highwaymen
and opened it and saw that the money was still inside,
and then I stuck it into the bundle of clothes and left
the room and crept down the hall until I reached the
narrow, enclosed staircase the servants used. It went
down to the basement and a small door that opened
onto the mews in back of the building.

I went down the stairs and unlocked the door and
opened it and stepped into the mews. It was black as
pitch out here, downright spooky, and I certainly didn't
relish sallying across London at night alone, but there
was nothing else to do. It wasn't safe, no, but it sure

wasn't safe for me to stay here either. Taking a deep breath, I hurried through the darkness to the thorough-fare at the end of the mews and turned and headed for Covent Garden as fast as I could.

Chapter Nine

Mellow rays of sunlight drifted lazily through the front windows, illuminating the large, littered, cozy workroom of Dottie's shop with its racks of costumes and cluttered work tables and wall of shelves jammed with ribbons and feathers and braids and boxes full of beads and spangles. Like a magpie's nest, it was. Everything seemed woefully disorganized, as did Dottie herself, but amidst all this chaos she managed to produce sumptuously beautiful, meticulously made costumes for almost every theatrical manager in London, including the great David Garrick himself. *We* managed to produce, for I had been working here for three months now, and Dottie often shook her head and stared dreamily into space and declared she had no idea how she had ever gotten along without me.

Sitting at my worktable, I carefully stitched the silver and white satin floral patterns onto the creamy pink satin skirt, sighing when I thought about edging each single pattern in white seed pearls. Hours and hours and hours it would take, but it was attention to details

like this that made Dottie's creations so spectacular.
Dottie employed four other seamstresses besides me,
but they all worked in the loftlike room upstairs, adjacent to her private living quarters. They were all quite
skillful, but Dottie couldn't stand their incessant chatter. Kept me working down here because she liked my
company and knew I wouldn't gush and carry on when
some glamorous theatrical notable came in to check on
a costume.

I had seen Mr. Garrick a number of times, a polite,
quiet-spoken gentleman in his late middle-age who
seemed rather drab and completely unremarkable. Davy
saved all his dazzle and dynamic personality for the
theater, Dottie told me. Away from the footlights, he
was a placid, domestic creature who was henpecked by
his wife and apt to forget things, but, ah, in his youth!
He'd been something then, he had. Dottie believed some
of his sparkle had vanished when Miranda James turned
him down and he married that retired Austrian dancer.
He was undeniably the greatest actor of the age, all
flashing magnetism on stage, but in his dull gray
breeches and shabby brown coat he would pass unno-
ticed on the street.

Another pattern stitched on. Another one begun. Only
three more left to do. It was routine work, and my mind
began to wander, as it tended to do when I was working
on something like this. I thought of that night four
months ago when I had fled Marie's Place, leaving an
unconscious Lord Meredith in the private room upstairs. A nightmare, that had been, me utterly terrified
as I ran through the dark streets, my heart beating
fast, but I had made it without having my throat slit
and dawn was breaking and the produce men were already setting up their stalls when I reached Covent
Garden. I asked one of them to direct me to Brinkley's
Wig Shop and he smiled, removed his greasy brown cap
and pointed and said he reckoned it was still right over
there on Henrietta Street just around that corner. A
sleepy but thoroughly delighted Megan had welcomed
me with open arms and we had drunk innumerable cups

of coffee and eaten a dozen cinnamon rolls and talked for hours, becoming as close as sisters almost at once.

I had been terribly nervous and apprehensive those first few weeks, for I knew full well that Marie could have me clapped into prison as an incorrigible minor as long as I was still her legal ward, and I knew she wouldn't hesitate, vindictive shrew that she was. I had caused her to lose a great deal of money, and nothing would please her more than to see me rotting away in a filthy cell in Newgate. I wouldn't be at all surprised if she hadn't marched herself down to Bow Street and filed a complaint and given them a description. The Runners were probably still keeping an eye out for the wretched girl who had assaulted a lord and run off into the night, and even now I was still a bit wary when on the streets. Megan assured me my fears were foolish. London was a huge place with thousands and thousands of people, a wonderful place to get lost in. Who would think to look for me in Covent Garden? Her words made good sense, but I still wouldn't feel completely safe for the next six months, when I would turn twenty-one. Until then I intended to keep low, never straying from the neighborhood.

But what a marvelous neighborhood it was. With its mellow old buildings, its piazza and arcades, its colorful fruit and vegetable stands and its stalls full of glorious flowers, Covent Garden was a magical place, warm and friendly and utterly unlike the rest of London. Throng-ing with flamboyant theater folk and artists, it had a casual, carefree air and a special ambience all its own. Covent Garden was weathered white marble columns and worn gray cobbles, pretty young soubrettes and swaggering actors, dusty velvet curtains and carts of cabbage. The noxious smell that pervaded the rest of London was missing here and the very air seemed cleaner and more invigorating. Shabby, scampish, cozy and not quite respectable, Covent Garden was like a bit of paradise, I felt, and I was proud to be a part of it.

The flat Megan and I shared over the wig shop was

large and roomy, with a run-down, dilapidated charm and battered furniture. We were never free of the smell of powder and scorched hair, but that was part of its raffish charm, and there were eating houses nearby where we could buy food to bring up to our rooms, as neither of us cared to cook. Looking out the windows, one could see the arcades across the way and the roof of the opera house with pigeons perching on the eaves. Dottie's establishment was but a short walk, down Southampton and around the corner to Tavistock Street. I loved rooming with Megan and loved working for Dottie, too, genial, eccentric soul that she was, and had it not been for the shadow of Newgate looming in my imagination I would have been wonderfully content with my new lot.

One more floral pattern to stitch on, and then time to start on the white seed pearls. A mote-filled ray of sunlight slanted across my table. I sighed and began to stitch the silver and white satin pattern onto the pink. I could hear Megan working in the stockroom beyond the curtained archway, rearranging bolts of velvet and satin and silk. She had been hired on as a super in a new production, got to wear a lovely blue satin gown with cream lace and simper on stage as a French courtesan in the crowd scenes, but the play had had a dismally short run and now she was back at Dottie's, good-natured as ever. Those French things never ran long, she declared. Give her a good thundering English drama every time. Duels, doxies and brooding heroes, that's what the public wanted. Bloodshed and battles.

The stairs at the other end of the room creaked noisily, and I glanced up to see Dottie descending, holding on to the wooden railing with one plump hand and looking distracted, as usual. In her wrinkled pale violet smock, her gray hair swept up in an untidy pompadour, Dorothea Gibbons was indeed something to see. Decidedly heavy, she had a round, amiable face and a fleshy double chin. Her plump cheeks were powdered, her small mouth cherry red with rouge, her eyelids smeared rather unevenly with shiny violet-blue shadow. Dottie had been a moderately successful actress thirty some odd years ago—"During the Peloponnesian War, dear," she declared—and saw no reason why she should stop using cosmetics merely because she was in her late fifties. Warm, generous, endearing, she reminded me of someone's cozy, eccentric old grandmother.

"I vow, those girls *do* chatter," she said wearily, shuffling over to my table in her comfortable purple felt slippers. "They've almost finished with the apple-green frocks trimmed with black lace. Eight actresses wearing apple-green and black lace all at the same time, in the same scene? I feel sure Mr. Foote has made a disastrous mistake, but I don't *order* the costumes, I merely make them."

Dottie sighed and patted her pompadour, which always seemed in danger of coming undone, despite the purple velvet bow fastening it in back. "My, you've done a lovely job with those flowers, dear. Almost finished, I see. How about a cup of tea?"

"No thank you, Dottie. I want to start on the seed pearls right away."

"Such a lovely gown," she said. "Costuming Shakespeare is always a delight, particularly *A Midsummer Night's Dream*. I feel certain young Mrs. Siddons will look enchanting in it as Hippolyta, particularly as Theseus is wearing silver, but I'm still worried about Titania—thin white gauze and a handful of spangles and nothing *else,* my dear."

"The spangles are strategically located," I reminded her.

"Even so, it's too near nude to my mind. Mr. Colman might just find himself in trouble, even if it *is* Shakespeare. When *I* did Titania—that was before your time, my dear, they had just invented the wheel—I wore a marvelous gown of silver-gray satin with silver and gold ribbons floating from the skirt and arms, very effective and *fully* covered."

"I tried out for Cobweb," came a voice from the stockroom. "Mr. Colman said I was altogether too provocative to be a fairy."

"Why didn't you try out for one of the wedding guests?" Dottie asked.

Megan stuck her head through the curtains, auburn waves gleaming. "I did. The supers had already been signed. The crushed gold velvet wasn't ready yet, Dottie. They won't have it until next week."

"Oh dear, that means some of us will be working till all hours if the costume is to be ready in time. Crushed gold velvet is all wrong for Mrs. Clive, with her sallow complexion, but that's neither here nor there."

Megan went back to work behind the curtains and Dottie shuffled across to pour herself a cup of tea from the pot kept ever ready on a small stove. Dottie was rarely without a cup of tea, drank it all day long. Nibbled on chocolate biscuits, too, a box of them always at hand. I got up to fetch the white seed pearls but couldn't find any in the boxes on the shelf. Dottie said they might be in back, so I stepped through the curtains into the large stockroom with its deep shelves crowded with hundreds of bolts of sumptuous cloth. Megan said she didn't remember seeing the seed pearls but there were all sorts of odds and ends stuck about, she'd help me look.

"I saw Larry again today, luv," she informed me.

"The journalist who followed you into Miller's?"

"The same. I was crossing the Strand, on my way back, and I saw him coming out of a shop with the *most* unusual blonde. I couldn't be sure of it, but I'd swear she was cross-eyed. Hanging onto his arm, she was, gazing up at him like he'd just hung the moon."

"You were jealous?"

"Not in the least," Megan replied, kneeling down to go through some boxes on the floor. "I just thought Larry had more *taste*. I do hope he's happy. He seemed very pleased with her."

"Did he see you?"

"I darted behind a tree. *Here* they are, a whole box full. I don't know what's happening to me," she declared, rising and handing me the box. "Four whole months without a serious romance. Next thing you know I'll be joining a *nun*nery."

"What about that handsome young actor you've been seeing now and then?"

"You mean Timothy? He's just a good friend, luv. I'd never allow myself to fall in love with an actor. Talk about ego—Lord, they're even worse than journalists!"

"Those who've come into the shop would certainly seem to be, although Mr. Garrick was nice."

"Always worrying about their looks—worry about bumps, worry about balding, worry about gaining weight. Worry about their voices, too. Most of them have hysterics when it's damp, won't go out unless they've got at least two or three scarves wrapped around their throats. Never, *never* fall in love with an actor."

"It's not likely I shall."

"Timothy's sweet, though, like a big brother. He's taking me to Ranelagh Pleasure Gardens on Saturday, luv. I wish you'd come along. You need to get out a bit—it isn't healthy, staying cooped up in the flat every night. Timothy'll get you an escort, he has ever so many chums, and you can wear a *mask*. Lots of ladies do at Ranelagh."

"We'll see," I said.

Megan shook her head. "I worry about you, Angela. I really do. A girl as lovely as you should have a dozen beaux, should be going out several times a week. I know you had a very unpleasant experience with that stableboy you told me about—the one who had his way with you and then skipped—and I realize your encounters with that handsome Lord Meredith weren't exactly thrilling, but not *all* men are like that."

"No?"

"Well—" Megan hesitated. "There are a few good ones out there, I feel *sure* of it."

I smiled. Megan did, too.

"You just have to keep looking for them," she said. "And neither of us is getting any *young*er, luv."

"I'd be content to be six months older."

Megan started to say something when a loud noise

out front startled both of us. Someone had slammed the
door so violently that boxes actually tumbled from the
shelves. *"Mrs. Gibbons!"* an angry voice roared. Megan
and I hurried to the curtain to peek out between the
central part. A very tall, very striking man in his mid-
thirties was standing in the middle of the shop, waving
a fist in the air and looking ready to commit several
murders. He had glossy, unruly brown hair and a wide,
full mouth and a slightly crooked nose that looked as
if it had been broken at least twice. His green-brown
eyes seemed to flash with emerald fire. "Mrs. Gibbons!"
he roared. *"Dottie!* Get your plump ass out here *at once!"*

"Who's that?" I whispered, peeking through the curtains.

"James Lambert, theatrical manager," Megan said
dryly. "The monster of Covent Garden."

"Oh, it's you, Lamb," Dottie said, strolling toward
him with her cup of tea and a chocolate biscuit. "I figured it must be. All that racket. I was right over there
all the time. You needn't have *thundered* so."

"I'm going to kill you!" he cried. "I really am. I'm
going to strangle you with my bare hands!"

"Tut," she said, taking a sip of tea.

"I mean it, Dottie! This time you've gone altogether
too far!"

Dottie was totally unperturbed. "What have I done?"
she inquired.

"What have you done? What have you *done!* You've
ruined me! My play is opening day after tomorrow, as
you bloody well know, every seat sold out, the most
ambitious, the most spectacular play I've ever mounted,
and today I plan the first dress rehearsal to see how
the costumes work and the enchanting Mrs. Tallent—
who has a decided *lack* of it but sells tickets nevertheless—takes down her first act costume and has a
shrieking fit and vows she won't put one foot on stage
in *gray* velvet!"

"Silver-gray," Dottie corrected him. "You selected the
cloth yourself, Lamb."

The man banged his fist on a worktable. A pair of

scissors fell to the floor with a noisy clatter. Megan repressed a giggle. I watched with horrified fascination as he picked up a bolt of velvet and hurled it to the floor. Dottie sipped her tea and nibbled her biscuit, letting him seethe. He wasn't at all handsome, not with that crooked nose, but he was undeniably arresting, crackling with virile presence. He wore black pumps and white silk stockings and knee breeches and frock coat of black broadcloth, his waistcoat rich plum-colored satin. His ruffled white jabot was limp. The garments were superbly cut but looked as though he'd slept in them. He banged his fist on the table again, his eyes still flaming green fire.

"I selected *blue!* Mrs. Tallent has *blue* eyes and wanted a *blue* gown and an aigrette of *blue* ostrich plumes and you do it in *gray!* Now the minx won't budge from her dressing room and vows she'll stay there until she gets a blue gown!"

"You told me she wanted blue, vivid blue, Lamb, I remember it distinctly, and I tactfully suggested that since she is a widow in the first act and supposedly in mourning a pretty gray velvet gown might be more appropriate. You agreed with me. You said you were bloody good and tired of that slut running the show and she'd wear gray and like it or you'd put a boot up her ass. You were quite definite about it," she added.

"You're lying! I said no such thing!"

"Don't snap those eyes at me, Jamie Lambert. Don't wave your fist in my face, either. I gave you your banana pudding when you hadn't a tooth in your mouth— fed you and your brother, too, I did—and I changed your wet nappies as well. If your father had any sense, I might well have been your mother instead of that poor creature who died giving birth to you."

"That has nothing to do with it!"

"How does Bobby like America?"

"Robert is doing brilliantly well in America. They love him. They love his company. Philadelphia is mad for him. Boston and New York, too. I well may be sailing for the Colonies my*self* if this mess isn't straightened out at once. What am I going to *do*, Dottie?"

"I suggest you put a boot up her ass, dear," she told him. "Coral Tallent is an ungifted amateur who hasn't a single thing going for her except a passably pretty face and a pair of remarkable breasts. The former is already beginning to show signs of wear and the latter have begun to sag. I told you when you signed her you'd having nothing but trouble."

"You *never* like my actresses."

"You never *hire* actresses. You hire pretty young nobodies you can bully and browbeat and terrify into giving a performance, and when they're successful you feel ever so important because you made them what they are, and when, inevitably, they rebel, you're totally befuddled and haven't an inkling *why*. It's happened time and time again."

"You make me sound like a monster!"

Dottie took a final sip of tea and set the cup down. "You *are* a monster, dear," she said fondly, "albeit most endearing. So was your father. I suppose that's why he was the only man I ever really loved. I will not make another gown in blue, Lamb. I couldn't possibly have it ready in time. If Mrs. Tallent persists in her demands seize her by the hair, drag her down the hall and boot her out the stage door."

Lambert lowered his lids, placed an index finger on his jaw and reflected a moment. "You know," he said thoughtfully, "I just might do that. I'd have to break down the dressing room door first, though."

"The exercise would do you good, dear."

James Lambert grinned, and at that moment he did indeed look most endearing, like a naughty, overgrown boy. He flung his arms out and grabbed Dottie in an exuberant hug, rocking her plump body and squeezing so tightly she gave a cry of protest. He released her, still grinning.

"You're so rough and rowdy," she grumbled, frowning quite unconvincingly. "You always were, even as a boy.

Don't know your own strength. You almost cracked my ribs, Jamie Lambert!"

He chucked her double chin. "They're well padded, love."

"Get out of here!" she said crossly.

Lambert gave her another quick hug and planted a noisy kiss on her cheek and started toward the door. "And get those clothes pressed!" Dottie called as he flung open the door, stepped outside and slammed the door shut. Another box tumbled off the shelf. My word, the man's a human tornado, I thought, letting the curtain drop back into place.

"So now you've seen the great James Lambert," Megan said in a dry voice. "He's been in a couple of times since you started work here, but you were apparently upstairs at the time. Lucky you," she added.

"You obviously don't care for him."

"I was a super in one of his productions a few seasons back—that Egyptian drama I told you about. Once was enough, believe me. A girl could get killed working for him."

"Oh?"

"Once I was a few seconds late making my entrance with the other slaves, my sandal had come loose, and when the act was over he grabbed me by the arms and shook me so savagely I thought my teeth would fall out. I had bruises on my arms for days. He's a terrible bully. *He* calls it being a perfectionist, of course."

"What kind of plays does he put on?" I inquired.

"His own. He's a playwright, too. Flamboyant melodrama invariably featuring a beautiful woman who claws and climbs her way to the top against some colorful historical background. An occasional risque comedy, though he's not as successful with those. His plays are very popular with the rowdier crowd, they flock to ogle his latest discovery. His latest discoveries rarely last more than a couple of seasons."

"Dottie seemed quite fond of him."

"Oh, Lambert has charm," Megan admitted. "When he chooses to employ it, that is. The women are wild for him, constantly chasing after him, as though he were some magnificent prize. More than one titled lady has lost her heart and her head over him. Treats them like dirt, he does, and they come running back for more."

"How odd," I remarked.

"Not really, luv. I loathe the man and will never step foot in his theater again, but I'll be the first to admit he's the most exciting man in Covent Garden. He's brilliant, volatile, mercurial—and rakishly good-looking as well."

"With that nose?"

"That nose keeps him from being *too* good-looking, makes his face all the more interesting. He's not my cup of tea, far from it, but I can see why women grow weak in the knees when he walks into a room. I've got to go pick up some more black lace, luv."

"And I've got to start sewing these seed pearls on."

"Do think about Ranelagh Pleasure Gardens on Saturday, Angela. We'll be leaving in the early afternoon and stay till midnight. You'll love the rotunda and the pavilion, and the gardens by moonlight are gorgeous. Timothy will find you a safe, charming escort and we'll have a marvelous time."

"Perhaps. I'll let you know."

The shop seemed unusually quiet after the thundering Mr. Lambert's departure. I picked up the boxes that had tumbled to the floor and put them up on the shelf. Dottie was at her table, carefully cutting a huge swath of gleaming pink and gold brocade. I resumed my work, painstakingly edging the floral patterns with the narrow strands of seed pearls, and I was soon immersed in the job. The rays of sunlight turned dark gold, began to fade, and I was surprised when Dottie tapped me on the shoulder and said it was time to close up. I could hear the other girls chattering as they came down the stairs. I told Dottie I'd like to finish the gown tonight and asked if it would be all right for me to take it home.

"Bless you, dear, it would be an enormous help—I'd like to get started on those fairy costumes tomorrow—

but I feel terribly guilty about it. You're always taking work home."

"I enjoy working, Dottie."

"I know, Angela, but there's more to life than work. A girl as pretty, as young as you should be having some fun as well. You should be jaunting about town with a good-looking young beau now and then, going out to the theater, going out to dine. I worry about you."

"You, too," I said wryly.

"Take the gown home if you wish, dear, but you're having the whole day off Saturday. Is that understood?" Dottie shook her head and stared dreamily into space. "I declare, I've no idea how I ever got along without you," she said once more.

I did take Saturday off, but I did not go to Ranelagh Pleasure Gardens. Megan was disappointed and looked regretful when she and the amiable Timothy departed around three. We had spent the morning cleaning the flat, had gone out and purchased a rather dilapidated second hand dusty-rose sofa which Timothy and a couple of his friends had hauled up to our large sitting room. I sat on it now, a book in my lap, but I didn't read. The flat seemed unusually still and, yes, lonely without Megan swirling about and making wry, humorous remarks. I almost wished I had gone with them. I *could* have worn a mask like some of the ladies did, and perhaps I would even have enjoyed myself. I needed to have some fun, Dottie and Megan insisted. Perhaps I did. How long had it been since I had really enjoyed myself? Not . . . not since Hugh Bradford abandoned me. Not since my father died.

I gazed at the patterns of sunlight playing on the uneven hardwood floor, fresh scrubbed but grayish-tan with age. We would have to buy a rug next, as soon as we had a pound or so to spare. I had spotted a dandy one at the used furniture shop, faded blue and pink with green leaves and Chinese chrysanthemums, only two pounds, but the sofa had temporarily depleted our funds. I should have asked the man to hold it for us, I reflected, and then I found myself on the verge of tears, and that disturbed me. I detested people who sat around feeling sorry for themselves. I had been very, very fortunate. I had a wonderful job, a comfortable flat in a charming part of London, new friends as well. Though still nervous about Marie and the possibility of being found and clapped into prison, I was content with my new life.

Content, yes, but not happy. I hadn't been truly happy since that night under the stars when Hugh Bradford made love to me.

I put the book aside and stood up, irritated with myself now. All right, Angela. That will be quite enough of that. You can sit here and grow misty-eyed and maudlin, or you can *do* something. Brushing the gathered folds of my dark pink skirt, I went to my bedroom, ran a comb through my hair, grabbed my reticule and then left the flat, going down the steep, enclosed wooden stairs that led to our private entrance. The door was a weathered green with Number 11 in tarnished brass. The door to Brinkley's Wig Shop, Number 12, was right beside it, and there were several wigs on oval-shaped white stands in the window. As I passed by, I could see old Brinkley busy with his curling irons in back of the shop. He happened to look up, his own wig askew. He waved at me and I waved back, smiling. Although he did a certain amount of business with balding gents, most of his trade came from the many theaters in the district, his wigs worn by all the actors.

Crossing the street, I strolled past St. Paul's with its tall white columns and mellowed rose-brown bricks. It was a beautiful old building, simple yet majestic in design, and some claimed it was Inigo Jones' masterpiece. St. Paul's had been deserted years ago by its fashionable, affluent congregation, and it was now known as the Actors' Church, even though its members were mostly market folk, actors being considerably less faithful in attendance. White marble tombstones stood in the churchyard, old and worn, some of them covered with moss. The murderer Robert Carr, a favorite of James I, was buried here, I knew, as well as many poets and painters, prostitutes and decent, God-fearing citizens. Moving leisurely across the square with its population of tiny brown sparrows and fat, cooing pigeons, I entered the Market, which wasn't at all busy this warm August afternoon.

What color, what beauty met the eyes, what marvelous smells assailed the nostrils. Bright red apples and vivid oranges, yellow squash and green broccoli, light green lettuce, dark maroon beets, pale brown potatoes arranged in pyramids in the carts. Artichokes. Hothouse-grown pineapples, the first one presented to Charles II over a hundred years ago, an exotic delicacy that was still much in favor. Hearty country faces smiling as you passed, robust country voices bidding you buy—"'Ere, luv, 'ave a bite, 'ave you ever seen such bleedin' red hap-ples?"—and carts of summer flowers, too, frothy pink banks of flowers, mauve, violet, pale blue, gold. Nell Gwynn had skipped over here to buy flowers when she was acting at the Drury Lane, burying her tilted nose in a bunch of violets. I strolled and smelled and savored the wonders of the Market, which was the very heart of Covent Garden, and eventually I purchased some sweet grapes and munched them as I left the Market and paused to gaze at the tall pillars of the Opera House.

Four months in Covent Garden and I had yet to attend any of the theaters that gave it such flavor and vitality. Hadn't even gone to see Megan in her blue satin gown with cream lace as she mimicked a French courtesan. Theaters weren't respectable, of course, and only harlots attended them without a male escort. I'd love to see a play, I thought, sauntering on, finishing my sweet grapes. I wandered leisurely through the maze of narrow, cobbled streets and finally found myself standing in front of the Lambert Theater, a large, unimposing gray stone building with soot-streaked white marble columns and portico. Hadn't planned it. Just happened to be here. I wondered how the bombastic Mr. James Lambert had handled the recalcitrant Mrs. Tallent. Had he dragged her down the hall by the hair and booted her out the stage door? Wouldn't be surprised if he had, but the play had opened four nights ago and she had worn the gray velvet and Dottie had said the evening was a disaster, poor Lamb had a dismal failure on his hands. Served him right, I thought, remembering what Megan had told me about the man.

I moved on, rather pensive, thinking of the long, lonely evening looming ahead. A solitary meal fetched from Hancock's around the corner. Reading on the cozy dusty-rose sofa. A cup of tea. A roomy flat smelling of powder and scorched hair. Silence within, while outside, in the night, people were making merry and laughing and courting and attending the theaters and disporting themselves with glee. Was it always going to be like this? What was I going to do with my life? I had made a promise to my father, but as yet I had done nothing that would have made him proud of me. Selling used clothes. Working in a gambling house. My work for Dottie was at least respectable employment, but there seemed little future in sitting at a table day after day, stitching silk tunics and cutting gauze wings and sewing spangles on tights. I turned, wandering down a narrow street empty of traffic. Count your blessings, Angela, I scolded myself. You're bloody fortunate to have such a job.

I would enjoy my solitary meal—a nice grilled chop and applesauce and steamed cabbage and hot buttered rolls—and I would enjoy my book, too. And the next time Megan asked me to go out with her I would bloody well go. Dottie was right, I *should* be having some fun. Lost in thought, I moved on down the pavement, vaguely aware of hooves clopping and wheels turning on the cobbles somewhere behind me, and then the elegant golden-brown carriage with its four gorgeous bays passed slowly and a man thrust his head out the window and peered at me and shouted "Stop!" and the driver in white and gold livery tugged on the reins and the short, jaunty footman riding on back almost lost his footing. I stopped, standing very still, my heart in my throat.

The man inside the carriage leaned his head out again, craning his neck.

"You, lass! Come closer. I want to have a good look at you."

Paralyzed, I was, unable to move a muscle, unable to yell for help. Not another soul in sight. Girls being abducted every day in London, snatched up off the streets and being drugged and put in houses, and me so scared I couldn't even run. The man had a plump, pleasant face with pink cheeks and friendly blue eyes and wore a powdered wig, looked exactly like someone's jolly old uncle, but that didn't mean a thing. A depraved old pimp, he was, pretending to be a nob, driving about in his fine carriage on the lookout for poor, defenseless girls.

"Do come closer, lass. I won't hurt you."

"Up your arse!" I cried, surprised I had a voice.

"Those eyes. Those cheekbones. That delicious mouth. That hair—glossy chestnut brown silk, rich highlights. I must paint you. I must. Who *are* you, lass?"

"None of your bleedin' business! Drive on! Leave me alone or—or I'll shriek bloody murder. You might grab other helpless girls off the street and sentence them to a fate worse than death, but you're not nabbing me!"

"Want me to fetch 'er for you, Mr. G.?" the footman asked.

I whirled around to glare at him. "You lay one hand on me and you'll be singing soprano for the rest of your life!"

He grinned and pretended to shiver. He had brick-red hair and twinkling brown eyes and a wide, saucy mouth. Considerably shorter than I, he was powerfully built, muscles bulging beneath the white and gold livery he wore with such cocky assurance.

"Feisty one, this 'un," he quipped. "Reckon she'd like to claw my eyes out!"

"You misunderstand my intentions, lass," the older man said. His voice was quite gentle, a kind voice, but those pimps were a devious lot. "I don't want to harm you, I merely want to—"

"I know what you want, and you're not getting it!"

"Be reasonable, lass. I must paint you. I'll pay you generously. I've never seen such glorious bone structure, such divine coloring, such radiance. Sir Joshua will turn green with envy. Come, let me talk to you. Let me tell you what I—"

"Sod off!"

"'Ey! Watch your mouth!" the footman called. "Mr. G.'s a bleedin' himport'nt gent, 'e is. Ain't no street wench gonna mouth 'im like that with *me* in 'is himploy!"

"Go bugger yourself, runt!"

Mr. G. sighed wearily. "I guess you'd better fetch her, Jenkins."

Jenkins leaped from his perch like the cocky bantam he was and moved toward me with a grin, and I tensed, claws unsheathed. He had an upturned nose and freckles and looked like a jaunty imp, but he moved like a tiger, he did, muscles rolling beneath the velvet coat. "Don't come any closer!" I warned. His grin widened and he sprang then and grabbed hold of my wrist and swung my arm up and out and had it twisted painfully behind my back quick as lightning and clamped a large, callused hand over my mouth before I could even draw breath to scream.

I struggled furiously, utterly terrified, and Jenkins chuckled in my ear and lifted me up so that I was kicking air and carried me over to the elegant carriage. Mr. G. opened the door and Jenkins hauled me inside and dragged me onto the padded pale gold velvet seat opposite Mr. G. and held me fast as the carriage began to move. This was it! I was being abducted by villains and I would never be heard from again! My heart was beating so rapidly I feared it would burst. Jenkins held me close, almost in his lap, his hand still covering my mouth, but somehow I managed to get it open and sink my teeth into his palm, biting as hard as I could. He let out a yowl and released me.

"Help!" I screamed, leaning out the window. "Help! I'm being abducted by villains!"

Jenkins hauled me back and slung his arm around my throat and choked me, squeezing so hard I began to black out.

"Easy, Jenkins," Mr. G. said calmly. "Give the wench some air. I want to immortalize her, not murder her."

"She bit my bleedin' 'and!"

"We'll bandage it later. Can you hold her still? I want to sketch her. Please don't be alarmed, lass. I know this is all a bit drastic, but I simply couldn't let a prize like you get away."

"You—you're taking me to a house!"

"Indeed I am, and I do hope you'll be able to stay for dinner. Reynolds is going to be green, all right. Hasn't painted anything but simpering aristocrats since they knighted him in '68."

"You're mad!" I cried.

Jenkins tightened his arm around my throat again and informed me that he would cheerfully squeeze my lights out if I didn't sit still, and I knew everything was lost, I had no chance, I was doomed to that fate worse than death. Mr. G. picked up a sketchpad and a piece of charcoal from the seat beside him, studied me intently for a moment and then began to sketch, humming to himself as he did so. He...he must be some kind of dreadful pervert. He wore a pair of white leather pumps with silver buckles and fine white silk stockings and breeches and frock coat of rumpled white satin, the coat embroidered with silver floral designs. His waistcoat was white satin, too, and the lace tumbling from his jabot and over his wrists was of the very finest quality. Certainly dressed like a nob, but maybe all pimps did. That benign, kindly face didn't fool me for a minute.

The carriage rumbled on, leaving Covent Garden far behind. I sat still, all struggle gone out of me now, all hope lost, and Jenkins loosened his hold and Mr. G. continued to sketch and after a while he held the pad up and examined it and nodded. His powdered wig listed slightly to the left. He turned the pad around so I could see it, and there I was on the paper, my face looking back at me big as life. I was dumbfounded! I stared at the image of myself captured so quickly, so expertly on the pad, and in a moving carriage as well.

"Why—you're an artist!" I exclaimed.

"The best in the country, Reynolds and that upstart Romney notwithstanding. Do let her go now, Jenkins."

The cocky footman let go of me and scooted over to the opposite side of the seat.

"No 'arm hin-tended, ducks," he told me. "Just doin' me job."

I gave him a hateful look and turned back to Mr. G.

"You're not a pimp?" I inquired.

"I've often been accused of prostituting my talent, but I've never been called a pimp."

He smiled, looking very genial and avuncular in his rumpled white satin coat and listing wig. He reached up to straighten the latter, his blue eyes twinkling with amusement. Plump, pink cheeked, he was probably in his early fifties. Maybe he *wasn't* a pimp.

"You really just want to paint me?"

"I must, lass. That marvelous bone structure, that coloring—to think I was returning from a visit with Sir Joshua when I spotted you!"

"What have you painted?" I asked suspiciously.

"Hundreds of landscapes—couldn't sell them, alas. In Bath I began to concentrate on portrait painting and had an immediate success. Came to London and had even *more* success."

"What's your name?"

"Thomas Gainsborough. You may call me Tom. We're going to be spending a lot of time together."

"Gainsborough?" I frowned. "Never heard of you."

Mr. G. looked hurt. "Perhaps you've seen my *Perdita.*"

"Perdita Robinson? The famous actress? You painted *her?*"

"Much reproduced, that painting. It's quite famous, I'm told. My *The Honorable Mrs. Graham* caused quite a stir, too, when it was hung at the Royal Academy. I'm one of the original members of the Academy, by the way, but I'm thinking of resigning. Don't like the way they've been hanging my paintings of late."

Bloke *seemed* respectable, but I still wasn't sure I believed him. Didn't seem reasonable members of the Royal Academy who painted famous actresses would go around snatching girls off the street. That sketch he'd done of me proved he could draw, and draw remarkably well, but maybe that was just a hobby. Maybe he made sketches of all his victims to...to show to prospective buyers! I tensed up again, eyeing the door. Maybe I could leap out when the carriage slowed down.

"Why—why would you want to paint me?" I asked. "My mouth's too big. My cheekbones are too high. My eyes are a peculiar color."

"Your mouth too big? Nonsense. It's a full, sensuous mouth, beautifully shaped, not one of those tiny rosebud mouths so much in vogue these days. Your cheekbones are divine, give you a cool patrician look few patrician women ever attain, and your eyes are incredibly arresting. You're undoubtedly the most beautiful woman I've ever seen."

I believed that. Sure. Bloke *was* a liar. Not to be trusted.

"More beautiful than Perdita?" I inquired.

"Far more beautiful. Perdita looks like an Afghan hound with her long neck and those sharp, pointed features. Thought so when I painted her. If you'll look closely at my portrait of her you'll *see* the resemblance."

The carriage was slowing down, and through the windows I could see that we had turned into an elegant square. Gracious white houses with tall white columns holding up the porticoes and fanlights over the doors. Smooth grassy green lawns and neat flower beds behind slender iron fences. Private drives. I eyed the door again as the carriage turned into one of the drives and came to a halt. Jenkins' hand clamped around my wrist, as though he were reading my mind.

"I'm going to scream," I threatened.

"Wouldn't advise it, ducks."

"It seems our guest is still a bit nervous, Jenkins.

Why don't you escort her to the studio. I'll just pop into the parlor and speak to the wife and join you in a few minutes."

Another footman had come outside and opened the carriage door, and Thomas Gainsborough, if, indeed, that was his name, scrambled out and climbed up the six flat marble steps and went into the house. Jenkins pulled me out of the carriage without undue gentility and told me I was bleedin' fortunate to 'ave a gent like Mr. G. take an hin-trest in me. I tried to pull free. His fingers tightened around my wrist. Place doesn't *look* like a brothel, I told myself. Looked even less like one inside. Jenkins dragged me down a lovely wide hallway with elegant white walls and a dark blue runner on the polished dark oak floor and a graceful white spiral staircase curling up to the floor above. A long mahogany table with pieces of porcelain and vases of flowers. A gorgeous chandelier with crystal pendants gleaming. Must be a huge amount of money in painting...or pimping. I intended to crack Jenkins over the head with something as soon as I spied the right object to grab.

He opened a door at the end of the long hall and pulled me into a large studio with windows looking out over a back garden. There was a skylight at one end of the room as well, a low wooden platform beneath it, and all those rays of sunlight streaming in emphasized the incredible disorder. Dozens of canvases leaning against the walls. Tables littered with tubes of paint and brushes in jars and dirty rags. Sketchpads, papers everywhere. An enormous wardrobe with doors standing open to reveal a bewildering array of garments, all crammed together, a dusty pyramid of hatboxes beside it. A large easel draped in cloth held what was obviously a work in progress, and other easels stood here and there holding paintings already finished. Jenkins closed the door and scowled at me.

"Goin' ter be'ave yourself," he said, "or ham I goin' to 'ave to get rough again?"

"You can let go of me, Jenkins," I said haughtily.

"You act up an' I'll clip-ya on th' jaw."

He let go of me and moved over to stand guard at the door, looking like a comical gremlin with that fierce expression, in that preposterous gold and white uniform. Wasn't a bit scared of him. Wasn't scared at all now that I was convinced Mr. G. really *was* a painter. Fancy him wanting to do a painting of *me*. I wandered about the studio, idly examining things and trying to ignore the strong smell of turpentine. I looked at the paintings that stood on easels—several landscapes with carts and cows and feathery green trees, one or two portraits of pretty-pretty ladies with haughty faces and gorgeous gowns and beplumed hats—and then I turned around and spied another painting that stood all by itself on an easel across the room.

I crossed over to the easel, drawn, it seemed, by those sad, thoughtful eyes, for the lad in the painting was so real he seemed about to speak to me. He had long dark brown hair and blue eyes and was dressed like a cavalier in a dark blue suit. One hand was resting on his hip, the folds of a blue cape draped over his arm, and the other hand hung listlessly at his side, holding a brown hat with a curling white plume that almost touched the floor. Never had I seen such vibrantly glowing colors—such sumptuous blues, such creamy whites, such rich browns—nor had I ever seen a portrait so touching. Were the boy to speak, I knew his voice would be sweet and dreamy, his words full of sadness.

"Like it?" Gainsborough asked at my side.

His voice startled me. I hadn't heard him come into the studio. Several moments passed before I could reply, so moved was I by the sad young man in blue.

"I—I think it's the most beautiful thing I've ever seen."

"The Boy in Blue, more commonly known as *Blue Boy.* One of my more successful efforts. That's a copy I made, by the way. The original canvas is much larger."

"You *must* be a great artist if you painted this."

"It's nothing compared to the painting I'm going to do of you," he informed me. "Come, lass, we'd best get started."

"You're going to paint me to*day?*"

Thomas Gainsborough chuckled at my ignorance. "Gracious no, lass. Today—while the light lasts—I'm just going to do some preliminary sketches. It will take weeks, maybe months to complete the painting. I'm going to have to work you in. I'm currently painting the Duchess of Devonshire—" He nodded toward the easel draped in cloth, "and time and the beauteous Georgiana wait for no one."

"Oh," I said, still a bit bewildered by all this.

"The wife is delighted we're having a guest for dinner tonight. You'll have her specialty—duck prepared after the Hittite manner."

"What's that?"

"A secret family recipe. Apparently it's been passed down from generation to generation for centuries. Mrs. G. won't even tell *me* how she makes it."

"I—I really don't know about dinner," I said nervously. "I have no idea how I'll get back to Covent Garden, and—"

"I'll send you back in the carriage," he said, leading me over to the wardrobe. "Come along, lass, let's find you something to wear. Pink isn't your color, by the way," he added, referring to my frock. "You need something bold, something dramatic. Purple, perhaps. Perhaps black velvet. I have a huge collection. What's your name, lass? I plain forgot to ask you earlier."

"Angela Howard. Do—do you often snatch girls off the street to pose for you?"

Gainsborough chuckled again, a merry sound. His blue eyes were twinkling. "Not often," he admitted, "but the minute I looked out the carriage and saw that remarkable face I knew I had to snatch *you*. I knew at once you were going to be the subject of my greatest masterpiece."

Mr. G. certainly thought highly of himself, I reflected, but I guessed anyone who had painted something like *Blue Boy* had a right to be confident. I liked the artist a great deal now, you couldn't help but warm to him, but I still felt a bit apprehensive.

"I—really, Mr. Gainsborough, I think maybe I— maybe I should just go home. I don't know anything about sitting for a painter and you're terribly busy with that Duchess and—"

"Nonsense. There's no need to be nervous, Angela. You and I are going to get along handsomely and have a grand time. I'm going to make you a very famous young woman."

Chapter Ten

My back ached terribly and my neck felt stiff and I longed to scratch my nose, but I didn't dare move. Mr. G. was an amiable soul, warm, wryly humorous, extremely considerate, but when he was at the easel he became an absolute tyrant and fretted irritably if I moved a muscle. Expected me to sit perfectly still and not complain and sitting that still wasn't a lark, believe me. Once I let out a sneeze and shattered his concentration and he flew into a frenzy. These artistic types were temperamental as could be. He stood at the easel now in a wrinkled brown frock coat and old gray breeches, palette in one hand, brush in the other, staring at the canvas, then staring at me, finally dabbing a bit of paint onto the canvas. His powdered wig was askew again, more gray than white, needed a new powdering, and his plump cheeks were pink.

A fire roared in the fireplace, but the room was still chilly, for it was early November now, the gardens in back bare of greenery, the sky a bleak gray, but enough sunshine spilled through the panes of the skylight overhead for Mr. G. to work. I sat on a stool on the low wooden platform beneath it, wearing a scarlet velvet gown with full elbow length sleeves worn off the shoulder and a form fitting bodice cut quite low. The plush skirt spread out in rich scarlet folds. I was turned slightly to the right, one hand in my lap, the other holding an unfurled fan of scarlet lace. My hair was stacked on top of my head in an elaborate arrangement of glossy chestnut waves with three ringlets dangling in back, one of them resting on my bare shoulder. It was bloody uncomfortable sitting like that, holding that fan, looking pensive. Hated it, I did, though I rarely complained aloud.

Didn't care for the dress, either. Too red, I thought, but it was better than the purple velvet I'd tried on, and the black had been all wrong. Gainsborough had been delighted when I finally put on the scarlet, declaring it absolutely perfect, bold, dramatic, extremely daring as well. All the other women he painted wore soft pastels and ribbons and laces, looked soft and dreamy and fragile, but this...this was revolutionary. Scarlet, deep, rich scarlet. Perfect! At first I had worn a wide-brimmed scarlet velvet hat dripping with black and white plumes, a gorgeous hat, I thought, but Mr. G. had decided it was too fussy, too traditional. They *all* wore beplumed hats. With glorious hair like mine, who needed a hat? So I sat on the stool without a hat and held the fan, a backdrop behind me depicting a pale, pearly gray sky with just a few wispy white clouds drifting about.

"Tilt your chin just a bit more, Angela," he said.

"Like this?"

"Not quite so much. There. That's it."

"I'm dying for a cup of tea."

"You'll have your tea in a few minutes, brat. Be quiet. Be still."

I stuck my tongue out at him. He made a face and resumed his work. When would it ever be done? I had been coming here to the studio four times a week for three months now—Gainsborough sent a carriage for me, sent me home in it as well—and I hadn't been allowed one peek at the painting. Covered it with a cloth as soon as he finished each afternoon, he did, said I could look at it when it was done. He gave me a pound for each sitting, a tremendous windfall. Dottie thought it was a great honor for me to be painted by such a famous artist and refused to dock my pay. I came in an hour early each morning and took work home at night, worked on the weekends, too, and she insisted that made up for the afternoons I came to the studio.

It was rather fun, I admitted, for a number of interesting people were always popping into the studio to chat while Gainsborough worked. Didn't bother him at all, long as *I* kept still. Several of the men—that horrid Boswell in particular—were extremely interested in me and wanted to know who I was, but I had told Mr. G. all about Marie and made him promise never to reveal my last name or where I lived and worked, so I was merely "Angela," a woman of mystery. That intrigued them all the more. David Garrick had come once, and I had been terrified he'd recognize me from Dottie's, but the actor had paid no attention to me. Sir Joshua Reynolds, Gainsborough's archrival, had come to call, too, come to *spy,* Gainsborough insisted, and he refused to let him in. Boswell had undoubtedly been blabbing, he grumbled. Should never have allowed *that* rascal to come, either, he declared, Boswell and Reynolds being thick as thieves, but who could resist the Scot's ebullient charm? Me, for one, I told him.

Once I had arrived a bit early and had encountered the beautiful Georgiana, Duchess of Devonshire, in the hall, departing after her own sitting for the artist. Two years younger than I and already notorious, the Duchess wore a pale lime green silk gown adorned with beige lace ruffles, beige plumes affixed to the side of her elaborate coiffure. Tall and willowy, she was absolutely breathtaking with her fair hair and cool blue eyes and perfectly chiseled features. The lady didn't deign to acknowledge my nod, sweeping on down the hall with her plumes aflutter. A compulsive gambler, she lost stag-

gering sums weekly, but her husband willingly paid
her debts, perhaps because he was so content with the
arrangement at home. Lady Elizabeth Foster, the
Duchess's best friend, lived with them, and both ladies
shared the Duke's bed. An open scandal, it was, but
because their blood was blue society chose to ignore the
ménage à trois, pretending it was merely "close friendship," though there was much whispering behind fans
when the trio appeared in public together.

Megan had told me this delicious bit of information
about Gainsborough's other current model, along with
an even more interesting item about Georgiana and
none other than Mr. James Lambert. Three years ago,
when she was scarcely sixteen and still Lady Georgiana
Spencer, the gorgeous, impetuous teenager had developed a passionate infatuation for the playwright-
theatrical manager, determined to have him at any cost.
Pursued him like a poodle in heat, Megan said, literally
throwing herself at him and once climbing through his
bedroom window in the middle of the night. Having no
interest whatsoever in the willful, deplorably spoiled
teenager, Lambert had turned the minx over his knees,
spanked her soundly and hurled her out of his flat,
whereupon she had slashed her wrists with the jagged
edge of a broken champagne glass. Quite an uproar *that*
had caused, Megan told me, but Lambert had survived
the scandal and Lady Georgiana married the Duke soon
after.

Wonder what she saw in him, I thought now, still
longing to reach up and scratch the side of my nose.
Would Gainsborough ever finish? The sky was beginning to turn a darker gray, the sunlight slanting down
through the skylight pale and silvery, growing dimmer.
Looked like it might snow soon. I held the pose, numb
all over, it seemed, and my tormentor continued to work,
humming to himself. Lambert's play had closed six
weeks ago after a disappointing run to half-empty
houses. Not in the least discouraged, he was busily writing another, according to Dottie, and we would soon be
making the costumes. Why should I be thinking about

him so often? I'd only seen him the one time and had been absolutely appalled by his loud, loutish manner. He *was* an interesting man, I admitted, but I certainly didn't look forward to seeing him again. He was altogether too disrupting.

"Well," Gainsborough sighed, stepping back from the canvas. "Guess I'll have to stop now. Light's gone."

"So am I," I said, arching my back. Tiny bones cracked. "Won't you let me have just a peek?"

"You'll have your peek when the painting's finished, not before, so don't keep pestering me."

"You're horrid."

"I'm a charming chap, and you bloody well know it." He thrust his brushes into a jar of turpentine and carefully lowered the cloth over the painting. "I'll summon Jenkins. He'll bring us a nice tea. You go ahead and change into your clothes."

I stretched. More bones cracked. My legs felt leaden.

"When will it be done?" I asked.

"The portrait? Shouldn't be long, now that I've finished with the delectable Duchess. Georgiana was most trying, chattering all the while, eating bonbons, having her friends come visit while she sat. Thought I was going to murder the woman. You, on the other hand, have been an angel."

"Your painting of her was lovely," I remarked, stretching again. Gainsborough had let me see the portrait before it was sent off to Devonshire House in Piccadilly. "She looked ethereal, like a goddess."

"A routine commission, a routine job. Plumes, pastels, luminous lighting and lace. She's quite happy, the Duke's delighted and I've put a whopping big sum in the bank. My portrait of you is entirely different, art, not artifice. Georgiana's portrait will hang in some musty, stately hall someday, while your portrait will be hailed as a masterpiece."

"Like *Blue Boy?*"

"It's going to be better than *Blue Boy.* Go ahead and change, Angela. We need food."

I moved behind the screen and took off the heavy red

velvet gown and carefully hung it up, then changed into the new violet-blue silk I had made for myself. Dottie had let me have the silk at cost and had given me the black lace I had used to make ruffles for the skirt. I adjusted the modestly low bodice, fluffed up the short puffed sleeves and took my hair down, chestnut waves spilling to my shoulders. I heard Jenkins coming in with the tea trolley and then heard footsteps coming down the hall and a hearty, jovial voice calling out in glee.

"Tom! Hark! It's me. Just in time for tea, I vow!"

Boswell! Damn, I thought, smoothing my hair. Why couldn't he have waited until after I was gone? I didn't really dislike him—one couldn't, he was much too jolly and, yes, engaging, too, in a vulgar sort of way—but if he attempted to pinch my bottom again I vowed I'd crack a plate over his head. Reluctantly I moved from behind the screen just as Mr. James Boswell came bursting into the room, radiating vitality and robust good nature.

"There she is! I haven't missed her after all. I stopped by the Burneys to return a book I'd borrowed and got caught up in one of those dreadful musical afternoons. Bach. Bah! Couldn't make heads or tails of it. Little Fanny was enchanting, of course. Sat quietly in a corner, scribbling in her diary. I had the feeling she was scribbling libelous things about *me*. A sly one, Miss Fanny. Claims she's going to become a lady novelist, like Miranda James. Minx probably *will!*"

"Hello, Boswell," Gainsborough said glumly.

"Perk up, Tom! I vow, Miss Angela grows lovelier each time I see her. I have a present for you, wench."

"I'm not a wench, you sod! What kind of present?"

"A very special book. A masterpiece, in fact. Several critics said so—I have the clippings, look at them often. *An Account of Corsica*, by Yours Truly. Lovingly inscribed by the author."

"Dreadful book," Gainsborough said.

"I resent that, Tom!"

"Too much about Boswell. Not enough about Corsica."

"It went through several editions. Sold out in all the shops. An enormous success! You'll adore it, Miss Angela, although it's—uh—a bit ribald. Like its author!"

I smiled at that. Bloke always made me smile, despite myself. He pulled the book from behind his back and handed it to me, and I thanked him politely. Boswell beamed. Robustly built, rather stocky, he had dark red hair and lively brown eyes and a full, decidedly sensuous mouth. He wore black pumps with silver buckles, gray silk stockings and knee breeches and frock coat of rich plum satin. His gray satin waistcoat was embroidered with plum silk flowers, and a row of silver buttons adorned his frock coat. Fancied himself a dandy, he did, yet somehow he always managed to look like a rowdy, overgrown boy playing dress-up.

"What luscious-looking tarts!" he declared. "Your wife's famous apricot tarts, I vow! Hot, buttered scones! Small slices of bread spread with cheese and olive paste! A veritable feast! Will your enchanting wife be joining us, Tom?"

"Not today, alas. She's busy putting up preserves."

"Such a marvelous cook. If you're not careful I'll snatch her right away from you. Will you pour, Miss Angela?"

"Why don't you make yourself at home?" I said dryly.

Boswell laughed and reached toward my backside and I deftly sidestepped, avoiding the intended goose. Gainsborough shook his head at his visitor's incorrigible behavior and sat down in one of the two old chairs covered in brown velvet. Boswell promptly took the other, crossing his legs and eyeing the heavily laden tea trolley with greedy anticipation. I poured the tea, served it, then took a chair safely out of reach.

"Painting almost finished?" Boswell inquired, reaching for a tart.

"Almost. I expect to exhibit it at the R. A. in January."

"Bound to create a sensation, Tom, if it's anything

like the model. Move your chair closer, Miss Angela. You look lonely over there."

"I bruise easily," I told him.

"Can't resist a fetching wench. Never could, and marriage hasn't changed me at all. Poor Margaret, pining away in Scotland. Misses me dreadfully, she does, but it's quite restful for her."

Boswell's amorous exploits were the talk of London. Parlor maids, aristocratic dames, serving wenches, actresses—he pursued them all with equal gusto and quite phenomenal success. Perhaps the gusto explained it, or his exuberant and unabashed delight in female flesh. Roistering rake though he was, his honest appreciation and boyish glee lent him a curiously innocent air, and I could never really be angry with him, no matter how outrageous his conduct.

"And how is the mighty Sir Joshua Reynolds?" Gainsborough asked.

"Terribly hurt that you wouldn't see him two weeks ago, Tom. Couldn't understand how you could be so rude to a fellow artist."

"I suppose he's painting another simpering grande dame."

"He's painting Hester Thrale, as a matter of fact."

"That woman! A chattering nitwit with a husband in *trade.*"

Boswell had a vast circle of friends, was welcomed in the grandest parlors and the lowest dives with like enthusiasm, but of all his friends the mighty Dr. Samuel Johnson of dictionary fame was the greatest. After studying for the law and taking an extended Grand Tour of Europe, the ebullient Boswell had penned a number of books and articles and began to court the thorny, irascible Dr. Johnson. Gainsborough claimed Boswell spent most of his time trotting about after Johnson with notebook in hand, scribbling down every word the Great Man uttered in order to preserve them for posterity. Seemed downright peculiar to me.

"More tea?" I inquired when Boswell had finished his anecdote.

"Please, and I'll just have another of those tarts, too. When are you going to let me take you out to dinner and the theater, Miss Angela."

"Never," I replied.

"I say! That's bloody unfair. Thousands of women in London, and the only one I'm interested in spurns my attentions. Tell me the truth, wench, is it my wicked reputation?"

"It's your groping hands."

"I could give you a grand time, wench."

"You could also give me a bad case of pox."

Gainsborough laughed, delighted by my retort. Boswell was taken aback for a moment, and then he laughed, too, and whipped out his notebook.

"Must tell Johnson!" he declared, scribbling down my words. "He'll get a grand chuckle out of it! Not only are you beautiful and mysterious, Miss Angela—you're witty as well."

"Not witty. Merely frank."

Boswell stuck notebook and pencil back into his pocket and grinned, reaching for yet another apricot tart. I finished my tea and stood up.

"I'd better be getting back now, Mr. G."

Boswell scrambled to his feet. "Let *me* take you home," he insisted.

"No, thank you," I replied. "I prefer to get there with everything still intact."

Couldn't resist that, even though it was stretching a point. Gainsborough laughed again and stood up, leading me into the hall. The cocky Jenkins handed me my cloak and scowled fiercely at Boswell, who had trotted along after us. I smiled at Jenkins as I slipped on the cloak. He came to fetch me on the afternoons I sat for Mr. G., always accompanied me back, too. We were great friends now and Jenkins had appointed himself my protector. I pulled my hood up, turning to Gainsborough. He handed me the copy of *An Account of Corsica*.

"Don't forget this. The author would be crushed."

"Be sure you *read* it," Boswell ordered.

"I shall. Next Tuesday, Mr. G.?"

"Next Tuesday it is, lass."

He gave me an affectionate hug, and Jenkins and I started down the hall.

"Who *is* she, Tom?" I heard Boswell ask. "An orange girl from Drury Lane? A noblewoman in disguise? A parson's daughter in hiding? I'm longing to know, and so are all the other chaps who've seen her. You *must* fill me in, Tom!"

I smiled, amused by his interest and knowing full well the artist wouldn't tell him anything. Jenkins took me back to Dottie's in the carriage, walked me to the door and asked if I'd like for him to give that bleedin' Boswell a taste 'uv 'is fists. I laughed and told him Boswell was perfectly harmless, and Jenkins scowled and said he was keepin' 'is eye on 'im all the same. I went on into the shop and back to work on the mauve and lime striped satin the modish and lively Mrs. Abington would wear in a revival of *The Way of The World*.

Snow covered the ground in the back gardens and James Boswell was not present when I sat for Gainsborough the following Tuesday. The studio was chilly, even though a fire roared in the fireplace, but Mr. G. didn't seem to notice it at all, working very intently, gravely, not even humming. No genial remarks today. No warm chuckles. I sat like a statue, aching all over, loathing the fan I held and certain my arm would drop off any minute now if he didn't give me at least a short break. How long had I been sitting here? An hour? Two? Gainsborough seemed to have lost track of time. He finally sighed heavily and moved back from the canvas and nodded, and then he put his brushes into a jar of turpentine and sighed again.

"All right, Angela, you can relax now. We're finished."

"Thank goodness!" I exclaimed. "I was about to keel over."

"Sorry about that, lass. I was concentrating, forgot

to give you a break. Why don't you go ahead and change now."

"We're through for the day?"

He nodded, gazing intently at the canvas, frowning. I stood up and arched my back and stretched and heard the tiny bones popping, and then I moved behind the screen and removed the scarlet velvet and put on my violet-blue silk, rather puzzled. It couldn't be much after four. We usually worked for a much longer time, unless the light started fading. There was plenty of light today, despite the snow. Was Mr. G. feeling bad? Was he worried about something? Wasn't himself at all, I thought, taking down my hair. I was startled to discover him still in front of the canvas when I stepped from behind the screen.

"Well," he said listlessly, "care to have a look?"

I was startled. "You—you mean it's finished?"

"Said so earlier. You must not have understood me."

I approached the canvas cautiously, a hollow feeling in the pit of my stomach. Had no idea why I should be so nervous, but I was, nervous as I could be. Rays of pale silvery-yellow sunlight streamed down through the skylight, one of them illuminating the painting. Gainsborough moved aside, and I stood in front of the easel, gazing at the portrait he had done, and I caught my breath, for I could not believe it was me, not that lovely, pensive creature. It was someone else, it had to be.

The young woman sat in the open, the sky behind her pale, pearly gray with just a few wisps of cloud floating about. She was turned slightly to the right on the stool completely hidden by the lush scarlet folds of skirt, and she held a scarlet lace fan, peering from the canvas with pensive violet-gray eyes that were full of secrets and sad wisdom. Her luxuriant chestnut-brown hair gleamed with rich highlights, one full ringlet resting on her bare, creamy shoulder, and her high cheekbones looked sculpted, her mouth beautifully shaped, not too large at all. The deep scarlet gown emphasized her creamy complexion and, strangely, made her seem somehow ethereal, the contrast bold, striking. I gazed at the painting in awe, for it was every bit as lovely, every bit as moving as his painting of the boy in blue.

"Like it?" Gainsborough inquired.

"It's—I can't believe it's me. She—she's beautiful."

"Of course she is. I painted her from life."

"But—"

"She's not a blue-eyed blonde with soft, pretty features, not beautiful in the vapid, traditional way, no. There's too much character in that lovely face, too much intelligence in those pensive eyes. She shall, I predict, set a whole new standard of beauty."

"Do—do I really look like that?"

"I painted exactly what I saw, I assure you."

"Her eyes are so—sad."

"I imagine you were thinking sad thoughts while you sat for me. What *were* you thinking about?"

"I—I was thinking of a man. Someone I—someone I used to know before I came to London. I tried not to, but I—I kept remembering a night when I was seventeen years old."

"And that night is there in the painting, in her eyes," Gainsborough told me. "It's the best work I've ever done, lass. For once I'm actually satisfied with one of my paintings. For once I'm actually proud."

"You have every right to be."

Gainsborough smiled. "I think we should celebrate," he said merrily.

He left the studio for a few minutes, and I went over to stand by the fire. I could see the painting from there, a large canvas, life size, and it was just as lovely, just as moving from a distance. Gainsborough returned with his wife, a slender, sweet-faced woman with fluffy silver-gray hair worn in a loose pompadour, a white cotton apron tied at the waist over her pale apricot linen gown. Mrs. Gainsborough smiled at me and went over to look at the painting. She said it was lovely indeed, his best work, but I could see she was far more interested in getting back to the kitchen than in discussing the painting.

"She never *has* appreciated me," Gainsborough complained, though his voice was full of affection. "Always said I should get some nice, dependable job and forget all this nonsense."

"I haven't said that in years, Thomas, and you know it," his wife protested. "I told you the painting was lovely. Why shouldn't it be with Angela sitting for it? I like it much better than those silly things you do of ladies in plumed hats. Did you enjoy those fruit tarts I made for your tea last time, Angela?"

"I'm afraid I didn't get one. Boswell ate them all up."

"Such a delightful young man. Big appetite. Appreciates good food. I've made almond cakes and blackberry tarts for tea this afternoon, turnovers, too, and some more of my cheese and olive paste."

"We shan't be having tea," Gainsborough informed her. "Jenkins is bringing in some champagne. I put it on ice earlier, suspecting I'd be finishing up this afternoon. You'll have some with us, of course."

"I must get back to the duck, Thomas. If you don't baste it just right it never comes out properly. As you'll not be having tea, I'll wrap up some goodies for you to take back with you, Angela," she told me. "Good-bye, dear."

She gave me a gentle hug, resting her cheek against mine, then left to attend to the duck. Gainsborough shook his head in mock exasperation, a smile on his lips.

"She *does* enjoy her cooking," he declared. "We could afford half a dozen cooks, but she insists on doing it all herself, takes as much care in preparing her duck as I do in painting a portrait. Ah, here's Jenkins!"

The jaunty red-haired footman sauntered in with three slender crystal glasses and an iced bucket of champagne on a tray. He set the tray down on a table, glancing around the room as though looking for someone.

"Could 'uv sworn you said there'd be three 'uv you. I brought three glasses."

"And we shall use all three," his employer informed him. "Mrs. G.'s much too busy with her duck to join our little celebration. You'll have a glass, my lad. After all, you're the one who nabbed my model for me."

"Oh, I ain't sure hit'd be proper," Jenkins protested. "Me drinkin' wine with my him-ployer. Make me jittery, hit would."

"You'll have a glass nevertheless," Gainsborough said, opening the bottle of champagne. The cork popped, flying almost to the ceiling, the wine fizzling as he poured it into the glasses.

"Here you are, Angela. Here, Jenkins, take the glass. Don't look so suspicious. I propose a toast," he said, lifting his glass. "To—" He hesitated, a slight frown creasing his brow. "To *Young Woman in Red?* Don't like that title at all. *Girl in a Red Dress?* No matter, we'll think of a title later on. To my Greatest Achievement!"

We clicked our glasses and drank, Jenkins sipping his cautiously and grinning when the bubbles tickled his nose. He became quite merry after a few more sips and sauntered over to the painting with his glass and said "Blimey! Hit's bleedin' like 'er, hit is!" and gulped down the rest of his champagne and vowed 'e'd never seen anything like hit. He accepted a second glass without protest, grinning broadly and already a bit unsteady on his bandy legs.

"I'm going to miss coming to the studio," I said wistfully.

"And I'm going to miss you, lass. Can't remember ever having a more pleasant working experience. The wife and I are taking a holiday, leaving for Bath this coming weekend to visit friends. Probably won't be back until early January, in time for me to oversee the hanging of your portrait at the Royal Academy. I'll write to you, lass, let you know when the exhibit opens."

We finished our champagne, and Gainsborough walked me out to the carriage, a sheepishly grinning Jenkins lurching along behind us. Mrs. Gainsborough came out and gave me another hug and a large white box full of goodies wrapped carefully in thin paper. Gainsborough hugged me, too. As the carriage pulled away I turned for a last look at that elegant white house

with its fanlight and marble portico. Gainsborough stood
on the front steps in his old brown frock coat, wig slightly
askew, his arm around his wife's aproned waist. They
waved, and I lifted my hand, feeling quite sad as we
drove on down the street.

I *did* miss going to the studio in the weeks that
followed, but several new plays were opening and we
were swamped with work at Dottie's, everything in constant upheaval with managers coming in with sketches
of costumes to be made up, actors and actresses dropping in for fittings, dozens and dozens of costumes in
various stages of completion. Mr. Foote's new production would be all in pinks and grays, performed against
a sky-blue backdrop with a few white clouds. Dottie
declared she was *sick* of pink, even sicker of gray. Mr.
Colman was doing a drama set in Tudor times, all those
fussy neck ruffs to make, all those cumbersome velvets,
while Garrick, bless him, was reviving *Hamlet* and
wanted Gertrude in cloth of gold and Ophelia in sea-
green gauze.

James Lambert's new production was to open soon,
too, and he came breezing into the shop one afternoon
in mid-December, stomping snow off his brown leather
knee boots and shaking snowflakes off his long brown
cloak that almost swept the floor. Dottie was upstairs,
supervising the girls, and I was sitting at my worktable,
carefully pinning a tissue-thin pattern onto a length of
pearl-gray velvet. Lambert stomped his boots a final
time, shook his shoulders and looked around, not at all
thunderous this afternoon, seeming, in fact, in a very
expansive mood. He spied me and strode over to the
table, his brown cloak billowing out like a pair of dark
wings.

"Dottie around?" he asked.

"She's upstairs," I said. "I'll go fetch her."

"There's no hurry," he told me. His voice was husky.

He was looking at me, really looking at me, examining me as he might examine a horse he was thinking
of buying. His eyes were indeed green, dark green,
flecked with golden-brown, interesting eyes, frank and

quite...quite attractive. His nose wasn't really all that crooked, just enough to keep him from being quite absurdly handsome. Skin stretched tautly across his broad cheekbones, and his lower lip was full and curving, undeniably sensuous. I felt myself coloring under his frank scrutiny, and I stood up, spilling a box of pins.

"Damn!" I exclaimed.

"Sorry," he said. "Guess I unsettled you."

"You don't unsettle me in the least, Mr. Lambert."

"Did anyone ever tell you you're a remarkably beautiful young woman?"

"Not recently," I retorted.

"I *do* unsettle you. You're blushing."

"I am *not* blushing."

"Your cheeks are as pink as a rosebud."

"Jesus! If that's the kind of dialogue you use in your plays it's no wonder they're so ghastly."

"Ghastly? Ghastly! *My* plays ghastly?"

"Melodramatic rubbish, I've heard."

"You listen to me, wench! I don't know who you've been *talk*ing to, but my plays are—they're marvelously entertaining, *huge*ly successful."

"Your last one wasn't," I reminded him.

James Lambert looked pained, and then he looked as though he longed to throttle me, his fingers actually clenching and unclenching. I gazed at him with a cool hauteur that belied my agitation. After a moment he reached up and ran his fingers through those rich dark brown waves, and then he smiled a devilishly engaging smile, murderous demeanor gone.

"Guess you put one over on me, wench. Got me good, you did. It was quite rude of me to stare at you like that, but I didn't mean any harm. I was studying your features, mentally casting you. Ever been on the stage?"

"I've never even been inside a theater."

He arched one dark brow. "*Real*ly?" He was clearly amazed.

"I work for my living. I have no time for frivolity."

"Frivolity? That what you think the theater is? It's bloody hard work, I assure you. Grueling, frustrating, backbreaking work that drains the very life blood out of you. You work, you slave, you hope, you pray, and when your nerves are in shreds and you're so worn you can't even think clearly you keep right on working until the production is finally mounted—and then it's in the hands of fate."

"Do you always talk like that?" I inquired.

"Like how?"

"In such a ridiculous fashion, like you're reciting awful dialogue."

James Lambert began clenching and unclenching his fingers again. "I may," he said, "I just *may* murder you."

"Shouldn't advise you to try it," I told him.

"Do you always insult Dottie's customers like this?"

"Only when they're insufferable," I said.

He grinned, delighted, those wonderful green-brown eyes full of wry amusement. He tossed the folds of his long cloak back over his shoulders, the brown silk lining gleaming darkly. His breeches and frock coat were brown broadcloth, superbly cut, and his dapper tan satin waistcoat had emerald and brown stripes. An emerald-green silk neckcloth was at his throat. Cut quite an impressive figure, he did, and he had much more presence than most of the actors who came for fittings. I wasn't nearly as put out with him as I pretended to be. Mr. James Lambert was rude and rather absurd, quite full of his own importance, but there was something undeniably engaging about him. He made one feel alert and alive, made one feel curiously stimulated.

"You think I'm insufferable?" he asked amiably.

"Quite," I said.

"Actually, I'm a delightful chap once you get to know me. I *do* have a temper—I admit it frankly—but I've been most dreadfully maligned. You shouldn't believe all the talk you hear about me."

"Oh?"

"Shouldn't bad-mouth my plays, either. Garrick and his kind produce plays the public ap*pre*ciate. I produce plays they enjoy. You'll have to come see my new one—

opens the day after Christmas, the most ambitious, the most spectacular play I've ever mounted—"

He had used the identical words to Dottie about his *last* production, I recalled. Obviously didn't spare the superlatives when describing one of his own productions. He was relating the plot with considerable enthusiasm when Dottie came down the stairs. Seeing him, she stopped and lifted her eyes heavenwards, less than enchanted at the prospect of dealing with the volatile theatrical manager whose nappies she used to change. Lambert cut himself off in midsentence and turned and forgot all about me, rushing over to greet Dottie with exuberant gallantry.

"Dottie, my love! You look radiant this afternoon! Such beauty blinds my eyes! That fulsome figure, those plump pink cheeks, that enchanting smile—my heart beats faster! Really should do something about your hair, though. About to tumble over your brow."

"I'm in no mood for your skylarking, Jamie Lambert. I've had a very difficult day, and—"

"And I've come to cheer you up! The costumes arrived and they're magnificent, love, each one a masterpiece. Willy Osborne is delighted with his second-act costume, says he'll really *feel* like a prince in that gold and white tunic, that white satin cape, and the temperamental Mrs. Tallent claims the purple and mauve gown is sheer magic. There's just one small problem—"

"I will not do it over in blue!"

"Would I ask you to do such a thing? Would I be so unreasonable?"

"You bloody well would, you rogue."

"You do me a terrible injustice, Dottie mine. Make me feel quite downcast and disconsolate. Here I come to rave about your wonderful skill and you start casting aspersions on my character. Problem is, love, the delectable Mrs. Tallent has been stuffing herself like a sow these past few weeks and her costumes no longer fit. *Could* you let them out a mite, love? I know it's asking a lot, you being so frightfully busy and all, but—"

I picked up the pins and put them in the box and went back to work, trying to ignore the argument that ensued. Mrs. Tallent had hardly been a sylph to begin with, Dottie protested, and if she wanted to appear on stage looking like a heifer it served him right for signing such a slut in the first place. She was much, much too busy at the moment to work on costumes that had already been delivered, carefully made to measurements, and ... of course he talked her into doing it, outrageously charming and persuasive. Dottie had no strength of character whatsoever, I thought, jamming a pin into the velvet.

I received a letter from Gainsborough a few days later. Bath was tiresome as could be, all those assemblies, all those teas. He was being horribly lionized by fluttery society women, all of whom wanted him to do portraits of their dreary young daughters, but he was on holiday and refusing all commissions, no matter how remunerative. Mrs. G. was baking like mad, you'd think she planned to feed everyone in the immediate vicinity. I wasn't surprised, therefore, when a box arrived for me the day before Christmas, containing wonderful rum cakes and small fruitcakes carefully wrapped in brandy-moistened cloths and several different kinds of cookies. Goodness, Megan declared, we'd look like Mrs. Tallent if we ate all those.

Timothy and four of his rowdy but charming chums raided the Market Christmas Eve, bringing vast quantities of holly and ivy to decorate our flat. Johnny brought a cooked goose as well, and Ian brought several bottles of wine. We had a splendid party, everything festive and bright, and all of Mrs. G.'s cakes were consumed, and all the cookies, too. It was after midnight when our guests departed, singing tipsily as they careened down the stairs, and Megan and I had a lovely time the next morning, opening our gifts. Dottie gave us both sumptuous bolts of cloth and several yards of lace. Megan gave me books and a lovely fan, and she was enchanted with the hooded deep blue velvet cloak I had secretly made for her. It was the loveliest Christ-

mas I had had in quite a long time, yet I was still a bit
sad, remembering other holidays, other years.

Blankets of glistening white snow covered the city
in January, and we bundled up heavily going to and
from work. Things were not so frantic at Dottie's, for
we had completed most of the costumes. Garrick's *Hamlet* was a huge success and several of the papers com-
mented on the beautiful and effective costuming of the
revival. James Lambert's new play received its usual
sneers from the critics, but it was doing good business,
Dottie reported, despite the fact that its leading lady
resembled a baby whale. Mrs. Tallent was a *very* unhappy woman and that was why she gorged herself with
pastries, Dottie said, and I thought to myself that any
woman who worked with a mercurial rogue like James
Lambert probably had good reason to be unhappy.

I hadn't heard from Gainsborough since before
Christmas and, on the morning of the tenth, was idly
wondering if he had returned to London when the front
door opened and the short, red-haired footman came in
waving an impressive-looking cream envelope. Jenkins
grinned, as cocky as ever, as comical in the white and
gold livery. 'Ad an hin-vitation for me, he did, a letter
from Mr. G. too. He handed me the creamy envelope
and another, smaller envelope and said hit was good to
be back in London, that bleedin' Bath was dreary as a
tomb. Dottie was fascinated by the jaunty footman and
insisted he have a cup of tea, but Jenkins said 'e 'ad to
be off, 'ad to pick up some bleedin' paints. Gainsborough's letter was brief. There was to be a private
showing of the new exhibit at the Royal Academy on
the afternoon of the twentieth, prior to its public opening. It would be primarily for journalists and artists
and society people but I might find it rather amusing.
The creamy envelope contained an engraved invitation
for "Miss Angela Howard and Guest."

"I can't go," I told Megan that evening. "I couldn't
possibly. I—what if someone recognized me as the girl
in the painting?"

"We'll go in dis*guise,* luv," Megan insisted, quite

thrilled with the idea. "We'll go disguised as society ladies—Dottie will loan us some costumes—and we'll wear masks! Lots of society ladies do."

"Really, Megan, I don't think—"

"We simply must go, luv. It'll be a lark!"

It was indeed a lark to Megan, and she blithely made all the arrangements. Dottie loaned us costumes from a forthcoming society drama, and Brinkley loaned us two elegant powdered wigs in the French fashion. Timothy and his chums were brought in on the conspiracy, and somehow they managed to acquire a lovely gold and white carriage for the afternoon of the twentieth. It pulled up in front of the wig shop, six white horses in harness, Timothy, in white velvet livery, perched on the driver's seat, Johnny riding on back in identical uniform.

"Lord," I said, peering out the window. "I hope they didn't *steal* it. I feel terribly nervous, Megan. I still don't think we—"

"We're going to have a grand time, luv!" she assured me. "You look absolutely gorgeous," she added.

She looked gorgeous herself in a sumptuous sky blue velvet gown with a low bodice and two enormous velvet flounces on the skirt that parted to display the underskirt of alternating rows of ivory and sky blue lace ruffles. A white satin mask concealed her eyes and nose, and the powdered wig had a high pompadour and several long ringlets dangling in back, two sky blue and one ivory plume affixed to one side of the coiffure with a false diamond clasp. My wig was identical, three tall pink plumes bobbing. The skirt of my low cut pink satin gown was very full, spreading out and parting in front to reveal a white satin underskirt embroidered with tiny pink roses. The wig was very uncomfortable, and my pale pink satin mask felt peculiar. My face was powdered, a heart shaped black satin beauty patch stuck on my right cheekbone, and my lips were painted a deep carnelian pink.

"We look like a couple of French courtesans," I said.

"Au contraire, luv. We've very *à la mode.* We'll fit right in. No one is going to *recognize* us, that's for sure."

Our skirts were so wide we had some difficulty managing the stairs, had to turn sideways to get out the narrow green door. Timothy grinned at us from his high perch, looking quite outrageous in the livery.

"Have to have it back by six o'clock," he called. "The Honorable Reggie Ashton will catch hell if his father finds out it's missing."

Johnny jumped down, made a deep bow and opened the carriage door, delighted to be part of the jolly hoax. I toyed with my large white lace fan adorned with tiny silk rosebuds, wishing I could feel as jolly about it as the rest of them. What if something happened to one of the costumes? Mrs. Clive and Mrs. Calder were to wear them on stage at the Haymarket in just two weeks. What if I tripped and fell flat on my face? What if my wig fell off? I fretted nervously as we drove through the congested streets, and when the carriage finally came to a halt I felt numb. Johnny opened the door for us, giving Megan a conspiratorial wink.

"Take a deep breath, luv," she told me. "Here we go."

We moved up the steps and past the marble columns and I handed my invitation to the man at the door. The huge gallery was full of people, all of them talking at once, it seemed. They wandered about, sipping the champagne served by liveried footman, chattering, pausing to look at the paintings. You're not Angela Howard, I told myself. You're an aristocratic lady, every bit as grand as any of these people, and there's no reason for you to be nervous. I tilted my chin at a haughty angle and fluttered my fan and tried to look blasé. Most of the women wore powdered wigs and plumes and gowns similar to ours, and some of them wore masks as well. We fit right in, I thought. Megan certainly knew what she was about.

"There's Garrick," Megan whispered, "over there by the column, chatting with Sir Joshua Reynolds."

"So that's Sir Joshua?" I said. "He *does* look a bit pompous."

"My word!" Megan exclaimed. "That gent who just passed us—the one in the purple silk frock coat with diamond buttons—he must be sixty and he just patted my behind!"

"Really?"

"These bluebloods aren't a bit different from any other men. A girl isn't *safe!*"

I smiled and, looking around the room, suddenly saw a familiar face.

"That's the Duchess of Devonshire over there—the one in cream satin embroidered with pink and blue flowers and tiny green leaves. Isn't she beautiful? That woman with her must be Lady Elizabeth Foster, what a lovely taffeta gown, pale aquamarine. The lethargic, sleepy-looking gentleman with them must be the Duke. I wonder what they see in him?"

"Money and position," Megan informed me.

A footman approached us with a tray of brimming champagne glasses. Megan took one casual as could be, as though she drank it every day. I didn't dare. We sauntered about, looking at the paintings—unusual still lifes, misty landscapes, dozens of portraits—and Megan sipped her champagne. A great mob was congregated at the end of the room, all of them gazing at a painting we couldn't see, all of them buzzing. A plump gentleman in back of the mob turned and spotted us in the throng and hurried over, a merry smile on his lips. He was wearing the white satin outfit he had worn the first time I ever saw him, and, of course, his freshly powdered wig was not quite straight.

"Here you are!" he exclaimed. "I was afraid you wouldn't come."

"How on earth did you recognize me?"

"The bone structure, lass. I studied it for over three months, remember? Couldn't miss those glorious cheekbones."

"This is my friend Megan Sloan, Mr. Gainsborough."

"How do you do, my dear?"

"I'm thrilled to be here. Where's the painting of Angela?"

He pointed to the mob. "Over there."

I was surprised. "You—you mean all those people are looking at the portrait of me?"

"It's creating an absolute sensation, lass. They're positively agog! No one's been able to talk about anything else. The chaps from Fleet Street have been driving me mad with their questions—everyone wants to know who you *are*. Refused to tell them anything, of course. Everyone vows it's the finest thing I've ever painted. Knew they would," he added.

Gainsborough beamed, delighted with his success. He guided us toward the mob, and we stood there, listening to the comments.

"Most beautiful woman I've ever seen. Makes all those pale-faced blondes with blue eyes and rosebud lips look drab. That hair—look at that hair, and those violet-blue eyes."

"Better than *Blue Boy*. Better by far."

"Where did he *find* her? I've never seen her before."

"It's a masterpiece. Unquestionably. A masterpiece."

"Gainsborough's going to clean up with this one. He'll get a fortune for the painting itself, and the reproduction rights will net him another fortune. Chap will be able to retire for life."

"Joshua Reynolds never did anything half as fine!" Mr. G. exclaimed in a loud, heavily disguised voice. "Neither did Romney!"

Megan giggled, and then she let out a gasp when some people moved and she had her first real glimpse of the painting. It hung in an ornate golden frame, and a shaft of sunlight touched it. The canvas seemed to glow with beauty and life. She *was* beautiful, I thought, for I couldn't associate myself with that dreamy young woman in red. She was solely Thomas Gainsborough's creation, his conception of me. I couldn't possibly look like that. Megan took my hand and squeezed it tightly, quite awed by the painting.

"It—it's amazing, luv," she whispered. "I always knew you were beautiful, but until now I never realized just how beautiful you *are*."

"It isn't me," I told her.

"It is, luv. How many times have I seen you with that sad, faraway look in your eyes? It's you, to the life."

There was a stir at the entrance, and I turned to see James Boswell entering with a great lumbering creature in a threadbare navy blue frock coat. The man had a jowly, pasty face pitted with pockmarks. His nose was enormous, his huge eyes myopic. His gray wig looked dirty. His black pumps were quite old, and his gray stockings sagged. His navy blue breeches were wrinkled and shiny with age, as was the frock coat. The man looked like a huge, disgruntled bear who had just come out of hibernation, but he was obviously someone very important. Talk grew hushed and people nodded respectfully as he shambled by them, scowling unhappily. A beaming Boswell strutted at his side, holding the man's arm in a proprietary manner and leading him forward.

"Ah, the Great Man has arrived," Gainsborough observed. "Now we'll know if we're to sink or soar."

"Who *is* that bizarre chap?" Megan asked.

"Boswell's intimate chum, Doctor Samuel Johnson. Johnson is the voice of London in matters of art and letters. His opinions are parroted by every hack on Fleet Street, his judgment the last word. Boswell, dear chap!" he cried, moving forward to greet them. "So pleased to see you, and I see you've brought Doctor Johnson."

"Much rather be home having my tea," Johnson grumbled. "Boswell dragged me here against my will, said I had to see your blasted painting. Seen enough paintings to last me a lifetime. I warn you, Gainsborough, if it's another of your pale, pretty dames in silk and plumes I'm going to be even unhappier than I am already. Tedious, these affairs, hate coming to 'em."

The mob of people around my portrait moved aside, and the whole room fell silent, waiting for the great Samuel Johnson to pass judgment on the painting that was causing such a sensation. Johnson scowled and Boswell led him toward the canvas like a little boy with a surly pet lion. Johnson clasped his hands behind his back and leaned forward, jutting his chin out and peering at the portrait with his myopic eyes. Several long moments passed, and the suspense was almost tangible as Johnson continued to stare, still scowling.

"Didn't I tell you?" Boswell exclaimed. "Isn't she glorious? Isn't she an angel?"

"Hummph!" Johnson snorted. "An angel in scarlet."

"An angel in scarlet," Gainsborough said thoughtfully. "I like the ring of that. That's what I'll call it. *An Angel in Scarlet*. Perfect! Thank you for giving the work a title, Johnson."

Doctor Johnson turned around and looked the artist in the eye. "I should thank *you*, Gainsborough, for painting this picture," he said gruffly. "Every connoisseur of great art should thank you. I rarely use the word masterpiece, but in this instance I must. You are indeed a master of your craft, sir, and this piece is your greatest achievement."

"Truer words were never spoken," Gainsborough said wryly. "You've got a keen eye, Johnson."

"Come along, Boswell," Johnson grunted. "I've seen the painting. Now I want my tea."

"There are several more paintings to see," Boswell protested. "Reynolds has one, and—"

"No point in seeing any more. They'd all pale in comparison to this one. My stomach's grumbling. If I don't have my tea I turn *very* unpleasant, as you well know."

Boswell sighed, defeated, and led Johnson away. The room buzzed with excitement as they left, and an even greater mob congregated around my portrait, their comments even more laudatory now that Johnson had placed his stamp of approval on it. Flushed with pleasure, Gainsborough led us away from the canvas and insisted we have a glass of champagne with him. Three journalists hurried over to us and bombarded him with questions, notebooks at the ready. Who was his model for *An Angel in Scarlet?* Where did she come from? Blue eyes twinkling, Gainsborough looked at me and in-

formed the gents from Fleet Street that she had been
sent to him from Heaven. He was in fine form, Gainsborough was, but he had every right to be. When the
journalists finally left, he finished his champagne and
gave me a merry smile.

"This is our success, Angela, yours as much as mine.
I'm so pleased you and Miss Sloan could come and share
the excitement—and what clever disguises. Two most
beautiful women here, even if you *are* wearing masks."

"Thank you, sir," Megan said, giving him a pert
curtsy.

"We'd better be leaving now," I told Mr. G. "Our friend
has to have the carriage back by six. Please give Mrs.
Gainsborough my regards. Tell her the Christmas cakes
were delicious."

Gainsborough escorted us to the door, waving to the
lovely Georgiana, who looked quite sulky because *her*
portrait wasn't on display. He nodded to David Garrick
and gave the pompous Sir Joshua Reynolds a triumphant smile, chuckling to himself as Reynolds grimaced.

"Stole *his* thunder," Gainsborough said happily. "By
this time tomorrow, all London will be talking about
An Angel in Scarlet—and the mysterious beauty who
posed for it."

"Do—do you really think so?" I asked.

"I know so, lass. We've created a furor."

We said our good-byes at the door. Megan was visibly
thrilled by our adventure, fluttering her fan quite rapidly.

"Lord, luv," she exclaimed as we started down the
steps, "it was really *some*thing, wasn't it? All those
important people talking about your portrait, wanting
to know who you are. Why, Angela, just think—you're
going to be famous!"

Chapter Eleven

Lord, what a to-do they were making over a simple painting, what a sensation it was causing. The public flocked to the Royal Academy in droves, mobbing it every day, and Fleet Street produced a veritable flood of words about the painting and the woman of mystery who had posed for it. I was amused to find myself identified as an Italian noblewoman living in England under an assumed name, as an obscure French actress, as the illegitimate daughter of an English noblewoman and a Russian Grand Duke, as a prostitute Gainsborough had picked up in St. Giles. A dozen histories were invented for me, all of them highly fanciful. I was repeatedly hailed as The Most Beautiful Woman of The Age, which did not sit at all well with celebrated beauties like Georgiana, Duchess of Devonshire, who heartily damned the painting and its artist as well. Gainsborough had sold reproduction rights for a huge sum to an enterprising print-shop owner, and thousands of prints were sold each week at sixpence a copy.

London had gone quite mad over *An Angel in Scarlet,*

the mysterious "Angel" setting a new standard in feminine beauty, just as Gainsborough had predicted I would. Blondes were no longer in favor. Shop girls and grand ladies alike began to dye their hair brown, with often disastrous results, and the more enterprising simulated high cheekbones with inventive applications of rouge and shadow. Scarlet velvet was all the rage, every single bolt sold out, frantic orders placed for more, and soft pastels were suddenly démodé. Hundreds of imitation Angels paraded about the city sporting the New Look, and the original went right on working at Dottie's, amused by the furor and, with hair down and wearing her everyday clothes, never once recognized on the street or by any of the people who came into the shop.

Gainsborough was riding the crest, turning down commissions by the dozen, and he merrily reported that Sir Joshua was gnashing his teeth. Mr. G. refused to divulge any information about me to Fleet Street, and Boswell kept his mouth shut, too, although he claimed he "knew the lady well" and intimated I had been his mistress! At first, I had been terrified that Marie might see the painting or one of the prints and recognize me and track me down, but after a few weeks, when nothing happened, I realized that my stepmother lived in an isolated world where art, fads or fashion had little or no impact. She would certainly never step foot inside the Royal Academy, nor was it likely she would ever see one of the reproductions. One of my stepsisters might, I realized, but I wasn't going to worry about it. It was late February now. I had turned twenty-one two days ago. Though she might still cause trouble, Marie was no longer the threat she once had been.

"Scarlet velvet!" Dottie said, shaking her head. "Mrs. Barry insists she have a scarlet velvet gown for the second act of *The Jealous Wife* and it's simply not to be had! She'll have to make do with purple."

"Has she dyed her hair yet?" I inquired.

"She has—had, rather—dark raven hair. She attempted to lighten it and now it's a curious shade of beige. She uses brown *boot* polish on it now. What madness have you *wrought,* my dear?"

"I find it all terribly silly," I told her. "It's merely a painting, you know."

"It's a phenomenon," Dottie corrected me.

"I still don't understand it. Why would anyone want to look like me?"

"Because you're absolutely lovely. Attractive, unusual, striking—if you had asked me before, those are the words I would have used to describe you. It took a great artist to show us just how beautiful you are."

"I don't *feel* particularly beautiful. I still think my mouth is too large and my cheekbones too high."

"I must say, Angela, you've certainly remained very levelheaded about all this excitement. Most young women I know would have a head this big—" Dottie spread her hands wide. "You, on the other hand, don't even want people to *know* you're the girl in the painting. Refuse to get caught up in the excitement. I find that very admirable."

"It'll die down," I said. "In a few weeks or so there'll be another sensation to take its place and 'Angel' will be quite forgotten. I prefer to keep a sensible perspective."

Dottie sighed and started sewing another gold tulle ruffle on the skirt of the gold satin ball gown we were working on. The gown had to be delivered first thing in the morning, and I had stayed late to help Dottie finish it. The other girls had left over an hour ago, and we had already lighted the candles. It was almost seven. Megan would probably be in the drafty basement dressing room at the Aldwych, getting ready with the rest of the supers. She had finally obtained another job in the theater and was ecstatic about it, even though it was merely a walk-on in a Restoration comedy.

"There!" Dottie said. "The last ruffle. Skirt's finished. We just have to gather it and fasten it onto the bodice."

"The bodice is done, too," I said, holding it up. "Those invisible hooks in back drove me mad. You look very tired, Dottie. Why don't you go on up and let me finish the gown? It'll only take an hour or so. I'll lock up."

"I wouldn't dream of it, my dear. You work much too hard as it is. I declare, I don't—"

"—know how I ever got along without you," I finished for her. "I *am* going to get a swelled head if you keep saying that, Dottie."

"It's quite true. I bless the day Megan brought you to me. *She*'s a treasure, too. I never had a better girl in the stockroom. So lively and amusing as well. She's such a dear to keep on helping me out for a few hours every afternoon even though she has found work at the Aldwych."

"I hope the play runs," I said.

"Oh, it'll have a good long run—they adore bawdy Restoration comedy, and those costumes we made are—"

Both of us were startled by the sudden pounding on the front door. Dottie cut herself short and slammed a hand over her heart, and I jumped. Someone was banging furiously and yelling something we couldn't make out. We were both paralyzed for a moment, and then Dottie clutched a pair of scissors and moved cautiously toward the door, peering through the glass pane. I felt myself growing tense. There was little crime in this neighborhood, but one needed to be careful nevertheless. Dottie squinted, leaning her forehead against the pane, and then she gave an exasperated sigh and threw open the door. A young man in his early twenties stumbled into the room, looking quite distraught.

"Andrew Dobson!" she exclaimed. "What's the meaning of this! Banging on the door like that! You gave us quite a turn! And you in a thin coat in weather like this. Nothing on your head, either. You'll catch your death."

"It's an emergency!" he cried.

"Get yourself over there by the stove this minute. You're having a cup of hot tea, too. This is Andy Dobson, Angela. He's stage manager at the Lambert, even though he *is* still wet behind the ears."

"I've no time to lose!" young Dobson said breath-lessly. "It really *is* an emergency, Mrs. Gibbons! Mrs. Tallent has split a seam in the side of her gown and curtain's going up in less than an hour and no one has any thread or— Lambert's in a fury! He grabbed my *throat* and told me to get myself over here and get you back fast with needle and thread or he'd *mur*der me!"

"Typical behavior," Dottie said calmly. "Lamb al-ways has gone in for histrionics. I altered those cos-tumes of hers once, Andy, and if Mrs. Tallent insists on stuffing herself like a pig—"

"That's what *he* said!" Dobson broke in. "He said she'd been stuffing herself like a pig, said she *looked* like one, said it was her own bloody fault the seam split open. Mrs. Tallent was in a fury, too, shrieking like a banshee. I thought they were going to kill each other!"

"Be a blessing if they did," Dottie observed. "I'm much too old and much too tired to go chasing about Covent Garden in weather like this. You can tell him I said so."

"You've got to come, Mrs. Gibbons! Lambert'll have my hide if I come back without you!"

Dottie poured herself another cup of tea. "It's entirely out of the question," she informed him.

Poor Dobson was filled with panic. His blond-brown hair was windblown and several locks tumbled across his brow. His light blue eyes were wide with apprehen-sion. His lower lip trembled. He was an attractive youth with an air of youthful innocence, and although I doubted Lambert would actually murder him, I was sure the lad would lose his job if he failed to bring Dottie back. She *was* too old and too weary to go rushing through the streets in this cold, but I wasn't. I squared my shoul-ders.

"I'll go, Dottie," I said. "I'll come in an hour earlier in the morning, and I'll finish the gown then."

"You don't have to go, dear. Let Lamb stew in his own—"

"Please come!" Dobson exclaimed. "It won't matter who comes just as long as the gown's sewn up."

"Which gown is it?" Dottie asked.

"The purple and mauve she wears in the first act."

"Very well," she sighed. "I'll put a few things in a bag for you, Angela. You'll need needles, scissors, purple thread, mauve, too, just to make certain, and I'll toss in a few scraps of cloth in case you need to do some patching. I intend to give Jamie Lambert a piece of my mind next time I see him, you can be sure of it!"

"You've saved my *life*," Dobson told me.

I smiled, liking the lad a great deal. A few minutes later we were hurrying through the labyrinth of cobbled streets toward the Lambert. Covent Garden was bustling with activity, despite the cold, despite the icy wind. I clutched my heavy cloak close about me as we rushed up Bedford Street and down King, passing the Market, turning up James Street, crossing Hart and making for Longacre as fast as we could. The streets were crowded with carriages bound for the theaters, and there was a congestion of them in front of the Lambert. Torches illuminated the soot-stained marble portico, and a noisy throng moved up the wide steps to the entrance.

"This way!" Dobson panted.

He led me around the side of the building to the dark alleyway in back and then to the stage door. My first sight of the inside of a theater was a large, dimly lighted area with dusty flats leaning against the walls and coils of rope on the floor. Discarded scenery and props were littered about, and there was a rack of old costumes mothy with age. Dobson led me up a narrow hall to a larger area in front where people bustled about in what appeared to be total confusion. I caught a glimpse of the stage, a garden set in place, white trellises draped with artificial leaves and flowers, a painted backdrop depicting distant green hills with trees, a misty blue sky, footlights bathing it all in extremely bright light. There were catwalks in the darkness above, a veritable jungle of ropes looped about, and the front curtains were closed. Looked quite shabby from here, I thought.

"This must be the wings," I said, dodging a chap in shirtsleeves who hurried toward the stage with two white lawn chairs. "I've often heard my friend Megan mention—"

"The table! Where's the bleedin' table?" a hoarse voice shouted. "Gotta have the pitcher and glasses, too. Quickly!"

"Twenty minutes! Twenty soddin' minutes! Shrubs! Bring on the shrubs at once!"

From the other side of the stage a man rushed on with a huge plaster statue of a Greek goddess, setting it in place, while another carried on four leafy shrubs and set them about. James Lambert came rushing into the wings with rich brown locks atumble, his green-brown eyes flashing dangerously. He wore brown breeches and a white shirt with the sleeves rolled up to his elbows and a natty green and yellow checked vest. Spotting Dobson, he stormed over and seized the youth by the shoulders and began to shake him vigorously.

"Where *is* she! I told you not to come back without her! I swear, Dobson, if you've failed me, I'll—"

"Mrs. G-Gibbons couldn't c-come," Dobson stammered. "She s-sent an assistant in her p-place."

Lambert released him and brushed a heavy brown wave from his brow and gave me a savage look.

"You!" he snapped. "Can you sew?"

"Of course not," I retorted. "Dottie merely hires me to insult the customers."

His eyes flashed with emerald fire. "Get her to the dressing room and get her to work!" he ordered Dobson. "It's less than twenty minutes till curtain! Everything is chaos! Inefficiency on all sides! How do I endure it? *Why* do I endure it? I'm surrounded by blithering incompetents!"

"I'll expect five pounds for the job," I said crisply.

"Five pounds! That's robbery!"

"I've been sorely inconvenienced, have missed my evening meal, have rushed through bitterly cold streets to get here in time, and—"

"You'll get your five pounds!" he shouted.

"Thank you," I said.

Dobson led me behind the painted backdrop, through a cluttered area and into the wings on the other side of the stage. We moved down another narrow hall, finally stopping in front of a door with peeling white paint. He knocked timidly. A heavy object crashed against the door from inside. There was a piercing shriek. Dobson gave me a worried look and shook his head. The door was opened by a middle-aged woman with gray hair and anxious blue eyes. She was wearing a black dress and a white apron and mobcap and was obviously a maid. A tall and decidedly statuesque blonde in a white silk petticoat and belted pink lace robe stood in front of a littered dressing table, fuming. She grabbed a box of powder and hurled it violently. A puffy white cloud filled the air as it exploded against the wall.

"How dare him!" she shrieked. "How dare him speak to me like that! I've made a bloody fortune for the son of a bitch and does he appreciate it, does he appreciate me? Not for a bloody minute! Treats me like I'm dirt under his sodding feet! Treats me like I'm some strumpet he picked up off the street! I'll show him! Call *me* a sow, will he? Mr. James bloody Lambert is going to regret he was ever *born!*"

She picked up a pot of face cream and hurled it, too. It crashed over the top of the doorframe. Dobson fled. The angry blonde noticed me standing there in the doorway.

"Who the hell are *you!*" she shouted.

"I've come to mend your gown," I said. "I think perhaps you'd better put it on so we can see how much damage there is and how much stitching will be required."

"There's no need to mend the bloody gown! I'm not wearing it! I'm not going on! I'll never step foot on that stage again as long as *he*'s in charge. I have my pride! I have my principles! Mr. James Lambert can find himself another leading lady! He can go straight to hell! He can *rot* there!"

Theatrical folk were certainly a volatile lot, I reflected. I wondered if any of them ever employed a normal voice or uttered a sentence not ending in an exclamation mark.

The maid began to wring her hands, eyes more anxious than ever.

"Now, Coral dear," she said, "you know you can't refuse to go on tonight. You wouldn't be hurting *him*, you'd be disappointing all those lovely people who have come out on a bitterly cold night just to see *you*."

"He'd be nothing without me! His bleeding play wouldn't last a week!"

"That's quite true, dear. Everyone knows it. Do calm yourself and put on the gown so this nice young woman can mend it for you. Let me get you a cup of hot tea."

"I don't want any tea! I want something to eat! I'm starving!"

"I tell you what, dear, you put on the gown and I'll go find that pleasant Mr. Dobson and have him send someone to Hatchard's Coffee House and buy some of those nice chocolate cream puffs. You can have them here in your dressing room during intermission."

"Oh, all right," Mrs. Tallent said petulantly, "but I'm not doing it for *him*. I'm doing it for my *pub*lic!"

She flung off her robe and pulled the purple and mauve gown from the rack. The maid shot me a relieved look and scurried away like someone just let out of an asylum. I took the sewing things out of the bag and removed my cloak as the actress struggled impatiently into the gown.

Although Carol Tallent *was* overweight, she certainly didn't resemble a sow, nor did she look like a baby whale. She was, instead, voluptuously hefty, like those women Rubens was always painting a hundred and fifty years ago. Her dark blonde hair was the color of honey, pulled back sleekly from her face with elaborate waves arranged in back. Her large brown eyes were sullen, her mouth petulant and provocative, a deep, rich pink. Though far from beautiful, she nevertheless had that potent sensual allure that drove men crazy. Made you think of cheap perfume and sweat and rumpled bedclothes, I thought.

"Well!" she snapped. "Are you going to hook me up?"

I stepped behind her and did up the tiny hooks in back. The purple velvet bodice had split along the seam on the right side, leaving a four inch gap, her white petticoat visible beneath.

"Shouldn't be at all difficult to mend," I told her. "No need for you to take the gown back off. If you'll raise your right arm I can sew it up easily. Just let me thread my needle."

"Hurry up! I've got to do my makeup after you've done. I don't know *why* I endure this!"

"You endure it for your public," I said sweetly.

"You're right. I can't let them down. One mustn't forget the little people, no matter *how* celebrated one becomes. They're the ones who buy the tickets. They're the ones who make it all happen. The indignities one has to suffer for one's art!"

I wondered if James Lambert had written that particular dialogue, too. It was certainly worthy of him.

"Just raise your arm up," I said. "Try to stand still. Wouldn't want to jab you. This is good, strong thread. It'll hold nicely. Gown'll be right as rain in a matter of minutes."

"If it had been done *right* in the first place this wouldn't have happened! I *begged* Lambert to use Mrs. Dane, she makes divine costumes, but no, he had to use that wretched Mrs. Gibbons who doesn't know sod about color or—"

Mrs. Tallent let out a bloodcurdling scream that must have startled humble folk on the outskirts of Plymouth.

"I'm *so* sorry," I said. "I told you to be still. These little accidents *will* happen."

"You bloody idiot! You've *wounded* me!"

"Just a teeny little jab with my needle. Let me see— is there any blood? Nary a drop. You're not hurt at all. Just a minute or so more now. It's coming along nicely indeed."

"Clumsy fool! It *hurts!*"

"You'll live, Mrs. Tallent. There. All done."

Mrs. Tallent jerked away from me and examined the

gown in the mirror, then gave me a murderous look as
I put the things back into the bag and picked up my
cloak. I smiled a sweet smile. Mrs. Tallent called me a
bumbling little bitch and said she intended to see I lost
my job. "Enjoy your cream puffs, Fatty," I said sweetly
and left, closing the door behind me. I heard something
splintering against it just as I got it shut.

Charming creature, Mrs. Tallent. Now to find James
Lambert and collect my five pounds. I moved back down
the hall to find the wings on the right side of the stage
crowded with men in handsome blue and white uni-
forms trimmed in golden braid. Sewed the braid on
myself, I had, made most of the white breeches as well.
The men were buckling on their sabers and milling
about, paying no attention to me as I moved through
their midst. I crossed behind the backdrop again and
found utter confusion prevailing on the other side of
the stage. A girl in blue with a white gauze apron was
giggling merrily as she lolled in the arms of two stagehands. A third stagehand was holding up an empty gin
bottle. Lambert was ranting, waving his arms in the
air.

"How did she *get* it! Who *gave* it to her! You all know
I never permit any kind of liquor backstage! My God!
There must be a full moon! Curtain's going up in less
than ten minutes and the little slut can't even *walk*
much less deliver her line!"

The girl tittered and kicked one leg high and tried
to grab the empty bottle. A plump, middle-aged woman
in black wig and luscious pink satin gown told Lambert
the girl's lover had deserted her that afternoon, and
Lambert glared at her and then placed his hands over
his temples and shook his head, looking woeful now,
looking tragic. "I'm cursed!" he cried. "Cursed!" Although Dottie had never mentioned it, I was willing to
bet a month's salary James Lambert had spent some
time as an actor. They probably booed him off the stage,
I thought. Lucky they didn't stone him.

"What are we going to *do?*" Dobson asked. "The house
is packed. We can't turn them out!"

"I don't *know* what we're going to do! I'll think of something."

I decided it was not a propitious time to collect my five pounds and started toward the hall leading to the stage door as unobtrusively as I could. Lambert looked up then. He saw me and stood up straight, suddenly galvanized with purpose.

"You!" he shouted. "Stop where you are!"

My heart leaped. I was terrified. He rushed over to me and fixed me with a hard stare and then nodded. He seized my cloak, seized the bag, tossing them aside. "Get that apron off her!" he ordered. "Bring it over here!" And then he reached up and pulled the puffed sleeves of my violet silk dress down off my shoulders. I should have slapped him across the face as hard as I could, but I was too stunned. I stumbled back. James Lambert clamped his fingers around my wrist and held on tightly.

"You'll do. You'll have to do! The dress is all wrong but the apron will help. Yes, I think it might work. *Get that apron over here!*"

"Let go of me!" I cried. "Have you lost your—"

"You've got to help us out, wench. It's an emergency. I want you to do a little favor for me. It's very, very simple, and I know you can do it, and you *will* do it, do you hear me? You're going to go onstage tonight. You're going to—"

"You're out of your bloody mind!"

I tried to pull free. His fingers tightened around my wrist. I was genuinely terrified now, and James Lambert saw it and sensed he'd better change his tactics and smiled a reassuring smile.

"There's absolutely nothing to be worried about," he assured me, speaking in that persuasive voice I had heard him use on Dottie. "When the curtain goes up the audience discovers Mrs. Tallent and Mrs. Pearson sitting at the table in the garden and you're in the background, you're the maid, you've been gathering flowers and—"

"I won't do it! I couldn't possibly! I—"

"—and you're just loitering there in front of the back-drop, enjoying the fresh air and sunshine. Mrs. Tallent and Mrs. Pearson are talking about Prince Karl whose armies have conquered the country. The Prince has requisitioned the villa and will soon arrive to take over. Mrs. Tallent looks fearful and shakes her head and says 'I fear we'll all be ravished' and when she says those words, you point stage right and say 'Lo! The Prince and his army approach!' and then you drop your flowers and flee stage left in terror."

"You're mad!" I protested. "I've never been on a stage in my life! I've never even been inside a theater until tonight! If you think I'm going to—"

"I know you're a bit nervous, wench, and that's understandable, but you've got absolutely nothing to worry about. No one is going to pay any attention to you, they're going to be looking at Mrs. Tallent and Mrs. Pearson and listening to their exchange of dialogue."

"I don't care! I—"

"You just have that one bit, that one line— 'Lo! The Prince and his army approach!' You can remember that! Then you just drop your flowers and run offstage and that's it, that's all."

"Let one of the supers do it!"

"I don't have any female supers. They're all men. They're all soldiers. You can't expect me to slap a dress on one of *them*."

"They did in Shakespeare's time!"

"This isn't Shakespeare!"

"*That*'s for bloody sure!"

A man came rushing up with the white gauze apron. Lambert seized it, eyes flashing dangerously. He jerked me to him and angrily tied the apron around my waist and then, fingers clamped on my wrist, dragged me toward the stage. I struggled furiously. "Be still!" he snapped. Mrs. Tallent and the middle-aged woman in pink satin and black wig were sitting down at the table onstage. James Lambert dragged me past the white plaster statue, past trellises and shrubs, finally stopping.

"You can do it," he said tenderly, wooing me with his voice. "I know you can. You just stand here and gaze at the sky and—"

"What the hell is going on!" Mrs. Tallent cried. "What's *she* doing here? Where's—"

"Shut up, sow! And when Mrs. Tallent says 'I fear we'll all be ravished,' you spot the army in the distance and point stage right and say your line, then drop your flowers and— Where are the bloody flowers! *Bring me the flowers!* I know you won't let us down, wench. I know you'll make us all very proud. Just think, this could be the start of a wonderful career in the theater."

"I don't want a career. I just want to go back ho—"

"Stop whining and do as you're told!" he ordered, seizing a bunch of artificial flowers from a panicky stagehand and thrusting them into my arms. "Curtain's going up in thirty seconds. We're *count*ing on you!"

He dashed offstage then and left me standing there with the bunch of flowers, and I was so stunned, so disoriented I didn't know what to do. I couldn't believe this was happening to me. Less than ten minutes ago I had been leaving the theater, and now...my heart was pounding. My throat was dry. Mrs. Tallent glared at me and then turned to Mrs. Pearson and picked up her purple lace fan and looked nervous, looked alarmed, getting into character, and then there was a creaking sound and a sudden cessation of the buzzing, humming noise I had paid no attention to before, noise made by over three hundred people sitting in the theater, quiet now as the pulleys creaked and the curtain slowly rose. The footlights were blinding, and behind them...My God! There they were! Hundreds of blurry faces in the darkness, all of them staring! I thought I was going to faint.

"It was a black day indeed when the invaders swarmed over this lovely land of ours," Mrs. Pearson declaimed in a deep, dramatic voice. "We have surren-

dered our freedom, and now we must surrender our villa
as well. They say Prince Karl is a demon."

"A demon with women," Mrs. Tallent replied. Her
voice was dramatic, too, phony as could be. "I'll not give
up, Lucinda! Somehow ... somehow I am going to save
our villa, save our honor, too!"

Lord! It was a wonder they didn't stone *her*. She was
abominable, but she *did* look stunning in the purple
and mauve gown. I began to relax a little bit, began to
catch my breath. You're a maid, Angela, and you've
been picking flowers and you're apprehensive about the
soldiers coming and this will all be over with in just a
few minutes. I swallowed and gazed at the imaginary
horizon and then lifted the flowers up and sniffed them.
They were dusty. I sneezed loudly. There were several
titters in the audience. They thought I was funny! I
sighed and then gazed at the horizon some more and
managed to look very apprehensive. There wasn't anything to this acting business, I decided. It was as easy
as could be. You just had to relax and pretend you were
someone else. I got up my courage and turned and casually peered at the audience and the first thing I saw
were two familiar faces there in the second row. I gasped.
Timothy and Johnny! What were *they* doing here? Both
of them were grinning broadly. Timothy waved. Without thinking, I waved back, and several people hooted
with laughter.

Mrs. Tallent was livid. I could tell. She kept right
on speaking, louder now, and there was an angry edge
to her voice that hadn't been there before. I suppose she
thought I was deliberately trying to undermine her
performance, if you could call it a performance. I gazed
at the horizon again, shading my eyes with my left
hand, clutching the flowers with my right, and Mrs.
Pearson started declaiming again and a curious hissing
noise began to spread in the audience and I realized
they were whispering. The whispering grew louder. Mrs.
Pearson was quite discomfited, fanning herself vigorously as she spoke her lines. What in the world were
they whispering about?

I could sense a wave of excitement sweeping through the audience. Puzzled me completely, it did. What were they excited about? Certainly not the dreary dialogue Mrs. Tallent was speaking now. She was afraid the villa would be thoroughly destroyed, burned to the ground, afraid we'd all be ravished. The hiss of whispers was even louder now, and people were shifting about in their seats. In the wings on the right the soldiers were all lined up, the actor playing the prince in front, in a long cape and a gleaming helmet. He was waving his hands at me and silently mouthing something, looking quite upset. Terribly distracting, it was. I pretended not to see, gazing at the imaginary horizon

"I fear we'll all be ravished!" Mrs. Tallent repeated angrily.

"Oh!" I cried.

"It's her!" a man shouted. "It *is* her! It's the Angel!"

"It's the *Angel in Scarlet!"* another yelled.

Oh, Lord! I was in a panic now as the audience grew more and more excited, more and more unruly. I desperately tried to remember my line, looking frantically about the stage as though to find it there. "Uh— Lo!" I cried nervously. "Here come the Prince! He's got his soldiers with him, too!" And then I threw the flowers down and rushed offstage and into the arms of the prince who seized me by the shoulders. "Not this way, you idiot! You exit stage *left!"* He gave me a shove and I stumbled back onto the stage and almost tripped and bumped into one of the artificial shrubs and sent it skittering across the stage. The audience roared with laughter, hearty, boisterous laughter that grew louder and louder, demolishing me completely.

"They're still coming!" I shouted.

I ran blindly across the stage and smack into one of the trellises. It toppled over with a noisy clatter and hit against the side of the pedestal on which the plaster statue stood. The Greek goddess wobbled precariously for a long moment, then fell with a deafening crash. "Bloody hell!" I exclaimed. The laughter was tumultuous now. People began to applaud. I leaped nimbly

over the shattered plaster and raced offstage again and
James Lambert grabbed me and held me fast as the
applause thundered. Mrs. Tallent and Mrs. Pearson were
still at the table, faces quite pale despite their heavy
stage makeup. Lambert's face was a chalky white, his
eyes a blazing emerald with brown flecks.

"I—oh, Jesus, I—I'm sor—I'm sorry!" I stammered.

"Shut up!"

The applause continued to thunder. The whole building seemed to shake with it. "Angel!" people began to
shout. "Angel! Angel! We want Angel!" And his mouth
tightened into a hard line and his fingers dug savagely
into my upper arms and he took a deep breath. I tried
to pull away. His fingers dug deeper, and I winced at
the pain. "Angel! Angel!" they yelled, and they were
stamping their feet now. "We want Angel!"

"Let go of me!" I cried.

James Lambert didn't seem to hear me. He was looking over my shoulder at a point in space, lost in thought,
and I could almost see the idea taking shape in his
mind. He took another deep breath and looked down
into my eyes as the furor continued.

"I am going to murder you," he said in a flat voice.
"You're going to die very slowly, very painfully, but first
you're going out on that stage and you're going to take
a bow. They think it was a stunt. They think it was all
planned. We'll let them go right on thinking that."

"I—I'm not going back out there! I—"

"You'll do as you're told," he said sternly.

"I'm not your bloody servant! I'm not one of your
employees, either. You've got no right to—"

He clamped a hand over my mouth, smothering my
protests. The audience continued to go wild. They'd start
ripping the seats out next, start throwing them at the
stage. I struggled with all my might as he slowly ma-
neuvered me over toward the stage, his hand still
clamped over my mouth.

"They love you," he murmured into my ear. "Listen
to that applause. I've never heard anything like it in
all my years in the theater. Go out there, Miss whoever-

you-are—I don't even know your name. Go out there and take a bow, let them love you."

He let go of me and placed his palm in the small of my back and shoved violently. I stumbled forward, and there I was in front of the footlights again and the people were standing and cheering. Never heard such a commotion in my life. And me the cause of it. They weren't angry. They were *happy*. They were cheering, not shouting. They liked me. I smiled a timid smile, and then I gave them a curtsy. They loved it. I curtsied again. I saw Timothy and Johnny yelling and stamping with the rest of them, undoubtedly the ringleaders of the brouhaha. I blew them a kiss. The audience roared. I blew kisses all around and made another curtsy, and then I turned and blew a kiss to Mrs. Tallent who looked like someone had just embalmed her.

James Lambert came out on stage then. He'd put on a brown frock coat and a green silk neckcloth and he was smiling warmly and carrying a bouquet of beautiful pink roses, real ones. Heaven knows where he got them in such a hurry. His wavy brown hair gleamed richly in the glow of the footlights. He looked impressive indeed, tall and striking and, yes, marvelously attractive, even though his nose was a bit crooked. He bowed to me and handed me the roses. I pretended to be overcome with gratitude. I sniffed them. I smiled. I pulled one out of the cluster and tossed it to Timothy. Lambert continued to smile.

"Don't overdo it, you little baggage," he said between his teeth.

"Sod off," I said sweetly.

I threw Johnny a rose, too, then tossed a few more just to defy him. After a few moments Lambert raised his arms up, asking for silence, and the crowd grew quieter and in a deep, beautifully resonant voice he told them he was frightfully pleased they'd enjoyed "our little jest" and begged them to let the drama resume. He took my hand. I made a final curtsy. He led me offstage and led me deep into the wings. The Prince and the soldiers marched onstage and Mrs. Tallent

screamed and Mrs. Pearson pretended to faint. I pulled
my hand free, feeling rather pleased with myself. I
handed the bouquet of pink roses to a passing stagehand
and began to take off the apron. Several people stood
around, staring at us. Andy Dobson looked shaken.

"Quite a performance," James Lambert said omi-
nously. "You and I have some things to discuss."

"We have nothing whatsoever to discuss," I said, "besides the five pounds you owe me."

I handed him the apron and went over to pick up my
cloak and put it on. He came storming after me. I gave
him a frosty look, enjoying myself immensely. I hadn't
felt quite so feisty since...in a very long time. I tied
the ribbons of the cloak around my neck and picked up
the bag of sewing things. Lambert was glowering. A
thick brown wave had tumbled over his brow, giving
him a curiously boyish look, and those marvelous green-
brown eyes were full of angry admiration. He thrust
out his lower lip in an attempt to look menacing.

"Why didn't you tell me who you are?" he demanded.

"I'm an humble seamstress who works for your friend
Mrs. Gibbons."

"You know bloody good and well what I'm talking
about. You're the toast of London. Every hack on Fleet
Street has written reams of copy about you. Prints of
your portrait are selling by the thousands."

"That's none of my doing," I said blithely. "If folks
want to make a fuss over Mr. Gainsborough's painting,
it has nothing to do with me."

"It has everything to do with you! You're *famous,*
wench. You saw how they carried on out there."

"It was something, wasn't it?"

"And you loved it! I saw your face when they were
cheering and applauding. You were glowing. The way
you curtsied, the way you tossed those roses—I've never
seen anyone take to the stage the way you did, nor have
I ever seen anyone with such natural stage presence.
With the right part, the right pro—"

"I'll take my five pounds now, Mr. Lambert."

His mouth tightened. His eyes flashed. He dug into

the pocket of his coat and pulled out some creased and rumpled bills and counted out five pounds, shoving them into my outstretched hand. I smiled politely and thanked him and started toward the hall. He scurried after me and seized my arm and jerked me around quite roughly. I was furious.

"You're not leaving!" he cried. "We've got things to talk about, plans to discuss. I'm going to—"

"You're going to let go of me this instant! I've had enough of your bullying, Mr. Lambert! You think you can just—just—"

"Calm down," he said pleasantly. "I have tremendous plans for you, wench. Come along. We're going to my office."

"I'm not going anywhere with you!"

He arched an eyebrow. "No?"

"No!"

He chuckled and took the bag out of my hand and gripped both my arms, smiling a wicked smile. My anger amused him. He was having a dandy time, relishing every minute of it. My anger rose. My cheeks flamed. I brought my knee up and made sharp contact and James Lambert yowled and staggered back, doubling over in pain. I balled my right hand into a tight fist and smashed it across his jaw as hard as I could and he reeled against the wall and crashed into a pile of flats. I picked up the bag and hurried down the hallway and out the stage door, feeling a strange exhilaration, feeling wonderfully, gloriously alive for the first time in years.

"I do hope you didn't do any permanent damage to the family jewels," Megan said the next afternoon. "Women all over London would go into mourning."

"I don't think I actually hurt him," I told her, "but I imagine it *smart*ed quite a bit."

Megan smiled. It was Saturday and we both had the afternoon off. Dazzling rays of sunlight streamed in through the front windows, making shimmery patterns on the floor. I was curled up on the dusty-rose sofa, wearing a light blue muslin frock, and Megan, in rust and cream striped linen, was pouring herself a cup of

tea. Her long auburn waves glistened with rich highlights in the sun. Timothy and Johnny had left a short
while ago after recounting *their* version of last night's
event with customary gusto.

"It seems James Lambert has finally met his match,"
Megan said, sitting on the other end of the sofa and
folding her legs under her. "I'd give anything to have
seen it."

"He's dreadful," I said. "Such a bully!"

"But exciting," she added. "There's a light in your
eyes when you mention his name, luv. You're fascinated. I can tell."

"He *is* fascinating, I won't deny it, but—I'm not at
all interested. I've got far too much good sense."

"Indeed?"

"A woman would have to be out of her mind to have
anything to do with a man like that."

Megan took a sip of tea, looking at me with those
vivid blue eyes that were so wise, so knowing. I felt a
bit uncomfortable, as though she had guessed some secret I didn't even know I had. She set down her teacup
and burrowed into the softness of the sofa.

"You know my feelings about James Lambert," she
said, "but it's high time *some*one made you forget about
the stableboy, luv. I haven't ever seen you look so radiant, so—excited. If Lambert can erase that sad look,
that pensive air, I'm delighted. You seem to be able to
handle him, and he's obviously interested in you."

"He's not interested in *me,* he's interested in 'Angel.'
Don't think for a minute I don't know what he's got in
mind."

"What's that?"

"He wants to capitalize on my 'fame.' He wants to
put me on the stage."

"Timothy said you seemed to be enjoying yourself
vastly, tossing roses and blowing kisses. He said your
'comic turn' was worthy of Peg Woffington, in her prime.
He said you took to the stage like a bird takes to air."

"It *was* rather fun," I confessed. "I was terrified at
first, felt sure I was going to faint, but—they *liked* me,

Megan. I could feel it. I felt waves of affection and good humor pouring over the footlights."

"They loved you," Megan said. "And why not? You're young and beautiful, you've got charm, spirit, an engaging personality. I think it's terribly exciting, luv! When you become a famous actress you can get parts for *me!*"

Both of us laughed, and then I gazed at the shimmery patterns on the floor and thought about the events of last night. I *had* enjoyed myself, there was no denying it, and yes, I was attracted to James Lambert. He was a rogue, a dreadful bully, a villain, but... he was a terribly exciting man, devilishly good looking and curiously engaging, despite his penchant for melodramatic behavior. Beneath all that bluster was a charming, insecure, immensely gifted man who was bound to have a great many virtues. Dottie adored him, and that was a definite credit in his favor. Of course I could never go on the stage. It was unthinkable. I was much too shy, much too serious, and after what I had done to James Lambert last night he would undoubtedly go out of his way to avoid me. Just as well, I thought. Megan and I exchanged looks as we heard someone coming up the stairs.

"Are you expecting someone?" I asked.

She shook her head. Someone began knocking on the door. I got up to open it, and he smiled a wonderfully engaging smile and handed me a giant bouquet of daffodils and daisies and mauve-blue iris and strolled past me into the room as though he owned it. Megan got up. She didn't seem at all surprised, but I was dumbfounded. Lambert gave her a friendly nod. He was carrying an enormous box of chocolates from the best shop in London.

"Daisies and daffodils in February?" I said.

"Hothouse grown," he told me. "Got them at the Market across the street. Cost me a fortune. So did these chocolates."

"How—how did you find out where I live?"

"Dottie. Had to choke the information out of her. Nice flat. What's that horrible smell?"

"Scorched hair and powder," Megan said. "I'll take the flowers, luv. We must have a vase around here somewhere."

She took the flowers from me and closed the door and left the room. James Lambert smiled again and handed me the box of chocolates. The box was blue and silver and quite heavy. I set it down on the table in front of the sofa, still dumbfounded. He was wearing a handsome black suit and a waistcoat of green and white striped satin and a white silk neckcloth. He looked dapper and expansive and wonderfully appealing with that rich brown wave tumbling over his brow. My pulses seemed to leap, and I found it difficult to compose myself.

"I can't believe Dottie would give you this address," I said.

"Did it against her will. I had to squeeze quite hard."

"I suppose I should thank you for the flowers and the chocolates, although I fear you've wasted your money— and your time. I know why you've come, and I might as well tell you right now that—"

"I came to apologize," he said glibly. "I'm afraid I was rather rough on you last night. You were rather rough yourself," he added.

"How—how are you?"

"I'll survive. There's a slight bruise on my jaw, as you'll notice if you look close enough, and I had a— uh—very uncomfortable hour or so, but I suppose I had it coming to me. I get carried away, you see."

"I've noticed."

"We made the newspapers," he told me. "A couple of journalists just happened to be in the audience last night. One of them came backstage afterwards, engaging fellow, full of questions. I told him your comic bit was all planned, said I was writing a play for you, said you were going to become the most exciting, the most glamorous personality on the London stage."

"How—how dare you!"

"I didn't give him your real name. I didn't know it. Dottie told me this afternoon. She also told me you were a sweet, sensible, levelheaded young woman who would flatly refuse to have anything to do with a scoundrel like me. I told her my intentions were strictly honorable. I don't intend to despoil you. I intend to make you rich and even more famous than you already are."

"I don't want to be famous!"

"Of course you do. Sit down. Have some chocolates. I *am* writing another play. It'll be the most ambitious, the most spectacular production I have ever mounted. It's set in the fifteenth century and based on the life of Jane Shore, the beautiful young goldsmith's wife who became the mistress of King Edward the Fourth and ruled his brilliant, profligate court with her charm and winsome beauty. It has everything—drama, color, pageantry, love sacred and profane. You are going to be my Jane Shore."

"I most certainly am not!"

Megan came back into the room and set the vase of flowers on the table beside the box of chocolates, and then she sat down in the cozy chair in front of the window and slung one leg over the arm, fascinated. I could tell she'd been eavesdropping.

"It's a magnificent part," Lambert continued. "There's not an actress in London who wouldn't kill for it."

"I'm not an actress!"

"You're going to be. I'm leaving for Tunbridge Wells next week, I've taken rooms there through May. I always go there to work—can't write in London, far too many distractions. You're coming with me. I intend to finish the play and teach you the rudiments of the acting profession. I'm a hard taskmaster, I must warn you, but I'm sure we'll get along swimmingly."

"You *are* out of your mind!"

Lord, now the sod had *me* using verbal exclamation marks. I tried my best to calm down. It wasn't easy. Megan lounged there in the chair with a knowing smile on her lips. I longed to slap her silly.

"I think you had better leave, Mr. Lambert," I said.

"You'll love Tunbridge Wells," he informed me. "It'll be quiet the first few weeks, but when spring comes there'll be a crowd—families, old folks come to take the waters. It's beautiful in springtime, green hills all around, flowers everywhere. We'll go for walks on the Pantiles and sit on the verandah and make a holiday of it."

"I am *not* going to Tunbridge Wells," I said.

James Lambert looked at me for a long moment with those magnificent green-brown eyes, and then he smiled.

"We'll see about that," he told me.

Chapter Twelve

Brilliant rays of early morning sunlight spilled across the verandah and through the open French windows to make radiant splashes on the polished hardwood floor. It was mid-April, and the sky was a pale, pure blue, the air soft and laden with the glorious smells of moist soil and flowers and new green leaves. I stretched and sighed, feeling lethargic this morning, feeling lazy, in no mood to work. I stepped to one of the windows and stood there for a moment, reveling in the sunlight and the air. Across the white banister of the verandah I could see leafy green treetops and the spire of the Church of King Charles the Martyr at the entrance to the Pantiles. People were already out strolling, on their way to take the waters at the spring or browse in the shops. Tunbridge Wells had a leisurely, serene air, everything quiet and calm and unhurried. It was much favored by cultured folk and the elderly and affluent who came to its famous spa. Our fellow lodgers in this elegant, spacious white house included a physician, a countess in her eighties, two wealthy matrons from Bath, a don

from Cambridge and Mr. Thomas Sheridan and his
daughter Betsy.

The house had been almost empty when we arrived
in late February, only the countess and the physician
in residence, and we had been given choice rooms. My
sitting room and bedroom upstairs were large and airy,
both opening onto the verandah, the sitting room done
in creams and tan and brown, the bedroom in shades
of blue and pale gray and white, with touches of violet.
The place had a mellow patina of slightly worn elegance, as did the widow who owned the house and took
in lodgers. The house was ultrarespectable and run with
calm efficiency by the widow and a fleet of servants.
James Lambert's bedroom and "studio" were on the
ground floor, overlooking the kitchen gardens, as remote from my suite as possible. He had been coming
here for years, and Mrs. Lindsey was quite fond of him,
but she was taking no chances. She wasn't thrilled with
the idea of my spending so much time in his studio
during the day, but Lambert assured her we were working and invited her to pop in and observe any time she
liked.

Sighing again, I slipped on my pale gray taffeta with
narrow violet stripes and sat down at the dressing table
to brush my hair. Dottie had been very sorry to lose
me, claimed she had no idea how she would ever get
along without me, and then she had informed me that
I hadn't a stitch suitable for Tunbridge Wells and insisted we create a complete new wardrobe, to be paid
for by Mr. James Lambert. That individual yowled like
a wounded buffalo when he received the bills, but he
paid them. Though she would miss me, Dottie loved the
theater and said she knew I would be a great success.
She also informed Lambert that his life wouldn't be
worth tuppence if he harmed a hair of my head. No
bullying, he promised her, no browbeating. He had an
investment in me. Lying through his teeth, the sod. He
had done nothing but bully and browbeat me ever since
we arrived, but he claimed I was making wonderful
progress.

Thought acting was simple, I had. Thought you just had to pretend you were someone else. How wrong I was. You had to know how to walk, how to sit, how to stand, how to speak, how to project. Thought I knew how to do those things. He informed me that I walked like a duck, sat like a hen, stood like an ostrich and had a voice that would shatter glass. I told him he could take a flying leap at the moon and said I was leaving for London at once. Lambert said I'd leave over his dead body. I said that might not be a bad idea. We fought quite viciously, and I was certain I had made a wretched mistake, but I finally agreed to let him begin his "training" and I did indeed learn how to walk, how to move gracefully, how to make simple, effective gestures without resembling a windmill. I learned to speak in a rich, melodious voice without sounding affected. That was extremely difficult, we were still working on it. He was determined to rid my voice of all traces of the country accent I hadn't even known I had. I was learning to project my voice without shouting.

Drawing the brush through my hair, I smiled. They had been grueling, those sessions. I had often been frustrated, often been furious, but I had never once been bored. James Lambert *was* a stern taskmaster, impatient, demanding, a terrible bully, but he knew what he was doing and he was a brilliant teacher, however brutal his methods. Being with him was marvelously stimulating, even elating, I admitted. Though he treated me like a recalcitrant, rather dim-witted child when we were working, away from the studio he was gallant, urbane, polite as he could be. Hadn't once tried anything improper. Treated me like a favorite sister, he did. Maybe all those stories I had heard about his romantic exploits were exaggerated, I thought.

And maybe I was more than a little disappointed.

There was a knock on my sitting room door. I set the brush aside and stood up. Gracefully. Not at all like an ostrich. I adjusted the tight elbow length sleeves of my frock. It had a modestly low bodice, a waistband of violet velvet and a full skirt that belled out over the half dozen pearl gray underskirts. He could wait, I thought, smoothing down the bodice. I felt that delicious anticipation I always felt of late, and I savored it as I toyed with my hair and deliberately delayed. There was another knock, louder, a bit impatient. I was on my own in the evenings—Lambert worked on his play then— but he always came up to escort me to breakfast, which we took in the spacious dining room downstairs. I delayed a bit longer, then left the bedroom, crossed the sitting room and opened the door, and, yes, that was definitely elation I felt as I looked at him standing there with a mock scowl on his face.

"Took your bloody time," he said.

"I wasn't quite ready."

"Why the fancy dress?"

"It isn't that fancy."

"Cost me a fortune, I wager. Worth it, though. You look quite enchanting, Miss Howard."

"Thank you, Mr. Lambert."

"In a saucy mood this morning, aren't you?"

"Saucy?"

"Perky. Pleased with yourself. Maybe it's the dress. You *do* look radiant this morning, Angel."

"I wish you wouldn't call me that."

"It's your new name. Get used to it. Angel Howard, the darling of the London stage."

I stepped into the hall and pulled the door shut behind me. Lambert smiled an amiable smile. He looked wonderfully attractive this morning in black breeches and frock coat and a waistcoat of brown and black striped satin, a dark brown neckcloth at his throat. His hair was neatly brushed, still a bit damp from his bath, and he smelled of soap and pine-scented shaving lotion. I had grown to admire that slightly crooked nose, so much more interesting than a boring, regular nose would have been, so much more appealing. In fact, when he wasn't in a temper, when he wasn't indulging in histrionics, James Lambert was the most appealing man I had ever met.

"Shall we go down to breakfast?" he said.

He crooked his arm and I placed my hand in it and we started down the wide, sunny hall toward the staircase. He took long, athletic strides, confident as a lord.

"It *is* going to happen, you know," he said as we started down the stairs. "You are going to be the darling of the London stage, no question about it. You have been an excellent student, a very hard worker, and you've made quite remarkable strides. I brought a lump of clay to Tunbridge Wells. I'll return to London with an actress."

"Thanks. Every girl loves being called a lump of clay."

"I meant it as a compliment," he assured me.

"That's what worries me," I said.

Lambert laughed quietly and patted my hand and led me into the dining room. The long mahogany sideboard was laden with silver-covered dishes and places were set at half a dozen small tables. The two matrons from Bath sat at one of them, sniffing with disapproval as we entered. Both ladies were convinced we were having a scandalous affair right under their noses, and Lambert went out of his way to agitate them, engaging them in long conversations, plying them with questions and pouring on the charm, delighted by their frigid responses. He waved to them now and bellowed a cheery good morning. Both ladies looked the other way. Betsy Sheridan sat at another table, busily scribbling one of her interminable letters to her sister Alicia in Dublin. Betsy was a charming, sprightly young woman devoted to fashion, gossip and books. Her father, Thomas, had been a great actor in his day, a rival to Garrick, and her brother Richard was interested in the theater, too, said to be busily penning a comedy that would make him one of England's greatest playwrights.

Lambert handed me a plate, took one himself and began to heap it with bacon and eggs and kippered herring and steamed mushrooms and buttered toast and chutney. I cringed, taking a couple of forkfuls of egg, one thin slice of ham, one sliver of toast. Lambert believed in a hearty breakfast to start the day, while I

was content with several cups of coffee. A servant
brought a pot to our table and, knowing my penchant,
left it after he had filled our cups. I toyed with my food,
drank the coffee with relish.

"You should eat more," Lambert scolded, spearing a
piece of herring. "You need fuel to start the body running properly."

"Hideous thought," I said. "At least I don't stuff myself with pastry and such, like some I could name."

"I'd bash your head in if you did. One sow's enough
for any man to have to cope with."

"Poor Mrs. Tallent. What's she doing now that your
play has folded?"

"It had a *very* respectable run," he retorted defensively. "The delectable Mrs. Tallent is, I believe, desperately seeking employment on the stage, without
resounding success. At last report she had put on another fifteen pounds."

"Poor dear. You probably drove her to it."

"I resent that, Miss Howard. I was the soul of patience with that harridan. Dottie was right. Coral Tallent was a mistake. Every man's entitled to one. I say,
is that strawberry preserves in that jar? Be delicious
on my toast. Shove it over, will you?"

I pushed the jar of preserves across the table. Lambert spread some on his toast and ate it with relish. I
sipped my coffee, longing to ask him more about Coral
Tallent. Had they had an affair? I assumed they had.
One heard he slept with all his leading ladies, and she
was certainly voluptuous. Would he attempt to sleep
with me? Would I resist if he did? I drove the thought
from my mind, telling myself that ours was strictly a
professional relationship. He wanted me to play the
lead in his new play and I thought it would be interesting to try my hand at acting and there was nothing
between us besides a . . . a rather refreshing feeling of
camaraderie. I finished my coffee and poured another
cup, trying to convince myself I was relieved he had
made no improper advances.

Young Miss Sheridan finished her letter and went

out to post it, pausing at our table to compliment me on my dress. The two matrons left shortly thereafter with noses in the air. Lambert had a second helping of eggs, a piece of sausage and more toast with jam, then declared himself wonderfully replete. He suggested we take a stroll, as it was such a glorious morning, and I agreed, rather puzzled as he was usually eager to get right to work. I placed my napkin beside my plate, and we left the dining room. A few moments later we were standing on the large, shady verandah in front of the house, looking out over the sun-splattered green lawn.

"I love this place," I said quietly. "It's so peaceful, so serene, like a haven after London."

"Glad you came?"

"Most of the time."

"I *have* been hard on you, haven't I?"

"You've been horrible," I told him.

"And you've learned a great deal," he said, leading me down the steps. "I am proud of you, Angel. There've been times, true, when I've longed to throttle you, a couple of times when I almost *did,* but as a whole you've been a marvelously satisfying student. Best I ever had."

"Oh?"

"Don't let it go to your head, wench. You've still got a lot to learn. We have to work on your voice—I still detect a trace of hayseed—and I'm not altogether satisfied with your projection. More exercises in order there. Tomorrow we'll begin work on interpretation of character."

"I thought you didn't want to begin that until you finished the play?"

"Plan to finish it this afternoon," he said casually. "Just need to touch up the last scene a bit, tighten the construction, hone the dialogue a bit. Tomorrow we'll read it aloud together and discuss Jane Shore's character—her motivations, her moods. Did you read those books I gave you?"

"All five of them," I replied. "I feel like I know her already, feel like I understand her."

"Good girl," he said, squeezing my arm.

We strolled past the gracious houses with their sunny lawns and vivid flower beds, past the shops and the Church of King Charles the Martyr. Dozens of people were parading slowly along the Pantiles—elderly ladies in pastel gowns and powdered wigs, querulous-looking gentlemen with gout, a scattering of young people here with their relatives. We joined the procession, strolling at a leisurely pace. With the colonnade on one side and a row of limes on the other, the Pantiles was a lovely walk, the surrounding hills spread with hazy purple and mauve shadows. Heads turned, for most of the people here knew that I had posed for *An Angel in Scarlet*. They were curious about me but much too genteel to intrude on my privacy.

"I received a long letter from Mr. Gainsborough in yesterday's post," I remarked. "The exhibit has finally closed down in order to make room for another. The painting has been sold."

"Oh? Who bought it?"

"Mr. G. didn't give his name. There was very heavy bidding, it seems. The gentleman who bought it wishes to remain anonymous and used a proxy to bid on it for him. He's a Lord and has a country estate—the painting will hang there in his drawing room. That's all Gainsborough would say. He's been sworn to secrecy. I find it quite odd."

"The painting is very valuable. The gentleman in question probably doesn't wish to alert potential thieves to his possession of it. I'd steal it myself if I thought I could get away with it."

"You would?"

"In a minute," he told me. "Alas, as I'm unable to own the painting, I'll have to make do with the company of the wench who sat for it. Not too difficult a task, I might add."

"You find my company pleasant?"

"When you're not being stubborn and temperamental," he said.

"Temperamental? Me?"

"Ah, you have the artistic temperament, wench. No

question about it. I've no doubt you'll turn into a monster, just like the rest of them."

"I could never be a monster."

"You've all the makings. Impudent, intractable, strong-willed, sassy, frequently foul-mouthed—you'll probably be worse than all the rest of them put together."

"Only if you drive me to it," I promised.

James Lambert laughed, and I felt lighthearted, felt joyous, felt much too happy just being with him, my arm in his. I wasn't in love with him. Of course I wasn't. I had far too much sense to allow myself to love a rogue like him. I wasn't in love with him, no, but I was attracted to him, strongly attracted, and I told myself that was only natural. James Lambert was a fascinating man, and I was only human. It had been a long, long time since that night under the stars. Lambert treated me like a sister. It was just as well.

"Want a drink?" he inquired when we reached the spring.

I shook my head and shuddered. Serious-faced grooms plunged tin dippers into an old stone fountain and filled the cups held out by the fashionably dressed crowd. The sulfurous, vile-tasting water was said to have marvelous medicinal powers, but the one time I had tasted it I had almost gagged, which had vastly amused Mr. Lambert. There were several older people in wheeled chairs, several using canes. In addition to the water, there were mud baths and a number of "treatments" available to the ailing and affluent. Betsy Sheridan dutifully carried a cup to her father who sat on a stone bench and looked glum indeed. Bored middle-aged women in modish gowns sipped the water as they strolled and gossiped about the latest scandals. Though sedate and respectable, Tunbridge Wells was a stylish resort for the *beau monde*.

"Get any other letters yesterday?" Lambert asked as we started back.

"Just a note from Megan. Her play is still running and she's still helping Dottie in the afternoons. Timothy has gone on tour with a repertory company and she has a new beau—nothing serious, she assures me."

"What about you? Do you have a beau?"

"Of course not."

"Why 'of course'? I should think a beautiful young woman like you would be constantly surrounded by randy bucks."

"I—I'm not interested in that sort of thing."

"I find that hard to believe. Hmm, perhaps I've made a mistake. The woman who plays Jane Shore should know something about love, should have a certain experience."

"I can play the role," I said dryly.

"So there *is* a man?"

"There was. A long time ago."

"You still love him?"

"I'm not sure. I—I haven't forgotten him."

"He hurt you," Lambert said.

"Badly," I replied.

He said nothing more, in a thoughtful mood as we returned to the house. We paused for a few moments on the verandah, enjoying the fragrance of flowers, the clean air and cloudless blue sky. He was still thoughtful, his hands thrust into his pockets, a rich brown wave slanting across his brow. His full pink mouth looked taut. I longed to reach up and stroke it. I brushed an imaginary bit of lint from my skirt. I smiled as the physician and the old countess came out onto the verandah. She nodded regally, wearing black silk and a fortune in rubies despite the hour. The physician was quite solicitous, holding her arm firmly as they moved slowly down the steps.

"Congratulations on your play," I said quietly. "I know you must be terribly pleased to have it so nearly finished."

"I must get back to work on it immediately. You, wench, shall have the day off. No lessons. No bullying. No shouting matches. You deserve a little free time. What shall you do with yourself?"

"I don't know. Betsy has been asking me to explore

the hills with her when I have some time. There's a particularly lovely spot she wants me to see. Perhaps I'll go with her today."

"See you this evening, then. If I finish the play we might just have a bottle of champagne with our dinner."

He went inside, and I sat on the verandah for a while, watching the morning sunlight spill over the railing, restless, a prey to conflicting emotions I knew had been gathering momentum ever since we left London. I listened to the pleasant drone of bees in the honeysuckle and tried to banish the emotions, and I was relieved when Betsy returned. The girl was delighted at the prospect of a hike, and after she had settled her father in his room we departed, taking a box lunch Mrs. Lindsey had generously packed for us.

Young Miss Sheridan was a charming companion, full of merry chatter, an intelligent and effervescent girl who was remarkably well read and *au courant* with all the latest news in fashion, society and the arts. We climbed Mount Ephraim, one of the gently sloping hills surrounding the town, and the exercise was invigorating. I felt rather nostalgic, remembering the long walks I had taken when I was Betsy's age. We reached the grove, which was lovely indeed, elms and planes spreading hazy gray-blue shadows over the sunny green grass sprinkled with small pink and mauve wildflowers. Through the trees, far below, we could see the town and the Pantiles and the race course where several riders exercised their horses, all of this looking tiny and toy-like from our vantage point.

We ate our lunch—boiled eggs, sliced tongue on buttered bread, delicious cheese, tiny oatmeal cakes with creamy white frosting—and drank the small jars of milk Mrs. Lindsey had thoughtfully put in. Betsy asked me all about modeling for Gainsborough, whose work she admired, and said she thought it was ever so exciting I was going to become an actress. She adored the theater and her brother did, too. He was going to be *very* famous one day soon, she confided. Betsy obviously worshiped this brother. Though still in his early twenties, he had already penned innumerable pieces for the theater and was working on a play to be called *The Rivals* which she just knew would make him immortal.

"Just think," she said. "He might write a play for *you* one day, Angel."

"Perhaps," I replied, indulging her.

We lolled in the sunshine for a while, Betsy chattering nonstop about various plays she had seen and books she had read, and then she gathered flowers to take back to her father who, she confided, was doing much better and yearned for the stage. When the theater was in your blood you could never shake the longing for greasepaint and footlights. We sauntered down the hill, Betsy carrying her flowers and still chattering. It was after three when we reached the house, and I thanked the girl for a pleasant afternoon. It had indeed been pleasant, and I felt much better as I went upstairs to my rooms. My attraction to James Lambert would be a problem only if I allowed it to be, I decided. I was grown up now, a mature woman, and common sense told me any relationship with him beyond our present working arrangement would be disastrous. I firmly intended to ignore those emotions his mere presence stirred so strongly.

As I moved down the hall I was surprised to see my sitting-room door standing open. I could have sworn I had closed it. Perhaps one of the maids left it open, I thought, stepping inside the room. I saw her sitting there on the cream sofa, a sneer on her lips, a triumphant gleam in her green eyes. I felt the color drain from my cheeks. She stood up.

"Well," she said, "you seem to be doing quite well for yourself."

"How—how did you—"

"It has taken me quite a long time to find you, Angela. I hired a man from Bow Street—a rather shady character, quite disreputable, a Runner I believe he called himself—and after several months he finally admitted he couldn't locate you. Charged me a very stiff fee, he did—for nothing. Then, three weeks ago, one of

the girls came in with a most interesting print, a reproduction of a portrait done by someone called Gainsborough."

She smiled a thin smile. Her lips were a bright crimson. Her plump cheeks were coated with powder and
rouge, a black satin beauty patch stuck on her right
cheekbone. Her eyelids were smeared with purple
shadow. She was wearing a purple silk gown, the bodice
trimmed in jet beads, a long black feather boa wrapped
around her arms. Marie had never looked so coarse, so
vicious. I told myself I had nothing to fear from her,
but my heart was palpitating nevertheless. I felt cold
all over.

"Betty happened to remember seeing something in
one of the papers about the girl in the painting appearing in a play by Mr. James Lambert. I didn't rely
on anyone from Bow Street this time. I went to the
theater myself and spoke to the doorman—slipped him
five pounds. He told me you had indeed been on the
stage several weeks ago. He said Lambert was writing
a play for you and had taken you to Tunbridge Wells
with him. As I said earlier, you seem to be doing quite
well for yourself."

The thin smile spread. Her eyes were glittering as
of old. She glanced at the elegantly furnished room as
though in confirmation, then adjusted the feathery black
loops about her arms.

"What do you want, Marie?" My voice was surprisingly level.

"I lost a great deal of money because of you," she
continued, ignoring my question. "Clinton Meredith was
quite understanding. He didn't demand a return of the
sum he had already advanced me—very reasonable of
him under the circumstances—but of course any future
profits were out of the question. You almost killed him,
by the way."

"I wish I had."

"He was in very bad shape when Blake found him.
We summoned a physician at once. He said he had no
intention of filing assault charges against you—again

he was very reasonable—but I just might file them
myself. I'm aware you're no longer my legal ward now
that you're twenty-one, so I can't clap you into prison
as an incorrigible minor, but you were working at my
establishment when that unfortunate incident took
place. You maliciously assaulted a customer. I'm quite
certain any magistrate would find that a grave offense
indeed."

I said nothing. My heart was no longer palpitating,
but I felt as though I were encased in ice. Marie reached
up to touch a bright henna curl, black feathers fluttering. Her glittery green eyes held mine, full of triumph.
She had me exactly where she wanted me, she believed.
She expected me to cringe, to cower. I gazed at her
coldly, showing not the least fear, but I began to tremble
inside and knew I couldn't maintain this calm demeanor much longer.

"The charge would never hold up," I said.

"You don't know the magistrates, my dear. They're
almost as corrupt as the criminals they sentence. For
a fee, they can be persuaded to be very accommodating.
There's also the matter of my diamond earrings. They're
missing. They've been missing ever since the night you
ran away. I can only assume you took them from my
room. Theft is a hanging offense," she added.

"If it's money you're after, Marie, I have none."

"You have something far more valuable," she told
me. "I'm not an unreasonable woman, my dear. I just
want my beloved stepdaughter to come back where she
belongs. Clinton Meredith is out of the picture now,
alas. He was in love with you, Angela—genuinely in
love with you, strange as that might seem. He blamed
himself for what happened. He left London some time
ago, but—there are a number of gentlemen far wealthier, far more important who would pay a king's ransom
to possess the celebrated Angel in Scarlet."

I stared at her—the coarse, jowly, painted face, the
outrageous red hair, the gaudy, vulgar clothes—and I
found it hard to believe such evil could exist. She had
always been this way, I realized, but her worst traits

had remained dormant when she was living with my
father. Coming to London and getting her hands on
large sums of money had turned her into some kind of
monster, for monster she was, as foul as the foulest
bawd in St. Giles. She had sold her own daughters, and
now she thought she was going to sell me.

"I'm not going to whore for you, Marie."

"Such an unpleasant word, my dear."

"Never," I said.

"Things haven't been going well of late," she continued. "We've had a number of losses at Marie's Place
and, frankly, the novelty has worn off, and we're not
getting the business we were. I'm losing money every
night, and, I'm sad to say, my arrangement with Mr.
Gresham has gone amiss. It seems he came back un-
expectedly from a business trip and found Janine in bed
with a soldier she had met the *one* time she decided to
take a walk in the park. Gresham threw her out. He
also demanded immediate payment of all the money
he says he *loaned* me so I could open Marie's Place—
he claims he'll have me in debtor's prison if the money
isn't forthcoming."

"That's too bad," I said.

Marie patted her hair again and smiled another tight
smile.

"He hasn't a prayer of getting it, of course. We signed
papers, and I feel sure they'd hold up in court, but I *do*
find myself in an awkward financial position. You can
understand why I was so delighted to locate you at last,
my dear. With your new and quite unexpected fame I
should be able to make a fortune—for both of us, my
dear. I wouldn't be a bit surprised if we snared a member of the Royal Family—they say the Duke of Cumberland is always scouting for new amusement."

"I think you'd better leave," I told her.

"I suggest you start packing. I believe there's a coach
leaving for London at six. I'd like for us to be on it."

"Get out, Marie. I'm not going anywhere with you."

"I think you'd better reconsider, my dear. If I leave
without you, I fully intend to go straight to Bow Street

and press charges. You stole my diamond earrings, pet. You'll hang for it."

"I think not," James Lambert said.

The door had been standing open all this time, and he marched into the room with a murderous expression on his face. His mouth was tight. His eyes flashed dangerously. There were two bright spots of pink on his cheekbones, the rest of his face chalk white. Marie stumbled back, startled out of her wits. He glared at her, and for a moment I thought he was actually going to murder her right before my eyes. He restrained himself. It took a great deal of effort. I could tell that. Nostrils flaring, fists clenched, he held back and gained control of himself and that hot rage slowly cooled into an icy anger that was even more intimidating.

"The lady asked you to leave," he said, and his voice was like steel. "I suggest you leave quickly, before I do something I wouldn't regret at all."

Still shaken, Marie managed to draw herself up with nervous hauteur. "Who the hell are *you?*" she demanded.

"I'm the man who happens to be a close personal friend of Mr. John Fielding who happens to be Chief Magistrate at Bow Street, in charge of *all* criminal prosecutions on the street. I'm the man who's going to call on my mate Fielding and file charges against you for blackmail, extortion, procuring and—oh yes, theft as well. Seems my gold watch fob is missing. I can and will provide four straw men who will testify they saw you lift it from my pocket. Theft is a *hang*ing offense, I believe, and I for one will cheer when I watch you swinging from Tyburn Tree."

These words were delivered in a cold, lethal voice, and Marie grew pale beneath the heavy layers of makeup. Lambert moved slowly toward her, pacing like a panther, and Marie stepped back, hitting the backs of her legs against the sofa and almost falling. She regained her balance and valiantly tried to regain some vestige of composure, but she was shaken to the core, the hideous makeup standing out in garish relief against her pallor. She fidgeted with the black feather boa and brushed at her purple skirt, the corners of her mouth quivering.

"You can't threaten me," she said.

"No?" he inquired.

"I know my rights. This—my stepdaughter caused me to lose a huge amount of money, and—and I intend to—"

He smiled. It was an absolutely chilling smile. Marie cut herself short. He was standing not two feet away from her, looming over her, smiling that chilling smile, his green-brown eyes gleaming with deadly purpose. Marie swallowed and leaned back, plopping down on the sofa. Lambert seized her arm roughly and jerked her to her feet.

"I meant every word I said," he informed her, and his voice was soft now, almost tender. "I'm a very powerful man, Mrs. Howard, and I have very powerful friends, and I'll destroy you quite cheerfully if you so much as breathe a word of accusation against this young woman. She's under *my* protection now, and believe me, madame, you don't want to have me for an enemy. Do you hear me? Answer me!"

The last two words lashed the air like a whip cracking. Marie was shaking now, her double chins bobbing. James Lambert tightened his grip on her arm and leaned down until his face was inches from her own.

"I told you to answer me," he said.

"I—I hear you," she stammered.

"I ought to go to Fielding anyway, just to make sure you don't cause trouble. He's a very moral man, very upright. Has an aversion to procuring. When he learns you've been running a brothel, when he learns you set your own daughters up with wealthy old men, he'll not be lenient."

"I—"

"When he learns you stole my gold watch fob, he's bound to sentence you to hang. Perhaps you and I both will take the six o'clock coach for London. Perhaps I should take you to London myself, take you directly to

Fielding's office and press charges. That way I won't have to worry about you."

"I—I won't—I didn't mean—"

"Come along!" he said sharply.

James Lambert strode purposefully toward the door, dragging her along with him. Marie tottered, stumbling. He jerked her into the hall and dragged her toward the staircase. I stepped to the door, watching, and I seemed to be in the middle of an ugly dream. He let go of her wrist and said something to her, and Marie seemed to be pleading. I couldn't hear her words. After a moment he nodded curtly, seized her shoulders, whirled her around and gave her a brutal push toward the stairs. She lurched forward and grabbed hold of the banister, and I turned and moved to the center of the room and stopped and closed my eyes, trying to shut the ugliness out of my mind.

"It's all right," he said.

He came into the room and moved behind me and rested his hands on my shoulders, gently massaging my flesh, and then he turned me around and pulled me into his arms and held me loosely, stroking the back of my head. I longed to let him console me, longed to melt against him and cling to his strength, but I was afraid of my own weakness. I pulled away.

"I'm fine," I said.

"You look pale. You were trembling."

"How—how much did you hear?"

"Enough. Dottie told me the whole story some time ago. I wanted to check a passage in one of those books I gave you. I came up to fetch it, and I heard her threaten you. I wanted to kill her."

"I—for a moment I thought you actually would."

"She's shaking like jelly," he told me, "convinced she's in danger of imminent arrest. Like most bullies, she's a sniveling coward when faced with superior strength. Put the fear of God in her, I did. Scared her good and proper. She won't bother you again, I promise."

"Do you really know John Fielding?"

"Never met him," he confessed, "but my father was

great friends with his brother Henry, the novelist-
magistrate. Chap who wrote *Tom Jones,* you know. I
remember Henry well—he used to take me and my
brother Robert into his lap and tell us most improper
stories. Are you all right now?"

I nodded, composed now. I asked him which book he
needed. He told me. I got it from the desk and handed
it to him. He took it silently and looked into my eyes
and somehow I knew he was thinking of those few moments when he held me in his arms. Neither of us spoke.
Something passed between us, something both of us
fully understood. I lowered my eyes. He said he would
see me at dinner. He left. I closed the sitting-room door
and turned, leaning against it, wondering how I would
cope with this new problem. I wanted him. I couldn't
deny it. I knew he wanted me, too.

I didn't go down to dinner. I wrote a brief note telling
him that I had a mild headache and preferred to stay
in my room. I gave it to one of the maids, and she took
it to him. I ordered a bath and soaked for a long time
in the water I had scented with essence of violet, reveling in the luxury of French soap which made my skin
feel silky to the touch. The water was hot, relaxing,
and I washed my hair as well, later drying it with a
soft towel and brushing it until it fell to my shoulders
in gleaming, luxuriant waves. The evening was mild.
I left the French windows open, and a gentle breeze
stirred the curtains, causing them to billow into the
room like thin silken sails.

The bath had helped a great deal, but I was restless,
filled with a tremulous feeling as though my whole body
tingled with a curious anticipation, flesh and bone and
blood aglow. At eleven I slipped into a nightgown of
white faille embroidered with minuscule, almost invisible blue flowers. There was an insert of pale blue ribbon that tied in a small bow beneath my breasts, the
gown spilling to my bare feet in a wispy cascade. It was
a fragile, frivolous garment, and, where it touched, the
cloth seemed to caress my skin. I blew out the candles.
Moonlight floated into the rooms, transforming both

into bowers of misty blue-gray shadow ashimmer with pale silver rays.

I couldn't sleep. I knew that. I didn't even try. Instead I stepped out onto the verandah and stood at the railing. The verandah extended all the way around this floor, a staircase at one side leading down to the gardens. It was a lovely night, moonlight coating the ground with pale silver, trees casting velvety black shadows. The house was quiet, as was the town, the silence strangely underlined by the soft rustle of leaves and the plaintive song of a solitary bird somewhere in the distance. The town was etched in black and pale gray and silver, while the surrounding hills were black, stained with purple. The night sky was a deep ash gray stained with amethyst and agleam with a thousand stars. The beauty of the night stirred me, seemed to beckon to a beauty dormant within me, craving release.

I don't know how long I stood there, bathed in moonlight and surrounded by shadow. The gentle night breeze stroked my bare arms and shoulders. The frail cloth of my nightgown molded itself against my naked body. I sighed, listening to the whisper of rustling leaves, aching with expectancy, and when I heard the soft pad of footsteps on the verandah I wasn't really surprised. I turned, and I saw him moving toward me, now in moonlight, now in shadow. He was carrying a bottle and two glasses, and as he drew nearer I saw that he was wearing a heavy satin dressing robe. He set the glasses and bottle on the railing and grinned, looking at me with mischievous eyes.

"I finished the play," he said.

"Did you?"

"Thought we should celebrate. I slipped down to the wine cellar and stole a bottle of Mrs. Lindsey's best, filched a couple of crystal glasses, too. The champagne is cold as ice—hope I didn't catch a chill in the cellar."

He picked up the bottle and worked with the cork until it popped loudly. He poured champagne into both glasses and set the bottle down and handed me one of the glasses, jaunty as a boy. I knew I should send him away or at least go inside and put on my clothes, but I didn't. I took the champagne and sipped it as he tightened the sash of the loose navy blue satin robe which kept threatening to spill open.

"Mrs. Lindsey would be very upset if she knew you were here," I said.

"That's why I slipped out through the gardens and up the staircase. I didn't want to disturb anyone. Good champagne, isn't it?"

"It's delicious. I—I shouldn't be drinking it."

"Why not?"

"Champagne does things to me—makes me quite giddy."

"Drink up," he said.

He grinned again, and I was suddenly very nervous.

"This—this is highly improper."

"Of course it is," he admitted. "I think it's time both of us stop being so bloody proper. I want you, Angel. You want me."

"That isn't—"

"Don't deny it. I've been very patient. I've been very proper. I've wanted you from the first."

"Ours is a business arrangement. We—"

"There's no reason why we can't enjoy ourselves as well. You need me, Angel. You were hurt very badly— I know all about the stableboy, you see—and you believe love is something grim and solemn and painful. It needn't be. It can be light and charming, even amusing."

"I'm not in love with you," I said.

"Nor am I prepared to pledge eternal vows, but I do find you an enchanting creature and I happen to be extremely fond of you. You're delectable, delightful, engaging, gorgeous—and I want you quite madly. I don't offer you solemn love nor soulful devotion. I offer you affection—and fun."

"I don't want to be hurt again."

"I don't want to hurt you. I want to make you happy. I want to make you smile, make you laugh."

His voice was seductive, ever so persuasive, and in

the moonlight his eyes gleamed darkly. He was standing very close. I could smell his skin, his hair, and I
could feel his presence. Like a magnet, it was, drawing
me to him, and I hadn't the will to resist, nor did I want
to. A smile played on his full lips, curving gently, a
lovely smile, and that errant wave had fallen across his
brow again. Moonlight spilled hazily over the railing,
bathing us both in soft silver. The bird continued to
sing its plaintive song, closer now, in a tree nearby. I
drank my champagne, looking at him, filled with a
delicious sense of expectancy I couldn't deny. He moved
nearer and touched my hair.

"It's time for you to forget the past. It's time for you
to start living, start savoring the joys of here and now."

"Is that from one of your plays?"

"As a matter of fact—I believe it is."

"You're a complete rogue."

"I don't deny it."

"I'd be an utter fool to get involved with you."

"Be a fool," he begged.

"I think I'd better have another glass of champagne."

"Do. Here, give me your glass."

"I suppose you think it'll be easier if you get me
drunk," I said, taking the brimming glass. "I suppose
you think I'm easy prey—a snap to seduce."

"You wrong me," he protested.

"You've treated me like a sister for weeks."

"I know. I didn't want to rush you. I wanted to give
you time. I wanted to be sure."

"And you're sure?"

"This afternoon, after I threw that horrible woman
out, when I held you in my arms, I knew. I knew you
wanted me as much as I wanted you. If that sounds like
something from one of my plays, I'm sorry."

"You haven't a sincere bone in your body."

"But I have an overwhelming yen for you," he purred.

Oh, he was wily, all right. He was smooth as silk,
an accomplished womanizer, but he was so engaging,
so appealing, and I was no longer a child. I wasn't fooled
for a minute. He wasn't taking me in. I had my eyes

wide open, and I knew exactly what I was doing. It wasn't the mood, the moonlight, the marvelous champagne. I was grown up, yes, and I was going to take a lover, because *I* wanted to. I did want to forget the past. I did want to start living. It was time, and he was a magnificent male, utterly irresistible in that slippery navy blue satin robe, with that heavy wave slanting across his brow.

"You're not seducing me," I informed him.

"Of course not. I wouldn't dream of such a thing."

I drank the rest of my champagne. He arched a brow, amused. I gave him a defiant look.

"I'm taking you as—as I would take a bonbon," I informed him, "purely for my own enjoyment."

"You're frightfully sophisticated," he said, "very much the woman of the world. Read a lot of novels, don't you?"

"You're mocking me."

"You're far too adorable to mock. I think we've talked enough now. We've much more delightful things to do."

He set his glass down on the railing and took mine and set it down too and then he pulled me loosely, lightly into his arms and kissed my hair and told me it smelled of violets and kissed my temple and said my skin was like silk. His lips were warm and moist and seemed to burn my flesh and a dozen delicious sensations exploded inside me as he drew me closer and buried his lips in the soft curve of my throat. I arched my back and slipped my arms around him and ran my palms over his broad back, satin smooth and slippery beneath my palms. He made murmuring noises and drew me closer still, our bodies melded together, his legs trapping one of my own between them, and I clung to him and closed my eyes, savoring the enchantment, savoring the bliss as his lips closed over mine and began to tease and torment, finally parting, possessing. I seemed to be spinning in a magical void of sensations, and the sensations grew and grew, stronger and sweeter by the moment until I was quite dizzy with delight.

"My God," I whispered when he pulled back.

"What's wrong?"

"You're not wearing anything under that robe."

"I came prepared."

"You're outrageous."

"Utterly," he said.

He smiled a sheepish smile, and I was absolutely enchanted. I touched his lean cheek with my fingertips and gently rubbed the skin and then examined that crook in his nose and finally traced the curve of his smile with the ball of my thumb, leaning back against the arm still curled around my waist. He pulled me closer and gave me several quick, fervent kisses and then lifted me up into his arms and carried me through the opened French window and the thin curtain enveloped us both for a moment and he stumbled and almost dropped me and I tried not to laugh, feeling deliciously lighthearted, feeling joyous, even as need surged inside.

He dropped me on the bed. I bounced. He wiped his brow from the exertion and sighed and looked down at me and smiled again and I smiled, too, completely uninhibited now, feeling inordinately fond of him, feeling playful, laughing as he struggled to untie his sash. He scowled and finally got it loose and chucked off the robe and stood there naked in the moonlight tall and, frankly, a bit too lean, though superbly muscled, and ready, too, unquestionably ready, throbbing with desire.

"You're too lean," I said.

"And you're too bloody heavy. Think I strained my back, carrying you like that."

"I am *not* heavy."

"You're no sylph, I assure you."

"I resent that!"

"Shall we fight?"

"Let's," I said.

And he pounced upon me and we wrestled vigorously and it was joyous and he pinioned me and the match continued and it was delightful and he entered me and I writhed and he bucked and I thrashed and he plunged and it was glorious, glorious, sensations shimmering, soaring, and I fought and he retaliated and I gave and he took and he gave and I took and sensations swelled and shattered and the victory was his but the reward was mine, ecstatic bliss that glowed inside like golden ashes long after the explosion was over.

Bedclothes atangle, moonlight spilling into the room like silver mist, his body lightly coated with perspiration, sprawling all akimbo, his right leg over both mine, his arm cradling me to him, his head on my shoulder, his hair moist, his breathing heavy as he slept. I stroked his hair and savored his weight and his warmth and the wonder of it all, and this wasn't love, no, not love, but he was endearing and engaging and I felt deep affection and it might not be solemn and forever but it was enchanting indeed. He had given back to me that part of myself I thought gone forever, and I was whole again. I slept finally and sometime during the night I woke up to find him nuzzling my throat and squeezing my breasts and I shifted position and he rolled atop me and I clasped his bare buttocks and we made love again, lazily, sleepily, and it was even more enchanting than our rowdy bout had been, wonderfully fulfilling.

Strong morning sunlight awoke me and I sighed and opened my eyes and struggled into a sitting position. He muttered angrily in his sleep, not pleased at being disturbed. He was spread out all over the bed, hogging it quite outrageously, on his back, chest bare, one leg sticking out of the tangle of sheets at his waist. Hair spilled over his eyes. I smiled and brushed it back and rested my hand on his cheek and he muttered and turned over, almost knocking me out of bed. I adjusted the bodice of my nightgown and smoothed the skirt and began to think of hot black coffee, and then I heard the noises. Servants were bustling about the house. People were strolling on the lawn, talking quietly. The clock across the room showed nine fifteen. I was horrified, then I was amused. I could barely restrain my mirth.

"Jamie," I said.

He grunted. I ran my fingers across his chest.

"I think you'd better get up," I said.

"Ummm," he moaned, grimacing.

I smiled. I poked him in the ribs with my fingertip.

He awoke with a start. He sat up. He heard the noises and saw the clock.

"My God!" he cried. "Everyone's up!"

"So it would seem."

"I could murder you, Angel! Why did you let me *sleep* so late?"

"It's not my fault. I just woke up myself."

"The halls are swarming with servants! People are mobbing the lawn! Mrs. Lindsey is probably lurking on the stairs! I'm stark naked and have nothing to wear but my robe! How in hell am I supposed to get back down to my rooms?"

"That's your problem," I said sweetly.

He grabbed my throat. Life with James Lambert might be hazardous and hectic, but it would certainly never be dull.

Book Three

Angel
London

Chapter Thirteen

The footlights blazed, illuminating the wonderfully authentic dressing room set with its mildewed walls and littered dressing table and rack of gaudy costumes. In tight plum-colored velvet breeches and a white silk blouse with full belling sleeves, I primped before the mirror, chestnut waves piled atop my head and concealed by a jaunty plum felt pirate's hat. I grinned and looked at the big box of chocolates and smothered a giggle. The audience grew hushed with expectancy as the dressing room door opened and Megan stepped onstage, a vision in golden brocade. There was a scattering of applause, for ever since her appearance in a minor role in *The Goldsmith's Wife* three years ago, Megan had been a favorite with the public, one of the most popular supporting players on the London stage. She paused, giving me a haughty look, then swept regally over to the mirror and began to fuss with her long auburn waves.

"How are you feeling, Moll?" I asked sweetly.

"Very well, thank you!" she snapped.

"You look a little yellow," I told her. "How's your stomach?"

"A bit nervous," she confessed, "but it isn't every night a girl goes to Whitehall. I must say, Nell, you're being very big about it. I know you hoped to attract the King yourself—capering about in those indecent tights—but he didn't even *see* you with me on hand."

"'Tis true," I said mournfully. "With the beautiful Moll Davis on stage, no one's going to notice little Nell Gwynn—not even the King. We've been rivals for a long time, Moll, but I *do* wish you success tonight. That's the reason I brought you the chocolates."

"So kind of you," she replied. "They're delicious—a most unusual flavor."

"Why don't you have another?" I suggested.

Megan took one of the chocolates and plopped it into her mouth, then began to unhook her gown. I scurried over to help her, repressing another giggle. A lout in the pit gave an appreciative whistle as she stepped out of the gown and smoothed down the bodice of the extremely revealing yellow silk petticoat. She hung the gown up on the rack and, suddenly, clutched her stomach in agony.

"Something wrong, Moll?" I inquired.

She stared at me and then stared at the box of chocolates, and realization dawned. I made a face at her. She lunged at me, knocking the hat off my head, seizing my hair.

"You're a whore, Nell Gwynn!"

"And tonight I'll be the King's whore! Moll Davis is going to be quite indisposed."

I pulled free and gave her a shove. She stumbled and almost fell and then lunged at me again, grabbing my shoulders, shaking me savagely. I made a fist, driving it into her stomach. She screamed and tumbled to the floor, pulling me down with her. We rolled about, fighting viciously and doing a most impressive job of it after weeks of rehearsal. She kicked and thrashed and pulled my hair and I rolled free. Megan stood up on wobbly legs and made a retching noise and then rushed offstage. I leaped nimbly to my feet, brushed myself off and then took the golden gown from the rack and held it up in front of me.

"I'll wear a hooded cloak over it," I said. "No one will be any the wiser. They'll think I'm Moll. Tonight Your Majesty is going to have a marvelous surprise. Little Nellie is going to Whitehall!"

The curtain fell to thunderous applause, and I hurried off into the wings. Megan caught me and gave me an exuberant hug, beaming.

"We did it, luv! I was afraid we'd never be able to pull it off properly. You were magnificent!"

"So were you," I assured her. "I thought you were actually going to pull my hair out by the roots."

"I think we have another success, luv. *My Charming Nellie* is bound to run for months!"

"Out of the way, ladies!" a stagehand barked. "We've got twenty minutes to dismantle the set and put up the next one. You're in the way!"

"Pardon us for breathing, luv," Megan told him. "You look a bit nervous, Angel."

"Opening nights always give me the jitters. I just know something is going to happen in the last act. Those damn spaniels! He *would* insist on using them."

"They behaved perfectly during rehearsals, luv. Come on, I'll walk you to your dressing room. Dottie will give you a cup of tea. You're going to be wonderful in the last act, though I'm not at all sure about that oaf who's playing the King. I never could understand why Lambert took him on in the first place. He's a complete boor, hasn't a jot of acting experience."

"He's terribly handsome, though," I teased.

"If you like the rugged, military type. I understand he was a soldier before he decided to try his hand at acting. He's far too tall," she continued, "and altogether too sure of himself. Thinks he's God's gift to the ladies. He accosted me in the Green Room after rehearsals last night, got very cheeky with me, tried to steal a kiss!"

"Oh?"

Megan shoved a long auburn wave from her temple

as we moved down the hall. "I gave him what for, I can assure you. Sent him packing good and proper. Six feet four if he's an inch, and the body of an athlete. I never *could* abide men with dark blond hair and roguish brown eyes, luv."

"Charles is a dear," I told her. "He might not be a consummate actor yet but the ladies in box, pit and gallery don't seem to mind a bit. You could actually hear them sighing when he stepped onstage in Act One. He's going to be very successful."

A door opened and the actor in question stepped into the hall, momentarily blocking our way. Charles Hart was indeed tall, and his brown eyes were indeed roguish, though his dark blond hair was currently concealed by the long, rolled brown wig he wore as King Charles II. In the silver-buckled royal blue pumps, the white silk stockings and the breeches and frock coat of royal blue brocade, he cut an impressive figure indeed. The frock coat was embroidered with silver floral designs, and silver lace spilled from his throat and cuffs. He smiled a most engaging smile and executed a low bow, exuding virility the elegant attire merely accentuated.

"Good evening, Mrs. Howard, Mrs. Sloan."

"Hello, Charles," I said. "Ready for our big scene?"

"A bit nervous," he confessed. "I still haven't got the hang of this acting business, I fear. Should never have let Lambert talk me into it. I know I made a fool of myself earlier."

"You certainly did!" Megan snapped. "Posturing like a peacock! I'm surprised they didn't boo you off the stage."

"That's very unkind, Megan," I scolded. "Untrue, too. The ladies adored you, Charles. You did a very competent job."

He thanked me with his eyes. I liked Hart a great deal. In his late twenties, he had a casual, confident air and none of the posturing artifice of most actors. Big, easygoing, good-natured, he was extremely attractive. Megan hadn't bothered to slip a robe over the revealing yellow petticoat. Those roguish brown eyes took in the breasts encased in fragile yellow lace, then looked back at me.

"Blew my lines twice," he said. "If Brown hadn't covered for me I'd have frozen completely."

"We all blow our lines now and then. You're going to be tremendous in the last act, Charles. Don't fret. We're going to knock them dead."

"Rather face a firing squad," he told me, and then he turned to Megan and smiled another smile. "You going to the party at Bedford's Coffee House afterwards, Mrs. Sloan?"

"Of course not," she said. "Since Lambert's giving it for the cast and crew, since this just happens to be the biggest role I've ever had, I thought I would go home alone and sulk."

"Hear you haven't got an escort. I'd be happy to take you."

"That's terribly sweet of you, luv, but I wouldn't feel right about breaking one of my cardinal rules."

"What rule is that?"

"Never associate with an actor outside the theater. We're in rather a hurry, Mr. Hart. Do you think you could let us pass? Angel has a costume change, and I have things to do."

Hart grinned, not at all put off by her snippy behavior. He reached up to rub the deep cleft in his chin, wide lips curling. He knew Megan was attracted to him—it had been obvious to everyone since the first day of rehearsal—and he was content to bide his time. He made another bow and stepped aside. Megan gave him a frosty look as we moved on past. Hart chuckled, strolling on toward the stage.

"The nerve of him!" Megan exclaimed. "Just because he looks like a rough hewn Adonis he thinks he can just snap his fingers and have any woman he wants! All the super girls might swoon at the sight of him, but I've got self respect. I've also got far too much good sense."

"How long *has* it been since Andrew left?" I inquired.

"Three months," she said. "The flat has been rather

lonely, but I'm well rid of him. Do yourself a favor, luv, never fall in love with a lawyer. They're always cross-examining you."

We reached the dressing room door. Megan gave me another hug, told me she would see me during curtain calls and hurried down the hall to the small dressing room she shared with Mrs. Perry, who played Castle-maine. I opened the door and stepped inside, astounded anew by the baskets of flowers that took up every foot of available space. There were pink roses from Gains-borough, lovely mauve hyacinths from Boswell, glo-rious blue larkspurs and purple iris from David Garrick and a gigantic basket of red-veined, pearly white tulips from Richard Sheridan, Betsy's brother, who wanted me to play the lead in his next play. Dottie looked up as I entered, the inevitable cup of tea in her hand.

"Here you are, dear. We've got—what? Twenty min-utes?"

"Thirty-five," I said. "I don't appear for the first fif-teen minutes of Act Two. Charles has an argument with Castlemaine and a confrontation with the Duke of Buckingham."

"We've plenty of time, then. I'll make you a cup of raspberry tea, dear. You look as though you need one. Nerves frayed?"

"Shredded," I confessed. "Thank God for you, Dottie. I could never make it through an opening night without you."

Dottie smiled and began to brew the tea, looking quite elegant in a watered gray silk gown with a white lace fichu and a purple velvet waistband, a purple vel-vet bow affixed behind her high gray pompadour. Her eyelids were coated with mauve shadow, her lips painted pale pink. Dottie had helped me dress when *The Gold-smith's Wife* opened three years ago—what a nervous fit I had been in *that* night—and, although I had a dresser of my own, Dottie had taken over the job every opening night since. It had become a tradition.

"Were you watching from the wings?" I asked.

"I saw most of the first act. It seems to be going beautifully. The audience loves it."

"I hate this play!" I snapped. I slipped off my pumps and perched on the edge of the dressing stool to remove my stockings. "It should be light and engaging, a comedy. It's altogether too ponderous and heavy-handed, too much emphasis on history. I *told* him so, but *he's* the playwright. It's the most ambitious, the most spectacular play he's ever mounted—I quote, of course. If he would concentrate less on spectacle and more on character he just might produce something critics would appreciate."

"He'd rather please the paying customers," Dottie said kindly. "It's going to be another huge success, dear, just like all six of the other plays you've done together. It seems the combination of Angel Howard and James Lambert invariably ensures success."

"It's *me* they come to see," I told her.

"That sounds suspiciously like something Coral Tallent would have said, my dear."

"I suppose it does. I'm sorry, Dottie. You know I'm always a horror opening nights. Poor Mrs. Tallent. I wonder what became of her."

"She's probably selling apples—or herself—on a street corner somewhere. I take it you and Lamb had a fight this afternoon."

"Last night," I said. "I begged him to abandon the spaniels. He insisted on keeping them in for historical verisimilitude—as if the public gives a damn about *that*. Charles the Second was always surrounded by a pack of frisky spaniels so we must have spaniels onstage during the last act. I can *smell* disaster."

I took off the white silk blouse and wriggled out of the plum velvet breeches. Dottie hung them up and handed me a blue silk robe which I slipped on, tying the sash around my waist. She stirred a spoonful of thick honey into my cup of raspberry tea and handed it to me. I sipped it slowly, sitting at the dressing table, studying my face in the mirror. I was twenty-four years old now, and little of the girl remained. The fresh glow of youth had been replaced by a patina of cool sophistication. Three years working in the theater and living with James Lambert gave a girl maturity, all right. Angela had been transformed into Angel, the girl into a woman.

"I look old," I complained.

"You look grown up," Dottie corrected me. "You're far more beautiful than you were three years ago, and you know it."

"So much has happened during those three years," I sighed.

"So much indeed. You've had the lead in six hugely successful plays. You've become the most famous, the most popular and the most beloved actress on the London stage—all because Lamb believed in you."

"I've worked like the devil," I said defensively.

"You have indeed."

"The critics say I have flair and style and a delicious light touch," I informed her. "They say I'm wasted in these turgid historical melodramas."

"I've read the reviews, dear."

"Davy Garrick wants me to join him at Drury Lane."

"So I've heard."

"Richard Sheridan wants me to do his next play. *The Rivals* was a glorious success with critics *and* the public. *The School For Scandal* ran for months last year."

"I know, dear. I did the costumes."

"Oliver Goldsmith bemoans the fact that I wasn't in the original production of *She Stoops To Conquer*. He wants me to play Kate Hardcastle in the revival he plans to do next November."

"You're very much in demand," Dottie agreed. "You clearly don't need Lamb any more. Why don't you accept one of those highly tempting offers?"

"One of these days I just might!"

Dottie smiled to herself and handed me a clean cloth, and I began to pat my face and freshen my makeup. When I had finished, I brushed my hair until it fell in gleaming chestnut waves. Dottie took my silver and violet gown from the rack, handling it with loving care.

It was the most elaborate, the most expensive gown she had ever done, and she was justifiably proud of her craftsmanship. I took off my robe and put on the silver-tissue petticoat with its half dozen full, spreading skirts. The bodice was cut quite low, leaving most of my bosom bare, the waist extremely snug. I stepped into the high-heeled violet slippers, and Dottie helped me into the gown.

"Where *is* Lamb?" she asked. "I haven't seen him tonight."

"He's skulking around the front foyer, tearing his hair, suffering the agonies of the damned, convinced the play will be a disastrous failure—you know how he is opening nights. He's never fit to live with until at least sixty people pound him on the back and assure him the play will run forever."

I slipped my arms into the short puffed sleeves and adjusted the bodice as Dottie began to do up the tiny hooks in back. This done, she spread the skirt out over the underskirts, smoothing it carefully, then stepped back. Framed by baskets of flowers, I stood in front of the full length mirror. The shimmering silver cloth was embroidered with tiny violet silk flowers, and the skirt parted in front, draped to display a sumptuous violet velvet underskirt. With the short puffed sleeves worn off the shoulder, the form-fitting bodice cut daringly low, the gown was a bold, magnificent creation.

"It's absolutely gorgeous, Dottie," I said. "It must have taken weeks to embroider all those delicate violet flowers. I—sometimes I still miss working at the shop."

"And I miss you, too, dear. I have the Simpson sisters now. They're very skillful, very efficient, work like Trojans but, alas, have all the personality of prunes. I get the work done, but the place isn't the same since you and Megan left. I'm proud of you both nevertheless."

"Megan's done wonderfully well. Jamie didn't want to use her for *The Goldsmith's Wife*—I had to fight for her—and then she almost walked off with the play. Audiences love her."

Andy Dobson rapped on the door and opened it to

inform me that the curtain was going up. I patted my hair and then put on the glittering diamond and amethyst necklace Dottie handed me. The loops of diamonds flashed with a shimmery fire, the amethyst pendants glowing a warm violet-pink. Although merely paste, they looked real enough, especially crafted by one of London's finest jewelers. I sighed, fastening the matching bracelet around my wrist.

"Mrs. Perry wears *real* diamonds as Castlemaine. Her lover, the Duke of Ambrose, gave them to her, and she insists on flaunting them."

"Most unwise of her, I should think, with Lord Blackie on such a rampage," Dottie said. "You can't open a paper nowadays without reading about another of his exploits. Captured the public's fancy, he has—haven't seen anything like it since the heyday of Jonathan Wild. One of these nights he's likely to break into Perry's flat and politely divest her of those diamonds."

"And it would serve the slut right. I can't abide the woman—always giving herself airs just because she's got a noble protector—but she *is* a gifted actress. I'd better go, Dottie."

"You're going to be marvelous, dear. I'll have a fresh cup of tea waiting for you after your curtain calls."

I moved back down the hall toward the wings, careful not to let my spreading skirts brush against the dusty flats. I stepped over a coil of rope, moved around fake marble columns the crew hadn't yet stored away. It was dim and shadowy back here, but I knew my way by heart. The Lambert was like a second home to me, every nook and cranny as familiar as the back of my hand, and I had grown so accustomed to the smell of dust and mildew, hemp, stale greasepaint and powder that I no longer even noticed it. I smiled at a stagehand and moved on into the wings, standing in the shadows and watching the activity onstage, fighting the panic as I always did.

Three years it had been since I made my debut in *The Goldsmith's Wife*. Six plays I had done. I was a seasoned actress now. I was a professional. I still felt

sheer terror every time I started to go onstage. My
throat tightened. My mouth went dry. I felt a hollow
sensation in the pit of my stomach. I was going to forget
all my lines. I was going to trip and fall flat on my face.
Everyone was going to laugh at me. I was going to make
a bloody fool of myself. I took several deep breaths.
You're going to be perfectly all right, I assured myself.
You're going to be fine. You *always* feel this way. You'll
go on and you won't trip over your skirts and you won't
forget your lines and you *will* control this trembling.
Why the hell do I *do* it? Why the hell did I let him talk
me into it in the first place? I hate acting. There's nothing glamorous or exciting about it. It's hellishly hard
work. It tears your nerves to shreds. I'm going to throw
up. I can't go on. I can't possibly. I'm ill. There's no way
I'm going to go out there and humiliate myself in front
of hundreds of people.

Charles II and the Duke of Buckingham were having
a heated confrontation in the King's private drawing
room, all done in ivory and gold and pearl gray, pale
violet upholstery covering chairs and sofa. The blasted
spaniels were curled up on a pile of sky blue cushions
near the King's chair. They looked jumpy and on edge.
I closed my eyes for a moment, valiantly struggling for
control. Buckingham confessed that he had indeed been
part of the conspiracy to discredit Nellie, to oust her
from Whitehall, and he admitted that Castlemaine was
behind it, afraid she would be supplanted. Charles sighed
and shook his head and said it was about time for the
beautiful Barbara to make a long visit to her country
estates. Buckingham left. Charles turned to the spaniels and informed them that these meddlesome women
were going to drive him mad with their jealous spats.
Nellie was different, though, he told them. Nellie didn't
give a damn whether he was a king or a pauper. She
was the only woman who had ever loved him for himself, and he'd be damned if he'd let those gorgeous bitches
drive her away... Oh God, he was going to hear the
knock and turn around... I took another deep breath
and swallowed and Angel Howard vanished.

I touched my hair. I brushed my skirt. I became bright, saucy Nellie, all vivacity and sass, still the mischievous scamp of Covent Garden despite the silver and violet gown, despite the jewels. The knock sounded. Charles II turned, arching one brow. I sallied onstage, not waiting to be announced, an engaging, capricious minx who was shockingly irreverent and refused to treat her handsome Charlie like the monarch he was. There were several oh's and ah's at my magnificent gown, then a round of noisy applause. I ignored it, just as I ignored the heat of the footlights and that vast darkness out there filled with staring eyes. I was Nell Gwynn, raffish orange girl and actress now become the King's favorite, and I greeted my King impishly and confessed that yes, I *had* put laxative in Moll Davis's chocolates in order to take her place and yes, I *had* smuggled the handsome lackey into Castlemaine's bedchamber and forged a note requesting Charles to come see her at once on urgent business.

"But I didn't know she was going to jump into bed with him, Sire," I added, ever so winsome. "I thought surely she'd send him away. Bet she was taken aback when you came sauntering into her bedchamber."

"Taken aback and *on* her back," he said solemnly, and then he grinned. "Ah, you're a sly minx, Nellie, a veritable imp."

"'Tis my nature, Sire."

The scene was going remarkably well. The spaniels were behaving themselves, and Charles Hart's casual, laconic delivery was perfectly suited for the role of Charles II. He certainly looked the part in the silver-embroidered blue brocade and long brown wig. He smiled indulgently as I made more confessions of pranks pulled on the beautiful but vicious Castlemaine. "But Sire," I said, "'twas done for love. Were I to lose my handsome Charlie, 'twould break my heart." He was touched by that, so touched he had to turn away—Megan really wasn't at all fair, Hart was quite good and had the makings of a superb leading man. He moved over to his chair and sat down, and I began my big scene wherein

I grew serious, pledged eternal devotion and shed real tears.

I had scarcely started when one of the spaniels got up from its cushion and wandered over to the chair. It sniffed about a moment and then blithely hoisted its hind leg and pissed all over the silk-clad ankle of Charles II. That noble personage turned a ghastly white and looked as though he might faint. The audience howled with boisterous laughter, which caused all four mutts to start barking and scampering about the stage in panic. I thought I might faint myself. I didn't. Murder in my heart, I watched the adorable creatures bounding about and tossed my curls, smiling another winsome smile.

"You *will* surround yourself with spaniels, Sire," I improvised. "Do allow me to remove them."

Charles II nodded regally, almost losing his heavy wig, and as the audience continued to howl. Charming Nellie in her gorgeous gown raced about the stage after the beasts, catching them, cuddling them, cooing and carrying the little horrors into the wings, thrusting them into the arms of their panic stricken trainer and an ashen Andy Dobson. I stepped back onstage and there was thunderous applause and rousing cheers and I desperately tried to remember where we'd been before the pup pissed. The Merry Monarch was gazing glumly at his soggy white silk stocking, still pale, and I smiled once more, vowing that James Lambert would not live to see the morning sun come up.

"'Twill quickly dry, Sire," I said. "A patch of piss never hurt anyone."

"'Tis bloody discomfiting, Nellie. Methinks I'll just take off my shoe and stocking. Will'st thou help me?"

"Sire, I am indeed your humble servant, your own charming Nellie, but there is no need. As I said, 'twill quickly dry. Sit there in your chair like a good King and contemplate the beauty of your Nellie and let her continue. Where were we, Sire?"

"Haven't a clue," he said.

The audience hooted. King Charles sat there in his

sumptuous attire, totally at a loss, and somehow, I know
not how, I managed to improvise until, finally, I picked
up the threads and got back into the scene. I told him
that I cared not if he sat on a throne or if he dwelled
in a hut, he was my handsome Charlie and I loved him
as I had never loved before or would again. Tears glistening prettily on my lashes, I made a low curtsy and
sank to my knees in front of my royal paramour. Deeply
moved, trying in vain to conceal his own emotions, he
rose and took my hand. "Arise, my charming Nellie,"
he commanded, and the curtain slowly fell amidst a
furor of deafening applause.

"Jesus, Angel!" Hart whispered. "I'm sorry!"

"It wasn't your fault, Charles. I *told* that son of a
bitch we shouldn't use those bloody animals, but would
he *listen* to me!"

"I thought I was going to pass out when that creature
lifted its leg."

"You almost did. He's going to pay for this."

"You were magnificent, Angel. The way you handled
yourself—I was ready to rush offstage and out of the
theater and join the Horse Guards again. They kept
laughing and you never once stepped out of character."

"I'm going to kill him," I said. "I'm going to *kill* him."

The curtain began to rise. I smiled at Hart. He smiled
at me and led me to the footlights and bowed to me. I
bowed to him. We bowed to the wildly applauding audience. Charles backed away, leaving me alone, and I
smiled and bowed and blew kisses and turned and held
out my hands, summoning the rest of the company.
They joined me, one by one, each modestly acknowledging their share of applause. Mrs. Perry simpered,
milking it, diamonds flashing. Megan received several
loud cheers. We all joined hands and bowed in unison
and the curtain came back down. The others scurried
into the wings and the curtain rose again to discover
me all alone in the center of the stage. The audience
was standing, cheering, stamping feet, and I bowed,
humbly accepting the boisterous tribute from my public. When they settled down somewhat, I made a charm-

ing speech, thanking them for their reception, and then
James Lambert strode out with a gigantic bouquet of
pink roses. I recognized them. They were the ones
Gainsborough had sent. The cheap son of a bitch had
removed them from my dressing room.

He smiled. He looked very elegant in his black
breeches and frock coat and white satin vest, frothy
white lace at throat and wrists. He handed me the roses.
I accepted them with a radiant smile. He bowed to me,
ever so gallant, and then *he* made a charming speech
in which he declared that his modest little drama would
be an abject failure without his magnificent leading
lady, who had brought it so brilliantly to life. I lowered
my eyes demurely as he rambled on about my talents
and his gratitude and when, at last, the curtain fell for
the final time I gave him a look that should have turned
him to stone. He grinned sheepishly. Temper, Angel, I
reminded myself. Keep your temper. Control. Dignity.
Don't let the sod see how furious you are.

"Mad at me?" he inquired.

"I don't wish to speak to you just now, James."

"You *are* angry. I can tell. You never call me 'James'
unless you're upset about something."

I started toward the wings. He trotted along beside
me. I pretended to ignore him.

"I was wrong about the spaniels," he said chattily.

I didn't reply. I thrust the bouquet of roses into the
arms of a startled stagehand. Several people were waiting in the wings to congratulate me. Seeing my expression, they decided to a man that it might be wise to
wait until later. I swept past them with my chin held
high, my silver skirt swaying, and Mr. James Lambert
was foolish enough to persist, infuriatingly affable,
trying his best to humor me.

"They *did* add an authentic touch," he said.

I said nothing. I moved around the fake columns. He
followed me, courting disaster. Now that the play was
over, lamps had been lighted backstage, and the area
looked even more shabby and disreputable. He caught
up with me and took my arm, forcing me to stop. I

turned and gave him another dangerous look. He wasn't at all intimidated. His green-brown eyes full of masculine appreciation, he treated me to one of those seductive smiles that had made many a woman grow weak in the knees and had, on occasion, had a similar effect on me. Not tonight however. Tonight I was completely immune to his potent male allure and rakish good looks.

"I'm sorry, love," he crooned. "I should have listened to you. I usually do—you have to admit that. We have a perfect partnership. I meant every word I said out there. My modest little drama would be an abject failure had you not brought it so brilliantly to life."

"Please let go of my arm, Mr. Lambert."

"You handled yourself magnificently, love. Professional all the way. I've always said that, while you might not be the *best* actress I've ever worked with, you're hands down the most professional, a terrific little trouper through thick and thin. You really proved your mettle tonight, didn't let it throw you at all, stayed right in character the whole time. I was in back, watching, I was *proud* of you, Angel."

Not the best? I was absolutely livid now.

"It won't happen again," he assured me. "The spaniels are out as of right now."

"Not the best?" I said in a lethal voice.

"Uh—" He realized his mistake and was momentarily at a loss. "That was a slip, love, an unfortunate choice of words. I didn't—uh—I didn't mean it to sound the way it must have sounded. You're upset. You're always this way after an opening. Go change and we'll join our friends at Bedford's and you'll unwind and feel much better."

He actually patted my arm. I casually lifted my skirts and kicked his shin as hard as I could. He let out a yelp and staggered back, hobbling. I moved on to my dressing room, feeling better already. I had learned quite early that the only way to deal with his bullying and bossiness was to fight back, and I fought back with a vengeance. We had had any number of rousing fights during these past three years. The fights were undeniably stimulating. The making up afterwards was invariably divine.

Dottie helped me out of the silver and violet gown and carefully hung it up as I slipped into a silk wrapper and removed my stage makeup. I washed my face and dried it and applied a touch of mauve shadow to my lids, a bit of pink rouge to my lips. I could feel the tension evaporating, anger disappearing, yet when Mr. Lambert opened the door and stuck his head in to ask if I was ready I hurled a pot of face cream at him. It smashed noisily against the wall, barely missing his skull, and he made a hasty retreat. Dottie shook her head. She considered both of us spoiled, unprincipled children and found our fights shockingly unprofessional. She scolded me roundly as she helped me into my crimson tulle petticoat with its multiple layers of skirt floating like soft red petals.

"You could have *killed* him if you'd hit him with that pot."

"I have perfect aim," I informed her. "I wasn't *try*ing to hit him."

"A perfectly good pot of face cream—ruined. And someone is going to have to clean up that mess. Not me, I can assure you. Really, my dear, I've come to expect such shenanigans from Lamb but I should think you'd have a bit more dignity and self-control."

"Dignity and self-control don't work with your friend Lambert. If I didn't hold my own he'd trample me under his feet. He knows just how far he can go and daren't go any further. I have to keep him in line."

"There are gentler means," she pointed out.

"Not with Jamie. Besides, both of us enjoy a good scrap. It relieves tension, and God knows there's enough of that in this crazy profession. Sometimes I wish I'd never taken it up."

"You love it," she retorted. "You were born for the stage. It's made you a very famous woman—a wealthy one as well."

"I never wanted to be famous, and as for wealth— most of my profits go into the next production. *My* money

is backing this play, as well as his. I own a huge chunk
of it."

"Oh?"

"He conned me into it. He invariably does. If this
play failed both of us would be in dire straits. Help me
with the gown, Dottie. Everyone will be waiting for us
at Bedford's."

The gown was a gorgeous crimson brocade with large
puffed sleeves worn off the shoulder, a low-cut bodice,
tight waist and very full skirt that spread over the
underskirts in gleaming folds. The sumptuous cloth was
embroidered all over with delicate flowers of a deeper
crimson silk. Dottie had created the gown for me. In
addition to costumes, she did a complete wardrobe for
me each season for which I happily paid a small fortune.
Angel of Covent Garden must have a bold, dramatic
wardrobe, and who better than Dottie to create it for
me? I fluffed up the sleeves and adjusted the heart-
shaped neckline as she stepped back to admire her
handiwork.

"How do I look?" I inquired.

"Stunning," she admitted. "Not too many women
could carry off a gown that bold. You do it with great
flair." She sighed and shook her head again. "What
became of that sweet, demure young woman who used
to work for me?"

"She grew up," I said. "Jamie claims he's created a
monster. *Have* I become a monster, Dottie?"

"I don't think I'd better answer that, dear."

Bedford Coffee House on King Street, just across from
The Market, was celebrated for its oysters and vastly
popular with theatrical folk. Jamie had taken it over
for the evening for a private party for cast, crew, friends
and journalists, the latter never averse to a free meal
and a plentiful supply of drink and frequently influ-
enced by same. Although it was only a short walk from
the theater, my usually thrifty partner had hired a carriage so that we could arrive in style. He and Dottie
chatted pleasantly during the ride, and he gave my
hand a squeeze as he helped me out of the carriage.

"You look smashing, love," he told me.

"Thank you," I said coolly.

"Wish we didn't have to attend this bloody party," he added. "I'd rather go home and fight some more."

"Oh?"

"Then we could make up," he murmured.

"They're waiting for us, Jamie."

There was a rousing burst of applause as we entered the coffeehouse. We were immediately surrounded and separated, and I found myself being ever so vivacious and charming to a pack of gents from Fleet Street who bombarded me with questions and compliments. Yes, I had been petrified when the pup pissed. No, it had not been planned to liven up the act, the act was lively enough, and the play was Lambert's best, didn't they agree? Yes, it was a delight to play Nell Gwynn, I found her utterly enchanting, and didn't Charles Hart make a wonderful Charles II? He was a dream to work with and was going to be tremendously successful. No, I was not going to go over to Drury Lane. I admired Mr. Garrick tremendously, but I was devoted to Mr. Lambert. Yes, Mr. Gainsborough was here tonight, but only as a friend. He always attended my opening nights. I had no plans to sit for him again any time soon. *An Angel in Scarlet?* It was privately owned, I understood, and I had no idea where it was currently hanging.

James Boswell rescued me, pulling me away from the journalists and handing me a glass of much-needed champagne. Brick red hair neatly brushed, brown eyes full of mischief, he glowed with robust health and exuded hearty charm, looking particularly spruce in a brown velvet frock coat and mustard silk neckcloth. I did a double step as his hand reached for my bottom.

"You haven't changed one bit," I said wryly. "That overactive libido of yours is going to get you into big trouble one of these days."

"Can't resist a well-shaped derriere," he confessed, "and yours, my dear Angel, is the shapeliest in London."

"Thank you for the flowers you sent. They're lovely. Thanks for rescuing me from Fleet Street, too."

"They adore you, those chaps. Always writing articles about Angel of Covent Garden, the most beloved actress in London, simple, unaffected, still does her own shopping at The Market and refuses to give herself airs. The only other person who gets as much coverage is Lord Blackie himself. You're the idols of London—the gentleman housebreaker who wears only black and the actress who is still one of the people."

"I'm not sure I care to be classed with a notorious criminal."

"Oh, Blackie's a hero. Robs only the aristocrats. Never commits violence and speaks in a soft, cultured voice behind that black hood he wears. Invariably gallant to the ladies whose jewels he lifts. Georgiana, Duchess of Devonshire, swears he actually kissed her hand before climbing out the window. Very romantic figure, Lord Blackie. Half the grandes dames in London secretly cherish the hope he'll steal into their bedchambers some lonely night."

I sipped my champagne, glancing around the crowded room, not at all interested in the habits of the much-written-about thief whose nocturnal jaunts were so avidly followed by the public. Boswell lifted a glass of port from the tray of a passing waiter and studied my decolletage with an appreciative eye.

"You, my dear, *have* changed," he informed me. "The beautiful, rather pensive girl I first met at Gainsborough's studio has turned into an incredibly alluring woman."

"Indeed?"

"Why don't you ditch that devilishly handsome rogue you're living with and run off with me?"

"Don't tempt me," I said.

Boswell grinned. "Fighting again? One hears of your frequent scraps, but you're still together, I see. Never known James Lambert to be faithful to one woman for so long."

"He wouldn't dare look at another woman," I said. "He values his health too much."

The Scot chuckled and, catching sight of a particularly buxom young blonde super in a low-cut pink gown, gave me an affectionate hug and headed in her direction. I finished my champagne. Dottie was chatting with David Garrick. Jamie was charming the gents from Fleet Street, plying them with goose-liver pâté and oysters baked in wine sauce and regaling them with humorous backstage anecdotes. The large room with its low-beamed ceiling, vast brick fireplace and white-washed walls hung with copper pans was filled to capacity, a festive air prevailing. Megan, exquisite in a yellow silk gown, was flirting amiably with a trio of actors and studiously ignoring Charles Hart, who stood by with lazy grace and observed her antics with wry amusement. A charming young girl in deep blue taffeta waved at me and came over, pulling along a stocky, ruggedly handsome young man in dapper brown suit and a rather startling pink silk waistcoat embroidered with orange and gold flowers.

"You were marvelous," the girl exclaimed. "I loved what you did with the spaniels."

"Thank you, Betsy."

"You've met my brother, of course?"

"Of course. How are you, Mr. Sheridan?"

"Disgruntled," the young playwright said. "I hate to see an actress with your talent wasted in a clunker like the one I just witnessed. You're far too gifted to be with Lambert. I'm still bitter about not getting you for *A School For Scandal*."

"It was a glorious play."

"Would have been better had you been in it."

"Richard's always been blunt," Betsy told me, giving her brother a disapproving look, "and he's much worse since his success. I *told* you he was going to be successful, remember?"

"I remember it well," I replied. "I'm sorry you disliked the play, Richard. I'm sure I could arrange to have your money refunded."

"The play was Lambert's usual melodramatic claptrap, but you were enchanting, as always, even if you were upstaged by a pack of spaniels. I'm writing a new play, Mrs. Howard, and I intend for you to play the lead, even if I have to challenge Lambert to a duel."

"I'm flattered, Sir. Where on earth did you get that waistcoat?"

"Like it?" he inquired. He grinned, the somber, arrogant playwright giving way to the brash youth of twenty-six. "Betsy says it's much too fussy, but I think it's elegant."

"You have distinctive taste," I said.

Young Mr. Sheridan blinked, not sure whether or not that was a compliment, and his sister smiled and led him over to the buffet tables laden with a tempting array of edibles. Gainsborough, in powdered wig and a sky blue frock coat, managed to extricate himself from the journalist pumping him with questions and came over to greet me. The wig, of course, was slightly askew, and the lace at his throat and wrists looked a little limp. He hugged me and rested his cheek against mine for a moment, and then he held me at arm's length in order to examine me more closely.

"Not the girl I painted," he observed. "Older and wiser—but even more beautiful. Maturity becomes you. When are you coming to visit us again? It's been months since you've been to the studio."

"I dare not visit too often. Mrs. G. keeps feeding me all those teas, and I have a figure to think of. Where is she, by the way?"

"Off to Bath for a short visit. She's sending you a package. Vanilla and chocolate truffles, I believe, filled with creamy nougat and bits of chocolate. Her latest enthusiasm."

"I'll be strong," I promised.

"The play was delightful, Angel. You were the very soul of Nell Gwynn. I loved the bit with the spaniels—haven't laughed so hard in ages. Very clever of Lambert to liven it up that way. Tell me—how ever did they train that mutt to piss on cue?"

"It was *not* in the script," I informed him, "and if I hear one more word about those bloody spaniels I'm going to scream. I told Jamie they were a mistake, but— I'm getting angry all over again. Let's have a bite to eat, Mr. G. You can tell me all about Sir Joshua Reynolds' latest masterpiece."

Mr. G. groaned at the mention of his archrival's name and followed me over to the tables. There were oysters on the half shell, smoked oysters, fried oysters, oysters baked in a variety of sauces, also sliced lamb, roast beef, baked chicken, ham, with all the trimmings. The journalists had already made quite a dent, I observed, and the liquor supply had already been replenished. The party was costing us a tidy sum, but cast and crew had earned it after long months of work, and the gents from Fleet Street would undoubtedly make the ticket-buying public well aware of *My Charming Nellie.* Mr. G. and I took our plates over to a corner table and he told me about his feud with the Royal Academy while we ate. They weren't hanging his paintings prominently enough and he was thinking about resigning. Who needed the R. A. anyway?

Dottie left early, around one, accompanied by David Garrick, who would see her home. Mr. G. left shortly thereafter, complaining that he was far too aged for these noisy, all-night theatrical parties and making me promise to come see him soon. Several of the journalists made friends with the super girls—there was a bevy of them in this particular production—and happily departed with an attractive new companion for the rest of the night. Boswell couldn't keep his hands off the young blonde in pink who, fortunately, was more than receptive to his hearty vulgarity and left with him at three, both of them pleasantly tipsy. I smiled when I saw Megan finally condescend to talk with the patient, lethargic Hart, who plainly intended to have her.

Jamie was moving around the room, attentive to all the women, slapping men on the back, radiating vitality and magnetism. Wavy brown hair tousled, green-brown eyes full of good humor, he grinned at an actor's wry remark and gave him a poke on the arm, then moved on to compliment Betsy on her gown. He was a magnificent host. He was a magnificent man, devastatingly appealing in his black and white attire. Catching my eye, he smiled that engaging smile and waved. I nodded coolly. I wasn't really angry with him, not any longer. It was impossible to stay angry with him. He was a rogue, bossy and overbearing, but I could easily hold my own, and if he had bullied me, he had also nurtured me and devoted all his energies to making me the success I had become. Beneath that rowdy facade, beneath all the bravado and emotional pyrotechnics was a thoughtful, utterly endearing man, and I considered myself the luckiest woman in London. Not that I'd ever let *him* suspect it.

I circulated, chatting with our guests, exhausted to the bone but charming nevertheless. Young Richard Sheridan had had far too much to drink and was vociferously declaring himself the greatest English playwright since Shakespeare, vowing he'd crack the skull of anyone who didn't agree. His sister managed to get some coffee into him and get him out of the place before fisticuffs occurred. I was drinking coffee myself when Megan came over, pouting prettily and pretending an outrage she was far from feeling.

"I can't get *rid* of him," she complained.

"Who?" I inquired.

"Charles Hart! He wants to take me home. I told him it was a very short walk, just across the piazza to Henrietta Street, but he insists. He claims it isn't safe with Lord Blackie on the prowl. I told him I'd take my chances with Lord Blackie, but the lout won't take no for an answer. What am I going to *do,* Angel?"

"Let him walk you home."

"He'll want to come up," she protested.

"I imagine he will."

"The place is a mess. He'll probably try to take *liberties.*"

"Undoubtedly."

"A hell of a lot of help *you* are. Very well, I'll let him escort me home, but if he thinks *I'm* going to flutter over him like those silly supers he's due a big surprise. He tries anything funny with me and he'll find himself nursing a black eye. Good night, luv. See you at the theater tomorrow evening."

"Have a nice time," I said sweetly.

It was almost four-thirty when the last guest finally staggered out, and I sighed with relief as Lambert gave a sheaf of bills to the weary proprietor and told him to pass them around among the help. He brought my long crimson velvet cloak and helped me into it, then draped a black cape around his shoulders with a dramatic flourish, white silk lining flashing. I was silent as he led me out into the night. The carriage was still waiting.

"It's a lovely night," he said. "Want to walk?"

"I suppose."

Lambert dismissed the carriage and took hold of my elbow and led me across the piazza. Moonlight brushed the stones with pale silver, and St. Paul's was a dim gray mass shrouded with velvety black shadows. Our footsteps rang on the stones, echoing in the stillness. The sky was a misty gray lightly tinted with violet and sprinkled with dimming stars. It would soon be dawn and The Market would be bustling as produce men set up their stalls and prepared for the day's business. Glancing up, I saw that a light was burning in the flat above Brinkley's Wig Shop, and I smiled to myself, suspecting that Megan had met her match at last.

"Very successful party," Jamie said as we started down Bedford Street.

"Very," I agreed. "I'm glad it's over. I plan to sleep forever."

"Saw you talking with Sheridan," he remarked. "I suppose he was trying to lure you away from me again?"

"You suppose right."

"Impudent rapscallion! Twenty-six years old and two phenomenally successful plays. Thinks he hung the moon."

"So do most of the critics," I taunted.

"You *could* play the lead in his next play, of course. We don't have a contract. You could become the critics'

darling. You have the talent. You don't have to settle
for mere popular success."

"I know."

"Of course, I'd kick you from here to Coventry if you
even considered such a step."

"You might try," I said.

We turned on Chandos Street, heading for St. Martin's Lane where the house we had taken three years
ago was located. The September night was pleasant and
cool without being chilly. The air was filled with all
those familiar smells I had come to love: mellow old
stone, lichen, ivy, crushed flower petals. Covent Garden
had its own atmosphere, its own aura, even at this hour.
Jamie slipped his arm around my waist, pulling me
closer to him, matching his stride to mine. I reveled in
his nearness, his strength, his warmth. I had been alone
for such a long time, and now I belonged, to this enchanting district, to this fascinating and infuriating
man who had changed my life.

"Still mad at me?" he asked.

"A little."

"You're an unreasonable wench."

"Sometimes," I admitted.

"Artistic temperament. You've more than your share.
I suppose *I* may not be the easiest person to get along
with myself."

"You have your moments," I told him.

"Oh?"

"Now and then," I said.

He chuckled and squeezed my waist. He was clearly
eager to kiss and make up. I thought that was a lovely
idea.

Chapter Fourteen

Rain pattered softly, softly, and I sighed in my sleep and turned and was aware of the emptiness there and opened my eyes. The sheets smelled of his body, the pillow was dented, but he was gone, and that was bewildering. I always woke up first and he was always there, sprawled out, tangled in the bedclothes, breathing deeply, and I always smiled and stroked his bare chest and he always grunted and curled his lips and I teased him until he woke up and he was always surly and groggy and usually he rolled over on me and I struggled and we made love before getting up, a divine way to begin the day. That emptiness beside me was disorienting now. I sat up, blinking, and I saw the dim gray light in the room and the rain slipping and sliding down the windowpanes in silver-gray patterns and saw the clock and saw that it was well after one in the afternoon. He had been undressing me as dawn broke. My crimson brocade gown was draped carelessly over a chair, the crimson tulle petticoat spreading on the floor like gigantic petals, his black frock coat hanging limply on the arm of another chair. I stretched and smiled, feeling the pleasant soreness in my limbs, remembering.

Jamie Lambert might have his faults, might be mercurial and temperamental, volatile and often over-bearing, but in the bedroom he was superlative, the most satisfying lover a woman could hope to have. He was rough and playful, greedy and gentle, teasing and tender, demanding and dominating and, always, as intent on my pleasure as he was on his own. Afterwards, he invariably curled arms and legs around me and slept soundly, making me his cushion, and that heaviness and warmth gave me a delicious sense of security. Yes, he was a superb lover, inventive and inciting, and I had no complaints on that score. I stretched again and listened to the rain pattering on the roof, wondering where he could be. I missed that nude, slumbering body, missed that warm skin, those unruly locks of dark brown hair moist with perspiration, those lips half-parted in sleep, ready to be kissed. Habit was deeply ingrained, and I didn't like waking up alone in bed. Those weeks he spent alone in Tunbridge Wells, working on his plays, were always hellish for me, always sorely dreaded.

Getting out of bed, I looked at the untidy litter in the bedroom and shook my head. Moving into the adjoining dressing room, I performed my ablutions and brushed my hair, then dressed, putting on a cream linen frock with narrow brown and gold stripes. Back in the bedroom, I hung up our clothing, put shoes away, straightened the piles of books, manuscripts and journals that covered the long table. Even in the dim gray light the room was snug and charming with its pale ivory walls, low-beamed ceiling and polished hardwood floor scattered with worn oriental rugs in soft hues. I made up the bed, smoothing down the heavy yellow-gold brocade counterpane. Curtains of the same brocade hung at the row of windows overlooking the walled herb garden in back of the house.

Yes, Angel of Covent Garden did all her own house-work, but I didn't mind at all. The house on St. Martin's

Lane was small, bedroom, dressing room and landing
on this floor, drawing room, study and kitchen below,
with staircase and foyer. It was very old, suffused with
character, and legend had it that it had belonged to
Aphra Behn over a hundred years ago. I liked to believe
that that colorful and determined lady had penned some
of her boisterous and scandalous plays within these
walls, that she herself had laid out the herb garden
with its intricate patterns.

Leaving the bedroom, I crossed the landing and moved
down the narrow staircase with its polished golden oak
railing and worn golden-brown runner. Posters of all
six plays I had done hung along the wall of the stairwell.
The foyer below was lined with golden oak bookcases,
each crammed to overflowing. Jamie was as avid a
reader as I and haunted Miller's on Fleet, invariably
returning with a plethora of dusty tomes. A lamp was
burning in the foyer. Raindrops dripped on the fan-
shaped panes above the large white door which, I noticed, was not locked. He had obviously gone out, not
bothering to lock the door behind him. I frowned as I
paused in the foyer, and my frown deepened when I
smelled the odor drifting strongly from the kitchen.
Something had been burning. What? Bacon? The odor
was overwhelming, and I rushed through the study and
into the kitchen in back of the house. The mess I encountered there made my blood turn cold.

Charred toast littered the old oak drainboard, along
with egg shells and a rasher of bacon. A skillet on the
large black stove contained a disgusting mess that might
possibly have been a madman's idea of an omelete. A
bellyful of red-orange coals still glowed in the stove,
and the mess in the skillet was turning even browner.
I seized a pad and removed it from the stove, then rushed
to open a window, rain or no rain. Pots, pans, dishes,
jars of preserves covered every surface. A canister of
flour had been overturned, spilling all over the counter
and onto the floor. I was going to murder him. Any
woman who had ever tried to keep a kitchen would

deem it justifiable homicide, and I would be very persuasive when I stood before the magistrate.

Fuming, I cleaned, cursing him every minute, and half an hour later I viewed my accomplishment with something less than bliss. The drainboard was clean and polished, the old oak gleaming, and the glazed brick floor gleamed too, dark red-brown. Copper utensils hung on the yellow-white walls as did strings of red pepper and mauve-white onions. A wicker basket of dried herbs hung from the low beamed ceiling. Most of the odor was gone now, and the window was shut. A pot of coffee perked merrily on the stove. Rain pattered. I wondered how I should do it. Poison? A knife between the ribs? A sharp blow on the head with a heavy object? Fetching a dark blue cup from one of the oak cabinets, I poured coffee and sipped it gratefully, and then I heard stamping on the porch.

I set down the cup and marched through the study and on into the foyer. He was just opening the door, wearing a long black cloak that was soaking wet. His hair was wet, too, plastered to his skull in sleek brown locks, and rain dripped down his face. His arms were laden with an immense pile of newspapers and several metal containers which he had attempted to keep dry under the heavy folds of his cloak. I glared at him. He gave me a sheepish look, kicking the door shut. A huge puddle of water was forming at his feet.

"Have you lost your mind!" I cried.

"Hello, love. Hoped you'd still be asleep."

"You wrecked my kitchen!"

"Discovered that, did you? I hoped I'd get back in time to clean it up before you found it."

"Whatever possessed you!"

"I woke up early," he said. "I thought it might be kinda nice if I cooked breakfast and brought it up to you. Breakfast in bed. Wanted to show my appreciation of you."

I didn't say anything. I was too moved.

"I can't cook," he confessed.

"You sure as hell can't!"

"So I decided to run over to Button's on Russell and buy some breakfast and bring it back. Have it here in these containers, still warm. While I was waiting for 'em to cook it I popped by Fleet to pick up the papers. We're a tremendous success, love."

"You're soaking wet!"

"Guess I am at that."

"Here, hand me those containers. Get yourself into the study and take that wet cloak off. I'll light the fire. My God, your boots are muddy. You're ruining the floor!"

"Sorry," he said.

I took the containers into the kitchen and lighted the fire in the study as he removed the sodden black cloak. He wore a white lawn shirt and black breeches beneath, and both were damp, the fine white cloth clinging to his chest and back, skin visible beneath. I made him sit down on the hearth. I helped him off with his boots and brought him a towel and ordered him to dry his hair, treating him like a bothersome child and trying not to show how moved I was that he had wanted to bring me breakfast in bed. What a beautiful, thoughtful man he was. What an idiot to go out in this rain in order to buy breakfast for me. I carried his muddy boots to the back hall, to be cleaned later, and I mopped up the puddle in the foyer and draped his cloak over the mantel so that it would dry, too, and he sneezed, vigorously toweling his hair.

"You're an idiot!" I snapped.

"I had good intentions," he protested.

"It took me forever to clean up that mess!"

"Bitch, bitch, bitch."

"You'll probably come down with a wretched cold."

"You can nurse me," he said.

"You'd better take off that shirt and those breeches. I'll go fetch a robe for you. Stay where you are! I want you in front of that fire until you're thoroughly dry."

"I'm roasting!"

"Don't give me any lip, Mr. Lambert. I'm in no mood for it."

I went upstairs and found an old brown satin dressing robe in the wardrobe, a disreputable garment that should have been discarded years ago. I carried it back down to the study. He had removed his shirt and was struggling out of the breeches which, wet, were like a second skin and not easy to remove. I couldn't resist helping him, peeling them down while he stood there patiently. He lifted first one foot, then the other, and I flung the breeches aside. He had obviously dressed in a hurry. He was quite naked, his tall, lean body burnished by the flickering firelight. I stroked his thigh. He grinned. I handed him the robe and told him to put it on.

"Your hair is still damp," I said crisply. "Here, take these cushions and sit back down on the hearth."

"You're a very bossy wench," he told me. "Reckon I ought to take you down a few pegs."

"Put the robe on, Jamie."

"Why don't you take *your* clothes off?"

I gave him a look and went into the kitchen and poured him a cup of coffee. He grinned when I handed it to him and tried to pull me down beside him. I gave his hand a slap. Back in the kitchen I opened the containers to discover fluffy eggs scrambled with cheese and herbs, juicy hot sausage patties, pieces of crisp bacon and buttered toast and wonderfully tempting cinnamon rolls baked with raisins and walnuts and glazed with creamy white icing. Remarkably enough, everything was still piping hot. I prepared a plate for him and carried it in along with knife, fork and tan linen napkin.

"You're not eating?" he inquired.

"I'll have a cup of coffee, perhaps one of the cinnamon rolls."

"All that food, all the trouble I went to, and you turn up your nose at it. I'm hurt."

"You know I never eat this early."

"It's two o'clock in the afternoon," he pointed out.

"Eat your food, Jamie."

I sat down on the floor a few feet away from him and leaned my back against one of the large brown leather chairs that flanked the fireplace. Propped up on one elbow he lolled there on the cushions before the fire like some indolent pasha, the old brown robe tied loosely at the waist, leaving much of his chest and most of his legs bare. He ate slowly, watching me with glowing green-brown eyes half-shrouded with drooping lids. I ignored those seductive looks and sipped my coffee. The rain was still pouring down, noisier now, drumming on the roof and splashing on the pavements.

"This is cozy," he said.

"Very," I agreed.

"Getting terribly warm in here."

"Think so?"

"You're wearing too many clothes."

"I'm quite comfortable."

"I'm getting more uncomfortable by the minute."

I loved it when he was in this playful, randy mood, but I managed to assume a prim expression and ignore his implication. He nibbled a piece of bacon, looking at me with darkly glowing eyes, and then he shifted position on the cushions and the slippery brown robe slipped even more, revealing a long, lean flank that was burnished by firelight. His hair was beginning to dry, fluffing up in feathery brown wisps, and I longed to move over there and smooth it down and kiss his temple. I took a bite of the cinnamon roll. It was sweet and rich and buttery, almost sinfully delicious. Jamie had another piece of sausage and finished his eggs and watched as I ate the rest of the roll and licked my fingers.

"They're delicious," I said. "You should have one."

"I'd rather have something else."

"I'll get you some more coffee," I told him.

I took his cup into the kitchen and refilled it and handed it to him and he reached up under my skirts and clasped my calf, fingers squeezing firmly, kneading the flesh. I pulled away easily enough and moved back and he gave me a disgruntled look and sipped his coffee, lolling back on the cushions exactly like a spoiled pasha. I stepped over to the huge, cluttered desk and picked up some of the papers and carried them over to the long wheat-colored sofa. Kicking off my shoes, I curled up on the sofa with legs beneath me and began to turn the pages. Jamie pushed his empty plate aside and sat up, folding his arms across his knees and looking at me in a most provocative way.

"Read them later," he said.

"Why not now?"

"There are better things to do."

"Indeed?"

He climbed lazily to his feet and tightened the sash of his robe and padded across the room and took the paper out of my hands. He caught my upper arms and pulled me to my feet and held me against him, and I pretended to be disinterested in his amorous maneuvers, trying to pull away. He clasped me close and began to kiss my brow, my temple, my cheek, the curve of my throat, murmuring deep in his throat as he did so. He was in no hurry, no hurry at all, and I tried to resist the warm, tingling sensations that crept over me. I didn't want to melt, not yet. Delay was delicious, and he was the master of it.

"Really, Jamie—"

"You're a tempting wench," he purred.

"I have a headache."

"I've got a great cure for it."

"You're impossi—"

His mouth covered mine and his arms tightened around me and my knees turned weak and I stumbled and he lost his balance and we almost toppled onto the sofa, swaying precariously until he got his footing. I clung to him for a moment until he had steadied himself and my own legs were steady too and then I placed my hands against his chest and pushed and he fell onto the sofa and looked startled and I smiled and he reached up and seized my wrist and gave it a savage jerk and I fell on top of him and he wrapped arms and legs around me and got me in a hold and I broke it and we wrestled and rolled and spilled onto the floor and he took hold of my hair and tugged it and covered my mouth with his again and I tried to shove him off me but he was too strong, too heavy, but I refused to give in just yet, the game too delightful, too divine.

He kissed me and made murmuring noises in his throat, pinioning me with his weight, and I ran my hands over his back and shoulders and felt the slippery satin and the muscle beneath and parted my lips and his tongue thrust savagely into my mouth and his body tensed, bone and muscle pressing down, hurting me until I managed to shift position and pretend submission and he relaxed and began rubbing my abdomen with that hot, hard tool as he continued to thrust his tongue in and out, jabbing the back of my throat. He raised up, straddling me with a knee on either side of my thighs, his hands reaching down to pull up my skirts, and I reared up then and he toppled over and I laughed again and he lunged for me as I crawled toward the fireplace.

He caught hold of my ankle and pulled and I fell flat as he caught my other ankle and held fast, pulling, and I slid on the floor and his hands moved higher and gripped my calves, my knees, and up came my skirts and over I turned and onto me he crawled and into me he plunged, filling me fully, strong, straining. I wrapped my legs around him and he reached out, groping, and got one of the cushions and positioned it under my hips and pulled back and plunged and pounded and repeated and I raised and reared and our movements matched and magic and marvelous sensations besieged us both.

Later there was sweet soreness and satiation and silence broken only by the gentle crackle of the fire and the splash and patter of rain outside. I cradled him in my arms, his head heavy on my shoulders, and he slept and I savored those ashes of aftermath and savored the weight and warmth of him and the lovely smell of his body. He stirred after a while and opened his eyes and looked into mine and smiled a sleepy smile and slept again, cradling me, and my heart filled with fondness and affection. The fire burned down, coals glowing a dim pink-orange, and the rain slowly ceased, although it continued to drip from the eaves with a monotonous plop-plop. I gently disentangled myself and put a cushion under his head and went upstairs, limbs aching, a wonderful languor in my blood.

My linen frock was deplorably wrinkled. Smiling, I removed it and washed thoroughly, then put on a tan muslin dress sprigged with gold and brown flowers. I brushed my hair, which was a tangled mess, and I thought about the man napping downstairs. I could have been the mistress of a Lord, could have had a luxurious apartment and jewelry and servants and a generous monthly allowance, and instead I was living with a mercurial, temperamental playwright and working like a slave under constant pressure and tearing my nerves to shreds and taking the money I earned and investing it in his plays. Marie would have said I had made a very bad bargain. I was more than content with my lot. I loved working in the theater, and I loved this charming old house in Covent Garden and ... and I was extremely fond of the man downstairs.

Did I love him? Not the way I had loved Hugh Bradford, with all my heart, all my soul, with anguished emotions and tender desperation. I thought of Hugh often, after all this time, and the feeling was still there, the pain, too, even though it no longer had the same stabbing impact. I wondered what had become of him, and I wondered if he remembered the girl I had been and the night under the stars. Jamie did not stir my soul. He stirred my wrath, my mirth, made me yell and made me laugh, made me frown and made me smile. He did not make me feel poetic and sad and sensitive. He made me feel exuberant and bawdy and gloriously, joyously alive. He drove me to distraction at times, particularly when we were working on a new play, made me so furious I longed to crack his skull, but I had never considered leaving him. Did I love him? Perhaps love wasn't the word for it. I was happy with our life together, and that was enough.

I went back downstairs to find him on the sofa in

breeches and robe, drinking a cup of coffee, eating a cold cinnamon roll and reading the newspapers he'd brought home. His hair was disheveled. There were faint gray smudges under his eyes. He looked lazy and replete, papers in his lap and scattered messily about the floor.

"Did you heat the coffee?" I asked.

He made a face. "Yeah. It tastes awful."

"I'll make fresh."

Engrossed in an article, he raised his cup into the air and I took it out of his hand and carried it into the kitchen. I made a new pot of coffee and carried cups for both of us back into the study. He didn't look up from the paper he was reading but raised his hand into the air again and gripped the cup that materialized. I wasn't his servant, no indeed, but I often enjoyed waiting on him, and I didn't scold now. I gathered up some of the papers and sat down on the other end of the sofa and sipped my coffee and read.

Our friends, the well-fed journalists, had written predictably laudatory articles about the enchanting Mrs. Howard who had surpassed herself in the role of Nell Gwynn and had done a delightful bit with the spaniels that had caused great merriment. Mrs. Howard was vivacious. Mrs. Howard was radiantly lovely. Mrs. Howard wore a stunning array of costumes. *My Charming Nellie* was a fine vehicle for London's best beloved actress. Praise was given to Charles Hart as well and to the engaging Mrs. Sloan. Even Mrs. Perry got her share. There was altogether too much about the spaniels, altogether too much about my private life and my shopping at The Market and nobbing with the common people. These puffery pieces would undoubtedly sell a great many tickets, but the actual reviews were considerably less kind. Mrs. Howard, a talented actress, was wasting herself in these turgid melodramas, of which *My Charming Nellie* was an apt example, a gaudy hodgepodge of history garishly mounted with leaden pace.

"It's going to run forever," Jamie said.

"You've read these?"

"Most of them. The party paid off. Our friends did us proud. The critics don't matter. Never have. What do they know? Those who want intellectual fare will go see Garrick do *Lear*. Those who want a good time will come see *My Charming Nellie*."

I could tell that he was hurt by the reviews. He always was. It hurt even more that they invariably praised me while damning his skills as a dramatist. I had to tread very cautiously, male pride, male ego being what they were. I gave a sigh and pushed the papers aside and told him we were bound to make a bleeding fortune.

"Bound to," he agreed, "even if it isn't a masterpiece."

"You weren't *try*ing to write a masterpiece," I told him. "You were trying to write a thundering good entertainment. You did. Sod the critics."

"Sod 'em," he said.

"If you wanted to write a masterpiece, I'm sure you could."

"Sure I could."

"And we'd promptly go bankrupt," I added.

Hurt, pride wounded, he had been prepared to sulk, but his fundamental good humor got the best of him and he had to grin at my remark. He shoved the papers out of his lap and took hold of my hand and pulled me close beside him and slung an arm around my shoulders. He told me I was a rather terrific lady and a good little actress even if I *had* flubbed the fight scene last night.

"Flubbed the fight scene! I was marvelous! So was Megan!"

"It looked false, looked staged. I told you a hundred times during rehearsals that I wanted the audience to *feel* those punches, *feel* that hair tearing at the roots. It's supposed to be a brawl, and the two of you were cavorting about like a couple of giggling schoolgirls on a picnic. We're going to have to *work* on it, love."

He was absolutely impossible! But, as usual, he was

right. We did work on the fight scene, putting in hours every afternoon before the performance, and it was much better, much more convincing, bringing spontaneous applause from a wildly enthusiastic audience. Megan and I both had a nice collection of bruises and scratches before we got it right but, as she wearily pointed out, it was all for our art. *My Charming Nellie* played to packed houses throughout September, October and November, and the usual Christmas slump didn't affect us at all. It was the most successful drama in London that winter, and by January production costs had been more than covered and Jamie and I were both earning tremendous profits. He was already researching the life of Mary, Queen of Scots and mulling over the dramatic possibilities therein. I was less than enthusiastic about playing that particular lady, whom I felt was a cold-hearted schemer and not at all sympathetic, even though she was beheaded, but he paid no heed to my protests and forged ahead with his researches.

He found an unexpected ally in Mrs. Perry who, born in Edinburgh and raised in that city, had been to Edinburgh Castle and seen Mary's apartment and considered herself an authority on the subject. Mrs. Perry saw Mary as a tragic heroine, as did Jamie, and recommended a number of books about her which he promptly found and read. Dumped by the Duke of Ambrose in early November, she had had to sell her diamonds in order to pay her debts and finance new living quarters, and she had ample time to discuss their favorite subject with Jamie. Thirty-five if a day, Perry frankly admitted to twenty-seven, had dark red-gold hair, deep blue eyes and a figure that was undeniably opulent. A foolish, affected woman heartily disliked by cast and crew, she was nevertheless a very competent actress who gave a commendable performance as Castlemaine. Though Megan warned me I had better watch out, the slut was after my man, I knew I had nothing to worry about on that score. They spent an inordinate amount of time together in the Green Room, true, but I knew they were discussing Mary and knew Jamie found Mrs. Perry tiresome and transparent, although he wasn't averse to picking her brains. Apparently she really did know a great deal about the Queen of Scots and had given him a number of good ideas for the play. Megan wasn't at all convinced.

"I still wouldn't trust her," she said.

"I don't," I replied, "but I do trust him, and I know how he is when he's researching a new play. He thinks of nothing else. Helen of Troy could wander in stark naked and he wouldn't give her a glance."

"If you say so, luv."

"Jamie doesn't even like the woman, he's merely using her. When he's finished researching he won't give her the time of day."

"I hope you're right."

"I know I am. I know Jamie."

February was cold and gray and dreary, and I was in low spirits, although I tried my best not to show it. Jamie was immersed in his research and completely preoccupied, reading constantly and making endless notes as he always did during this particular stage of creation. Megan was preoccupied too—with Charles Hart. The man was impossibly persistent and bold as brass. In early January he had simply brought all his clothes over and moved into the flat above Brinkley's Wig Shop and she couldn't get *rid* of him. He wanted to *domes*ticate her, wanted her to settle *down* and, really, wasn't at all like any of the other actors she'd ever known. He was phenomenal in bed and quite engaging in his calm, lethargic way, but he wasn't that much *fun*, luv. She had no idea what she was going to do with him, but she threatened to scratch his eyes out if he so much as glanced at one of those simpering supers who still fluttered around him. I saw very little of her outside the theater. This was one of Dottie's busiest periods, preparing costumes for the new spring productions, and I saw even less of her.

I was feeling particularly low when I arrived at the theater on the evening of my birthday. Twenty-five years old, and no one remembered. Perhaps it was just as

well. Twenty-five years old, a quarter of a century! I
didn't ex*pect* a fuss to be made, of course, but it would
have been rather nice if someone had remembered and
given me flowers, maybe, or maybe a box of candy. Jamie
was so immersed in Mary he rarely remembered I was
in the house except when he climbed into bed at night,
and Dottie and Megan and everyone else had their own
affairs to think about. I tried my best to give a vivacious
performance, but as I returned to my dressing room
after the first act I knew I had been less than inspired.
I was surprised when Peg, my dresser, greeted me with
an engraved calling card and a look of intense excitement.

"A lady wants to see you after the show," she exclaimed, "a *real* lady! A duchess! Her footman knocked
on the door and gave me this card and said he'd be back
to see if it was all right. Wearin' powder blue satin, he
was, laces, too, and one of them fancy white wigs! Plumb
intimidated me, he did, so cool and proper."

I took the card from her. It was a rich, creamy white,
rimmed with silver, with *The Duchess of Alden* in elaborate silver script. Nothing else. The Duchess of Alden?
Although the name seemed vaguely familiar, I was certain I didn't know the lady and wondered what she
could possibly want with me. I told Peg to inform the
footman I would see her, and then I promptly forgot all
about it until after the curtain calls when I was returning to my dressing room in the silver and violet
gown. Peg opened the door for me, jittery as could be,
her plain face flushed with nervous excitement.

"The Duchess of Alden!" she announced.

The Duchess had been sitting in the large white velvet chair. She stood up and nodded at me. Her hair was
powdered a silvery-white and worn in the French style
with high pompadour in front and three long ringlets
in back. A pale gold and two soft white plumes were
affixed to one side of her coiffure with a flashing diamond clasp. Her face was exquisitely made-up, lids
shaded a subtle blue-gray, lips a soft shell-pink, cheeks
delicately tinted with a heart-shaped black satin beauty

patch on the left cheekbone. Her gown was magnificent, creamy pale gold satin with tight elbow-length sleeves and a low heart-shaped bodice. Delicate golden-white lace adorned the bodice and edged the sleeves, and the spreading, puffed skirt parted in front to reveal an underskirt of row upon row of the same delicate lace. More diamonds sparkled at her ears and throat, and she carried a gorgeous gold and white lace fan. I hadn't seen her in almost five years, and I actually didn't recognize her at first.

"Happy birthday," she said.

Alden? Alden. Of course, Solonge had been kept by the Duke of Alden, that was why I remembered the name, but... I frowned.

"Solonge?"

"Surprised to see me?"

"It—it really *is* you!"

The greenish hazel eyes sparkled and the lovely mouth curled with a suggestion of the old pixie smile, but this elegant, dignified creature bore little resemblance to the piquant, vivacious girl I remembered. She was the very epitome of aristocratic poise, beautiful and refined. Peg was gaping openly, and I dismissed her. She left reluctantly, shutting the door behind her. I stared at my stepsister, scarcely able to believe the transformation. Solonge seemed to read my mind.

"I know it's hard to believe," she said, "but you've undergone some rather startling changes yourself. Who would have thought gawky little Angie would be painted by Gainsborough and become The Great Beauty of our day?"

Even her voice was aristocratic, cool and mellifluous. She must have taken lessons.

"You—you married the Duke," I said. "You actually *are* a duchess."

Solonge smiled again, a wry, worldly smile. "Not quite," she replied. "I married Bartholomew—poor, dear, dull Bartholomew who pined for me all the time I was his father's mistress. I knew the Duke would never allow us to marry, but I knew the Duke couldn't last

forever, so I bided my time. I educated myself in the
ways of the aristocracy, took lessons in voice and de-
portment, developed cultivated tastes, and when the
dear Duke drew his last breath, I was ready to step into
my new role. Bart became the new Duke of Alden, and
I became his bride."

There was a light knock on the door. To my surprise,
Solonge opened it, admitting the footman Peg had described. He bore a tray holding a bottle of champagne
in a silver bucket and two gold-rimmed crystal glasses.
He set it down on the low table beside the white chair,
deftly uncorked the bottle and poured champagne into
the glasses, handing one to each of us. Putting the bottle
back into its nest of ice, he left, and Solonge closed the
door, smiling again.

"One of the advantages of being extremely wealthy,"
she said blithely. "I thought champagne might be nice
on your birthday. There was quite a lot of talk when
we married," she continued. "The Duke had been very
discreet, never introduced me to any of his friends, so
no one actually *knew* I had been his mistress, but there
were rumors. Bart and I faced them down. There are
so many skeletons in aristocratic closets that no one
quite dared rattle this one, for fear one of their own
might be exhumed."

"So Marie's dream came true," I said. "One of her
daughters actually married into the aristocracy."

I sat down on the dressing stool, violet and silver
skirts spreading. Solonge was silent for a moment, a
thoughtful look in her eyes.

"I'm going to do right by Bart," she told me. "We're
moving to Italy next week. A very important diplomatic
position is soon to be open in Naples—I intend to see
that Bart gets it. I'm going to make something of him,
and I'm going to be the most refined, most respectable
Duchess who ever drew breath, which means I could
never acknowledge any kind of kinship with a shockingly common actress."

I smiled at that. Solonge sat down in the white chair
and took another sip of champagne, relaxing, allowing

some of the old warmth to shine through the elegant facade.

"I know we haven't been in touch, darling, but I've been following your career with a great deal of pride— and I simply had to see you before leaving for Italy."

"I'm so glad you came, Solonge. I—I've thought of you often."

"And I of you. You've made an enormous success of yourself, Angie. I saw the play. You deserve all the acclaim you've received."

"I've worked very hard."

"I know you have, darling. Your father would have been proud, too."

She said the words quietly, sincerely, and I felt a terrible tugging inside and knew I mustn't give in to the feelings they stirred. Yes, Father would have been proud. I had achieved no great accomplishment, had made no great contribution, but I brought pleasure to thousands of people and, through my work, employment for dozens of others. He would rather see me playing Ophelia to Garrick's Hamlet, of course, but I sensed he would appreciate my Nell Gwynn and smile when I pranced in my tights and pulled pranks on Moll and Castlemaine.

"Oh," Solonge said, suddenly remembering something, "I brought presents, too. Your dresser put them over there behind the screen."

"Presents?"

"It *is* your birthday, darling, though how you could be twenty-five when I'm only twenty-six defies logic."

"You don't look a *day* over twenty-six," I assured her.

"You always were a wretched liar. Get them, darling. Open them. I was in a terrible quandary—I had no idea what to get you. I do hope you're not disappointed."

I fetched the presents from behind the screen, all beautifully wrapped with gold paper and cloth-of-silver ribbon. I opened them to discover a seven volume set of the works of Aphra Behn, a gorgeous amethyst lace shawl ashimmer with silver thread and a glossy light blue box of chocolates exactly like the box Janine had

had in the parlor that day years ago when I came home
from my first encounter with Hugh Bradford in the
gardens at Greystone Hall. I stared at it in amazement,
remembering that day—Janine in sky blue, lolling on
the sofa and popping bon bons into her mouth, Solonge
in pink, at the window, so full of life and devilment.

"You *used* to like that kind," she said.

"You—you remembered."

"Had a devil of a time finding them, too. I read in
one of the papers that you lived in the house that once
belonged to Aphra Behn, and I had the bookseller find
a set for me and had it rebound in blue leather. I imagine you probably already have the books."

I shook my head. "We— Father used to have a set,
but they were sold, and I have never been able to locate
another. I—I'm terribly pleased, Solonge. Damn it, I
want to cry."

"Please don't, darling. I thought the shawl would go
with your eyes. It's exquisite, isn't it—not my color,
though. I wear only soft pastels now, creamy pinks and
pale blues and golds and soft limes, nothing bold and
dramatic. I have a new image to project, alas. You must
drink some more champagne. Hand me your glass."

I did so. She refilled it and gave it back. "Solonge,"
I said hesitantly, "what—what became of Marie?"

Solonge frowned. "I heard about what she tried to
do to you, darling, and I fear that was the last straw
as far as I was concerned. She lost Marie's Place, you
know, and naturally she came to me for money—a pack
of howling creditors at her heels. I paid them, and I
settled a sum of money on her on the condition she leave
the country and not pester me *or* you any longer. She
went back to Brittany and opened a boardinghouse. I
hear from her occasionally—asking for money, of
course."

"She runs a boardinghouse?"

"And scrubs her own floors, from all reports. I could
do more for her, particularly now, but I have no incli-
nation to do so. Call me a monster if you like but she

has no real need and I want nothing more to do with her. She's out of my life and I plan to keep it that way."

"And—Janine?" I asked.

"Janine went to Brittany with her. She married a French cobbler and, according to my informant, is as big as a house. Spends her days eating pastry and napping over the shop while her husband mends shoes. Don't look so distressed about it, darling—she's probably happier than you or I will ever be."

"She probably is," I agreed.

Solonge sighed, glancing at the clock I kept on the dressing table. "How do you get home, darling?"

"I generally walk. It's only a short distance."

"It's safe?"

"In Covent Garden it is. Everyone knows me—even the pickpockets. They'd never let harm come to their Angel."

"I'll take you home in my carriage tonight. This will be the last time I'll see you for—a very long time. If things go as I hope, we'll probably settle in Italy with only an occasional trip back to see after the properties here."

"I'd better change," I said. "Would you unhook me?"

Solonge unfastened the tiny hooks in back of the bodice and I stepped behind the screen, removed gown and petticoat and put on my white faille petticoat and a silk wrapper.

"Bart was— He wasn't terribly exciting, as I recall," I said, sitting down at the dressing table to remove my stage makeup, "but I remember him being very nice."

"He's dull as ditch water, darling, but he's much brighter than anyone gives him credit for being, and he's a genuinely good person. All his life he's lived under the shadow of his father. Now he's going to step into the sun and a lot of people are going to be surprised by the new Duke of Alden."

"He'll have you behind him."

"Every step of the way," she said. "I've sown my share of wild oats as you know, but I'm almost thirty, darling—don't you dare tell anyone—and it's time to settle

down. I'm going to be faithful to him. I'm going to give
him an heir. I'm going to make him happy."

"I—I'm sure you will."

"Count on it, darling."

Makeup removed, my face washed and dried, I applied a bit of pink lip rouge and brushed my hair out,
then put on the black and white striped taffeta gown
I'd worn to the theater. It had a red velvet waistband,
complementing my high-heeled red slippers and heavy
red velvet cloak. Solonge and I chatted as I dressed,
and we finished the champagne. Her elegantly attired
footman removed glasses, bucket and tray, then returned to carry my presents out to the waiting carriage.
I told the doorman good-night, and we stepped outside
a few minutes later.

It was a lovely night, cool and clear, the sky a deep
blue-black. Moonlight bathed the front of the theater
and created deep shadows in the recesses. Torches held
by the linkboys illuminated the carriage, and it was
every bit as splendid as I expected, white and gold with
the Alden crest on the door. Four strong, handsome
white horses stood in harness, stamping impatiently. I
gave the driver directions, and the footman opened the
door for us and handed us inside. The interior was
sumptuous, too, seats padded white velvet, cloth of gold
curtains hanging at the windows. It was the grandest
carriage I'd ever been inside, and I was duly impressed.
Solonge settled back against the cushions, clearly accustomed to such luxury. I was pleased for her and glad
that, against all odds, she had made so fabulous a match.
With linkboys running alongside to light the way, the
carriage began to move through the twisting cobbled
streets of Covent Garden.

"Tell me about your man," Solonge said. "Is he really
as handsome, as brilliant and wicked as they claim?"

"He's very handsome," I replied, "even with his
crooked nose, and he's unquestionably brilliant, though
not at all wicked. He has a wretched temper which he
makes no effort to control and he's impatient and stub-

born and willful and impossibly demanding, but—quite endearing in his way."

"He must have something. You've been with him for three years."

"He has something," I said. "Definitely."

"You're in love with him?"

"I—I'm not sure. I don't think so. I'm terribly fond of him."

"Three years is a long time to stay with someone of whom you're merely fond, darling."

"We work well together. We've formed a theatrical partnership. We're interested in the same things, have the same goals."

"Even so—"

"I suppose 'fond' isn't a strong enough word. I suppose I do love him, in a way, but—" I hesitated.

"Not the way you loved Hugh Bradford," Solonge said. "It's just as well, Angie. That kind of love comes but once—it's overpowering, overwhelming, obsessive, altogether too intense to endure more than once. It makes you a captive of your emotions and you're no longer free. You survive it, but you never feel with quite that degree of intensity again. Thank God," she added.

"I forgot—you loved him, too."

"I was tougher than you, darling. I cured myself of it before a serious infection could occur."

"I—I often wonder what became of him."

"They followed his trail to Plymouth," she told me, "but lost track of him there. It's reasonable to assume he boarded some ship and left the country, although they were never able to prove it—he undoubtedly sailed under an assumed name. He's probably in the Colonies now, fighting on the side of the Rebels. It would certainly appeal to him, hostile as he was."

"He had reason to be hostile," I said quietly.

We were both silent for a few moments as the carriage bowled down the street with linkboys trotting alongside, flames wavering in the dark like ragged orange banners. As horse hooves clopped smartly on the cobbles, I gazed out the window and thought about the moody, dark-eyed youth I had loved, and then I deliberately forced those thoughts out of my mind.

"I suppose you heard about Clinton Meredith," Solonge said.

I shook my head. "I haven't heard anything about him since—since he wanted to set me up in an apartment. That was four years ago."

"He was in love with you, darling. Did you know that? He was desolate when you vanished without a trace. He blamed himself—felt quite guilty about it."

"So Marie said. I imagine he got over it."

"He went back to Greystone Hall and, believe it or not, he reformed—or at least he seemed to. He gave up his wild ways and settled down and began to take a sincere interest in the estate. He married Lady Julia Robinson, a demure young woman with a sweet nature and, unfortunately, very poor health. She succumbed to the fever only a few weeks ago. He's been in deep mourning ever since."

"I'm sorry to hear that," I said. "Clinton was— He wasn't really wicked, just spoiled and unprincipled. He was too wealthy, too good-looking. He had too much of everything and thought the world should pay obeisance to him."

"Perhaps he's grown up," Solonge said. "People do change. I'm the living proof of it."

Both of us smiled, and the carriage came to a halt in front of the house and the footman opened the door. Moonlight gilded the front steps and the small portico sheltering the narrow porch. A light was burning in the study, a misty gold square against the shadows. Jamie was undoubtedly working on his notes. Solonge told the footman to take my presents, and I asked him to put them on the table in the foyer, adding that the door was sure to be unlocked. Solonge and I looked at each other, both of us far more moved than we cared to admit. It was hard to associate this elegant creature with her silvery hair and gold and white plumes and diamonds and gorgeous pale gold and lace gown with the vibrant, feisty girl I had known, but the bond was still there between us.

"I do wish you'd come in and meet Jamie," I said.

"I'd better not, darling. Bart's waiting for me at Grosvenor Square, and he always gets restless when I'm not there."

"Thank you for the presents, Solonge. You've made this the nicest birthday I've had in a long time."

"Take my advice, darling—stop having them."

I smiled. "Good-bye, Solonge."

"Good-bye. I'll send you a letter from Italy."

"Please do."

I climbed out of the carriage and, casting aristocratic poise aside, Solonge climbed out after me and caught me to her. We hugged tightly, emotionally, both of us remembering those days gone by. "Take care," she whispered. "You, too," I said. We clasped each other for another moment, and then she sighed and let me go, brushing a tear from her cheek. The footman helped her into the carriage and shut the door and ascended his perch on back of the vehicle. I climbed the steps and turned. Solonge held the curtain back and waved as the carriage pulled away, linkboys trotting alongside with torches held high. Brushing away my own tears, I went inside. The past was a part of all of us, and I knew I would never be entirely free of my own.

Chapter Fifteen

Glorious golden marigolds, lovely yellow and white daisies, bronze chrysanthemums, just what I needed, and, yes, a huge bouquet of those daffodils as well. The flower woman assured me I had made the perfect selection, her flowers were the loveliest in th' 'ole bloomin' Market. I paid her, and she began to twist sheets of thin green paper around the stems of the bunches of flowers, talking all the while. It was an 'onor 'avin' me buy 'er blooms. She 'adn't seen one of my plays 'erself, 'adn't 'ad th' pleasure, but everyone knew Angel. Wudn't 'oity-toity like some of them actresses, I wudn't. A real person, it was well known. She placed the flowers carefully into the large, flat basket hooked on my arm, and I smiled and thanked her.

"Would you *like* to see one of my plays, Annie?" I inquired.

"Lor', luv, me—I ain't got th' means to go squanderin' money on theater tickets, though if I *'ad*, it'd be your play I'd go ta see."

"You come to the box office tomorrow night, Annie.

Bring a friend. I'll have two tickets waiting there for you—the best seats in the house. Compliments of Mrs. Howard."

"You mean, you mean—" Annie was dismayed. "Lor', you *are* an Angel!"

"And be sure to come backstage after the play is over. We'll have a cup of tea in my dressing room."

She thrust a large bunch of flame-colored hibiscus into the basket, smiling a broad smile and wiping gnarled brown hands on her soiled white apron. I thanked her again and moved on through The Market with my heavily laden basket. Friendly greetings assailed me on every side. I smiled and nodded, acknowledging them, feeling the waves of affection. Actresses were supposed to be temperamental and exclusive, haughty creatures who were surrounded by sycophants and had nothing to do with the common folk. That might be very well for women like the pretentious Mrs. Perry and her ilk, but I considered myself a working woman, and I worked bloody hard, finding precious little glamor in my position as London's Favorite Actress. Being so successful just meant you had to work twice as hard in order not to disappoint your public.

"'Ow 'bout some fine cabbage, Angel?" a burly man cried.

"Not today, Ed. They're lovely, though. Those last you sold me were wonderfully crisp."

"Only th' best for Angel of Covent Garden."

"'Ear, 'ear," his companion called. "Our very own Angel, gracin' us today with 'er presence. Three cheers for Angel!"

Hearty cheers rang out all around, and I acknowledged this tribute with a gracious smile, slightly embarrassed as I always was by such displays of adulation. Gone were the days when I could saunter through Covent Garden with anonymity, but I refused to barricade myself and live in elegant seclusion with a staff of servants to protect me from the public, as did most prominent theatrical folk. My freedom and mobility were far too important to me, and I realized full well that my

accessibility was one of the major reasons for my popularity. Leaving The Market, I crossed the piazza. Plump
blue-gray pigeons scurried on the stones, searching for
crumbs, and radiant sunlight bathed the facade of St.
Paul's. It was late April, a glorious afternoon, and I
savored the clear blue sky and the fresh new greenery
as I strolled toward St. Martin's Lane.

Spring was here and the air was soft and scented
and flower beds were full of varicolored blossoms and
Jamie was leaving tomorrow for Tunbridge Wells. I was
going to be bright and cheerful. I was going to make
our last day together pleasant and fun. I was not going
to be sad. I would fill the house with the flowers I had
bought and I would be light and merry and this evening
after I returned from the theater I was going to cook a
splendid midnight supper and open a bottle of the superb wine I had ordered and give him something to
think about while he was away. He would only be gone
for two or three weeks, but it would seem an eternity,
I knew. Damn the bloody play, and damn Mary, Queen
of Scots, too. I was thoroughly sick of her and had no
desire to portray her onstage, but Jamie assured me I
would adore the play once he had finished it.

I sighed, turning the corner of Chandos Street and
starting down St. Martin's Lane with its rows of mellow
old stone houses. There was a carriage in front of our
own, brown and battered, obviously hired, sturdy chestnuts standing patiently in the sunshine while the driver,
in a worn green coat, slouched on his seat and munched
a crusty roll. I wondered who could possibly be visiting
at this hour. Moving up the steps, I opened the door
and stepped into the foyer, and I felt an iciness inside
me as I heard that rich, resonant, affected voice I knew
so well and had come to detest.

"—see no reason why we *shouldn't* have a meeting
between Mary and Elizabeth, even though they never
actually met face to face. An artist is permitted to take
liberties with history, after all—*Shake*speare did—and
it would make a stunning curtain for the second act."

"The dramatic possibilities are endless," Jamie agreed.

"The two cousins, face to face, Mary proud and poised, refusing to humble herself, Elizabeth cold and scornful—'I expect no mercy for myself, Cousin, but I plead with you to release my beloved Bothwell'—and the third act opens on the eve of her execution. She has learned that Bothwell has gone insane in his Danish prison, her son has become her sworn enemy and the poor darling has nothing else to live for. All her hopes, all her dreams have turned to ashes, but she is going to face her death like the noble, majestic soul she is. It's going to be mag*nif*icent, James!"

"Maybe you should write it for me," he said.

"Dear me," Mrs. Perry protested, "*I* could never write a play—I merely interpret those lines written by my betters, but if I have provided some small inspiration to *you* I'm more than satisfied. Our discussions have been so *very* stimulating, James, and I trust they've been helpful as well."

"They've been helpful indeed."

"I know *Angel* doesn't like the material, but I feel in my heart this play is going to be your greatest achievement. Charles Hart will be superb as Bothwell, he has such magnetism, and though she's really not *mature* enough to play Mary, I'm sure Angel will give a perfectly competent performance. You couldn't dream of doing the play without her, of course. The public expects her to be in all your plays, even if she's not right for the part."

This last was said in a velvety, commiserating voice, indicating her sympathy with his problem, and I actually looked around for a pistol to shoot the slut with. Seeing none, I shut the door rather emphatically and stamped noisily on the floor of the foyer. Silence fell in the study. I sailed blithely in, basket of flowers on my arm, a radiant smile on my lips.

"What a *lovely* surprise!" I exclaimed. "Mrs. *Per*ry. How *nice* it is to see you. So unex*pec*ted. You must

forgive me if I'm a bit breathless. It's a good walk from
The Market."

Jamie was standing by the fireplace in tall black
knee boots, tight black breeches and a loosely fitting
white lawn shirt with full belling sleeves, the tail tucked
carelessly into the waistband of his breeches and bag-
ging over it. He was holding some manuscript pages
and looked both startled and wryly amused by my dramatic, ingenue entrance.

"Mrs. Perry stopped by to bring me a couple of books
I wanted to borrow," he told me. "I'll need them in Tunbridge Wells."

"How *lovely* of her," I said.

I flashed another radiant smile. Mrs. Perry smiled,
too, a tight, carefully controlled smile. She was looking
particularly opulent in a deep honey-colored satin gown.
The edge of the extremely low-cut bodice was trimmed
with black fox fur, as was the hem of the full skirt. The
sleeves were short, and she wore a pair of long black
velvet gloves. A wide-brimmed black velvet hat slanted
across her head, one side dripping amber and black
plumes. Full lips a lush pink, deep blue eyes half-veiled
by heavy mauve lids with dark, luxuriant lashes, Mrs.
Perry exuded that ripe, slightly bruised sensuality that
most men find irresistible. I gave her that. She might
be *old,* but she was loaded with allure. She was a good
actress, too, perfect as Castlemaine. I tried to remember
that now as we smiled at each other.

"What a stunning gown," I remarked. "A bit extreme
for this time of day I should think, but it suits you
divinely."

"Thank you. Been shopping?"

"I always select my own flowers."

"My maid does all my shopping. I feel it would be
rather unseemly for an actress of my stature to appear
at The Market—all those people."

"An actress of your stature could appear at The Market without the slightest danger of being bothered by
all those people," I said sweetly.

Her smile tightened even more as the dart struck

home. I set the basket of flowers down on one of the low tables, still the ingenue and playing it to the hilt. Shoving a long chestnut wave from my temple, I brushed a speck of imaginary lint from my sprigged muslin skirt and sighed.

"We'll be having tea soon. Won't you stay?" I asked.

"I really mustn't. I have to think of my figure."

I glanced at it pointedly. "Of course," I said.

Jamie chuckled. Both of us whirled around to glare at him and he quickly sobered and immersed himself in the pages he was holding. Mrs. Perry reached up to pat the plumes dripping from her hat brim and said she really must be going. I said that was a pity, she must come back soon, and Jamie put down the pages and said he was very grateful for the books. She said it was no trouble at all and gave him a smile so warm it would have melted ice and he grinned at her and said he'd show her to the door. I watched them leave the room and listened to the words they exchanged at the door, and then I went into the kitchen and took vases from the cabinet and carried them back to the study. I was arranging the flame-colored hibiscus in one of them when Jamie came back, that heavy brown wave slanting across his brow. I ignored him, reaching for another hibiscus.

"No need to be upset," he said.

"Upset? Me? I'm not upset. Whyever should I be upset?"

"I didn't ask her to come by. She just showed up. I thought she'd leave the books at the theater for you to bring home."

"Very thoughtful of her to bring them," I said.

"As a matter of fact, it was."

"Pity I came home so soon."

"What's that supposed to mean?" he demanded.

I finished with the hibiscus, fluffed them a bit, set the vase on the table and began to arrange the giant marigolds in a shallow white vase, sticking daisies among them.

"I asked you a question," he said. "Are you implying—My God! Are you implying I planned to *sleep* with the woman?"

"That's what *she* had in mind, I can assure you. She came dressed for it. That gown—at four o'clock in the afternoon? Oh yes, she came prepared. The hook was baited and no doubt she'd have pulled you in if I hadn't arrived when I did."

"I resent that! I have no interest whatsoever in—"

"Spending hours with her in the Green Room, discussing your beloved Mary, *that* I can tolerate, but when she brazenly comes to my home dressed like an expensive Piccadilly whore and tries to undermine me with her sly remarks I draw the line!"

"You're *jealous!*" he exclaimed. He looked pleased.

"Jealous? Of an inconsequential supporting player pushing forty and losing her looks? Don't be absurd! I'm not jealous, don't flatter yourself, you sod. Wipe that grin off your face. I just happen to know that bitch would like to take my place!"

"Sure." he said.

"She wants to supplant me!"

"Of course she does."

"You ad*mit* it!"

"Why shouldn't I? She's wretchedly obvious, love, transparent as a sheet of glass. Think I don't know what she's been up to? Think I'm that dense and dim-witted? Sure she'd like to take your place. What actress with any ambition wouldn't? I was on to her little ploys from the first, but she *has* been helpful, Angel, she *does* know a great deal about Mary, and she's given me some very good ideas."

"I'll bet she has!"

He smiled a slow, pleased smile and came toward me and I stiffened and he paused and shook his head, very amused by my anger. I stuck the last marigold into the vase and picked up the large bunch of golden-yellow daffodils and debated whether I should put them in the tall, fluted white vase or the shorter, rounded cut-glass container.

"She hadn't a prayer," he told me.

"Indeed?"

"No one could ever take your place, love."

I ignored that remark and put the daffodils in the tall white vase, and I heard his exasperated sigh but didn't look up. I was being totally unreasonable, I knew that, my anger was at her, not him, but he was so... so exasperating! And he was going to leave in the morning and I would be alone, wake up alone in the mornings, and he would not be there to touch and tease and delight. I put the bronze chrysanthemums in the cut-glass container and fetched a brass pitcher with a long spout from the kitchen and filled it with water and poured water into all the vases of flowers. Jamie watched as I placed the vases at various points around the room.

"Finished?" he inquired.

"For the moment."

My voice was cool, but that didn't deter him. He came over to me and put his hands on my shoulders and squeezed gently and gazed down at me with sleepy seductive green-brown eyes and I smelled the musky, male smell of him and felt his warmth and felt his strong fingers kneading my flesh, one hand reaching up to lift my hair and curl around the back of my neck, but I was still irritated and I wasn't going to melt and give in just because he had a magnificent body, just because he had a full curving mouth and a wonderful crooked nose that was endearing and kept him from being too handsome, just because he was a superlative lover and knew how to make me feel such glorious, wicked feelings inside, even now, when I didn't want to feel them at all. I had had such plans for today, his last day home, such delicious plans for tonight, and now they were in ruins and I was quite put out.

"I *hate* Mary, Queen of Scots," I snapped.

"You'll love the Mary I'm going to write for you."

"I wanted you to do a play about Aphra Behn. She was a strong, independent lady who made her own way in a man's world and became a huge success. Her life was full of romance and adventure, too. I don't know why you can't write *that* play for me."

"Maybe I'll write it later," he said huskily.

"I'm not in the mood, Jamie."

"Hunh?"

"You heard me. Stop rubbing your thighs against me."

"Just delivering a message."

"I got the message. I'm not interested."

"You don't have to leave for the theater for hours. I thought—"

"I know what you thought and I'm not in the mood. I suggest you read the books Mrs. Perry so thoughtfully brought, or, better yet, go see her. Pay her a visit. She'd love to receive your message."

"Sometimes you're an awful bitch, Angel."

"I don't deny it."

"I don't know why I put up with you."

"Nor I with you, you sod."

He squeezed the back of my neck. "Sure you're not in the mood?"

"Positive."

"Guess I'll have to work on it," he purred.

He did and I resisted and we fought and he won but he had to work for it. The victory was mine, of course, even though he overpowered me and I submitted against my will, and it was glorious, even though he was rough and unruly, and it was even better later, lying on the sofa, his arms around me, the afternoon sunlight drifting through the windows and fading on the floor, he murmuring in my ear and growing amorous again and slowly, gently, lazily loving me anew and rebuilding the bliss we had so splendidly shared a while before. We loved and we had tea and the sunlight vanished and lamps were lit and all too soon I had to bathe and change and leave for the theater.

Jamie walked me to the Lambert, a long gray cloak draped around his shoulders, his fingers curled around my elbow, and he left me at the stage door and gave me a perfunctory kiss and told me he'd be waiting for me when I got back. I watched him saunter away and then went to my dressing room and left my cloak and went to the Green Room to join Megan. We had formed the habit of meeting there for a chat before the performance a long time ago, and both of us looked forward to this opportunity to catch up on gossip and exchange the latest news. With its faded, pale lime-green walls, worn beige carpet and large comfortable chairs, the Green Room was pleasant and full of atmosphere with framed posters hanging about and two glass cases full of theatrical memorabilia.

"Well, luv," Megan announced when she came in a few moments later, "the handwriting is on the *wall*."

"Oh?"

"This morning I was in the kitchen, making coffee for him, spreading butter on his toast, and the charming Mr. Hart saunters in looking thoughtful and holding a pair of stockings and casually informs me they need mending, would I mind terribly patching them for him when I finished making breakfast. You can *imagine* my reaction!"

"You told him what to do with the stockings."

"In very explicit language."

"And then you mended them," I said.

"Not until after I finished making breakfast, luv."

Both of us smiled and Megan shook her head as though in dismay at her own gullibility. Though she was loath to admit it, she was very much in love with the lethargic, good-natured, handsome blond actor, and it showed. There was a new radiance about her, a glow to her creamy complexion, a sparkle in her vivid blue eyes. Her abundant auburn hair tumbling about her shoulders and glistening with dark red-gold highlights, she looked absolutely stunning in a gown of royal blue taffeta with narrow gold, silver and turquoise stripes. Snug at the waist, low at the bodice, with puffed sleeves worn off the shoulder, it admirably displayed her superb figure.

"It really wasn't all that much trouble," she confessed, "and he looked so pathetic and helpless, gazing at the stockings. Lord, luv, I'm absolutely hopeless. I suppose I'll *never* learn."

"Charles is very good to you," I pointed out.

"That's what worries me, luv." She sank into one of the chairs. "By the way, he's borrowing a carriage and we're driving out to the country on Sunday, taking a picnic hamper. We want you to come along."

"We'll see," I said.

"You'll enjoy it, Angel, and you know how lonely you always are when Lambert's away."

"If it weren't for this bloody play I'd go with him. I'm bored to tears being cheeky and winsome six nights a week, even if it does mean more money in the bank."

"Maybe we'll be in a failure next time," Megan said.

"We very likely will, if he persists with this Mary, Queen of Scots play. She's going to be impossibly noble, impossibly virtuous—I can tell from his notes."

"Lord, we'll have to wear heavy velvets and those cursed starched ruffs," she said. "I look dreadful in ruffs. You can imagine what those velvets will feel like under the heat of the footlights. I suppose Mrs. Perry will be happy, though—she's been so supportive I assume he'll write a part for her."

"Undoubtedly," I said.

"You look less than enchanted with the idea."

I told her what had happened that afternoon and what I had overheard when I was standing in the foyer, and Megan was, of course, fascinated. Furious as well, for she was the most loyal of friends and detested Mrs. Perry with a passion. She told me what she would do if the actress dared try her wiles on *her* man and added that it was a bloody wonder they hadn't already killed each other, sharing a dressing room as they had all these months. Both of us fell silent as the subject of our conversation strolled into the Green Room, lush and seductive in a cinnamon colored satin gown spangled in gold, her dark red gold hair pulled back sleekly and worn in a twist on back of her head, a glittering gold wire spray affixed to one side.

"I *thought* I might find you here," she announced.

"Why he*llo*, Mrs. Perry," I said.

"I knew you and Mrs. Sloan make a habit of coming

here to chat while some of us meditate and try to get into character for the play. I wanted to speak to you, Mrs. Howard."

"You're doing just that, Mrs. Perry."

"I—" She smiled her tight smile and reached up to pat the gold spray on the side of her coiffure. "I just wanted to explain the—uh—the little incident this afternoon. I wouldn't want you to get the wrong idea."

"How kind of you."

"I knew James needed the books and I wanted to make sure he got them, and so I took them over, fully expecting you to be there as well. We weren't having a *tête-à-tête,* darling, we were just discussing the play."

"I'm so glad you clarified that."

"We *have* spent a lot of time together, it's true, but I assure you we've done nothing unseemly. James is the kind of man who needs a woman to inspire him, and in this instance I've been able to be of service as you're so terribly negative about the play. You might say I've been his muse."

"You might," I replied.

"But nothing more, darling. I just wanted you to know that."

My smile was as tight as her own. Mrs. Perry gave me a gracious nod and left the room in a swirl of bespangled cinnamon satin. Megan and I exchanged looks. My smile tightened even more.

"I may shoot her," I said.

"Better drive a stake through her heart, luv. One can't be too careful these days."

Jamie left the next morning, and I was light and bright and smiled radiantly and told him to take care of himself and not work too hard and remember to eat properly and added that he'd bloody well better write at least twice a week or he'd be sorry indeed when he got back. He endured all this patiently and gave me a quick, distracted kiss on the front steps, eager to be gone. I watched the carriage drive away and then went inside and told myself I wasn't going to be silly and feel sad, but I did. Without him the charming house on

St. Martin's Lane felt curiously empty, as though the life force had gone out of it. I was going to miss him terribly, as I always did, not because I was so deeply in love with him, that wasn't it at all. I was ... I was merely accustomed to him, used to his being there, and it was perfectly natural that I should feel this sense of emptiness and loss.

I did go with Megan and Charles on Sunday, and the countryside was beautiful with the hawthorn blooming pink and white and the rhododendrons red and purple and mauve. Lofty trees spread soft blue-gray shadows over the sun-silvered green grass, and there was a cool, clear brook that actually babbled as it flowed swiftly over its pebbled bed. We had our picnic beside the brook, and Megan took off her shoes and lifted her skirts and went wading, splashing merrily, and after much cajoling Charles took off his boots and stockings and joined her. It was lovely watching them together, his calm, lethargic manner the perfect foil for her vivacity and wit, but their closeness, their obvious joy in each other's company made me feel even lonelier.

The ebullient James Boswell came to call on me the following Tuesday afternoon and wittily recounted all the latest gossip about Dr. Johnson and his circle and expounded on his theories about Lord Blackie who, after lying low for several months, had made another spectacular foray the week before, relieving Countess Bessborough of her diamond and emerald necklace and, if the lady was to be believed, her honor as well. He had scampered nimbly over the rooftops and climbed in through a maid's open window, all in black, of course, a black silk hood over his head, moving so quietly the sleeping maid didn't even wake up. The rascal was quite obviously a nobleman himself, Boswell informed me, and he had been on the Continent for the past few months, which explained the lack of forays during that time. Boswell had definite ideas about Lord Blackie's true identity, had, using the process of elimination, drawn up a list of four names, and he assured me it was only a matter of time until one of these gentlemen was caught in the act.

We had tea and buttered scones and sliced tongue, and the red-haired Scot made the mandatory attempt to pinch my bottom and I did my usual sidestep and he chuckled and told me I was the great love of his life and I told him I was flattered and, that game over with, he was the entertaining, affable fellow I had come to enjoy so very much. He said he was looking forward to writing the greatest book of all time, a life of his friend Samuel Johnson, and I said it would be a great book indeed if his writing was as energetic and witty as his speech. Boswell gave me a hug and scampered off to visit Mrs. Piozzi who, he confided, was the silliest woman in London but a veritable storehouse of scandalous gossip, which he adored and always recorded in his journal.

I dined with the Gainsboroughs two nights later—we ate early so that I could get to the theater on time—and Mrs. G. fussed over me and fed me wonderful things and Mr. G. took me into the studio to show me his work in progress, a misty landscape with feathery trees and an ox cart crossing a dilapidated stone bridge, a painting he was doing for his own pleasure. We talked about the past and my posing for him and I said I often wondered where *An Angel in Scarlet* was hanging. Gainsborough looked rather uneasy. He straightened his wig, brushed the lapels of his light blue satin frock coat and tried to change the subject. I wouldn't let him.

"You *know* where it is," I said. "I know you were sworn to secrecy, and I can understand why the buyer wouldn't want the world to know he owns so famous a painting, but surely it wouldn't hurt to tell *me* who he is."

"Afraid I can't, Angel. I gave my word."

"Does he think *I'll* try to steal it?"

"Wouldn't surprise me."

"I know he's a nobleman with a country estate, and I assume he's wealthy or he couldn't have afforded to outbid everyone else. Is he famous as well? Would I recognize his name?"

"Not another word, wench."

"You're positively infuriating, Mr. G."

"But I *do* keep my word," he told me.

I got a short, unsatisfying letter from Jamie the next day that informed me he had arrived and was working hard and had forgotten to pack his favorite old black leather slippers and missed them sorely. The sod didn't say a word about missing me. His next letter, which arrived on Monday, informed me that he had come down with a cold and was miserable and needed his slippers, never felt comfortable writing without them, would I send them by the next post? I was tempted to send a bomb instead. He got his bloody slippers and a snippy letter from me letting him know I was having a marvelous time and seeing dozens of people and enjoying the peace and quiet that prevailed on St. Martin's Lane.

I missed him dreadfully. The days were not so bad, for I had the house to keep tidy and shopping to do and friends to see, but the evenings, after I returned from the theater, were bad indeed. I climbed into bed and read till dawn every night, going through book after book, reading omnivorously, obsessively while candlelight flickered and books piled beside the bed. I had to go to Miller's to replenish my stock, and it was there that I stumbled upon Oliver Goldsmith, almost literally, for he was hunched on the floor in one of the dusty aisles, peering at titles on the lower shelf. That affable, absentminded charmer with his blinking owl eyes and gentle, lopsided smile and his shabby, oversized coat with pockets stuffed full of notes to himself told me he was looking for Virgil, as though Virgil were a lost dog. I helped him search and we eventually located a copy of the *Georgics,* and Goldy thanked me effusively if somewhat absentmindedly, gazing over my shoulder at the volumes on the shelf behind me.

The most lovable of men and one of the most eccentric, Goldsmith was always in debt and always being evicted from his quarters, despite the huge popularity of *The Vicar of Wakefield,* one of my favorite novels, and the tremendous success of *She Stoops to Conquer* in '73, hailed by one and all as the comic masterpiece of the English stage. Goldy was forgetful, fanciful, improvident, an incurable optimist who refused to take himself or life too seriously. Clutching his Virgil, he cheerfully informed me that he had been evicted again and was staying with friends and had faith that next November's revival of *She Stoops to Conquer* would make his fortune.

"Particularly if you'll be my Kate, Angel," he added in that soft, fuzzy voice his friends found so endearing. "Everyone agrees you're the only one to play the part."

"I'd love to play Kate, Goldy," I told him. "It's probably the most delightful part ever written for a woman, and *She Stoops to Conquer* is sheer enchantment, but— I have other commitments."

"But no contract," he said blithely, "that's encouraging. I'm the most honorable of men, ask anyone, but if I could steal you away from Jamie Lambert I'd do so in a minute."

"So would Garrick," I replied.

"Oh, Davy's much too stuffy. You don't want to go over to Drury Lane and do Shakespeare and such. Playing Kate would be *fun*."

"It would indeed," I agreed.

Goldy prowled around the dusty aisles with me while I selected some books to read, and I took him home with me and gave him a generous tea complete with buttered bread, cheese, sliced ham, grapes and some delicious honey cakes Mrs. G. had sent over by the irascible Jenkins. All of his friends had a protective feeling toward Goldy who was so sweet, so inept, so befuddled and incompetent, scribbling away in his dusty rented rooms, producing reams of hack articles for Fleet Street and an occasional masterpiece. He was an utterly endearing man, and I enjoyed his company immensely. After our tea his eyes began to blink and his voice grew drowsier and drowsier and he finally gave me a sleepy smile and nodded off on the sofa. I let him nap and cleared up and eventually it was time for me to dress for the theater and he was still dozing happily, a contented expression on his mellow, aged face. I lighted a lamp, spread a rug over him and left, feeling quite maternal.

Goldy was gone when I got back, but there was a note pinned to the sofa: *Thank you, Dear Angel* in handwriting as gentle and hazy as he. I smiled to myself, folding the rug. Goldy would continue to scribble his wry, amusing articles and move from room to room and write notes to himself and stuff them into the pockets of that oversized brown coat and he would find himself penniless and be evicted and one of his friends would take him in and feed him and care for him and feel pleased to be of service to the brilliant, bewildered genius who had given the world so much pleasure through his pen. The revival was sure to restore his fortune and the money would undoubtedly slip through his fingers like water and he would be living in another dusty rented room before many months passed.

I wished it were possible for me to play Kate Hardcastle, the wry, aristocratic lass who pretends to be a maid in order to win the debonair Marlow. It was a marvelous part, one that would give full range to my talents, and the lavish revival at the Haymarket was bound to be a tremendous critical and popular success. I longed to play comedy, knew I would be far better at it than I was in melodrama, but, of course, I couldn't think of taking the part. Jamie and I didn't have a written contract, true, and there was no legal reason why I couldn't go elsewhere when *My Charming Nellie* finally shut down, but there was a silent understanding between us. I could never be disloyal, not even for a plum like Kate. Goldy would have to find another actress, alas, but I felt honored that he wanted me. Perhaps Mary wouldn't be as dreary and stilted as I feared. Jamie was convinced the play would be a triumph.

A full week passed without a letter from him, and when, the following Friday, one finally arrived, it was distressing indeed. His cold had grown worse, Mrs. Lindsey had nursed him back to health with mustard plasters and hot chicken soup, and he was just now getting back to work on the play. Mary was giving him problems, the whole play had to be restructured and he probably wouldn't be home for another three weeks. Another three weeks! The page shook in my hand. It would be almost June before he got back home! I was in a wretched mood when I got to the theater that evening, impatient with my dresser, blowing a line in the first act, finding it difficult indeed to be blithe and capricious as Nell. The enchanting Mrs. Perry didn't help matters one bit.

We all took our curtain calls together and the audience applauded enthusiastically and the others left the stage and I stood alone and smiled and bowed. A rowdy group of young bucks from Oxford stood and cheered and threw a somewhat tattered bouquet of red roses onto the stage. I picked it up and sniffed the blooms and smiled again and pulled out one rose and tossed it to the ringleader of the group, a strapping blond. I was still in a wretched mood. I blew him a kiss. Lord, would they ever stop applauding and carrying on? I had a dreadful headache and knew I was going to stomp offstage if they didn't stop soon. The curtain came down, came up again, and I was humble and demure and grateful, giving a performance far superior to the one I had just given as Nellie. The curtain came down for the final time and I sighed with relief, giving the roses to the stagehand and moving into the wings.

Mrs. Perry was waiting for me, wearing the luscious pink and black striped satin she wore in the last act. It had a very full skirt and a very low bodice that left most of her bosom bare. One black and two pink plumes were fastened to the side of her coiffure with a large false diamond clasp. The diamonds she wore at her throat and on her wrists were false, too, and almost as gaudy as the real ones she had worn when the play opened last year. She smiled a very sweet smile that literally oozed malice.

"A bit off tonight, weren't you, dear?"

"On the contrary, I was brilliant. You should observe more closely. You might learn something."

"I doubt seriously there is anything I could learn from you, Mrs. Howard," she replied.

It was open warfare. Both of us knew it.

"I'm *so* relieved that James is feeling better," she told me. "I was very concerned about him, but apparently those mustard plasters did the trick. Mrs. Lindsey must be a dear soul, nursing him as she did."

Keep your temper, Angel. Don't let the bitch know she's scored a hit. So he wrote her a letter? Why shouldn't he? He's perfectly free to write to anyone he cares to, and I'm going to kill him when he returns.

"He's always been one of her favorites," I said. "He's been going to Tunbridge Wells for years, and he always takes rooms there."

"So I gather. It's so very peaceful there, with no one to bother him and distract him from his work. He needs that."

"Indeed he does."

"At least he keeps in touch," she added. "I've received a letter almost every day this week—*long* letters. All about the play, of course. He's going to restructure it, and he wanted my opinion about the new scenes."

"So kind of you to take an interest," I said.

"Isn't it," she replied.

She flashed that sweet, malicious smile and turned and left, and Megan, in her street clothes, came looking for me and saw my expression and was immediately concerned.

"Lord, luv, what *is* it? You look awful. Can I do something?"

"Yes," I said tightly. "You can find me that stake."

I was absolutely livid as Peg helped me out of the silver and violet gown. I snapped at her and apologized and she said that was all right, pet, she understood artistic temperament and, besides, it was difficult being without my man, wasn't it? When her Herb wasn't around, he frequently took trips to visit his brothers in Kent, when he wasn't around she got as jittery as could be and wasn't herself at all, not at all, and Mr. Lambert had been gone a long time, hadn't he, it must be awfully hard on me, us being so close and all. I knew that if she didn't shut up I was going to crack a vase over her head so I smiled and told her that would be all, she could go, I'd finish dressing myself. Peg left and I put on a silk wrapper and sat at the dressing table and removed the stage makeup and washed my face and dried it.

I knew what she was up to, of course. She was trying to drive a wedge between Jamie and me so that she could step in and console him and play Mary herself. *I* knew that and *Jamie* knew that, he had told me so himself, the slut wasn't fooling anyone, so why did the son of a bitch have to write long letters to her? Almost every day! *I* sent him his bloody slippers and *I* worry myself sick about his cold and he pens a short note to me and writes reams to her! I could kill him, I really could, and I just might do it. I brushed my hair angrily until it fell in gleaming chestnut waves about my shoulders and then I hurled the brush across the room and it crashed against the wall.

Getting angry accomplished nothing, and that was exactly what the slut had intended to do, make me angry. I took several deep breaths and controlled myself and, eventually, managed some semblance of composure. I felt drained now, bone weary through and through. I wasn't getting enough sleep. I wasn't eating properly. I was growing edgy and snappish and shrewish. I sighed heavily, dressing, adjusting the low-cut bodice of the amethyst silk, spreading the full skirt over the silver-gray petticoat skirts beneath. I slipped on my cloak of silver-gray velvet, pulled the hood up over my head and left the theater, dreading going back to the empty house.

Perhaps... perhaps I hadn't been fair to Jamie, I thought as I strolled toward St. Martin's Lane. I *had* been negative about the new play from the very beginning, had made it quite clear that I had no desire to play Mary, and I had given him none of the encouragement, none of the support I always gave him when he began a new project. I had kept insisting he write the Aphra Behn play instead, and ... and if he had turned to Mrs. Perry for encouragement and support, I had no one to blame but myself. He was an artist. He was temperamental. He was far more sensitive than his confident, swaggering manner would lead one to suspect, was, in fact, quite vulnerable beneath all the histrionics, all the noise. I knew that, and I suspected he was hurt by my lack of interest, my negative remarks. He was determined to prove me wrong, to prove he was capable of writing a play that would make the critics take notice.

That was very important to him. Jamie was proud of my success, for it was his success as well, but it stung when I received wonderful notices for my acting while his skills as a playwright were constantly denigrated. One critic had gone so far as to say that without Angel Howard to bring in the customers James Lambert would undoubtedly be sweeping stalls for a living. Although he claimed it didn't bother him one bit, that critics were a vile, envious lot, frustrated playwrights all, he had been in a foul mood for weeks afterward, sulky and bad tempered. It stung, too, that others eagerly sought me, that Garrick wanted me to act at Drury Lane, that Sheridan wanted me for his next play, that Goldsmith wanted me for the revival. Jamie had *created* Angel of Covent Garden, a fact I never denied, and it hurt that I no longer needed him. The male ego is a fragile thing indeed.

Poor darling. I decided I wouldn't kill him when he returned. I would be light and loving and I'd try my damndest to like the bloody play and be enthusiastic about playing Mary. Covent Garden was all moonlight and shadows and yellow light spilling out of Coffee Houses and windows. Couples strolled together and tipsy revelers staggered on the pavements and discreet prostitutes, many of them part-time actresses and supers, discreetly plied their trade. A pickpocket nimbly lifted a watch from a stout, drunken gentleman and, seeing me, waved. I blew a kiss and turned down St. Martin's Lane. Moonlight silvered the steps in front of the house and flooded the foyer when I unlocked the door and opened it. I reached for the candlestick on the table beside the door, struck a match and lighted the candle.

A pool of wavering gold light surrounded me and shadows sprang against the walls. I closed the door and locked it and stood there for a few moments holding the candlestick, frowning. I could feel the emptiness all around me, and I had a peculiar sensation that the house was...was waiting, watching me, holding its breath, as though it were an animate thing. I felt a curious chill in my blood, and my frown deepened. Get hold of yourself, Angel, I scolded. It's a little late in the game for you to get spooked now, after staying by yourself for weeks. You've been reading too many of those scary novels Walpole made so popular with *The Castle of Otranto*. There is no one in the house but you, and you're not going to get nervy now. I squared my shoulders and went upstairs to the bedroom and lighted candles there and removed my cloak, and I still had the spooky feeling that something was wrong, that the atmosphere had been disturbed somehow.

My first instinct was to lock the bedroom door and barricade it and huddle here in terror until dawn, but I wasn't about to do that. I knew that if I let myself give in I'd be a mass of nerves all night long. You're going to go down to the kitchen and make yourself a cup of nice hot tea and find some snacks and come back up here and read and put this nonsense out of your mind. If there *is* a ghost in the house it's Aphra Behn's, and she's bound to be a dear soul, full of benevolence. I picked up the candlestick and left the bedroom and stood at the top of the stairs, peering down into the shadowy darkness below, and it was one of the bravest things I had ever done.

The house waited, watched, and it seemed to whisper as well, a soft, barely audible whispering. I held the candlestick high, and wavering golden light spilled around me and intensified the darkness, and I knew there was nothing on earth that would induce me to go down those stairs, into the study and kitchen. I didn't *need* tea. I wasn't really hungry. Oh, no, Angel, you're not going to back out now. This is positively absurd. You've never been frightened before. There is nothing wrong. I tried to convince myself of that as I took another deep breath and started slowly down the stairs. My amethyst silk skirts made a loud rustling noise. The fourth step down creaked loudly, seemed to squeal out in the silence. I paused, gripping the pewter candlestick tightly. Go on. Go on down. If you let this silly nervousness get the best of you you'll be nervous every night, afraid to stay alone.

Someone was down there. In the darkness. I sensed it. I knew it. Someone was watching me. I could feel eyes staring, an almost physical sensation. There, by the bookcase, a dark form, darker than the darkness surrounding it, a man, waiting, watching me. The heavy candlestick shook in my hand. The candle flame waved wildly, shadows leaping on the wall. The dark form moved, merging into the darker shadows, vanished, and I knew my imagination was playing tricks on me. Damn Walpole. Damn all those scary novels I'd been consuming. Aphra, if it's you, I'm coming down and I'm making myself some tea, and if you want to watch, fine. I moved on down the stairs and golden light washed over the bookcases lining the foyer, and there was no one there, of course, never had been. I sighed with relief and moved through the doorway into the study.

I had only taken a few steps into the room when a gust of wind caused the draperies to billow. The candle blew out. Darkness engulfed me like a tangible thing, like a heavy black cloak suddenly thrown over my head, and I was in a world of inky blackness, alone with the thing that watched. I could feel it again, and my skin seemed to prickle. My heart pounded. I couldn't breathe. I knew a moment of sheer, stark terror and I thought I was going to faint. My knees grew weak. I could feel myself beginning to reel, and I steadied myself, willed myself to hold the hysterics at bay. A gust of wind blew the draperies into the room and blew out the candle and there was positively no reason to be alarmed. But

...why was the window open? It had been shut, been securely locked when I left for the theater. Hadn't it? Had I opened it this afternoon to get some fresh air and forgotten to close it? My heart still pounded. I caught my breath.

Several moments passed and each one seemed an eternity. I couldn't stand here in the darkness all night, clutching the candlestick and imagining I wasn't alone in the room. I had to relight the candle. We kept a box of matches on the mantelpiece above the fireplace. I started toward it and stumbled, my foot slipping on a rug, and I knew I was likely to fall and break my neck if I tried to grope around in this inky blackness. I turned and took two steps and reached the window and pulled the draperies open. Shafts of silvery moonlight flooded the center of the room and left everything else in shadow but at least I would be able to see my way to the fireplace without falling and... I saw him then.

He was leaning against the wall beside the fireplace. He was dressed all in black—black boots, black breeches, black frock coat—and where his face should have been there was black, too, shiny blackness, a black silk hood covering his head. His arms were folded across his chest. He unfolded them and stood up straight and stepped into the moonlight and stood there staring at me through the eyeholes in the hood. I was paralyzed, frozen with horror, looking at him as he stood there, staring, staring. My throat was tight. I couldn't possibly scream. He took another step toward me and paused and tilted his head to one side.

"Hello, Angel," he murmured.

Chapter Sixteen

I stared at him, still paralyzed, unable to speak, but the terror I had felt a moment before vanished completely. The unseen, the unknown, the imagined had chilled my blood and caused that stark terror, but the reality didn't frighten me at all. I was shaken, yes, alarmed, too, and I was mad as hell, but I wasn't at all frightened as I stood there by the window and stared at Lord Blackie. My heart stopped palpitating. I took a deep breath and tried to control the anger that steadily mounted. How dare he break into my house! How dare he give me such a fright! I glared at him, and I had the curious feeling that he was smiling beneath that black silk hood, amused by my obvious fury.

"If you've come for jewelry, you've come to the wrong house!" I snapped. "The only jewelry I own is paste, and it's at the theater. There isn't a single valuable object in the place—no gold, no silver, no plate and no money, either, besides a small amount I keep on hand for household expenses. I'll be happy to give *that* to you!"

He didn't speak, merely stared at me, and that ired

me all the more. He was extremely tall, with a lean, muscular build, and he stood with arms folded across his chest, utterly relaxed, in a kind of lazy slouch. Silver moonlight gilded the high black leather boots and gave the heavy black silk hood a shimmery sheen. There was nothing at all menacing about this man, no sinister vibrations. I felt somehow that he was indeed a gentleman, and I was certain he meant me no harm. Remembering all the stories about his gallantry to the ladies, I couldn't help but be intrigued.

"You scared the bloody hell out of me!" I said irritably.

"I'm sorry about that," he crooned.

"I'm afraid you've wasted your time. I suggest you leave right now—and close the bloody window behind you!"

"You're as spirited as ever, I see."

"I'm not afraid of you, if that's what you mean! Petty thieves who break into—into respectable people's houses hold no terror for me. Take my household money if you like and—and get the hell out of my house or I—I'll yell like a banshee!"

"I wouldn't do that if I were you," he murmured.

His voice was low, melodious, a soft caress, and I had the feeling he was deliberately disguising it. In complete control of myself now, I took another deep breath and tossed my head, shaking a long wave from my cheek. Lord Blackie continued to gaze at me, feasting his eyes. He seemed to be savoring each and every feature. If the bloody sod was so fascinated by me he could bloody well buy a ticket and come to the theater. I told him so. He chuckled softly to himself.

"I've seen you perform several times," he said.

"Oh? I suppose I should be flattered."

"You're quite good on stage—magnificent presence—even if the material you chose to do leaves much to be desired."

"Jesus," I said, exasperated. "*Every*one's a critic."

"I've been tempted to come backstage and see you

any number of times, but I could never bring myself to do so."

"Good thing you didn't. I'd have turned you over to Bow Street in a minute."

"You wouldn't have known I was Lord Blackie. I never wear these garments except when I'm on a job."

"Smart man," I retorted. "Look, it's late, I'm exhausted and although I find this conversation utterly fascinating I'm really in no mood to chat. I'm going to light this candle and then I'm going to make myself a pot of tea, and if you're not gone by the time I'm finished I fully intend to go to the window and yell my head off."

"Oh?"

"There's lots of constables around, Runners, too. You'll find yourself spending the night in the nearest roundhouse."

"Feisty, unafraid—utterly gorgeous. The painting by Gainsborough doesn't do you justice. I own a reproduction. Not a day passes that I don't look at it and—remember."

"That's lovely, Sir, and I'm thrilled beyond words that you're such an admirer, but, like I said, it's quite late and I'm not in a sociable mood. Get your ass *out* and I'll forget this ever happened."

I moved toward the mantel to fetch the matches. He caught hold of my arm to restrain me and, instinctively, without thinking, without consciously planning to do so, I swung the heavy pewter candlestick and slammed it against the side of his head. He gave a startled cry then, slowly, still holding onto my arm, began to crumple, his knees giving way, his tall body swaying to and fro. I pulled my arm free just before he toppled, landing on the floor with a heavy thud. He was very still, stretched out there in the moonlight like a gigantic crumpled doll. My God, I thought, I've killed him! I stumbled into the shadows and fumbled nervously for the box of matches on top of the mantel, and it seemed to take me forever to find them.

Somehow, hands shaking, I managed to light the candle, and then I lighted several more and set the candlestick down and stood there looking at the still form sprawled out on the study floor. Lord, I *had* killed him. He wasn't even breathing. Was he? Was his chest rising and falling ever so slightly? Gnawing my lower lip, I stepped closer and, summoning all my courage, kneeled down and took his right wrist between thumb and forefinger. Yes, thank God, there was a pulse, a slight one, and he *was* breathing, through his mouth apparently. The black silk covering his face rippled faintly at the level of his lips. I could see two closed lids through the circular eyeholes. I dropped his wrist and stood up, moving back.

I hope he isn't *hurt,* I thought. Lord! Angel of Covent Garden captures Lord Blackie. What a news story *that* would be, and what a boon to the box office. With all the new spring productions opening, *My Charming Nellie* was beginning to suffer, and we hadn't played to a full house for several weeks. We wouldn't be able to *print* enough tickets now. What did I do now? Rush out into the night and try to find a constable? He might wake up and get away while I was gone. Find some cord or scarves or something and tie him up? I had no idea how you went about tying someone up and, besides, the idea was repugnant to me. So what are you going to do? I asked myself. Just stand here and wait for him to come to and then request him to come along peacefully to the roundhouse? Some heroine you are. He gave a faint moan, twitched. I jumped. You have him, love. What are you going to do with him?

I didn't really *want* to turn him in. Somehow it didn't seem quite fair. He hadn't really *hurt* anything, and he'd been ... well, rather polite to me, soft spoken, gallant. Said I was utterly gorgeous, he had. Came to the theater several times. If I turned him in they were bound to hang him and I would feel terrible about it. You're one tough lady, love. Hard as nails. The man is a seasoned criminal, broke into your house, scared the wits out of you, and you want to pat him on the back and thank him for calling. He looks so uncomfortable there on the floor. He's probably in pain. He moaned again, and so, of course, I fetched a cushion and kneeled down and carefully lifted his head, placing the cushion under it, and then I went to get Jamie's brandy. He would need some when he came to. Putting the decanter of brandy and a glass down on the table in front of the sofa, I moved over to one of the wing chairs and sat down, patiently watching my guest.

He didn't move. A good fifteen minutes passed, the clock over the mantel ticking loudly in the quiet house. He was so still, hadn't moaned again, hadn't even twitched. I began to worry. Maybe...maybe he *had* died. Maybe he wouldn't ever come to. I got up and went over to him and checked and, yes, he was still breathing, but his pulse didn't seem any stronger than it was before. I had slammed the candlestick against his head with considerable force. His injury might be...might be serious indeed. He might be bleeding under that hood. I would have to remove it. There was no way around it. Of course my curiosity about what he looked like had nothing whatsoever to do with my decision to remove the hood. Carefully, I lifted his head. He moaned again and mumbled something incoherent as I took hold of the top of the hood and pulled. Shiny black silk slipped away, revealing his features.

I didn't gasp. I didn't faint. My heart didn't leap. Calmly, I stared, and I seemed to have no feeling whatsoever. I saw the lean, foxlike face and noted that it was a bit fuller than before, not quite so sharp and thin. His mouth was wide and full, the lower lip with that cruel curve I remembered, and the sleek black eyebrows slanted up from the bridge of his nose to a high arch and then swept back down. Though still dark, his skin wasn't as deep a tan as it had been, but his hair was as thick, as black, the rich blue-black of a raven's wing. There was an ugly mauve bruise above his temple darkening to purple-blue. I must tend to that, I thought, ever so calm, completely objective. I had seen his face so often in my dreams that seeing it now, even after all this time, had no effect whatsoever on me.

Or so I believed.

I went upstairs and found a clean cloth and the bottle of rubbing alcohol we kept in a cabinet in the dressing room. I returned to the study and bathed the bruise. The skin wasn't broken, and there was only a slight swelling. He wasn't seriously hurt, although he was going to feel wretched when he came to. He moaned. His eyelids fluttered. He opened his eyes and they were so deep a brown they seemed almost black, confused now as they gazed up at me. "Angie," he moaned, a low, aching moan that seemed to hurt his throat, and then he shut his eyes and drifted back into unconsciousness. I finished bathing his temple and eased his head back down onto the cushion and spread a cloak over him, and I poured myself a glass of brandy and sat back down in the wing chair and wondered how I could possibly be so very calm and objective, feeling nothing whatsoever.

I sipped the brandy. An hour passed, two, and the memories came and with them the emotions I hadn't felt earlier and I wanted another brandy, needed it badly, but I didn't have one. I went into the kitchen and made tea and another hour passed and the feelings I wanted so desperately to deny swept over me, and I knew that love was not dead, was still very much alive inside me. I was sad, so sad, remembering that sensitive girl, that moody youth, knowing it was too late for both of us, for both of us had changed, though the love was still alive. Dawn came and he awoke and I helped him onto the sofa and told him not to talk and made another pot of tea and made him drink it, and I was composed, cool, in complete control of the emotions raging inside. He finished his second cup of tea and set the cup aside and rubbed the side of his head and grimaced.

"How do you feel?" I asked. My voice was crisp.

"I suppose I'll live. I've had worse bumps. I had to come, Angie. For weeks I've been trying to build up enough courage. They claim Lord Blackie is brave and dauntless, the boldest man in London, but I suffered agonies while I waited for you to come home last night."

"Indeed?"

"I was afraid—afraid to see you. I had stayed away for so long a time, but I couldn't stay away any longer. What I said about that portrait is true, Angie. Every day I look at the reproduction and I remember and—"

"It's too late, Hugh."

"You remember, too," he told me.

"Yes, I remember."

Pink-orange light streamed into the room, growing brighter by the moment. I got up and put out the candles and opened all the curtains. Hugh watched me with brown-black eyes full of unspoken emotion.

"You must leave," I said.

"Not yet. We have to talk."

"There's nothing to talk about, Hugh."

"I love you. I've never loved anyone else. When I escaped I longed to come to you, to see you just one more time before—" He paused, a deep frown creasing his brow. "It wasn't possible. I had to get away. I went to sea. I intended to make enough money to get to Italy and gather the proof I needed to establish my legitimacy and bring my case to court, but there is very little money to be made when you're a lowly sailor. I found that out early on, but I dared not come back to England. Eventually, when I felt it was safe, I returned. I discovered that Clinton was married and living at Greystone Hall—in my house, with my title—and I discovered that you had become the celebrated Angel Howard. I was penniless. I knew I couldn't approach you until I—until I had a future to offer you."

"So you became Lord Blackie," I said. "You became a thief."

"Out of necessity, Angie. I had to have a great deal of money in order to accomplish my goal, and there was no way I could earn it honestly. I became a thief, yes, but I only robbed the rich, the gentry, lifting bright baubles from empty-headed women who wouldn't suffer from the loss. I never committed an act of violence, never hurt anyone. I feel no remorse."

"I don't imagine you do," I said.

He didn't like my tone of voice. He frowned again,

looking then remarkably like the sullen youth I had known. I sat down wearily in the wing chair and caught sight of myself in the mirror across the room. My face was drawn, faint shadows under my eyes, and my hair looked limp, all atumble. It didn't matter. I was utterly weary. I wanted to be alone. I wanted to forget, and I knew I never could.

"It took me quite some time to get the money I needed," he told me. "I lifted many valuable jewels, true, but their value decreased drastically when I took them to the fence—the best fence in London, I might add. When, finally, I felt I had enough, I went to Italy and began my search. It was very expensive. I had to hire people to help me, bribe clerks, pay people to dig through records, and then we found out that the records I needed were lost in a fire. Or so we thought. Some of them had been saved, transported to another place, and I have men searching for them now. I have someone else looking for the priest who performed the ceremony. He is still alive, they say, and I hope he may remember, may have records of his own."

"I see."

"I ran out of money. I had to come back. Once I have the proof I need, it will take a great deal of money to present my case properly in court. It takes money to fight money, and Clinton is a very wealthy man."

His voice was low and full of determination, and I looked at him and saw the resolution in his eyes and knew he still clung to the dream. He still believed he would become Lord Meredith and live in the house he hadn't been allowed to enter as a youth. He still believed the stableboy would become the master. It was an obsession with him. I understood, and I was sad for him, sad for all the disappointment, all the loss, all the bitterness he had lived with since childhood. I fought the compassion welling up inside, fought the urge to go to him and hold him to me and give him the love he had been denied all his life.

"You intend to go on stealing," I said.

"Until I have what I need. Two or three more jobs and Lord Blackie will retire."

I stood up, hardening myself. I brushed my amethyst skirt and looked at the clock. It was after seven.

"You must go now," I told him.

"Angie—"

"I'm not Angie," I said, and my voice was cool. "I'm Angel Howard now. The girl you knew is— She no longer exists."

Hugh got to his feet, a bit unsteady on his legs. The swelling had gone down, but the bruise was an ugly purple-gray. His face was drawn, too, taut, skin tight across those wide, sharp cheekbones. Morning sunlight gleamed on his thick, tousled hair, bringing out deep blue-black highlights. He looked at me with dark eyes. His full pink mouth was tight.

"I don't believe that," he said harshly.

"It's true."

"I love you, Angie. You're the only person I've ever loved, and I don't intend to lose you again. You love me, too. You can't deny it. I see it in your eyes."

"You're wrong, Hugh."

"No."

The anger was there, the old anger, and he took a step toward me and his knees gave way and I rushed to him and caught hold of his arms before he fell and eased him back down onto the sofa. "Damn!" I said. He was still weak. The blow on the side of his head had clearly done more harm than either of us suspected. I poured a glass of brandy and gave it to him and ordered him to drink it, and I stood watching him with a hard expression on my face. I knew I had to get him out of the house before I gave in to the emotions raging inside, and I knew he couldn't make it on his own. He leaned back on the cushions, pale now, trying to keep his eyes from closing.

"Stay here!" I snapped.

I left the house and hurried down St. Martin's Lane to the Strand, and I found a cabbie there, dozing on his seat while the horses stood listlessly in harness. I woke him up and ordered him to take me back to the house and wait while I fetched another passenger. He yawned, blinked his eyes and then said "'Op in, luv, 'Oward Finney at yer service." Minutes later I was back in the study, pulling Hugh to his feet. His face was still pale. He was still unsteady. I curled one of his arms around my shoulders, holding his wrist, and I felt his weight and felt my own knees sag and told him he'd bloody well better walk as I wasn't about to carry him. He smiled at that and, staggering, we moved into the foyer and out of the house.

"'Ad a mite too much to drink, didn't 'e?" the cabbie said.

"Yes," I snapped. "Give him your address, Hugh."

"The Blue Stag. It's on Holywell Street, near Lincoln's Inn Fields, and Holywell is just off Fleet."

"Know th' place well, Guv. Need any 'elp gettin' 'im in my cab?"

"I think we can make it," I said crisply.

We climbed in and Hugh sank back against the dusty leather seat, sighing heavily, looking woozy indeed. I pulled the door shut and the cabbie snapped the reins and we started back toward the Strand which, after passing the little church of St. Clement Danes, ran into Fleet. Hugh wiped his brow, beaded with moisture, and I was afraid he might pass out again. The son of a bitch would probably die on me and wouldn't *that* be a dandy thing to have on my conscience. Why the hell hadn't he stayed away? Why the hell hadn't I summoned a constable immediately, without even removing his hood? I had dreamed about him all these years, had longed for him, and now that he was here beside me I found that I didn't want him in my life again. There had been too many changes in both our lives.

"Sorry about this," he said weakly. "I feel a fool."

"It's my own bloody fault for hitting you so hard."

"It was quite a whack," Hugh agreed. "I seem to be having some kind of delayed reaction."

"You'll probably *die* on me."

He managed a chuckle at that and took my hand

and squeezed it. The sensations that stirred within as those strong fingers squeezed mine were alarming indeed. I pulled my hand away. I tried to ignore the nearness of him, the smell of him, the wild exhilaration that swelled within me despite all my efforts to stem it. The carriage rattled noisily over the cobbles and swayed and his weight was thrown against me and I felt bone and muscle and closed my eyes and prayed for strength. It was too late, too late, much too late. The girl he had known really didn't exist any longer, just as I had said, and the youth I had loved with such fervor no longer existed either. We were different people, with only the past and the dream of first love to bind us.

We passed the church of St. Clement Danes and moved down Fleet and eventually turned and stopped. The Blue Stag was a huge building in Tudor style with plaster and exposed beams and an archway with rooms over it opening into the central courtyard. The carriage stopped. The cabbie hopped down to open the door for us. I asked him to wait for me. Hugh was still unsteady on his feet and his face was still pale, moist. He gave me instructions and I took hold of his arm and led him into the courtyard and over to the door he pointed out. I opened it to discover a dim foyer and a narrow wooden staircase.

"How many flights?" I inquired.

"Three," he said apologetically.

"Wonderful. Can you make it?"

"With your help."

"Put your arm around my shoulders, lean on me. There, I'll slip my arm around your waist. Jesus, this is going to be fun. You *would* have rooms on the third floor."

He smiled weakly. "You shouldn't have hit me so hard."

I ignored this attempt at light banter and started up the stairs. Hugh leaned heavily on me, and I was bearing most of his weight. I was exhausted before we reached the second flight but, gritting my teeth, forged on, feeling him grow weaker by the moment. I'd probably have to *drag* the son of a bitch up the other flights. His arm clutched my shoulders, curling tightly, his body pressing against mine. He had put on a great deal of weight during the past eight years, all of it solid muscle, it seemed, and I felt my knees giving way. I stumbled, almost fell. I hadn't had a wink of sleep. I hadn't eaten. I feared I was going to pass out myself. I didn't. Somehow I got him up the stairs and leaned him against the wall beside his door and opened the door with the key he dug out of his pocket.

The two rooms were pleasant and airy, the walls a light gray with white wood trim around the doors and windows. A shabby, dark blue carpet covered most of the sitting-room floor, and chairs and sofa were upholstered in faded blue and gray striped brocade. There was a small white brick fireplace, and over the mantel, framed in gilt, hung a large and obviously expensive reproduction of *An Angel in Scarlet*. Although it lacked the vibrant color and glow of the original, it was quite good, dominating the room. What changes that painting had brought about in my life. Had I not been walking down the street that day, had Gainsborough not seen me as he rode past, my life would undoubtedly have taken an entirely different course. Where would I be now? What would I be doing?

Hugh sank into one of the chairs and looked at me with dark brown eyes, heavy black locks spilling over his forehead. I felt a new weakness within as I gazed at those sharp, taut cheekbones, that full pink lower lip with its cruel curl. I remembered that mouth on mine. I remembered the feel of his arms holding me tight, drawing me nearer, remembered the warmth of his skin, the weight of his lean, bony body. He watched me. He seemed to be reading my mind.

"I'll fetch the doctor," I said. "I'll send him here."

He shook his head. "I don't need a doctor poking over me. All I need is some rest."

"Very well," I said. I moved to the door. "Good-bye, Hugh."

"I'll see you, Angie."

I gave him a cold, hard look. "No," I told him. "I don't want to see you again. I intend to—to forget this ever happened. There's no place in my life for—for the past. It's over, Hugh."

"I think not," he said.

I opened the door and left, moving resolutely down the stairs. The cabbie was still waiting for me and he took me home and I went upstairs and undressed and climbed into bed and, because I was so weary, I managed to sleep a few hours and then I bathed and dressed and forced myself to eat something and left early for the theater. I gave a competent performance that night. The house was only two thirds full. Megan noticed that I was distracted and asked if anything was wrong. I smiled brightly and said I was perfectly all right, I was just missing Jamie, and it was true, I was, I needed him desperately to hold me and keep me safe from the past.

I kept very, very busy during the days that followed. I spent a lot of time with Megan and Charles and paid several visits to Dottie, sitting in the shop with her, helping her cut and trim, savoring the security of her presence. I was not looking at all well, she informed me. There were mauve shadows on my lids and I looked too thin, seemed edgy, out of sorts. I said I would be fine when Jamie got back. Dottie shook her head, concerned. The days I could fill, but the nights were hell. Reading didn't help. I lived in terror he would return, and when, two weeks later, he finally appeared in my dressing room after the performance, I was almost relieved. At least the suspense was over.

"He said he was an old friend," Peg told me. "I told him he couldn't come in here, but he insisted. I was—" She looked nervously at Hugh, and her voice dropped to a whisper. "I was afraid to make a fuss. There's something scary about him. Do you want me to go fetch Andy and a couple of the stagehands?"

"That won't be necessary, Peg. You may go. I won't need you tonight."

"But—"

"You may go," I said firmly.

Peg left, shutting the door behind her, and I looked at my visitor with a cool, level gaze. He was wearing polished black knee boots and elegantly cut black broadcloth breeches and frock coat and a vest of dark-maroon satin embroidered with tiny black fleurs-de-lis, his white silk neckcloth expertly folded. His hair was neatly brushed, pulled back and fastened with a black ribbon at the nape. He looked fully recovered. He looked like a gentleman. No, I thought, with those wickedly arched eyebrows and that cruel pink mouth he looked like some cynical buccaneer masquerading as a gentleman.

"How dare you intimidate my dresser!" I snapped.

"I didn't do a thing," he protested. "I was as polite as could be."

"You undoubtedly curled your lip at her. You glared at her with those eyes. She was afraid to throw you out."

"I can't help it if I have that kind of face."

"I told you I didn't want to see you again, Hugh."

He smiled. "Tell me that you haven't thought about me every day since we parted. Tell me you haven't longed to see me."

"Get out, Hugh."

"I have a carriage waiting. I'm taking you to dinner."

"I'm going home."

"Afraid?" he inquired.

There was challenge in his voice, in his eyes as well. I looked at him for a long moment before replying.

"No, Hugh," I said, "I'm not afraid. I'll go out to dinner with you, if only to prove that there is nothing left between us. Kindly wait for me out in the hallway. I have to change."

I joined him twenty minutes later, cool, composed, polite. I was wearing a low-cut cream satin gown printed with tiny blue and violet flowers and minuscule brown leaves. The small puffed sleeves were worn off the shoulder and the full, spreading skirt parted in front to reveal an underskirt of alternating rows of blue and brown lace ruffles. Dottie had delivered it here at the

theater a week ago, and I was glad I had it on hand.
The simple pink linen frock I had left the house in would
hardly have been appropriate for a midnight supper.
Hugh looked at me with approval as I slipped on a pair
of elbow-length brown lace gloves.

The eating house he had selected was near St. James
Square and extremely elegant, filled with sumptuously
attired ladies and gentlemen, the majority of them in
powdered wigs. Crystal chandeliers glittered. Gilt sparkled on the ivory walls. Our entrance caused quite a
stir, for I was recognized, of course, and a number of
the customers seemed affronted that a common actress
would dare appear in their aristocratic establishment.
I held my head high, both amused and irritated by
Hugh's obvious efforts to impress me. A nice grilled
chop and steamed red cabbage at Button's would have
done nicely but the former stableboy had to show me
he could mingle with the bluebloods with ease. I was
not surprised when the waiter showed us into a small
private room aglow with candlelight from gilt and crystal wall sconces.

"I hope you can afford this," I said.

"I can," he assured me. "Champagne?"

I nodded. Hugh was polite and attentive throughout
the meal, handling himself with undeniable polish. No
one observing him would have questioned his right to
be here. The meal was magnificent, flawlessly served,
the conversation deliberately light and impersonal. He
had learned to ape the gentry to perfection, but the
beautiful clothes and carefully cultivated manner didn't
deceive me at all. No, the surly stableboy was still ev-
ident in the curl of that lower lip, the slant of the brows
and in those moody dark brown eyes that watched me
so closely, revealing far too much. He wanted so badly
to show me how he had changed, but the essentials
hadn't changed at all. He was still obsessed, still bitter,
still tormented by all he felt had been denied him. The
raw edges had been polished but the raw emotions still
surged inside, as strong as ever.

Poor Hugh, I thought. I felt the old compassion and

wanted to take his hand and tell him it didn't matter.
That was dangerous, I knew, as dangerous as the stir-
rings caused by the desire smoldering in those eyes, the
taut curve of that wide mouth. I remembered, and the
memories were potent, and I pushed my dessert plate
aside and told him that it had been a very long day, I
was very tired. Hugh summoned the waiter and settled
the bill immediately and then led me out to the carriage
he had hired for the night.

Moonlight streamed through the windows of the carriage. Sitting across from him, I studied his face in the
soft silver light. He was in a thoughtful mood, silent,
his brown eyes full of memories, his mouth held in a
tight line. His was not a handsome face, no, by no means,
but it was striking and perversely attractive: lean, sharp,
intriguing. I had seen it in my dreams, so often, and
this seemed like a dream, too. I couldn't believe that,
if I wanted to, I could reach across and rest my hand
on that sharp cheekbone and caress that lean cheek. I
wanted to. I wanted to love him and comfort him and
heal all those wounds he carried inside. I hardened
myself against the yearnings that were like a physical
ache within me.

The carriage stopped in front of the house and Hugh
helped me down, his hand squeezing mine. He walked
me to the door and I gave him my key and he unlocked
the door.

"Thank you for the meal, Hugh," I said. "It was
lovely."

"I'm glad you enjoyed it. You see, I *can* be a civilized
fellow on occasion."

"I've never doubted that. Do you plan to do another
job?"

The abrupt question startled him. "Eventually. I have
a number of prospects lined up."

"I see," I said coldly. "I have something for you. Please
wait here. I'll be right back."

I stepped inside and returned a few moments later
and silently handed him the neatly folded black silk
hood. He glanced at it and then stuffed it into the pocket

of his frock coat and looked into my eyes, frowning. We
stood there in front of the door for several moments
without speaking. He placed his hands on my bare
shoulders. I pulled away.

"Did it ever occur to you that you might get caught?"
I asked sharply. "Did it ever occur to you that if—if
you're caught you'll be carted off to Tyburn and hanged?
Is that dream of yours so important? Is it worth risking
your life to—to prove you're not a bastard?"

"It means everything," he said in a flat voice. "I want
what is mine. I love you, Angie. I want to give you the
world. I want to give you a title, an estate, luxury for
the rest of your life."

"Those things aren't important, Hugh."

"They are if they've been denied you through treachery."

"Hugh—"

"I want to marry you, Angie."

He pulled me into his arms and covered my mouth
with his own and kissed me for a long time, tenderly,
thoroughly, and my head seemed to swim and the sweet
sensations exploded and I tried to resist but I was too
weak. I cried inside, sad for all that was lost, all that
could never be. I clung to him, overcome by emotion,
and when he finally let me go I was trembling. It was
some time before I could speak.

"I don't want to see you again, Hugh."

"I'm going to marry you. I'm going to make you Lady
Meredith."

"Go on with your life of crime," I said. "Pur—pursue
your obsession if you must, but I—I want no part of it.
There's no place in my life for you, Hugh. It's too late.
I have my career, and I— There's someone else. I live
with him."

"Lambert," he said. "I know about that."

"I love him."

"A moment ago, in my arms, you proved that you
still loved me."

I didn't reply. I wished with all my heart I could deny
it, could look at him coolly and say it wasn't true, but

I couldn't. Hugh glared at me with dark, intense eyes that challenged me to tell him it wasn't so. Neither of us spoke. Moonlight spilled over the steps. Shadows brushed the walls. On the street the horses stamped impatiently. Hugh waited and time passed and I summoned all my strength and called on all my training and somehow managed to speak in a cool, level voice.

"I meant what I said. I don't want to see you again. The past is over and I'm no longer the girl you knew. I want no part of you. I mean that. Good-bye, Hugh."

He continued to glare at me, anger in his eyes now, pain as well, and I knew I had hurt him and knew I must hold fast and not let him suspect what I felt inside. I met his glare with icy composure. After a moment he scowled and pressed his lips tight, and then he turned and went back to the carriage and snapped an order to the driver and climbed inside. The carriage pulled away, wheels grinding over the cobbles, hooves ringing loudly in the silence of the night. I stood in front of the door, my lower lip trembling, lashes moist, and it was a long time before I found the strength to go inside.

I slept very little that night.

The days that followed were bright and sunny and warm. June was almost here. London would soon be hot and stifling, and those who could afford to would leave the city. Audiences were growing sparser by the night, the empty seats seeming to glare at us in silent accusation as we moved through our paces in front of the footlights. Jamie would probably close the play when he came back, and he would be back any day now. There had been no more letters, but he was terribly busy, finishing the play. If Mrs. Perry received any letters, I didn't want to know. I avoided her as though she were carrying the plague, fuming silently each time she flashed one of her smug, knowing smiles. The woman was *not* going to draw me into a cat fight, which was precisely what she wanted.

On a Tuesday, nine days after I had dined with Hugh, I was restless and decided to bake a walnut cake, simply to fill the hours until it was time to leave for the theater.

I was out of flour, and I would need shelled walnuts, too. I went to The Market and bought some oranges and a lovely bunch of silver-mauve onions as well, strolling home leisurely with the wicker basket on my arm. It was the last day of May. The sky was a cloudless blue, swimming with silvery sunlight, and the trees were thick with dark green leaves. It was very warm, and I was glad to get back to the relative coolness of the house, its thick walls keeping much of the heat out. I put the things away and sighed, not really in the mood now to heat up the large black iron stove and bake.

He stepped into the kitchen. I whirled around, startled. He grinned. I frowned, furious at him for sneaking up on me like that. I looked around for something to throw at him. He sauntered over to me and lazily pulled me into his arms and I pulled away, still furious. The amusement left his eyes and he frowned.

"I—I'm sorry," I said. "You gave me a frightful turn."

"Since when have you been such a nervous type?"

"Since spending the last month alone!"

"I'm back now." His voice sounded strange, studiedly casual.

"I see that now. You still smell of sweat and horses."

"Got back half an hour ago, took my bags upstairs, expecting to find you waiting with open arms. Been out somewhere?"

"I went to The Market."

Jamie reached for one of the oranges I had piled in a bowl on the table and began to peel it. "Glad to see me?" he inquired.

"You could have written, you sod. You could have let me know when you were coming back."

"Too busy," he said, plopping an orange section into his mouth. "Hadn't any time for letter writing."

I let that pass. "Did you finish the play?"

"Still have a bit of tidying up to do, a few minor changes to make. It should be ready for you to read in a couple of days. I wanted to get back, have a look 'round at the theater. I hear audience attendance is dropping off drastically."

And just how had he heard that? I wondered. "We're probably losing money keeping it open," I said. "The nightly receipts probably aren't paying our overhead. We've had a good long run."

"Longest ever," he agreed.

We went into the study. Jamie licked the orange juice off his fingers. He had removed coat and vest and was wearing dusty brown boots and snug fawn-colored breeches and a loose white lawn shirt open at the throat and faintly moist with perspiration. I fussed with a vase of golden-yellow daffodils on one of the tables, rearranging them. I kept thinking about the long letters he had written to Mrs. Perry. I had to bite my tongue to keep from mentioning them.

"I see you've recovered from your cold," I said. "How was your stay otherwise?"

"All right, I suppose. Betsy Sheridan was there, that damnable brother of hers, too. We almost engaged in a bout of fisticuffs in the dining room. He called me a hack. I called him an insolent young pup who happened to get lucky. We'd have battered each other for sure if Mrs. Lindsey hadn't intervened. She gave us both a tongue-lashing."

"You shouldn't have let him bait you."

"Can't abide the fellow. *Are* you glad to see me, Angel?"

"Of course I am," I said quietly.

"You've a strange way of showing it, love."

"I—I have a headache, Jamie, and I'm out of sorts. I'm sorry if I'm not as enthusiastic as you expected me to be. You—shouldn't have crept up on me like that."

He didn't reply, merely gave me a strange look I couldn't quite fathom. His green-brown eyes were sober, seemed to be examining me as though looking for some change. It made me quite uncomfortable, and I felt a sudden twinge of alarm.

"I see," he said after a while, and again his voice was much too casual. "Well, I guess I'll go upstairs and clean up and get into some fresh clothes. I want to get to the theater early, go over the receipts, see how we stand. We'll talk later."

He left the room, and I listened to his footsteps moving up the stairs, disturbed by that peculiar look he had given me. I frowned. Something was wrong. I could sense it. It was as though an invisible wall had sprung up between us, and it had nothing to do with his creeping up on me and my angry reaction. He had looked at me as though he thought I might be hiding something, as though...as though that close scrutiny might provide an answer to some question in his mind. Puzzled, bewildered, upset, I glanced at the clock. It was barely two, hours before time to go to the theater. I sighed and then went back into the kitchen. It was going to be a very long day. I might as well bake the goddamn cake.

Jamie was remote during the days that followed. He was very polite and considerate, and that was somehow much worse than harsh words or anger would have been. He spent most of his time at the theater, working on the play in his office there, and although we slept in the same bed at night, we did not make love, not once. After almost four years I was accustomed to his moods, his insecurity, his frequent outbursts of temper, but he had never been like this before. The strain was almost unbearable, and I hadn't the least idea what had caused it. Too proud to confront him, to ask him what was wrong, I was as polite, as considerate as he, even after I saw Mrs. Perry leaving his office one afternoon when I arrived at the theater earlier than usual.

After studying the receipts and observing the decreasing number of people in the audience on successive nights, Jamie decided to close the play after Saturday night's performance. I, for one, was sick and tired of playing the winsome Nell, as delightful as the role had been in the beginning. The rest of the cast seemed relieved as well. Megan declared that she was ready for a few weeks of rest and Charles said he would be glad to see the last of that bloody heavy wig he wore onstage every night. Nevertheless, there was an air of sadness backstage after the final curtain call Saturday night.

We had all been working together for almost a year, and there had been a strong feeling of camaraderie among us, despite Mrs. Perry. That was over now, and all of us felt a sense of loss.

On Sunday morning I was in the kitchen at ten, making eggs and buttered toast and bacon. I was just putting them on the table when Jamie sauntered in, already dressed in brown frock coat and green and white striped vest and a green silk neckcloth. That surprised me, but I made no comment, pouring a cup of coffee and handing it to him as he sat down at the table. I sat down across from him and remarked that it was a lovely day and he said yes, lovely, if a bit warm, and I asked if he were going out and he replied that he was going to his office at the Lambert and would be gone most of the day, and we ate in silence after that.

Jamie finished his toast with strawberry preserves and took a final sip of coffee, then stood up, dropping his napkin beside his plate.

"By the way," he said. "I finished the play a couple of days ago. I left the manuscript in the study, in case you'd care to read it."

"I'll read it today," I told him.

He left the kitchen. I heard the front door open and close a few minutes later. I finished my coffee. I had another cup. I washed the dishes, put things away, deliberately delaying the time when I would have to pick up that manuscript and read. I wanted to like it, fervently wanted to like it, but I already had severe reservations about the subject matter and I knew he would want my opinion and knew I would have to be honest. Finally, when the kitchen was sparkling, when I could delay no longer, I walked into the study and saw the manuscript on the table in front of the sofa and felt a terrible apprehension as I curled against the cushions and picked it up.

I read slowly, carefully, trying to visualize each scene onstage, trying to imagine how it would play, reading some dialogue aloud to hear how it would sound. Three hours later I set the manuscript aside and stared at the empty fireplace without seeing it. The play was bad. It was incredibly bad, far and away the worst thing he had ever committed to paper. The structure was sound enough, but the whole second act was devoted to an emotion-charged encounter between Mary and Elizabeth, who had never met in real life, and it was violently melodramatic, would never, never play convincingly. Elizabeth was a caricature, not a character, while Mary was so good, so pure, so noble she was totally unbelievable. The curtain scene, her execution, might have been effective and quite moving had the dialogue not been so stilted and had one been able to care one way or the other. The play was a ponderous, tedious bore, and I dreaded having to tell him so.

Jamie came home at six, looking weary and a bit rumpled, the green silk neckcloth untidy, his brown frock coat creased. I had bathed and washed my hair and changed into a deep rose brocade gown embroidered with flowers in a darker rose silk. Megan and Charles had asked us to dine with them tonight, and I intended to go whether Jamie came or not. I hoped he would. I hoped we could have a pleasant evening and not discuss the play, not just yet. It was not to be. He came into the study and saw the manuscript wasn't on the table where he had left it and looked at me, prepared to battle.

"You read it?" he inquired.

"Yes, Jamie. I read it."

"You don't like it. I can tell from your tone of voice."

"It— I know you worked very hard, Jamie, and I know you had high hopes for it, but—" I hesitated.

"You think it stinks," he said sharply.

He was angry, and I could feel my own anger beginning to mount. I was prepared to discuss it calmly, objectively, but I wasn't about to be bullied and have him put words into my mouth.

"It stinks," I said.

"Would you care to elucidate?"

"If you like. It's ponderous. It's tedious. It's leaden. The scenes are much too drawn out, and the dialogue is incredibly stilted, like nothing ever spoken by the human tongue. Elizabeth is a stereotype villainess, without a single redeeming feature, and Mary is so absurdly noble you might just as well give her a harp and a pair of wings."

"What did you think of the handwriting?"

"Spare me your sarcasm, Jamie! I'm trying to be objective. I'm trying to be honest. You asked for my opinion and I gave it to you. It will never play. If you attempt to produce it you're going to have a full-scale disaster on your hands."

He didn't explode. He looked at me with a faint, deprecatory smile on his lips and stepped over to pour himself a glass of brandy. His manner was infuriatingly calm and superior as he glanced at the liquor in his glass and swirled it, the smile still playing on his lips.

"Some think it's a brilliant piece of work," he re-marked.

"Some? Who do you mean by *some?*"

"Mrs. Perry," he replied.

I had been sitting in one of the wing chairs. I stood up, and I could feel two spots of color burning on my cheeks.

"You gave it to her? You let *her* read it before I did?"

"She loves it."

"God*damn* you, Jamie!"

"She thinks it's the best thing I've ever done," he said calmly.

"She would! The bitch wants to play Mary! If you respect her opinion so goddamn much, let her play it! Produce it. Lose your shirt. Become the laughingstock of London. Not one penny of *my* money will go into it, let me assure you."

"I don't need your money," he informed me, still speaking in that calm flat voice. "I got along quite nicely for a number of years without you, Angel, and I imagine I can do so in the future."

"Be careful, Jamie," I warned. "Don't force the issue. Don't say anything you'll regret. I don't know what's happened, why you've been so cold and remote this past

week, but—I've had just about all the strain I intend
to take."

"You don't have to play Mary," he continued, as
though I hadn't said a word. "You've had offers from
half the managers in London. They're panting for you,
waving offers left and right. Garrick wants you. Goldsmith wants you. Sheridan wants you for his next play.
You certainly don't need *me* any longer."

"I damn sure don't!"

"That's it, then, I guess."

"I guess it is," I said.

We faced each other, that invisible wall between us,
and I felt a terrible pain inside, felt tears I was too
proud, too angry to shed. Jamie drank his brandy and
set the glass down, still calm. I couldn't believe this
was happening. I couldn't believe it was ending. I wanted
to scream at him and shake him and make him see how
foolish, how unnecessary this was, but I didn't say anything. My damnable pride prevented it.

"I'll pack a few things," he said. "You can stay in the
house. We'll settle all business and financial matters
later."

"No," I replied. "You signed the lease. I'll leave. I'll
spend the night with Megan. I'll collect my things as—
as soon as I've found another place."

"As you wish," he said. "I hope you and your new
lover will be very happy."

"My new lover? What are you talking about?"

"Don't bother to pretend, Angel. I know all about it.
He came to the theater for you. He took you to dinner
at Eldridge's. You were seeing him all the time I was
at Tunbridge Wells. Apparently he's very wealthy, one
of the gentry, a striking-looking fellow from all reports."

I saw then. I understood. I understood everything.

"These reports," I said, "I assume they came from
Mrs. Perry."

"She wrote me. She told me all about it."

"And—and you believed her." My voice was trembling with anger. "You trusted me so much, had so much
faith in me that you—you accepted the word of that

woman without question. After four years, you had such a high opinion of me you were perfectly willing to believe I'd be unfaithful, perfectly willing to believe I could blithely sleep with another man while living with you. That you could even think me capable of such conduct is—is—" I cut myself short, trying to control the fury.

"A man did come to the theater," I continued after a moment, "and I did go out to dinner with him, but—"

"You don't have to explain yourself," he told me.

"You're right," I said.

I stepped over to him and slapped his face so hard I feared I had broken my wrist. He stumbled back, almost falling, absolutely appalled, and his face turned white, a vivid pink hand print burning on his left cheek. I gave him a savage look and marched to the door leading into the foyer, and then I turned and looked at him again.

"Good-bye, Jamie," I said, "and good luck with your new leading lady. God knows you're going to need it."

Chapter Seventeen

I hadn't counted on the chickens and the cow. The cottage I had rented for the summer was only five miles from London and charming indeed with a thatched roof and mellow cream stucco walls with exposed brown beams and blue morning glories climbing the trellis around the front door. There were flower beds and ancient oaks and, in back, a pleasant kitchen garden. There were also chicken pens and a cow and I had agreed to tend to the animals during the three months I would be staying here. I had grown quite fond of Matilda, the cow, an amiable creature who stood patiently swishing her tail while I milked her, who nuzzled my arm when I brought her feed, but the chickens were a hateful querulous lot who clucked and flapped and carried on quite rudely when I fed them, the hens giving me accusatory looks when I gathered their eggs.

The cottage belonged to a friend of Mrs. Gainsborough's who was visiting a sister in Cornwall for the summer, and Mrs. G. had arranged this rental for me. She and Thomas had stayed in the cottage several times in the past, he painting bucolic landscapes while she went merrily berserk with her baking, elated by the plentitude of eggs and milk. I had been here for two and a half weeks now, and the peace and solitude was wonderfully welcome after the rush and noise of London. I hadn't realized just how hard I had been working or how weary I was until the activity ceased. I spent my days reading, cooking simple meals, taking long walks about the countryside or strolling to the nearby village for provisions. Instead of staying up all night, I went to bed quite early, awakening at dawn to the sound of birds chirping in the boughs of the oaks. It was pleasant and restful and it helped. The anger and resentment and pain were still strong inside, but somehow they were easier to bear here in the country, away from Covent Garden.

My books, much of my wardrobe and most of my personal belongings were presently stored in the spare room of the flat Megan and Charles shared. They had helped me remove them from the house on St. Martin's Lane, and I was glad Jamie hadn't been there at the time. I hadn't seen him since that Sunday night I had left the house. I had no desire to see him. I was still too bitter, too hurt. My fear of accidentally encountering him in Covent Garden was one of the main reasons I had decided to take the cottage. I needed to be away from everything associated with the past four years. Being alone had definite advantages, for I didn't have to put on a front, didn't have to pretend, didn't have to answer questions or make explanations.

Bag of feed in hand, I strolled past the kitchen garden now, past the well with its old oaken bucket, approaching the chicken house at the end of the property, the yard carefully fenced in. Oak boughs groaned quietly overhead, thick leaves rustling. Seeing me from the adjacent field where she was grazing, Matilda mooed plaintively. I called to her and opened the gate and stepped into the chicken yard. The nasty creatures immediately went into convulsions of excitement, swarming around me and clucking greedily and flapping their wings for attention. I tossed handfuls of grain into the air, and they scrambled for it, squabbling viciously, pecking angrily. The rooster crowed, shaking his bright red wattle and driving a cluster of hens away from a particularly large pile of grain.

The chickens were making such a racket I didn't hear the rig coming up the lane, didn't hear the knocking on the front door or the footsteps moving around the side of the cottage. Bag empty at last, I brushed the skirt of my blue cotton frock and shoved a long chestnut wave from my temple and turned, and it was then that I saw him standing there on the path beside the kitchen garden. Somehow I wasn't at all surprised. Calmly, I checked the trough to see that there was enough water, and, finding it half full, I opened the gate and stepped out, securing it behind me. He watched, arms folded across his chest, a gentle summer breeze ruffling his raven-black hair. He was wearing tall black knee boots and snug black breeches and a fine white silk shirt with full bell sleeves. He unfolded his arms and rested his hands on his thighs as I approached.

"How did you find me?" I asked.

"I made inquiries."

"I see."

His dark eyes studied me, and even though my hair was tousled and my face was probably smudged and my dress was dusty, I could see that he was pleased by what he saw. The girl feeding the chickens was far more appealing to him than the glamorous Angel Howard in her satin gown. There was admiration in his eyes, and love, and I felt a wonderful elation awakening inside. I hadn't wanted to see him again, had hoped he would stay away forever, but now that he was here I wanted to weep with joy. Hugh would never know that, of course. I couldn't afford to let him know. I mustn't give him any encouragement whatsoever.

"How did you get here?"

"Rig I hired for the summer. It's out front."

"Did you have any trouble finding the place?"

"I stopped in the village, got directions there."

I looked at him, loving him, yet when I spoke my voice was cool. "Why did you come, Hugh?"

"We both know the answer to that," he said.

Yes, we both knew. I was still bitter and disillusioned and hurt over the breakup with Jamie, and I wanted to be alone. I didn't want to love anyone ever again, and Hugh had come and we both knew why and I wondered if I could find the strength to send him away. Matilda mooed and the chickens clucked and the rich, loamy smell of the kitchen garden wafted on the air as we stood under the boughs of the oak tree, looking at each other.

"I was just going to make some lunch," I said. "Will you join me?"

"That would be nice," he replied.

"Eggs," I said. "I have a plethora of eggs. Will eggs do?"

"Eggs will do nicely," he told me.

I led the way and he followed me through the back door and into the kitchen with its cool stone floor and mellow beige walls and low-beamed ceiling. He sat down at the old oak table and watched as I tied an apron around my waist and began to stoke the fire in the belly of the old iron stove. I cracked eggs, dumping them into a wooden bowl, beating them with a little cream, adding some herbs and then pouring them into the skillet that had been heating on the stove. Hugh stretched his long legs out and tilted his chair back, and it seemed so natural, so right for him to be here. I chopped ham and grated cheese and added them to the skillet, carefully folding the cooked egg over them.

I served the omelete with buttered bread and poured fresh coffee into heavy brown cups, and Hugh ate with relish. Afterward I cut him a slice of the almond cake I had baked the day before. It was rich and buttery and he claimed he had never eaten better cake. There was no strain, none whatsoever. It didn't bother me that I was wearing the old dress, that my hair wasn't brushed, that my forehead was moist from standing over the hot stove. Hugh finished his cake and drank the glass of milk I handed him, and it felt good to have him here, to wait on him. He continued to loll at the table while I washed the dishes and tidied up the kitchen, and I was pleasantly aware of his eyes on me the whole while.

We went into the parlor in front of the house, a cozy room with shabby pink sofa and chairs and a worn gray oriental carpet with green and blue and pink designs, the colors faded. A vase of wildflowers sat on the low mahogany table in front of the sofa, another on the mantel above the fireplace. Hugh examined the books I had brought along with me and stacked on one of the tables. He asked me if I still read a great deal and I nodded and said that reading was a great comfort.

"Haven't had much time to read myself," he told me. "I used to when I was a boy. I fairly devoured the books your father loaned me."

"He—he told me about that," I said.

"He was a remarkable man, Angie, the only man I ever truly respected. When everyone else shunned me, considered me some kind of wild animal, he was kind to me. He believed in me."

"I know."

I believed in you, too, I thought. I believed you could make something of yourself, on your own, through your own efforts, without the inheritance you believe should be yours, and what have you become? A thief, a criminal. I should send you away, Hugh, this very minute, before it's too late. Hugh put down the book he had been examining and looked at me with those dark brown eyes and I was unable to speak the words I knew I should speak, unable to do the thing I knew I should do.

"I've missed you, Angie," he said.

"Have you?"

"These past weeks have been hellish, knowing you were so close, knowing you were living with another man. When I learned that you had left the house on St. Martin's Lane, when I learned you and Lambert were no longer together I couldn't stay away. I love you, Angie."

"I believe you do," I said quietly.

He came over to me and took me into his arms and I shook my head and pulled away, and he didn't persist. He stepped back, patient, content to wait. I knew what I should do, true, my head told me in no uncertain terms, but my heart told me something else and I mustn't listen, I mustn't. I was very vulnerable at the moment, hurt, disillusioned, lonely, and it would be so easy to turn to Hugh and take comfort in the love he offered, but I sensed that that would merely lead to more pain, more disillusionment, far worse than that I felt now.

"You're afraid," he said.

"Yes," I admitted.

"I would never hurt you, Angie."

"Not intentionally," I said.

"I want to give you the world."

"I don't want the world," I told him. "I don't want a title, a grand estate, riches. The things that matter to you aren't important to me."

"You're all that matters to me," he said.

I looked at him, and I wanted so desperately to believe him. I glanced out the window and saw the open one-seat rig he had arrived in standing in the lane beyond the low gray stone wall, a beautiful bay in harness, waiting patiently in the shade of an oak tree. I saw his bags on the seat of the rig, and I knew he had come to stay. Send him away, Angel. Now. Tell him there is no future for us. There isn't. You know that. Tell him he must go.

"You gave up your rooms at the Blue Stag?" I asked.

He nodded. "The Gainsborough reproduction, a few other things were put into storage. Everything else I own is in those bags you see."

"The horse? The rig?"

"For a modest fee the innkeeper at the village will stable the horse for me and keep the rig in the carriage house. I made tentative arrangements with him before I came on out here."

"Tentative," I said. "You weren't sure."

"I hoped, Angie."

His voice was quiet, his dark brown eyes were grave, and in the hazy, softly diffused light streaming in through the windows his face seemed sculpted by a master artist, the lean, sharp lines with their own special beauty, the curve of his full lower lip taut, expectant. His hair gleamed, so rich a black, brushed back neatly and fastened at the nape of his neck with a black ribbon. He was so hard, so harsh, so vulnerable. He was the love of my life.

Instead of giving him an answer I suggested we take a walk, and we left the cottage and strolled slowly down the lane. There were rhododendrons growing on either side, mauve and pink and purple, and that brought back memories of another time, another lane. We left the lane and crossed a field, and it was spotted with wild daisies. That brought back memories, too, and time seemed to shimmer, evaporate, and the present disappeared and I was seventeen again and in love for the very first time, filled with poignant emotions as vibrant and tender as they had been all those years ago. Hugh was silent, grave, walking beside me, waiting for me to say the words he so wanted to hear.

We strolled back to the cottage, the sunlight pale silver, the sky a cloudless blue, and as we reached the low gray stone wall festooned here and there by strands of morning glories, I was at peace with myself and my decision was made. I suggested he carry his bags inside and drive the rig to the inn. Hugh didn't say anything. He pulled me to him and kissed me lightly on the lips and held me for a moment, and then he fetched the bags and took them inside and came out and took hold of the side of the rig and swung nimbly up onto the black leather seat and gathered up the reins. I watched him drive away, a tremulous joy inside me, and though I knew I might regret it, that joy was all that mattered now.

I went out to the well and drew buckets of water and heated it, filling the small porcelain hip bath. I scented the water and bathed and washed my hair and reveled in the luxury of love, my whole body seeming to tingle with anticipation of his touch. I dried myself with a soft towel and toweled my hair dry and put on a frail white silk petticoat with rows of delicate lace ruffles on the swirling full skirt. I brushed my hair until it fell to my shoulders in loose gleaming waves, and then I slipped on a pair of soft tan kid slippers with high heels and a pale tan muslin frock sprigged with small dark gold flowers and tiny brown leaves. It was fetching indeed with its small puffed sleeves and low bodice and snug waist, the full skirt spreading out over the petticoat beneath. Looking in the mirror, I saw a girl with glowing complexion and sparkling violet-gray eyes. The glamorous, sophisticated actress had disappeared.

I went down into the cellar and fetched a bottle of cool amber wine, and in the kitchen I sliced chicken and ham and arranged slices on a plate and buttered bread and washed grapes and peaches and placed them in a bowl. The sunlight was beginning to fade slightly when I heard footsteps coming up the walk. I went to the front door and greeted him with a smile. He was a bit dusty from the walk, his thin white shirt moist with perspiration, clinging to his skin, but that didn't matter at all when he drew me to him and kissed me again, lightly, tenderly, there in the cool, dim foyer. His lips caressed mine and his arms held me loosely and I rested my hand on the back of his neck and gently stroked the warm skin and then ran my hands over his shoulders and back, feeling the smooth, hard muscle beneath the damp silk.

I pulled back when his lips became more urgent, demanding. I smiled again and told him we had all the time in the world and he grinned and his eyes glowed darkly and he said yes, perhaps he'd better wash up. I caressed his lean cheek and stroked his lower lip and he captured the ball of my thumb between his teeth and bit the soft flesh gently. I pulled my thumb away, and he lightly encircled my waist, drawing me to him again, and I ran my hands along those lean, muscular thighs tightly encased in black broadcloth, and I felt

the bulge in his breeches pressing against my abdomen
and smiled once more as he rubbed, straining against
me, silently informing me of his need.

"Later," I whispered.

He leaned his head down and planted warm lips
against the base of my throat and made a low, moaning
noise and then, reluctantly, he released me and sighed
a heavy sigh. I went into the kitchen and placed the
food on the table and opened the wine, and he joined
me a short while later, smelling of soap, wearing another thin white shirt, lawn, with lace at the wrists, a
lace jabot dripping at his throat, and that small vanity
pleased me. He sat down at the table and glanced at
the food, hungry, but not for food, and I reveled in the
delicious torment of anticipation, pouring the wine, sitting down myself. We ate slowly, looking at each other
the whole while, silent, anticipating, savoring the sensations building, mounting inside.

Utterly enthralled, I watched him eat chicken, his
strong white teeth tearing the flesh apart, and it was
thrilling, tantalizing. I observed the way his neck muscles worked when he swallowed his wine, and that was
thrilling, too, and I watched with fascination as his
large brown hand reached out, fingers wrapping around
a fuzzy golden-pink peach, clutching it. He took up a
knife and carefully peeled the peach and divided it into
sections and ate them one by one, gleaming brown eyes
devouring me as he did so. The tip of his tongue slipped
out and slowly licked the peach juice from his lips, and
then he took another swallow of the cool amber wine.
He set the glass down and rested his hands on the edge
of the table, fingertips drumming the oak.

He was impatient now, eager, finding it difficult to
contain the smoldering need inside. I felt the same need,
but I wanted to savor this delicious anticipation, knowing it would make eventual release all the more satisfying. I asked him if he wanted another slice of cake.
Hugh shook his head. The sunlight was dimmer now
and the kitchen was beginning to fill with hazy blue-
gray shadows. I cleared the table, stacking the dishes

on the drainboard, and Hugh climbed slowly to his feet and came up behind me and wrapped his arms around my waist, drawing me to him.

"I've waited a long time for this," he murmured.

"I'm afraid you must wait a little longer. I must bring Matilda in."

"Matilda?"

"The cow. I must put her in the barn."

Hugh sighed and, resigned, followed me out the back door. The sky was pale gray, softly smeared with fading orange and gold banners in the west. Heavy oak boughs groaned overhead, leaves rustling, and the chickens were quiet now, roosting in the henhouse. Matilda looked up expectantly as I moved across the field toward her, followed by the tall, lean stranger with the disgruntled expression. I stroked her soft velvety nose and, taking hold of the lead rope, led her slowly toward the small barn behind the henhouse. I talked to her and stroked her as I put her in her stall, promising to see her first thing in the morning. The barn was dim, smelling of hay and manure. Hugh stood in the hallway silhouetted against the light behind him, and I knew he was remembering the stables at Greystone Hall and the bitter, unhappy boy who had tended them.

"Quite finished?" he inquired.

I patted Matilda a last time and joined him at the door. "For now," I replied, carefully closing the barn door.

"I suppose hundreds have told you how beautiful you are," he said.

"I never believed them. I keep remembering that gawky adolescent girl."

"You were beautiful back then, Angie. You were the most captivating child I had ever seen, the most beautiful young woman, gentle and graceful and totally unaware of your beauty."

"And now?"

"You're even lovelier," he said.

"You just want to sleep with me," I accused.

"You're right about that!"

I smiled and he slung his arm around my shoulders
and we walked back to the house, passing the kitchen
garden with its pungent smells. The house was filled
with shadows now, all hazy, dreamlike as we moved
down the hall to the foyer and climbed up the worn
wooden stairs to the bedroom above with its low-beamed
ceiling and whitewashed walls now a soft mauve-gray
at twilight. Impatient before, Hugh was strangely sub-
dued and hesitant now, as though this really were a
dream, as though he couldn't believe we were truly
together at last and free to communicate the love living
inside us all these years. His dark eyes glowed with
that love as he gazed at me now.

Oak leaves rustled outside the opened windows. Hazy
white light grew dimmer still, deeper mauve shadows
spreading over the walls. His face was solemn, brushed
with shadow, cheekbones prominent, lips slightly parted.
I put my hands on his shoulders and stood up on tiptoe
to lightly caress those lips with mine. He tilted his head,
leaning forward, wrapping one arm around my waist,
responding to my kiss with a passionate fervor that was
still incredibly tender. I held on to his shoulders as my
senses reeled, as so many dreams suddenly materialized into a shattering reality. It was real, it was real,
he was here, his strong arms holding me to him, his
lips tenderly, urgently devouring my own, his warmth,
his smell, his lean, sinewy body real, mine, no dream
to disappear at dawn.

Need, desperate need, became a torment inside, for
me, for Hugh, our bodies crying for immediate release,
but it was not to be, for Hugh had waited too long to
plunge and thrust and squander this precious time with
instant gratification. Gently, firmly, he held me away
from him, and he smiled and kissed my throat, my chin,
the corner of my mouth, my cheek, my brow. He stroked
my hair and lifted it with his hands to savor its weight
and silky texture, and all the while I was trembling
inside, a weak, hollow feeling in the backs of my knees,
the pit of my stomach, warmth glowing and spreading
throughout my body as he tugged at my hair and tilted

my head back and finally covered my lips with his once again, kissing me tensely, tenderly, holding me tight.

Shadows spread and light faded and the walls were dark gray now and the air was filled with a blue-mauve haze that deepened by the moment. Slowly, expertly Hugh unfastened the back of my bodice and I stepped out of my high-heeled shoes, kicking them aside. I freed my arms from the sleeves and Hugh pulled the bodice down slowly, bunching the muslin in his hands, sliding it over my hips. I moved slightly and the dress fell to the floor to be pushed away with my bare foot. I closed my eyes, certain I would swoon, and my breasts swelled, nipples tight and straining against silk, and suddenly the silk was no longer there and my breasts were free and silk was slipping over my skin, falling to my feet. His right arm curled firmly around my waist, supporting me, he caressed my breasts gently with his left hand, fingers stroking, squeezing, and then he cupped his palm under my right breast and lifted it and leaned down to kiss the taut pink nipple and then lifted the left and encircled the nipple with his teeth and bit down lightly and licked it with his tongue.

My knees gave way then and Hugh gathered me up into his arms and carried me over to the old brass bed. He carefully lowered me onto the quilted white satin counterpane and the satin was cool and slippery beneath me and I arched my body, lifting my arms, and he stood at the side of the bed gazing at me with something like awe, and I knew he loved me, really loved me, as I loved him, and I knew he had dreamed of this moment, as I had, and couldn't believe it was ours now after so many years. He placed one knee on the bed and leaned over and began to kiss me, those warm, moist lips covering every inch of my body, pausing here to savor the smoothness of inner thigh, lingering there to nuzzle the softness of my belly with his nose, my legs writhing, my arms thrown back, fingers curling tightly around the cool brass bars of the headboard.

Sweet, sweet torment, delirium of bliss, delay divine torture that must end soon or sanity would shatter. Lips

ANGEL IN SCARLET

413

warm, burning my skin, hands stroking flesh, kneading
it gently, an urgent ache inside, swelling, spreading, a
moan escaping, another, smothered by his mouth, his
tongue thrusting inside mine, the weight of his body
pinioning me, my hands clutching his buttocks and feeling the hard muscle beneath black broadcloth, feeling
soft silk as my hands slipped up his back, clutching his
shoulders, my body undulating beneath him, my legs
spreading as he kneeled and tugged at his breeches,
the room in darkness now, now the warm hardness of
him entering slowly, slowly, plunging then to fill, holding for a moment and then slowly withdrawing, so
slowly, plunging again, flesh filling flesh, his hard and
strong as steel and soft as velvet, my own clutching,
clinging, my body arching to meet him, to bring him
closer still, the first pale rays of moonlight streaming
into the room as senses soared, higher, higher, building,
bursting, soft silver brushing the walls of the room as
his teeth sank into my shoulder and the oblivion of bliss
claimed us both.

And in the night, more love, he nude now, lazy, lethargic, loving leisurely as, outside, the leaves rustled
in the darkness, and in the morning a thin gold-pink
light streamed into the room and he was asleep, sprawled
over me, clutching me, and it was right, it was real, no
dream, yet I still couldn't believe he was here, his leg
thrown over mine, his skin warm, moist with perspiration, his hair damp, too, his breathing deep, even. He
opened his eyes and looked at me, and I smiled. He
kissed me sleepily and I felt him swell, felt him grow
harder, grow longer, and I shifted beneath him and he
shifted too and there was more splendid love as the
sunlight grew stronger and a bird chirped merrily in a
tree outside. And later, in the kitchen, dressed in last
night's garments, the ashes of aftermath glowing within,
limbs sweetly sore, I cooked breakfast and he came into
the kitchen, looking weary and worn and wonderful in
black breeches and wilted white silk shirt with limp
laces. He looked with some consternation at all the food
I had prepared.

"I can't possibly eat all that," he said.

"You're going to need your strength," I told him.

Hugh was with me now, and never, never had I known such happiness as during the weeks that followed. London and the life I had lived there seemed the dream now, seemed to have happened to someone else. Hugh was with me, and we fed the chickens and he watched critically as I milked Matilda, squirting him once after he made a sarcastic remark about my technique. We took long walks over the countryside and discovered a dilapidated stone bridge spanning a small stream, and I recognized it from one of Gainsborough's paintings. Hugh told me about his life at sea, and I told him about my life in the theater, but neither of us mentioned Lord Blackie, nor did he ever refer to Italy and his dream of becoming Lord Meredith. We went to the village on market day, and he bought me bright ribbons and I bought him a red gypsy scarf he immediately tied around his neck. We watched the Punch and Judy show and the trained birds and came home with fresh fruit and vegetables and a lovely glazed ham and a set of dishes I couldn't resist.

The days were long and warm and filled with simple pleasures. I cooked for him, delicious meals, and he put on some weight and looked better although still too lean. How content I was, beating eggs, adding sugar and cream and flour and pouring the batter into a pan, baking it in the black iron stove, washing sheets and hanging them out to dry in the sunlight, gathering wildflowers and arranging them in bowls, simple domestic tasks suddenly suffused with meaning because Hugh was here and he would eat the cake and sleep on the sheets and admire the flower arrangements. We made love, in the barn, on the damp hay, beside the stream after a picnic one day, the summer sunlight bathing his bare buttocks as he plowed away with breeches tangled about his knees, in the kitchen and in the parlor, in the broom closet once when he caught me putting away mop and pail. It was joyous, and it was beautiful, and often he simply gazed at me with love in his eyes and took my hand and squeezed it, conveying his love without words.

Frequently, in the evenings, after dinner and after Matilda had been put in her stall, we would sit in the parlor and read, me curled up on the pink sofa, a novel in my lap, Hugh sitting at the small mahogany desk, poring over a newspaper he had purchased from the stationer's in the village, both of us quiet, content to share the silence and serenity. The post brought letters from Megan and Dottie, from Boswell and Gainsborough and others, but I wasn't at all interested in theatrical gossip, in chatty news of doings in London. That busy, frenetic, frenzied world full of tensions and temperaments, crises and conflict held absolutely no appeal for me now. I was through with it. I knew what living was all about, knew my reason for being here, and, as June melted into July and day followed day, I began to nourish dreams of a future that would be as serene, as fulfilling as these weeks had been.

In all this time Hugh had never once mentioned Greystone Hall or his dreams of proving his legitimacy and claiming the estate, and I began to hope that perhaps, during these past weeks, he had finally seen the futility of his obsession and given it up. Nevertheless, I was still hesitant about discussing the future with him, not wanting anything to endanger the harmony between us. It was with some apprehension that I brought up the subject one afternoon in late July. We had lunched, had taken some surplus eggs to a family living in a nearby cottage, and we were strolling idly back down the lane. It was an overcast day, the sky a misty gray, promising rain. A cool breeze ruffled the purple and mauve rhododendroms, a few blossoms drifting to the ground. After all the warm days, this cool spell was most welcome. Hugh was silent, lost in thought. He had seemed preoccupied all day long.

"Thinking?" I inquired.

"About us," he said.

"These past weeks have been wonderful, haven't they?"

He nodded. "The happiest weeks of my life, Angie."

"There—there's no reason why it can't always be like this," I said carefully. "You love the country as I do. We could buy a place of our own, a farm. You could work it. We could have chickens and cows and—and horses and everything. We could have a large, lovely house and a few tenant farmers to help you with the crops."

"You actually believe you could be happy living like that?"

"If—if I had you," I replied. "I'm a wealthy woman, Hugh. I received a letter last week from Richard Bancroft, my banker. Jamie—" I hesitated a moment, biting my lower lip. "My former partner has made an accounting of profits from *My Charming Nellie*, and my portion has been deposited in my name. I could easily afford to buy a place, a fine place."

Hugh didn't reply at once. He thrust his hands into his pockets and kicked a stone out of his path, walking in a long, lanky stride. "I want more for you, Angie. I want to see you in silks and velvets, not cotton dresses with an apron around your waist. I want to see you pouring tea in a lovely drawing room, not tossing feed in a chicken yard. I want your hands to be white and as smooth as silk, not red and rough from peeling potatoes and scrubbing floors. I want you to have servants and carriages and jewels. I intend to give them to you."

"When you win your case," I said.

"When I win my case and acquire what is mine."

He hadn't given it up at all. The obsession was still there, held in abeyance these past weeks, and a voice deep inside told me that I had been living in a fool's paradise. Nothing had changed, nothing at all. He loved me, yes, but the dream of inheritance meant more to him than the happiness we had shared, and he was prepared to risk that happiness in order to see the dream through, no matter the odds against it. He had been a pariah in his youth, reviled and taunted because of his birth, and he had to prove to himself and to the world that he was worthy, a person of note. I understood, I understood all too well, but that didn't make it any easier.

"Give it up, Hugh," I said quietly.

"I can't do that, Angie."

"I know what it means to you, Hugh, but—you don't have to prove anything. Can't you see that? It isn't *who* a person is that counts, it's what a person is inside. It isn't who you were born, it's what you make of yourself. Wealth, a title, an estate—those things aren't important. What's important is what we have right now—our love, our health, our ability to work and make a future for ourselves. We don't *need* anything more."

"I'm going to win," he told me.

His voice was solemn, and I saw that it would be futile for me to say more. The dream obsessed him, and my words might as well have been spoken to the wind. We went on home, and a light summer rain began to fall. I cooked a lovely meal, and later we sat in the parlor reading, the rain pattering down, and later still we went upstairs and made love. Everything was as peaceful, as pleasant as ever during the days that followed, but I felt as though an invisible cloud hung over our happiness now, and I sensed it was only a matter of time until it ended altogether. I felt a sad resignation inside, even as we strolled hand in hand over the sunny fields and through the woods, even as we kissed before the dilapidated stone bridge and made love in a small clearing lavishly bestrewn with wild crimson poppies. When, a week later, he walked into the kitchen in the morning and told me he was going to London, I went right on buttering the toast, beautifully composed.

"I assume you'll have breakfast," I said.

He nodded. "I'll walk to the village and take the horse and rig. I should be gone most of the day."

"You intend to come back, then?"

He gave me a look, surprised. "Of course I'm coming back. I have some business I need to tend to, that's all."

We ate breakfast and he left, and I milked Matilda and put her out to graze. I fed the chickens and came inside and tidied the house and time seemed to creep, each hour an eternity. What was he doing in London? Was he planning to pull another robbery? Not today. Lord Blackie worked only under cover of darkness. He had "business to tend to." What kind of business? Did it have something to do with Italy, with the people he had working for him there? Why, after all of this time, did he have to make a trip to London? The afternoon stretched ahead of me, and I thought I might as well answer the latest letters from Megan and Dottie. I discovered I was out of stationery, and that gave me an excuse to walk to the village. At the stationer's I purchased elegant creamy-tan paper and envelopes and, on impulse, one of the London papers, although I hadn't bothered to read the ones Hugh had bought earlier.

Back at the cottage, I wrote to Megan and wrote to Dottie, bright, cheerful letters that belied my true state of mind. I sealed them and sighed and glanced at the clock. It was barely four. Would the afternoon never end? I picked up the newspaper and began to turn the pages idly. What cared I what was happening at court, what was happening in the Colonies, what Lady Claymore had worn to the opera, who Lord Duff had visited in Scotland? I turned the page and scanned one of the articles and started another . . . and then I began to read closely, carefully, gripping the paper with hands that suddenly began to tremble. Who is Andrew Dawson, the writer asked his readers, where is he now? Is he Lord Blackie? Andrew Dawson was the name Hugh had been using at The Blue Stag.

The writer then recounted, in vivid prose, the events of June the eighteenth, when Lord Blackie had scaled the wall of Newark House on Grosvenor Square and climbed into an attic window and made his way through the darkened rooms to the chamber where blonde and lovely young Lady Newark was fast asleep, her jewel case on the dressing table. As he was removing the exquisite diamond and ruby bracelet and earrings her doting husband had recently given her, Lady Newark awoke and let out a terrified shriek that brought her husband and two stalwart footmen running. The thief

in black tackled one of the footmen, shoved Lord Newark aside and made his escape down the staircase and
out the front door, the second footman in hot pursuit.

A chase through the streets of London ensued, and
the footman lost sight of his quarry. He continued to
prowl around, searching, and later on he thought he
saw a man in black slipping into the courtyard of The
Blue Stag, a huge building on Holywell, off Fleet, hous-
ing some two hundred tenants. Bow Street was alerted
and inquiries were made the next day. One of the tenants, a woman named Rose Pickering, a plump middle-
aged blonde in pink wrapper with maribou trim, hostess
by trade, said yes, she 'ad seen a gent in a black suit,
'e was comin' 'ome just as she was, but it was only that
nice Mr. Andrew Dawson, 'andsome chap, real refined.
Yes, it was around two in the mornin' and no, 'e 'adn't
been wearin' no black silk 'ood, 'ow'd she be able to
recognize 'im if 'e 'ad been? The journalist succinctly
captured Rose Pickering's character and did a splendid
job of reproducing her speech.

Accompanied by Miss Pickering and the hefty, disgruntled concierge, the gentlemen from Bow Street went
up to Dawson's rooms, only to discover that they had
been hastily vacated, all personal belongings removed.
Dawson had disappeared, no trace of him to be found
anywhere in the city, and while this provided no con-
clusive proof of guilt, the journalist writing this article
firmly believed that if Bow Street found the mysterious
gentleman calling himself Andrew Dawson, they would
find Lord Blackie. I set the newspaper aside, gazing
into space, thinking about what I had just read. The
events so vividly described had taken place on the night
of June the eighteenth, and ... yes, Hugh had arrived
here on the morning of the nineteenth. He had undoubtedly begun to pack soon after meeting Rose Pickering on the stairs, leaving The Blue Stag before dawn,
renting horse and rig when the livery opened, under
another assumed name, of course, paying in cash, then
storing the reproduction and his other personal effects
under the same name and driving directly out here.

The time elements fit perfectly. Andrew Dawson had disappeared, leaving not a trace, and... and Hugh had come to stay with me here in the country not because of his undying love for me but because he felt it was no longer safe for him to remain in London.

Shafts of dark red-gold sunlight slanted through the windows, making blurry pools on the carpet. It faded even as I watched, red-gold to pink-gold to pale silvery-gray. I went outside and put Matilda in the barn. The sun was gone now and the sky was slate gray, growing darker, a purple-gray haze settling over the country-side. Crickets rasped in the cracks between the flag-stones leading to the back door. Shadows spread. Oak leaves rustled quietly. I went inside and made myself a light meal and forced myself to eat, and I waited. I knew it would be better, far better, if Hugh didn't re-turn, if he never came back, if I never saw him again, yet as the clock ticked solemnly in the parlor I grew tenser and tenser, desperately afraid he wouldn't re-turn, desperately afraid something had happened to him. The clock struck nine, nine-thirty, ten, and the sadness and pain inside were almost impossible to bear.

I heard his footsteps on the lane. I leaped to my feet, relief flooding my soul. It was only through the greatest exercise of will that I prevented myself from rushing out to meet him. The gate opened, closed. Somehow, I know not how, I managed to compose myself, and when he came into the parlor I greeted him casually, as though he had just come in from the barn. I had put the news-paper away. I did not mention the article to him, nor did I question him about his trip to London. I knew that I loved him. I knew that this love for him was my ob-session, as Greystone Hall was his, and I knew I would continue to hold him to me for as long as possible. Those things unspoken must remain unsaid, for I hadn't the strength nor the character to confront him and send him away.

July ended and August began warm and sultry. We bathed naked in the stream and lay on the bank and let the sun dry our bodies. We took long walks together and picked wildflowers and Hugh helped me with the chores and it was serene and peaceful and wonderful, having him there, loving him, his body next to mine when I awoke in the mornings, his presence bringing joy even when we were sitting together in silence, reading in the parlor. It was a fool's paradise, yes, I was fully aware of that, and I was aware that it must inevitably end, but I intended to savor each joy as it came and cling to what happiness I could until the inevitable happened. And so the days passed, one melting pleasantly into the next, a fool's paradise better than none at all.

I received a long, chatty letter from Megan. Lambert would soon be starting rehearsals of the new play, she informed me, and Charles Hart would be playing Bothwell to Mrs. Perry's Mary. Megan herself had been offered a strong supporting part, but she had flatly refused to take it. Hell would freeze over before she'd go onstage with that woman in the lead. La Perry had been intolerable before with her airs and affectations, but now she was downright impossible, convinced she was the greatest actress who ever trod the boards and making everyone around her miserable. Megan wasn't sure just *what* she'd be doing in the new season, but something was bound to turn up. Now that I was no longer with him, she had no desire to work for Mr. James Lambert.

The letter I received from Dottie a few days later was both astonishing and delightful. *She* was going back on the boards, after all these years. Goldsmith had popped into the shop to talk to her about costumes for the revival. He told her he remembered her well as Mrs. Malaprop and said he wished there were someone like her around to play Mrs. Hardcastle, Kate's mother. He paused, blinked his large owl eyes, tilted his head to one side and started to nod, growing more enthusiastic by the moment. Why settle for someone *like* Dottie? Why not Dottie herself? She had been dumbfounded, had informed him that she had long since retired, but Goldy persisted. Once the idea occurred to him, nothing else would do but that she take the role. It was a lively, exuberant comic part for an older actress, and he simply couldn't see anyone else in the role. Wore her down, he did, finally got her to accept, and although she pretended to be blasé about it, I could tell that Dottie was excited about returning to the theater in such a spla⌐y, flamboyant role. It had been years since she'd donned greasepaint and wig, but it might be a lark, she confided. Goldy was such a dear, and they were certain to have a rollicking good time even if she *was* a disaster.

"Do you miss the theater?" Hugh inquired when I told him about the letter. "I detect a rather wistful note in your voice."

"I don't miss it at all," I replied.

I didn't. Not at all. Did I? Of course not. All that tension, all that noise, all that confusion and strain, the constant pressure, the constant crises night after night. Of course I didn't miss it. The peace and serenity of these past two and a half months gave me a wonderful perspective, made me see just how frantic the past four years had been. They had been exciting, yes, and challenging, glamorous, too, but who needed all the stress and temperament? The life I was leading now was much more appealing, and with all the money I had made I didn't *need* to work.

Although I told myself I couldn't care less what happened, I was human, and I couldn't help but be curious about Jamie's new production. Much of my bitterness was gone now, and ... and I really couldn't blame Jamie for what had happened. Men were notoriously weak when under the influence of a conniving female like Mrs. Perry, the male ego no match for the feminine wile. I couldn't bring myself to wish him ill. I never wanted to see him again, true, but I wished him luck. I hoped his play was the success he wanted it to be, although its chances were slim indeed. He was a complex, volatile, brilliantly gifted man who needed constant assurance of his genius. Perhaps Mrs. Perry would provide it. They deserved each other, I thought ruefully, and then I smiled at my own lack of charity. No one deserved Mrs. Perry, but Jamie, it seemed, was stuck with her. It served him right, poor sod.

It rained during the last week of August, a heavy deluge pouring from a sky the color of pewter, and afterwards it was much cooler, the air fresh and clean, the countryside vivid, trees a newly washed green, fields gold and tan and misty gray. I came downstairs early one morning wearing a pale blue cotton frock with narrow pink and lavender stripes, my hair brushed and gleaming, feeling at peace with myself, with life, content with my fool's paradise. The study was littered and I decided to tidy it up before cooking breakfast—Hugh was still in bed upstairs, fast asleep. I put away the books I had taken down and put away the stationery I had used and fluffed the cushions on the old pink sofa and stacked the cups and saucers and picked up the London paper Hugh had been reading last night with such concentration. It was folded open to an article he must have read at least two or three times and, idly, my eyes began to scan the lines of print. I felt the color leave my cheeks.

It was a society item, the kind relished by humble folk who thrived on gossipy news of their betters. The Duke of Herron and his lovely Duchess had gone to the opera last week, the Duke in powder-blue satin and lace and diamond studded shoe buckles, the Duchess in a stunning confection of pink taffeta and silver lace, dazzling one and all with her newly acquired diamonds. The tiered diamond necklace with seventeen grape-sized diamond pendants suspended had been designed especially for Maria Theresa, Empress of Austria, but, in a rare burst of economy, that lady had decided it was far too costly for the state coffers and it had been placed on the market, snapped up at once by the extravagant Duke of Herron. Although they would soon be leaving for the castle in Scotland, the Duke and his Duchess were currently snugly ensconced at Herron House, their elegant town house on Leicester Square. I put the paper down. I carried the cups and saucers into the kitchen. When Hugh came downstairs half an hour later, breakfast was ready. He looked at the mound of fluffy eggs scrambled with cheese and cream, the buttered rolls, pot of honey and jar of plum preserves, the plate of ham and crisp bacon and informed me that I was much too good to him. He ate with gusto. I sipped a cup of black coffee, watching him eat, knowing full well what he planned to do, knowing I could no longer keep silent.

"By the way," he said casually, "I'll be going up to London sometime this afternoon. Business matters. I probably won't be back until tomorrow morning. Early," he added.

"Don't go, Hugh," I said.

My voice was flat. He gave me a surprised look.

"Whyever not?" he inquired.

"For one thing, it's too risky. Herron House is certain to be well guarded with footmen everywhere, perhaps even dogs. If you're caught, you'll hang. And it's wrong, Hugh. It's wrong. I—I can't countenance it. I can't let you go, knowing—knowing you'll be deliberately committing a crime."

"How did—" He paused, frowning. "You saw the newspaper."

"I saw it. I knew at once. It's wrong, Hugh," I repeated.

"It's something I have to do," he said.

I began to clear the table, stacking the dishes on the drainboard. "You'd risk being hanged?"

"I'd risk anything."

"It means that much to you?"

"It means more than anything."

"More than me," I said.

Hugh didn't answer. Sitting there at the table in his fine white shirt open at the throat, a wave of sleek raven hair slanting across his forehead, he looked pained, dark brown eyes full of indecision. We couldn't go back now. Both of us knew that. Those things unspoken had been brought into the open, and we couldn't ignore them any longer. I took the pot of honey and jar of jam off the table and set them in the cabinet, my manner cool, icily composed. Hugh sighed and brushed the wave from his brow.

"You don't understand, Angie."

"I understand perfectly," I said. "We could be happy, Hugh. We could buy a place in the country. We could— we could have what we've had this summer for the rest of our lives. We don't need anything more. *I* don't."

"You'd soon be miserable," he told me.

"No, Hugh."

"You'd soon grow to hate me."

"I'm asking you not to go, Hugh."

"I must."

I hesitated a moment, and then I took off the apron I'd tied around my waist earlier. I hung it up and turned to look at him, a tremulous feeling inside as I contemplated what I had to do, what I had to say.

"If—if you go, Hugh, I don't want you to come back. I want you to pack up your things and take them with you. If you leave, if you—if you do what you're planning to do, I don't want to see you again. Ever."

He stood up, eyes full of alarm. "You don't mean that, Angie," he said in a tight voice.

"I mean every word."

"I love you. You know I love you."

"Apparently not enough," I said.

I went outside and took Matilda out of the barn and took her out to pasture, stroking her velvety tan forehead and trying hard not to cry as we stood there in the grassy tan-green field under a pure pale blue sky. She nuzzled my arm, looking at me with large, mournful eyes, as though she sensed my grief. I patted her flank and moved away, leaving her to graze, and then I fed the squawking chickens and filled their water trough. Slipping on a pair of old white gloves and a wide brimmed white straw hat, I weeded the kitchen garden, heedless of the dirt stains I was getting on my skirt. An hour passed, another, and it was nearing noon when I finally went back inside.

The house was still, silent. I sat down at the kitchen table and snapped a bowl full of crisp green beans, killing time, not strong enough yet to face up to the truth. I must keep busy every moment, and maybe the pain wouldn't sweep over me in searing waves. Maybe I would stay numb, unfeeling. Maybe I could endure it if I just kept busy. He was gone. I knew that. I hadn't heard a sound since I had come back inside. He was gone, and I would never see him again, and it was best, I would survive, somehow I would survive. It was only in novels that people died of love. The clock struck twelve, and almost at the same moment I heard the sound of horse hooves and wheels on the lane.

I went into the foyer. His bags were by the door. He had gone to the village for the horse and rig, and now he had come back to pick up his bags. I saw him stop out front, saw him climb down and open the gate and come up the walk toward the open door, and it seemed to be happening in a dream, everything slightly blurred, seen through a fine haze. He was wearing black breeches and frock coat and a deep wine-colored vest, a frothy lace jabot at his throat. His raven hair was pulled back sleekly and tied at his nape with a thin black ribbon. His deeply tanned face was drawn, skin stretched taut across those sharp cheekbones. His mouth was held in a tight line, and his dark brown eyes were expressionless as he stepped inside and took up the bags. He looked at me for a long moment, and then he turned to go.

I followed him out to the porch. He hesitated, gripping the handles of the bags so tightly his knuckles showed white. Neither of us spoke. Sunlight slanting through the oak boughs caused shadows to dance all around us on the porch. I wanted to beg him to give it up, give it up, but I couldn't. Pride and self-respect were all I had left now. He frowned and his eyes grew pained again, and at that moment the mature, splendidly attired gentleman resembled the moody, unhappy youth I had first loved so many years ago.

"You're sure this is what you want?" he asked.

"You've made your decision, Hugh," I said. My voice was surprisingly calm. "I hope you realize your dreams. Mine have just been demolished."

"I'm sorry, Angie."

"Good-bye, Hugh."

He left. I stood on the porch and watched him drive away, and it seemed my heart would break. It didn't. It never does, not for love. I got through the day and through the night with stubborn determination, refusing to give in to the anguish, refusing to cry, and I got through the next day and the next after that. I knew I would continue to go on. I would survive. One does. Time would help. Time wouldn't heal, it never does, but time would help. I kept very, very busy. I worked in the gardens and worked in the house, purposely exhausting myself, ignoring the anguish, refusing to acknowledge it. It was not easy. It was not at all easy, but determination saw me through.

On the fourth day I went to the village and bought a London paper, and, yes, there was a long, lurid story about Lord Blackie's latest exploit. It was filled with dramatic details about his bold rooftop entry into Herron House and his narrow escape. The Duke of Herron and his nineteen-year-old heir heard a noise, got up to investigate and came upon Lord Blackie in a downstairs hall, just as he was leaving, the Maria Theresa diamonds in his pocket. The Duke held a pistol, aimed it at the thief and ordered him to halt. Moonlight streamed through the windows, gleaming on the pistol barrel. Lord Blackie lunged, grabbed the heir in a deadly stranglehold and promised to break his neck if the Duke didn't drop the pistol at once. The Duke hesitated. The thief applied brutal pressure. The heir began to make gurgling noises and flap his arms in panic. The Duke threw the pistol aside and, using the heir as both shield and hostage, Lord Blackie made his exit, hurling the heir into a clump of bushes and fleeing into the darkness. I put the paper down. So he got away with it. It was, I knew, Lord Blackie's very last job. He was probably on his way to Italy now. At least he wouldn't hang.

Another week went by, and it was time for me to start thinking about the immediate future. My lease would be up in three days. Mrs. Gainsborough's friend would be returning from Cornwall. I would have to find another place to stay. I supposed I would return to London and stay with Megan and Charles or Dottie until I could make some other arrangement. Two days later I began to gather up my personal belongings and pack them away, books, hairbrushes, toilet articles. I had a moment of stabbing pain when, in a drawer in the bureau, I came upon the bright colored ribbons Hugh had bought for me on market day in the village. It passed. I couldn't bring myself to throw the ribbons away. Folding them carefully, I put them into the bag spread open on the bed, then I went downstairs to make myself a cup of tea.

Hearing creaking wheels and the clop of hooves on the lane a short time later, I stepped to the front door and peered out, astonished to see an ancient farm wagon loaded with hay stopping in front of the gate. On the wooden seat in front of the hay, immersed in lively conversation with the farmer, sat Oliver Goldsmith in shabby, oversized brown coat, wrinkled olive green breeches, disreputable gray stockings and cracked brown pumps. He continued to chat with the farmer for several minutes before climbing down. I had stepped out onto the porch, and, seeing me, Goldy waved, opened the gate and shambled toward me as the wagon pulled away, trailing bits of hay behind it.

"Well, lass," Goldy said, "I hope you've started packing. Chap's coming back for us at five. He'll drive us back to the village, and we'll catch a coach on into the city. Interesting chap. Had a most illuminating talk with him, all about crop rotation and manure—never know when such information'll come in handy. I must say, Angel, you're looking a bit peaked. This fresh country air will do you in every time."

"Goldy, what—what are you *do*ing here?"

Goldy blinked, surprised that I should ask so irrelevant a question. "I've come to get you, of course. Understand the owner of this charming abode is returning first thing in the morning, and you need a ride back to London. We begin rehearsals Monday morning, by the way."

"Rehearsals? I—"

"Useless to argue with me, Angel. You're going to be my Kate. No one else will possibly do. Your friend Mrs. Gibbons is going to play Mrs. Hardcastle—I fully expect her to steal the play—and I've signed Mrs. Sloan to play Constance Neville. Marvelous cast! What a jolly time we'll have, working together. *Have* you started packing, lass?"

"As a matter of fact, I have, but—"

"Splendid, splendid! Come, I'll help you finish. You've been rusticating out here altogether too long, lass. Dottie tells me you've actually been feeding chickens and milking a cow. Wonder it hasn't wrecked you completely. You belong in London, lass, in the theater. Covent Garden without its Angel is a grim place indeed. We've all missed you sorely. Come on, let's get inside. Don't dawdle! A few more whiffs of this damnable fresh air and I'll be ill for a week!"

Chapter Eighteen

I wondered if there would be another rose tonight. The first had arrived Monday night, waiting in my dressing room when I got to the Haymarket. A single rose, soft and velvety, pink, perfect, in its own slender crystal vase. The note accompanying it merely said "From An Admirer" in elegant copper script on a creamy beige card. There had been another rose on Tuesday night, on Wednesday, Thursday and Friday, each pink, each perfect, in its own vase, accompanied by a beige card identical to the first. If my admirer's purpose was to intrigue me, he had certainly succeeded. I was pleased and impressed by his unique and elegant approach and consumed with curiosity about his identity. It was Saturday now, my birthday, and as the private carriage drove me through the icy February streets, I thought about my secret admirer and tried to picture him in my mind.

He would be mature, of course. No callow youth could have come up with so novel an idea. He would be wealthy, too. Extremely. The crystal vases alone must have been terribly expensive, and the price of those perfect pink roses, in midwinter, must be exorbitant. He was a man of taste, that went without saying, and the elegant copper script on those creamy beige cards suggested great breeding and refinement. I fancied he might even be a member of the aristocracy. So I had a secret admirer who was mature, wealthy, tasteful, refined, perhaps aristocratic. The chances of his being handsome as well were very slim, I knew, but in my mind's eye I saw him as a suave and virile Adonis, a storybook hero in his mid-thirties ready to woo and win a maiden's heart. I smiled wryly at the foolishness of this image. You're twenty-six years old tonight, Angel—twenty-six, it doesn't seem possible—and far removed from maidenhood. You may still be a romantic at heart, but God knows you've no illusions left. Your secret admirer is probably a lean, balding rake panting to get into your bedroom.

The carriage came to a halt in front of the Haymarket and the driver leaped down to hold the door open for me. I smiled, thanked him politely and told him I wouldn't be needing him this evening after the play as I was going out with my friends, and then I went on into the theater. The private carriage was just one of the luxuries Goldy had insisted his leading lady be granted. It picked me up early each evening at the small, charming house I had taken in Leicester Fields, brought me to the theater, took me home after the play. My dressing room was a dream, all done in shades of white and pale gray and blue with subtle violet accents, especially redecorated for me, and there was always a bottle of very fine chilled white wine and a tray of tempting snacks awaiting me when I arrived each evening. Megan and Dottie were accorded treatment almost as grand. The management had vehemently protested all these added expenses, but Goldy had calmly informed them that we were worth it. As the house had been sold out every single night since the play opened four months ago, one of the biggest successes of the decade, the management no longer groused about the extra expense.

The revival of *She Stoops To Conquer* was a gigantic success, all right, but not merely because the critics had deemed me "a consummate comedienne, sheer perfection as Kate." Megan was magnificent as Constance Neville, playing the role with a light, droll touch that enchanted audiences. Derek Stuart as Marlow and Jack Wimbly as the bumbling Tony Lumpkin had received enthusiastic plaudits from critics and public alike, but, as Goldy had predicted, it was Dottie who blithely walked off with the play. Her comic turn in Act Five when, in her own garden, she believes she is lost in the woods and mistakes her own husband for a treacherous highwayman always brought the house down. Dottie invariably received more curtain calls than any other member of our close-knit ensemble, and all London had taken her to their hearts. A whole new career had blossomed for her and she was besieged by offers from rival managements who longed to capitalize on her immense popularity, but Dottie staunchly refused to let her head be turned and continued to run her shop, "moonlighting" at the Haymarket each night.

"Here you are," she exclaimed, meeting me in the hallway outside our dressing rooms. She gave me an exuberant hug, rubbing her cheek against mine. "Happy birthday, dear. You don't look a day over eighteen."

"You lie divinely," I retorted. "Won't you come in for a sip of wine before you start changing?"

"Alas, dear, at my age it takes me *hours* to apply enough makeup to conceal the ravages of time, and I always have trouble with that bloody red wig. We'll celebrate afterwards, at the party. My girl delivered your gown to the theater this afternoon. It's hanging in your wardrobe. There's no bill, dear. It's my birthday gift to you."

"Dottie, that gown cost a fortune. I can't let you—"

"And I'm *earn*ing a fortune by making a fool of myself onstage every night. The business has never been better, either—seven girls working for me now, all of them with more work than they can do. You'll accept the gown with my compliments, dear, and dazzle 'em in it at the party."

I returned her hug, too touched for words. She patted her pompadour, gently shoved me away and told me she had best start plastering on the paint. Dottie moved down the hall to her dressing room door, and I opened mine and stepped inside.

I saw the roses at once. They stood on a low white table in a magnificent cut-glass vase, at least three dozen of them, long stemmed, each as pink and perfect and velvety as the others had been. Their fragrance filled the room, and I moved over to them as to a fire, warming myself in their glory. Touching one of the soft pink petals, I found that it did indeed feel like velvet, caressing the ball of my fingertip as I stroked it. Never had I seen such beautiful roses, so delicate, so rich and glorious a pink. It was as I was admiring them that I saw the large flat white leather box and the card. I picked up the latter.

Happy Birthday, it read. *May I see you after the play? Your Admirer.* The copper script was elegant against the beige. He knew this was my birthday. He must be . . . must be someone who knew me. The date of my birth was not general knowledge, had never been given in any of the newspapers. Like every other woman over twenty-one, I was acutely aware of age and, with future subtractions in mind, kept quiet on the subject. Who did I know who was mature, wealthy, tasteful, refined, perhaps aristocratic? No one I could think of fit all the particulars. Puzzled, I put down the card and opened the white leather box.

The jewels seemed to blaze with a life of their own, shimmering brilliantly against a background of gleaming white satin. There were three scalloped loops of diamonds suspended from a diamond band, a dozen pear-shaped sapphire pendants dangling from the loops, each framed with smaller diamonds. The diamonds glittered with silver and violet fire, and the large sapphires were of a unique violet blue, the most gorgeous I had ever seen. I took the necklace out of the box and it shimmered all the more, gem fires flashing, darting, dancing from my fingertips.

The door opened. Megan stepped into the room, her eyes widening with shock when she spied the gems.

"My God!" she exclaimed. "They're real!"

"They certainly are. Have—have you ever seen anything so gorgeous?"

"Never. Your secret admirer?"

I nodded. "He—he knows me, Megan. He knows this is my birthday, and he picked out these stones especially to go with my violet-gray eyes. See, the sapphires have a violet flame trapped inside the indigo."

"I wish he knew *me*, luv," she said. "The last gift Charles gave me was a new pair of scissors, and then only because he wanted me to do some mending. Do you have any idea who he *is?*"

"Not a clue."

"It doesn't matter," she said sagely. "String him along, luv, at least until he gives you a bracelet and earrings to match. Lord, he must be as rich as Croesus to be able to buy a necklace like that."

"He wants to see me after the play," I said.

"*See* him," she implored.

"I intend to. I'll have to give this back."

Megan frowned and laid her palm against my forehead. "You don't *seem* ill," she told me, "but I'm convinced you've recently had a severe blow to your head. It's addled your brains."

"I couldn't keep it," I protested.

"I want you to count backwards, very slowly, starting with ten," she said in a concerned voice. "I'll go fetch an ice pack, luv. I'm sure it's not anything fatal."

I put the necklace back onto its nest of satin and closed the box. "Roses are one thing, Megan. Jewelry like this is altogether different."

"You've got *that* right, luv."

Megan examined the tray of delicate snacks sent over each evening from Button's and finally selected a tiny square of bread spread with white cream cheese, a curl of pink salmon on top. I opened the bottle of chilled white wine, pouring a glass for each of us. Megan took another snack and sipped her wine, sinking into the overstuffed pale blue chair and gazing at the roses.

"I suppose, being you, you do have to give it back," she said. "I do hope he's presentable, though, someone you can see now and then. You *need* someone in your life, luv. It's been six months since that Hugh Bradford left you. You've been living like a nun ever since you returned to London."

I had told Megan about Hugh. She knew he was the man I had fallen in love with years ago, that he had spent the summer with me, had left me, but of course I had mentioned nothing about his criminal activities or the real reasons why he had departed. Time did help. I could think of him now without the pain sweeping over me. It was still there, locked inside, but I had learned to keep tight control over my emotions.

"I've been extremely busy, as you know," I told her, "and I've been able to see more of my friends than I have in ages. My Sundays At Home have been wonderfully stimulating."

"Sundays come just once a week," she replied, "and friends are no substitute for a man in your life. Maybe this secret admirer of yours will sweep you off your feet."

"Maybe he will."

Megan set her wine glass aside and got up to fetch another snack, selecting a square of dry toast spread with goose-liver pâté with minced truffle. She offered the tray to me. I shook my head.

"Do you ever think about Lambert?" she inquired.

"I try not to," I said dryly.

"Pity about his play. The audience didn't actually throw stones on opening night, nor did the critics rush onstage brandishing knives and axes, but it was a total disaster. Seven performances, the last four to empty houses. I have it on good authority that Mrs. Perry was burned in effigy and received hate letters from the critics. Lambert lost a fortune on that particular production."

"I'm not surprised."

"He's living in grubby rooms on High Holborn, feverishly writing a new play and looking for backers to finance it."

"He—he isn't in *need*, is he?"

"I imagine he has enough to eat, luv, but The Lambert is closed up tight as a tick, and until he can open it with a new play and get some revenue coming in, he's going to have to count every penny. He sank almost everything he had into *Mary, My Queen.*"

"The most ambitious, the most spectacular play he ever mounted. The idiot! I *told* him it was doomed as soon as I read the script."

"Sure you did, luv, but Mrs. Perry assured him it was brilliant, and that's what he wanted to hear. Men! Who can figure them out? Thank God Charles finally got another part, replacing Dick Philips in *The Henchman*. During those weeks *I* was working and he wasn't, he was impossible to live with, said he felt like a kept man."

"I suppose you told him he was worth keeping."

"He is, luv. I'm holding *on* to this one."

Millie, my dresser, arrived and Megan went to her own dressing room, and an hour later we were both onstage, breezily performing Goldy's masterpiece. In a towering red wig and utterly outlandish green and black taffeta gown, our friend Dottie proceeded to steal the play again, causing the house to howl with delight as she went through her paces as the daffy, befuddled Mrs. Hardcastle. She was a wonder, her timing perfect, every bit of stage business executed with flawless aplomb, and she made it all seem as natural as breathing. I wanted to step out of character and applaud her myself. We received a standing ovation that night, and I thought the very rafters would collapse when Dottie took her bows, so loud were the cheers.

"I love Dottie dearly," Megan remarked as we left

the stage, "but I don't think I'd care to appear in another play with her."

"I know what you mean," I said.

I had left word with Millie that if a gentleman asked permission to see me after the play, she was to grant it, and when I entered my dressing room she informed me that I would indeed be having a visitor. I hastily removed my costume and stage makeup, cleaned my face, dried it and applied a touch of shadow to my lids, a suggestion of subtle pink rouge to my lips. I put on my white silk petticoat and Millie helped me into the sumptuous gown Dottie had created especially for me. It was a gorgeous, creamy white satin embroidered all over with delicate violet and sapphire-blue flowers. The small puffed sleeves were worn off the shoulder, and the heart-shaped neckline left much of my bosom bare. The bodice was formfitting, the full, spreading skirt parting in scalloped flounces to reveal an underskirt of row upon row of white lace ruffles. Millie stepped back and gazed at me with something like awe.

"Loveliest gown I ever saw. You look breathtakin', Miss Angel."

"Thank you, Millie. You may go now. I'll see you Monday evening."

Millie nodded and left and I stepped over to the mirror to examine my hair. No time to do anything with it. I'd just have to let it fall to my shoulders in loose, natural waves. I was inordinately nervous, felt as skittish as a schoolgirl, and that, of course, was ridiculous. He would come in and I would be very polite and thank him for the roses and return the necklace and that would be it. Then, with Dottie and Megan and the rest of the cast, I would drive to the newly redecorated flat over Brinkley's where Megan and Charles were giving me a party, complete with champagne and food sent in from Button's. No reason for my pulses to leap like this. No reason at all. There was some white wine left. I longed to have a glass and had just decided to pour it when he knocked on the door. It was several moments before I could bring myself to open it.

He looked at me with glorious gray eyes the color of smoke. He smiled, the full pink lips curving gently. I stared, at a complete loss for words. He wore white kid pumps with silver buckles, white silk stockings and breeches and frock coat of gorgeous sky-blue velvet. His white silk vest was embroidered with silver leaves, and delicate white lace spilled from his throat and over his wrists. This elegant attire accentuated his virile beauty, for beautiful he was. He *did* look like a storybook hero. I had thought so the first time I laid eyes on him fourteen years ago in the garden at Greystone Hall.

"Hello, Angela," he said.

His deep, throaty voice was still incredibly seductive, but there was a husky rasp to it now and, too, an edge of sadness. The radiant bloom of youth that had made him so dazzling years ago had faded, and the handsome face had mellowed. The arrogance was gone and there was character in its place, a lived-in look that made it even more attractive. His thick blond hair was paler than I remembered, pulled back and tied at the nape of his neck with a thin white ribbon. His heavy lids drooped slightly over eyes that, I saw now, seemed sad too. I gazed at him, and a full minute must have passed before I replied.

"Hello, Lord Meredith."

"I wouldn't blame you at all if you refused to see me," he said. "I still feel wretched about the way I treated you—what? Five and a half years ago? My conduct was inexcusable."

"It was indeed," I replied.

"Do you want me to go away?"

"It was a long time ago. Come in, Clinton," I said.

He stepped into the dressing room and I shut the door, remembering, surprisingly unresentful. He had changed. With the exception of physical features, the man I was looking at now bore no resemblance to the arrogant, randy youth who had attempted to bed me all those years ago. Maturity became him well, I thought. I offered him a glass of wine. Clinton shook his head.

"I—I heard about your wife's death," I said quietly. "I'm sorry."

He didn't reply. The gray eyes darkened with sadness for a moment, and then he frowned slightly. I felt awkward, sorry that I had brought it up. He sighed, shaking off the mood. His eyes held mine.

"I've thought of you often," he told me.

"Have you?"

He nodded. "I've thought about how I treated you and wondered if you could ever forgive me. I felt very guilty, Angela. I felt even guiltier after Julia died, for—you see, I never loved her. I was fond of her, I tried to be a good husband to her, but—I was still in love with you."

His frankness startled me. He could see that, and a faint smile curved on his lips.

"I'm not being very subtle, I fear, but—it took a great deal of nerve for me to come here tonight. I decided to tell you how I feel at once, without playing clever word games. I love you, Angela. Do you want to slap my face?"

I slowly shook my head, still startled.

"I wouldn't blame you if you did. I didn't know if I would ever have courage enough to come, Angela. I've been in mourning, and most of the time I sat in the drawing room at Greystone Hall, thinking about myself and not very pleased by the picture that emerged. You were a comfort to me, Angela. I looked up at the painting over the mantel and took comfort, knowing that you were doing so well in London."

"Painting?"

"An Angel in Scarlet. It's my prized possession."

"So you're the one who bought it," I said.

Both of us seemed to have run out of words. We were silent, looking at each other, and I felt a curious warmth for this man I had every reason to despise. A woman is always flattered to learn a man is in love with her, and I could tell he was completely sincere. As remarkable as it might be, Lord Clinton Meredith was in love with me. It sometimes happened that way, without any real logic. After a brief encounter, sometimes at first sight, love came, and it was as real and as potent as love that develops over a long period of time. He loved me, had loved me for years. I was dumbfounded, but I wasn't at all displeased.

"I had hoped you might let me take you to a late supper," he said finally.

"I—I think I might enjoy that," I replied, "but I'm afraid it isn't possible tonight. My friends are giving a party for me, and—"

"I understand. I didn't really expect you to accept."

"It's my birthday, you see, and— You knew that," I added, suddenly remembering the necklace.

"I made it a point to find out."

I moved over to the table, picked up the white leather box and turned, handing it to him.

"It was—it was very thoughtful of you to send me the necklace, very generous as well, but I couldn't possibly accept it."

Clinton didn't reply at once. He opened the box, removed the necklace, set the box aside, holding the necklace out between his hands. The fiery gems shimmered brilliantly, seeming to burn with glittering life. He examined them closely, then sighed.

"I had this created especially for you," he told me. "It took the jeweler months to locate just the right sapphires with violet fire—these came from Africa, I believe. I wanted them to go with your eyes. You won't accept the necklace as a token of my admiration?"

"Surely you can see why I couldn't."

"You have given the gift of your beauty and talent to thousands, Angela, and you have brought them great joy. Will you not permit me the joy of giving you a small gift in return?"

"I—"

"There will be no obligation, I assure you. If you wish me to, I will leave tonight and never see you again. Knowing you have the necklace will give me much pleasure. Don't deny me that."

"You're extremely persuasive," I said.

"Then you'll accept it?"

I hesitated, and, looking into his eyes, I saw that he was sincere, saw that he would be hurt if I refused his gift. Finally, reluctantly, I nodded, and Clinton smiled a beautiful smile and carefully put the necklace back into the box. I hoped I hadn't made a very bad mistake.

"You've made me very happy," he said, setting the box aside. "Your friends will be waiting for you, I expect. I'd better leave now. Thank you for seeing me, Angela."

"It's been my pleasure."

He looked at me. "You mean that?"

I nodded. I did mean it.

"Do you think we might be friends?" he asked.

"I think it highly possible. I'm sorry I couldn't have dinner with you tonight. I would have enjoyed it. Per-perhaps you could come to see me tomorrow afternoon. I have an At Home every Sunday from two until five. My friends drop in any time between those hours. I'd love to have you come. I live in Leicester Fields, Number Ten, a small white house with light tan shutters."

"I'll be there," he promised.

I showed him out, and Megan burst into my dressing room a few moments later, a stunned expression on her face.

"My God, luv, I saw him! I was lurking in the hallway deliberately, I admit it, hoping to catch a glimpse of him. I couldn't believe my eyes! He's the most gorgeous man I've ever seen. And rich! You kept the necklace. *Please* tell me you kept the necklace."

"I kept it," I said.

"And you're going to see him again?"

"I'm going to see him tomorrow."

"Hallelujah," she said.

Although the house in Leicester Fields was small, the drawing room was large and airy with windows looking out over the square. Done in shades of white, pale tan and gold, with a lovely pearl-gray carpet on the floor, it was an ideal place for entertaining, roomy enough to accommodate several people while small enough to give a sense of cozy intimacy. My Sunday At

Homes had come about almost by accident. As it was my day of leisure, friends had started dropping by to visit, enjoyed themselves, came back the following Sunday, and it had become habit. Journalists frequently referred to "Mrs. Howard's Sunday salon," but that was putting far too grand a name to it. Friends simply came by and stayed to enjoy one another's company, and if they all chanced to be writers, painters and actors that was pure happenstance.

Tabitha, my saucy but efficient maid, helped me put the finishing touches on the buffet table and then scowled at the lavish array of food. "Seems a shame to waste it on that lot," she remarked. Tabitha had red hair, large brown eyes and a turned-up nose, her cheeks liberally sprinkled with freckles. She had been in my employ ever since I took the house, had her own room upstairs and took marvelous care of the house and me, too. Though only nineteen, she fussed over me like a mother hen, seeing that I got the proper rest, the proper food and all the services suitable to "a lady of the theater." Tabitha did not approve of the crowd who came on Sundays. They ate far too much and got much too rowdy, particularly that 'orrible Boswell and that pompous young Mister Sheridan who was always quarreling with everyone.

"I believe that's someone at the door, Tabby," I said.

"I 'eard, Miss Angel. I'll go fetch 'em in."

She flounced out, pert as could be in her salmon-pink dress, white apron and mob cap. I checked my appearance in the mirror. I was wearing a simple buttercup-yellow muslin frock sprigged with small dark gold flowers, a gold velvet sash around my waist. My hair, newly washed, gleamed with rich brown high-lights, and my complexion looked quite fresh, despite the fact that Charles hadn't brought me home from the party until almost four o'clock in the morning. A sulky Tabby had been waiting up for me. There were faint mauve-brown shadows on my eyelids, but the effect was not unattractive. Sighing, I turned away from the mirror to greet my first guests.

"I say, Tabby," I heard Gainsborough remark in the hall, "my man Jenkins has been asking about you."

"'Im!" Tabby snapped. "It'll be a cold day in 'ell before I spend my afternoon off in '*is* company, I can tell you for certain."

"I told him to go around to the kitchen. I figured you might give him a cup of tea when you aren't too busy with your duties."

"That's all I'm givin' 'im, I promise you."

Gainsborough chuckled as she led them into the drawing room, the artist in a slightly rumpled white satin suit, his wig askew, his wife in a very becoming sky-blue taffeta gown with white lace fichu. She was carrying a large tray.

"I brought some small iced cakes, two dozen in fact," Mrs. Gainsborough announced, "and some sliced tongue, too. I'll just set this tray on the table. I had hoped to bring a ham glazed with sweet mustard, but, alas, I didn't have time to bake it."

"And *I* brought your birthday present," her husband informed me, holding up a brightly wrapped package. "Sorry we couldn't come to the party last night, but Mrs. G. is *much* too old to keep such hours."

"Speak for yourself, Thomas. I can stay up as late as anyone, Angel, but he starts to nod off as soon as the sun goes down. No fun at all these days. It's frightfully dreary being married to such a man."

"Open your present, Angel," Gainsborough said grumpily.

He handed it to me, and I removed the bright paper to discover a small drawing in ink and pastels depicting a rustic landscape I recognized immediately from my summer in the country: a daisy-strewn field behind a broken stone wall, a line of feathery trees in the background. It was beautifully framed in dark, polished wood. Gainsborough beamed when he saw my delight.

"I—I walked over that field several times," I said. "It's magnificent, Thomas. I'll treasure it always."

"I did it year before last when we were at the cottage. I thought you might like it."

I gave him a hug and, with Tabby's help, promptly hung the landscape up over a side table between two windows with long tan silk curtains. As I did so, Gainsborough stared out a window at Sir Joshua Reynolds' house across the square, hoping to catch him in some mischief, perhaps. Mr. G. wasn't at all pleased that I lived so near his archrival and feared that I might sit for him. Sir Joshua had, indeed, asked to paint me, but I had told him that I was far too busy to have another portrait done just now.

Megan and Charles arrived a few minutes later, Megan fetching in a new frock of beige and brown striped silk, Charles looking unusually handsome in brown velvet breeches and frock coat, eyelids drooping lethargically over his sleepy eyes, his dark blond hair charmingly tousled. When, several weeks after the fiasco of *Mary, My Queen,* Charles had replaced an ailing Dick Philips in *The Henchman,* that rather lackluster production had turned into a great success. With his striking good looks and potent sexual magnetism, Charles was perfect as the amoral, womanizing rogue and had become the idol of the ladies. They were constantly writing passionate letters to him, hiding themselves in his dressing room, throwing themselves at him. While Charles took it all with easygoing good humor, Megan found it considerably less amusing. It wasn't *easy* living with a man every other woman in London longed to sleep with, she informed me.

She took me aside, blue eyes full of excitement. "Is he *com*ing?" she asked me.

"He said he would. It's early yet."

"I don't mind telling you, luv, if I didn't have Charles on tap I'd give you some *strong* competition for Lord Clinton Meredith. I can hardly wait to see him again. Grab him, luv. Men like that are few and far between, and they're *never* rich to boot."

I smiled and told her I had no intentions of becoming romantically involved. Megan gave me an exasperated look and then went over to ask Mr. G. when he was going to break down and paint a portrait of *her*. Boswell

arrived, as boisterous as ever and full of bawdy anecdotes about his doings in the city, and Goldsmith came
in shortly thereafter, looking uncharacteristically affluent in a new brown frock coat and a rather startling
tan vest with bold orange stripes. Sir Joshua walked
over, which put Thomas into a snit, and Betsy Sheridan
came at two-thirty, sporting a feathered pink bonnet
and without her brother who, she explained, was spending the day with Perdita Robinson, the clever and ambitious actress who had been monopolizing his time of
late. Betsy rushed over to Charles Hart, gazing up at
him with rapt adoration.

By three-thirty things had become lively indeed.
Thomas and Sir Joshua were having a heated discus-
sion about the merits of their respective techniques,
while Boswell was scandalizing Mrs. G. with a vivid
account of a hanging he had recently witnessed at Tyburn. Dottie was sipping tea and talking with Jack
Wimbly, the actor who played Tony Lumpkin, and Megan was charming a couple of journalists and keeping
an eye on Charles who was dazzling Betsy and the pretty
young actress who had come with Jack. Tabby scurried
about refilling glasses and teacups and passing out
snacks. Goldy was snoozing quite contentedly in a large
tan chair, unable to keep his eyes open after two glasses
of wine.

Gazing out the window, I saw an elegant coach pull
up in front of the house, and I motioned to Tabby. Putting down a tray, deftly avoiding Boswell's straying
hand, she went into the foyer and, a few moments later,
returned with Lord Clinton Meredith in tow. He was
wearing light gray velvet breeches and frock coat and
a white silk vest with narrow indigo stripes, a sky blue
neckcloth at his throat. His pale blond hair was pulled
back and tied at the nape with a light gray velvet ribbon. A shy smile played on his beautifully shaped pink
lips as I hurried over to greet him. Could this quiet,
almost retiring man really be the arrogant buck I had
known in years past? Could a man really change all

that much? Lord Clinton Meredith was the living proof
of it.

"I'm so glad you could come," I said, taking his hand.

"I'm glad to be here. You have a charming house."

"Come, I'll get you a glass of wine and introduce you
to my friends."

Clinton smiled, a bit ill at ease, but he soon relaxed.
Dottie took him under her wing, all friendly warmth,
and Mrs. Gainsborough insisted he have some of the
sliced tongue she had brought. Impressed by his title,
Boswell was most engaging and chatted about shooting
in the country and various London clubs. Clinton seemed
to enjoy himself, but I noticed a certain reserve in his
manner. Though there was nothing snobbish or haughty
in his manner, I suspected he found us all rather too
exuberant and outgoing.

"He's charming," Megan told me a while later after
talking with him. "Terribly polite and well bred. I can
hardly believe he used to be the randy hellion you described."

I gazed at Lord Meredith, engaged in conversation
with Betsy Sheridan across the room. "People change,"
I said. "People grow up. It's been five and a half years
since—since I cracked him over the head with a champagne bottle and left him on the floor at Marie's Place.
After that he returned to Greystone Hall and settled
down, married, took an interest in the estate, and then
he lost his wife. He's a different man."

"Some men sow their wild oats early, get it out of
their system. I guess he falls into that category, although I must say, luv, there's still a lot of randiness
remaining. That voice, those heavy eyelids drooping
over those smoky eyes—he's wonderfully virile, despite
that polite reserve."

"You noticed," I said.

"So did you, luv."

"I'm human, Megan. I noticed."

"And?"

"And, as I said earlier, I have no intention of becoming involved with him. He's an aristocrat. I'm an ac-

tress, quite beyond the pale. I won't refuse his friendship, but anything else is out of the question."

"We'll see," she said.

People began to depart around four-thirty, and by five everyone had gone except Megan and Charles and Clinton. Charles said he was still a mite hungry and suggested we finish the food. Megan gave him a stern look and informed him they had plenty to eat at home, then shoved him toward the door. She told Clinton how very pleased she was to have met him, gave me a hug and left with Charles in tow. Tabby had tactfully disappeared. Clinton smiled.

"I like your friends," he said.

"I've been very blessed when it comes to friends," I replied. "They've all been wonderful to me."

"You've made quite a life for yourself," he told me. The smile lingered on his lips. "The schoolmaster's daughter from a small village in Kent has come a long way."

"I've worked very hard."

"I admire that," he said quietly.

"Are—are you going to be in London long?" I inquired.

"I've opened the house on Hanover Square. I don't know how long I'll stay. That—depends on a number of things."

There was a moment of silence. Both of us were rather ill at ease now, the implication of his last words all too clear. I smoothed a lock of hair away from my temple and asked if he would like another glass of wine, and Clinton shook his head.

"I must be going myself. I—uh—I was wondering if you might like to come riding with me tomorrow. I ride in the park every morning at eleven, then have a light lunch back at the house."

"You ride in this weather?" I was surprised.

"It's very invigorating. One dresses warmly. Will you come, Angela?"

"I—I'm afraid I don't ride," I confessed. "In fact, I've never even *been* on a horse."

He smiled again, amused by my tone of voice. "Then I will have the pleasure of teaching you," he replied. "I have a beautiful little mare in my stable, extremely gentle. You'll love her. I also have a ladies' riding saddle. Let me give you your first lesson tomorrow."

"I—I don't know."

"Come, Angela," he said teasingly. "Be adventuresome. You might be a little sore from the experience, but I can assure you you'll enjoy yourself."

"Well—"

"My carriage will pick you up at ten-thirty. All right?"

"I'll be ready," I said.

He was right. I did enjoy myself, and I was indeed sore after the first lesson. Very. It was a lovely day, crisp and cold, but the sun was shining brightly. I wore a long sleeved blue velvet gown, black kid gloves, black boots and a heavy black velvet cloak with violet silk lining, the hood pulled up over my head. Clinton looked handsome in his black riding habit and white silk stock. The mare he had selected for me was a gentle chestnut named Cynara, and I did love her, at once. Nevertheless, I was a bit nervous as Clinton helped me up into the saddle. He was wonderfully patient, giving me careful instructions and correcting me when I made an error. There were few people in the park that chilly day, and we were soon moving under the ice-encrusted tree limbs at a leisurely trot, Clinton firmly restraining his powerful gray stallion who longed to gallop. It was frightening at first—I was certain I would fall off—but after a time I managed to relax and enjoy myself thoroughly.

Returning to Hanover Square, we had a light, lovely lunch in the dining room of the small, beautifully appointed town house. Soup was followed by fillets of fish cooked in wine sauce and served with asparagus, with cheese and fruit afterward. The food was excellently cooked by his chef, flawlessly served by a footman in livery. We had coffee in the small drawing room, in front of a crackling fire, both of us relaxed and feeling quite exhilarated after the exercise. Clinton said I had the

makings of a fine horsewoman and said we must definitely continue the lessons.

"Tomorrow," he added.

"Isn't—isn't that a bit soon?"

"You have to keep right at it. And, as I've been so
exemplary an instructor, I think I should have a reward."

"Oh?"

"I think you should let me take you out to dinner
tonight after the play."

"I can scarcely refuse," I told him.

And so I learned to ride. Dottie made me a beautiful
riding habit of garnet velvet with a wide-brimmed garnet velvet hat to match, black plumes sweeping down
over one side of the brim. I wore it with my black kid
gloves and boots, feeling quite elegant, cutting a dashing figure, I felt. Clinton was quite pleased with my
rapid progress, said I was a natural horsewoman, said
I had a perfect seat. I told him I'd never had any complaints. He grinned at that. March was mild, pure blue
skies soaring overhead, brilliant sunlight spilling over
the pathways in the park, and in April, as the trees
began to green, as the first daffodils opened up delicate
yellow faces to the sun, Cynara and I were racing right
alongside Clinton and his stallion, aptly named Hercules. We rode almost every day, and it was wonderfully
invigorating.

We lunched together at Hanover Square, having long,
leisurely, relaxed talks afterward, and he took me out
after the theater four or five nights a week. How lovely
it was to have so polite, attentive and considerate a
companion. That he was wealthy and as handsome as
a young god made it all the more enchanting. Although
he made no secret of his feelings toward me, Clinton
was completely proper and treated me with the utmost
respect. He was content, it seemed, merely to be in my
company. At first I was pleased that he made no advances, that he left me at the door with a squeeze of
the hand and a fond good night, but after a while I
began to wonder if I wasn't just a little disappointed. I

was not at all immune to his dazzling good looks and the potent sensuality held in tight control behind that careful reserve. Although I certainly didn't love him, I couldn't deny the strong physical attraction I felt, and although I truly had no intention of becoming romantically involved, I couldn't help but wonder how long it would be before he took me into his arms and kissed me. His restraint was much more titillating than any overt move could have been.

"He *still* hasn't kissed you?" Megan asked me one evening before the play.

"He's been a perfect gentleman," I told her.

"I find that terribly *odd,* luv."

"He respects me."

"And he's madly in love with you—it's as plain as anything. I would have thought he'd have made a move long before this. I suppose after what happened at your stepmother's place all those years ago he's afraid he might scare you off if he got too randy."

"Maybe so," I said. "He—he *is* in love with me. I know that."

"And you, luv? How do you feel about him?"

"I—I'm quite fond of him. I enjoy his company a great deal. He's everything a woman could want in an escort."

"A woman wants more than an escort, luv," she said sagely. "Despite rumors to the contrary, we have needs, too—just like men."

"I'm content with things as they are, Megan."

"Oh?" she inquired.

"Perfectly," I said.

I tried to sound convincing.

I was thinking of all this one afternoon in early May as I walked to the stationer's on Great Queen Street, off Drury Lane. Clinton and I had not gone riding that morning, as he had business to attend to, but he was taking me out after the play tonight to an elegant new dining establishment where he planned to introduce me to the delights of Russian caviar. Smiling to myself, I stepped into Lavvy's and selected new cream note paper and envelopes and dawdled a bit, examining the prints for sale. There was a new series by young Thomas Rowlandson, who did satiric drawings in the vein of Hogarth, as well as prints of the latest works by Gainsborough, Reynolds, and "that upstart" Romney, who both men claimed was stealing their style. I was looking at a print of Romney's portrait of Countess Bessborough when I became aware of someone staring at me, the stare so intense it was almost like physical touch.

Putting down the print, I turned ever so casually, and I felt my pulses leap when I saw him standing there at the counter as Lavvy wrapped up the ream of writing paper he had just purchased. His rich brown hair was unruly, tumbling untidily over his forehead, and there were smudgy gray shadows beneath the green-brown eyes that stared at me with such intensity. His face looked pale and drawn, making the slightly crooked nose more pronounced, and I observed that he could use a fresh shave. Though his clothes were clean, they looked a bit shabby, looked as though he might have slept in them. The brown broadcloth frock coat was superbly cut but well past its prime, and his emerald green neckcloth was carelessly folded. The fingers of his left hand were ink stained. He gave me a curt nod, then paid Lavvy for the paper and took the bundle from him. I moved over to the counter, feeling strangely light-headed.

"Aren't you going to speak, Jamie?" I asked.

"Hello, Angel," he said. "You're looking quite fit."

"I wish I could say the same for you."

"I suppose you think I look like hell?"

"As a matter of fact, you do."

"I've been working."

"I'm pleased to hear that."

"Damn! I've dreaded this. I've lived in fear I'd run into you accidentally one day."

"I've lived with the same fear," I told him. "Isn't that a little ridiculous? We're both adults, after all. I'm not going to bite you, and I seriously doubt you'll bite me."

"You never can tell," he said grumpily.

I had to smile at that. Jamie scowled. I paid Lavvy

for the note paper and envelopes and brazenly asked Jamie if he would like to go with me to Button's for coffee and some cheesecake. He hesitated, scowling, clearly not enchanted by the idea, and I waited, my eyes holding his with a challenging look. After a moment he shrugged, said he guessed it couldn't hurt anything and opened the door for me. He was silent all the way to Button's, walking in long, limber strides, clutching the ream of paper under his arm. I found his brusque, rude manner extremely irritating, but I could understand why, rumpled as he was, he wouldn't be overjoyed to see me.

Eyebrows were raised and there was a buzz of whispers as we entered Button's together, for it was the favorite haunt of theatrical London and, of course, both of us were immediately recognized by its inhabitants. Covent Garden would be rustling with rumors tomorrow, I reflected, waving to a trio of journalists, smiling at a table of actors. Jamie's mood didn't improve one bit as we were shown to a choice corner table. Scowling, eyes belligerent, he tugged at his already untidy green neckcloth and glared at the waiter who brought the coffee and cheesecake I had ordered.

"Mrs. Gainsborough claims this is the best cheesecake in all London," I remarked. "She's been trying to get them to give her the recipe for ages, but they stoutly refuse to divulge it."

"*Must* you keep chattering on and on like a bloody magpie?"

"Those happen to be the first words I've addressed to you since we left Lavvy's. I don't know why you're so *nervous*, Jamie. Just because we no longer live together doesn't mean we can't be civil, does it?"

"So you think I'm uncivil, do you?"

"I think you're acting like an absolute ass."

He scowled, looking quite murderous, and then, after a few moments, he emitted a deep sigh and reached up to shove the dark brown locks from his brow. The gray smudges under his eyes had a faint mauve tint, and there were slight hollows beneath his cheekbones. He hadn't been getting enough sleep, I thought. Probably hadn't been eating properly either. He was like a little boy in so many ways, one of those men who definitely needed someone on hand to take care of him. According to Megan he was quite alone in those grubby rooms on High Holborn.

"I guess I have been acting like an ass," he admitted. "This isn't exactly easy for me, Angel."

"Nor is it a picnic for me," I said, "but we can't spend the rest of our lives living in fear we'll run into each other. Covent Garden isn't that large. It's bound to happen occasionally. I—" I hesitated, trying to find the right words. "I just thought it might be nice if we could be grown-up about things. I thought we might even be friends."

Jamie didn't reply. He took a sip of his coffee and gazed moodily about the room. He wasn't going to make it easy for either of us, I thought. I toyed with my cheesecake, wishing I'd never asked him to come. After several moments of silence he took another sip of coffee, set the cup down and looked at me with frosty green-brown eyes.

"You were right about *Mary, My Queen,*" he said in a flat voice. "I imagine you were quite pleased with yourself when it failed so abysmally. I imagine you gloated for weeks."

"On the contrary, I was very sorry. I had hoped it would be a great success for you."

"'Mrs. Howard wisely declined the part,'" he quoted.

"I can't help what the journalists wrote. I know how much it meant to you, Jamie. I wanted you to have a success."

A bitter smile played on his lips. He pushed his plate of cheesecake aside. "You've certainly done well for yourself. I've rarely read such plaudits. 'Free of lugubrious melodrama, Mrs. Howard proves herself a consummate comedienne, pure perfection as Kate. She radiates vitality, wry good humor and overwhelming charm in a performance that is sheer enchantment.'"

"They were very kind," I said.

"Not kind. Factual. You deserve every word of praise they gave you. Your Kate *is* perfection. You've proven yourself one of the greatest actresses of the age. All you needed was a role worthy of your talents."

Something I was never able to give you, he implied. I made no reply, knowing anything I said would be taken the wrong way. I took another sip of the hot, aromatic coffee and made another stab at the creamy cheesecake with the prongs of my fork.

"I hear there hasn't been an empty seat since it opened," he said. "Had a hard time getting a ticket myself. Is it true you're closing in June?"

I nodded. "It was originally planned for a limited run of three months. We extended the run to six, and then the management decided to let it run until June the first. *The Tempest* will move into The Haymarket then."

"And what will you be doing next?" he asked.

"I—I have no idea. There've been offers, of course, but—nothing I find particularly interesting. Megan tells me you're writing a new play."

"Finished it last week," he told me. "I'm making a few revisions now. I'm pretty sure I've got a backer, a rich textile merchant from Leeds with more money than good sense. Thinks it might be fun to invest in the theater. Actually enjoys lugubrious melodrama."

"You're terribly unfair to yourself, Jamie. You're—at what you do, you're the best there is. The public loves your plays."

"Yeah. They simply adored *Mary, My Queen*."

I let that pass. "What is the new one about?"

"It's a comedy set in Shakespeare's England," he informed me. "It's about a winsome, capricious young lady-in-waiting who falls madly in love with Richard Burbage when Shakespeare's troupe comes to perform for Good Queen Bess. She flees the palace, disguises herself as a boy and, with Will Shakespeare's help, becomes a member of the troupe, playing Ophelia to Burbage's Hamlet—with all the predictable romantic and comedic complications."

"It—it sounds delightful, Jamie!" I exclaimed, genuinely enthused. "What a clever idea!"

"It's a romp, really, pure entertainment, with no heavy historical overtones to muck up the pace. Much of the action will take place at The Globe, backstage and on. Jack Wimbly, your Tony Lumpkin, has already said he'll play Shakespeare, and I'm hoping to get Hart for Burbage if *The Henchman* ever shuts down. With the right actress to play young Lady Amelia I'm relatively sure we'll have a long and healthy run."

"A lot will depend on her," I said.

He nodded. "The whole play revolves around her."

"She must be very good."

He nodded again, watching me.

"I—I'd love to read it, Jamie."

Jamie looked at me for a long moment, and then he got to his feet. A wintry smile flickered on his lips.

"I'm afraid that would be a waste of your time, Angel. You're far too distinguished an actress to sully yourself by appearing at The Lambert again. What would your beloved critics think? Thanks for the coffee—I believe it *is* your treat? I must get back to work now. Nice seeing you."

He turned and left, moving purposefully toward the door with the ream of paper under his arm. He might as well have slapped my face. Never had I felt such utter humiliation. I was sure my cheeks were burning, and I could feel unwanted tears welling on my lashes. Oh, Jamie, I thought, that wasn't necessary. That really wasn't necessary at all. If your intention was to wound me, then you have succeeded beyond your wildest dreams. I forced the tears back and forced myself to finish my coffee, acutely aware of the eyes watching me. Finally, composed, I paid for our coffee and cheesecake and left, waving to the journalists once again and smiling at the actors, giving the best performance of my life.

"You're very quiet tonight," Clinton said nine hours later.

It was after one o'clock in the morning and we were

driving back to Leicester Fields in his lovely white and
gold carriage. I was sitting across from him, the wide
skirt of my violet-gray satin gown spread out on the
seat. I was wearing the diamond and sapphire necklace
Clinton had given me, and he was pleased by that, for
this was the first time I had worn it. Moonlight streamed
through the windows of the carriage. The silver haze
burnished his pale blond hair, gleamed on the lapels of
his white satin frock coat, softly brushed his handsome
face.

"Forgive me," I said. "I—I haven't felt too vivacious
tonight."

"Perhaps you didn't enjoy the Russian caviar," he
suggested.

"The caviar was magnificent, Clinton. I could de-
velop a taste for it quite easily."

"Perhaps it was the champagne."

"The champagne was delicious."

"Perhaps it was the company, then," he said.

"The company was the best of all. I—I can't tell you
how much your kindness, your courtesy, your thought-
fulness have meant to me tonight. I must be the most
fortunate woman in London to have so—so wonderful
a companion."

"I'd like to be more than a companion, Angela," he
said quietly. "Surely you must know that."

I looked at him, feeling very vulnerable, feeling very
grateful for all his kindness, all his patience, and I knew
I couldn't refuse him, nor did I want to. I had loved two
men, foolishly, fervently—for, yes, I had loved Jamie,
too, I admitted that now—but neither of them had loved
me like this man did, nor had either of them shown one
tenth the consideration or concern for my happiness. I
didn't love him, no, but I wanted very much to make
him happy.

The carriage turned quietly into Leicester Fields and
pulled up in front of Number Ten. The footman leaped
down and held the door open for us, and Clinton handed
me down, holding my hand lightly. Moonlight silvered
the yard. My satin skirt rustled softly as he led me up

the pathway to the door. A light was burning in the foyer. Tabby was undoubtedly waiting up for me, but she would vanish discreetly when she saw I had a guest. We stopped in front of the door. The lilacs were blooming, scenting the air with their fragrance.

Neither of us spoke. Clinton took my hand and pressed it gently and looked into my eyes. He saw my answer there. He let go of my hand and rested his on my shoulders and then, tilting his head slightly, leaning down, he kissed me and I curled my arms around his shoulders, returning the kiss with a tenderness that matched his own. I felt his need, felt mine as well. Clinton pulled back, and I rested my hand on his cheek.

"Come inside, Clinton," I said.

"No, Angela."

I looked at him, puzzled. He reached up and took my hand and gently kissed my palm, then lowered it. He rested his hands on my shoulders again and I trembled slightly as his fingers began to massage my bare flesh.

"This isn't what I want," he said. "Not this way."

I didn't speak. He smiled at my puzzlement.

"I want to marry you," he said. "I want to make you Lady Meredith."

"You—you can't mean that."

"I love you very much, Angela."

His voice was low, melodious, with that husky rasp, and his eyes gleamed in the moonlight, so gentle, full of love. I could scarcely believe this was really happening. I remembered a precocious little girl of twelve who had scrambled up the garden wall and scooted along the tree limb to spy on the handsome, randy young heir who had pinched the lovely Laura's pink nipple and kissed her hungrily. Now, fourteen years later, he was standing here with his hands on my shoulders, and he wanted me to become his wife.

"You're an aristocrat," I said. "I'm the schoolmaster's daughter, grown up to become a notorious actress. Men—men of your class make mistresses of women like me, but they don't marry them. Your friends—society—I would never be accepted. You'd be ostracized yourself."

"Do you seriously believe that would matter to me?"

"It should."

"Nothing matters to me but you, Angela."

I could see that he meant it. If only Hugh had felt the same way.

Clinton continued to massage my shoulders, his fingers surprisingly strong, the tips pressing gently into my flesh. His eyes held mine, and his lips curved in a quiet smile, a beautiful smile. How I wished I loved him, but unfortunately I didn't. Deep affection, fondness, admiration were not enough, and I knew I had to be completely honest with him.

"I—I'm very fond of you, Clinton," I said, and there was a tremor in my voice. "I'm deeply moved by your proposal, but I couldn't marry you. I don't love you, you see, and it—it wouldn't be fair. You deserve someone who—"

He curled the fingers of his left hand around the side of my neck, the ball of his thumb resting lightly against the base of my throat. "I believe I could make you love me," he said.

I looked at him for a long moment there in the moonlight and then I nodded. "Yes," I whispered, "I believe you could."

"I'm leaving for Greystone Hall tomorrow morning, Angela. There are estate matters that need to be tended to. I'll be gone for two weeks. Your play will be closing. You will have had time to think about it. I would like for you to give me your answer when I return."

"Very well," I said.

"I hope it will be yes, Angela."

I hoped so, too.

Book Four

Lady Angela

Kent

Chapter Nineteen

Clinton folded his napkin and placed it neatly beside his empty plate, smiling at me as I sipped my second cup of black coffee. On the sideboard in the dining room, under silver covers, were fluffy scrambled eggs, crisp bacon, stewed mushrooms, kippered herring, delicious sausage links, but I wasn't to be tempted. A piece of toast from the silver rack, perhaps, perhaps a bit of marmalade spread on it, but I couldn't bring myself to eat anything more substantial this early in the day. Clinton, like most men, ate a hearty breakfast, and he couldn't understand how I could make do with so little. He nodded as a footman entered with fresh coffee in a silver pot. The footman poured coffee into his delicate blue and white porcelain cup with its gold rim, and Clinton lifted it to his lips. From distant regions of the enormous house came the sounds of banging and bustle as the fleet of workmen started early on the renovations being made to Greystone Hall.

"Please leave the pot, Robert," I said. "I'll probably want another cup when I finish this one."

"Yes, Milady."

"Chef is going to be terribly distressed, you know," Clinton informed me. "He takes your not eating breakfast as personal criticism of his fare. Yesterday, when you turned down his plovers' eggs poached in wine sauce, he actually burst into tears, I hear."

"I suppose I'll have to go to the kitchen and compliment him again on the dinner he prepared last night. Why are chefs so temperamental?"

"They're artists," he explained, "and they're usually French. Henri is less temperamental than most, though he still smarts at having to prepare such mundane dishes as eggs and bacon for breakfast. Sure you won't have some sausage?" he asked teasingly.

"Quite sure," I said.

"Then I'll leave you to your coffee. I've a lot of work to do today. I have to go over the books with Jenson, and I want to inspect the Langley place myself. Jenson claims they don't really need a new roof, but it's going to be a rainy fall, and I want to make sure."

Although he had a very efficient bailiff and a number of able assistants, Clinton considered running the estate a full-time job, and the concerns of his tenant farmers were his own concerns. Because of this attitude, the farms had never been so productive. While they greatly envied his success, most of his fellow landed aristocrats considered Clinton's work habits unseemly and highly eccentric. Chap actually rode about the fields and supervised work, inspected the plows, got dirty, sweated like a menial. No way for a Lord to act. Set a very bad example. Clinton, of course, didn't care a fig what the rest of the gentry thought, but the welfare of his farmers was most important to him.

He stood up now, tall and superbly built, wearing black knee boots, tight gray breeches and a loosely fitting shirt of thin white lawn, the sleeves full gathered, the tail tucked carelessly into the waistband of his breeches. Pale blond hair pulled back and tied with a thin gray ribbon, his handsome features thoughtful as he contemplated the day's duties, he stood there for a moment beside the table, and I looked at him with admiration, telling myself once again how very fortunate I was. We had been married for four and a half months now, returning to Greystone Hall immediately after the small, quiet ceremony in mid June, and I had no cause to regret the decision I had made. My husband sighed and, catching me looking at him, smiled.

"Don't forget to take your cloak," I said. "Even though the sun is shining, it's bound to be nippy outside. I don't want you catching cold."

"No?"

"I want you strong and healthy," I told him.

The smile curled, and his lips lifted slightly at one corner, lids drooping seductively over his smoky gray eyes. Although I hadn't meant it to sound provocative, Clinton interpreted it that way, recalling, no doubt, the private times together when his being strong and healthy was definitely an asset. His politeness and gentility notwithstanding, Clinton was a potently sensual male, and in the bedroom he was superlatively aggressive and masterful. That aspect of our marriage could not possibly have been improved. Moving around the table, he leaned behind me, encircled me with his arms and rested his cheek next to mine.

"There's no time," I said. "You have to go over the books. You need to inspect the Langley place."

"It *could* wait."

"You're incorrigible, Clinton."

He caught my earlobe between his teeth and bit it gently. "And you're absolutely delectable in your light blue frock. I wonder what you're wearing under it."

"Behave yourself, Clinton. Robert may come back in any minute."

"He's the soul of tact. He'd go right back out again. If he didn't, I'd thrash him. You know, we've never *done* it in the dining room."

"And we're not about to this morning. I thought I was marrying a gentleman, not a savage."

"Are you complaining?" he inquired.

"I'd like to be able to finish my coffee in peace."

Clinton chuckled, nuzzled his cheek against mine and released me, standing up straight. I turned around in my chair and gazed up at him, taking his hand in mine. He pulled me to my feet, gathered me into his arms and kissed me very chastely on the brow.

"Happy, Lady Angela?"

"Very."

"No regrets?"

I shook my head, leaning back against his arms.

"You don't miss London, the theater, your friends?"

"We'll be going to London frequently, the theater can do without me and I keep in close touch with my friends. I have a passionate, attentive husband, a marvelous staff of servants and—everything I could possibly want. I am a very fortunate woman."

"I'm the fortunate one," he said.

He smiled, kissed me gently on the lips and stepped back, reluctantly letting me go.

"Don't forget to speak to the chef," he reminded me. "I'd like to have a decent lunch, and when he's sulking he deliberately serves things he knows I dislike."

"Spinach?"

"And hard-boiled eggs. See you in a few hours, Milady."

Clinton left, and I finished my coffee, and then I sighed and went to the kitchen and told Henri how much Lord Meredith had enjoyed the wonderful breakfast, how much I had enjoyed the superlative dinner last night. I asked him how on earth he was able to cook sole so tender, prepare such a magnificent sauce and added that he simply had to stop baking such delicious tortes or I would be unable to get into my clothes. Surrounded by his pots and pans, helpers scurrying about, an aromatic soup bubbling on the stove, Henri beamed and asked if I would perhaps prefer a croissant instead of toast tomorrow morning as I was so "delicate" at breakfast. I said that would be wonderful and left him planning a "great surprise" for our lunch.

That accomplished, I decided to make the long trek to the ballroom to see how the work was progressing there. When I had arrived at Greystone Hall four and a half months ago it had seemed to me a great gloomy place with a labyrinth of dark, depressing rooms filled with ugly Jacobean furniture. Clinton admitted that it was less than cozy and said I was free to make any changes that I cared to make. Expense, he added generously, was no object. I immediately contacted the noted Scottish architect, Robert Adam, whom I had met in London, asking if he would come look at Greystone Hall. Adam had arrived a week later with his brother James and, after expressing their horror, the brothers promptly began to draw plans. A veritable fleet of workmen arrived, overrunning the place, and, under the supervision of Adam himself, walls were torn down, small rooms turned into spacious chambers.

Dark oak panelling was ripped out, replaced by soft creamy plaster painted in shades of white or by light, subtly patterned wall coverings. Immense, ugly fireplaces were transformed into the simple, elegant creations done in various light marbles for which Adam was famous. Floorboards black with age were either bleached and polished or replaced with gleaming new parquets, lovely Oriental carpets in pale pinks, tans, grays and yellow spread over them. Heavy velvet draperies, dark and dusty, were yanked down, silk hangings in soft pastels hung in their stead, and hideously ornate carved furniture was banished to the attics, lorries arriving from London with new pieces from the workshops of Hepplewhite and Chippendale.

My long consultations with Adam had been quite stimulating, and I had enjoyed selecting the fabrics for draperies and upholstery and going through the glossy catalogues to select carpets and furniture. It had kept me busy indeed during those first weeks, and Clinton had left everything to me, saying he had complete faith in my decisions. He had been wonderfully patient about the invasion of workmen and artisans, the perpetual confusion, the chaos, the noise, spending most of his time away from the house and enduring all of the inconvenience with sunny good humor. He professed himself delighted with the new look gradually transforming the place, and I could tell he was sincere. He had experienced a great deal of sadness here at Greystone Hall, and the sad memories were banished along with the dusty velvet drapes and Jacobean armchairs. All the work had been completed now except in the ballroom, and Adam promised that would be finished in less than two weeks.

The men were busily at work when I entered, and the noise was quite deafening. On the south side of the house, the ballroom was large, though not as immense as many in houses this size. Scaffolding had been set up around three sides, swarming now with men, while others worked on ladders. Robert Adam was personally supervising the placement of one of the marble panels, a rare light orange-pink marble that had come from Italy. The walls, newly plastered, now gleamed a rich cream-white, interspersed with the marble panels, and the ceiling had been painted a pale salmon a few shades lighter than the panels. Italian artisans were carefully gilding the delicate molding in gold leaf. Adam saw me and nodded curtly, and I made my way around ladders to join him, almost tripping on the heavy burlap cloths covering the polished golden-oak floor.

A stockily built man not quite as tall as I was, Adam had dark brown hair and rather blunt features, his gray eyes shrewd. Brusque, assertive, he was a perfectionist who brooked no nonsense. There was nothing at all elegant about this man who had brought such light, graceful beauty into English homes. His clothes were drab, sensible, the lapels of his heavy brown coat sprinkled with marble dust. Though I would have enjoyed having him at the house, Adam stayed at the local inn, firmly refusing to socialize with any of his customers. It wasn't good business, he claimed, and this brilliant, intimidating man was all business, the very best there was.

"It's coming along beautifully," I exclaimed. "I can't believe it used to be so dim and gloomy. You've filled it with light, made it seem more spacious. Cream and light salmon and a few touches of gilt—it's going to be the most beautiful ballroom in England."

"I think it may well be," he agreed soberly. "Your choice of colors was ideal, Lady Meredith."

"You're the one who suggested the salmon and said we could probably match it with the marble from Siena. I can't tell you how pleased I am with the way it's turning out."

"Fine," he said. "Be careful with that sheet of marble!" he bellowed. "Ease it up gently, men. Gently, I say! I'm glad you're pleased, Lady Meredith. If you'll excuse me, I'll get back to my men. This is a very crucial step. One slip and an irreplaceable sheet of marble would be rubble."

I nodded, ignoring his rudeness. The dour Scot had insulted the majority of his aristocratic clientele, causing counts to grind their teeth and leaving haughty duchesses apoplectic, but so great was his vogue, so elegant his work, they would have endured twice the insults. Feeling like an intruder in my own home, I made my way out of the ballroom, almost colliding with one of the ladders and causing an Italian artisan with palette of gold leaf to emit a highly volatile curse.

Wending my way through the corridors, I entered the drawing room in front of the house, off the main foyer. It was done in shades of white, light gray and sky blue, with sapphire blue velvet covering the graceful Chippendale sofa and chairs. Over the lovely white and blue-gray marble Adam fireplace hung *An Angel in Scarlet,* the focal point of the room. I gazed at the painting, marveling anew at the rich, glowing colors and the sad expression in the eyes of that beautiful young woman who seemed a stranger to me now. So much had happened since I had posed in Gainsborough's cluttered studio over five years ago. This painting had changed the entire course of my life, and the woman standing now in the drawing room of Greystone Hall scarcely recognized the pensive girl in deep scarlet velvet. I was no longer the same person who had posed for the famous portrait.

Sighing, I turned just as Mrs. Rigby came into the room, her black taffeta skirts rustling crisply, the keys at her waist making a merry jangle. Mrs. Rigby was the housekeeper, a plump, efficient woman with clear blue eyes and a number of silver streaks in her severely bunned black hair. A pleasant, tactful woman who had done all she could to make things easy for me, she was a tyrant with the staff of maids, seeing that all work was done promptly, correctly and as unobtrusively as possible. While others might have been martyred by the invasion of workmen, Mrs. Rigby took it in her stride without a complaint. She and I met here in the drawing room every day at nine so that she could receive "instructions" for the day. They generally consisted of her suggestions that today might be a good day to clean the chandeliers or polish the silver or air the linens in the upstairs cupboards and my agreeing that yes, that would be a dandy idea. Mrs. Rigby was eager to acknowledge my authority and pleased that I had no intentions of usurping her own.

Greystone Hall employed some twenty-seven servants, including footmen and grooms, and Mrs. Rigby and Putnam, the butler, ran things so smoothly that one was rarely aware of their presence except when they were serving. Putnam had been with the family for thirty years, rising from footman to his present exalted rank, while Mrs. Rigby had only been here for twelve. I considered myself fortunate indeed to have so splendid a staff, but I often thought longingly of Tabby, whose bossy ways had kept me in line at Leicester Fields. That cheeky young lady was now working for the Gainsboroughs and making life hell for Jenkins, whom she had married shortly after Clinton and I were wed. Mrs. Gainsborough's letters were full of humorous descriptions of the newlyweds' antics, and I invariably smiled when I thought of them together.

Having listened to Mrs. Rigby's tactful suggestions for the day, I agreed to them all and dismissed her. It was nine-fifteen, and I had three hours to fill before Clinton came back for lunch, another four after that before he was through for the day. While I was pleased that Clinton took his duties so seriously, I had to admit that time frequently hung heavy on my hands. Adam didn't want me underfoot, the house was run beautifully without my lifting a hand and there was precious little for me to do. It had been several weeks since I had been to see Eppie, and I decided to pay her another call this morning, although the other visits had been curiously strained and uncomfortable.

Fetching my heavy cloak, I left the house and went around to the stables. Ian, the brawny young groom, greeted me with a wide grin and told me 'e'd 'ave Cynara all saddled up an' ready quick as a flash. With his sun-streaked brown hair, lively blue eyes and sunny disposition, Ian was a particular favorite of mine, always polite and prompt but never obsequious. He was a merry lad, not quite eighteen but already a rogue with the ladies, causing quite a stir among the pretty housemaids. It was Ian who had picked out the right saddle for me when I had decided to ride astride, abandoning the fine leather sidesaddle. I found riding astride much more natural and comfortable, although Clinton wryly informed me that I was scandalizing the countryside. Ladies, it seemed, didn't ride astride like red Indians. It wasn't done.

Standing there in the sunny cobbled yard in front of the stables, I could smell damp hay and horseflesh, old leather and manure, an earthy, not unpleasant odor that invariably reminded me of Hugh. I tried not to think about him, but it was difficult not to do so. His ghost seemed to haunt the stables, the grounds. I carefully avoided that section of the garden with rose trellis and marble bench where, from my perch in the tree, I had first seen him and he had called off the dogs. Over a year had passed since he had left me there at the cottage I had taken for the summer, and although I told myself that I was completely over him, the memories were still painful.

Poor Hugh, traveling around Italy at this very moment no doubt, driven by his obsession, spending his ill-gotten gains searching for evidence that had never existed. Happiness could have been his, could have been ours, if only he had been willing to give up that futile quest. How supremely ironic it was that I was now living at Greystone Hall and had the title, the wealth, all the luxuries he had claimed I couldn't be happy without. And I *was* happy, I assured myself, not because of the material things but because, for the first time in my life, I was loved by a man who put me first. I didn't love Clinton with that consuming passion I had felt for Hugh, nor did he make me feel the wild exhilaration and joyous abandon Jamie had stirred within me, but love him I did, in my way. It was a quieter love, much more genteel, and, ultimately, much more satisfying, without the emotional highs and lows that took so heavy a toll. I was very lucky to have him, and I was determined to make him happy.

"'Ere she is, Milady!" Ian announced, bringing Cynara around. "An' full of spirit this mornin'!

Cynara whinnied with delight when she saw me, prancing quite outrageously on the cobbles. Her chestnut coat gleamed with glossy highlights in the morning sun. I patted her cheek, told her to behave herself and, with Ian's help, swung up into the saddle, arranging my skirts demurely around me. Ian handed me the reins, and I was soon on my way, leaving house and grounds behind, riding at a brisk gallop down the road, amidst countryside I knew so well. There were the woods where I had climbed trees and searched for mushrooms as a child and there the fields where I had picked wildflowers, there the old gray wooden stile I had used to get over the low stone wall. Up ahead, branching off the road, was the familiar lane with its masses of rhododendrons, and as I rounded a curve I could glimpse the rooftops of the village in the distance.

I rarely went to the village except for an occasional trip to Blackwood's to pick up the newest books. As a child I had known everyone, been readily accepted as the schoolmaster's daughter, but there had been a complete change in the villagers' attitude toward me. I had left the village, and I had gone to wicked London. I had become an actress, which most of them equated with becoming a prostitute, and now I had returned as Lady Meredith and all those people who had welcomed young Angie with a smile weren't about to be friendly with me now. Oh, they were polite enough. They called me "Milady" and "Lady Angela," but there was a distinct reserve and, I suspected, a bit of resentment as well. I was no longer one of them. I was an outsider, and I was treated as such. I was rejected by my own class, and Clinton's had never accepted me in the first place.

Our marriage had, of course, caused a furor of talk among those affluent, beribboned, beplumed and powdered dames and dandies who thought themselves the select few of this world. Though there wasn't a closet not crammed with skeletons, as Solonge had pointed out, and though their behavior set new standards in rudeness and frequently in depravity as well, a common actress would never, never be welcome in their drawing rooms and salons. One *slept* with an actress and bought her bright baubles and kept her in a plush apartment, but one never *married* her. Lord Clinton Meredith had done the unthinkable, and his friends and fellow aristocrats were deliciously scandalized. Not a single one of them had come to visit since we had returned to Greystone Hall, nor had we been invited to any of their hunts or balls. It mattered not a jot to me, but I was rather concerned for Clinton's sake.

Clinton told me not to worry. We would win them over, he assured me. As soon as they met me they were sure to respond to my beauty, my charm, my natural breeding. They hadn't come to call, true, but as soon as the renovations were finished we would give an elaborate ball and invite them all. They would all come, he promised, out of curiosity if for no other reason, and they would find the new Lady Meredith enchanting and welcome her into the ranks with open arms. I had my doubts about that, but I wasn't going to argue. How free and easy, friendly and caring Covent Garden seemed now that I had left it. There were no class distinctions in the theater, and wit, talent and personal accomplishment were the only criteria by which one was judged. Would that the rest of the world could be as tolerant.

It was a bright, crisp morning as Cynara and I sped along, my hair bouncing about my shoulders, the cloak billowing out behind me. Gently tugging the reins, I directed Cynara onto a side road and we passed more fields and a bank of trees, and then I saw the McCarry place in the distance. The farmhouse was seriously in need of a new coat of paint. The roof could stand repair. Three small boys were playing in the front yard, and a little girl sat on the porch, gently cradling a beautiful doll. The boys stopped playing and stared when I rode up and stopped, slipping out of the saddle. The little girl clutched her doll as though she feared I might take it away from her. No more than three, she had large blue eyes, a dirty face and fluffy pale blonde hair.

"Hello, Millicent," I said. "My, what a beautiful doll."

Millicent lowered her eyes shyly, holding the doll even closer. The oldest little boy came over and, taking the reins, informed me that he would take care of Cynara. I thanked him and turned as the front door opened. Eppie was wearing a yellow cotton dress sprigged with tiny brown flowers, a garment that had seen better days. Her hair, a listless blonde now, was stacked on top of her head, stray locks spilling down, and the enormous brown eyes had lost that lively sparkle. Her face was sadly lined. Eppie was exactly one year older than I, and she looked forty. Smiling a shy smile, she led me inside.

"So nice of you to call, Lady Angela," she said.

"It's Angie, Eppie," I told her. "I thought I made that clear last time I was here. We're old friends."

She nodded, still shy and ill at ease. What had become of that vivacious silly goose of a girl who resembled a giraffe with her long neck and lean, angular body? She had married her handsome Jamie McCarry and moved to this farm and given birth to four children. The vitality and zest for life had vanished long ago. It seemed a tragedy to me. Eppie had gotten exactly what she wanted from life and was quite content with her lot. Perhaps that was the greatest tragedy of all. She led me into the "parlor" of which she was so proud, a small, spotlessly clean room with cheap, shiny furniture. A vase of wildflowers, the colored shawl spread over the sofa and the seven blue and gold plates hanging on the wall made a rather pathetic attempt at elegance.

"I'll just run make some tea, Lady An-Angie. Won't take a minute."

"It's really not necessary, Eppie. I just finished breakfast. I thought we might just—visit for a while."

Eppie smiled again and asked me to sit down, indicating the sofa. When I was comfortably settled, she sat down herself in one of the armchairs. Eppie and I had grown up together and she had been my closest friend for years. Now she was uncomfortable around me, clearly in awe.

"I—I want to thank you for the things you sent the children," she said shyly. "The boys loved their presents, and Millicent hasn't let that doll out of her sight. I must thank you for—for the things you sent me, too. I never had such a lovely dress. I'm keeping it to wear on special occasions. You didn't have to send all those things, Angie."

"I wanted you and the children to have them."

"Lord Meredith takes wonderful care of his tenant farmers, has ever since he came back from London and settled down at Greystone Hall, but people didn't expect you to take an interest in 'em, too. Expected you to be flashy and affected, they did, all paint and put-on. Angie ain't like that, I told 'em. I wudn't at all surprised when I heard about all the nice things you've done for people. Folks in the village might be standoffish, but the wives of the farmers think you're a regular Lady Bountiful."

"I haven't done that much," I said.

"You took medicine to Claire Weatherford when she was down with the fever and nursed her yourself. You bought shoes for all the Miller kids and a brand new stove for Anna Henderson. You've taken an interest in all the families of the tenant farmers, ain't too good to go visit 'em, stay for a cup of tea. No other Lady of Greystone Hall ever did that."

"I have a lot of time on my hands," I told her.

Eppie didn't reply. She toyed with her hands in her lap, her brown eyes thoughtful. I could tell she was remembering earlier days.

"I—I guess we both did pretty well for ourselves, Angie," she said after a while. "I got Jamie McCarry— all the other girls were after him, but I was the one who got him, and he's still as handsome as ever. I've got my four kids and a nice house and a lot of pretty things—you noticed my plates, didn't you? Jamie bought 'em for me one at a time. And you—you became a Lady. Who'd of thought it when we were girls?"

"Who indeed," I said. "I'm so glad you're happy, Eppie."

"Me, I wasn't ever ambitious like you. I wasn't ever special, never wanted to set the world on its ear. You were always different, Angie. I knew it way back then when we were gadding about the village and giggling at the boys. You had something. Didn't surprise me at all when you became a famous actress in London. Didn't surprise me when you married Lord Meredith, either. He always had an eye for you. Remember that time we were sitting in the square and he came riding by on his horse and tried to get you to go off with him and you were so lippy?"

"I remember."

"Funny how people change," she said. "He was something back then, handsome as a god and randy as a ram, only one thing on his mind. And he grows up to be such a fine man, sober and fair-minded, admired by everyone. Life sure is full of surprises, isn't it?"

"It is indeed," I replied.

I left Eppie's a short while later and, without really planning to do so, circled around the village and rode past the square with its sun-warmed benches and rusty cannon, then came to the weathered old church, its pale tan stone walls brushed with shadow from the oaks, its tarnished copper spire soaring up toward the pale blue-gray October sky. I dismounted and opened the gate, moving into the churchyard. Several of the old white marble tombstones were toppling and covered with moss, but my father's was brand new, of the finest marble. Fresh pink flowers stood in the white marble vase. Clinton had ordered the new tombstone, had given instructions that fresh flowers were to be placed on the grave each week. He had done all this without consulting me, and I had been deeply touched. Clinton hadn't known my father, but he knew his reputation and knew that we had been very close.

Late morning sunlight slanted through the boughs of the oaks, making patterns on the ground, flecks of sunshine alternating with shadow. I stood beside the grave for a long time in silent communion, remembering. Once, a long time ago, I had vowed that I would make my father proud of me, and in my heart I knew that he would indeed be proud of me now. He would be proud of Clinton, too, pleased that I had married so fine a man. The title, the wealth wouldn't have impressed him, but the man and his integrity would have had his approval. I had been dubious of this marriage, had hesitated quite some time before giving Clinton my answer, afraid I might be making a dreadful mistake, but I knew now my decision to say yes was the wisest I had ever made.

Bidding my father a silent farewell, I left the churchyard, mounted Cynara and rode home to join my husband for lunch.

Work on the ballroom was completely finished by the first of November and Adam and the workmen departed, the architect declaring himself more than satisfied with the job he had done on Greystone Hall. Five days later three dozen beautifully embossed invitations were mailed to all the neighboring gentry and a number of Clinton's aristocratic friends, requesting their presence at a grand ball to be held at Greystone Hall on the evening of November fifteenth. Mrs. Rigby and her

staff were in a positive flurry, making preparations, and
Henri and staff were in a flurry, too, planning the menu,
ordering foodstuffs. Twelve cases of the finest champagne were delivered, stored in the wine cellar, and on
the morning of the fifteenth three lorries arrived from
the hothouses in the next county, loaded with literally
thousands of white and salmon pink roses and huge
sheaves of white fern as delicate as lace, with four florists to see to the arrangements. Everything was in
chaos, it seemed. Nothing would possibly be ready in
time.

Clinton was completely unperturbed at breakfast,
enjoying his eggs and bacon, having an extra piece of
toast spread with strawberry preserves. I was a mass
of nerves, drinking cup after cup of black coffee and
working myself into a state almost as bad as those on
opening nights. He calmly informed me that there was
nothing for me to worry about, the ball would be a huge
success, and then he left to go supervise the repair of
a stone fence in one of the fields. That didn't help at
all. The house was bustling with activity, the silver
being polished, the Sevres china being washed, flowers
being arranged, dozens of last minute tasks being seen
to. I thought I just might possibly go mad.

The day seemed interminable. Clinton returned for
lunch and told me all about mending the fence and said
the men had done a damned fine job and I told him that
was absolutely marvelous. He smiled at my sarcasm
and told me to relax, and then he suggested I take a
nice long nap so that I would be fresh and lovely for
our guests. I didn't throw the sugar bowl at him, staying
my hand just in time. My dear husband would never
know just how close he came to being crowned. He finished his meal, said he had to spend the rest of the
afternoon in his office and, coming around the table to
give me a kiss on the brow, left the room. Oh, he was
very supportive, very understanding, going blithely
about his business when I was on the verge of a nervous
collapse. I stared at my untouched crabmeat salad with
loathing and pushed it aside. Hours to fill, and nothing

for me to do. Everything was under perfect control Mrs.
Rigby assured me as she hurried past me in the hall a
few minutes later. The florists were almost finished
with the arrangements and the footmen were setting
up the small gilt chairs around the ballroom. She bustled on down the hall, taffeta skirts crackling, and I
moved glumly up the stairs.

The musicians arrived at four-thirty and began to
set up their stands and tune their instruments in the
ballroom. In three hours our first guests would begin
to arrive. Holding back the panic that threatened to
grip me, I ordered a bath and luxuriated in the hot,
perfumed water and washed my hair, drying it with a
fluffy towel. Wearing only my thin pale violet silk petticoat, I spent almost an hour with my hair, brushing
it until it gleamed like glossy chestnut silk, pulling it
away from my face, arranging it in an elaborate roll in
back, a simple, elegant style that, I fancied, made me
look older and more dignified. I used cosmetics spar-
ingly, applying a pale pink to my lips, a mere suggestion
of lighter pink blush to my high cheekbones, rubbing
a subtle mauve shadow onto my lids. The effect was
natural, not at all theatrical. If they expected to meet
a gaudy, painted actress, they were due a surprise.

Polly, my personal maid, came in to help me with
the gown. A shy lass of seventeen with long flaxen hair
and blue-gray eyes, she exclaimed in wonder at the
gown and said she'd never seen anything so beautiful.
It had arrived from London a week ago, one of Dottie's
loveliest creations designed especially for the ball. It
was a deep violet-blue velvet, the cloth rich and sumptuous, making a soft rustling sound as I put it on. Polly
fastened it up in back, deftly hooking the tiny, invisible
hooks, and I stood before the mirror, examining myself
with a critical eye. The short, narrow sleeves were worn
off the shoulder, and the form-fitting bodice was cut
low, though not as extreme as fashion decreed. The waist
was snug, the deep violet-blue skirt parting in draped
panels to display an underskirt of watered gray silk

with narrow violet stripes. It was a gorgeous gown, tasteful and demure yet absolutely spectacular.

"You look a vision, Milady," Polly said in an awed voice.

"Thank you, Polly. You may go now."

Polly bobbed a curtsy and left. I fetched my jewel box and took out the necklace Clinton had given me in London. The diamonds and sapphires seemed to vibrate with shimmering life as I fastened the necklace around my neck. Dottie had selected a velvet only a few shades deeper than the sapphires, and the necklace beautifully complemented the gown. I vividly remembered that evening Lord Clinton Meredith had come back into my life, remembered the gorgeous pink roses and my reluctance to accept this gift. Only eight months ago, that was, and now I was Lady Meredith and waiting in terror to meet his friends and aristocratic neighbors. Gazing into the mirror, I took a deep breath and squared my shoulders. You're an actress, Angela, I reminded myself, and you're going to carry it off with perfect aplomb. You're going to hold your head high and be gracious and charming and every inch a lady and if they don't like you they can all go sod themselves.

"Thinking of me?" Clinton inquired.

He walked into the room, looking positively dazzling in black velvet knee breeches and frock coat and a white satin vest with narrow black stripes, delicate lace cascading from his throat and spilling over his wrists. His stockings were of fine white silk, and diamond buckles gleamed on his black leather pumps. His pale blond hair gleamed in the candlelight, and his gray eyes were full of fond amusement. It was hard to believe that he had been working most of the day.

"Actually, I wasn't," I said. "I was thinking of our guests."

"Still nervous?"

"Terrified," I confessed.

"They're going to love you," he told me.

"I'll probably make a dozen dreadful faux pas. I'll probably stumble and fall flat on my face. This is worse than any opening night I've ever had. I think I may just run away."

"No, you won't. You'll charm them one and all. Before the night is over you'll have the haughtiest duchess eating out of your hand."

"Will there be haughty duchesses?"

"At least a brace of 'em. Frightful old dragons, breathing real fire. I forgot to warn you about 'em."

"You're teasing," I said sulkily.

"And you're being a perfect ninny, my darling."

"How—how do I look?" I asked.

Clinton tilted his head to one side, studying me with narrowed eyes. "I suppose you'll do," he said, frowning. "There—uh—there seems to be something missing, though."

"Something missing?" I was puzzled.

He studied me for a moment longer, the frown still creasing his brow, and then, light dawning, he snapped his fingers and told me he'd be right back. I frowned myself as he darted out of the room. He returned a few moments later, a merry grin on his lips and a large white leather box in his hand. Making an exaggerated bow, he handed the box to me, and I opened it to discover a gleaming pair of diamond and sapphire earrings and a magnificent silver wire spray, each curving wire studded with diamonds and sapphires. The diamonds had a violet-white shimmer, and the sapphires were identical to those in the necklace, deep violet fires flashing within the indigo.

"Damn you," I said. "Now I'm going to cry."

"You don't like them?"

"I don't deserve them. I—I've never done anything to deserve a husband like you."

Clinton smiled, pleased with my reaction. "I think I should be the judge of that," he said.

"I *am* crying. It's going to spoil my face."

I stepped to the mirror and blotted the silvery tear from my cheek with a white cloth. I wanted to sob, so moved was I, but I managed to control myself and face him with some semblance of composure. The smile was still curving on his beautifully chiseled pink lips. I went over to him and placed my hands on his shoulders and stood up on tiptoe and brushed those lips with my own. His arms curled around me, drawing me nearer, and my right hand rested on the back of his neck. After a few moments, most reluctantly, he drew back and eased me away.

"Let's not start anything we can't finish in five minutes," he said amiably. "We have to go downstairs and greet our guests."

"Damn the guests," I murmured.

He smiled again, delighted. "Why don't you put on your new things," he suggested. "The spray, I believe, goes on the side of your head. I was going to buy a tiara but tiaras are for plump dowagers. The jeweler assured me this hair piece would be quite the thing."

Lifting the shimmering spray from its nest of white satin, I carefully secured it to the side of my head, just behind the temple, the silver wires curving up and around in a half circle, each wire studded with exquisite diamonds and sapphires blazing with fiery life. It went perfectly with my new coiffure, as did the pendant earrings I put on next. Clinton nodded his approval, and I felt another tear trailing down my cheek. He brushed it away and took my hand and led me out of the room.

"I feel something fluttering in my stomach," I said.

"Nonsense."

"I know now exactly how the early Christians felt as they were waiting to face the lions."

Clinton chuckled quietly and led me down the curving white staircase Adam had recently installed. My velvet skirt rustled. A footman in gold and white livery and powdered wig stood at the foot of the staircase. Clinton asked him to fetch us some champagne, and he obliged, returning a few moments later with two slender crystal flutes on a tray. Clinton took them, nodded his thanks to the footman and handed me a flute. I sipped it gratefully, still feeling tremulous inside. It was seven twenty-five. Our first guests would be arriving at any moment.

"Ready?" Clinton inquired.

"I'd prefer to be shot."

"I'm looking forward to showing you off," he said. "I want everyone to see what a beautiful, charming, enchanting wife I have."

I didn't reply. Clinton sipped his champagne, looking at me over the rim of the glass with fond smoky gray eyes. I straightened my shoulders, and suddenly the tremors were gone and I was filled with a steely resolve. I was going to carry it off. I was going to win over each and every one of them, for Clinton's sake. Although he pretended not to care that his peers had shunned him since our marriage, that there had been no calls, no invitations, I sensed that he was deeply disappointed, even hurt.

We chatted about inconsequential things, waiting. The delicate porcelain and gilt clock on the table across the hall chimed seven-thirty. Clinton finished his champagne and motioned to the footman who came and took our glasses. How proud I was to be standing beside him, so handsome in his elegant clothes, so dignified and self possessed, and, as I had reason to know, so very virile. I linked my arm in his. He looked down at me and smiled. We waited. Several more minutes passed. I listened for the sound of carriage wheels on the drive outside, composed now, ready for the onslaught.

The clock chimed again. It was seven forty-five. My legs were beginning to feel a bit stiff. No one wanted to be the first to arrive, of course, but surely by this time... I gave Clinton a reassuring smile. He told me I was going to dazzle them. Five minutes passed, ten, and then it was eight o'clock and I had a terrible premonition. No, I prayed. Please, no. It doesn't matter for my sake, but please, please don't let him be hurt. The clock struck eight-fifteen, and no carriages circled the drive, and finally it struck eight-thirty and Clinton turned to me, beautifully composed.

"It seems our guests have been detained, my darling," he said quietly.

"So—so it seems." My throat was tight.

"I believe Henri has prepared quite a spread. Shall we dine?"

I nodded, afraid to speak again.

Taking my hand, he led me into the grand dining room where liveried footmen stood behind the long buffet tables covered with snowy linen cloths, laden with a gorgeous array of food. There were glazed hams and golden-brown roasted turkeys and two sides of beef, pink and juicy. There were mounds of shrimp and pails of oysters and fillets of sole cooked in white wine sauce and a porcelain tureen of turtle soup. There were vegetables of every variety, wonderfully cooked, tempting salads and one table devoted exclusively to a seductive display of desserts, glorious cakes and tortes, miniature fruit pies, individual dishes of pudding topped with swirls of whipped cream.

"Henri has done himself proud," Clinton remarked.

"He certainly has," I agreed.

He handed me one of the magnificent pink and white Sevres plates delicately patterned in gold, and we moved slowly down the line with the footmen serving us. I wasn't hungry. I couldn't possibly eat. I smiled at Clinton and said the prawns looked delicious, said I must try some of that aspic. When we had made our selections, we took our plates over to the immense table with its banks of roses and gleaming silver candelabra. Clinton set his plate down at the head of the table and helped me into the seat at his left. A footman came to fill our glasses with fine white wine. Clinton lifted his in a toast.

"To you, my darling," he said.

I smiled and sipped my wine. I wasn't going to cry. I wasn't. I was going to be as calm, as composed as he. I took a bite of aspic and said that it was marvelous. Clinton said that the ham was tasty indeed. We ate and sipped our wine and chatted as though nothing at all was amiss. Clinton said that he was very pleased with the renovations Adam had made and complimented me on the colors I had chosen, the furniture I had selected. He said that his wife had exquisite taste. The footman

removed our plates and we selected our desserts. Coffee
was poured into our delicate Sevres cups.

"You should taste this cake," Clinton said.

"My torte is divine," I told him.

When we were finished, when we had drunk our
coffee, Clinton helped me to my feet. He spoke briefly
to one of the footmen, telling him to see that the food
was removed to the servants' hall downstairs where
they were having their own party, and then he took my
hand and led me out into the foyer and down the corridors to the ballroom. The chandeliers hanging from
the pale salmon-pink, lightly gilded ceiling blazed,
crystal pendants glittering brightly. Enormous white
wicker baskets full of pink and white roses stood around
the cream walls with their pale pink-orange marble
panels, scenting the air with a lovely fragrance. The
huge expanse of golden oak floor gleamed, the musicians stationed at one end in front of a spectacular bank
of roses and white fern.

"May I have this dance, Milady?" Clinton inquired.

"You may, Sir," I said.

He signaled to the musicians, and they began to play,
sweet, sublime music tinkling, rising, swelling, filling
the room with a beauty as touching, as intangible as
the fragrance of the roses. Clinton took my hand and
led me onto the floor and looked into my eyes and smiled
and we began to dance. He was a marvelous dancer,
executing each step with graceful perfection, and we
moved to the music and my skirts swayed, rustled, and
somehow the sadness and disappointment vanished and
there was only beauty and joy, this man, the music, the
movement, crystals shimmering above, roses blurred
bits of pink and white velvet as we danced around the
great, empty floor.

That first dance was followed by a second, a third,
a fourth, and Clinton maintained eye contact, smiling,
silently informing me of his love, his pride, his passion.
The room seemed to swirl, the pale salmon ceiling with
its delicate gilt patterns seemed to blur, chandeliers
swaying as I threw my head back and gave myself en-

tirely to the magic of the moment. The music stopped and my husband drew me to him and kissed me tenderly there in the middle of the floor and led me over to one of the gilt chairs as the music began again. A footman brought us champagne and I sat and sipped mine and Clinton stood behind me and rested one hand on my shoulder and I tilted my head back to look up at him and he smiled again and leaned down to brush my lips with his, banks of roses surrounding us, music floating on the air.

"Happy?" he asked.

"Very," I said.

"Your cheeks are pink. Your eyes are gleaming. You look radiant."

"Because of you."

He lifted a brow. "Because of me?"

"Because you are a wonderful man."

"A lucky man," he amended.

He took my empty glass and set it aside, leading me onto the floor again. We danced, and the music was soft and lilting, and it seemed to lilt inside of me as well, music and emotion becoming one, filling me with a sweet, warm glow that grew as his hand squeezed mine, as his body gracefully turned, guiding me along, as those glorious gray eyes gazed intently into mine and that full pink mouth curved in a tender smile. Time seemed to melt, meaningless, and Clinton seemed tireless, dancing on and on, smiling, guiding me through the steps, and it was well after one and the glow suffused me when, finally, he signaled to the musicians and the music ceased.

He held me loosely, looking at me, gray eyes aglow.

"Want to dance some more?" he asked.

I shook my head.

"More champagne?"

I shook my head again.

"Want to go upstairs?"

I nodded. He kissed me lightly and curled an arm around my shoulders and led me out of the magic ballroom and down the dim corridors and up the curving white staircase and into our bedroom. He let go of me and I stood wearily and watched as he blew out all the candles and a haze of moonlight slowly streamed in through the windows. There were roses here, too, vases of them, their perfume heavenly, heady. He came back to me and drew me into his arms and kissed me once again, and I melted against him, my hands moving over the sculpted muscles of his back and shoulders.

"You know," he murmured, "I think this was the best ball I've ever attended."

"It was a beautiful ball," I whispered.

"And the evening has just begun."

"Oh?"

"The best is yet to come."

"Is it?"

He smiled. "May I have this dance, Milady?" he asked, and he had another kind of dance in mind, with its own rhythm, its own steps, its own swelling splendor. "You may, Sir," I said, and he held me closer and covered my mouth with his and we danced until dawn.

Chapter Twenty

Although the November sky was a rather forbidding gray, it wasn't all that cold as Megan and I strolled leisurely over the grounds. A light wind billowed our cloaks and brushed our cheeks, and the bare limbs swayed slightly. The gardens were bare of the riotous blossoms and greenery of spring, but there were bushes of late-blooming pink and white roses and formal evergreen trees and the lovely white marble benches. I told Megan that we were planning extensive changes in the spring, adding more flower beds, a knot garden, but I could tell from her expression that she found our gardening projects less than fascinating. Wearing a cream and rust striped linen frock and a rust velvet cloak, she had a worried look in her eyes and kept listening for the sound of horse hooves.

"I do wish they'd come back," she complained. "They've been gone since early morning and I didn't like the look of that stallion Charles mounted. Men are so careless, such show offs, always trying to top each other—bag the most quail, leap the most fences, take the most risks."

"Charles is a superb horseman," I reminded her.

"Sure he is. So is Clinton. Don't you worry about *him?*"

"Sometimes," I admitted. "Hercules is such a powerful stallion and Clinton is rather reckless, charging across the fields like a red Indian and bounding over stone fences."

"That's what I *mean,* luv. Charles is just as bad. Why did they have to go hunting in the first place? Who *needs* quail?"

"Men enjoy these things," I said. "It'll do them both good. They'll return all flushed and triumphant and pleased with themselves. Having the two of you here has been nice for Clinton. He and Charles get along wonderfully well, don't you think?"

"Hearty mates from the first day. Charles has enjoyed himself tremendously, and he needed to get away from London for a while after *Amelia Mine* closed. Such a disappointment that was—everyone expected it to run every bit as long as *My Charming Nellie*. It *was* a delightful play, luv."

"I know," I said quietly. "Dottie sent me a copy."

We stopped at the foot of the gardens and turned, looking up past the terraced beds of pink and white rose bushes to Greystone Hall, immense and impressive with its weathered gray walls and leaded windows and the multilevel gray-green rooftops. Megan's hood fell back and a skein of auburn hair blew across her cheek. I gathered my dark blue cloak closer about me, thinking about Jamie and the bitterness I knew he must be feeling.

"Amelia Mine was the best thing he's ever written," I observed. "It's a shame it didn't run longer."

"The critics loved the play," Megan said. "For the first time in his career Lambert receives brilliant notices—'clever, inventive, a delightful romp of a play'—and it closes after two and a half months. Charles was positively marvelous as Burbage, the ladies practically fell out of their seats during the love scenes, and Jack Wimbly was inspired as Shakespeare, best performance he's given, but the play needed a very strong actress in the lead. Young Mrs. Thayer simply hadn't the experience to carry it off."

I was silent, remembering the newspaper clippings Dottie had sent me after the play opened. *A part tailor-made for Mrs. Howard. An actress of Mrs. Howard's stature would have done the role justice. While charming, Mrs. Thayer is no Angel Howard, for whom the part was obviously written. Lambert's brightest play demanded the presence of his brightest actress, Mrs. Howard, who was sadly missing.* How these comments must have stung Jamie, for, had I played the part, and I would have had he given me the least encouragement that afternoon at Button's, he would likely have had the success he so badly wanted. The success he so badly needed.

"You should have played Amelia," Megan said.

"That was out of the question, Megan."

"Poor Lambert. He had so much in his favor—a genuinely fine play, full of wit and verve, a superb set, gorgeous costumes, a perfect leading man, an excellent supporting cast—and, alas, a weak leading lady. Mrs. Thayer gave it a good try, but the part was too much for her."

"I know Jamie must have been terribly disappointed."

"He was devastated, luv."

"What—what is he doing now?" I asked.

"Hurting," Megan replied. "I don't know who he got to put up the money for the production, but they lost it all, and rumor has it that Lambert is deeply in debt."

"He'll pull through," I said. "He always does."

We started slowly back toward the house, moving up the levels of terraces, the fragrance of roses scenting the cool November air. The sky seemed a darker gray, the color of slate, and I suspected we might soon have snow. Megan emitted a sigh and gazed at the roses.

"It's lovely here," she remarked.

"Very," I agreed.

"And so *quiet*. Do you miss it, luv?"

"Miss what?"

"The theater. The excitement, the vitality, the color. The greasepaint, the applause."

"I'm very happy here, Megan."

"That doesn't answer my question."

"I—I have nothing to complain about. Clinton is wonderful. I love him very much."

"But?"

"There really—there really isn't all that much to do," I confessed. "I have hours and hours each day when—when I find myself restless, at a loss. I don't mean to sound like an awful bitch—Clinton couldn't be kinder, couldn't be more considerate—but—I'm used to being *involved* in something."

"Exactly," Megan said.

"At first I was kept busy with the house—going over the plans with Adam, selecting colors and fabrics, picking out furniture—but after that—" I hesitated, feeling terribly disloyal. "I visit the tenant farms now and then and perform small acts of charity. I take long rides. I read a great deal. When Clinton is around, it's fine, but—the estate takes up so much of his time. I must sound dreadfully ungrateful."

"Not at all, luv."

"I *do* miss the theater, yes, I'll admit it, but I—I'll soon get used to this new way of life."

"I'm sure you will."

"It—it's simply a matter of adjustment. It wouldn't be so bad if we had some kind of social life, but Clinton's class has turned a cold shoulder on him ever since our marriage."

"Dottie told me about the ball," Megan said.

"It's much harder on Clinton than it is on me. I say sod 'em, but Clinton grew up in that world. Those are his friends, his colleagues. He never says a word about it, but I know he's been deeply wounded. I feel it's my fault."

"You shouldn't," she told me. "Clinton wanted *you,*

luv, and he knew full well what he was letting himself in for. You matter far more to him than a lot of powdered fops and their haughty dames. He loves you, and, I must say, I've never seen a man who seemed happier with his lot."

"I want him to be happy," I said quietly. "It's the most important thing in the world to me."

"Things will brighten up when you get to London," Megan said. "Clinton's friends might be bloody snobs, but he's certainly tolerant of *your* friends. He has been a marvelous host, luv. Charles and I both adore him."

"And he's fond of you. Having you here has been marvelous."

Reaching the top level, we paused for a moment. The lawn here directly behind the house was smooth rolled and edged with flower beds that in spring were full of daffodils and daisies. Tall evergreens shivered in the breeze. Megan smoothed back her auburn hair, running her fingers through the lustrous coppery brown waves. Since Charles, she seemed more settled, I thought. The vitality and sparkle were still there, as lively and engaging as ever, but the restlessness was gone, and there was a new maturity in those vivid blue eyes. Both of us had changed a great deal since that day at Miller's on Fleet when she begged me to help her hide from her former lover. That seemed a lifetime ago.

"Has—has Clinton ever mentioned Hugh Bradford, luv?" she asked, pulling up her rust velvet hood.

I shook my head. "His name has never come up."

Megan knew the whole story, even the fact that Hugh was the notorious Lord Blackie. I had finally told her about that, and Megan had been intrigued. She was the only person I had dared confide in, but I needed to talk to someone about it and knew I could trust Megan completely.

"Clinton doesn't know about you and Hugh?"

"He hasn't an inkling," I replied, "and—he must never know. There was bad blood between them when they were youths. It—it would upset Clinton terribly if he were to find out."

"I can see why, luv," Megan said. "Do you think Hugh will return to England?"

"I haven't any idea. I hope he doesn't. It could only mean trouble for everyone."

"You're over him," she said.

"I just want to forget. Hugh belongs to—to a past that is firmly behind me."

Hearing shouts, laughter and the sound of horse hooves pounding on the cobbles, Megan and I circled around the back of the house to the stables, arriving just as Charles and Clinton were dismounting. Both men were dusty, disheveled and flushed with the ruddy glow of male satisfaction. Charles was dressed all in brown, a crumpled burnt-orange neckcloth at his throat, his dark blond locks attractively tumbled. Alighting nimbly from the powerful chestnut he had been riding, he proudly held up a clump of quail all strung together, at least seven of them. Megan gave him a look of total disgust. Clinton, in black knee boots and navy blue breeches and coat, chuckled at her reaction to the dead birds and slipped out of the saddle, his sky blue neckcloth as crumpled as Charles'. Hercules stamped and let out a wicked snort as Ian took the reins and led him into his stall for feed and grooming. Another groom led the chestnut away.

"Quite a day!" Charles exclaimed. "Seven quail! Bagged four of 'em myself!"

"Bully for you," Megan said dryly. "Slaughtering innocent birds isn't my idea of heroism."

"A man has to eat," he protested.

"*I'm* not eating one of those poor creatures, I assure you. You've got a streak of dirt on your cheek. You look a mess."

"I feel marvelous! Give us a hug."

"Not a chance. You smell of blood."

Charles turned to Clinton and grinned broadly. "Women!" he seemed to say. Clinton grinned back. Both men were inordinately pleased with themselves. One of the footmen came out to take charge of the string of quail, his powdered wig and velvet livery looking quite incongruous. His expression stoic, he bore the birds away, and I could imagine Henri's outburst when those bloody corpses were carried into his kitchen. Clinton handed the guns to yet another servant with instructions that they were to be cleaned and oiled, and then he brushed a spot of mud from his elbow.

"I could use a strong port," Charles said.

"You could use a bath," Megan told him.

"Can't a man have *any* fun?"

"You call that fun? I call it senseless slaughter. I suppose you think it's terribly manly to shoot helpless little birds."

"It's more manly than slapping paint on your face and plopping a heavy wig on your head and prancing before the footlights, spouting romantic nonsense and acting the fool."

"That pays the bills," she informed him, "and you happen to be marvelous on stage. Come along, you need a good scrub, and then you can have your port. *If* you behave yourself. Do you realize you could have been killed, riding that fierce beast over strange terrain, handling that *gun?* I was worried sick about you, you lout. You're *not* going hunting again, do you hear me?"

"Are you trying to tell me what I can or can't do?"

"You bet your arse I am. Come along now!"

She led a chastened, amiably grinning Charles away. Clinton smiled at me. I rubbed a speck of dust from his chin, and he slung an arm around my shoulders and I felt a rush of warmth and affection and gratitude. We strolled leisurely toward the house, Megan still scolding Charles up ahead.

"She's dreadfully rough on him," I remarked.

"And he adores every minute of it," Clinton replied. "Men like to know their women care."

"Maybe I should have scolded *you.* I do worry about you, you know. Hercules is so powerful and you're so bloody reckless."

"Been riding all my life," he told me.

"I don't know what I'd do if something happened to you, Clinton."

He smiled, tightening his grip around my shoulders. "So you *do* care?" he said.

"You know I do, you silly sod, and if you want proof of it, you'll have to wait until our guests have retired for the night."

"You'll furnish proof then?"

"*If* you behave yourself."

Megan seemed unusually quiet at dinner that evening, seemed rather nervous and distracted, fidgeting with her wine glass. She was gorgeous in a gown of exquisite bronze velvet, cut provocatively low, her lustrous auburn hair artfully styled on top of her head with three long ringlets dangling in back, a pearl studded gold wire hair spray affixed to one side. She wore a matching gold and pearl bracelet, both pieces of jewelry given to her by Charles who had apparently decided a pair of scissors now and then wasn't enough to keep a girl happy. Handsome in dark brown velvet frock coat and a cream silk vest embroidered with dark brown leaves, that gentleman was as expansive and hearty as Megan was withdrawn. Something had clearly happened between them since they were upstairs together, and I was eager to hear about it. I hadn't long to wait. Megan gave me a look that informed me she had very important news to impart.

"—not much hunting in London," Charles was saying, "but there's plenty to keep a fellow occupied. When you get to London, Clinton, I'll introduce you to all my favorite haunts."

"I'm not at all sure I want my husband *go*ing to your haunts, Mr. Hart," I said.

"It sounds intriguing," Clinton told him.

"Better than those stuffy clubs you aristocrats frequent. A man wants redblooded fare—hearty companions, buxom wenches, stout ale, lively fun."

"I agree wholeheartedly," Clinton said.

Megan and I exchanged exasperated looks.

"I haven't heard from Dottie in at least two weeks," I remarked, changing the subject. "How is she?"

"Still fighting off the theatrical managers," Charles

replied. "Garrick has offered her a small fortune, but she staunchly refuses to sign with anyone. I'm too *old* to tie myself down, she claims. All this attention is flattering, I'm sure, but I've got a business to run. If the right role comes along she'll consider it, she says, but in the meantime she's perfectly content creating costumes and running them up."

"Quite sensible of her," I said. "Dottie has her feet firmly planted on the ground. Her head's not easily turned."

"You should have seen the outfits she had me got up in for *Amelia*—forest green tights and tunic, skintight, a green cape lined with bronze taffeta—I had to wear a codpiece! Bloody embarrassing, appearing in that get-up. I felt like a fool."

"I'm sure the ladies loved it," I said.

"They did," Megan said dryly. "The Harlequin outfit, too."

"White silk shirt with bell sleeves, pink and green striped tights, another codpiece," Charles grumbled. "I know I heard snickers as I stepped out in front of the footlights."

"One woman actually swooned and fell out of the balcony," Megan informed me. "She wasn't injured, but it made wonderful copy for the papers. I believe she was with a circus—I saw Lambert giving her five pounds after the show."

"He knows his business," I remarked.

"Is *this* any way for a grown man to make his living, I asked myself. Burbage was a brilliant part, can't deny that, I gave my best performance yet, but those costumes—I think Dottie did it deliberately to get back at me for teasing her about her age."

"She knows her business, too," I said. "How does it feel to be adored by half the women in London?"

"Bloody uncomfortable."

"It's a trial he bears with amazing fortitude," Megan said. "I suggest we change the subject. All this theatrical talk must be boring Clinton dreadfully."

"On the contrary," Clinton said. "I find it fascinating. I'd pay quite a sum to see you in those tights, Charles."

"It'll never happen, mate."

Dessert was brought in—a marvelous brandied souffle, served with sweet, hot sauce—and I could see that Megan was impatient to impart her news. When coffee came, Clinton was telling Charles about his extensive gun collection. I suggested they go look at it. The men gulped down their coffee in record time, excused themselves and hurried away like two little boys on a lark.

"They'll be occupied for hours," I said. "It *is* an extensive collection. Shall we adjourn to the drawing room?"

Megan nodded, pushing her coffee cup aside.

We walked to the drawing room, her full bronze velvet skirt swaying like a great bell, rustling softly. I was wearing velvet, too, pale gray with a light violet sheen. A footman stood on duty in the luxurious foyer, striking in his handsome livery and powdered wig. When we reached the drawing room, Megan went directly over to the exquisite white Chippendale liquor cabinet and poured herself a glass of brandy, nervous and agitated.

"What *is* it?" I asked, concerned.

"He wants to *marry* me," she said.

"Charles?"

"No, luv, the Duke of Cumberland. Of *course* Charles. We came in this afternoon and I was still scolding him when we got to our room and he grinned and said I sounded exactly like a nagging wife and I said *some*one had to look after him and he said since I was going to *act* like a wife I might as well *be* one and you could have knocked me over with a feather."

"So?"

"I'm terrified, luv. He wants to *marry* me."

"I fail to see what the problem is," I said.

Megan took a drink of her brandy and gave me an exasperated look as though I were being particularly dense. "Marriage, luv," she said, "commitment, no way out, forever and ever."

"Is that so bad?"

"Darning stockings, cooking meals, stroking egos, muddy boots in the hallway and bread crumbs in bed. Freedom and independence gone and someone else always there."

"When that someone happens to be Charles Hart, the tragedy is considerably less dire."

"You have a point," she admitted.

"What did you tell him?"

"I didn't say anything. I just burst into tears. Me! Frightfully out of character. I just started sobbing and he pulled me to him and held me and then he said he loved me."

"And that surprised you?"

"No one's ever *said* it to me before, luv. Men adore me, they have a jolly good time with me, think I'm a wonderful carefree spirit and loads of fun to be with, by they never *love* me."

"Charles does."

"I can't believe it."

"You love him, too," I said.

"I know," she admitted, "and it scares the hell out of me. What if something goes wrong? What if he grows tired of me? What if he discovers that I'm not really the vivacious, flip, smart-mouthed creature he thinks I am but a woman who secretly *loves* cooking his breakfast?"

"I imagine he'd be able to sustain the shock."

"Me," she said, "married. I can't see it, luv. He's marvelously handsome and incredibly magnetic and a superlative lover and making a great deal of money now and becoming very famous and he could have any woman in London and he wants *me.*"

"Congratulations," I said.

Megan set the brandy down and gave an exasperated sigh and stepped over to the fireplace, the gold and pearl hair piece gleaming against her auburn locks, her blue eyes thoughtful as she gazed up at the painting of the girl in scarlet velvet. The colors glowed richly in the candlelight, the dark gold frame softly burnished. Megan gazed at it for several moments, and then she sighed again and turned to me.

"It all began that day Gainsborough spotted you on the street," she said. "If he hadn't painted this portrait, if you hadn't become a successful actress, I wouldn't have gotten good parts, wouldn't have met Charles. Thomas Gainsborough has a hell of a lot to answer for."

"He does indeed."

"He still won't paint me, incidentally. Says I'm too piquant, not ethereal enough. I'm deeply wounded."

"You've a right to be."

"It's this damned pert nose. The bane of my existence."

"Charles likes it," I pointed out.

"There's that," she agreed. "What am I going to *do*, luv?"

"Marry him, of course."

"I suppose I'll have to," she said wearily. "He'll pester me to death if I don't."

We heard the men coming down the hall, their footsteps heavy, their voices hearty as they discussed stocks and barrels and range and such. Megan made a face and brushed her bronze velvet skirt. I smiled and, moving over to her, gave her a hug. She sighed once more and assumed that wry, sophisticated expression I knew so well.

"The son of a bitch is *in* for it now, luv," she told me. "He opened his mouth and asked the question and if he thinks he can back out of it now he has a huge surprise in store. I might as *well* marry him. Someone has to protect him from all those adoring women who're always hurling themselves at his feet. Someone has to pick up after him and see that he eats the proper meals and remind him it's time to go to the theater. It might as well be me."

"Might as well," I agreed.

"I love him, Angel."

"I know you do, darling."

"I never thought it would happen," she said. "A girl

like me—turning respectable. Next thing you know I'll
be baking cookies."

"I rather doubt that."

Megan stepped away from me and placed her hands
on her hips. "Well, it's about *time* you got back to us,"
she scolded as the men walked into the room. "Leaving
us alone all this time while you were looking at a lot
of guns! How rude and thoughtless can you get? We've
been frightfully lonely, pining away the whole time."

"I'll bet," Charles said.

"No lip from you, Charles Hart. I've had just about
enough of your sauce for one day. Shall we play some
whist? Angel and I will take on the two of you, and
tonight we're playing for high stakes and real money.
There's a hat I fancy in London and it costs a bloomin'
fortune. I'm going to win enough tonight to buy it—a
new pair of shoes as well."

"Oh?" Clinton inquired.

"Just you watch, sweetheart."

It snowed that night, and fluffy white flakes were
slowly swirling in the air as I dressed the next morning.
Everything outside was blanketed in a pure glistening
white, the gardens transformed into a spectacular wonderland. Sitting at the dressing table, I brushed my
hair, feeling happy and replete after a marvelous night
with Clinton. Megan and I *had* won at whist and she
had been saucy and triumphant and Charles had accused her of cheating and accused me of being a cardsharp and there had been a wonderfully stimulating
scrap, Charles threatening to haul us both off to Bow
Street, Clinton grinning, vastly amused by our shenanigans. Later, in the privacy of our bedroom, he had
taken me into his arms and kissed me for a very long
time, a tantalizing prelude to pleasures that would soon
follow.

Setting the hairbrush aside, I pushed gleaming
chestnut brown waves away from my face and stood up,
my silk petticoats rustling. I was wearing a dusty rose
frock of fine linen with a low, square-cut neckline and
a full, spreading skirt. Stepping over to a window, I

gazed out at the wonderland of new snow. Sunlight reflected on the glistening white, creating lovely silver-violet sunbursts. Clinton sauntered into the room, tucking the tail of his loose white silk shirt into the waistband of his snug gray trousers. His pale blond hair was tousled, his eyes still sleepy. I smiled. He grinned at me and finished tucking his shirt in.

"Up early, aren't you?" he said.

"It's almost nine."

"I slept that late?"

"You had a very active night," I told him.

"Seems like I remember that."

"And you owe me twenty-four pounds."

"Charles was right about you," he grumbled. "You *are* a cardsharp, and you taught Megan everything you know."

"I hate a sore loser," I replied. "I intend to collect from Charles too before they leave this afternoon."

He joined me at the window and, moving behind me, slipped his arms around my waist. I leaned my head back against his shoulder, and we watched the snow swirl slowly in the air.

"You've really enjoyed their visit, haven't you?" he asked.

"Tremendously."

"I've enjoyed it, too. Seeing you with them, so bright and vivacious, so full of fun, makes me realize just how dreary these past months must have been for you."

"I haven't complained."

"Indeed you haven't, but it's hardly been a picnic for you with me so involved with the estate and gone so much of the time and you with nothing to do for hours on end."

"I take rides. I read. I—"

"It's been dreary for you, darling, don't try to say it hasn't. It's going to be better, I promise. We'll leave for London the first of December and stay through the holidays. You'll be able to see all your friends, go to the theater, give parties at Hanover Square. We'll have a grand time."

"I'm having a grand time right now," I told him. "Just being with you is enough to keep me quite content. I don't need anything else."

"A little outside stimulation wouldn't hurt, though. Besides, you probably need some new clothes."

"I have all the clothes I need."

"What? You expect me to believe that? A woman never has enough clothes, at least that's what I've been led to believe. Everything will soon be caught up here. We'll leave for London in a couple of weeks."

"If you insist."

"What time did you say it was?"

"A little after nine now. Breakfast at nine-thirty."

"Damn," he said. "Logistics are against it."

"Against what?"

He pulled me closer. "Guess."

"Too bad," I said. "Megan and Charles will be expecting us. It took me a good twenty minutes to dress, and—"

"That's what I mean," he complained. "Not enough time."

"It'll keep, darling."

"What time are they leaving?"

"Around two, I believe."

"We've got an appointment at two-thirty. Same time. Same place. We'll stand here in front of the window and I'll hold you like this and you'll turn around and give me one of those looks and I'll smile and we'll adjourn to the bedroom."

"At two-thirty in the afternoon? The servants will be horrified."

"To hell with the servants," he said.

"I think you'd better go wash your face with cold water, darling, then I suggest you brush your hair and think of something terribly mundane and unexciting for a few minutes. Those breeches are very snug."

Clinton glanced down, saw the bulge, grinned and gave me a quick, affectionate kiss and then sauntered off to his own dressing room. Twenty minutes later, as we entered the breakfast room, he wore a neat gray frock coat matching his breeches, a handsome dark blue vest stitched with black fleurs de lis and a dashing light gray silk neckcloth, very much the country gentleman with no telling bulge to mar the fit of those snug breeches. Our houseguests had already come down, Charles heaping his plate with sausage and eggs and slices of ham, Megan seated, buttering one of Henri's flaky croissants.

Charles made his official announcement as we were having coffee. I wasn't at all surprised, of course, although I pretended to be. Clinton was delighted and said we must have champagne. At this hour? I inquired. At this hour, he insisted. Robert fetched a bottle from the wine cellar. It was deliciously cool. Clinton poured the bubbly wine and toasted our guests.

"It's about time," I told Charles.

"Don't know what came over me," he confessed. "It must be something in the air down here. I didn't *intend* to propose, the words just came out. I'm having second thoughts already."

"Too bloody bad," Megan said.

"And when is the happy event to occur?" Clinton asked.

"I had in mind sometime next spring—April, May, somewhere around then, but Miss Sloan informed me that if we're going to do it, we're going to do it promptly, so we've decided to do it next month, before the holidays. She isn't giving me a chance to back out."

"Bloody right I'm not."

"That leaves precious little time to plan a trousseau," I said. "Dottie will have a fit."

"She'll manage," Megan replied.

"What about the wedding gown?"

"Something simple. White, naturally. Dottie will know exactly what to run up. An antique lace veil perhaps, and orange blossoms from The Market of course."

"Listen to them," Charles told Clinton. "They've already forgotten the groom."

"We're coming up to town on the first," I said. "I'll be able to help you with all the arrangements. What fun, Megan! Do you remember that wedding gown Dottie made for *The Inconstant Wife* a few years ago? Creamy white satin, I believe, overlaid with fragile lace, with tiny white satin rosebuds stitched onto the veil."

"I don't want anything quite that fancy. She might modify the design a bit. I *did* love the veil."

"More eggs?" Clinton asked.

"Might as well," Charles said. "They'll go nicely with this champagne. Might have a bit more of that sausage, too."

"And I'd like some more buttered wheat toast. I like a hearty breakfast to start the day."

"Me, too."

"Maybe pale mica sequins on the veil instead of rosebuds," I suggested. "Remember that veil Titania wore in *Midsummer?* Of course it was yellow, with gold sequins, but you could get the same effect with mica on white. It would be stunning with your auburn hair."

"I have a feeling this is going to cost me a fortune," Charles said.

"I have a feeling you're right," Clinton replied.

Megan and I were both rather tearful as the four of us stood outside under the front portico, waiting as the footmen strapped bags on top of the carriage. It had stopped snowing, but the snow covering the ground was dazzling white with a soft blue tinge, the sky a cloudy gray-white. Megan was wearing a dark golden velvet gown with matching golden velvet cloak trimmed in golden brown fur, the hood pulled up over her head. She took my hand and gave it a tight squeeze. Charles and Clinton were chatting idly about their afternoon of shooting. The footmen secured the last bag and scrambled down. The driver climbed up onto his perch and took up the reins, and the four strong grays stamped impatiently, eager to be off. The men shook hands. Megan and I exchanged hugs, and then Charles gave me a brotherly kiss.

"I like your husband, love. Be good to him."

"I intend to be."

They climbed into the carriage. Clinton slipped his

arm around my waist and we stood on the steps, waving as the carriage pulled around the drive and drove through the graystone portals, and then we went upstairs to keep our appointment. It was lovely and leisurely, the bedroom windows frosted from the snow, a fire crackling quietly in the fireplace. A delicious languor possessed us both afterwards, and we dined late on chilled lobster soup and wonderful goose-liver pâté and retired quite early for another appointment.

The snow lasted a week and was replaced by rain that seemed to fall constantly from a bleak, dark gray sky. As we would soon be leaving for London, Clinton found it necessary to spend a great deal of time in his office, going over the accounts. The Meredith holdings were extensive, I learned, with tin mines in Cornwall, a textile mill in Leeds and a pottery factory outside Coventry, these efficiently managed by trusted employees and requiring very little personal attention from Clinton, whose main interest was the tenant farms. Although he rarely inspected these other holdings in person, he received regular reports on all transactions and kept an eye on everything, which meant a huge amount of paperwork to catch up with before we left for the holidays.

I was in the library late one afternoon, leafing through a volume of sixteenth-century prints and listening to the rain splattering against the leaded windowpanes. Although the Merediths had never been big readers, the towering floor to ceiling shelves were crammed with thousands of volumes. Adam had stained the shelves a rich golden brown and installed an elegant gold and brown marble fireplace, and I had decided to keep the comfortable leather sofa and chairs, scattering Oriental carpets patterned in gold, brown and green on the dark oak floors. Despite its size, the library was still quite cozy, with that musty, dusty smell of old books I found so pleasant. A fire crackled in the fireplace. I turned a page of the heavy leather-bound volume and then, sighing, closed it and watched the rain making slippery patterns on the windowpanes. The day had seemed interminable, and it would be at least two hours before dinner. I missed my morning rides. Would the rain never end?

"Been missing me?" Clinton inquired.

I looked up, startled, for I hadn't heard him enter the room. His white lawn shirt was open at the throat, the full sleeves rolled up over his forearms. His pale blond hair was mussed, and there were faint shadows under his eyes. He looked weary, I thought, which wasn't at all surprising, for he had been working in his office most of the day. Many of the landed gentry might live idle, pampered lives in luxurious surroundings, but I didn't know anyone who worked harder than my husband.

"Actually, I was missing Cynara," I said. "I haven't been able to ride her in over a week."

"This rain's been hard on you, I know. It should end soon."

"You look tired, darling."

Clinton smiled wearily and moved over to the fireplace to warm his hands. "I have things pretty well under control—some problems with the pottery factory, missing orders, I won't bore you with the details, some major reenforcement work on the tin mines in Cornwall, profits down—" He sighed and turned his hands over, warming the backs. "How I hate it all. I'd much rather just concentrate on the land, but it's a necessary evil."

"Did your uncle take an active interest in the holdings?"

He shook his head. "Left it all to hirelings, rarely glanced at the accounts. Things were in quite a tangle when I took over—some of those hirelings had been robbing us blind."

"Was he interested in the land?"

"He never sullied his hands, never visited any of the tenant farms. He let his bailiff handle any problems. Later on he turned the work over to his bastard."

"Hugh," I said.

Clinton looked at me sharply. "You knew him?"

"I— Everyone in the village knew about—what went on at the big house, darling. I seem to recall Hugh Bradford managing the farms for a while, before he ran away. It—it was a very long time ago."

"He managed the farms, yes," Clinton said, "and he did a damn fine job of it, I'll have to admit that, but—" He cut himself off, scowling darkly. I had rarely seen him look that way.

"There was bad blood between you, wasn't there?" I asked quietly.

"You might say that. Yes, you just might. He was an arrogant, surly, impertinent lout, seething with hatred and resentment—the disposition of a cur dog and every bit as vicious. I tried to make friends with him when both of us were boys, felt sorry for him, but he would have none of my friendship. He hated me, felt I had usurped his rightful position."

"He— I understand your aunt wouldn't allow him in the house."

"Quite true. Would you want a vicious cur inside your house? He was insolent and hateful to her, snarled at her every time she tried to make things pleasant for him. She finally told my uncle she could take no more of it and he was given rooms over the stables. My aunt was not the most admirable person I've ever met—she was a miserable shrew, in fact—but she was perfectly justified in banishing him from the house."

"I—see," I said. "She accused him of stealing her jewels, I believe. After your uncle died, she claimed he had taken her emeralds—something like that. I—I can't remember the details. Hugh had to flee, with Bow Street in hot pursuit."

Clinton nodded, still scowling. "I'm not particularly proud of that little episode," he told me. "Hugh Bradford caused my uncle's death, as surely as if he'd shot him, and my aunt wanted to have him arrested. When she found she couldn't she hid her emeralds and accused him of stealing them. I helped her press charges, was eager to see him arrested myself—I actually believed he *had* stolen the emeralds, you see."

"You weren't—in league with your aunt?"

"I hated the bastard, blamed him for my uncle's death and wanted to have him hang for it, but I wouldn't have set him up like that. Later on, when I discovered my aunt's treachery, I insisted all charges be dropped. I wasn't the most admirable character myself back then— I was spoiled and headstrong and very full of my own importance—but I was never a villain."

No, my darling, you weren't, I thought. You weren't nearly as bad as I believed you were. You were spoiled, true, and you were indeed full of your own importance, but your youth and your upbringing had a lot to do with that. You were an inveterate womanizer too, but why wouldn't you be, looking like a young god, women hurling themselves at you. You were never a villain, only a willful youth who eventually grew up and took on responsibilities and matured into a remarkable man. The rain splattered on the windowpanes, still making slippery patterns. The fire crackled, tiny flames consuming the log. Clinton's eyes were hard as he thought of those days gone by. I only saw one side of the picture, I thought, Hugh's side, and it was always colored by his bitterness and hatred.

"Hugh Bradford was consumed by his own obsession," my husband informed me. "Somehow or other he had convinced himself that he was not illegitimate at all, that he was the rightful heir to Greystone Hall, that all the rest of us, his father included, had conspired to take it from him. It turned him into a vicious cur, as I said, and no one could help him. A cur only snaps at the hand that tries to pet or feed."

"I—understand," I replied.

"I detested him, I freely admit it, and I had good reason. We got into some rousing fights when we were children—I fear I taunted him, called him a beggar boy, a bastard. Children can be very cruel. When he wouldn't allow us to become friends, I decided we might as well be enemies—and we were. I just ignored him later on. I had more interesting things to do with my time than bait the sullen boy who cleaned the stables and lived over them."

"And now?" I asked.

"Now?"

"How—how do you feel about him now?"

Clinton hesitated a moment, his gray eyes thoughtful as he considered my question. His mouth tightened. "I try to be charitable," he said, "but in his case it's difficult. I suppose I should feel pity for Hugh Bradford, for he was a pitiful figure, but I don't. I could never forgive him for what he did to my uncle. I haven't given it much thought in recent years, but I suppose I still hate his guts. Not very admirable of me, I'll admit, but that's the way I feel."

His eyes were cool now, his mouth still tight, and I felt a chill inside me. He must never, never know about Hugh and me. It was the one thing he could never accept, I realized, the one thing that could seriously jeopardize our relationship. As gentle, as compassionate and understanding and intelligent as Clinton was, he could never come to terms with the fact that his wife had been in love with his bastard cousin, the man he held responsible for his uncle's death. Seeing the tight set of his mouth, the uncharacteristic coldness in his eyes, I felt the chill and felt afraid and felt a tremulous quiver in the pit of my stomach. I stood up, my skirts rustling crisply. All my years on the stage came to my aid, but I still found it difficult to speak in a normal, casual voice.

"You *do* look terribly tired, darling. You've been working much too hard these past few days. Why don't you have a nice hot bath, and then we'll have dinner. Henri is preparing pressed duck with orange sauce, I believe, with a salad of lettuce and marinated artichoke hearts—your favorite."

"Sounds delicious. And after dinner?"

I moved over to him. I rested my palm on his cheek. His eyes were no longer cold. They were warm now, full of affection, and his mouth curved in a playful smile.

"We'll find something to do," I said.

"I imagine we will."

"I love you, Clinton," I said. There was a catch in my voice. "I love you very much."

"Convince me."

He pulled me into his arms and tilted his head and kissed me for a long, long time, and I clung to him and finally pulled back. Heavy eyelids drooped over his eyes. His lips were parted, ready to savor mine again. I gently extricated myself from his arms.

"A bath first," I said, "and then dinner and then, if you're not too weary, we might continue this upstairs."

"You can count on it," he told me.

It rained again the next day and the next, and then the gray sky cleared and the rain was gone and the land had a new-washed look and the air was full of the pungent scents of wet soil as I rode Cynara, both of us exhilarated by the exercise. The sky was a lighter gray, pale and pearly, cloudless, with a faint violet hue, and the earth was brown and gray and black with a few green accents. It was glorious to be out again, the cool breeze in my face, lifting my cloak behind me, my hair tumbling and flying. Clinton had apparently forgotten our talk about Hugh Bradford and was concentrating on finishing his paperwork so we could enjoy our stay in London. Orders had been forwarded to the staff on Hanover Square, and everything would be ready for us when we arrived a week from now.

"Enjoy your ride, Milady?" Ian asked when I returned to the stable.

"It was wonderful, Ian."

He took my hand, helping me from the saddle.

"Cynara enjoyed it, too, I wager. Looks perky, she does. Did 'er good to get out. 'Is Lordship 'ad me take 'Ercules out for a bit of exercise this mornin', too, as 'e wasn't able to ride 'im 'imself."

"I imagine Hercules appreciated that."

"Appreciated it more that I did, I can tell you. Beast is so big an' so powerful, 'ad a 'ard time holdin' 'im back. Thought 'e was goin' to throw me off for sure. I was

relieved as all get out to find all my bones intact when
we got back."

"Hercules *is* a bit frightening," I said, handing him
the reins. "I often worry he'll get too excited and bolt
when my husband is riding him."

"Oh, 'Is Lordship never 'as any trouble with 'im, Milady. 'E's the best rider I ever seen, 'andles 'Ercules like
'e was a baby."

I stroked Cynara's damp cheek before Ian led her
away. "Give her an extra portion of oats after you've
groomed her, Ian. She's earned it."

"I'll do that, Milady."

Crossing the cobbled yard, I entered the house
through the side door and took off my cloak, hanging
it on a rack in the back hall, feeling flushed and glowing, feeling wonderful. It was almost time for lunch,
and Clinton would be meeting me in the drawing room
at twelve. A footman nodded to me as I entered the
front foyer. I heard voices coming from the drawing
room. Clinton was already there and...my word, we
must have a guest! Who could it possibly be? I felt a
moment of panic. My hair was still all atumble, and
the hem of my garnet riding habit was spotted with
flecks of mud. I couldn't conceivably meet anyone looking like this. As I moved toward the staircase, intending
to go up and change, Clinton and another man came
out into the foyer, both their faces grave indeed.

"—feel sure we haven't got anything to worry about,"
the stranger was saying, "but it's going to be a dreadful
nuisance, Milord, and it's going to consume a tremendous amount of your time."

"He claims he has proof?"

"He claims to have, yes, but I've no doubt we'll be
able to prove it insubstantial. He has a great deal of
money, it seems, and he's hired the best advocates money
can provide."

"He hasn't hired you, Burke. I feel confident we'll
win."

"Thank you, Milord. I feel confident, too."

Both of them saw me standing there by the staircase

then. The stranger seemed embarrassed. Clinton looked
vaguely perturbed, but good breeding came to the fore
and, moving over to me, he took me by the hand and
led me over to the stranger and performed introduc-
tions. The man's name was Jonathan Burke, and he
was an advocate from London. Tall, lean, rather stern,
he had coppery-red hair and grave brown eyes and looked
to be in his early forties. He was soberly dressed in
brown, a dark green neckcloth at his throat.

"I'm delighted to meet you, Mr. Burke," I said. "You're
my husband's legal adviser?"

"I have that honor, Milady."

"There—there isn't any problem, is there?"

"A minor matter," Clinton said quickly. "Burke came
down from London to apprise me of it. He was just
leaving."

"Surely you'll stay for lunch, Mr. Burke?"

"I'm afraid there's no time, Milady. I'm sorry about
that. I would enjoy it immensely."

His voice was deep and melodious and full of sin-
cerity. Although still grave, his brown eyes were friendly.
Burke might have a sober demeanor, but he was neither
cool nor disapproving. I could tell that he admired me,
and I suspected that he had seen Angel Howard perform
on stage a number of times, a suspicion he confirmed
later on. He said that it had been a pleasure meeting
me and that he hoped to see me in London. I said I
would look forward to it. Clinton led him to the door
and stepped outside with him, and I moved on into the
drawing room, both puzzled and disturbed.

I moved over to the fireplace, a terrible dread growing inside me. When Clinton came in, the expression
on his face did nothing to reassure me. His eyes were
a stony gray. His lips were pressed into a tight line.
His cheeks were ashen. Burke had obviously arrived
soon after I left for my ride. What had been important
enough to bring him all the way from London for so
brief a conference? Clinton stepped over to the liquor
cabinet without speaking and poured himself a shot of

brandy. I noticed that his hand was trembling as he lifted the glass to his lips. I had never seen him so upset.

"Clinton, what—what *is* it?"

He didn't answer. He drank the brandy and set the glass aside, and then he made a valiant effort to control himself. He took a deep breath and ran a hand across his brow, and then he sighed. When he spoke, his voice was calm, but each word might have been chiseled from ice.

"Hugh Bradford," he said. "He has returned to England."

Oh, dear God, I thought. Dear God, no.

"He's been in Italy, it seems, looking for proof that my uncle was legally wed to his mother. It took him almost two years, but he feels sure he has finally found that proof."

"That—that's why Burke came to see you."

He nodded curtly. "Bradford claims that he's the rightful heir to Greystone Hall and all the holdings."

I thought sure my knees would give way beneath me. They didn't.

"My bastard cousin has gotten together a shrewd team of legal advisers," Clinton said. "They're taking the case to court. The son of a bitch thinks he's going to become the new Lord Meredith."

Chapter Twenty-One

It's going to be all right, I told myself as I straightened the lapels of his dark gray frock coat. Everything is going to be all right. This will pass. Hugh will lose. He's bound to lose. Burke says his proof is tenuous at best, and there's no reason why Clinton should ever find out about Hugh and me. He sighed now as I fussed with his deep blue silk neckcloth and reminded me that the carriage was waiting, that he was due at Burke's office at ten and it was nine forty-five now. We were in the foyer of the house on Hanover Square. I gave the neckcloth a final pat and moved back. Seeing the worried look in my eyes, Clinton reached for my hand and gave it a tight squeeze.

"There's no reason for you to be so worried, my darling. We're going to win—it's a foregone conclusion. Burke just wants to go over some matters with me today. The case won't come to court for at least three months."

"I know, but—"

"I'll be gone most of the day, won't be back until four

at the earliest, and then, I promise, we'll concentrate on enjoying ourselves. No more legal conferences until after the holidays."

"We've been here for three days already, and you've spent every day with Burke. I—I can't help but worry."

"Today will be the last day," he told me. "I don't like this any more than you do, darling, but it's necessary."

"I suppose it is," I said, resigned.

He squeezed my hand again. "And what are you going to do all day while I'm going over tedious legal details with Burke? Something exciting?"

"I'm lunching with Megan," I replied, "and then we're going to Dottie's for the final fitting of her wedding gown. The wedding's next week, you know, and—"

"I know, darling. I must rush now, really."

He pulled me to him, kissed me thoroughly and then released me, reaching for the heavy gray cloak he had draped over a chair earlier. Swirling it in the air, he draped it around his shoulders and adjusted the long folds. Putnam, who had accompanied us to London along with Mrs. Rigby, opened the front door for him, and, giving me a reassuring smile, Clinton strolled outside and to the waiting carriage. I stood there in the foyer for a few moments, deeply perturbed, and Putnam asked me if there was anything I required. I shook my head and went back upstairs to get dressed for Megan, who would be here at eleven.

I washed thoroughly and made up my face, using a faint blush on my pale, drawn-looking cheekbones, applying a deeper pink to my lips. My eyes were a worried violet-gray as I rubbed a suggestion of mauve shadow onto my lids. I *must* try to put it out of my mind. Clinton had complete confidence in Burke, was certain we would win, and, as he had pointed out, the case wouldn't go to court until sometime in February. As I arranged my hair, I finally admitted to myself that it wasn't the court case that worried me so much. It was the fact that Hugh Bradford was here in the city at this very moment, that he undoubtedly knew I had married his archrival and become Lady Meredith, that he might decide to do something impulsive and Clinton would discover we had been lovers.

Megan arrived at eleven fifteen, radiant, vivacious, stunning in a topaz silk frock. Her merry chatter was irresistible, and my spirits lifted considerably. We had a delightful lunch at Button's, various theatrical folk stopping by our table to congratulate Megan and tell me how much they'd missed me the past few months, how lovely I was looking. It was glorious to be back in Covent Garden again, in my own milieu. No, I reminded myself, not my milieu any longer. Jack Wimbly gave me an exuberant hug and told me about the marvelous new role he would soon be rehearsing.

"Play a lovable scamp, I do," he informed me. "Actually get the girl at the end of the show. The lead! Can you believe it? No more supporting parts for our boy Jack."

"I'm thrilled for you, Jack. I know you'll be wonderful."

"Always am, luv. Always am. Marriage agrees with you, Milady. You've never looked more delectable."

"What about *me?*" Megan inquired.

"With that turned up nose? Can't imagine what Charles wants with a drab like you, luv. Must be out of his blinkin' mind."

Jack grinned a wide, enchanting grin, tugged her hair playfully and then moved jauntily away to join his friends. Megan stuck her tongue out at him. They adored each other, of course, and Jack was going to be Charles' best man next week. There was no camaraderie like that among theater people, I reflected, eating Button's delicious steak and kidney pie. How I loved the jovial give and take, the generosity of spirit, the breezy, carefree attitude hiding a fervent dedication to their craft. Megan continued to talk excitedly about the forthcoming wedding and the reception Clinton and I were giving afterward at Hanover Square.

"Charles is growing more and more nervous," she confided, signaling a waiter. "His face grows paler by the day, and he looks frightened of his own shadow.

Yesterday, as a lark, I sneaked up behind him and yelled 'Boo!' and he almost jumped out of his skin."

"Poor Charles."

"He's afraid *I*'ll back out of it—can you imagine that? I told him I'd be at the church even if they had to carry me on a pallet. He's such a darling, really. We're going to give up the flat over Brinkley's after all this time and buy a *house*. And he wants me to go on acting, too. We'll do plays together, he says. How did I *get* so lucky, luv?"

"Clean living, I suppose."

The waiter came over to our table. "Dessert, luv? No? You're sure? I guess I won't have any either. We're not due at Dottie's for another half an hour, we've time for coffee. Two coffees, George, and, oh hell, bring me one of those divine raspberry cream tarts. I've been eating everything in sight, luv," she confided as the waiter left. "Nerves. Dottie will *scream* if I've put on any weight. Promise me you'll have half the tart."

The air was crisp and cool and invigorating as we left Button's and, moving across the piazza, passed St. Paul's, where the wedding would take place. Even in winter Covent Garden had its rakish, colorful atmosphere, vendors selling hot roasted chestnuts and gingerbread men, pretty young ingenues walking with their beaux, The Market as busy as ever with fruit, vegetables and lovely hothouse flowers. "Angel's back!" a man yelled, seeing me on the street. I smiled and waved, loving the recognition. I hadn't realized quite how much I missed all this, though of course I was wonderfully happy with my new life. Being Lady Angela might not be as much fun as being Angel Howard, but my husband's love for me was more than compensation.

"I'm wonderfully blessed," I mused aloud.

"What's that, luv?"

"To have Clinton," I said.

"Of course you are. We've both been blessed. Maybe it *is* clean living, luv. Can't think of any other reason why we've been so fortunate."

Dottie was brisk and businesslike when we got to the shop, taking us into the fitting room, making Megan strip to her chemise and slip into the billowy pale peach gauze petticoat she would wear beneath her wedding gown. Megan took a deep breath, trying to disguise the fact that the waist was a mite too snug, but Dottie's shrewd eyes missed nothing.

"You've gained at *least* three pounds!" she accused.

"Couldn't help it, Dottie. I've been so *ner*vous."

"I'll have to let the waists out!"

"No you won't. I won't eat a bite until the wedding, I promise. Not a single bacon roll with mustard, not a single slice of chocolate cake."

"Let's try on the gown. I just don't understand it, Megan. Here I work my fingers to the *bone* getting all these things ready for you, seven complete new outfits, *plus* your wedding gown, and you stuff yourself like a pig. It's bloody inconsiderate."

"Oh, stop being so dramatic, Dottie," I told her. "You're not onstage now."

"I must say *you*'re looking splendid, Milady. Slim as ever. You're going to be needing some new things, too, I daresay, and now that you're a member of the aristocracy I intend to charge the sky. No more courtesy rates to the profession, I can assure you. I have a living to make."

She took a sip of raspberry tea and reached for a chocolate biscuit, her eyes narrowing critically as Megan slipped on the sumptuous wedding gown over the petticoat. They had decided against white, too conventional and not terribly appropriate as Megan was far from virginal. The gown they had finally agreed upon was pale peach-colored velvet, the skirt and large off-the-shoulder puffed sleeves overlaid with pale, transparent peach gauze appliqued with white velvet lilies outlined in white seed pearls. The wedding veil would be of matching peach gauze.

"I can hardly breathe," Megan protested as Dottie hooked the gown up in back.

"It's your own fault, you little slut. I don't suppose

it's *too* tight, and you've just eaten lunch, of course. At any rate, there's no time to let everything out."

"It's gorgeous, Dottie," Megan said, looking into the full-length mirror. "You've surpassed yourself. Oh God, I think I'm going to cry."

"Don't you dare. You've tried my patience quite enough for one day. We need to work on that hem a bit—here, let me put a few more pins in. Do be still! The yellow silk you're wearing to the reception is already finished, stayed up till three in the morning last night, doing all the work myself. I don't know why I bother," she complained. "No one appreciates it."

"Listen to her," Megan told me. "One season on the boards and she's a prima donna—everything's a drama."

"Hands off my box of biscuits!" Dottie thundered. "Davy Garrick is going to revive *The Country Wife* next spring. He wants me to play Lady Fidget. It's a marvelous part."

"Perfect for you," I agreed.

"I may do it, though I haven't decided for sure yet. Davy claims he'll completely redecorate the largest dressing room for me and provide all of the amenities. I've always longed to play the Drury Lane. Never made it when I was younger. Davy wasn't around then."

"Davy hadn't even been *born* then," Megan said dryly.

Dottie gave her a murderous look and, taking my arm, led me out front to have a cup of tea while Megan changed back into her topaz silk frock. I felt a nostalgic tug as I looked at the shelves of ribbons and laces, the bolts of cloth draped over the tables, the cozy litter I remembered so well. I could hear Dottie's girls working upstairs, their chatter a muted background. How I had loved working here, sewing on costumes, meeting the colorful, fascinating people who came into the shop. How young I had been then.

"Here's your tea, my dear," Dottie said, handing me a cup. "I put some honey in it. Something's worrying you," she added.

"What—what makes you think that?"

"You're a gifted actress, dear, but I can always tell

when you're giving a performance. You've something on your mind—it was bothering you all the time we were carrying on back there."

I took a sip of tea, still standing. Dottie swept a length of turquoise brocade off a table and began to fold it up. I hadn't told either Dottie or Megan about Hugh's return or the pending court case. I didn't want to spoil Megan's high spirits with the bad news, and there hadn't been time to discuss it with Dottie. She laid the turquoise brocade aside and spread a length of ivory velvet in its place.

"Something's come up," I told her. "There's no time to discuss it now, and I don't want to dampen Megan's effervescent mood. After the wedding I'll tell you all about it."

"Is everything all right between you and Clinton?"

I nodded. "Clinton and I are very much in love and getting along beautifully. This is—something else. I just hope Fleet Street doesn't get wind of it. They will eventually, I suppose. It's inevitable."

Dottie didn't press. "Well, dear, you know I'm always here and you know that if there's anything I can do you've only to ask. Ah, here's Megan—and with my box of chocolate biscuits! I *knew* I shouldn't have left them in the room with her."

It was almost three when I returned to Hanover Square. Putnam met me at the door, took my cloak and solemnly informed me that a gentleman was waiting to see me in the drawing room. A gentleman? I was puzzled. A Mr. Black, he said regally. I frowned. Mr. Black? I didn't know a Mr. Black, at least I didn't think so. I thanked Putnam, dismissed him and then moved over to the mirror to tidy my hair. I was wearing a dark blue silk gown, the full skirt draped back over an underskirt of light blue and cream striped silk. Whoever Mr. Black was, I wished I had had a bit more notice. Giving my hair a final pat, I moved down the foyer and stepped into the drawing room.

He was standing before the fireplace, his back to me. He turned around. I stopped, the words of polite greeting freezing in my throat. He looked at me, perfectly composed, the moody brown eyes taking in every detail of my appearance. He was superbly dressed in glossy black pumps with silver buckles, fine white silk stockings, black velvet knee breeches. His black velvet coat was exquisitely tailored, and his waistcoat was of shiny white satin embroidered with silver and black silk patterns. Lovely white lace spilled over his wrists and fell in a frothy cascade from his throat. His deep raven hair was pulled back sleekly and fastened with a ribbon at the nape of his neck. His lean, foxlike face was deeply tanned, and he had that sleek, polished patina of great affluence and social ease, every inch the gentleman.

"Hello, Angie," he said, "or should I say Lady Angela now?"

I didn't answer him. I couldn't. For a moment I was totally incapable of speech, my throat tight, my body numb. I stared at him, so sleek, so confident, so devilishly attractive in his elegant clothes, and I remembered the last time I had seen him and those weeks we had spent together in the country and the anguish I had suffered when he drove away. I tried to hate him now, but I couldn't. The old feeling was still there— God help me, it was still there, deep inside me, stirring to life again at the sight of him—and I was shaken to the core. I took a deep breath, willing the emotions away, gazing at him with a cool composure I was far from feeling.

"How dare you come here," I said.

"Surely you knew I would?"

"You must leave at once. My husband—"

"Your husband is with his legal counsel, Jonathan Burke, and they are in Burke's office—they've been cloistered there for hours. I checked before I came here. I didn't wish to cause you any embarrassment, Angie. I even gave your butler an assumed name."

"That was very thoughtful of you."

His wide pink mouth curled into a smile, and his eyes never left my own. "You're looking unusually beautiful, Angie."

"And you're looking unusually prosperous," I replied. "I suppose the Maria Theresa necklace must have fetched a fortune—even from your fence."

"I had the necklace broken up and sold the diamonds individually. They did indeed net me a tidy sum, more than enough to meet my needs. You seem a bit upset, my dearest."

"You must leave at once," I repeated, "before Clinton returns. If he found you here—"

"He'll be with Burke for at least another hour, I should think, and that gives us ample time to talk."

"We have nothing to talk about, Hugh."

My voice was firm, as cool as ice, but I was trembling inside now, and I was desperately afraid I couldn't maintain this control much longer. Looking at that wide, curving pink mouth, those sharp, angular cheekbones, those dark moody eyes, I remembered, and the memories brought no joy, only pain and confusion. Hugh sensed my discomfort. The ghost of a smile played on his lips, and he strolled over to examine a painting hanging on the wall...the landscape Gainsborough had given me on my last birthday, depicting a daisy-strewn field behind a broken stone wall, feathery trees in the distance. I had hung it here in Hanover Square after Clinton and I were married, and a blush tinted my cheeks as I realized that Hugh and I had made love in that very field a year and a half ago.

He recognized it. He remembered, too. He gazed at it for a long time, and then he turned around to look at me. The confident, almost arrogant manner he had had before seemed to have vanished. His expression was strained, serious, his eyes dark with emotion, and he looked strangely vulnerable. He didn't speak, just gazed at me with longing and pain and bitter regret, and I wanted to go over to him and take his hand and tell him it would be all right. I detested myself for feeling anything at all for this man who had hurt me so badly, who would willingly destroy the husband I loved with all my heart, but the feelings were there. I might not welcome them, but I couldn't deny their existence. Compassion, concern, strong sexual attraction don't go away simply because one no longer wants to feel them.

"We had a good thing, Angie," he said at last.

I nodded, not trusting myself to speak. Hugh tilted his head toward the painting behind him.

"I remember that afternoon—the slant of the sunlight on the field, the smell of the grass, the way the daisies grew in clusters. I remember it all, and those memories sustained me during the months that followed. You remember, too. I can see it in your eyes."

"I remember, yes."

"Those days should never have ended."

"You made your choice, Hugh."

"It was something I had to do. I explained that. I hoped you would understand."

"I understood all too well," I told him. "I—I really don't care to discuss it, Hugh. I just want you to go. You should never have come here in the first place. It was a foolhardy thing to do."

"You've succeeded beautifully, Angie," he said.

"Succeeded?" I didn't understand.

"I left you and you were hurt and you wanted to hurt me, too. I can understand that—we're only human, after all. You tried to think of the thing you could do that would hurt me most and so you married Clinton Meredith—to spite me."

"Is that what you think?" I asked.

"Why else *would* you have married him?"

"I happen to love him, Hugh."

"I don't believe you," he said sharply.

"It's true."

He shook his head, unwilling to believe it, and when he saw the truth in my eyes his cheeks paled. He looked utterly lost, utterly bereft, and for a moment I thought he might actually faint. Never had I seen such naked grief in a man's eyes, and the fact that I was responsible for it made it even more painful to behold. Several long moments passed as he stared at me with that terrible anguish, and then he sought to control himself. It took a tremendous effort, but he finally succeeded. His cheeks were still ashen. His eyes were hard now, more black than brown.

"I love you, Angie," he said.

"Don't. Just—please, Hugh, just go."

"I've always loved you. There's been no one else. Ever. It's always been you. You love me, too."

"I did. Once. I love my husband now."

"I came here today to ask you to come away with me. Isn't that supremely ironic? I was going to take you away with me and help you arrange to get a divorce. It wouldn't be easy to obtain one, true, but it could be accomplished. You would be free then and we would live happily ever after. That's what I believed. That's what I was fool enough to believe."

"I'm sorry, Hugh."

"All my life he's had everything—everything that should rightfully be mine—and now he has you as well."

"Give it up, Hugh," I said.

"My position, my title, my estate—and now the woman I love. It's too much—" His voice trembled with passion, and the striking gentleman in velvet and lace became a youth again, the fervent, embittered stable-boy with mud on his boots and dark fire in his eyes. "I could kill him! I could kill him with my bare hands. I'm going to win, Angie. I'm going to beat him. I'm going to get back everything that belongs to me—and that includes you."

"I love my husband, Hugh. I intend to stand by him. I—I suggest you drop this folly before you do even more harm. The 'proof' you think you have is tenuous at best—the word of a doddering old priest who can hardly remember his own name, the yellowing pages of a daily journal, not a single bit of evidence that could be called substantial. Clinton's legal team will rip you apart in court. Give it up," I repeated. "Don't—don't cause your-self any more grief."

He didn't seem to hear me. "He'll be penniless," he continued, and his voice was full of conviction. "He'll be a pauper. You'll come to me then. We'll be married, and you'll still be Lady Meredith. We'll live in Greystone Hall together. We'll have everything I ever wanted for us."

He fell silent then, looking at me, waiting for me to answer. I didn't say anything, and my own silence was far more effective than words could have been. Hugh frowned, stubbornly refusing to accept defeat. He drew himself up, passion contained now, emotion held in check. I stepped over to the door and stood beside it, waiting for him to leave. He touched his lace jabot and straightened the lapels of his black velvet frock coat, that confident facade back in place.

"Please leave, Hugh," I said. "Clinton might return any minute now. I don't want him to find you here."

"He doesn't know, does he?"

"He has no idea. It—it would distress him terribly if he were to find out."

"I can understand that," Hugh said.

"Please leave," I repeated.

He hesitated a moment, then nodded curtly. He followed me into the foyer, and I was relieved to find that Putnam wasn't on hand. Hugh opened the front door and paused, looking at me with cool black-brown eyes that nevertheless reflected a fierce determination.

"It isn't over between us, Angie," he told me. "It will never be over between us."

He left then and a moment later I heard a carriage pulling away. I felt a wave of relief, far more shaken by his visit than I had first realized, but when Clinton returned half an hour later I was beautifully composed, at least on the surface. He was in a very good mood, more confident than ever that we would win the case with ease. We celebrated that evening by going out to the theater and for a late dinner afterward, and by the time we finally got back home I felt much better, convinced that Hugh would make no further attempt to see me. Caught up in the excitement of Megan's wedding, helping her with all the arrangements, I had little time to think of Hugh's visit in the days that followed, but, addressing invitations to the reception from a list

Megan had given me, I had good reason to think about someone else.

Oh, God, will my past never stop haunting me, I thought as I saw Jamie's name on the list. Naturally he would be on the list. Megan and Charles had been in a number of his plays, and he and Charles were jolly good friends. I hesitated, feathery quill poised over silver inkwell, the elegant cream envelopes stacked in front of me. He would have to be invited, no question about it, and it could mean a tricky situation indeed. Clinton knew about him, of course—our relationship had scarcely been a secret during those years I had performed at The Lambert—even though neither of us had ever referred to it. Frowning, I dipped the quill into the inkpot and addressed the envelope. All three of us were adults, all three highly civilized, and if Jamie came to the reception all three of us would be terribly polite. Clinton would undoubtedly shake his hand and welcome him warmly, pretending Jamie was merely another guest, and, moody and volatile though he might be, Jamie would never dream of doing or saying anything that might cause me embarrassment. He would be the perfect gentleman.

Slipping the invitation into the envelope, I sealed it and put it on top of the others I had already addressed. They went out early the next morning, each hand-delivered by footman in the Meredith livery. Henri and his helpers arrived from Greystone Hall three days later to take over the kitchen and begin preparations for the variety of dishes to be served at the reception. My husband was wonderfully tolerant of the chaos that seemed to prevail as cases of champagne were delivered, as florists arrived, as Mrs. Rigby bustled about riding herd on a flock of housemaids. I was reminded of the preparations for our ball. At least this time I could be sure our guests would arrive.

Thursday dawned cool and clear, the December sky over London a pale gray-white, winter sunlight sparkling vividly. Charles and Jack Wimbly arrived at Hanover Square at two, having apparently consumed a liquid lunch, I observed. Jack was full of lively good humor, cracking bawdy jokes, and Charles wore an inebriated grin, looking sleepy and lethargic and rather dazed. They were to don their wedding attire here and drive to St. Paul's with Clinton while Dottie and I got Megan ready for her big day. As a footman took my own wedding attire out to the carriage, Clinton suggested to the men that they all have a glass of champagne. Jack greeted this suggestion with enthusiasm. Charles grinned tipsily and sat down heavily.

"Black coffee might be better," I said dryly. "Charles looks like he's already had quite enough."

"You go on about your business, luv," Jack told me. "We'll get him to the church."

"Sure we will," Clinton added.

"It might be nice if he were able to stand at the altar."

"Doomed," Charles groaned. "Doomed."

"Cheer up, mate," Jack said. "More champagne's on the way."

I arrived at their flat thirty minutes later. There was a new selection of wigs in the windows of Brinkley's and the old green door beside them needed a new coat of paint, but everything else looked the same. I felt another tug of nostalgia as I climbed the dark enclosed stairs, the footman following with my clothes. Dottie opened the door for us, looking thoroughly exasperated. She took the garments from the footman and, when he had gone, informed me that Megan was being absolutely impossible.

"Flatly refuses to come out of her room," she said.

"Doesn't surprise me at all," I replied. "It's going to be a very long day."

I went down the hall and pounded on the bedroom door while Dottie put my clothes in the guest bedroom.

"Megan, dear," I called. "It's me. If you don't come out of there immediately Dottie and I are both leaving. You have exactly two minutes to get your ass into the living room."

Dottie and I were having a cup of her perennial raspberry tea when, sulky, resentful, our friend dragged herself into the living room. She was wearing a ruffled white cotton petticoat, and her hair, newly washed, spilled over her shoulders in glistening auburn waves. She smelled of scented soap, and I was relieved to know that at least we wouldn't have to bathe her. Dottie ignored her, taking another sip of tea.

"You both might as *well* leave," she said. "I'm not getting married today."

"Oh?" I inquired.

"It's entirely out of the question. Who *needs* to be married? I'm much too young to be tied down. It'll be better for everyone concerned if I just pack my things and sneak out of town. Charles will be a bit disappointed, of course, but it won't take him long to find a replacement."

"It probably won't," I agreed.

"That pretty Mrs. Leigh has her eye on him," Dottie remarked, "has had for a long time. She'll be delighted. I don't believe you've ever met her, Angel. She has silver-blonde hair and huge brown eyes and the kind of figure men go wild over—looked enchanting in that pink velvet gown I made for her to wear in *Calista*. An ingenue, barely eighteen."

"Eighteen my ass!" Megan protested. "The little slut's a *good* twenty-seven."

"Anyway, my dear, I'm sure she'll appreciate your giving up Charles this way, leaves the field open for her. When I was fitting her she confided that she'd do anything to get him—those brown eyes of hers were positively gleaming with anticipation."

Dottie smiled sweetly and took another sip of tea. Megan shot her a murderous look and then emitted a disgusted sigh.

"I suppose I might as well marry the son of a bitch," she told us, "if only to save him from the likes of her. Come on, Angel, my things are in the dressing room. I shouldn't have washed my hair—I can't do a thing with it. You'll have to help, luv. A French twist, maybe?"

An hour and a half later, calm as could be, looking spectacularly lovely in the pale peach velvet gown, Me-

gan examined herself in the full length mirror and gave
a satisfied nod. I had arranged her hair into a gleaming
stack of auburn waves on back of her head, weaving in
fragrant orange blossoms, and now I handed her the
transparent peach gauze veil appliqued with smaller
velvet lilies than those on her overskirt. The tiny seed
pearls outlining them glistened as she put the veil over
her head and adjusted it.

"Well," she said, "I suppose this will have to do."

"You look beautiful, Megan."

"I really do, don't I? It's the gown, of course. The son
of a bitch is damned lucky to get me."

"He truly is."

"What if I faint, luv?"

"You won't," I assured her.

"Where's my bouquet of orange blossoms?"

"Dottie has it."

"You know what he did? He bought a house. Day
before yesterday. It's on Maiden Lane, right on the street
with no front yard, just two marble steps. White with
gray shutters and a steep green roof and a garden in
the back yard where, he says, we can grow vegetables."

"It sounds enchanting, darling."

"Me growing vegetables! Can't you just picture it?
He didn't lease the place, luv, he bought it. That seems
so permanent." Megan adjusted the hang of the veil,
turning this way and that to study the effect. "It's being
repainted inside—the breakfast room is being done in
sunny yellow, the drawing room in white. We'll be moving in next Tuesday. Yesterday we went shopping for
furniture. Charles has suddenly become frighteningly
domestic. You should have seen him picking out chairs."

"I'm sure he was adorable, darling, but we only have
thirty minutes, and I'd better go get dressed myself."

The gown I had selected was of creamy pale tan velvet with short, narrow sleeves worn off the shoulder, a
low-cut neckline and a full, sumptuous skirt that spread
out over half a dozen champagne-colored underskirts.
With a thin violet velvet ribbon tied around the waist,
it was exquisitely simple and extremely elegant. My

hair was pulled back from my face, ringlets falling down in back, and I fastened a small spray of real violets on one side, just above my temple. The effect was understated and, I thought, quite charming. Megan and Dottie expressed their approval as I joined them in the living room. Dottie had changed into mauve velvet and looked lovely herself.

I glanced at the clock. "Is everyone ready?"

"You two go ahead," Megan said. "I'm staying here."

"Do, dear," Dottie said. "I'm sure Mrs. Leigh will be glad to fill in for you."

"You know, Dottie, at heart you're an awful bitch. I've always suspected it."

"Come along," I said. "We don't want to be late."

"Speak for yourself, luv. For God's sake, hold my hand as we cross the piazza. My legs have just turned to water."

We moved slowly down the narrow steps and out the green door, our velvet skirts making a soft, rustling noise. The air was cool, but we hadn't wanted to be bothered with cloaks. Old Brinkley stepped out of his wig shop, grinning broadly. He wished Megan good luck. She told him to sod off. Crossing the street, we started across the piazza toward the church. Groups of people from The Market had come out to watch the bride pass by, and they cheered and waved. Megan scowled grumpily and tried to shoot them a stiff middle finger. I slapped her hand. St. Paul's, the Actors' Church of Covent Garden, looked mellow and worn in the late afternoon sunlight, and we could hear organ music coming from the opened door. The guests had already arrived. Megan gave me a terrified look and tried to halt. Dottie and I prodded her on and finally got her up the steps and into the vestibule where Clinton was waiting.

"Ah," he said, "the radiant bride."

"Go to hell," she snapped.

Clinton grinned and kissed her on the cheek. The music swelled, filling the shabby old church with sonorous beauty, then gradually grew softer. Megan's eyes grew moist. She hugged me tightly and hugged Dottie and then wiped a shiny tear from her cheek and straightened her veil. She composed herself, even managed a smile, and she did indeed look radiant. Dottie handed her the bouquet of orange blossoms. The music was softer now, eventually fading away, and when it began again it would be time for Megan to make her entrance on the arm of Lord Meredith, who was giving her away. Megan emitted a heavy sigh and linked her arm in his as the first strains pealed out.

"Let's get this bloody show over with," she said.

Despite all the tension and nervous turmoil beforehand, the wedding went beautifully, the ceremony simple, the principals wonderfully poised. Charles looked handsome and impressive, showing no sign of inebriation. He smiled as Megan joined him at the altar banked with lilies and peach-colored roses, and she smiled back. Dozens of tall white candles were burning, creating a softly diffused glow as they exchanged vows. Charles slipped the ring on Megan's finger. His was a mite too small, and he winced as she jammed it up over his knuckle. Dottie dabbed at the corner of her eye with a lace handkerchief as the organ music swelled, as the groom kissed the bride, and in no time at all they were sweeping up the aisle, Charles smiling a proud smile, Megan looking vastly relieved.

"Thank goodness that's over with," I said as Clinton and I stepped outside.

"You had problems with Megan?"

"That's putting it mildly," I replied.

A carriage had already whisked Megan and Charles away to Hanover Square, where they would change and prepare for the reception. Clinton took my arm, guiding me down the steps and past the old tombstones in the yard. Behind us wedding guests continued to stream out of St. Paul's, rich, theatrical voices creating a merry, excited babble. Dottie had stopped to chat with David Garrick, who would bring her to the reception later on, and Clinton and I walked slowly across the piazza toward our waiting carriage, pausing now and then as people greeted me. Rupert Guild, a plump, ruddy-cheeked, red-haired character actor famous for his Falstaff blocked our way, blue eyes atwinkle.

"Angel, pet!" he cried. "Smashing to see you! When are you returning to the theater?"

"I'm quite retired, darling. This is my husband, Lord Meredith. Rupert Guild, Clinton. You may remember his Falstaff."

"Pleased to meet you, Milord. How does it feel to be a thief?"

Clinton arched a brow, amused. "Thief?" he said.

"Robbed us all of London's brightest light. Theater isn't the same without our Angel. Have to rush, pet," he told me. "I'm playing Caliban at the York tonight and it takes me hours to make myself ugly. Won't be able to get to the reception. Give Megan a big bearhug for me."

Inside the carriage, Clinton wrapped a heavy cloak around my bare shoulders and scolded me for venturing out without one even if St. Paul's *was* just across the street. I sighed, drawing the velvety folds around me. He was in a pensive mood as we rode home, and I knew that Rupert's words, though spoken in jest, had bothered him. Clinton loved me so much and wanted me to be happy, and he felt marriage to him might seem dreary after the color and excitement of the theater. I did miss it, true, and there were indeed times when I felt bored and restless, but I had tried my best to hide it. I reached over and took his hand now, squeezing it tightly. Clinton looked up, surprised by the gesture.

"I wish we weren't having this bloody reception," I said.

"I thought you were looking forward to it. You'll see all your friends, have an opportunity to catch up on all the gossip."

"The gossip doesn't interest me and I've seen quite enough of my friends for a while. I'd much rather be alone with you."

"You would?"

"You—you're the most important thing in the world to me, Clinton. I'm so glad you married me."

"I'm rather glad myself," he told me.

"After this reception, I want us to spend a lot of time alone together," I said.

Clinton smiled. "I'm on to you, my darling. Christmas is coming up and you want to be especially nice to me, hoping I'll give you something very expensive and grand."

I touched the spray of violets in my hair and rearranged the folds of my tan velvet skirt, pretending to be found out. "Well, as Megan would say—a girl can't help trying."

"You're a clever minx, aren't you?"

"Think big for Christmas," I said. "I've also got a birthday coming up in a couple of months."

Clinton chuckled, clambered across to my side of the carriage and pulled me rather violently into his arms. When the carriage stopped in front of the house on Hanover Square, the violets I'd been wearing had fallen to the seat, my bodice had slipped askew and my skirts were deplorably rumpled. Clinton's jabot was crushed flat and there was a smear of pink lip rouge on the side of his mouth. I wiped it off and managed to straighten my bodice before a footman opened the carriage door for us. Clinton gave my backside a rude pat as I climbed out. My sensitive, thoughtful husband was a wonderfully sensual animal as well, that being a bonus I reveled in. Taking my hand, he led me into the house.

"My gown is quite ruined," I complained. "It's a good thing I was planning to change anyway."

"I suppose there's no time to—"

"You have to change yourself, darling," I reminded him, "and our first guests will be arriving soon. Megan and Charles are already here."

"Damn," he grumbled.

An hour later, hair sleekly brushed, expression serene, he was making polite conversation with two actors who had just arrived. In his black velvet breeches and frock coat and silver-gray satin vest, frilly white lace lavishly festooning throat and wrists, he shook hands with a new arrival and introduced himself, the

perfect, genial host. The tatterdemalion theatrical folk
who had been skeptical about their welcome at the mansion on elegant Hanover Square were put immediately
at ease by Clinton's warmth. He didn't seem like a bleedin' Lord at all. Seemed just like a regular person. Our
haughty neighbors might look askance at the colorful,
noisy types invading their turf, but here they were made
to feel right at home. Megan and Charles were greeting
guests too, Megan a vision in yellow silk brocade embroidered with golden flowers, Charles handsome in
brown velvet. I had changed into a gown of pale amethyst satin with narrow silver stripes, a silver hair spray
affixed to the side of my coiffure.

"Here are the Gainsboroughs," Megan announced.
"Thomas, you old rogue, I still expect you to paint me.
I'm a respectable married lady now. Can you believe
it? Your wig's on crooked, luv. Just thought I'd mention
it."

Gainsborough straightened his wig and brushed the
lapels of his wrinkled white satin frock coat while Mrs.
G. gave the bride a warm hug. Young Richard Sheridan
arrived, looking out of sorts, a vivacious Betsy trotting
in behind him. As I greeted him, the arrogant playwright informed me that he had just completed another
masterpiece. I said I wasn't at all surprised. Megan told
him she was currently at liberty and would simply love
to read his play. "My, what a pretty dress you're wearing," he told her and then rushed off to find a drink.
Jack Wimbly came jaunting in with a striking brunette
ingenue in pink silk. The outrageous comic actor made
several bawdy jokes about newlyweds until Charles finally told him to sod off. In full makeup and crackling
purple taffeta, Dottie arrived with a sober, polite Davy
Garrick in tow, an ebullient James Boswell right behind
them.

Guests continued to arrive during the next half hour.
I smiled and made pleasantries and shook hands and
wondered when Jamie would show up. I hadn't seen
him at St. Paul's, but there had been a crush and I had
been too nervous about the ceremony to pay much at-

tention to who was there. Expecting him to step through the door at any minute, I felt a growing tension. What would he say? What would I reply? Both of us would be painfully polite, of course, but there was bound to be some strain. I dreaded that first encounter, even as I anticipated seeing him again. I had no hard feelings, none whatsoever. I thought of him with ... with great fondness, remembering only the excitement and stimulation, the frolics and fun. It had been a tumultuous relationship, yes, but ... there had been so many good times.

"—desperately need a glass of champagne," Megan was saying. "If anyone else arrives, Putnam can show them in."

"I could use some champagne myself," Charles agreed. "I hope that rotten Wimbly hasn't drunk it all up."

"The receiving line is officially closed," Clinton announced. "Let's go have that champagne."

"Coming, luv?" Megan asked me.

"What? Oh—oh, yes. Of course."

"You look disappointed about something."

"Disappointed? Nonsense. I—I'm just a little tired."

"Nothing wears you out like being charming," she agreed. "If I have to smile one more time I'm going to scream."

The house was thronging with bright, engaging people who wandered around from dining room to foyer to drawing room to sitting room, chatting vivaciously, greeting old friends, exchanging news. Liveried footmen circulated with trays of champagne, and there was a sumptuous buffet in the dining room every bit as lavish as that prepared for the ill-fated ball. A merry, festive mood prevailed, growing rowdier as the evening progressed. Megan and Charles were in fine form, the bride absolutely scintillating, the groom jovial, accepting congratulations with a broad grin. Clinton was wonderful, moving from group to group, smiling, chatting, putting everyone at ease. I did the same, telling myself I wasn't at all disappointed Jamie hadn't come, telling myself it was for the best.

"Splendid fellow, your husband," Boswell said, coming over to me in the dining room. "Had a most interesting talk with him. I happened to mention I was going back to Scotland in mid-January, and he invited me to stop by Greystone Hall on the way, spend the night."

"You must, Boswell," I told him. "We have very few guests. It will be a treat for both of us."

"Just might do it. I'll tell you all about my visits to Seven Dials and the fascinating underworld figures I've met there. Thieves, assassins, forgers—the place is a hotbed of vice and corruption, wonderful material for a student of human nature."

"Like you," I said.

"Like me. I say, who's that stunning brunette in pink?"

"I believe she belongs to Jack Wimbly."

Boswell grinned. "Not for long. What a derriere! Wonderful party, Angel. See you later."

The audacious red-haired Scot bustled off to charm Wimbly's ingenue, and I moved on out into the foyer where guests stood talking in bright groups under the radiant chandelier. Others sat on the steps with plates of food, the convivial informality of Covent Garden spilling over to Hanover Square. Dottie waved and continued her chat with Richard Sheridan. I went into the drawing room and paused to have a glass of champagne with David Garrick who saw a copy of one of Miranda James's novels on the bookshelf and talked wistfully of the days when he had known her.

Another hour passed. I saw Clinton across the way, charming a character actress, saw Charles grinning tipsily and stumbling as Jack pounded his back, saw Megan fluttering amidst the crowd like a splendid butterfly in her yellow and gold gown. I chatted with Mrs. G. I laughed with a group of rowdy young actors from the Haymarket. I listened to Betsy's witty account of her visit with the Burneys and smiled at Gainsborough who, surrounded by a bevy of pretty actresses, looked like a beaming, bewigged pasha, relishing the adulation. Merry babble filled the air. Noisy laughter rang out. The buffet table was decimated, footmen bringing more smoked salmon, more caviar, more sliced ham. Champagne was downed with abandon, trays emptying almost as fast as they were filled. The reception was a tremendous success, the radiant look in Megan's eyes making it all worthwhile.

Smiling, nodding, I moved down the foyer and stepped into the small sitting room, relieved to see that it was empty, hoping for a moment to catch my breath. I sighed, passing a hand across my brow, and then I noticed the pair of legs stretched out in front of the blue wing-backed chair. Scuffed black pumps, white silk stockings encasing well-turned calves, black knee breeches. The legs moved. The man stood up. The noise of the party seemed to recede, became a mere background to the pounding of my heart. He looked at me. His green-brown eyes were full of yesterdays. He nodded. Why was my heart pounding like this? Why did I feel this wild elation, this awful dread? Why did I want to cry, want to shout with joy? Why, suddenly, did I feel gloriously, vibrantly alive?

"Hello, Angel," he said.

"Jamie," I said. "I didn't know you were here."

Was that my voice? Could that regal, polite, perfectly controlled voice possibly be mine? It sounded alien to my ear, so different from the voice inside that cried out at the sight of him looking so drawn, looking so sad, his handsome face so very grave. He was too thin. There were faint shadows under his eyes, and the slight twist to his nose looked more pronounced, looked endearing. I recognized the frock coat. It was a bit the worse for wear. I recognized the green neckcloth, too. It was slightly rumpled. Poor darling. He needed someone to take care of him.

"I arrived late," he told me. "I was working, you see, lost track of time. You know how it is when I'm involved with a new play."

I nodded, smiling, remembering. Jamie smiled too, a hesitant, tentative smile, as though he weren't sure if we were enemies or friends. I moved over to him and took both his hands in mine and squeezed them.

"It's good to see you, Jamie. I'm so glad you came. Have you seen Megan and Charles?"

"I spoke to them when I arrived. I also spoke with your husband. Seems like a fine fellow, Angel."

"He is," I said.

"He's a very fortunate man."

His voice was low, that unique, exciting voice I remembered so well, and those green eyes flecked with brown held mine, still full of yesterdays, conveying far more than words. I was still holding his hands. I let go of them and stepped back, feeling awkward and embarrassed, covering it with a polite, artificial smile that didn't deceive him at all.

"What—what are you doing back here by yourself?" I asked. "Have you eaten? Would you like a glass of champagne?"

"I was back here by myself because I wanted to be alone for a while, because I saw you across the room and felt a terrible loss and didn't feel like speaking to anyone. I'm not hungry, and no, I wouldn't like a glass of champagne."

"I see."

"I shouldn't have said that, Angel. I didn't mean to. I intended to be proud and arrogant and indifferent, to show you I didn't give a damn you were married, that you didn't mean a bloody thing to me, but I—I'm not that good an actor."

"Jamie—"

"I'm sorry. Please forgive me. I didn't mean to embarrass you. I went for five years without ever telling you what you meant to me, without telling you you were the world to me, and it's hardly fitting for me to tell you now. I lost you. Because of my goddamned pride and artistic temperament I let you get away, and that was the greatest mistake of my life."

"You—"

"I love you, Angel. I always did. Fool that I am, I never told you. I took you for granted. I was jealous of your success, had the crazy notion it threatened me, threatened our relationship. I—I was desperately afraid you would leave me, and you did. I drove you away. I was the world's greatest fool. I suppose I deserved to lose you."

"I—I'm sorry, Jamie."

"It was my own bloody fault."

I was deeply moved, and I was frightened, too, frightened by what I felt and what I saw in his eyes. There was a loud burst of laughter in the doorway as a group of jolly young actors and their girlfriends came spilling into the room, all of them a bit the worse for champagne. Jamie scowled, and I smiled graciously at the intruders and asked if they were having a good time. The boys grinned. The girls giggled. A husky young lad with merry blue eyes said it was the best party ever, best champagne, too, and I really *was* an angel for having them. I smiled again and took Jamie's hand and led him out of the room.

"You may not want any," I said, "but I could definitely *use* some champagne."

We moved down the foyer, through the colorful, noisy crowd. I let go of his hand. He was still scowling, already regretting his lapse, no doubt, and wishing he had never spoken. Dottie saw us together and arched a brow. Jamie gave her a curt nod, the temperamental playwright beholden to no one, that damnable pride of his securely in place again. We went into the dining room and I fetched a glass of champagne and sipped it as we stood near the buffet, the party swirling around us.

"I'm sorry about *Amelia Mine,* Jamie," I said. "It was a glorious play. Dottie sent me a copy. It—it should have been a huge success."

"It would have been if the woman I wrote it for had done the lead. That was my fault, too. That afternoon at Button's—" He paused, the scowl deepening. "I had to show you I didn't need you."

"I know," I said.

"Shakespeare said it all. 'What fools these mortals

be.' We pay dearly for it. I think I *will* have a glass of that champagne."

He went to fetch one, pausing to speak with Jack Wimbly who came over to greet him. They chatted for a few moments and then Jack stumbled away, looking for the stunning brunette who had mysteriously vanished. As had Boswell. Before he could get back to me with his champagne, Jamie was stopped by several other people. He had become something of a recluse in recent months, and all his friends were delighted to see him again. The scowl had vanished when he returned. He gave me a rueful smile.

"Sorry I took so long," he said.

I smiled. Both of us were relaxed now.

"Poor Jack," I said. "I fear James Boswell has made off with his girlfriend."

"Striking brunette in pink? I saw them slipping out together as I came in. Don't know what the bloke has, but the ladies dote on it."

"You mentioned a new play, Jamie. Is it coming along well?"

He nodded. "It's writing itself, it seems. Full of drama, full of comedy, very little melodrama and lots of human interest. It's going to be the most—"

"—spectacular, most ambitious play you've ever mounted," I said. "Is it another historical drama?"

"In a way. I'm writing the Aphra Behn play, Angel."

The play I had begged him to write for me, the role I had wanted so badly to play. The son of a bitch! It was *my* play. It had been my idea in the first place. I remembered the lively discussions we had had about it, my enthusiasm and encouragement, my disappointment when he decided to do the awful Mary, Queen of Scots play instead. I felt a sharp pang now. Bitterness? Resentment? Regret? A combination of all three, with a healthy dose of anger as well. I longed to stomp on his foot and throw my champagne into his face. I smiled instead. It was a very tight smile.

"I'm sure it will be marvelous," I said.

"You always wanted me to do this play."

"I know."

"It's going to be my best, Angel. I—I'm having a few financial difficulties at the moment, but I'm sure I can get it mounted. It's going to put me back on top again."

His voice was determined, full of conviction. He had no idea I was angry and was so bloody dense and insensitive it would never even dawn on him that I might be. He hadn't changed one bloody bit. I seethed silently, and then I realized how silly I was being. Poor Jamie. He would always have the power to rile me and set the sparks flying. My anger vanished, and I felt ashamed of myself for being so petty. I wished him well. I really did. I hoped the play would be an enormous success for him.

I smiled again, warmly this time. Jamie smiled back.

"You've done very well for yourself, Angel," he said.

"I—I suppose I have."

"A title, wealth, a place in the country, a mansion on Hanover Square—" He shook his head. "It's a far cry from the house on St. Martin's Lane."

"It is indeed."

"Do you love him?" he asked.

I nodded. "He—he's a wonderful man. He's been very good to me. I'm very, very happy."

"I'm glad," he said. His voice was quiet now, and the sadness was back in his eyes. "I love you, Angel. I suppose I always will, but I let you get away and—I'm glad you're happy," he continued. "I'm glad you have all the things I could never give you."

I'm not going to cry, I told myself. I'm not. I won't.

"Thank you, Jamie," I said.

"Guess I'd better leave now. Have to get back to that third act. Wish me luck."

"I—I wish you all the best," I whispered.

He smiled a brave, heartbreaking smile and looked into my eyes, and then he nodded and set down his champagne glass and left. I stood there, watching him move through the crowd, leave the room, and the party continued to swirl, bright and festive, colors blurring, everything misty, and I have no idea how many minutes may have passed before Megan came up to me and took my hand, her eyes full of concern.

"Are you all right, luv?" she asked nervously.

"I—why, yes. I'm fine."

"I saw you talking with him. I should never have placed his name on the list. I should have known seeing him would upset you. Here, take this handkerchief. Wipe your eyes. I don't think anyone else noticed. They're all too tipsy."

I took the handkerchief and dabbed at my eyes. Megan frowned.

"Was he awful to you?" she asked.

"Not at all. He—he was— Oh, Jesus."

"Let's go upstairs, luv. You need—"

"No," I said. I gave the handkerchief back to her. "I'm fine now. It just— I'm all right now."

"You're sure?"

I nodded. I squeezed her hand. Then I went to find my husband.

Chapter Twenty-Two

The January sky was gray and dreary and frost was gathering on the windowpanes, but in the breakfast room at Greystone Hall everything was bright and cheerful. In Boswell Clinton had a table companion who could match him dish for dish, and they had already devoured a mound of eggs, a plate of sausages, half a ham, innumerable hot rolls with butter and preserves. Dottie contented herself with a kippered herring and a piece of toast, and Goldsmith nodded at the table like a sleepy owl, occasionally blinking at his plate of food and taking a bite. With coffee cup in hand and a silver pot nearby, I marveled at Boswell's heartiness, Clinton's enthusiasm. We had all stayed up very, very late last night talking, and I for one would have been content to sleep later, but Boswell and Goldsmith were leaving at ten this morning and good manners demanded I see them off.

"Have some more bacon, Goldy," I said. "You've hardly eaten anything at all."

Goldy blinked, yawned, smiled, nodded off again.

Wearing the familiar old brown coat that was deplorably rumpled and much too large, a shabby mustard-colored neckcloth at his throat, he looked like a lovable, befuddled derelict, as indeed he had been of late. After the largess of the Haymarket revival slipped through his incompetent fingers, he had disappeared into another of those dusty rooms to scratch away at his articles, forgetting to attend Megan's wedding and failing to tell any of his friends where he was staying. They eventually discovered his whereabouts and rescued him, and now Boswell was taking him to Scotland for a few weeks in hopes the trip would clear out the cobwebs. Poor Goldy seemed to have little say in the matter, amiably shambling along in the wake of the dynamic Scot.

"—not at all worried," Boswell was saying, "go where I please without a care. People in Seven Dials have a code, just like we do, and as long as you don't break that code, you're safe as houses. Thief in Seven Dials might slit a throat for tuppence, but he'd never squeal on a mate. I get along splendidly with all of 'em—they know I've got a sympathetic ear. Every man loves to gab about himself. Denizens of Seven Dials are no different. I've heard some hair-raising tales, I assure you."

"We heard quite enough of them last night," Dottie informed him. "I, for one, would like to finish my breakfast without hearing about body snatchers and murderous fiends. Not *all* of us are fascinated by crime and criminals, my dear sir."

Boswell gave her an exasperated look. "You women are such squeamish creatures," he complained, forking another sausage. "Very well, I won't tell you about the severed heads—chap I met had a whole collection of 'em, let me examine the lot—but I must, I simply must tell you about The Grand Cyprus. Without question the most amazing fellow I've ever met. A great artist. I'd even go so far as to employ the word genius."

Dottie sighed and gave *him* a look. "I'm sure we'll be enthralled," she said dryly.

"Lives in a hovel in Seven Dials, he does, dark, filthy

place reeking with foul odors—both his rooms piled high with old papers and bottles of ink and a variety of exotic tools. He's a forger. Show him a document, he can duplicate it. Tell him what you want, he can run it up—so perfectly executed it'd fool the greatest expert. Wills, birth certificates, bank notes—man's incredible. Has his own press and a secret process for aging paper. You want something two hundred years old, he'll fix it for you, paper'll be yellow and brittle, foxed, you'll swear it's genuine."

"Fascinating," Clinton said.

"Utterly," Dottie added.

"The man's an artist, I tell you. Does a brisk business and you'd be surprised at his customers. Some of the noblest names in the country have visited that filthy hovel, incognito, of course. Johnson lost a very important document a few weeks ago, and it was imperative he have it for his lawyer. He was in an uproar, making everyone miserable. I slipped off to Seven Dials and paid The Grand Cyprus a visit—next night Johnson located the document between the pages of a book. Fake, naturally. He never knew it. Neither did his lawyer. Problem solved simple as that. Really put one over on him. Irony is he found the original a week or so later."

"And?" Clinton inquired.

"Raised bloody hell with me when I confessed what I'd done, then he roared with laughter. Couple of nights later I took him down to meet the man. Two of them hit it off at once, of course."

"Kindred souls," Dottie observed.

"Expedition made a fascinating entry in my journal—The Grand Cyprus like a ragged Buddah, Johnson like a bear, the two of them huddled together over the printing press, gabbing about type and techniques."

"When are we going to read these incredible journals you're always talking about?" Dottie asked.

"Oh, they'll *never* be published. Much too frank and racy, keep 'em for my own edification. Enumerate all my sins, all the foibles of my friends. Some spicy entries about *you*, Angel. Wrote about the first time I ever saw you sitting on the dais in Gainsborough's studio, looking like a goddess in your scarlet velvet gown. I made a cheeky remark—remember?—and you told me I could go take a—" He deliberately cut himself short, grinning broadly. "Thought my ears would burn. Gainsborough actually blushed."

"Tell us more," Clinton pleaded.

"Don't you dare," I warned.

"You were an adorable minx back then—haven't changed one bit. I have to confess, Lord M., I've always been madly in love with her, tried my best to win her. Wench wouldn't give me a tumble. The minute I saw· her I knew she was going to take London by storm— as, indeed, she did."

"It's just as well those journals of yours are not going to be published," I remarked.

"It would be disastrous," he said proudly. "Half my friends would be after me with cleaving knives. The other half would be quietly leaving the country. Inflammatory material! Soon as I finish one, I stash it away in a hiding place—have a secret cache of them in a castle in Scotland. No, the journals of James Boswell will never see the light of day."

Goldy snored loudly and tilted sideways, almost tumbling out of his chair. Boswell frowned and propped his friend back up and we finished breakfast shortly thereafter. At ten Clinton and I accompanied our literary guests out to the coach Boswell had hired for the trip. That gentleman was still chattering volubly, and Goldy was still nodding on his feet. Boswell shook hands with Clinton and gave me a kiss on the cheek. Goldy grinned and hugged me warmly, looking bemused. Both men thanked us for our hospitality.

"Hope everything goes well with your case," Boswell told Clinton. "Chap doesn't have a prayer of winning. Harassment, pure and simple. They'll throw it out of Justice High Court in record time—I know something about law, as you know. Shame the papers are making such a big to-do about it."

"It was inevitable they get hold of it," Clinton re-

plied. "I threw three chaps from Fleet Street off the
property myself two days ago. One of them was actually
trying to break into the house. Blacked his eye for him,
marched him to the gates. Bradford can court them all
he likes, give them interviews every other day, but I
prefer to maintain my dignity."

"Smart decision. Stick to your guns. Case is coming
up when—sometime in early March, right? I'll be back
in plenty of time to sit in on the proceedings. Can't wait
to see those six sober judges in their scarlet robes and
long white wigs boot the bastard out of court."

He bustled Goldy into the coach and clambered in
himself, closing the door and leaning out the window
for a final good-bye. The coach pulled away a moment
later, and Clinton and I waved, standing there on the
front steps as slate gray clouds roiled in the darker gray
sky. Clinton had enjoyed their brief visit, I knew, but
he seemed preoccupied now, his brow furrowed, his eyes
dark, the wind ruffling his blond hair. He was thinking
about Hugh, thinking about the forthcoming court battle and brooding about the endless stories that had been
appearing in the London papers. Involving as it did a
Lord of the Realm married to a celebrated actress and
a wealthy, mysterious stranger who claimed he was the
genuine heir, the Meredith Case contained all the elements Fleet Street thrived on, and it had caused a sensation, driving even the bloodiest murders off the front
pages.

Hugh delighted in the attention he was getting and
was constantly inviting journalists to the plush, luxurious apartment he had rented and giving them new
fuel for their stories. I lived in terror he would reveal
his former relationship with the new Lady Meredith.
Wouldn't the gents from Fleet love *that* little item. I
took Clinton's hand now and held it firmly as we watched
the coach disappear around a curve in the drive. Although Clinton ignored the newspaper articles as best
he could and tried to go on about his business as though
nothing were amiss, I could sense the tension building
up in him. An even-tempered man, he was finding it

more and more difficult to contain his steadily mounting anger against the man who was trying to destroy him.

"It's chilly out here," I said. "We'd better go back inside."

"What's that?"

Lost in thought, he hadn't paid any attention to my words. I squeezed his hand and then linked my arm in his, leading him back into the foyer. He sighed and shook his head, smiling apologetically. I stood up on tiptoe and gave him a light kiss.

"Sorry to be so distracted," he said. "Had something on my mind."

"I understand, darling."

"Where's Dottie?" he inquired.

"In the sitting room, I believe. Said it was much too cold for her to go traipsing outside just to tell those two scoundrels good-bye. She made her farewells earlier."

"I'm so glad she's come down to keep you company for a while, what with me being so busy with Burke. He's coming down again this afternoon, incidentally, wants to go over some family records with me. He'll be staying the night."

"I'll tell Henri. I—I'll be so glad when this is over."

"There's no need for you to worry, my love. Burke and his team have been working around the clock, as you know, breaking down Bradford's 'evidence.' As Boswell said, he hasn't a prayer."

"Even so, it—it's been a terrible strain on you."

"One copes," he said, "and I fear I've been terribly moody of late. All those newspaper articles, all those bloody journalists sniffing around—it *has* been a strain, I admit it, but it will soon be over. Until then, I hope you'll bear with me."

"You've been wonderful, Clinton."

"I've been a moody brute," he said, drawing me to him, "but I'll make it up to you when this is over."

"Oh?" I said lightly.

"We've never had a honeymoon. Immediately after the wedding we came back here and I immersed myself in estate work. Dreadfully unfair of me. I'm surprised you didn't leave me."

"I'd never leave you."

He kissed my cheek, the tip of my nose. "Come spring, we'll take a trip, go someplace very romantic. Intimate candlelight dinners. Luxurious lodgings. Long, lazy days strolling hand in hand beside some sparkling blue lake. Long, lovely nights on silken sheets."

"It sounds divine."

He kissed the tip of my nose again and let me go. "But now alas, I need to go to my office and get things ready for Burke. I won't be having any lunch today, not after that enormous breakfast. You and Dottie will have to do without me."

"What about afternoon tea? Will you and Burke be joining us?"

"Depends on how things go. At any rate, I'll see you at dinner this evening. Wear something lovely to impress Burke. I believe the fellow's smitten with you."

He grinned and gave me a quick kiss, then sauntered off toward his office. I found Dottie in the small, cozy sitting room in back of the house. It was an intimate room, snug and informal, books and papers scattered about, a fire burning in the fireplace, a row of windows looking out over the back gardens. Dottie had ensconced herself on the comfortable deep blue sofa, sewing in her lap, a battered and much-annotated copy of *The Country Wife* on the table in front of her.

"They get off?" she inquired.

I nodded. "I enjoyed their visit. Poor Goldy—I hope the trip to Scotland wakes him up."

"He's probably plotting another masterpiece," Dottie said. "He'll wander about in a daze for months on end, then hide himself away in one of those dusty rooms and write something like *She Stoops To Conquer* or *The Vicar of Wakefield*. Befuddled and absentminded he might be, but the man's a genius."

"And utterly endearing."

"Which is more than I can say for your friend Boswell. How that man loves the sound of his own voice.

He's a brilliant conversationalist, of course, but the man *does* go on. You look a bit distracted, dear. Is something bothering you?"

I stepped over to the fireplace to warm my hands. "I'm just worried about Clinton. This has all been very hard on him, Dottie. I—somehow I feel responsible."

"That's ridiculous, my dear. You're in no way responsible. Hugh Bradford would have pursued this even if you weren't Lady Meredith."

"That may well be, but I feel he—he's been much more vindictive because I *am* married to Clinton. All those stories he's given to Fleet Street about being neglected and abused and living in the stables while 'the golden boy' lived in splendor. Those stories about Lord Meredith's cruelty, his wife's drinking, Clinton's wild youth and wenching—" I cut myself short, frowning. "It's all so sordid."

"And most of it is true," Dottie pointed out gently. "Clinton was hardly a saint in his youth—you've told me so yourself—and Bradford did live over the stables. It's in wretched taste, of course, but you really can't blame him for making the most of it, vying for sympathy."

"I suppose you're right," I said.

Dottie set her sewing aside. Her gray watered-silk skirts crackled. The purple velvet bow fastened to her pompadour was slightly crooked, and her mauve eye shadow was smeared. A heart-shaped black satin beauty patch was affixed to her left cheekbone. Her lips were a vivid pink. The eccentric theatrical makeup somehow seemed natural on her, emphasizing her mellow warmth, the compassion in those wise and lovely eyes. I was so glad she had decided to come spend the month with us. Her presence was a great comfort, easing the strain for Clinton and me both.

"It has been hard on Clinton," she said, "and he has been moody—angry, too, though he's tried his best to contain it. That's perfectly understandable under the circumstances, and all the more reason why you must be strong and supportive. He needs you."

"I know that," I replied. "I—I mustn't let him know how much all this upsets me. I must be as bright and cheerful as possible."

"You're an actress, dear. It shouldn't be too difficult."

Leaving the fireplace, I stepped over to the windows and peered out at the bleak gray sky filled with clouds. A breeze caused the evergreens to shiver in the gardens. The white marble benches looked bare and abandoned. Dottie got up to pour herself a cup of raspberry tea. She poured one for me as well, adding a spoonful of honey.

"You and your raspberry tea," I said fondly, taking the cup. "The remedy for all ills."

"It can't hurt, dear," she informed me. "This will all be over with soon enough," she added. "I have great faith in that man Burke. A solid, sensible type, most reassuring."

She settled back down on the sofa, and I sat down in one of the overstuffed gray velvet chairs, feeling better already.

"I have faith in him, too," I told her. "I've no doubt we'll win. The priest Hugh brought back to London to testify for him is eighty-nine years old and his memory is almost completely gone. He claims he married Lord Meredith and Hugh's mother, yes, but Burke says any testimony he might give will be virtually worthless because of his senility. He did keep a daily journal— somehow or other Burke got a look at it, says it's genuine—but there's no record of a wedding ceremony, only a mention of the fact that the couple came to visit him and a notation of the sum of money Lord M. gave him 'for services rendered.' That's inconclusive, to say the least."

"I should think so."

"There's also a yellowing guest registration book from a hotel in Naples. It's signed 'Lord and Lady Meredith' in Lord Meredith's handwriting, but again that proves nothing. How many men take a woman to an hotel or inn for illicit purposes and sign her in as his wife?"

"Legions, I should think. And that's all he has?"

"Basically. Burke says that in order to win the case

he'd have to have a legitimate record of his parents'
marriage, a record of his own birth as well. No such
documents exist, and I'm convinced they never did."

"So there you are," Dottie said.

She finished her cup of tea and took up her sewing
again, her needle darting in and out of a piece of violet
silk brocade. She told me about the visit she had made
to Number Seven, Maiden Lane just before leaving London. The newly married Harts were firmly established,
the rooms freshly painted, furniture all in place. Megan
was not much of a housekeeper, Dottie confided, which
was no surprise to me, but a bit of dust and disorder
only made the place seem homier. They had a cat, Kitty,
to keep out the mice, and Charles himself had been
putting new carpeting on the staircase, wielding the
tack hammer with aplomb. He would be opening in
April at the York, playing a dashing brigand in *Her
Secret Lover,* and Megan had been offered several substantial parts, too, although she hadn't as yet decided
which one she would take. They were, of course, blissfully happy, bickering at each other constantly and loving every minute of it. It was, Dottie said, a match made
in heaven.

"Megan's proud as can be of that gorgeous set of
Sevres china and the silverware you and Clinton gave
them for Christmas," she added. "She refuses to use it,
keeping it for 'special occasions.' They eat off the old
cracked pottery they used at the flat."

"I look foward to seeing them when we're in London.
Dottie—" I hesitated a moment. "Have—have you seen
Jamie? How is he doing?"

Dottie took a final stitch and then put her sewing
down again. It seemed to me her expression grew
guarded. "I saw him two days before I left London," she
said carefully. "He came by the shop. He's finished his
play. He let me read it. It's magnificent, Angel, far and
away the best thing he's ever written. It's witty and
bright in places, delightfully droll, and there's genuine
feeling in the dramatic scenes."

"I'm so pleased for him."

It was true. I *was* pleased. I hoped he had a great success and received all the plaudits he deserved. He'd be impossible, of course, strutting around with an ego that would make Sheridan's look small. I smiled to myself, visualizing him preening at Button's, standing everyone to drinks. Perhaps he'd buy some new clothes, I thought, he sorely needed them, and perhaps, at long last, he would feel secure about his talent. I felt a tender warmth inside as these thoughts took shape, and the smile lingered on my lips. Dottie got up to pour herself another cup of tea.

"It will probably never be produced," she said.

I looked up, startled. "What do you mean?"

She poured her tea and added a spoonful of honey, stirring it thoroughly. A frown creased her brow. "I didn't intend to tell you this," she said hesitantly. "I didn't want to upset you—you've got enough on your mind at the moment."

"Tell me what?"

She looked at me with sorrowful eyes, and I felt a sudden chilliness in my blood. It quickly grew into panic, and I gripped the arms of the chair tightly, so tightly my knuckles grew white.

"What *is* it, Dottie? Is— He's not ill? He's—"

I stood up. I could feel the color leaving my cheeks.

"He's perfectly all right," she said, "although I daresay he's not taking proper care of himself. He's thin as a rail, and there are shadows under his eyes. He's got a pallor, too, looks like he hasn't had enough sleep, but that's not what I was referring to. He's in trouble, Angel."

"Trouble?"

"Financial trouble."

Relief swept over me. I sighed, irritated with Dottie for alarming me so badly. Financial trouble! That was nothing new. He was *al*ways in financial trouble, and somehow he always managed to pull through. Damn Dottie with her sorrowful eyes and hesitant voice, frightening me that way. I gave her an exasperated look and sat back down while she took a sip of tea. I didn't really *care* if he was having financial trouble. Served the sod right. Jamie Lambert and his troubles were no affair of mine, hadn't been for some time. He'd pull through and find backing somehow and the play would be produced and some other actress would play Aphra Behn, the role I might seriously have considered killing for a year ago.

"It's serious this time," Dottie said.

"It's always serious," I said wryly.

"You don't understand, Angel."

"I lived with him for years. I understand perfectly."

"He's going to lose The Lambert," she said.

"Lose The Lambert?" That took me aback. "How could he possibly lose The Lambert? It's his theater. It was his father's before him. It—why, it's the very corner-stone of his life and career. It's been shut down a couple of times when times were bad, but—"

"He mortgaged it," she said. "In order to finance *Amelia Mine* he put The Lambert up as collateral. The textile magnate from Leeds didn't come through, Angel, backed out at the last minute, and Jamie went to a group of 'private investors' from The City, smooth, shrewd types who happily advanced him the money he needed in exchange for his signature on several papers."

"He didn't?" I said.

"He did."

"The idiot. The bloody idiot."

"He has until the end of the month to repay the loan, with interest. Had *Amelia Mine* succeeded, there would have been no problem, but—" She shook her head. "It was a foolhardy thing to do, granted, but he was so certain the play would succeed."

"The bloody *idiot*," I repeated.

I sat there fuming while Dottie gave me all the details of the transaction, providing names and specifics, and the picture grew bleak indeed. Whoever held those papers Jamie had signed owned The Lambert for all practical purposes, and unless he could come up with two thousand pounds by the end of the month, those smooth, shrewd gentlemen with offices on Thread-needle Street would boot him out completely and take over the theater themselves. I went white when Dottie told me the interest being charged. He would have done better had he gone to one of the criminal sharks in Seven Dials. Two thousand pounds! The son of a bitch was living in a squalid room and eating sardines when he ate at all and he didn't have two pounds to rub together, much less two thousand. I longed to crack a vase over his head for being such a blithering fool.

"This will destroy him," Dottie said grimly.

"It probably will."

"If he loses The Lambert he'll lose all his spirit, all his will to go on. He'll give up completely. He'll become a ruin."

"It serves him right," I snapped.

"You don't mean that, dear."

"I do, too. He *deserves* to be ruined!"

I was furious with him, absolutely furious, for I knew in my heart that it would indeed destroy him if he lost his theater, knew he would be a broken man, all those dreams of his turned into dust. It was his own bloody fault for being such an idiot, of course, but that only made me angrier. I seethed all afternoon long, and by six I had begun to blame myself. If I hadn't been so successful in *She Stoops To Conquer,* if he hadn't been so determined to show me he could succeed without me, he'd never have done anything so foolhardy as signing those bloody papers. It was totally unreasonable of me to feel in any way responsible, I knew that, but the feeling persisted, along with the anger, and as I went upstairs to dress for dinner I had determined what I must do and decided just how I would carry it off.

I dressed very carefully, selecting a rich red silk brocade with tiny flowers embroidered in a deeper red. The gown had full puffed sleeves worn off the shoulder, a low-cut neckline and formfitting bodice. The waist was snug, the skirt spreading out in luxurious folds over half a dozen red gauze underskirts. The gown was bold and dramatic, most unsuitable for Lady Angela but perfect for Angel Howard, and Angel was going to be giving a performance tonight. Opening my jewel box, I took out the diamond and ruby necklace Clinton had given me for Christmas. It was exquisite, large pear-shaped ruby pendants framed with diamonds and suspended from diamond loops, the rubies glowing with deep red fires, the diamonds flashing brilliantly. I put it on and fastened the matching ruby and diamond bracelet around my wrist, and then I stepped back to examine myself in the mirror.

My hair was carefully styled with gleaming chestnut waves arranged artfully atop my head and three long ringlets dangling down in back. My makeup was perfect, eyelids brushed with subtle blue-gray shadow, high cheekbones accentuated with rouge, lips a deep pink. The jewels were stunning and, though undeniably provocative, the gown was spectacular. I felt rather wicked as I moved down the gracefully curving white staircase. Clinton was waiting for me at the foot of the stairs, and when I saw the look in his eyes I knew that I had chosen the right strategy.

"Jesus!" he exclaimed. "You look incredible."

"Is that a compliment?"

"Definitely. That gown— I don't believe you've ever worn it before."

"Not since we've been married," I said demurely. "You said I should wear something lovely to impress Burke."

"The poor man's going to be dazzled. I'm dazzled myself. Don't know how I'm going to concentrate on dinner. I'm going to be thinking very, very wicked thoughts and counting the minutes until we can be alone."

"Perhaps I should go back up and change into something a bit more demure," I said.

"No time," he said cheerfully. "Burke will just have to suffer, as will I. Did anyone ever tell you you were a positively delectable specimen of feminine allure?"

"Not in those precise words."

"You *are*, my love. Believe me."

"You're not entirely without appeal yourself."

He arched a brow. "Oh?"

"I suggest we join our guests," I said.

Dottie and Jonathan Burke were waiting for us in the library. Burke stood up, solemn in dark brown suit and black vest and a jabot of starched white ruffles. His brick-red hair was pulled back and tied at the nape with a black ribbon. A sober, serious-minded man very much aware of his own dignity, Burke was always in control of himself, guarded in his responses, but I could see that he was indeed dazzled. A woman always can. Dottie looked at the gown, looked at me, lifted one brow and frowned, clearly wondering what I was up to. I stepped over to Burke and took his hand in both my own and told him how delighted I was to see him again. He made a polite reply, slightly discomfited by my effusive greeting. Dottie coughed. I let go of Burke's hand. He stepped back and began to fidget with his jabot. He was going to present no problem. I knew that at once. Like many men who led quiet, relatively uneventful lives, he was intrigued by the colorful, glamorous world of the theater, which I represented to him, and though he might not react openly, he was not at all immune to feminine charms.

I deliberately set about charming him. While the role I was playing might be best suited to the talents of a Mrs. Perry, I played it to the hilt but with considerably more finesse than that lady would have employed. Clinton was delighted that I was so vivacious, so considerate of Burke, so attentive. Dottie kept casting me dark looks throughout dinner, not taken in for a minute. Conversation centered around the theater—neither man cared to discuss the forthcoming legal battle—and I regaled Burke with bright and amusing anecdotes and he finally confided that he had seen almost all my plays and had been an admirer for years. Later, over dessert, he unbent enough to confess he had actually purchased a reproduction of *An Angel in Scarlet.*

"A remarkable painting," he observed. "I wish I could have seen the original."

"You mean you've never seen it? My husband purchased it—it's hanging in the drawing room. I'll show it to you myself."

After the dessert plates had been removed I asked Clinton to escort Dottie to the library, where we would take our coffee, and, linking my arm in his, led Burke to the drawing room. Candles glowed brightly, the light imbuing the portrait with vibrant life. The pensive girl in scarlet velvet looked down at us, and I released Burke's arm so that he could move closer. He inspected the portrait for several moments, silent, and then he turned to look at me. The woman in red silk brocade smiled quietly, her eyes attractively troubled. Burke saw the troubled eyes, and his own were immediately concerned.

"Is something wrong, Lady Meredith?" he inquired.

I nodded, the helpless, hopeful female now. "I'm so glad to have this opportunity to speak to you alone. There—" I paused, a deliberate, theatrical pause that made him even more attentive. "There's something I'd like you to do for me if—if it's possible. I don't know all the legalities involved or even if you *could* do it, but—"

I paused again, looking at him with beseeching eyes. Jonathan Burke grew guarded. The man was no fool and, admire me though he did, he certainly wouldn't undertake any job that might compromise his integrity. I realized that. I respected him for it. I didn't want him to do anything unethical, I just wanted him to do it secretly, without my husband's knowledge.

"Perhaps you'd better tell me what the problem is, Milady," he said.

"It—it involves a friend of mine, a man to whom I owe a great deal. He is having serious financial difficulties, and—well, I happen to be in a position to help him, but I—I wouldn't want him to know I was the one helping him out of his difficulties."

"I see."

"I wouldn't want my husband to know, either," I said. "He has so much on his mind right now—I wouldn't want to bother him with this. I happen to have a great

deal of money of my own, under the name Angel Howard. It's in the Bank of England. A Mr. Richard Bancroft
handles my affairs there."

"I know Bancroft well. What exactly is it you want
me to do for you, Lady Meredith?"

I told him. I gave him names and details, and he
listened carefully, nodding now and then, his expression
extremely grave. When I finished, he was silent, a frown
creasing his brow, and I could see that he was not at
all certain he wanted to undertake my little commission.

"Legally, there would be no problem whatsoever," he
said finally. "All I would require would be a letter of
authorization in your handwriting, giving me power to
act as your representative."

"Then—"

"I'm your husband's lawyer, Lady Meredith. I'm not
at all sure I could do this without his knowledge."

"Clinton would want to help," I said. "He would want
to use his own money—that's the primary reason I
haven't told him about it. This is something I want to
do myself. I—I don't want to bother him with it at this
particular time."

Burke started to say something, hesitated. I could
see him weakening.

"I thought I could rely on your help, Mr. Burke, but
if you feel you can't undertake the job, I—perhaps I
could write to Mr. Bancroft. Perhaps he could recom-
mend someone who might—"

I let the sentence dangle in air, looking hurt, looking
brave. Burke weakened even more, and then he tightened his lips and nodded curtly, his decision made.

"That won't be necessary, Lady Meredith," he said.

"You—you'll help me?"

He nodded again. "I'll need that letter of authorization."

"I'll see that you have it before you leave in the
morning. I can't tell you how grateful I am."

"The pleasure is mine, Milady."

I smiled and, taking his hands, squeezed them. Burke

relaxed, his reservations gone, delighted now to be of service. We went to join the others in the library, where coffee was served. The men had port afterward, and while they were talking together with glasses in hand Dottie came over to the sofa where I was sitting and plopped down beside me. Her voice low and inaudible to the men, she informed me that I didn't fool her one bloody bit and demanded to know just what the hell I was up to. I gave her a fond look and patted her hand.

"I'll tell you later, darling," I said.

Burke left the next morning with the letter of authorization I had secretly passed to him after breakfast, and the following Monday he returned to Greystone Hall for another consultation with Clinton. I managed to speak to him in the drawing room before he joined Clinton in the office, and Burke proudly handed me a sheaf of very official-looking documents. He informed me that for all practical purposes I now owned The Lambert Theater. James Lambert had been informed that the papers were now in the possession of "an interested party," who would not press for payment, and that the same party was eager to provide financial backing for his new play.

"Was— Did he seem pleased?" I asked.

"He seemed dumbfounded," Burke replied. "He didn't press me for a name," he added, "but he was most interested to know when he would get the money. I took the liberty of drawing up a contract for your protection. The chap signed it promptly, didn't even read it thoroughly—it's included in the sheaf of papers. The money has already been transferred into an account under his name at the Bank of England. As financial backer, your share of the profits will be—" He paused when I waved my hand.

"The details aren't important," I told him. "The important thing is that he'll be able to produce the play."

"If the play is successful, you stand to make a considerable sum," Burke said. "The contract is very carefully worded. If you'd care for me to go over it with you—"

"That won't be necessary. Are—are you sure he has no idea who his mysterious benefactor is?"

"Positive. Frankly, he didn't seem to care. I must say, the chap isn't very *business* minded."

"He's an artist," I replied.

Dottie was on the sofa in the back sitting room, her favorite spot, sewing beside her, an expression of deep concentration on her face as she made another annotation in her copy of *The Country Wife*. A fire was crackling pleasantly in the fireplace, and, once again, the sky outside was wet and gray. A tear slid down her cheek when I told Dottie what had transpired. She put her book down, giving me an irritable look that was nevertheless full of affection.

"You've made me spoil my makeup," she grumbled, brushing the tear aside. "You're an exasperating minx, Angel, you always have been—letting me stew all this time, letting me worry. There are times when I'd like to shake you. Why didn't you *tell* me what you were doing?"

"I wanted to be sure Burke could carry it through. It's done now. Legally, I own The Lambert."

"And you're financing the new play. It must have taken—"

"Every cent I had," I told her, "and there was a lot. The money isn't important. I—I couldn't see him lose The Lambert, Dottie."

"Of course you couldn't."

"He must never know what I've done—his bloody pride. He'd think it was charity. It—it was the least I could do, Dottie. I want him to succeed. I want him to see all his dreams come true. He's a brilliant man—a wonderful man, too, in his way. There were dozens of times I would cheerfully have murdered him, but—"

I cut myself short. Dottie looked at me with those wise, wonderful eyes, seeing so much, seeing, perhaps, more than I saw myself, but she didn't say anything. She gathered her sewing into her lap and quietly began to stitch, and I poured myself a cup of tea and stepped over to the windows and gazed out at the wet gray sky, remembering, a poignant feeling welling inside. A long time went by before I finally sighed and set the cup down and went to see about lunch.

It rained that evening and all the next day and Wednesday as well. Thunder rumbled in the distance on Thursday morning, sounding like ominous drumrolls, but the rain had temporarily ceased. I shall never, never forget the events of that day, each detail sharp and clear. Clinton was cheerful at breakfast, Dottie in an inordinately chatty mood, telling us just how she would interpret the role of Lady Fidget, which she had definitely decided to do. It was a marvelous part and she would really be foolish to pass it up and it would be a wonderful challenge to act with Davy though she knew a thing or two about scene stealing herself and had no doubt she could hold her own. She would make all of the costumes, of course, and she thought a pink and silver striped silk with silver lace would be ideal for Act Two, didn't I agree? I drank my third cup of black coffee and nodded listlessly and wondered how anyone could possibly be so talkative so early in the morning.

I had my meeting with Mrs. Rigby in the drawing room and she tactfully mentioned that all the silver needed polishing and said it might be a good idea for the maids to polish today after the floors were done and the furniture all dusted. The Blue Room needed to be turned out, and those Boulle cabinets in the upstairs hall could use a thorough cleaning with turtle oil. I gave her "instructions" to do what she had already decided to do today and she gave me a cheerful nod and bustled out, black taffeta skirts rustling. Thunder still rumbled, louder now, it seemed, and it was so grim and gray outside we had candles burning at nine-thirty in the morning. As I stood there in the drawing room after Mrs. Rigby departed, a flash of lightning illuminated the gloom outside. Apparently the rain we had had the past two days was only a prelude to the downpour to come later on today.

Clinton had several reports to read and accounts to

go over, and he had already gone to his office, where he planned to spend most of the day catching up. Two large cartons of books I had ordered had arrived from London a few days ago, and they were still on a table in the library, unopened. I decided to spend the rest of the morning sorting out the books and putting them on the shelves. Dottie decided to keep me company. She brought her copy of *The Country Wife* along and thought it might amuse me if she read the play aloud while I worked. I took the books out of the cartons and examined them idly and put them on the shelves, and Dottie moved about the room with book in hand, reading the play and declaiming Lady Fidget's lines with considerable brio. She wore full theatrical makeup and a dusty-rose frock trimmed with black lace, a black velvet bow affixed to her pompadour. My lack of attention deterred her not one whit, and when, finally, the books were all shelved, she concluded with a flourish and frankly admitted that she was going to be *marvelous* in the part.

Clinton joined us for a light lunch at one. He looked weary after poring over papers all morning and was unusually quiet, preoccupied, no doubt, with estate matters. A thick, pale blond wave spilled across his brow, and there were faint gray-mauve shadows beneath his eyes. He was wearing comfortable old black leather knee boots, snug gray breeches and a fine white lawn shirt opened at the throat, the sleeves rolled up over his forearms. Poor darling, I thought. He worked so hard, and he endured Dottie's bright chatter with a polite show of attentiveness, although his mind was clearly on other things. I took his hand as we left the dining room, and he gave me a gentle smile.

"Your fingers are ink-stained," I said, entwining my own around them.

"I've been making notes and writing letters of instruction to various of my trusty lieutenants. Tedious work, but necessary if we're to continue to live in the style that so admirably suits us."

"I thought perhaps you'd like to take a break this afternoon."

The gentle smile reappeared. "Is that an invitation?"
"Definitely."

"I'd love to accept, my darling, but I really do need to get all this paperwork finished. Disappointed?"

"Very." I squeezed his hand.

"I'll try to make amends later on."

He kissed me lightly on the brow and then went to check on the post, always arranged on a table in the foyer by the ever-efficient Putnam. There were several letters for him, which he carried off to his office. There were letters for Dottie as well and, tired from her bravura reading this morning, she told me she was going to spend the afternoon up in her bedroom, reading her letters, answering them and resting till tea. She went on upstairs, dusty-rose skirts making a silken rustle. I felt rather at a loss with the whole afternoon to fill. Going back into the library, I browsed for a while and eventually took down one of the new books I had examined earlier and carried it over to a large, comfortable chair near the fire.

I tried to read. I couldn't. Thunder rumbled constantly, and there were repeated flashes of lightning like violent silver-blue demons hurling themselves against the windowpanes. Half an hour must have passed before I finally put the book aside and stood up, feeling restless, feeling vaguely disturbed, although I usually wasn't bothered by storms. Stepping over to the window, I looked out at the sky. It was a much darker gray, tinged with purple, and clouds roiled about in dense profusion, puffy and black. Skeletal silver fingers ripped at the sky, and, for an instant, the earth was a blinding silver-blue, then gray again. The window looked out over the side of the house, and I saw the old gray stone wall, the tree limb, the trellis with a marble bench beneath it, and the memories came flooding back.

As I looked out, it seemed I could see a little girl crawling out onto that limb, and two figures entwined on that marble bench, a lovely lady in blue and a handsome blond youth who looked like a prince. The wind roared savagely, sweeping the couple away, and another figure appeared, a boy with black hair and belligerent expression, three large greyhounds bounding about at his heels. Lightning flashed and then the greyhounds were gone and the little girl was no longer in the tree, she was on the marble bench, across the boy's knees, his hand lifting to smack that round little bottom. I shut my eyes, willing the ghosts away, and when I opened them again the bench was bare. It had all begun that day, so very long ago. The little girl hiding in the tree had come to love both youths she spied on, the handsome blond prince in sky blue satin, the stableboy in muddy boots, our lives inextricably entwined down through the years.

A clap of thunder shook the earth. The windows rattled. Another flash of lightning exploded, shattering the gray with blazing silver-blue, but still rain didn't come. I moved back, disturbed by the elements, disturbed by the emotions inside. I went out into the foyer and stopped in front of the mirror to shove a chestnut wave from my temple and brush the skirt of my low cut violet blue gown. Thunder rumbled, rumbled, moving closer, and there was another deafening clap so powerful it seemed the house shook. Poor Dottie. She couldn't possibly rest in weather like this. I decided to go up and see if she was all right. I turned, frowning, and then I saw Clinton.

He was standing not ten feet away, a sheet of paper in his hand. He looked at me with troubled gray eyes that seemed to be seeking the answer to some burning question. His cheeks were ashen. He didn't speak, just stood there staring at me as another fusillade of thunder rumbled outside, sounding like mighty cannons being fired.

"I want to talk to you," he said at last.

His voice was calm, much too calm, carefully modulated, and that frightened me. I looked at the sheet of paper in his hand, and I knew. It had happened at last. I felt a weak, tremulous feeling inside, and I knew I couldn't give in to it. I was afraid my knees were going

to give way. They didn't. I took a deep breath, and when
I spoke my voice was as calm as his own had been.

"Is something wrong?" I asked.

It was a foolish question. I knew. I knew. I wanted
to burst into tears. I wanted to turn and flee up the
stairs. I stood facing my husband with perfect composure. A heavy blond wave had fallen across his brow.
He shoved it back. The tail of his white lawn shirt was
tucked carelessly into the waistband of his snug gray
trousers.

"I received a letter," he said.

"Oh?"

"From him."

"Him?"

"From Hugh Bradford, Angela."

It was what I had feared, what I had been dreading
all these weeks, and now that it had actually happened
I felt, perversely, something very like relief. I was almost glad it was out in the open, for nothing could be
much worse than the constant dread I had been living
with since Hugh Bradford's return.

"I see," I said.

"Do you?"

"I think so. He—he told you about our— He told
you that we had been together."

"He said that you had been lovers, that you are still
in love with him. He said that the only reason you
married me was to get back at him for leaving you. He
said you had merely used me to hurt him."

"That isn't true, Clinton."

"No?"

"You know it isn't true."

He didn't reply at once. He continued to look at me.
His cheeks were no longer ashen. His face was hard,
the muscles tight, and his gray eyes were hard too. The
hurt, troubled man who had come into the foyer was
now stiff, unyielding, a Clinton I didn't know. That
alarmed me. The tremulous feeling returned, worse than
before. The fear returned as well.

"Clinton—"

"Then the letter is a lie," he said.

"Not—not all of it," I said, and for all my skill as an actress I couldn't keep the tremor out of my voice. "I—I did love him. When I was seventeen I—we slept together, and I thought he was the world. When Lord Meredith died and Hugh vanished I—I thought I would never get over my grief."

Another clap of thunder shook the earth. The whole house seemed to tremble as though besieged by a battering ram. There was a moment of silence and then a shrieking, splitting explosion of noise in back. Lightning must have struck one of the small trees, I reflected, but it was an idle thought. My whole being was concentrated on my husband, on convincing him of my love.

"I—I went to London," I continued. "I began a whole new life. You know about that. You know about Jamie. I never tried to hide our relationship. We had a falling out and I left him and—and Hugh came back into my life. I took a cottage in the country and Hugh came to stay with me and we resumed our affair and I thought—"

I hesitated, trying to find the proper words. He continued to stare at me with those hard eyes, the eyes of an enemy, and my heart seemed to stop beating. I couldn't lose him. I couldn't. I loved him with all my heart and soul, and I must convince him of that. The thunder ceased. There was an eerie silence outside, as though the earth were holding its breath, all sound, all motion ceased. It was the calm before the storm.

"He planned to go to Italy. He wanted to gather evidence to—to prove he was the rightful heir. I tried to dissuade him. I told him it was folly, but he wouldn't listen, he was obsessed. I told him that if he left it would all be over between us, but that—that didn't matter to him. He left and it *was* over, Clinton."

"And then you met me again," he said.

"I know what you're thinking, but it isn't true. It isn't. I fell in love with you, Clinton. I thought you were the gentlest, the kindest, the most compassionate man I had ever met—I couldn't help falling in love with you.

I never told you about Hugh because—because there seemed to be no reason for me to tell you."

Clinton crumpled the sheet of paper into a ball and tossed it into the corner. He looked away from me, staring at a point in space. The silence outside seemed far more ominous than the thunder had been.

"You can't believe what he wrote," I said, and my voice trembled. "I married you because I loved you. It had nothing to do with Hugh. You must believe me. He—he just wanted to hurt you."

Clinton looked at me again. His eyes were expressionless.

"No," he said, "he wanted me to call off Burke and give up the fight. He informed me that if I didn't he would tell Fleet Street all about his passionate affair with the new Lady Meredith."

He looked at me for a long moment and then turned around and started toward the back of the house. My heart was breaking. I couldn't let him go, not like this, not with him thinking...Hesitating just a second to catch my breath, I hurried after him.

"Clinton—"

"Leave me alone, Angela. I need to think."

He tossed these words over his shoulder without losing stride. I caught up with him and took hold of his arm and he stopped and looked down at me with eyes that were still flat and expressionless.

"Clinton, we—we can't leave it like this. Please," I pleaded. "We must talk. You must let me explain—"

"We'll talk later," he said curtly.

He pulled his arm free and strode away and I leaned against the wall, tears spilling down my cheeks. Everything grew blurry, and I seemed to be watching my whole world crumbling to pieces. In the distance I heard a loud retort, and it was a moment before I realized it was the sound of a door slamming shut. He had gone outside. In this weather. He had gone outside, and that could only mean he intended to ride Hercules. He always went riding when something was bothering him. He rode with reckless abandon over the fields and...I had to stop him! It was going to storm! Filled with a new panic now, I rushed on down the foyer and through an archway and into the back hall. I heard footsteps clattering behind me. Someone was calling my name. I hurried on, stumbling on a rug, almost falling. Reaching the back door, I hurled it open and cried out sharply as I saw him tearing across the cobbled yard on Hercules. Ian came rushing out of the stables, looking distraught, shouting words that were torn asunder by the wind that rose suddenly, sweeping across the yard with a fierce roar.

"Clinton!" I called.

I started to rush outside. Hands caught me, held me, pulled me back, and I whirled to find Dottie. She was shaking her head, speaking words I couldn't hear for the pounding of my heart. The wind roared and there was another deafening clap of thunder like a fusillade of cannons and lightning split the purple-gray sky. I tried to pull free. Dottie held me firmly, telling me to be calm, be still, it would be all right, and then I was babbling and trying to explain. I had to go after him! I had to stop him! It was going to storm! Dottie crooned more soothing words I didn't hear and gently, firmly led me into the nearby back sitting room. She eased me into a chair and poured a glass of brandy and stood over me, forcing me to drink.

The brandy seemed to set my insides afire and gradually the fire turned into a pleasant warmth and with the warmth hysteria abated and then some semblance of calm returned. I handed Dottie the half-emptied glass and shook my head, indicating I could drink no more, and she set the glass down and looked at me with deeply concerned eyes, her brow creased, and I told her I was all right now. My voice seemed to belong to someone else, a flat, hollow, defeated voice that came from a great distance. My body seemed to belong to someone else, too, numb now, all energy, all life force seeped away. The windows rattled violently and lightning flashed repeatedly as though some maniacal god flicked blinding silver-blue light on and off, on and off, accompanied by rumbling crashes of thunder. Dottie picked up the glass and drank the rest of the brandy herself.

"I've lost him, Dottie," I said.

"Nonsense, dear."

"Hugh sent him a letter. Clinton believes—"

"No, dear. Don't worry yourself about it. It will all work out."

"You don't understand. He—"

"I heard, Angel. I couldn't rest with all that bloody thunder. I started downstairs and heard your voices and didn't want to interrupt. I wasn't actually eavesdropping, I just couldn't help hearing—"

"I've lost him," I repeated.

"He loves you. He knows that you love him. He's upset, but he'll get over it. Don't fret, my dear."

Several long minutes passed as claps of deafening thunder boomed and lightning flashed and, somewhere in the distance, there was a shattering explosion as lightning struck a tree. Clinton was out there, on Hercules, charging over the roads and fields. I gripped the arms of the chair, starting as another explosion sounded nearby. Dottie was wringing her hands, worried sick herself, moving about the room restlessly, pausing now and then to stare out the window with apprehensive eyes. Clinton had been gone perhaps ten minutes when we heard shouting outside, in the stableyard. The back door flew open. Loud footsteps pounded in the hall. There were loud, excited voices yelling words we couldn't quite make out and then there was a moment of silence and the voices were lowered. I was already on my feet, my face white. Dottie gripped my hand, the color draining from her own cheeks. Both of us seemed paralyzed. Putnam stepped into the sitting room, clearly shaken but somehow maintaining his regal composure.

"Milady," he said. "I fear there's been an accident."

"What is it? What's happened?" My voice was a hoarse whisper.

"No one is quite certain, Milady. His Lordship's horse has returned to the stables, dragging the reins, the saddle empty. It—it seems Lord Meredith has had a mishap. I sent four of the men out to search for him—" Even as he spoke we heard the sound of horse hooves pounding on the cobbles. "I also instructed one of the footmen to ride to the village and fetch the doctor in—in the event Lord Meredith has sustained some kind of injury."

I stared at him, unable to speak, and after a moment Putnam nodded and left the room. Dottie squeezed my hand tightly. Thunder rumbled. Lightning flashed with dazzling brilliance and then there was a pause, several moments of silence, and the rain began to fall. It fell strongly, steadily, without any particular violence, splattering noisily on the ground. I pulled my hand loose. I headed blindly for the door. Dottie rushed after me, caught hold of my arm.

"I must go to him," I told her, and it was someone else speaking, someone I could barely hear. "I must find him. He's out there. Clinton is out there. I must mount Cynara and go find him."

"No, dear, no. The men will find him. You mustn't go out in this. Clinton wouldn't want you to. He—he's had a fall, that's all. He'll probably come hobbling back on his own two feet any minute now."

"Dottie—"

"I'm not going to let you go out there, Angel."

Her voice was firm. I looked at her. She folded me to her and held me for a long time, held me tightly, and then she led me back over to the chair and set me down and sat on the arm of the chair and held her arm around my shoulders and I saw the worry in her eyes and the tears spilling over her lashes. Rain splattered and the fire crackled pleasantly and time passed, each moment agony, and I prayed silently and calm came and with it strength and when I heard the men come in I stood up, composed now, ready to face whatever might be. They brought him into the room, bundled up in a blanket, his pale blond hair plastered wetly over his brow, and I told them to put him on the sofa.

"We found him on the side of the road, Milady," Ian said gravely. "A 'uge oak was blockin' the road, the trunk still smoking. Apparently lightning struck the tree and the tree fell and startled the 'orse and it reared up and threw 'im off. 'E—'e's been moanin', but 'e 'asn't regained consciousness."

"Thank you, Ian," I said. "Please tell Putnam to bring the doctor here as soon as he arrives."

Ian nodded and the men left and I was on my knees beside the sofa, smoothing the damp locks from his brow. He moaned and his body twitched and I knew he was in terrible pain. There was no blood, no bruises. The injuries were internal. I reached for his hand, took it, held it tightly, and he moaned again, his eyelids fluttering. His lips parted. His cheeks were flushed. His lashes were all wet and stuck together in short spikes. Dottie handed me a cloth. I wiped his face gently. He opened his eyes. I smiled a tender smile and touched his cheek.

"An—Angela—" he stammered.

"I'm here, darling. You—you've had a little accident. The doctor will be here in a few minutes. Don't—don't try to talk, my darling. Just try to relax."

"My—my back— can't feel—"

"Hush, my darling. Hush."

"Don't—don't leave me. Please—don't—"

"I'm here. I'll always be here. I love you, Clinton."

"Cold. Can't—can't feel anything. H-hold me, Angela."

He struggled into a sitting position and I sat down on the sofa and wrapped my arms around him and eased him back, his head resting against my shoulder. He looked up into my eyes and I smiled again and felt him relax, saw him wince. He closed his eyes for a moment and the color fled from his cheeks and he trembled. I held him close and he seemed to sleep and then his eyes flew open and he gazed at me as though through a fog, peering intently, squinting, and then he found me and his lips curved into a weak smile and I held him closer.

"Love—love you," he murmured. "My fault— shouldn't have doubted—forgi-forgive me—"

"My darling, my darling, it's all right. The doctor will be here. You'll be—you'll be fine."

"Love—you," he repeated, his voice fainter now.

"And I love you. I love you with all my heart and soul."

He nodded and the weak smile reappeared and then his eyes filled with panic and he trembled and his torso jerked and he grew rigid. The rain splattered on the windowpanes and the fire made spluttering noises as a log snapped and began to flake apart. The room was dim and I was vaguely aware of Dottie standing beside the chair but everything was misty. I felt something warm and salty on my lashes. The tears streamed down my cheeks. Clinton relaxed in my arms, resting his damp head against my shoulder. His eyes opened and they were clear and gray and filled with tenderness and then concern when he saw my tears.

"No-no," he murmured. He frowned. "Don-don't cry. You mustn't cry. I want you to be happy. Prom-promise me you'll be happy, my darling."

I couldn't speak. I nodded. The smile curved tenderly on his lips, and he looked at me with love and then he frowned and squinted and tried desperately to find me in the fog. His body jerked again and grew rigid in my arms and then he gasped and went limp and I knew that he was gone. I held him close, feeling his weight and his warmth for the final time as tears streamed, blinding me. I gently rocked him as the rain fell and finally there were voices in the hall, and I knew I had to turn loose, give up, with only emptiness ahead. I eased him back onto the cushions and Dottie helped me to my feet. I looked at her for a moment without words and then sobbed wildly and threw myself into her open arms.

Chapter Twenty-Three

Winter was over and already, in mid-March, the air held a promise of spring. A lovely pale blue sky arched over London, and the trees in the garden in back of the house on Maiden Lane were studded with tiny nubs that would soon burst into delicate light jade leaves. It was not quite ten o'clock. Megan, Charles and I had had breakfast below in the charming yellow breakfast room, and I had come up to dress. Jonathan Burke would be here shortly and we would go together to Justice High Court where, he assured me, I would make my statement and we would be free before noon. I gazed at my reflection with level violet-gray eyes, and I was amazed at the calm and composure of the woman in the glass. The anguish and grief that had tormented me for weeks were nowhere in evidence. The woman in the glass looked cool, self-assured, determined.

Megan tapped at the door of the guest room and called my name. I told her to come in. She entered apprehensively, a worried look on her face. She wore a fetching sky blue frock with narrow sapphire blue stripes, a sapphire sash at the waist. I put the brush down, gave my chestnut waves a final pat and stood up, the folds of my black velvet grown rustling softly. I smiled at Megan, and she frowned, still apprehensive.

"Has Charles gone?" I inquired.

She nodded. "He had to be at rehearsal early. They're opening the first of April, you know, and everything's still in shambles."

"And when do you start rehearsing?"

"Not for another two weeks. Sheridan's still doing revisions on the third act. I bowled him over when I auditioned, luv—he didn't think I could handle the part. Everyone in the theater burst into spontaneous applause when I finished reading. Betsy went into raptures. Her brother scowled and reluctantly admitted I was marvelous. It's my very first lead, luv. I hope I have what it takes to carry it off."

"You'll be superb, darling."

"Sheridan and I are sure to fight like cats and dogs, but I intend to give my all, if only to show Charles he's not the only star in the family. Dottie's doing the costumes, busy as she is, and I'll wear a powdered wig and satin gowns that will take your breath away. Angel—"

Megan hesitated, frowning. We had merely been making small talk, ignoring what was really on our minds. She looked at me, eyes full of concern.

"I still wish you'd let me go with you, luv," she said. "You might need someone to—to give you moral support. I just don't feel right about your going alone, Angel."

"I won't be alone," I pointed out. "Burke will be with me."

"I know, but—"

"I'll be perfectly all right, Megan."

I picked up the hat I had selected and put it on. It was of black velvet with a wide, slanting brim, black egret feathers spilling down one side. I had contemplated wearing the delicate black lace veil I had worn to the funeral but had finally decided against it. I wanted

those six judges to see my face when I gave my testimony. Adjusting the tilt of the brim, I secured the hat
pin and sighed.

"I just want to get it over with," I told her. "Burke
assures me it will not take long. The judges have already seen the documents and Hugh's attorneys have
already been briefed. It's a mere formality."

I began to pull on a pair of delicate black lace gloves.
Megan moved over to the bed and sat down, rumpling
the smooth lilac satin counterpane and watching as I
stretched the frail lace over my fingers.

"The carriage I've hired will be waiting for me," I
continued, "and I'll go directly to Greystone Hall."

"I don't like the idea of your being there by yourself."

"I shan't be by myself, darling. The servants will be
there. It shouldn't take me long to—to gather up the
rest of my things and say my farewells. I'll be on my
way back before sundown. I should get back here before
midnight. There's no need for you to concern yourself."

"Still—"

"It's something I have to do, darling," I said in a
quiet voice, "and I have to do it alone. You and Charles
and Dottie have been—you've been wonderful, but I—
I have to stand on my own two feet."

"I understand, luv."

She got up from the bed and we hugged. Tears glistened in her eyes. She brushed them aside and, hand
in hand, we went downstairs to wait for Burke. It was
warm in the front drawing room, a small fire burning
in the fireplace. The room was pleasant with its beige
wallpaper delicately flowered in blue and pale orange,
its blue rugs and comfortable chairs and sofa upholstered in brown. We stood near the fireplace, waiting
for the sound of a carriage pulling up out in front. Megan took the brass poker and jabbed at the log. Tiny
sparks shot up as the log flaked.

"Are you certain about this, Angel?" she asked.

I nodded, smoothing one of my gloves.

"It's still not too late, you know. You could tell Burke.
He could prove the documents were forged—you weren't

ever directly involved, the court needn't know how it came about. It—what I'm trying to say, luv, is—"

"I know what you're trying to say, Megan, and I appreciate your concern."

"I—I just don't want you to do something you'll regret for the rest of your life."

"I shan't regret it."

"It doesn't seem fair. He—" She hesitated, gnawing her lower lip. "He was indirectly responsible for Clinton's death, and now he's being *rewarded* for it."

"Sometimes getting what you want is no reward at all," I replied. "Sometimes it's the worst kind of punishment."

We heard the carriage coming down Maiden Lane, heard it stop in front, and we stepped into the foyer together. Megan gave me another tight hug before she opened the door. Jonathan Burke stood on the doorstep, looking very solemn in brown, looking very unhappy, as well he might. His brick-red hair gleamed copper in the morning sunlight. His dark eyes were grim. Megan asked if he would like to come in for a cup of coffee before we left. He shook his head and consulted his pocket watch and said we'd best leave at once. I took Megan's hand and squeezed it and told her I would see her around midnight.

"We'll be waiting up for you, luv," she said, tearful again.

I kissed her cheek and followed Burke out to the carriage and he helped me inside. A few moments later we were on our way to Justice High Court, the carriage rumbling over the cobbles, caught up in the congestion of traffic as soon as we left Covent Garden. Burke sat across from me, silent, unhappily pondering the recent turn of events that had cost him a certain victory in court. He had been positive that we would win when the case came to trial. Now there was to be no trial. I would simply make my statement to the judges and answer some questions and it would all be over.

"I'm dreadfully sorry about all of this, Lady Meredith," Burke said after a while. "Had those documents not turned up, you would have inherited everything yourself. There was no other male issue, as you know, and by law and the terms of Lord Meredith's own will, you would have received the lot as his widow."

"But the documents turned up," I said.

He nodded, his lips tight.

"I couldn't very well destroy them," I continued. "One—one has to be honest, no matter what the cost."

Burke nodded again, totally unaware of the supreme irony of my words. The carriage left the Strand, turned past Charing Cross and started down Whitehall, moving toward Westminster. St. James Park was beginning to green, filled this sunny morning with a mob of strollers and noisy children. Inigo Jones' Banqueting House, all that remained of Whitehall Palace after the destruction of 1698, was majestic in the sunlight, though weathered and sooty. The Thames was sluggish, filled with filth, the noxious odors filling the air. I lifted my black lace handkerchief to my nostrils. Burke frowned when we were caught up in the congestion and had to stop while a cart with a broken wheel was hauled out of the street amidst much shouting, cursing and lashing of whips. We eventually began to move again and I soon saw Westminster Abbey looming up ahead, huge and brown and ancient, dominating the whole area.

A swarm of journalists from Fleet Street were waiting outside the building when we arrived. Burke took my elbow and deftly ushered me inside, scowling at the cocky chaps who fired questions at me. Inside was dim and cool and vaguely imposing, and I began to feel nervous for the first time. What...what if I faltered when they began questioning me? What if they could tell I was lying? Burke led me down a long dim corridor and into an anteroom and settled me on a bench and asked me to wait. The room was small, windowless. I felt as though I were in a prison cell. I paced back and forth, trying to control my nerves, and finally I sat back down on the bench, willing myself to be calm.

I was doing the right thing, I was certain of that. It would be different if Clinton were still alive, but he was gone, and nothing would bring him back. I had not married him for his wealth, for his estate, and I didn't want them now. Greystone Hall and the house on Hanover Square were filled with poignant memories. I could never live in either of them again. I had loved my husband and I had tried my best to make him happy, but I didn't feel eight months of marriage entitled me to an estate that had been in his family for two hundred years. I hadn't a drop of Meredith blood, whereas Hugh ... Yes, I was doing the right thing.

When Burke came to fetch me, looking quite different in his black robe and long white wig, I was completely composed. I followed him down another corridor and into a large, dusty room that wasn't nearly as stately or impressive as I had expected. It was paneled in dark oak and shafts of sunlight streamed in through windows set very high in the east wall. There were benches and tables and a witness box up front set on a raised platform behind a wooden railing, as was the table where the six solemn-faced judges sat in their long scarlet robes and curly white wigs. I felt a sense of unreality as Burke showed me to a seat near the back and moved off to speak to two more men attired in black robes and wigs like his. I assumed they were Hugh's counselors. There were no more than twenty people in the room, including the judges, and I was relieved to discover I would not have a large audience. The public had not been admitted, nor were there any representatives from Fleet Street.

Hugh sat at a table up front with yet another counselor. He wasn't aware that I had come in. His face, in profile, was stony and grave, his raven hair pulled back sleekly and fastened at the nape with a thin black silk ribbon. He wore an elegant black frock coat and black silk vest, fine white lace cascading from his throat and over his wrists. His strong brown hands nervously shuffled some papers in front of him. He was clearly not sure what the outcome of this hearing was going to be. Hadn't his counselors told him what had happened? He pushed the papers away and began to tap the table with the fingers of his right hand, drumming nervously, impatiently. He turned his head. He saw me sitting in back. His cheeks paled. I felt nothing.

Motes of dust swirled slowly in the shafts of sunlight. The room was warm and stuffy, despite its size. It seemed to take forever for the procedures to begin, and the legal rituals seemed inane and meaningless. I paid little attention, my mind wandering, the grief that had demolished me for weeks threatening to resurface. I toyed with my black lace handkerchief and was surprised to look down and see that I had torn it to shreds. They called my name. I looked up, startled. Everyone seemed to be waiting for me to do something. The room was very quiet. Burke hurried over and took my hand and led me to the witness box. I sat down in the large, uncomfortable wooden chair and Burke closed the wooden railing that opened and shut like a gate. He went back to his table and another man took his place, his black robe a size too large, his long white wig rather frayed.

Hugh was staring at me. His face was still pale. The judges were staring at me, too. Their faces seemed to blur. The room seemed to blur into a brown haze, and I was aware only of the man in front of me, his face lean and haggard and pasty gray, aged, his blue eyes scrutinizing me with alarming intensity. I gazed at him coolly. He held up two ancient, creased, yellowing sheets of parchment spotted with brown fox marks and, in a cracked, rasping voice, asked me if I had ever seen them before. I nodded.

"I must ask you to speak up, Lady Meredith," he admonished.

"Yes," I said, "I have seen them before."

"Would you describe for the court the circumstances under which they first came to your attention?"

You don't want me to do that, dear counselor. No indeed. Megan and Charles had been absolutely horrified at my proposal and Charles had flatly refused to have anything to do with it. They had both railed at me, told me I was out of my mind, refused to listen when I tried to explain my reasons for wanting it done. Finally, when I threatened to go to Seven Dials alone and unaccompanied, Charles had reluctantly agreed to accept the commission. He took two stalwart ex-guardsmen with him, and he wore shabby old clothes and a gray wig, his handsome face heavily disguised with greasepaint. The Grand Cyprus hadn't been at all interested in his identity, only in his gold, and for an exorbitant fee had agreed to forge the papers Charles requested. Charles returned for them a week later, and they were perfect. The Grand Cyprus was indeed a genius, every bit as clever as Boswell had claimed that morning at the breakfast table. I looked at the papers now, aware that the counselor was growing impatient.

"Milady?" he said.

"I was cleaning out my husband's desk in his office at Greystone Hall," I said, "and I noticed one of the drawers seemed to be stuck. It wouldn't open all the way. I tugged and strained and finally I employed a nail file and gave it a jerk. There was a tiny cache in back, obviously a secret compartment, and the papers were there, rolled up and tied with a rotten brown ribbon, completely covered with dust. I took them out and examined them, and when I discovered what they were I turned them over to my advocate, Mr. Burke."

The counselor nodded decisively and looked at the judges, as though to determine that they had heard properly, and then he turned to me again. "I see," he said, "and do you think your late husband was aware of their existence?"

"I'm certain he wasn't," I replied, and my voice was full of conviction. "As I said, they were completely covered with dust and clearly hadn't been disturbed for a great many years."

"Tell me, Lady Meredith—" He hesitated a moment. "Do you have any idea how the papers might have come to be in this compartment you describe?"

"I feel sure that Lord Meredith, my husband's uncle, placed them there for reasons of his own."

"And what might those reasons have been?"

It was an impertinent question. Both of us were aware of that. I gazed at him with cool eyes.

"I don't feel I'm qualified to answer that question," I said crisply. "I would imagine you and the rest of Mr. Bradford's counselors have a theory which you will establish in due course."

"Ah hummm ... yes, well, uh, would you describe the papers to us for the benefit of the court."

"One appears to be a certificate verifying the legal marriage of Lord Meredith and one Teresa Guiccoli. The other would seem to be a certificate registering the birth of their legitimate son, the date entered approximately seventeen months after that on the first certificate."

The counselor was quite pleased with my statement. He brushed one of the long, billowing sleeves of his robe and looked at the judges again, beaming. I was acutely aware of Hugh's eyes staring at me but I refused to look at him. I was growing restive and prayed that it would soon be over. The counselor gave me his attention, and when he spoke his cracked, raspy voice was portentous and full of drama.

"Lady Meredith, you discovered these papers yourself. Have you any doubts about their authenticity?"

"None whatsoever," I lied.

"You turned them over to your legal counselor, fully aware of their import. Would you tell the court what you believe they signify?"

"I believe they signify that the man known as Hugh Bradford is unquestionably the legitimate son of my late husband's uncle and his Italian wife and, as such, the rightful heir to all his father's estate."

"To which you have no legal claim!" he cried triumphantly.

"A fact I have no intention of contesting," I said.

"Thank you, Lady Meredith. I am sure the court appreciates your integrity and your honesty in these matters. That will be all."

There were excited murmurs in the room as I opened the railing and stepped down. Hugh had leaped to his feet, his expression exultant. He called my name as I moved past. I paid him no mind. My part of the proceedings was over, and I did not intend to stay for the rest. Burke took my arm and led me out of the room and down the corridor and past the anteroom and down yet another corridor to the front of the building. The carriage I had hired was waiting for me, and so were the gentlemen from Fleet. A furor broke out when I appeared.

"Lady Meredith! Angel! What happened? Tell us! Give us the story! Do you keep the estate? Does Bradford get it? Come on, Angel! You've always cooperated before!"

I smiled politely and maintained a discreet silence as they swarmed around me. Burke fended them off as best he could and led me over to the waiting carriage. The journalists shouted and waved and leaped about trying to get my attention. Burke opened the door for me and brutally shoved aside a husky fellow who tried to leap inside. I climbed in and Burke closed the door firmly, looking at me through the window. I reached out and took his hand and squeezed it, thanking him silently amidst the uproar. He nodded and I released his hand and he stepped back. The carriage pulled away, surrounded by journalists who hotly pursued it for several minutes.

I was tense. The streets were terribly congested. It seemed to take forever to get out of the city, and it was only when the countryside began to clip past the windows that I finally relaxed. I sat back against the cushions, gazing out at the trees, the fields, the gentle hills already a hazy green against the vivid blue sky. Now that it was over, I had no regrets whatsoever. I had done what I felt I must do, and now . . . now I could get on with my life. We passed through a small village with thatched cottages and an ancient brownstone church with tarnished copper steeple. A little girl with flaxen hair was leading a flock of geese across the green. The carriage moved on, wheels rumbling, horse hooves clopping heavily on the road. There were more trees, more fields, several more villages. The journey seemed interminable. It was midafternoon when the carriage turned into the drive of Greystone Hall.

Putnam himself came out to open the carriage door for me. Although he was as stately and reserved as ever, there was a new kindness in his eyes, and as he helped me out of the carriage he did so with concern, as though I were fragile. I smiled at him, thanking him with my eyes, and Putnam nodded and gave the driver instructions to go around to the stableyard. Mrs. Rigby was in the front hall, waiting for me. She made a deep curtsy, looking as though she might begin to cry at any moment.

"I've packed all the clothes you left, Milady," she said. "The bags are in the back hall. One of the footmen will carry them out to the carriage. The boxes of books you packed before you left are ready, too. I—I wasn't sure if you would want tea or not, but I've prepared it anyway."

"Thank you, Mrs. Rigby. I'll take it in the back sitting room."

"Will you be staying long, Milady?"

"Not long," I replied. "An hour or two at most. I—I would like you to thank all the staff for me, Mrs. Rigby. You all have been wonderful to me from the first, and it has meant a great deal. I'll miss you all."

The housekeeper took out a handkerchief and brushed a tear from the corner of her eye. "Then—then—this means you won't be coming back?"

The servants, of course, were fully aware that I was to go to court today, and they were all most eager to know the outcome. I handled it as tactfully as I could, knowing Mrs. Rigby would spread the news promptly.

"There is a new Lord Meredith, Mrs. Rigby. I would imagine he will be arriving in a day or so to look at the property, and he will undoubtedly want you all to stay on. He will be depending on you, and I hope you will give him all the help and consideration due him."

"Of—of course, Milady," she said hesitantly.

I thanked her again and went back to the sitting room. Robert brought the tea trolley in a few minutes later. He was wearing his best livery, and he had clearly already heard the news. He poured for me himself and, before leaving, told me that it had been a pleasure serving me. Henri had prepared all of the things I liked, but I ate very little, sitting there near the fire and drinking my tea, trying not to look at the sofa where Clinton had drawn his last breath. After a while I went over and picked up one of the soft cushions and held it to my bosom, staring out the windows for a long time, and then I tenderly replaced the cushion and left the room.

There was very little for me to pack, a few wedding gifts, a few of my personal possessions. Most of my things had already been sent on to Maiden Lane, where Megan was storing them for me. The jewels Clinton had given me were in a safe at Dottie's. I had leased space in a stable near the park in London, and Cynara was already there. I couldn't leave her behind. Ian had gone to London with her, hiring on at the stable and assuring me she would receive the best of care. I packed the few things remaining. Robert took the bag to the back hall and it would soon be strapped atop the carriage along with the others.

The sunlight was beginning to fade, long shadows spreading on the lawn. I went into Clinton's dressing room and opened the wardrobe and took out his favorite navy blue satin dressing robe, holding it to me, resting my cheek against the smooth, cool cloth, and then I put it back and went into our bedroom, resting my hand on the curve of one of the bedposts, remembering, storing away memories that would remain forever. I had loved him with a gentle love that would always have a place in my heart, and my grief would always be there too, locked deep inside me. I went downstairs and wandered through the rooms so beautifully renovated by Adam, silently saying my good-byes. I stepped into the elegant empty ballroom where we had danced all alone the night of the ball, remembering that night, his wonderful composure, the love that had glowed in his eyes as we glided around that polished golden-brown floor to the lilting strains of music. The tears came at last, and I let them fall for several minutes.

Putnam met me in the foyer twenty minutes later. I had dried my eyes, and I was completely composed. He informed me that the bags had all been strapped on top of the carriage, and I asked him to have it brought around. I went into the drawing room, so tastefully done in shades of white, pale gray and sky blue, rich sapphire blue velvet covering the graceful Chippendale furniture. Fading rays of sunlight slanted through the windows, hazily illuminating the beautiful Adam fireplace and the painting above it. *An Angel in Scarlet* glowed with rich color, vibrant and alive, and I gazed for a final time at that pensive girl who was no more. I was vaguely aware of the sound of wheels and horse hooves and I heard footsteps entering the foyer, but, lost in reverie, I paid no mind. Someone came into the room. Gazing at the portrait, I didn't turn around.

"It *is* beautiful," he said. "After all these years of looking at reproductions, I can hardly believe I now own the original."

Somehow I was not surprised. I turned slowly, and Hugh smiled at me, his dark eyes filled with triumph ... and love. He loved me. He genuinely loved me, with every fiber of his being, and now that his dark obsession had ended in victory that love was ready to blossom and grow and supplant everything else in importance. I saw that, and I was sorry. He was wearing the elegant attire he had worn in court, both of us in black, his relieved by exquisite white lace at throat and wrists.

"I would have arrived sooner, Angie, but those chaps from Fleet waylaid me as I was leaving. I took them all to a coffee house nearby and bought a round of drinks, answered all their questions. One of them called me 'Lord Meredith' for the first time. I can't tell you how that made me feel."

He looked younger. He looked exultant. The sullen, brooding Hugh I had known had been transformed by his triumph, and now there was something youthful and buoyant about him. He was like a little boy who has been given a room full of brightly wrapped presents and can hardly contain his joy. The foxlike features were not nearly so sharp. He had put on some weight and it was quite becoming to him. The lean, surly buccaneer look was gone, and, always striking, he could now almost be called handsome. The smile played lightly on those wide pink lips—he had smiled so rarely in the past—and the brown-black eyes were glowing. I noted all this coolly, objectively, without emotion.

"We've won, Angie!" he exclaimed.

"You've won," I corrected him.

"Everything I always wanted, everything I always dreamed of having—it's mine now. And all because of you. If you hadn't found those documents, if you hadn't turned them over to Burke, I would never have won. I admit that freely now. My own advocates had given up. I had no real proof, they claimed. They wanted me to drop my suit, but I wouldn't. I couldn't. I had to prove who I was."

"I know," I said.

"I owe it all to you, Angie."

"I did what I had to do," I told him.

Hugh came over to examine the portrait more closely—yes, there was buoyancy in his stride as well, it was almost jaunty—and he clasped his hands behind his back, standing there in front of the fireplace and gazing up at Gainsborough's masterpiece which now belonged to him. After a few moments he turned to look at me, and the joy, the love in his eyes was painful to behold. I felt no reflection of those emotions stirring within me. I felt nothing at all for this man, neither love nor hate. My feelings for him had once been the most important thing in my life, but they were gone, nothing whatsoever remaining now. The last feeble spark had died away the day my husband received that fatal letter.

"Gainsborough captured you to the life," he said. "So young, so beautiful, so wistful. You look so pensive in the portrait. What were you thinking of when he was painting you?"

"I was thinking of—of love lost," I replied.

"You're even more beautiful now. I—" He smiled again. "I'm so happy, Angie—so very happy. Dreams really do come true."

"Some do," I said. "Others are lost forever."

"It's not just winning—it's *know*ing. Knowing I was right, knowing I was indeed cheated out of my inheritance, just as I always believed. I will admit now that there were times when—when I sometimes began to doubt, began to believe I really might *be* a bastard, but I carried on nevertheless. Those documents you found proved I was right all along."

I looked at him, wondering if I could tell him, wondering if I could be so cruel. I remembered the letter he had posted to my husband.

"The documents are forgeries, Hugh," I said. "I had them done myself by a master criminal in Seven Dials."

His eyes filled with disbelief. The color slowly left his cheeks. Those brightly wrapped presents had just been taken away. I was immediately sorry I had told him. I could at least have left him his illusions. Several moments went by in silence, and I heard my carriage come round and stop in front of the house.

"You did it—you did it for me," he said.

I didn't answer. Hugh peered at me, as though to find one.

"You did it for—for us, because of our love."

"I did it because it seemed the right thing to do. I never wanted a title or great wealth or an estate—those things were never important to me. I told you that once, Hugh. I don't think you believed me. You turned your back on the things that mattered to me, and—" I hesitated, not wanting to continue in this vein. "I married Clinton because I loved him," I went on. "He was the last of his line and, legitimate or no, you are your father's son with Meredith blood in your veins. You're far more entitled to the estate than Clinton's widow—who has no desire to keep it."

"It will still be yours," he said, "ours."

"No, Hugh."

"Angie—"

"I'm leaving now. I have no desire to see you ever again."

"Angie!"

It was a cry from the depths of his soul. He was utterly distraught, utterly demolished. His eyes were full of panic, his cheeks ashen, all that earlier youthful elation vanished—perhaps forever. He shook his head repeatedly, his complexion even paler now. I knew that he loved me, and I knew what he was feeling now. I had been there before.

"You have what you always wanted, Hugh," I said quietly. "You have the title, you have the wealth, you have the estate—and no one will ever question your right to them now."

"I wanted them for us—for you. I love you, Angie. I love you! You're the only person in the world I've ever loved! You love me, too. You *must* love me! All these years—I've plotted, schemed, struggled, worked because—because you would be there in the end. I did it for *you!* You can't leave me now, Angie. Without you—" His voice broke, and it was several moments before he could go on. "Without you to share it with it means—it means nothing."

"You're Lord Meredith now, Hugh, and a very wealthy man. I have no doubt you'll eventually find someone else to share it with you. In the meantime, you have the painting to remind you of what might have been."

"You—you can't leave me," he said hoarsely.

"I really must. I want to be back in London by midnight. You have what you always wanted, and I genuinely hope it makes you happy."

"I love you. I—"

"Good-bye, Hugh."

"Angie!"

That anguished cry seemed to ring throughout the house as I left the room. I went outside and climbed into the waiting carriage. He did not follow me. I tapped on the roof with my knuckles, signaling the driver, and the carriage began to move slowly down the drive. I did not look back. The last rays of sunlight were fading on the lawn. We turned onto the road, and before we had gone ten miles night had fallen and the land was shrouded in misty black and the sky was a deep purple-gray ashimmer with stars. The carriage bowled along, carrying me away from the past, taking me toward the future. It was a long, uncomfortable, uneventful ride, and bells were tolling midnight when we entered London. Charles and Megan were waiting up for me, as promised, and Charles helped the driver unload the bags and boxes and bring them inside. I was utterly exhausted, and, seeing this, Megan led me straight upstairs to the guest bedroom. I undressed and put the candle out and climbed into bed and, undisturbed by the noises downstairs, went to sleep immediately.

A bird was singing in the gardens, warbling throatily and lustily and with excessive volume. I moaned and opened my eyes, and the sunlight streaming into the room was dazzling, making bright patterns on the polished floor. The window was open—Megan must have opened it earlier—and a warm breeze caused the white faille curtains to flutter. I struggled into a sitting position, resting my shoulders against the headboard, still groggy and disoriented. The bird continued to sing. I could have done without the noise just now, however pleasant it might be. There was a cheerful rap on the door and Megan came swirling into the room bearing a tray with coffeepot, cup, a plate of buttered toast. Wearing a fetching yellow frock, her long auburn waves falling to her shoulders and glistening with rich golden-red highlights, she looked disgustingly chipper.

"I see you're finally awake, luv. I was beginning to worry. I've brought your breakfast up—or what passes for your breakfast. You really should eat more in the morning, Angel. It's the most important meal of—"

"Please," I protested.

"I won't tarry, luv. I know you're always a grump until you've had several cups of coffee. It's a glorious day, warm as can be. Spring is early this year."

She placed the tray across my knees, smiled perkily

and left, informing me that she would be downstairs when I was ready to join the living. I sighed and poured my coffee and drank it, waiting for the sadness to come as it always did when I first awakened, presaging the rest of my day. The damnable bird outside kept right on singing and the curtains stirred gently and I could feel the warm breeze on my bare arms and cheeks and the sadness did not come. The grief was still there, would always be there, but it was contained now and instead of the sadness there was a sense of acceptance. I ate a slice of toast and drank another cup of black coffee, and then I set the tray aside and got out of bed and performed my ablutions, washing thoroughly. Wearing only a thin white silk petticoat, I went over to the window and looked out.

The tight, tiny buds studding the tree limbs had burst open, and the limbs were covered with fragile, pale jade-green leaves, and, gracious, the daffodils had opened already, bobbing delicate yellow silk heads in the breeze. The hyacinths were blooming, too, pink and mauve and pale purple, and it was only mid-March! The bird warbled in the sunlight, a plump robin with an apricot-colored breast, celebrating this phenomenon with its song. I smiled, and it was as if a great weight had lifted from my shoulders. Yes, yes, it was time... time to go on living. *You mustn't cry,* he had said. *I want you to be happy. Promise me you'll be happy, my darling.*

I intended to keep that promise, for I knew it was what Clinton had wanted for me. I went over to the wardrobe and opened the doors, examining the frocks hanging there. No more black velvets and silks. It was time to put my mourning away. I took down a turquoise silk and put it on. Solonge had worn a turquoise frock once, I recalled, years ago when she was a golden-haired siren intent on mischief. Mine was bold and dramatic with a low heart-shaped neckline and short puffed sleeves worn off the shoulder. The waist was snug, the skirt full and flaring out over my petticoat. It made me look younger. It made me look... almost like a girl myself. I sat down at the dressing table, brushing my hair

until it fell in glossy chestnut waves, and I could feel
the joy in my heart. I wanted to sing myself. I *was*
young, and I was alive, and the future was mine to
shape as I would.

"Angel!" Megan cried as I came downstairs.

"It's time, darling," I told her.

"Oh, luv, I—I'm so glad! You look radiant."

"I feel radiant. I'm going out," I added.

Megan rushed over and caught me up in a tight hug,
and then she moved back and smiled a wonderfully wry
smile.

"Give him hell, luv," she said.

"I intend to do just that."

I left the house without a cloak, but I didn't need
one. The air was warm and soft, laden with all those
marvelous smells that come with spring. The sky was
a pure translucent blue, silvery sunlight spilling down
in brilliant profusion. A sense of elation, of expectation
filled me as I went down Maiden Lane. I turned on
Bedford and again on Henrietta, and Covent Garden
seemed to welcome me back. Wonderful, worn, mellowed by age, shabby and raffish and not quite respectable, it had its own unique character and color, and I
was part of it. I belonged here, as I had never belonged
at Greystone Hall, and I was a member of its aristocracy, an aristocracy far more lively and interesting than
that which had haughtily refused to have anything to
do with Lady Angela Meredith, who had married into
its ranks. This charming, tatterdemalion neighborhood
with its Market and run-down shops and busy theaters
was, to me, the heart of London, and it was good to be
back home.

I paused in front of Brinkley's Wig Shop, looking
through the dusty window at the display of wigs. Old
Brinkley, in back of the shop, looked up and spotted me
and waved. Immersed in his own little world of powder
and curling irons and hair, he had probably never been
aware I had been away. Moving on past the green door
that led to the apartment Megan and I had shared, I
smiled to myself and wondered if the new tenants had

grown accustomed to the smell of powder and scorched hair. I crossed the street. Plump blue-gray pigeons strutted on the sun-warmed stones of the piazza, and St. Paul's had its own faded majesty. The Market seemed to be bustling, carts full of flowers and vegetables being pushed through the portals, customers coming and going. "Angel!" someone cried, and I turned to see a hefty woman with an armload of flowers hurrying toward me. I stopped and smiled. Pigeons scuttled out of the way as Annie made her rapid approach.

"Angel! You're back! Lor', luv, you look glorious!"

"Thank you, Annie. You're looking fit yourself."

"Me? Go on! I look like a weather-beaten old 'arridan an' well I know it. All-a us were sorry to 'ear about your loss, luv. We were all 'opin' you'd be comin' 'ome an' you *'ave!* She's *our* Angel, I told everyone. She ain't stayin' with them 'igh-falutin' folk now that 'er 'usband's gone. 'Ere—" She thrust the flowers into my arms. "These are for you, luv."

"Why—why, thank you, Annie."

"Pink roses, blue delphiniums, white and gold daisies—best th' 'ot 'ouses 'ave to offer, though we'll soon be 'avin' 'em out of th' gardens. Never in all my days seen spring come so early. And you're back! Covent Garden wudn't th' same without you, luv."

Annie grinned, made me an awkward curtsy and started back to her stall in The Market. I stood there in the middle of the piazza with my armload of fresh flowers, pigeons cooing, sunlight splashing all around, and my eyes misted with tears, so touched was I by Annie's gesture. It seemed like an omen, and I had the feeling that this was the very first day of a glorious new life. Brushing the tears away, I left the piazza and walked up King and turned on James, heading toward Longacre. People called to me, waved, and, clutching the flowers to my bosom with one arm, I waved back and smiled and returned greetings, a joyous elation welling inside.

The Lambert was ugly and gray, its white marble portico deplorably stained with soot, but to me it was the loveliest sight in the world. I walked around to the stage door and went inside, savoring the wonderful smell of greasepaint and powder, dust and damp rope. It was very dim back here, but I knew the way well, and I moved past piles of painted flats and a rack of dusty old costumes, recognizing the silver and violet gown I had worn as Nell Gwynn. I could hear voices onstage, one familiar voice soaring angrily above the others. Someone moved briskly toward me when I reached the wings, prepared to deal sternly with an intruder. I gave the flowers to a startled Andy Dobson and, before he could exclaim aloud, placed a finger to my lips, cautioning him to silence. Awkwardly holding the bunches of flowers, Andy beamed and nodded, and I went on toward the stage.

"You call *this* your best work!" he roared, slapping a sketch he clutched in his other hand. "I asked you to design a backdrop representing Covent Garden in 1660, and you show me a sketch of a few indeterminate buildings obscured by mist! I want to see The Market! I want to see Drury Lane in the distance! I want to *feel* Covent Garden as it was back then! There are going to be orange girls strolling in front of that backdrop, cavaliers in plumed hats, flower sellers with carts of real flowers, pickpockets in rags, high-born harlots in silk gowns and jewels! This is going to be the most ambitious, the most spectacular production I've ever mounted, and, by God, I'll have the proper backdrop or you two gentlemen will be out on the streets begging for work!"

The two gentlemen in question cringed and nodded and nervously assured him he'd have a satisfactory sketch before the week was out. James Lambert scowled furiously, tore the existing sketch to shreds and hurled the pieces away. They fluttered in the air like thin white birds and drifted slowly to the stage. He jammed his hands into the pockets of his breeches and continued to scowl as the two worried gentlemen scurried off into the wings on the other side. When they were out of sight he gave an exasperated sigh, shook his head and turned, looking extremely harried.

He saw me standing in the wings but, because of the dim light, he couldn't distinguish my features. I stepped out onto the stage, my turquoise skirt making silken music. Jamie stared at me, so startled he was momentarily robbed of speech. An unruly lock of glossy brown hair had tumbled across his brow. His green-brown eyes were wide with surprise. The slightly twisted nose was as engaging as ever, adding character and appeal to that handsome face, and the full pink lips were parted in dismay. I smiled to myself, delighted to be catching him off guard like this.

"Hello, Jamie," I said sweetly.

"What do *you* want!" he snarled.

"Is that any way to speak? I want a job, if you must know. I understand you haven't cast Aphra yet, and I'd like the part. As you may have read in the morning papers, I am no longer Lady Meredith. I haven't a penny to my name. I have to work for my living again."

"I—uh—I was sorry to hear about your husband's death, Angel. I meant to write, but—well, I've been very busy planning this new production. I was sorry about the other, too—lost everything, didn't you? Tough break, that. This chap Bradford must be an utter sod, turning you out in the cold. I—uh—I wish there were something I could do for you, Angel, I really do, but—"

He hesitated, very uncomfortable.

"But?" I prompted.

"But I feel an artist of your caliber would be much happier with Davy Garrick or one of the more prestigious managers."

"You do, do you?"

"Besides, I visualize someone a mite younger in the part."

"Younger? *Younger!*"

"You are getting on, my dear," he said kindly.

I stared at him, my cheeks flaming, and he looked back at me with triumph, delighted to see that he had scored. It took every ounce of restraint I had to keep from slapping that smug grin off his mouth. I was ab-

solutely furious, and I would happily have murdered
him at the moment, but that joyous elation I felt earlier
continued to well nevertheless. I felt the familiar exhilaration, felt vibrantly, gloriously alive with every
fiber of my being. Jamie Lambert might be an infuriating scoundrel but he was the only man who had ever
made the blood dance in my veins.

"I could play sixteen tonight," I said with admirable
control, "and you bloody well know it!"

"Maybe so, but—"

"You son of a bitch! I was *born* to play Aphra Behn,
and I mean to do just that."

He gave me a pitying look. "I'm sorry, Angel, but
this is *my* play, *my* production, and I don't intend to see
it turned into another vehicle for the celebrated Angel
Howard. I don't *need* you. I can make it on my own and
that's exactly what I mean to do. When they write their
reviews, they're going to write about James Lambert's
brilliant production, not Angel Howard's superlative
performance."

"You and your bloody pride!" I exclaimed. "You really
would risk another fiasco like *Amelia Mine* just because—just because you're so bloody unsure of your
own talents. Well, I have news for you, Mister Lambert,
it isn't going to happen!"

"No?" he said calmly.

"No! I'm going to play Aphra, and *our* production is
going to be the biggest success of the season. It may be
your play, but it happens to be *my* theater."

"What?"

"I also happen to be financing the whole bloody show."

"What!"

"You heard me, you sod! If you don't believe me I can
show you the papers to prove it. I happen to have an
enormous investment in this production, and I don't
intend to let you diddle it away because you're so goddamned stiff-necked and stubborn you can't see the—
the two of us *together* are an unbeatable combination!"

We stood there on the empty stage, glaring at each
other, and then a peculiar expression passed over his

face. The anger vanished, and he looked bewildered, looked perplexed. My own anger melted, too, replaced by another emotion that had been there from the very beginning. I had loved three men, each in a different way, but this was the man who made my soul sing.

"You—you're the one," he said in a strained voice. "You're the one who paid off the mortgage and took the papers and put up the money to—to finance the production."

"And it took every penny I had in the bank—money that was there in the first place because of you and your plays and your faith in me when I was a totally inexperienced seamstress's assistant who— Goddamn you, Jamie, if I start crying I intend to black both your eyes!"

"Why?" he asked quietly. "Why did you do it?"

"You know bloody well why I did it. Do you think I could sit back and see you lose The Lambert when I knew full well it's the most important thing in the world to you?"

Jamie didn't reply. He looked at me for a long moment, caught up by emotions he could no longer conceal behind stubborn pride and thorny posturing. I thought I might expire with joy when he moved closer and took both my hands and held them tightly and looked deep into my eyes, his own reflecting everything I felt in my heart. He would never change. He would always be moody and mercurial and volatile and I would always be feisty and as willful as he and we would always fight ... but oh how glorious the making up would be.

"You're wrong about that," he said. "The Lambert isn't the most important thing in the world to me. It's the *second* most important thing."

"Indeed?"

"A close second," he admitted.

"And what would be the first?"

"Do you really have to ask? Do I really have to show you?"

"It might be rather amusing," I said.